OXFORD POCKET
CLASSICS

°

THE MILL ON
THE FLOSS

OXFORD POCKET
CLASSICS

○

THE MILL ON
THE FLOSS
'In their death they were not divided'

○

GEORGE ELIOT

AVENEL BOOKS
NEW YORK

The Mill on the Floss was first published in 1860, and in Oxford World's Classics in 1903.

This edition first published in 1986 by Avenel Books, distributed by Crown Publishers, Inc.

produced by

Chancellor Press
59 Grosvenor Street
London W1

under licence from

Oxford University Press
Walton Street
Oxford

ISBN 0 517 62635 7

Printed in Shenzhen, China

h g f e d c b a

CONTENTS

BOOK FIRST

BOY AND GIRL

BOOK SECOND

SCHOOL-TIME

BOOK THIRD

THE DOWNFALL

BOOK FOURTH

THE VALLEY OF HUMILIATION

BOOK FIFTH

WHEAT AND TARES

Contents

BOOK SIXTH

THE GREAT TEMPTATION

BOOK SEVENTH

THE FINAL RESCUE

BOOK FIRST

BOY AND GIRL

I

OUTSIDE DORLCOTE MILL

A WIDE plain, where the broadening Floss hurries on
between its green banks to the sea, and the loving tide,
rushing to meet it, checks its passage with an impetuous
embrace. On this mighty tide the black ships—laden with
the fresh-scented fir-planks, with rounded sacks of oil-
bearing seed, or with the dark glitter of coal—are borne
along to the town of St. Ogg's, which shows its aged,
fluted red roofs and the broad gables of the wharves
between the low wooded hill and the river brink, tinging
the water with a soft purple hue under the transient
glance of this February sun. Far away on each hand
stretch the rich pastures, and the patches of dark earth,
made ready for the seed of broad-leaved green crops, or
touched already with the tint of the tender-bladed autumn-
sown corn. There is a remnant still of the last year's
golden clusters of beehive ricks rising at intervals beyond
the hedgerows; and everywhere the hedgerows are studded
with trees: the distant ships seem to be lifting their masts
and stretching their red-brown sails close among the
branches of the spreading ash. Just by the red-roofed town
the tributary Ripple flows with a lively current into the
Floss. How lovely the little river is, with its dark, changing
wavelets! It seems to me like a living companion while I
wander along the bank and listen to its low, placid voice,
as to the voice of one who is deaf and loving. I remember
those large dipping willows. I remember the stone bridge.

And this is Dorlcote Mill. I must stand a minute or two
here on the bridge and look at it, though the clouds are

threatening, and it is far on in the afternoon. Even in this leafless time of departing February it is pleasant to look at—perhaps the chill damp season adds a charm to the trimly-kept, comfortable dwelling-house, as old as the elms and chestnuts that shelter it from the northern blast. The stream is brimful now, and lies high in this little withy plantation, and half drowns the grassy fringe of the croft in front of the house. As I look at the full stream, the vivid grass, the delicate bright-green powder softening the outline of the great trunks and branches that gleam from under the bare purple boughs, I am in love with moistness, and envy the white ducks that are dipping their heads far into the water here among the withes, unmindful of the awkward appearance they make in the drier world above.

The rush of the water, and the booming of the mill, bring a dreamy deafness, which seems to heighten the peacefulness of the scene. They are like a great curtain of sound, shutting one out from the world beyond. And now there is the thunder of the huge covered waggon coming home with sacks of grain. That honest waggoner is thinking of his dinner getting sadly dry in the oven at this late hour; but he will not touch it till he has fed his horses—the strong, submissive, meek-eyed beasts, who, I fancy, are looking mild reproach at him from between their blinkers, that he should crack his whip at them in that awful manner, as if they needed that hint! See how they stretch their shoulders up the slope towards the bridge, with all the more energy because they are so near home. Look at their grand shaggy feet that seem to grasp the firm earth, at the patient strength of their necks, bowed under the heavy collar, at the mighty muscles of their struggling haunches! I should like well to hear them neigh over their hardly-earned feed of corn, and see them, with their moist necks freed from the harness, dipping their eager nostrils in the muddy pond. Now they are on the bridge, and down they go again at a swifter pace, and the arch of the covered waggon disappears at the turning behind the trees.

Now I can turn my eyes towards the mill again, and watch the unresting wheel sending out its diamond jets of water. That little girl is watching it too; she has been standing on just the same spot at the edge of tne water ever since I paused on the bridge. And that queer white cur with the brown ear seems to be leaping and barking in ineffectual remonstrance with the wheel; perhaps he is jealous because his playfellow in the beaver bonnet is so rapt in its movement. It is time the little playfellow went in, I think; and there is a very bright fire to tempt her; the red light shines out under the deepening grey of the sky. It is time, too, for me to leave off resting my arms on the cold stone of this bridge. . . .

Ah, my arms are really benumbed. I have been pressing my elbows on the arms of my chair and dreaming that I was standing on the bridge in front of Dorlcote Mill, as it looked one February afternoon many years ago. Before I dozed off I was going to tell you what Mr. and Mrs. Tulliver were talking about as they sat by the bright fire in the left-hand parlour on that very afternoon I have been dreaming of.

II

MR. TULLIVER, OF DORLCOTE MILL, DECLARES HIS RESOLUTION ABOUT TOM

'What I want, you know,' said Mr. Tulliver—'what I want is to give Tom a good eddication; an eddication as 'll be a bread to him. That was what I was thinking of when I gave notice for him to leave the academy at Ladyday. I mean to put him to a downright good school at Midsummer. The two years at th' academy 'ud ha' done well enough, if I'd meant to make a miller and farmer of him, for he's had a fine sight more schoolin' nor *I* ever got: all the learnin' *my* father ever paid for was a bit o' birch at one end and the alphabet at th' other. But I should like Tom to be a bit of a scholard, so as he might be up to the tricks o' these fellows as talk fine and write with a flourish. It 'ud be a help to me wi' these lawsuits, and arbitrations, and things. I wouldn't make a down-right lawyer o' the lad—I should be sorry for him to be a raskill—but a sort o' engineer, or a surveyor, or an auctioneer and vallyer, like Riley, or one o' them smartish businesses as are all profits and no outlay, only for a big watch-chain and a high stool. They're pretty nigh all one, and they're not far off being even wi' the law, *I* believe; for Riley looks Lawyer Wakem i' the face as hard as one cat looks another. *He's* none frightened at him.'

Mr. Tulliver was speaking to his wife, a blond comely woman in a fan-shaped cap (I am afraid to think how long it is since fan-shaped caps were worn—they must be so near coming in again. At that time, when Mrs. Tulliver was nearly forty, they were new at St. Ogg's, and considered sweet things).

'Well, Mr. Tulliver, you know best: *I've* no objections. But hadn't I better kill a couple o' fowl and have th' aunts and uncles to dinner next week, so as you may hear what sister Glegg and sister Pullet have got to say about it? There's a couple o' fowl *wants* killing!'

'You may kill every fowl i' the yard, if you like, Bessy; but I shall ask neither aunt nor uncle what I'm to do wi' my own lad,' said Mr. Tulliver defiantly.

'Dear heart!' said Mrs. Tulliver, shocked at this san-guinary rhetoric, 'how can you talk so, Mr. Tulliver? But it's your way to speak disrespectful o' my family; and sister Glegg throws all the blame upo' me, though I'm sure I'm as innocent as the babe unborn. For nobody's ever heard *me* say as it wasn't lucky for my children to have aunts and uncles as can live independent. Howiver, if Tom's to go to a new school, I should like him to go where I can wash him and mend him; else he might as well have calico as linen, for they'd be one as yallow as th' other before they'd been washed half-a-dozen times. And then, when the box is goin' backards and forrards, I could send the lad a cake, or a pork-pie, or an apple; for he can do with an extry bit, bless him, whether they stint him at the meals or no. My children can eat as much victuals as most, thank God.'

'Well, well, we won't send him out o' reach o' the carrier's cart, if other things fit in,' said Mr. Tulliver. 'But you mustn't put a spoke i' the wheel about the washin', if we can't get a school near enough. That's the fault I have to find wi' you, Bessie; if you see a stick i' the road, you're allays thinkin' you can't step over it. You'd want me not to hire a good waggoner, 'cause he'd got a mole on his face.'

'Dear heart!' said Mrs. Tulliver, in mild surprise, 'when did I iver make objections to a man because he'd got a mole on his face? I'm sure I'm rether fond o' the moles; for my brother, as is dead an' gone, had a mole on his brow. But I can't remember your iver offering to hire a waggoner with a mole, Mr. Tulliver. There was John Gibbs hadn't a mole on his face no more nor you have, an' I was all for having you hire *him*; an' so you did hire him, an' if he hadn't died o' the inflammation, as we paid Dr. Turnbull for attending him, he'd very like ha' been driving the waggon now. He might have a mole somewhere out o' sight, but how was I to know that, Mr. Tulliver?'

'No, no, Bessy; I didn't mean justly the mole; I meant it to stand for summat else; but niver mind—it's puzzling work, talking is. What I'm thinking on, is how to find the right sort o' school to send Tom to, for I might be ta'en in again, as I've been wi' th' academy. I'll have nothing to do wi' a 'cademy again: whativer school I send Tom to, it shan't be a 'cademy; it shall be a place where the lads spend their time i' summat else besides blacking the family's shoes, and getting up the potatoes. It's an uncommon puzzling thing to know what school to pick.'

Mr. Tulliver paused a minute or two, and dived with both hands into his breeches pockets as if he hoped to find some suggestion there. Apparently he was not disappointed, for he presently said, 'I know what I'll do— I'll talk it over wi' Riley: he's coming to-morrow, t' arbitrate about the dam.'

'Well, Mr. Tulliver, I've put the sheets out for the best bed, and Kezia's got 'em hanging at the fire. They aren't the best sheets, but they're good enough for anybody to sleep in, be he who he will; for as for them best Holland sheets, I should repent buying 'em, only they'll do to lay us out in. An' if you was to die to-morrow, Mr. Tulliver, they're mangled beautiful, an' all ready, an' smell o' lavender as it 'ud be a pleasure to lay 'em out; an' they lie at the left-hand corner o' the big oak linen-chest at the back: not as I should trust anybody to look 'em out but myself.'

As Mrs. Tulliver uttered the last sentence, she drew a bright bunch of keys from her pocket, and singled out one, rubbing her thumb and finger up and down it with a placid smile while she looked at the clear fire. If Mr. Tulliver had been a susceptible man in his conjugal relation, he might have supposed that she drew out the key to aid her imagination in anticipating the moment when he would be in a state to justify the production of the best Holland sheets. Happily he was not so; he was only susceptible in respect of his right to water-power; moreover, he had the marital habit of not listening very closely, and since his mention of Mr. Riley, had been apparently occupied in a tactile examination of his woollen stockings.

'I think I've hit it, Bessy,' was his first remark after a short silence. 'Riley's as likely a man as any to know o' some school; he's had schooling himself, an' goes about to all sorts o' places—arbitratin' and vallyin' and that. And we shall have time to talk it over to-morrow night when the business is done. I want Tom to be such a sort o' man as Riley, you know—as can talk pretty nigh as well as if it was all wrote out for him, and knows a good lot o' words as don't mean much, so as you can't lay hold of 'em i' law; and a good solid knowledge o' business too.'

'Well,' said Mrs. Tulliver, 'so far as talking proper, and knowing everything, and walking with a bend in his back, and setting his hair up, I shouldn't mind the lad being brought up to that. But them fine-talking men from the big towns mostly wear the false shirt-fronts; they wear a frill till it's all a mess, and then hide it with a bib; I know Riley does. And then, if Tom's to go and live at Mudport, like Riley, he'll have a house with a kitchen hardly big enough to turn in, an' niver get a fresh egg for his breakfast, an' sleep up three pair o' stairs—or four, for what I know—an' be burnt to death before he can get down.'

'No, no,' said Mr. Tulliver, 'I've no thoughts of his going to Mudport: I mean him to set up his office at St. Ogg's, close by us, an' live at home. But,' continued Mr. Tulliver after a pause, 'what I'm a bit afraid on is, as Tom hasn't got the right sort o' brains for a smart fellow. I doubt he's a bit slowish. He takes after your family, Bessy.'

'Yes, that he does,' said Mrs. Tulliver, accepting the last proposition entirely on its own merits; 'he's wonderful for liking a deal o' salt in his broth. That was my brother's way, and my father's before him.'

'It seems a bit of a pity, though,' said Mr. Tulliver, 'as the lad should take after the mother's side i'stead o' the little wench. That's the worst on't wi' the crossing o' breeds: you can never justly calkilate what'll come on't. The little un takes after my side, now: she's twice as 'cute as Tom. Too 'cute for a woman, I'm afraid,' continued Mr. Tulliver, turning his head dubiously first on one side and then on the other. 'It's no mischief much while she's a little un, but an over-'cute woman's no better nor a long-tailed sheep—she'll fetch none the bigger price for that.'

'Yes, it *is* a mischief while she's a little un, Mr. Tulliver, for it all runs to naughtiness. How to keep her in a clean pinafore two hours together passes my cunning. An' now you put me i' mind,' continued Mrs. Tulliver, rising and going to the window, 'I don't know where she is now, an' it's pretty nigh tea-time. Ah, I thought so—wanderin' up an' down by the water, like a wild thing: she'll tumble in some day.'

Mrs. Tulliver rapped the window sharply, beckoned, and shook her head, a process which she repeated more than once before she returned to her chair.

'You talk o' 'cuteness, Mr. Tulliver,' she observed as she sat down, 'but I'm sure the child's half an idiot i' some things; for if I send her up-stairs to fetch anything, she forgets what she's gone for, an' perhaps 'ull sit down on the floor i' the sunshine an' plait her hair an' sing to herself like a Bedlam creatur', all the while I'm waiting for her down-stairs. That niver run i' my family, thank God, no more nor a brown skin as makes her look like a mulatter. I don't like to fly i' the face o' Providence, but it seems hard as I should have but one gell, an' her so comical.'

'Pooh, nonsense!' said Mr. Tulliver, 'she's a straight black-eyed wench as anybody need wish to see. I don't know i' what she's behind other folks's children; and she can read almost as well as the parson.'

'But her hair won't curl all I can do with it, and she's so franzy about having it put i' paper, and I've such work as never was to make her stand and have it pinched with th' irons.'

'Cut it off—cut it off short,' said the father rashly.

'How can you talk so, Mr. Tulliver? She's too big a gell, gone nine, and tall of her age, to have her hair cut short; an' there's her cousin Lucy's got a row o' curls round her head, an' not a hair out o' place. It seems hard as my sister Deane should have that pretty child; I'm sure Lucy takes more after me nor my own child does. Maggie, Maggie,' continued the mother, in a tone of half-coaxing fretfulness, as this small mistake of nature entered the room, 'where's the use o' my telling you to keep away from the water? You'll tumble in and be drownded some day, an' then you'll be sorry you didn't do as mother told you.'

Maggie's hair, as she threw off her bonnet, painfully confirmed her mother's accusation: Mrs. Tulliver, desiring her daughter to have a curled crop, 'like other folks's children,' had had it cut too short in front to be pushed behind the ears; and as it was usually straight an hour after it had been taken out of paper, Maggie was incessantly tossing her head to keep the dark, heavy locks out of her gleaming black eyes—an action which gave her very much the air of a small Shetland pony.

'O dear, O dear, Maggie, what are you thinkin' of, to throw your bonnet down there? Take it upstairs, there's a good gell, an' let your hair be brushed, an' put your other pinafore on, an' change your shoes—do, for shame; an' come an' go on with your patchwork, like a little lady.'

'O mother,' said Maggie, in a vehemently cross tone, 'I don't *want* to do my patchwork.'

'What! not your pretty patchwork, to make a counterpane for your aunt Glegg?'

'It's foolish work,' said Maggie, with a toss of her mane, 'tearing things to pieces to sew 'em together again. And I don't want to do anything for my aunt Glegg—I don't like her.'

Exit Maggie, dragging her bonnet by the string, while Mr. Tulliver laughs audibly.

'I wonder at you, as you'll laugh at her, Mr. Tulliver,' said the mother, with feeble fretfulness in her tone. 'You encourage her i' naughtiness. An' her aunts will have it as it's me spoils her.'

Mrs. Tulliver was what is called a good-tempered person —never cried, when she was a baby, on any slighter ground than hunger and pins; and from the cradle upwards had been healthy, fair, plump, and dull-witted; in short, the flower of her family for beauty and amiability. But milk and mildness are not the best things for keeping, and when they turn only a little sour, they may disagree with young stomachs seriously. I have often wondered whether those early Madonnas of Raphael, with the blond faces and somewhat stupid expression, kept their placidity undisturbed when their strong-limbed, strong-willed boys got a little too old to do without clothing. I think they must have been given to feeble remonstrance, getting more and more peevish as it became more and more ineffectual.

III

MR. RILEY GIVES HIS ADVICE CONCERNING A SCHOOL FOR TOM

THE gentleman in the ample white cravat and shirt-frill, taking his brandy-and-water so pleasantly with his good friend Tulliver, is Mr. Riley, a gentleman with a waxen complexion and fat hands, rather highly educated for an auctioneer and appraiser, but large-hearted enough to show a great deal of *bonhommie* towards simple country acquaintances of hospitable habits. Mr. Riley spoke of such acquaintances kindly as 'people of the old school.'

The conversation had come to a pause. Mr. Tulliver, not without a particular reason, had abstained from a seventh recital of the cool retort by which Riley had shown himself too many for Dix, and how Wakem had had his comb cut for once in his life, now the business of the dam had been settled by arbitration, and how there never would have been any dispute at all about the height of water if everybody was what they should be, and Old Harry hadn't made the lawyers. Mr. Tulliver was, on the whole, a man of safe traditional opinions; but on one or two points he had trusted to his unassisted intellect, and had arrived at several questionable conclusions; among the rest, that rats, weevils, and lawyers were created by Old Harry. Unhappily he had no one to tell him that this was rampant Manichæism, else he might have seen his error. But to-day it was clear that the good principle was triumphant; this affair of the water-power had been a tangled business somehow, for all it seemed—look at it one way—as plain as water's water; but, big a puzzle as it was, it hadn't got the better of Riley. Mr. Tulliver took his brandy-and-water a little stronger than usual, and, for a man who might be supposed to have a few hundreds lying idle at his banker's, was rather incautiously open in expressing his high estimate of his friend's business talents.

But the dam was a subject of conversation that would

keep; it could always be taken up again at the same point, and exactly in the same condition; and there was another subject, as you know, on which Mr. Tulliver was in pressing want of Mr. Riley's advice. This was his particular reason for remaining silent for a short space after his last draught, and rubbing his knees in a meditative manner. He was not a man to make an abrupt transition. This was a puzzling world, as he often said, and if you drive your waggon in a hurry, you may light on an awkward corner. Mr. Riley, meanwhile, was not impatient. Why should he be? Even Hotspur, one would think, must have been patient in his slippers on a warm hearth, taking copious snuff, and sipping gratuitous brandy-and-water.

'There's a thing I've got i' my head,' said Mr. Tulliver at last, in rather a lower tone than usual, as he turned his head and looked steadfastly at his companion.

'Ah!' said Mr. Riley, in a tone of mild interest. He was a man with heavy waxen eyelids and high-arched eyebrows, looking exactly the same under all circumstances. This immovability of face, and the habit of taking a pinch of snuff before he gave an answer, made him trebly oracular to Mr. Tulliver.

'It's a very particular thing,' he went on; 'it's about my boy Tom.'

At the sound of this name, Maggie, who was seated on a low stool close by the fire, with a large book open on her lap, shook her heavy hair back and looked up eagerly. There were few sounds that roused Maggie when she was dreaming over her book, but Tom's name served as well as the shrillest whistle: in an instant she was on the watch, with gleaming eyes, like a Skye terrier suspecting mischief, or at all events determined to fly at any one who threatened it towards Tom.

'You see, I want to put him to a new school at Midsummer,' said Mr. Tulliver; 'he's comin' away from the 'cademy at Ladyday, an' I shall let him run loose for a quarter; but after that I want to send him to a downright good school, where they'll make a scholard of him.'

'Well,' said Mr. Riley, 'there's no greater advantage you can give him than a good education. Not,' he added, with polite significance—'not that a man can't be an excellent miller and farmer and a shrewd sensible fellow into the bargain, without much help from the schoolmaster.'

'I believe you,' said Mr. Tulliver, winking, and turning his head on one side, 'but that's where it is. I don't *mean* Tom to be a miller and farmer. I see no fun i' that: why, if I made him a miller an' farmer, he'd be expectin' to take to the mill an' the land, an' a-hinting at me as it was time for me to lay by an' think o' my latter end. Nay, nay, I've seen enough o' that wi' sons. I'll never pull my coat off before I go to bed. I shall give Tom an eddication an' put him to a business, as he may make a nest for himself, an' not want to push me out o' mine. Pretty well if he gets it when I'm dead an' gone. I shan't be put off wi' spoon-meat afore I've lost my teeth.'

This was evidently a point on which Mr. Tulliver felt strongly, and the impetus which had given unusual rapidity and emphasis to his speech, showed itself still unexhausted for some minutes afterwards, in a defiant motion of the head from side to side, and an occasional 'Nay, nay,' like a subsiding growl.

These angry symptoms were keenly observed by Maggie, and cut her to the quick. Tom, it appeared, was supposed capable of turning his father out of doors, and of making the future in some way tragic by his wickedness. This was not to be borne; and Maggie jumped up from her stool, forgetting all about her heavy book, which fell with a bang within the fender; and going up between her father's knees, said, in a half-crying, half-indignant voice—

'Father, Tom wouldn't be naughty to you ever; I know he wouldn't.'

Mrs. Tulliver was out of the room superintending a choice supper-dish, and Mr. Tulliver's heart was touched; so Maggie was not scolded about the book. Mr. Riley quietly picked it up and looked at it, while the father laughed with a certain tenderness in his hard-lined face, and patted his little girl on the back, and then held her hands and kept her between his knees.

'What! they mustn't say any harm o' Tom, eh?' said Mr. Tulliver, looking at Maggie with a twinkling eye. Then, in a lower voice, turning to Mr. Riley, as though Maggie couldn't hear, 'She understands what one's talking about so as never was. And you should hear her read—straight off, as if she knowed it all beforehand. And allays at her book! But it's bad—it's bad,' Mr. Tulliver added, sadly, checking this blamable exultation: 'a woman's no business wi' being so clever; it'll turn to trouble, I doubt. But, bless you!'—here the exultation was clearly recovering the mastery—'she'll read the books and understand 'em better nor half the folks as are growed up.'

Maggie's cheeks began to flush with triumphant excitement: she thought Mr. Riley would have a respect for her now; it had been evident that he thought nothing of her before.

Mr. Riley was turning over the leaves of the book, and she could make nothing of his face, with its high-arched eyebrows; but he presently looked at her and said:

'Come, come and tell me something about this book; here are some pictures—I want to know what they mean.'

Maggie with deepening colour went without hesitation to Mr. Riley's elbow and looked over the book, eagerly seizing one corner, and tossing back her mane, while she said:

'O, I'll tell you what that means. It's a dreadful picture, isn't it? But I can't help looking at it. That old woman in the water's a witch—they've put her in to find out whether she's a witch or no, and if she swims she's a witch, and if she's drowned—and killed, you know—she's innocent, and not a witch, but only a poor silly old woman. But what good would it do her then, you know, when she was drowned? Only, I suppose, she'd go to heaven, and God would make it up to her. And this dreadful blacksmith with his arms akimbo, laughing—oh, isn't he ugly?—I'll tell you what he is. He's the devil *really*' (here Maggie's voice became louder and more emphatic), 'and not a right blacksmith; for the devil takes the shape of wicked men, and walks about and sets people doing wicked things, and he's oftener in the shape of a bad man than any other, because, you know, if people saw he was the devil, and he roared at 'em, they'd run away, and he couldn't make 'em do what he pleased.'

Mr. Tulliver had listened to this exposition of Maggie's with petrifying wonder.

'Why, what book is it the wench has got hold on?' he burst out, at last.

'"The History of the Devil," by Daniel Defoe; not quite the right book for a little girl,' said Mr. Riley. 'How came it among your books, Tulliver?'

Maggie looked hurt and discouraged, while her father said:

'Why it's one o' the books I bought at Partridge's sale. They was all bound alike—it's a good binding, you see—and I thought they'd be all good books. There's Jeremy Taylor's "Holy Living and Dying" among 'em; I read in it often of a Sunday' (Mr. Tulliver felt somehow a familiarity with that great writer because his name was Jeremy); 'and there's a lot more of 'em, sermons mostly, I think; but they've all got the same covers, and I thought they were all o' one sample, as you may say. But it seems one mustn't judge by th' outside. This is a puzzlin' world.'

'Well,' said Mr. Riley, in an admonitory patronizing tone, as he patted Maggie on the head, 'I advise you to put by the "History of the Devil," and read some prettier book. Have you no prettier books?'

'O yes,' said Maggie, reviving a little in the desire to vindicate the variety of her reading, 'I know the reading in this book isn't pretty—but I like the pictures, and I make stories to the pictures out of my own head, you know. But I've got "Æsop's Fables," and a book about Kangaroos and things, and the "Pilgrim's Progress." . . .'

'Ah, a beautiful book,' said Mr. Riley; 'you can't read a better.'

'Well, but there's a great deal about the devil in that,'

said Maggie triumphantly, 'and I'll show you the picture of him in his true shape, as he fought with Christian.'

Maggie ran in an instant to the corner of the room, jumped on a chair, and reached down from the small bookcase a shabby old copy of Bunyan, which opened at once, without the least trouble of search, at the picture she wanted.

'Here he is,' she said, running back to Mr. Riley, 'and Tom coloured him for me with his paints when he was at home last holidays—the body all black, you know, and the eyes red, like fire, because he's all fire inside, and it shines out at his eyes.'

'Go, go!' said Mr. Tulliver peremptorily, beginning to feel rather uncomfortable at these few remarks on the personal appearance of a being powerful enough to create lawyers; 'shut up the book, and let's hear no more o' such talk. It is as I thought—the child 'ull learn more mischief nor good wi' the books. Go, go and see after your mother.'

Maggie shut up the book at once, with a sense of disgrace, but not being inclined to see after her mother, she compromised the matter by going into a dark corner behind her father's chair, and nursing her doll, towards which she had an occasional fit of fondness in Tom's absence, neglecting its toilette, but lavishing so many warm kisses on it that the waxen cheeks had a wasted, unhealthy appearance.

'Did you ever hear the like on 't?' said Mr. Tulliver, as Maggie retired. 'It's a pity but what she'd been the lad—she'd a been a match for the lawyers, *she* would. It's the wonderful'st thing'—here he lowered his voice—'as I picked the mother because she wasn't o'er 'cute—being a good-looking woman too, an' come of a rare family for managing; but I picked her from her sisters o' purpose, 'cause she was a bit weak, like; for I wasn't agoin' to be told the rights o' things by my own fireside. But you see when a man's got brains himself, there's no knowing where they'll run to; an' a pleasant sort o' soft woman may go on breeding you stupid lads and 'cute wenches, till it's like as if the world was turned topsy-turvy. It's an uncommon puzzlin' thing.'

Mr. Riley's gravity gave way, and he shook a little under the application of his pinch of snuff, before he said:

'But your lad's not stupid, is he? I saw him, when I was here last, busy making fishing-tackle; he seemed quite up to it.'

'Well, he isn't not to say stupid—he's got a notion o' things out o' door, an' a sort o' common-sense, as he'd lay hold o' things by the right handle. But he's slow with his tongue, you see, and he reads but poorly, and can't abide the books, and spells all wrong, they tell me, an' as shy as can be wi' strangers, an' you never hear him say 'cute things like the little wench. Now, what I want is to send him to a school where they'll make him a bit nimble with his tongue and his pen, and make a smart chap of him. I want my son to be even wi' these fellows as have got the start of me with having better schooling. Not but what, if the world had been left as God made it, I could ha' seen my way, and held my own wi' the best of 'em; but things have got so twisted round and wrapped up i' unreasonable words, as aren't a bit like 'em, as I'm clean at fault, often an' often. Everything winds about so—the more straightforrard you are, the more you're puzzled.'

Mr. Tulliver took a draught, swallowed it slowly, and shook his head in a melancholy manner, conscious of exemplifying the truth that a perfectly sane intellect is hardly at home in this insane world.

'You're quite in the right of it, Tulliver,' observed Mr. Riley. 'Better spend an extra hundred or two on your son's education, than leave it him in your will. I know I should have tried to do so by a son of mine, if I'd had one, though, God knows, I haven't your ready money to play with, Tulliver; and I have a houseful of daughters into the bargain.'

'I dare say, now, you know of a school as 'ud be just the thing for Tom,' said Mr. Tulliver, not diverted from his purpose by any sympathy with Mr. Riley's deficiency of ready cash.

Mr. Riley took a pinch of snuff, and kept Mr. Tulliver in suspense by a silence that seemed deliberative before he said:

'I know of a very fine chance for any one that's got the necessary money, and that's what you have, Tulliver. The fact is, I wouldn't recommend any friend of mine to send a boy to a regular school if he could afford to do better. But if any one wanted his boy to get superior instruction and training, where he would be the companion of his master, and that master a first-rate fellow—I know his man. I wouldn't mention the chance to everybody, because I don't think everybody would succeed in getting it, if he were to try; but I mention it to you, Tulliver—between ourselves.'

The fixed inquiring glance with which Mr. Tulliver had been watching his friend's oracular face became quite eager.

'Ay, now, let's hear,' he said, adjusting himself in his chair with the complacency of a person who is thought worthy of important communications.

'He's an Oxford man,' said Mr. Riley sententiously, shutting his mouth close, and looking at Mr. Tulliver to observe the effect of this stimulating information.

'What! a parson?' said Mr. Tulliver, rather doubtfully.

'Yes, and an M.A. The bishop, I understand, thinks very highly of him: why, it was the bishop who got him his present curacy.'

'Ah?' said Mr. Tulliver, to whom one thing was as wonderful as another concerning these unfamiliar phenomena. 'But what can he want wi' Tom, then?'

'Why, the fact is, he's fond of teaching, and wishes to keep up his studies, and a clergyman has but little opportunity for that in his parochial duties. He's willing to take one or two boys as pupils to fill up his time profitably. The boys would be quite of the family—the finest thing in the world for them; under Stelling's eye continually.'

'But do you think they'd give the poor lad twice o''

pudding?' said Mrs. Tulliver, who was now in her place again. 'He's such a boy for pudding as never was; an' a growing boy like that—it's dreadful to think o' their stintin' him.'

'And what money 'ud he want?' said Mr. Tulliver, whose instinct told him that the services of this admirable M.A. would bear a high price.

'Why, I know of a clergyman who asks a hundred and fifty with his youngest pupils, and he's not to be mentioned with Stelling, the man I speak of. I know, on good authority, that one of the chief people at Oxford said, "Stelling might get the highest honours if he chose." But he didn't care about university honours. He's a quiet man—not noisy.'

'Ah, a deal better—a deal better,' said Mr. Tulliver; 'but a hundred and fifty's an uncommon price. I never thought o' payin' so much as that.'

'A good education, let me tell you, Tulliver—a good education is cheap at the money. But Stelling is moderate in his terms—he's not a grasping man. I've no doubt he'd take your boy at a hundred, and that's what you wouldn't get many other clergymen to do. I'll write to him about it, if you like.'

Mr. Tulliver rubbed his knees, and looked at the carpet in a meditative manner.

'But belike he's a bachelor,' observed Mrs. Tulliver in the interval, 'an' I've no opinion o' housekeepers. There was my brother, as is dead an' gone, had a housekeeper once, an' she took half the feathers out o' the best bed, an' packed 'em up an' sent 'em away. An' it's unknown the linen she made away with—Stott her name was. It 'ud break my heart to send Tom where there's a housekeeper, an' I hope you won't think of it, Mr. Tulliver.'

'You may set your mind at rest on that score, Mrs. Tulliver,' said Mr. Riley, 'for Stelling is married to as nice a little woman as any man need wish for a wife. There isn't a kinder little soul in the world; I know her family well. She has very much your complexion—light curly hair. She comes of a good Mudport family, and it's not every offer that would have been acceptable in that quarter. But Stelling's not an everyday man. Rather a particular fellow as to the people he chooses to be connected with. But I *think* he would have no objection to take your son—I *think* he would not, on my representation.'

'I don't know what he could have *against* the lad,' said Mrs. Tulliver, with a slight touch of motherly indignation, 'a nice fresh-skinned lad as anybody need wish to see.'

'But there's one thing I'm thinking on,' said Mr. Tulliver, turning his head on one side and looking at Mr. Riley, after a long perusal of the carpet. 'Wouldn't a parson be almost too high-learnt to bring up a lad to be a man o' business? My notion o' the parsons was as they'd got a sort o' learning as lay mostly out o' sight. And that isn't what I want for Tom. I want him to know figures, and write like print, and see into things quick, and know what folks mean, and how to wrap things up in words as aren't actionable. It's an uncommon fine thing, that is,' concluded Mr. Tulliver, shaking his head, 'when you can let a man know what you think of him without paying for it.'

'O my dear Tulliver,' said Mr. Riley, 'you're quite under a mistake about the clergy; all the best schoolmasters are of the clergy. The schoolmasters who are not clergymen, are a very low set of men generally. . . .'

'Ay, that Jacobs is, at the 'cademy,' interposed Mr. Tulliver.

'To be sure—men who have failed in other trades, most likely. Now a clergyman is a gentleman by profession and education; and besides that, he has the knowledge that will ground a boy, and prepare him for entering on any career with credit. There may be some clergymen who are mere book-men; but you may depend upon it, Stelling is not one of them—a man that's wide awake, let me tell you. Drop him a hint, and that's enough. You talk of figures now; you have only to say to Stelling, "I want my son to be a thorough arithmetician," and you may leave the rest to him.'

Mr. Riley paused a moment, while Mr. Tulliver, somewhat reassured as to clerical tutorship, was inwardly rehearsing to an imaginary Mr. Stelling the statement, 'I want my son to know 'rithmetic.'

'You see, my dear Tulliver,' Mr. Riley continued, 'when you get a thoroughly educated man, like Stelling, he's at no loss to take up any branch of instruction. When a workman knows the use of his tools, he can make a door as well as a window.'

'Ay, that's true,' said Mr. Tulliver, almost convinced now that the clergy must be the best of schoolmasters.

'Well, I'll tell you what I'll do for you,' said Mr. Riley, 'and I wouldn't do it for everybody. I'll see Stelling's father-in-law, or drop him a line when I get back to Mudport, to say that you wish to place your boy with his son-in-law, and I dare say Stelling will write to you, and send you his terms.'

'But there's no hurry, is there?' said Mrs. Tulliver; 'for I hope, Mr. Tulliver, you won't let Tom begin at his new school before Midsummer. He began at the 'cademy at the Ladyday quarter, and you see what good's come of it.'

'Ay, ay, Bessy, never brew wi' bad malt upo' Michaelmas day, else you'll have a poor tap,' said Mr. Tulliver, winking and smiling at Mr. Riley with the natural pride of a man who has a buxom wife conspicuously his inferior in intellect. 'But it's true there's no hurry—you've hit it there, Bessy.'

'It might be as well not to defer the arrangement too long,' said Mr. Riley quietly, 'for Stelling may have propositions from other parties, and I know he would not take more than two or three boarders, if so many. If I were you, I think I would enter on the subject with Stelling at once: there's no necessity for sending the boy before Midsummer, but I would be on the safe side, and make sure that nobody forestalls you.'

'Ay, there's summat in that,' said Mr. Tulliver.

'Father,' broke in Maggie, who had stolen unperceived to her father's elbow again, listening with parted lips, while she held her doll topsy-turvy, and crushed its nose against the wood of the chair—'Father, is it a long way off where Tom is to go? shan't we ever go to see him?'

'I don't know, my wench,' said the father tenderly. 'Ask Mr. Riley; he knows.'

Maggie came round promptly in front of Mr. Riley, and said, 'How far is it, please sir?'

'O, a long, long way off,' that gentleman answered, being of opinion that children, when they are not naughty, should always be spoken to jocosely. 'You must borrow the seven-leagued boots to get to him.'

'That's nonsense!' said Maggie, tossing her head haughtily, and turning away, with the tears springing in her eyes. She began to dislike Mr. Riley: it was evident he thought her silly and of no consequence.

'Hush, Maggie, for shame of you, asking questions and chattering,' said her mother. 'Come and sit down on your little stool and hold your tongue, do. But,' added Mrs. Tulliver, who had her own alarm awakened, 'is it so far off as I couldn't wash him and mend him?'

'About fifteen miles, that's all,' said Mr. Riley. 'You can drive there and back in a day quite comfortably. Or—Stelling is a hospitable, pleasant man—he'd be glad to have you stay.'

'But it's too far off for the linen, I doubt,' said Mrs. Tulliver sadly.

The entrance of supper opportunely adjourned this difficulty, and relieved Mr. Riley from the labour of suggesting some solution or compromise—a labour which he would otherwise doubtless have undertaken; for, as you perceive, he was a man of very obliging manners. And he had really given himself the trouble of recommending Mr. Stelling to his friend Tulliver without any positive expectation of a solid, definite advantage resulting to himself, notwithstanding the subtle indications to the contrary which might have misled a too sagacious observer. For there is nothing more widely misleading than sagacity if it happens to get on a wrong scent; and sagacity, persuaded that men usually act and speak from distinct motives, with

a consciously proposed end in view, is certain to waste its
energies on imaginary game. Plotting covetousness, and
deliberate contrivance, in order to compass a selfish end,
are nowhere abundant but in the world of the dramatist:
they demand too intense a mental action for many of our
fellow-parishioners to be guilty of them. It is easy enough
to spoil the lives of our neighbours without taking so
much trouble: we can do it by lazy acquiescence and lazy
omission, by trivial falsities for which we hardly know a
reason, by small frauds neutralized by small extrava-
gancies, by maladroit flatteries, and clumsily improvised
insinuations. We live from hand to mouth, most of us,
with a small family of immediate desires—we do little
else than snatch a morsel to satisfy the hungry brood,
rarely thinking of seed-corn or the next year's crop.

Mr. Riley was a man of business, and not cold towards
his own interest, yet even he was more under the influence
of small promptings than of far-sighted designs. He had
no private understanding with the Rev. Walter Stelling;
on the contrary he knew very little of that M.A. and his
acquirements—not quite enough perhaps to warrant so
strong a recommendation of him as he had given to his
friend Tulliver. But he believed Mr. Stelling to be an
excellent classic, for Gadsby had said so, and Gadsby's
first cousin was an Oxford tutor; which was better ground
for the belief even than his own immediate observation
would have been, for though Mr. Riley had received a
tincture of the classics at the great Mudport Free School,
and had a sense of understanding Latin generally, his comprehension of any particular Latin was not ready. Doubtless there remained a subtle aroma from his juvenile
contact with the *De Senectute* and the Fourth Book of
the *Æneid*, but it had ceased to be distinctly recognisable
as classical, and was only perceived in the higher finish
and force of his auctioneering style. Then Stelling was an
Oxford man, and the Oxford men were always—no, no,
it was the Cambridge men who were always good mathe-
maticians. But a man who had had a university education
could teach anything he liked; especially a man like Stelling

who had made a speech at a Mudport dinner on a political
occasion, and had acquitted himself so well that it was
generally remarked this son-in-law of Timpson's was a
sharp fellow. It was to be expected of a Mudport man,
from the parish of St. Ursula, that he would not omit to
do a good turn to a son-in-law of Timpson's, for Timpson
was one of the most useful and influential men in the
parish, and had a good deal of business, which he knew
how to put into the right hands. Mr. Riley liked such
men, quite apart from any money which might be diverted,
through their good judgment, from less worthy pockets
into his own; and it would be a satisfaction to him to say
to Timpson on his return home, 'I've secured a good
pupil for your son-in-law.' Timpson had a large family
of daughters; Mr. Riley felt for him; besides, Louisa
Timpson's face, with its light curls, had been a familiar
object to him over the pew wainscot on a Sunday for
nearly fifteen years: it was natural her husband should
be a commendable tutor. Moreover, Mr. Riley knew of no
other schoolmaster whom he had any ground for recommending in preference: why, then, should he not recommend Stelling? His friend Tulliver had asked him for an
opinion: it is always chilling in friendly intercourse, to
say you have no opinion to give. And if you deliver an
opinion at all, it is mere stupidity not to do it with an
air of conviction and well-founded knowledge. You make
it your own in uttering it, and naturally get fond of it.
Thus, Mr. Riley, knowing no harm of Stelling to begin
with, and wishing him well, so far as he had any wishes at
all concerning him, had no sooner recommended him than
he began to think with admiration of a man recommended
on such high authority, and would soon have gathered so
warm interest on the subject, that if Mr. Tulliver had in
the end declined to send Tom to Stelling, Mr. Riley would
have thought his 'friend of the old school' a thoroughly
pig-headed fellow.

If you blame Mr. Riley very severely for giving a
recommendation on such slight grounds, I must say you
are rather hard upon him. Why should an auctioneer and

appraiser thirty years ago, who had as good as forgotten his free-school Latin, be expected to manifest a delicate scrupulosity which is not always exhibited by gentlemen of the learned professions, even in our present advanced stage of morality?

Besides, a man with the milk of human kindness in him can scarcely abstain from doing a good-natured action, and one cannot be good-natured all round. Nature herself occasionally quarters an inconvenient parasite on an animal towards whom she has otherwise no ill-will. What then? We admire her care for the parasite. If Mr. Riley had shrunk from giving a recommendation that was not based on valid evidence, he would not have helped Mr. Stelling to a paying pupil, and that would not have been so well for the reverend gentleman. Consider, too, that all the pleasant little dim ideas and complacencies— of standing well with Timpson, of dispensing advice when he was asked for it, of impressing his friend Tulliver with additional respect, of saying something, and saying it emphatically, with other inappreciably minute ingredients that went along with the warm hearth and the brandy-and-water to make up Mr. Riley's consciousness on this occasion—would have been a mere blank.

IV

TOM IS EXPECTED

It was a heavy disappointment to Maggie that she was not allowed to go with her father in the gig when he went to fetch Tom home from the academy; but the morning was too wet, Mrs. Tulliver said, for a little girl to go out in her best bonnet. Maggie took the opposite view very strongly, and it was a direct consequence of this difference of opinion that when her mother was in the act of brushing out the reluctant black crop, Maggie suddenly rushed from under her hands and dipped her head in a basin of water standing near—in the vindictive determination that there should be no more chance of curls that day.

'Maggie, Maggie,' exclaimed Mrs. Tulliver, sitting stout and helpless with the brushes on her lap, 'what is to become of you if you're so naughty? I'll tell your aunt Glegg and your aunt Pullet when they come next week, and they'll never love you any more. O dear, O dear! look at your clean pinafore, wet from top to bottom. Folks 'ull think it's a judgment on me as I've got such a child—they'll think I've done summat wicked.'

Before this remonstrance was finished, Maggie was already out of hearing, making her way towards the great attic that ran under the old high-pitched roof, shaking the water from her black locks as she ran, like a Skye terrier escaped from his bath. This attic was Maggie's favourite retreat on a wet day, when the weather was not too cold; here she fretted out all her ill-humours, and talked aloud to the worm-eaten floors and the worm-eaten shelves, and the dark rafters festooned with cobwebs; and here she kept a Fetish which she punished for all her misfortunes. This was the trunk of a large wooden doll, which once stared with the roundest of eyes above the reddest of cheeks; but was now entirely defaced by a long career of vicarious suffering. Three nails driven into the head commemorated as many crises in Maggie's nine years of earthly struggle; that luxury of vengeance having been suggested to her by the picture of Jael destroying Sisera in the old Bible. The last nail had been driven in with a fiercer stroke than usual, for the Fetish on that occasion represented aunt Glegg. But immediately afterwards Maggie had reflected that if she drove many nails in, she would not be so well able to fancy that the head was hurt when she knocked it against the wall, nor to comfort it, and make believe to poultice it, when her fury was abated; or even aunt Glegg would be pitiable when she had been hurt very much, and thoroughly humiliated, so as to beg her niece's pardon. Since then she had driven no more nails in, but had soothed herself by alternately grinding and beating the wooden head against the rough brick of the great chimneys that made two square pillars supporting the roof. That was what she did this morning on reaching the attic, sobbing all the while with a passion that expelled every other form of consciousness—even the memory of the grievance that had caused it. As at last the sobs were getting quieter, and the grinding less fierce, a sudden beam of sunshine, falling through the wire lattice across the worm-eaten shelves, made her throw away the Fetish and run to the window. The sun was really breaking out; the sound of the mill seemed cheerful again; the granary doors were open; and there was Yap, the queer white-and-brown terrier with one ear turned back trotting about and sniffing vaguely, as if he were in search of a companion. It was irresistible. Maggie tossed her hair back and ran down-stairs, seized her bonnet without putting it on, peeped, and then dashed along the passage lest she should encounter her mother, and was quickly out in the yard, whirling round like a Pythoness, and singing as she whirled, 'Yap, Yap, Tom's coming home!' while Yap danced and barked round her, as much as to say, if there was any noise wanted he was the dog for it.

'Hegh, hegh, Miss, you'll make yourself giddy, an tumble down i' the dirt,' said Luke, the head miller, a tall broad-shouldered man of forty, black-eyed and black-haired, subdued by a general mealiness, like an auricula.

Maggie paused in her whirling and said, staggering a little, 'O no, it doesn't make me giddy, Luke; may I go into the mill with you?'

Maggie loved to linger in the great spaces of the mill, and often came out with her black hair powdered to a soft whiteness that made her dark eyes flash out with new fire. The resolute din, the unresting motion of the great stones, giving her a dim delicious awe as at the presence of an uncontrollable force—the meal for ever pouring, pouring—the fine white powder softening all surfaces, and making the very spider-nets look like a faery lace-work—the sweet pure scent of the meal—all helped to make Maggie feel that the mill was a little world apart from her outside everyday life. The spiders were especially a subject of speculation with her. She wondered if they had any relatives outside the mill, for in that case there must be a pair ful difficulty in their family intercourse—a fat and floury spider, accustomed to take his fly well dusted with meal, must suffer a little at a cousin's table where the fly was *au naturel*, and the lady-spiders must be mutually shocked at each other's appearance. But the part of the mill she liked best was the topmost story—the corn-hutch, where there were the great heaps of grain, which she could sit on and slide down continually. She was in the habit of taking this recreation as she conversed with Luke, to whom she was very communicative, wishing him to think well of her understanding, as her father did.

Perhaps she felt it necessary to recover her position with him on the present occasion, for, as she sat sliding on the heap of grain near which he was busying himself, she said, at that shrill pitch which was requisite in mill-society—

'I think you never read any book but the Bible—did you, Luke?'

'Nay, Miss—an' not much o' that,' said Luke, with great frankness. 'I'm no reader, I aren't.'

'But if I lent you one of my books, Luke? I've not got any *very* pretty books that would be easy for you to read; but there's "Pug's Tour of Europe"—that would tell you all about the different sorts of people in the world, and if you didn't understand the reading, the pictures would help you—they show the looks and ways of the people, and what they do. There are the Dutchmen, very fat, and smoking, you know—and one sitting on a barrel.'

'Nay, Miss, I'n no opinion o' Dutchmen. There ben't much good i' knowin' about *them*.'

'But they're our fellow-creatures, Luke—we ought to know about our fellow-creatures.'

'Not much o' fellow-creaturs, I think, Miss; all I know—my old master, as war a knowin' man, used to say, says he, "If e'er I sow my wheat wi'out brinin', I'm a Dutchman," says he; an' that war as much as to say as a Dutchman war a fool, or next door. Nay, nay, I aren't goin' to bother mysen about Dutchmen. There's fools enoo—an' rogues enoo—wi'out lookin' i' books for 'em.'

'O, well,' said Maggie, rather foiled by Luke's unexpectedly decided views about Dutchmen, 'perhaps you would like "Animated Nature" better—that's not Dutchmen, you know, but elephants, and kangaroos, and the civet cat, and the sun-fish, and a bird sitting on its tail—I forget its name. There are countries full of those creatures, instead of horses and cows, you know. Shouldn't you like to know about them, Luke?'

'Nay, Miss, I'n got to keep count o' the flour an' corn—I can't do wi' knowin' so many things besides my work. That's what brings folks to the gallows—knowin' everything but what they'n got to get their bread by. An' they're mostly lies, I think, what's printed i' the books: them printed sheets are, anyhow, as the men cry i' the streets.'

'Why, you're like my brother Tom, Luke,' said Maggie, wishing to turn the conversation agreeably; 'Tom's not fond of reading. I love Tom so dearly, Luke—better than anybody else in the world. When he grows up, I shall keep his house, and we shall always live together. I can tell him everything he doesn't know. But I think Tom's clever, for all he doesn't like books: he makes beautiful whipcord and rabbit-pens.'

'Ah,' said Luke, 'but he'll be fine an' vexed, as the rabbits are all dead.'

'Dead!' screamed Maggie, jumping up from her sliding seat on the corn. 'O dear, Luke! What! the lop-eared one, and the spotted doe that Tom spent all his money to buy?'

'As dead as moles,' said Luke, fetching his comparison from the unmistakable corpses nailed to the stable-wall.

'O dear, Luke,' said Maggie in a piteous tone, while the big tears rolled down her cheek; 'Tom told me to take care of 'em, and I forgot. What *shall* I do?'

'Well, you see, Miss, they were in that far tool-house, an' it was nobody's business to see to 'em. I reckon Master Tom told Harry to feed 'em, but there's no countin' on Harry—*he's* an offal creatur' as iver come about the primises, he is. He remembers nothing but his own inside—an' I wish it 'ud gripe him.'

'O, Luke, Tom told me to be sure and remember the rabbits every day; but how could I, when they didn't come into my head, you know? O, he will be so angry with me, I know he will, and so sorry about his rabbits—and so am I sorry. O, what *shall* I do?'

'Don't you fret, Miss,' said Luke soothingly, 'they're nash things, them lop-eared rabbits—they'd happen ha' died, if they'd been fed. Things out o' natur' niver thrive: God A'mighty doesn't like 'em. He made the rabbits' ears to lie back, an' it's nothin' but contrairiness to make 'em hing down like a mastiff dog's. Master Tom 'ull know better nor buy such things another time. Don't you fret, Miss. Will you come along home wi' me, and see my wife? I'm a-goin' this minute.'

The invitation offered an agreeable distraction to Maggie's grief, and her tears gradually subsided as she trotted along by Luke's side to his pleasant cottage, which stood with its apple and pear trees, and with the added dignity of a lean-to pig-sty, at the other end of the Mill fields. Mrs. Moggs, Luke's wife, was a decidedly agreeable acquaintance. She exhibited her hospitality in bread and treacle, and possessed various works of art. Maggie actually forgot that she had any special cause of sadness this morning, as she stood on a chair to look at a remarkable series of pictures representing the Prodigal Son in the costume of Sir Charles Grandison, except that, as might have been expected from his defective moral character, he had not, like that accomplished hero, the taste and strength of mind to dispense with a wig. But the indefinable weight the dead rabbits had left on her mind caused her to feel more than usual pity for the career of this weak young man, particularly when she looked at the picture where he leaned against a tree with a flaccid appearance, his knee-breeches unbuttoned, and his wig awry, while the swine, apparently of some foreign breed, seemed to insult him by their good spirits over their feast of husks.

'I'm very glad his father took him back again—aren't you, Luke?' she said. 'For he was very sorry, you know, and wouldn't do wrong again.'

'Eh, Miss,' said Luke, 'he'd be no great shakes, I doubt, let's feyther do what he would for him.'

That was a painful thought to Maggie, and she wished much that the subsequent history of the young man had not been left a blank.

V

TOM COMES HOME

TOM was to arrive early in the afternoon, and there was another fluttering heart besides Maggie's when it was late enough for the sound of the gig-wheels to be expected; for if Mrs. Tulliver had a strong feeling, it was fondness for her boy. At last the sound came—that quick, light bowling of the gig-wheels—and in spite of the wind, which was blowing the clouds about, and was not likely to respect Mrs. Tulliver's curls and cap-strings, she came outside the door, and even held her hand on Maggie's offending head, forgetting all the griefs of the morning.

'There he is, my sweet lad! But, Lord ha' mercy! he's got never a collar on; it's been lost on the road, I'll be bound, and spoilt the set.'

Mrs. Tulliver stood with her arms open; Maggie jumped first on one leg and then on the other; while Tom descended from the gig, and said, with masculine reticence as to the tender emotions, 'Hallo! Yap—what! are you there?'

Nevertheless he submitted to be kissed willingly enough, though Maggie hung on his neck in rather a straggling fashion, while his blue-grey eyes wandered towards the croft, and the lambs, and the river, where he promised himself that he would begin to fish the first thing to-morrow morning. He was one of those lads that grow everywhere in England, and, at twelve or thirteen years of age, look as much alike as goslings—a lad with light-brown hair, cheeks of cream and roses, full lips, indeterminate nose and eyebrows—a physiognomy in which it seems impossible to discern anything but the generic character of boyhood; as different as possible from poor Maggie's phiz, which Nature seemed to have moulded and coloured with the most decided intention. But that same Nature has the deep cunning which hides itself under the appearance of openness, so that simple people think they can see through her quite well, and all the while she is secretly preparing a refutation of their confident prophecies. Under these average boyish physiognomies that she seems to turn off by the gross, she conceals some of her most rigid, inflexible purposes, some of her most unmodifiable characters; and the dark-eyed, demonstrative, rebellious girl may after all turn out to be a passive being compared with this pink-and-white bit of masculinity with the indeterminate features.

'Maggie,' said Tom confidentially, taking her into a corner as soon as his mother was gone out to examine his box, and the warm parlour had taken off the chill he had felt from the long drive, 'you don't know what I've got in *my* pockets,' nodding his head up and down as a means of rousing her sense of mystery.

'No,' said Maggie. 'How stodgy they look, Tom! Is it marls (marbles) or cobnuts?' Maggie's heart sank a little, because Tom always said it was 'no good' playing with *her* at those games—she played so badly.

'Marls! no; I've swopped all my marls with the little fellows, and cobnuts are no fun, you silly, only when the nuts are green. But see here!' He drew something half out of his right-hand pocket.

'What is it?' said Maggie in a whisper. 'I can see nothing but a bit of yellow.'

'Why it's . . . a . . . new . . . guess, Maggie!'

'O, I *can't* guess, Tom,' said Maggie impatiently.

'Don't be a spitfire, else I won't tell you,' said Tom, thrusting his hand back into his pocket, and looking determined.

'No, Tom,' said Maggie imploringly, laying hold of the arm that was held stiffly in the pocket. 'I'm not cross, Tom; it was only because I can't bear guessing. *Please* be good to me.'

Tom's arm slowly relaxed, and he said, 'Well, then it's a new fish-line—two new uns—one for you, Maggie, all to yourself. I wouldn't go halves in the toffee and gingerbread on purpose to save the money; and Gibson and Spouncer fought with me because I wouldn't. And here's hooks; see here! . . . I say, *won't* we go and fish to-morrow down by the Round Pool? And you shall catch your own fish, Maggie, and put the worms on, and everything— won't it be fun?'

Maggie's answer was to throw her arms round Tom's neck and hug him, and hold her cheek against his without speaking, while he slowly unwound some of the line, saying, after a pause:

'Wasn't I a good brother, now, to buy you a line all to yourself? You know, I needn't have bought it if I hadn't liked.'

'Yes, very, very good . . . I *do* love you, Tom.'

Tom had put the line back in his pocket, and was looking at the hooks one by one, before he spoke again.

'And the fellows fought me, because I wouldn't give in about the toffee.'

'O dear! I wish they wouldn't fight at your school, Tom. Didn't it hurt you?'

'Hurt me? no,' said Tom, putting up the hooks again, taking out a large pocket-knife, and slowly opening the largest blade, which he looked at meditatively as he rubbed his finger along it. Then he added:

'I gave Spouncer a black eye, I know—that's what he got by wanting to leather *me*! I wasn't going to go halves because anybody leathered me.'

'O how brave you are, Tom! I think you're like Samson. If there came a lion roaring at me, I think you'd fight him —wouldn't you, Tom?'

'How can a lion come roaring at you, you silly thing? There's no lions, only in the shows.'

'No; but if we were in the lion countries—I mean in Africa, where it's very hot—the lions eat people there. I can show it you in the book where I read it.'

'Well, I should get a gun and shoot him.'

'But if you hadn't got a gun—we might have gone out, you know, not thinking—just as we go fishing; and then a great lion might run towards us roaring, and we couldn't get away from him. What should you do, Tom?'

Tom paused, and at last turned away contemptuously, saying, 'But the lion *isn't* coming. What's the use of talking?'

'But I like to fancy how it would be,' said Maggie, following him. 'Just think what you would do, Tom.'

'O don't bother, Maggie! you're such a silly—I shall go and see my rabbits.'

Maggie's heart began to flutter with fear. She dared not tell the sad truth at once, but she walked after Tom in trembling silence as he went out, thinking how she could tell him the news so as to soften at once his sorrow and his anger; for Maggie dreaded Tom's anger of all things—it was quite a different anger from her own.

'Tom,' she said timidly, when they were out of doors, 'how much money did you give for your rabbits?'

'Two half-crowns and a sixpence,' said Tom promptly.

'I think I've got a great deal more than that in my steel purse up-stairs. I'll ask mother to give it you.'

'What for?' said Tom. 'I don't want *your* money, you silly thing. I've got a great deal more money than you, because I'm a boy. I always have half-sovereigns and sovereigns for my Christmas boxes, because I shall be a man, and you only have five-shilling pieces, because you're only a girl.'

'Well, but, Tom—if mother would let me give you two half-crowns and a sixpence out of my purse to put into your pocket and spend, you know; and buy some more rabbits with it?'

'More rabbits? I don't want any more.'

'O, but, Tom, they're all dead.'

Tom stopped immediately in his walk and turned towards Maggie. 'You forgot to feed 'em, then, and Harry forgot?' he said, his colour heightening for a moment, but soon subsiding. 'I'll pitch into Harry—I'll have him turned away. And I don't love you, Maggie. You shan't go fishing with me to-morrow. I told you to go and see the rabbits every day.' He walked on again.

'Yes, but I forgot—and I couldn't help it, indeed, Tom. I'm so very sorry,' said Maggie, while the tears rushed fast.

'You're a naughty girl,' said Tom severely, 'and I'm sorry I bought you the fish-line. I don't love you.'

'O, Tom, it's very cruel,' sobbed Maggie. 'I'd forgive you, if *you* forgot anything—I wouldn't mind what you did—I'd forgive you and love you.'

'Yes, you're a silly—but I never *do* forget things—*I* don't.'

'O, please forgive me, Tom; my heart will break,' said Maggie, shaking with sobs, clinging to Tom's arm, and laying her wet cheek on his shoulder.

Tom shook her off, and stopped again, saying in a peremptory tone, 'Now, Maggie, you just listen. Aren't I a good brother to you?'

'Ye-ye-es,' sobbed Maggie, her chin rising and falling convulsedly.

'Didn't I think about your fish-line all this quarter, and mean to buy it, and saved my money o' purpose, and wouldn't go halves in the toffee, and Spouncer fought me because I wouldn't?'

'Ye-ye-es . . . and I . . . lo-lo-love you so, Tom.'

'But you're a naughty girl. Last holidays you licked the paint off my lozenge box, and the holidays before that you let the boat drag my fish-line down when I'd set you to watch it, and you pushed your head through my kite, all for nothing.'

'But I didn't mean,' said Maggie; 'I couldn't help it.'

'Yes, you could,' said Tom, 'if you'd minded what you were doing. And you're a naughty girl, and you shan't go fishing with me to-morrow.'

With this terrible conclusion, Tom ran away from Maggie towards the mill, meaning to greet Luke there, and complain to him of Harry.

Maggie stood motionless, except from her sobs, for a minute or two; then she turned round and ran into the house, and up to her attic, where she sat on the floor, and laid her head against the worm-eaten shelf, with a crushing sense of misery. Tom was come home, and she had thought how happy she should be—and now he was cruel to her. What use was anything, if Tom didn't love her? O, he was very cruel! Hadn't she wanted to give him the money, and said how very sorry she was? She knew she was naughty to her mother, but she had never been naughty to Tom—had never *meant* to be naughty to him.

'O, he is cruel!' Maggie sobbed aloud, finding a wretched pleasure in the hollow resonance that came through the long empty space of the attic. She never thought of beating or grinding her Fetish; she was too miserable to be angry.

These bitter sorrows of childhood! when sorrow is all new and strange, when hope has not yet got wings to fly beyond the days and weeks, and the space from summer to summer seems measureless.

Maggie soon thought she had been hours in the attic, and it must be tea-time, and they were all having their tea, and not thinking of her. Well, then, she would stay up there and starve herself—hide herself behind the tub, and stay there all night; and then they would all be frightened, and Tom would be sorry. Thus Maggie thought in the pride of her heart, as she crept behind the tub; but presently she began to cry again at the idea that they didn't mind her being there. If she went down again to Tom now—would he forgive her?—perhaps her father would be there, and he would take her part. But, then, she wanted Tom to forgive her because he loved her, not because his father told him. No, she would never go down if Tom didn't come to fetch her. This resolution lasted in great intensity for five dark minutes behind the tub; but then the need of being loved, the strongest need in poor Maggie's nature, began to wrestle with her pride, and soon threw it. She crept from behind her tub into the twilight of the long attic, but just then she heard a quick footstep on the stairs.

Tom had been too much interested in his talk with Luke, in going the round of the premises, walking in and out where he pleased, and whittling sticks without any particular reason, except that he didn't whittle sticks at school, to think of Maggie and the effect his anger had produced on her. He meant to punish her, and that business having been performed, he occupied himself with other matters, like a practical person. But when he had been called in to tea, his father said, 'Why, where's the little wench?' and Mrs. Tulliver, almost at the same moment, said, 'Where's your little sister?'—both of them having supposed that Maggie and Tom had been together all the afternoon.

'I don't know,' said Tom. He didn't want to 'tell' of Maggie, though he was angry with her, for Tom Tulliver was a lad of honour.

'What! hasn't she been playing with you all this while?' said the father. 'She's been thinking o' nothing but your coming home.'

'I haven't seen her this two hours,' says Tom, commencing on the plumcake.

'Goodness heart! she's got drownded,' exclaimed Mrs. Tulliver, rising from her seat and running to the window. 'How could you let her do so?' she added, as became a fearful woman, accusing she didn't know whom of she didn't know what.

'Nay, nay, she's none drownded,' said Mr. Tulliver. 'You've been naughty to her, I doubt, Tom?'

'I'm sure I haven't, father,' said Tom indignantly. 'I think she's in the house.'

'Perhaps up in that attic,' said Mrs. Tulliver, 'a-singing and talking to herself, and forgetting all about meal-times.'

'You go and fetch her down, Tom,' said Mr. Tulliver, rather sharply, his perspicacity or his fatherly fondness for Maggie making him suspect that the lad had been hard upon 'the little un,' else she would never have left his side. 'And be good to her, do you hear? Else I'll let you know better.'

Tom never disobeyed his father, for Mr. Tulliver was a peremptory man, and, as he said, would never let anybody get hold of his whip-hand; but he went out rather sullenly, carrying his piece of plumcake, and not intending to reprieve Maggie's punishment, which was no more than she

deserved. Tom was only thirteen, and had no decided
views in grammar and arithmetic, regarding them for the
most part as open questions, but he was particularly clear
and positive on one point—namely, that he would punish
everybody who deserved it: why, he wouldn't have minded
being punished himself, if he deserved it; but, then, he
never *did* deserve it.

It was Tom's step, then, that Maggie heard on the
stairs, when her need of love had triumphed over her pride,
and she was going down with her swollen eyes and dis-
hevelled hair to beg for pity. At least her father would
stroke her head and say, 'Never mind, my wench.' It is a
wonderful subduer, this need of love—this hunger of the
heart—as peremptory as that other hunger by which
Nature forces us to submit to the yoke, and change the
face of the world.

But she knew Tom's step, and her heart began to beat
violently with the sudden shock of hope. He only stood
still at the top of the stairs and said, 'Maggie, you're to
come down.' But she rushed to him and clung round his
neck, sobbing, 'O Tom, please forgive me—I can't bear it
—I will always be good—always remember things—do love
me—please, dear Tom!'

We learn to restrain ourselves as we get older. We keep
apart when we have quarrelled, express ourselves in well-
bred phrases, and in this way preserve a dignified alienation, showing much firmness on one side, and swallowing
much grief on the other. We no longer approximate in our
behaviour to the mere impulsiveness of the lower animals,
but conduct ourselves in every respect like members of a
highly-civilized society. Maggie and Tom were still very
much like young animals, and so she could rub her cheek
against his, and kiss his ear in a random, sobbing way;
and there were tender fibres in the lad that had been used
to answer Maggie's fondling; so that he behaved with a
weakness quite inconsistent with his resolution to punish
her as much as she deserved: he actually began to kiss her
in return, and say:

'Don't cry, then, Magsie—here, eat a bit o' cake.'

Maggie's sobs began to subside, and she put out her mouth for the cake and bit a piece: and then Tom bit a piece, just for company, and they ate together and rubbed each other's cheeks and brows and noses together, while they ate, with a humiliating resemblance to two friendly ponies.

'Come along, Magsie, and have tea,' said Tom at last, when there was no more cake except what was down-stairs.

So ended the sorrows of this day, and the next morning Maggie was trotting with her own fishing-rod in one hand and a handle of the basket in the other, stepping always, by a peculiar gift, in the muddiest places, and looking darkly radiant from under her beaver-bonnet because Tom was good to her. She had told Tom, however, that she should like him to put the worms on the hook for her, although she accepted his word when he assured her that worms couldn't feel (it was Tom's private opinion that it didn't much matter if they did). He knew all about worms, and fish, and those things; and what birds are mischievous, and how padlocks opened, and which way the handles of the gates were to be lifted. Maggie thought this sort of knowledge was very wonderful—much more difficult than remembering what was in the books; and she was rather in awe of Tom's superiority, for he was the only person who called her knowledge 'stuff,' and did not feel surprised at her cleverness. Tom, indeed, was of opinion that Maggie was a silly little thing; all girls were silly—they couldn't throw a stone so as to hit anything, couldn't do anything with a pocket-knife, and were frightened at frogs. Still he was very fond of his sister, and meant always to take care of her, make her his housekeeper, and punish her when she did wrong.

They were on their way to the Round Pool—that wonderful pool, which the floods had made a long while ago: no one knew how deep it was; and it was mysterious, too, that it should be almost a perfect round, framed in with willows and tall reeds, so that the water was only to be seen when you got close to the brink. The sight of the old favourite spot always heightened Tom's good-humour,

and he spoke to Maggie in the most amicable whispers, as
he opened the precious basket, and prepared their tackle.
He threw her line for her, and put the rod into her hand.
Maggie thought it probable that the small fish would come
to her hook, and the large ones to Tom's. But she had
forgotten all about the fish, and was looking dreamily at
the glassy water, when Tom said, in a loud whispering,
'Look, look, Maggie!' and came running to prevent her
from snatching her line away.

Maggie was frightened lest she had been doing something wrong, as usual, but presently Tom drew out her
line and brought a large tench bouncing on the grass.

Tom was excited.

'O Magsie! you little duck! Empty the basket!'

Maggie was not conscious of unusual merit, but it was
enough that Tom called her Magsie, and was pleased with
her. There was nothing to mar her delight in the whispers
and the dreamy silences, when she listened to the light
dipping sounds of the rising fish, and the gentle rustling,
as if the willows and the reeds and the water had their
happy whisperings also. Maggie thought it would make a
very nice heaven to sit by the pool in that way, and never
be scolded. She never knew she had a bite till Tom told
her; but she liked fishing very much.

It was one of their happy mornings. They trotted along
and sat down together, with no thought that life would
ever change much for them: they would only get bigger
and not go to school, and it would always be like the
holidays; they would always live together and be fond of
each other. And the mill with its booming—the great
chestnut-tree under which they played at houses—their
own little river, the Ripple, where the banks seemed like
home, and Tom was always seeing the water-rats, while
Maggie gathered the purple plumy tops of the reeds, which
she forgot and dropped afterwards—above all, the great
Floss, along which they wandered with a sense of travel,
to see the rushing spring-tide, the awful Eagre, come up
like a hungry monster, or to see the Great Ash which had
once wailed and groaned like a man—these things would

always be just the same to them. Tom thought people were at a disadvantage who lived on any other spot of the globe; and Maggie, when she read about Christiana passing 'the river over which there is no bridge,' always saw the Floss between the green pastures by the Great Ash.

Life did change for Tom and Maggie; and yet they were not wrong in believing that the thoughts and loves of these first years would always make part of their lives. We could never have loved the earth so well if we had had no childhood in it—if it were not the earth where the same flowers come up again every spring that we used to gather with our tiny fingers as we sat lisping to ourselves on the grass—the same hips and haws on the autumn hedgerows—the same redbreasts that we used to call 'God's birds,' because they did no harm to the precious crops. What novelty is worth that sweet monotony where everything is known, and *loved* because it is known?

The wood I walk in on this mild May day, with the young yellow-brown foliage of the oaks between me and the blue sky, the white star-flowers and the blue-eyed speedwell, and the ground ivy at my feet—what grove of tropic palms, what strange ferns or splendid broad-petalled blossoms, could ever thrill such deep and delicate fibres within me as this home-scene? These familiar flowers, these well-remembered bird-notes, this sky, with its fitful brightness, these furrowed and grassy fields, each with a sort of personality given to it by the capricious hedgerows—such things as these are the mother tongue of our imagination, the language that is laden with all the subtle inextricable associations the fleeting hours of our childhood left behind them. Our delight in the sunshine on the deep-bladed grass to-day, might be no more than the faint perception of wearied souls, if it were not for the sunshine and the grass in the far-off years which still live in us, and transform our perception into love.

VI

THE AUNTS AND UNCLES ARE COMING

IT was Easter week, and Mrs. Tulliver's cheese-cakes were more exquisitely light than usual: 'a puff o' wind 'ud make 'em blow about like feathers,' Kezia the housemaid said, feeling proud to live under a mistress who could make such pastry; so that no season or circumstances could have been more propitious for a family party, even if it had not been advisable to consult sister Glegg and sister Pullet about Tom's going to school.

'I'd as lief not invite sister Deane this time,' said Mrs. Tulliver, 'for she's as jealous and having as can be, and's allays trying to make the worst o' my poor children to their aunts and uncles.'

'Yes, yes,' said Mr. Tulliver, 'ask her to come. I never hardly get a bit o' talk with Deane now: we haven't had him this six months. What's it matter what she says?— my children need be beholding to nobody.'

'That's what you allays say, Mr. Tulliver; but I'm sure there's nobody o' your side, neither aunt nor uncle, to leave 'em so much as a five-pound note for a leggicy. And there's sister Glegg, and sister Pullet too, saving money unknown—for they put by all their own interest and butter-money too; their husbands buy 'em everything.' Mrs. Tulliver was a mild woman, but even a sheep will face about a little when she has lambs.

'Tchuh!' said Mr. Tulliver. 'It takes a big loaf when there's many to breakfast. What signifies your sisters' bits o' money when they've got half-a-dozen nevvies and nieces to divide it among? And your sister Deane won't get 'em to leave all to one, I reckon, and make the country cry shame on 'em when they are dead?'

'I don't know what she won't get 'em to do,' said Mrs. Tulliver, 'for my children are so awk'ard wi' their aunts and uncles. Maggie's ten times naughtier when they come than she is other days, and Tom doesn't like 'em, bless him—though it's more nat'ral in a boy than a gell. And there's Lucy Deane's such a good child—you may set her on a stool, and there she'll sit for an hour together, and never offer to get off. I can't help loving the child as if she was my own; and I'm sure she's more like *my* child than sister Deane's, for she'd allays a very poor colour for one of our family, sister Deane had.'

'Well, well, if you're fond o' the child, ask her father and mother to bring her with 'em. And won't you ask their aunt and uncle Moss too? and some o' *their* children?'

'O dear, Mr. Tulliver, why, there'd be eight people besides the children, and I must put two more leaves i' the table, besides reaching down more o' the dinner-service; and you know as well as I do as *my* sisters and *your* sister don't suit well together.'

'Well, well, do as you like, Bessy,' said Mr. Tulliver, taking up his hat and walking out to the mill. Few wives were more submissive than Mrs. Tulliver on all points unconnected with her family relations; but she had been a Miss Dodson, and the Dodsons were a very respectable family indeed—as much looked up to as any in their own parish, or the next to it. The Miss Dodsons had always been thought to hold up their heads very high, and no one was surprised the two eldest had married so well—not at an early age, for that was not the practice of the Dodson family. There were particular ways of doing everything in that family: particular ways of bleaching the linen, of making the cowslip wine, curing the hams, and keeping the bottled gooseberries; so that no daughter of that house could be indifferent to the privilege of having been born a Dodson, rather than a Gibson or a Watson. Funerals were always conducted with peculiar propriety in the Dodson family: the hat-bands were never of a blue shade, the gloves never split at the thumb, everybody was a mourner who ought to be, and there were always scarfs for the bearers. When one of the family was in trouble or sickness, all the rest went to visit the unfortunate member, usually at the same time, and did not shrink from uttering the most disagreeable truths that correct family feeling

dictated: if the illness or trouble was the sufferer's own
fault, it was not in the practice of the Dodson family to
shrink from saying so. In short, there was in this family
a peculiar tradition as to what was the right thing in
household management and social demeanour, and the
only bitter circumstance attending this superiority was a
painful inability to approve the condiments or the conduct of families ungoverned by the Dodson tradition. A
female Dodson, when in 'strange houses,' always ate dry
bread with her tea, and declined any sort of preserves,
having no confidence in the butter, and thinking that the
preserves had probably begun to ferment from want of due
sugar and boiling. There were some Dodsons less like the
family than others—that was admitted; but in so far as
they were 'kin,' they were of necessity better than those
who were 'no kin.' And it is remarkable that while no
individual Dodson was satisfied with any other individual
Dodson, each was satisfied, not only with him or her self,
but with the Dodsons collectively. The feeblest member of a
family—the one who has the least character—is often the
merest epitome of the family habits and traditions; and
Mrs. Tulliver was a thorough Dodson, though a mild one,
as small beer, so long as it is anything, is only describable
as very weak ale: and though she had groaned a little in
her youth under the yoke of her elder sisters, and still
shed occasional tears at their sisterly reproaches, it was
not in Mrs. Tulliver to be an innovator on the family ideas.
She was thankful to have been a Dodson, and to have one
child who took after her own family, at least in his features
and complexion, in liking salt and in eating beans, which
a Tulliver never did.

In other respects the true Dodson was partly latent in
Tom, and he was as far from appreciating his 'kin' on the
mother's side as Maggie herself; generally absconding for
the day with a large supply of the most portable food, when
he received timely warning that his aunts and uncles were
coming; a moral symptom from which his aunt Glegg
deduced the gloomiest views of his future. It was rather
hard on Maggie that Tom always absconded without letting

her into the secret, but the weaker sex are acknowledged to be serious *impedimenta* in cases of flight.

On Wednesday, the day before the aunts and uncles were coming, there were such various and suggestive scents, as of plumcakes in the oven and jellies in the hot state, mingled with the aroma of gravy, that it was impossible to feel altogether gloomy: there was hope in the air. Tom and Maggie made several inroads into the kitchen, and, like other marauders, were induced to keep aloof for a time only by being allowed to carry away a sufficient load of booty.

'Tom,' said Maggie, as they sat on the boughs of the elder-tree, eating their jam puffs, 'shall you run away to-morrow?'

'No,' said Tom slowly, when he had finished his puff, and was eyeing the third, which was to be divided between them—'No, I shan't.'

'Why, Tom? Because Lucy's coming?'

'No,' said Tom, opening his pocket-knife and holding it over the puff, with his head on one side in a dubitative manner. (It was a difficult problem to divide that very irregular polygon into two equal parts.) 'What do *I* care about Lucy? She's only a girl—*she* can't play at bandy.'

'Is it the tipsy-cake, then?' said Maggie, exerting her hypothetic powers, while she leaned forward towards Tom with her eyes fixed on the hovering knife.

'No, you silly, that'll be good the day after. It's the pudden. I know what the pudden's to be—apricot roll up—O my buttons!'

With this interjection, the knife descended on the puff and it was in two, but the result was not satisfactory to Tom, for he still eyed the halves doubtfully. At last he said:

'Shut your eyes, Maggie.'

'What for?'

'You never mind what for. Shut 'em, when I tell you.' Maggie obeyed.

'Now, which'll you have, Maggie—right hand or left?'

'I'll have that with the jam run out,' said Maggie, keeping her eyes shut to please Tom.

'Why, you don't like that, you silly. You may have it if
it comes to you fair, but I shan't give it you without.
Right or left—you choose, now. Ha-a-a!' said Tom, in a
tone of exasperation, as Maggie peeped. 'You keep your
eyes shut, now, else you shan't have any.'

Maggie's power of sacrifice did not extend so far; indeed,
I fear she cared less that Tom should enjoy the utmost
possible amount of puff, than that he should be pleased
with her for giving him the best bit. So she shut her eyes
quite close, till Tom told her to say which, and then she
said, 'Left-hand.'

'You've got it,' said Tom, in rather a bitter tone.

'What! the bit with the jam run out?'

'No; here, take it,' said Tom firmly, handing decidedly
the best piece to Maggie.

'O, please, Tom, have it: I don't mind—I like the other:
please take this.'

'No, I shan't,' said Tom, almost crossly, beginning on
his own inferior piece.

Maggie, thinking it was no use to contend further, began
too, and ate up her half puff with considerable relish as
well as rapidity. But Tom had finished first, and had to
look on while Maggie ate her last morsel or two, feeling
in himself a capacity for more. Maggie didn't know Tom
was looking at her; she was seesawing on the elder bough,
lost to almost everything but a vague sense of jam and
idleness.

'O, you greedy thing!' said Tom, when she had swallowed the last morsel. He was conscious of having acted
very fairly, and thought she ought to have considered this,
and made up to him for it. He would have refused a bit
of hers beforehand, but one is naturally at a different point
of view before and after one's own share of puff is
swallowed.

Maggie turned quite pale. 'O, Tom, why didn't you ask
me?'

'*I* wasn't going to ask you for a bit, you greedy. You
might have thought of it without, when you knew I gave
you the best bit.'

'But I wanted you to have it—you know I did,' said Maggie in an injured tone.

'Yes, but I wasn't going to do what wasn't fair, like Spouncer. He always takes the best bit, if you don't punch him for it ; and if you choose the best piece with your eyes shut, he changes his hands. But if I go halves, I'll go 'em fair—only I wouldn't be a greedy.'

With this cutting innuendo, Tom jumped down from his bough, and threw a stone with a 'hoigh!' as a friendly attention to Yap, who had also been looking on while the eatables vanished, with an agitation of his ears and feelings which could hardly have been without bitterness. Yet the excellent dog accepted Tom's attention with as much alacrity as if he had been treated quite generously.

But Maggie, gifted with that superior power of misery which distinguishes the human being and places him at a proud distance from the most melancholy chimpanzee, sat still on her bough, and gave herself up to the keen sense of unmerited reproach. She would have given the world not to have eaten all her puff, and to have saved some of it for Tom. Not but that the puff was very nice, for Maggie's palate was not at all obtuse, but she would have gone without it many times over, sooner than Tom should call her greedy and be cross with her. And he had said he wouldn't have it—and she ate it without thinking—how could she help it? The tears flowed so plentifully that Maggie saw nothing around her for the next ten minutes ; but by that time resentment began to give way to the desire of reconciliation, and she jumped from her bough to look for Tom. He was no longer in the paddock behind the rick-yard—where was he likely to be gone, and Yap with him? Maggie ran to the high bank against the great holly-tree, where she could see far away towards the Floss. There was Tom ; but her heart sank again as she saw how far off he was on his way to the great river, and that he had another companion besides Yap—naughty Bob Jakin, whose official, if not natural, function of frightening the birds, was just now at a standstill. Maggie felt sure that Bob was wicked, without very distinctly knowing why ;

unless it was because Bob's mother was a dreadfully large fat woman, who lived at a queer round house down the river; and once, when Maggie and Tom had wandered thither, there rushed out a brindled dog that wouldn't stop barking; and when Bob's mother came out after it, and screamed above the barking to tell them not to be frightened, Maggie thought she was scolding them fiercely, and her heart beat with terror. Maggie thought it very likely that the round house had snakes on the floor, and bats in the bedroom: for she had seen Bob take off his cap to show Tom a little snake that was inside it, and another time he had a handful of young bats: altogether, he was an irregular character, perhaps even slightly diabolical, judging from his intimacy with snakes and bats; and to crown all, when Tom had Bob for a companion, he didn't mind about Maggie, and would never let her go with him.

It must be owned that Tom was fond of Bob's company. How could it be otherwise? Bob knew, directly he saw a bird's egg, whether it was a swallow's, or a tomtit's, or a yellow-hammer's; he found out all the wasps' nests, and could set all sorts of traps; he could climb the trees like a squirrel, and had quite a magical power of detecting hedgehogs and stoats; and he had courage to do things that were rather naughty, such as making gaps in the hedgerows, throwing stones after the sheep, and killing a cat that was wandering *incognito*. Such qualities in an inferior, who could always be treated with authority in spite of his superior knowingness, had necessarily a fatal fascination for Tom; and every holiday-time Maggie was sure to have days of grief because he had gone off with Bob.

Well! there was no hope for it: he was gone now, and Maggie could think of no comfort but to sit down by the holly, or wander by the hedgerow, and fancy it was all different, refashioning her little world into just what she should like it to be.

Maggie's was a troublous life, and this was the form in which she took her opium.

Meanwhile Tom, forgetting all about Maggie and the sting of reproach which he had left in her heart, was hurrying along with Bob, whom he had met accidentally, to the scene of a great rat-catching in a neighbouring barn. Bob knew all about this particular affair, and spoke of the sport with an enthusiasm which no one who is not either divested of all manly feeling, or pitiably ignorant of rat-catching, can fail to imagine. For a person suspected of preternatural wickedness, Bob was really not so very villanous-looking; there was even something agreeable in his snub-nosed face, with its close-curled border of red hair. But then his trousers were always rolled up at the knee, for the convenience of wading on the slightest notice; and his virtue, supposing it to exist, was undeniably 'virtue in rags,' which, on the authority even of bilious philosophers, who think all well-dressed merit over-paid, is notoriously likely to remain unrecognised (perhaps because it is seen so seldom).

'I know the chap as owns the ferrets,' said Bob, in a hoarse treble voice, as he shuffled along, keeping his blue eyes fixed on the river, like an amphibious animal who foresaw occasion for darting in. 'He lives up the Kennel Yard at Sut Ogg's—he does. He's the biggest rot-catcher anywhere—he is. I'd sooner be a rot-catcher nor anything —I would. The moles is nothing to the rots. But Lors! you mun ha' ferrets. Dogs is no good. Why, there's that dog, now!' Bob continued, pointing with an air of disgust towards Yap, 'he's no more good wi' a rot nor nothin'. I see it myself—I did—at the rot-catchin' i' your feyther's barn.'

Yap, feeling the withering influence of this scorn, tucked his tail in and shrank close to Tom's leg, who felt a little hurt for him, but had not the superhuman courage to seem behindhand with Bob in contempt for a dog who made so poor a figure.

'No, no,' he said, 'Yap's no good at sport. I'll have regular good dogs for rats and everything, when I've done school.'

'Hev ferrets, Measter Tom,' said Bob eagerly, 'them

white ferrets wi' pink eyes; Lors, you might catch your own rots, an' you might put a rot in a cage wi' a ferret, an' see 'em fight—you might. That's what I'd do, I know, an' it 'ud be better fun a'most nor seein' two chaps fight—if it wasn't them chaps as sold cakes an' oranges at the Fair, as the things flew out o' their baskets, an' some o' the cakes was smashed. . . . But they tasted just as good,' added Bob, by way of note or addendum, after a moment's pause.

'But, I say, Bob,' said Tom, in a tone of deliberation, 'ferrets are nasty biting things—they'll bite a fellow without being set on.'

'Lors! why, that's the beauty on 'em. If a chap lays hold o' your ferret, he won't be long before he hollows out a good un—*he* won't.'

At this moment a striking incident made the boys pause suddenly in their walk. It was the plunging of some small body in the water from among the neighbouring bulrushes: if it was not a water-rat, Bob intimated that he was ready to undergo the most unpleasant consequences.

'Hoigh! Yap—hoigh! there he is,' said Tom, clapping his hands, as the little black snout made its arrowy course to the opposite bank. 'Seize him, lad, seize him!'

Yap agitated his ears and wrinkled his brows, but declined to plunge, trying whether barking would not answer the purpose just as well.

'Ugh! you coward!' said Tom, and kicked him over, feeling humiliated as a sportsman to possess so poor-spirited an animal. Bob abstained from remark and passed on, choosing, however, to walk in the shallow edge of the overflowing river by way of change.

'He's none so full now, the Floss isn't,' said Bob, as he kicked the water up before him, with an agreeable sense of being insolent to it. 'Why, last 'ear, the meadows was all one sheet o' water, they was.'

'Ay, but,' said Tom, whose mind was prone to see an opposition between statements that were really quite accordant—'but there was a big flood once, when the Round Pool was made. *I* know there was, 'cause father says so. And the sheep and cows were all drowned, and the boats went all over the fields ever such a way.'

'*I* don't care about a flood coming,' said Bob; 'I don't mind the water, no more nor the land. I'd swim—*I* would.'

'Ah, but if you got nothing to eat for ever so long?' said Tom, his imagination becoming quite active under the stimulus of that dread. 'When I'm a man, I shall make a boat with a wooden house on the top of it, like Noah's ark, and keep plenty to eat in it—rabbits and things—all ready. And then if the flood came, you know, Bob, I shouldn't mind. . . . And I'd take you in, if I saw you swimming,' he added, in a tone of a benevolent patron.

'I aren't frighted,' said Bob, to whom hunger did not appear so appalling. 'But I'd get in an' knock the rabbits on th' head when you wanted to eat 'em.'

'Ah, and I should have halfpence, and we'd play at heads-and-tails,' said Tom, not contemplating the possibility that this recreation might have fewer charms for his mature age. 'I'd divide fair to begin with, and then we'd see who'd win.'

'I've got a halfpenny o' my own,' said Bob proudly, coming out of the water and tossing his halfpenny in the air. 'Yeads or tails?'

'Tails,' said Tom, instantly fired with the desire to win.

'It's yeads,' said Bob hastily, snatching up the halfpenny as it fell.

'It wasn't,' said Tom loudly and peremptorily. 'You give me the halfpenny—I've won it fair.'

'I shan't,' said Bob, holding it tight in his pocket.

'Then I'll make you—see if I don't,' said Tom.

'You can't make me do nothing, you can't,' said Bob.

'Yes, I can.'

'No, you can't.'

'I'm master.'

'I don't care for you.'

'But I'll make you care, you cheat,' said Tom, collaring Bob and shaking him.

'You get out wi' you,' said Bob, giving Tom a kick.

Tom's blood was thoroughly up: he went at Bob with a

lunge and threw him down, but Bob seized hold and kept
it like a cat, and pulled Tom down after him. They
struggled fiercely on the ground for a moment or two, till
Tom, pinning Bob down by the shoulders, thought he had
the mastery.

'*You* say you'll give me the halfpenny now,' he said
with difficulty, while he exerted himself to keep the command of Bob's arms.

But at this moment, Yap, who had been running on
before, returned barking to the scene of action, and saw
a favourable opportunity for biting Bob's bare leg not
only with impunity but with honour. The pain from Yap's
teeth, instead of surprising Bob into a relaxation of his
hold, gave it a fiercer tenacity, and, with a new exertion of
his force, he pushed Tom backward and got uppermost.
But now Yap, who could get no sufficient purchase before,
set his teeth in a new place, so that Bob, harassed in this
way, let go his hold of Tom, and, almost throttling Yap,
flung him into the river. By this time Tom was up again,
and before Bob had quite recovered his balance after the
act of swinging Yap, Tom fell upon him, threw him down,
and got his knees firmly on Bob's chest.

'You give me the halfpenny now,' said Tom.

'Take it,' said Bob sulkily.

'No, I shan't take it; you give it me.'

Bob took the halfpenny out of his pocket, and threw it
away from him on the ground.

Tom loosed his hold, and left Bob to rise.

'There the halfpenny lies,' he said. 'I don't want your
halfpenny; I wouldn't have kept it. But you wanted to
cheat: I hate a cheat. I shan't go along with you any
more,' he added, turning round homeward, not without
casting a regret towards the rat-catching and other pleasures which he must relinquish along with Bob's society.

'You may let it alone, then,' Bob called out after him.
'I shall cheat if I like; there's no fun i' playing else; and I
know where there's a goldfinch's nest, but I'll take care
you don't. . . . An' you're a nasty fightin' turkey-cock,
you are. . . . .

Tom walked on without looking round, and Yap followed his example, the cold bath having moderated his passions.

'Go along wi' you, then, wi' your drownded dog; I wouldn't own such a dog—*I* wouldn't,' said Bob, getting louder, in a last effort to sustain his defiance. But Tom was not to be provoked into turning round, and Bob's voice began to falter a little as he said:

'An' I'n gi'en you everything, an' showed you everything, an' niver wanted nothin' from you. . . . An' there's your horn-handed knife, then, as you gi'en me. . . .' Here Bob flung the knife as far as he could after Tom's retreating footsteps. But it produced no effect, except the sense in Bob's mind that there was a terrible void in his lot, now that knife was gone.

He stood still till Tom had passed through the gate and disappeared behind the hedge. The knife would do no good on the ground there—it wouldn't vex Tom, and pride or resentment was a feeble passion in Bob's mind compared with the love of a pocket-knife. His very fingers sent entreating thrills that he would go and clutch that familiar rough buck's-horn handle, which they had so often grasped for mere affection as it lay idle in his pocket. And there were two blades, and they had just been sharpened! What is life without a pocket-knife to him who has once tasted a higher existence? No: to throw the handle after the hatchet is a comprehensible act of desperation, but to throw one's pocket-knife after an implacable friend is clearly in every sense a hyperbole, or throwing beyond the mark. So Bob shuffled back to the spot where the beloved knife lay in the dirt, and felt quite a new pleasure in clutching it again after the temporary separation, in opening one blade after the other, and feeling their edge with his well-hardened thumb. Poor Bob! he was not sensitive on the point of honour—not a chivalrous character. That fine moral aroma would not have been thought much of by the public opinion of Kennel Yard, which was the very focus or heart of Bob's world, even if it could have made itself perceptible there; yet, for all that, he was not utterly a sneak and a thief, as our friend Tom had hastily decided.

But Tom, you perceive, was rather a Rhadamanthine personage, having more than the usual share of boy's justice in him—the justice that desires to hurt culprits as much as they deserve to be hurt, and is troubled with no doubts concerning the exact amount of their deserts. Maggie saw a cloud on his brow when he came home, which checked her joy at his coming so much sooner than she had expected, and she dared hardly speak to him as he stood silently throwing the small gravel-stones into the mill-dam. It is not pleasant to give up a rat-catching when you have set your mind on it. But if Tom had told his strongest feeling at that moment, he would have said, 'I'd do just the same again.' That was his usual mode of viewing his past actions; whereas Maggie was always wishing she had done something different.

VII

ENTER THE AUNTS AND UNCLES

THE Dodsons were certainly a handsome family, and Mrs. Glegg was not the least handsome of the sisters. As she sat in Mrs. Tulliver's arm-chair, no impartial observer could have denied that for a woman of fifty she had a very comely face and figure, though Tom and Maggie considered their aunt Glegg as the type of ugliness. It is true she despised the advantages of costume, for though, as she often observed, no woman had better clothes, it was not her way to wear her new things out before her old ones. Other women, if they liked, might have their best thread-lace in every wash; but when Mrs. Glegg died, it would be found that she had better lace laid by in the right-hand drawer of her wardrobe, in the Spotted Chamber, than ever Mrs. Wooll of St. Ogg's had bought in her life, although Mrs. Wooll wore her lace before it was paid for. So of her curled fronts: Mrs. Glegg had doubtless the glossiest and crispest brown curls in her drawers, as well as curls in various degrees of fuzzy laxness; but to look out on the week-day world from under a crisp and glossy front, would be to introduce a most dreamlike and unpleasant confusion between the sacred and the secular. Occasionally, indeed, Mrs. Glegg wore one of her third-best fronts on a week-day visit, but not at a sister's house; especially not at Mrs. Tulliver's, who, since her marriage, had hurt her sisters' feelings greatly by wearing her own hair, though, as Mrs. Glegg observed to Mrs. Deane, a mother of a family, like Bessy, with a husband always going to law, might have been expected to know better. But Bessy was always weak!

So if Mrs. Glegg's front to-day was more fuzzy and lax than usual, she had a design under it: she intended the most pointed and cutting allusion to Mrs. Tulliver's bunches of blond curls, separated from each other by a due wave of smoothness on each side of the parting. Mrs. Tulliver had shed tears several times at sister Glegg's unkindness on the subject of these unmatronly curls, but the consciousness of looking the handsomer for them, naturally administered support. Mrs. Glegg chose to wear her bonnet in the house to-day—untied and tilted slightly, of course—a frequent practice of hers when she was on a visit, and happened to be in a severe humour: she didn't know what draughts there might be in strange houses. For the same reason she wore a small sable tippet, which reached just to her shoulders, and was very far from meeting across her well-formed chest, while her long neck was protected by a *chevaux-de-frise* of miscellaneous frilling. One would need to be learned in the fashions of those times to know how far in the rear of them Mrs. Glegg's slate-coloured silk-gown must have been; but from certain constellations of small yellow spots upon it, and a mouldy odour about it suggestive of a damp clothes-chest, it was probable that it belonged to a stratum of garments just old enough to have come recently into wear.

Mrs. Glegg held her large gold watch in her hand with the many-doubled chain round her fingers, and observed to Mrs. Tulliver, who had just returned from a visit to the kitchen, that whatever it might be by other people's clocks and watches, it was gone half-past twelve by hers.

'I don't know what ails sister Pullet,' she continued. 'It used to be the way in our family for one to be as early as another—I'm sure it was so in my poor father's time—and not for one sister to sit half an hour before the others came. But if the ways o' the family are altered, it shan't be *my* fault—*I'll* never be the one to come into a house when all the rest are going away. I wonder *at* sister Deane—she used to be more like me. But if you'll take my advice, Bessy, you'll put the dinner forrard a bit, sooner than put it back, because folks are late as ought to ha' known better.'

'O dear, there's no fear but what they'll be all here in time, sister,' said Mrs. Tulliver, in her mild-peevish tone. 'The dinner won't be ready till half-past one. But if it's long for you to wait, let me fetch you a cheese-cake and a glass o' wine.'

'Well, Bessy!' said Mrs. Glegg, with a bitter smile, and a scarcely perceptible toss of her head, 'I should ha' thought you'd known your own sister better. I never *did* eat between meals, and I'm not going to begin. Not but what I hate that nonsense of having your dinner at half-past one, when you might have it at one. You was never brought up in that way, Bessy.'

'Why, Jane, what can I do? Mr. Tulliver doesn't like his dinner before two o'clock, but I put it half an hour earlier because o' you.'

'Yes, yes, I know how it is with husbands—they're for putting everything off—they'll put the dinner off till after tea, if they've got wives as are weak enough to give in to such work; but it's a pity for you, Bessy, as you haven't got more strength o' mind. It'll be well if your children don't suffer for it. And I hope you've not gone and got a dinner for us—going to expense for your sisters, as 'ud sooner eat a crust o' dry bread nor help to ruin you with extravagance. I wonder you don't take pattern by your sister Deane—she's far more sensible. And here you've got two children to provide for, and your husband's spent your fortin' i' going to law, and's likely to spend his own too. A boiled joint, as you could make broth of for the kitchen,' Mrs. Glegg added, in a tone of emphatic protest, 'and a plain pudding, with a spoonful o' sugar, and no spice, 'ud be far more becoming.'

With sister Glegg in this humour, there was a cheerful prospect for the day. Mrs. Tulliver never went the length of quarrelling with her, any more than a waterfowl that puts out its leg in a deprecating manner can be said to quarrel with a boy who throws stones. But this point of the dinner was a tender one, and not at all new, so that Mrs. Tulliver could make the same answer she had often made before.

'Mr. Tulliver says he always *will* have a good dinner for his friends while he can pay for it,' she said, 'and he's a right to do as he likes in his own house, sister.'

'Well, Bessie, *I* can't leave your children enough out o' my savings to keep 'em from ruin. And you mustn't look to having any o' Mr. Glegg's money, for it's well if I don't go first—he comes of a long-lived family; and if he was to die and leave me well for my life, he'd tie all the money up to go back to his own kin.'

The sound of wheels while Mrs. Glegg was speaking was an interruption highly welcome to Mrs. Tulliver, who hastened out to receive sister Pullet—it must be sister Pullet, because the sound was that of a four-wheel.

Mrs. Glegg tossed her head and looked rather sour about the mouth at the thought of the 'four-wheel.' She had a strong opinion on that subject.

Sister Pullet was in tears when the one-horse chaise stopped before Mrs. Tulliver's door, and it was apparently requisite that she should shed a few more before getting out, for though her husband and Mrs. Tulliver stood ready to support her, she sat still and shook her head sadly, as she looked through her tears at the vague distance.

'Why, whatever is the matter, sister?' said Mrs. Tulliver. She was not an imaginative woman, but it occurred to her that the large toilet glass in sister Pullet's best bedroom was possibly broken for the second time.

There was no reply but a further shake of the head, as Mrs. Pullet slowly rose and got down from the chaise, not without casting a glance at Mr. Pullet to see that he was guarding her handsome silk dress from injury. Mr. Pullet was a small man with a high nose, small twinkling eyes, and thin lips, in a fresh-looking suit of black and a white cravat, that seemed to have been tied very tight on some higher principle than that of mere personal ease. He bore about the same relation to his tall, good-looking wife, with her balloon sleeves, abundant mantle, and large be-feathered and be-ribboned bonnet, as a small fishing-smack bears to a brig with all its sails spread.

It is a pathetic sight and a striking example of the complexity introduced into the emotions by a high state of civilization—the sight of a fashionably drest female in grief. From the sorrow of a Hottentot to that of a woman in large buckram sleeves, with several bracelets on each arm, an architectural bonnet, and delicate ribbon strings—what a long series of gradations! In the enlightened child of civilization the abandonment characteristic of grief is checked and varied in the subtlest manner, so as to present an interesting problem to the analytic mind. If, with a crushed heart, and eyes half-blinded by the mist of tears, she were to walk with a too devious step through a door-place, she might crush her buckram sleeves too, and the deep consciousness of this possibility produces a composition of forces by which she takes a line that just clears the doorpost. Perceiving that the tears are hurrying fast, she unpins her strings and throws them languidly backward—a touching gesture, indicative, even in the deepest gloom, of the hope in future dry moments when cap-strings will once more have a charm. As the tears subside a little, and with her head leaning backward at the angle that will not injure her bonnet, she endures that terrible moment when grief, which has made all things else a weariness, has itself become weary; she looks down pensively at her bracelets, and adjusts their clasps with that pretty studied fortuity which would be gratifying to her mind if it were once more in a calm and healthy state.

Mrs. Pullet brushed each doorpost with great nicety, about the latitude of her shoulders (at that period a woman was truly ridiculous to an instructed eye if she did not measure a yard and a half across the shoulders), and having done that, sent the muscles of her face in quest of fresh tears as she advanced into the parlour where Mrs. Glegg was seated.

'Well, sister, you're late; what's the matter?' said Mrs. Glegg rather sharply, as they shook hands.

Mrs. Pullet sat down—lifting up her mantle carefully behind, before she answered:

'She's gone,' unconsciously using an impressive figure of rhetoric.

'It isn't the glass this time, then,' thought Mrs. Tulliver.

'Died the day before yesterday,' continued Mrs. Pullet; 'an' her legs was as thick as my body,' she added with deep sadness, after a pause. 'They'd tapped her no end o' times, and the water—they say you might ha' swum in it, if you'd liked.'

'Well, Sophy, it's a mercy she's gone, then, whoever she may be,' said Mrs. Glegg, with the promptitude and emphasis of a mind naturally clear and decided; 'but I can't think who you're talking of, for my part.'

'But *I* know,' said Mrs. Pullet, sighing and shaking her head; 'and there isn't another such a dropsy in the parish. *I* know as it's old Mrs. Sutton o' the Twenty-lands.'

'Well, she's no kin o' yours, nor much acquaintance as I've ever heared of,' said Mrs. Glegg, who always cried just as much as was proper when anything happened to her own 'kin,' but not on other occasions.

'She's so much acquaintance as I've seen her legs when they was like bladders. . . . And an old lady as had doubled her money over and over again, and kept it all in her own management to the last, and had her pocket with her keys in under her pillow constant. There isn't many old *pa*rish'ners like her, I doubt.'

'And they say she'd took as much physic as 'ud fill a waggon,' observed Mr. Pullet.

'Ah,' sighed Mrs. Pullet, 'she'd another complaint ever so many years before she had the dropsy, and the doctors couldn't make out what it was. And she said to me, when

I went to see her last Christmas, she said, "Mrs. Pullet, if ever you have the dropsy, you'll think o' me." She *did* say so,' added Mrs. Pullet, beginning to cry bitterly again; 'those were her very words. And she's to be buried o' Saturday, and Pullet's bid to the funeral.'

'Sophy,' said Mrs. Glegg, unable any longer to contain her spirit of rational remonstrance—'Sophy, I wonder *at* you, fretting and injuring your health about people as don't belong to you. Your poor father never did so, nor your aunt Frances neither, nor any o' the family as I ever heared of. You couldn't fret no more than this, if we'd heared as our cousin Abbot had died sudden without making his will.'

Mrs. Pullet was silent, having to finish her crying, and rather flattered than indignant at being upbraided for crying too much. It was not everybody who could afford to cry so much about their neighbours who had left them nothing; but Mrs. Pullet had married a gentleman farmer, and had leisure and money to carry her crying and everything else to the highest pitch of respectability.

'Mrs. Sutton didn't die without making her will, though,' said Mr. Pullet, with a confused sense that he was saying something to sanction his wife's tears; 'ours is a rich parish, but they say there's nobody else to leave as many thousands behind 'em as Mrs. Sutton. And she's left no legacies, to speak on—left it all in a lump to her husband's nevvy.'

'There wasn't much good i' being so rich, then,' said Mrs. Glegg, 'if she'd got none but husband's kin to leave it to. It's poor work when that's all you've got to pinch yourself for;—not as I'm one o' those as 'ud like to die without leaving more money out at interest than other folks had reckoned. But it's a poor tale when it must go out o' your own family.'

'I'm sure, sister,' said Mrs. Pullet, who had recovered sufficiently to take off her veil and fold it carefully, 'it's a nice sort o' man as Mrs. Sutton has left her money to, for he's troubled with the asthmy, and goes to bed every night at eight o'clock. He told me about it himself—as free as could be—one Sunday when he came to our church.

He wears a hare-skin on his chest, and has a trembling in his talk—quite a gentleman sort o' man. I told him there wasn't many months in the year as I wasn't under the doctor's hands. And he said, "Mrs. Pullet, I can feel for you." That was what he said—the very words. Ah!' sighed Mrs. Pullet, shaking her head at the idea that there were but few who could enter fully into her experiences in pink mixture and white mixture, strong stuff in small bottles, and weak stuff in large bottles, damp boluses at a shilling, and draughts at eighteenpence. 'Sister, I may as well go and take my bonnet off now. Did you see as the cap-box was put out?' she added, turning to her husband.

Mr. Pullet, by an unaccountable lapse of memory, had forgotten it, and hastened out, with a stricken conscience, to remedy the omission.

'They'll bring it up-stairs, sister,' said Mrs. Tulliver, wishing to go at once, lest Mrs. Glegg should begin to explain her feelings about Sophy's being the first Dodson who ever ruined her constitution with doctor's stuff.

Mrs. Tulliver was fond of going up-stairs with her sister Pullet, and looking thoroughly at her cap before she put it on her head, and discussing millinery in general. This was part of Bessy's weakness, that stirred Mrs. Glegg's sisterly compassion: Bessy went far too well drest, considering; and she was too proud to dress her child in the good clothing her sister Glegg gave her from the primeval strata of her wardrobe; it was a sin and a shame to buy anything to dress that child, if it wasn't a pair of shoes. In this particular, however, Mrs. Glegg did her sister Bessy some injustice, for Mrs. Tulliver had really made great efforts to induce Maggie to wear a leghorn bonnet and a dyed silk frock made out of her aunt Glegg's, but the results had been such that Mrs. Tulliver was obliged to bury them in her maternal bosom; for Maggie, declaring that the frock smelt of nasty dye, had taken an opportunity of basting it together with the roast-beef the first Sunday she wore it, and finding this scheme answer, she had subsequently pumped on the bonnet with its green ribbons, so as to give it a general resemblance to a sage cheese garnished with withered lettuces. I must urge in excuse for Maggie, that Tom had laughed at her in the bonnet, and said she looked like an old Judy. Aunt Pullet, too, made presents of clothes, but these were always pretty enough to please Maggie as well as her mother. Of all her sisters, Mrs. Tulliver certainly preferred her sister Pullet, not without a return of preference; but Mrs. Pullet was sorry Bessy had those naughty awkward children; she would do the best she could by them, but it was a pity they weren't as good and as pretty as sister Deane's child. Maggie and Tom, on their part, thought their aunt Pullet tolerable, chiefly because she was not their aunt Glegg. Tom always declined to go more than once, during his holidays, to see either of them: both his uncles tipped him that once, of course; but at his aunt Pullet's there were a great many toads to pelt in the cellar-area, so that he preferred the visit to her. Maggie shuddered at the toads, and dreamed of them horribly, but she liked her uncle Pullet's musical snuff-box. Still, it was agreed by the sisters, in Mrs. Tulliver's absence, that the Tulliver blood did not mix well with the Dodson blood; that, in fact, poor Bessy's children were Tullivers, and that Tom, notwithstanding he had the Dodson complexion, was likely to be as 'contrairy' as his father. As for Maggie, she was the picture of her aunt Moss, Mr. Tulliver's sister, —a large-boned woman, who had married as poorly as could be; had no china, and had a husband who had much ado to pay his rent. But when Mrs. Pullet was alone with Mrs. Tulliver up-stairs the remarks were naturally to the disadvantage of Mrs. Glegg, and they agreed, in confidence, that there was no knowing what sort of fright sister Jane would come out next. But their *tête-à-tête* was curtailed by the appearance of Mrs. Deane with little Lucy; and Mrs. Tulliver had to look on with a silent pang while Lucy's blond curls were adjusted. It was quite unaccountable that Mrs. Deane, the thinnest and sallowest of all the Miss Dodsons, should have had this child, who might have been taken for Mrs. Tulliver's any day. And Maggie always looked twice as dark as usual when she was by the side of Lucy.

She did to-day, when she and Tom came in from th
garden with their father and their uncle Glegg. Maggi
had thrown her bonnet off very carelessly, and, coming in
with her hair rough as well as out of curl, rushed at once t
Lucy, who was standing by her mother's knee. Certainly
the contrast between the cousins was conspicuous, and, t
superficial eyes, was very much to the disadvantage o
Maggie, though a connoisseur might have seen 'points' i
her which had a higher promise for maturity than Lucy'
natty completeness. It was like the contrast between
rough, dark, overgrown puppy and a white kitten. Luc
put up the neatest little rosebud mouth to be kissed: every
thing about her was neat—her little round neck, with th
row of coral beads; her little straight nose, not at a
snubby; her little clear eyebrows, rather darker than he
curls, to match her hazel eyes, which looked up with sh
pleasure at Maggie, taller by the head, though scarcely
year older. Maggie always looked at Lucy with delight
She was fond of fancying a world where the people neve
got any larger than children of their own age, and she mad
the queen of it just like Lucy, with a little crown on he
head, and a little sceptre in her hand . . . only the quee
was Maggie herself in Lucy's form.

'O Lucy,' she burst out, after kissing her, 'you'll sta
with Tom and me, won't you? O kiss her, Tom.'

Tom, too, had come up to Lucy, but he was not going t
kiss her—no; he came up to her with Maggie, because i
seemed easier, on the whole, than saying, 'How do you do ?
to all those aunts and uncles: he stood looking at nothin
in particular, with the blushing, awkward air and sem
smile which are common to shy boys when in company—
very much as if they had come into the world by mistak
and found it in a degree of undress that was quite embarras
sing.

'Heyday!' said aunt Glegg, with loud emphasis. 'D
little boys and gells come into a room without takin
notice o' their uncles and aunts? That wasn't the wa
when *I* was a little gell.'

'Go and speak to your aunts and uncles, my dears,' sai

Mrs. Tulliver, looking anxious and melancholy. She wanted to whisper to Maggie a command to go and have her hair brushed.

'Well, and how do you do? And I hope you're good children, are you?' said aunt Glegg, in the same loud emphatic way, as she took their hands, hurting them with her large rings, and kissing their cheeks much against their desire. 'Look up, Tom, look up. Boys as go to boarding-schools should hold their heads up. Look at me now.' Tom declined that pleasure apparently, for he tried to draw his hand away. 'Put your hair behind your ears, Maggie, and keep your frock on your shoulder.'

Aunt Glegg always spoke to them in this loud emphatic way, as if she considered them deaf, or perhaps rather idiotic: it was a means, she thought, of making them feel that they were accountable creatures, and might be a salutary check on naughty tendencies. Bessy's children were so spoiled—they'd need have somebody to make them feel their duty.

'Well, my dears,' said aunt Pullet, in a compassionate voice, 'you grow wonderful fast. I doubt they'll outgrow their strength,' she added, looking over their heads with a melancholy expression, at their mother. 'I think the gell has too much hair. I'd have it thinned and cut shorter, sister, if I was you: it isn't good for her health. It's that as makes her skin so brown. I shouldn't wonder. Don't you think so, sister Deane?'

'I can't say, I'm sure, sister,' said Mrs. Deane, shutting her lips close again, and looking at Maggie with a critical eye.

'No, no,' said Mr. Tulliver, 'the child's healthy enough—there's nothing ails her. There's red wheat as well as white, for that matter, and some like the dark grain best. But it 'ud be as well if Bessy 'ud have the child's hair cut, so as it 'ud lie smooth.'

A dreadful resolve was gathering in Maggie's breast, but it was arrested by the desire to know from her aunt Deane whether she would leave Lucy behind: aunt Deane would hardly ever let Lucy come to see them. After various reasons for refusal, Mrs. Deane appealed to Lucy herself.

'You wouldn't like to stay behind without mother,
should you, Lucy?'

'Yes, please, mother,' said Lucy timidly, blushing very
pink all over her very little neck.

'Well done, Lucy! Let her stay, Mrs. Deane, let her stay,'
said Mr. Deane, a large but alert-looking man, with a type
of physique to be seen in all ranks of English society—bald
crown, red whiskers, full forehead, and general solidity
without heaviness. You may see noblemen like Mr. Deane,
and you may see grocers or day-labourers like him; but the
keenness of his brown eyes was less common than his
contour. He held a silver snuff-box very tightly in his hand,
and now and then exchanged a pinch with Mr. Tulliver,
whose box was only silver-mounted, so that it was naturally a joke between them that Mr. Tulliver wanted to exchange snuff-boxes also. Mr. Deane's box had been given
him by the superior partners in the firm to which he belonged, at the same time that they gave him a share in the
business, in acknowledgment of his valuable services as
manager. No man was thought more highly of in St. Ogg's
than Mr. Deane, and some persons were even of opinion
that Miss Susan Dodson, who was once held to have made
the worst marriage of all the Dodson sisters, might one day
ride in a better carriage, and live in a better house, even
than her sister Pullet. There was no knowing where a man
would stop, who had got his foot into a great mill-owning,
ship-owning business like that of Guest and Co., with a
banking concern attached. And Mrs. Deane, as her intimate
female friends observed, was proud and 'having' enough:
she wouldn't let her husband stand still in the world for
want of spurring.

'Maggie,' said Mrs. Tulliver, beckoning Maggie to her,
and whispering in her ear, as soon as this point of Lucy's
staying was settled, 'go and get your hair brushed—do, for
shame. I told you not to come in without going to Martha
first; you know I did.'

'Tom, come out with me,' whispered Maggie, pulling his
sleeve as she passed him; and Tom followed willingly enough.

'Come up-stairs with me, Tom,' she whispered, when

they were outside the door. 'There's something I want to do before dinner.'

'There's no time to play at anything before dinner,' said Tom, whose imagination was impatient of any intermediate prospect.

'O, yes, there is time for this—*do* come, Tom.'

Tom followed Maggie upstairs into her mother's room, and saw her go at once to a drawer, from which she took out a large pair of scissors.

'What are they for, Maggie?' said Tom, feeling his curiosity awakened.

Maggie answered by seizing her front locks and cutting them straight across the middle of her forehead.

'O, my buttons, Maggie, you'll catch it!' exclaimed Tom; 'you'd better not cut any more off.'

Snip! went the great scissors again while Tom was speaking; and he couldn't help feeling it was rather good fun: Maggie would look so queer.

'Here, Tom, cut it behind for me,' said Maggie, excited by her own daring, and anxious to finish the deed.

'You'll catch it, you know,' said Tom, nodding his head in an admonitory manner, and hesitating a little as he took the scissors.

'Never mind—make haste!' said Maggie, giving a little stamp with her foot. Her cheeks were quite flushed.

The black locks were so thick—nothing could be more tempting to a lad who had already tasted the forbidden pleasure of cutting the pony's mane. I speak to those who know the satisfaction of making a pair of shears meet through a duly resisting mass of hair. One delicious grinding snip, and then another and another, and the hinderlocks fell heavily on the floor, and Maggie stood cropped in a jagged, uneven manner, but with a sense of clearness and freedom, as if she had emerged from a wood into the open plain.

'O, Maggie,' said Tom, jumping round her, and slapping his knees as he laughed, 'O, my buttons, what a queer thing you look! Look at yourself in the glass—you look like the idiot we throw our nut-shells to at school.'

Maggie felt an unexpected pang. She had thought beforehand chiefly of her own deliverance from her teasing hair and teasing remarks about it, and something also of the triumph she should have over her mother and her aunts by this very decided course of action: she didn't want her hair to look pretty—that was out of the question —she only wanted people to think her a clever little girl, and not to find fault with her. But now, when Tom began to laugh at her, and say she was like the idiot, the affair had quite a new aspect. She looked in the glass, and still Tom laughed and clapped his hands, and Maggie's flushed cheeks began to pale, and her lips to tremble a little.

'O Maggie, you'll have to go down to dinner directly,' said Tom. 'O my!'

'Don't laugh at me, Tom,' said Maggie, in a passionate tone, with an outburst of angry tears, stamping, and giving him a push.

'Now, then, spitfire!' said Tom. 'What did you cut it off for, then? I shall go down: I can smell the dinner going in.'

He hurried down-stairs and left poor Maggie to that bitter sense of the irrevocable which was almost an every-day experience of her small soul. She could see clearly enough, now the thing was done, that it was very foolish, and that she should have to hear and think more about her hair than ever; for Maggie rushed to her deeds with passionate impulse, and then saw not only their conse-quences, but what would have happened if they had not been done, with all the detail and exaggerated circum-stance of an active imagination. Tom never did the same sort of foolish things as Maggie, having a wonderful instinctive discernment of what would turn to his advan-tage or disadvantage; and so it happened, that though he was much more wilful and inflexible than Maggie, his mother hardly ever called him naughty. But if Tom did make a mistake of that sort, he espoused it, and stood by it: he 'didn't mind.' If he broke the lash of his father's gig-whip by lashing the gate, he couldn't help it—the whip shouldn't have got caught in the hinge. If Tom Tulliver whipped a gate, he was convinced, not that the whipping of gates by all boys was a justifiable act, but that he, Tom Tulliver, was justifiable in whipping that particular gate, and he wasn't going to be sorry. But Maggie, as she stood crying before the glass, felt it impossible that she should go down to dinner and endure the severe eyes and severe words of her aunts, while Tom, and Lucy, and Martha, who waited at table, and perhaps her father and her uncles, would laugh at her,—for if Tom had laughed at her, of course everyone else would; and if she had only let her hair alone, she could have sat with Tom and Lucy, and had the apricot pudding and the custard! What could she do but sob? She sat as helpless and despairing among her black locks as Ajax among the slaughtered sheep. Very trivial, perhaps, this anguish seems to weather-worn mortals who have to think of Christmas bills, dead loves, and broken friendships; but it was not less bitter to Maggie —perhaps it was even more bitter—than what we are fond of calling antithetically the real troubles of mature life. 'Ah, my child, you will have real troubles to fret about by-and-by,' is the consolation we have almost all of us had administered to us in our childhood, and have repeated to other children since we have been grown up. We have all of us sobbed so piteously, standing with tiny bare legs above our little socks, when we lost sight of our mother or nurse in some strange place; but we can no longer recall the poignancy of that moment and weep over it, as we do over the remembered sufferings of five or ten years ago. Every one of those keen moments has left its trace, and lives in us still, but such traces have blent themselves irrecoverably with the firmer texture of our youth and manhood; and so it comes that we can look on at the troubles of our children with a smiling dis-belief in the reality of their pain. Is there anyone who can recover the experience of his childhood, not merely with a memory of what he did and what happened to him, of what he liked and disliked when he was in frock and trousers, but with an intimate penetration, a revived consciousness of what he felt then—when it was so long from one Midsummer to another? what he felt when his schoolfellows shut him out of their game because he would pitch the ball wrong out of mere wilfulness; or on a rainy day in the holidays, when he didn't know how to amuse himself, and fell from idleness into mischief, from mischief into defiance, and from defiance into sulkiness; or when his mother absolutely refused to let him have a tailed coat that 'half,' although every other boy of his age had gone into tails already? Surely if we could recall that early bitterness, and the dim guesses, the strangely perspectiveless conception of that life that gave the bitterness its intensity, we should not pooh-pooh the griefs of our children.

'Miss Maggie, you're to come down this minute,' said Kezia, entering the room hurriedly. 'Lawks! what have you been a-doing? I niver *see* such a fright.'

'Don't, Kezia,' said Maggie angrily. 'Go away!'

'But I tell you, you're to come down, Miss, this minute your mother says so,' said Kezia, going up to Maggie and taking her by the hand to raise her from the floor.

'Get away, Kezia; I don't want any dinner,' said Maggie, resisting Kezia's arm. 'I shan't come.'

'O, well, I can't stay. I've got to wait at dinner,' said Kezia, going out again.

'Maggie, you little silly,' said Tom, peeping into the room ten minutes after, 'why don't you come and have your dinner? There's lots o' goodies, and mother says you're to come. What are you crying for, you little spooney?'

O, it was dreadful! Tom was so hard and unconcerned; if *he* had been crying on the floor, Maggie would have cried too. And there was the dinner, so nice; and she was *so* hungry. It was very bitter.

But Tom was not altogether hard. He was not inclined to cry, and did not feel that Maggie's grief spoiled his prospect of the sweets; but he went and put his head near her, and said in a lower, comforting tone:

'Won't you come, then, Magsie? Shall I bring you a bit o' pudding when I've had mine? . . . and a custard and things?'

'Ye-e-es,' said Maggie, beginning to feel life a little more tolerable.

'Very well,' said Tom, going away. But he turned again at the door and said: 'But you'd better come, you know. There's the dessert—nuts, you know—and cowslip wine.'

Maggie's tears had ceased, and she looked reflective as Tom left her. His good nature had taken off the keenest edge of her suffering, and nuts with cowslip wine began to assert their legitimate influence.

Slowly she rose from amongst her scattered locks, and slowly she made her way down-stairs. Then she stood leaning with one shoulder against the frame of the dining-parlour door, peeping in when it was ajar. She saw Tom and Lucy with an empty chair between them, and there were the custards on a side-table—it was too much. She slipped in and went towards the empty chair. But she had no sooner sat down than she repented, and wished herself back again.

Mrs. Tulliver gave a little scream as she saw her, and felt such a 'turn' that she dropt the large gravy-spoon into the dish with the most serious results to the table-cloth. For Kezia had not betrayed the reason of Maggie's refusal to come down, not liking to give her mistress a shock in the moment of carving, and Mrs. Tulliver thought there was nothing worse in question than a fit of perverseness, which was inflicting its own punishment by depriving Maggie of half her dinner.

Mrs. Tulliver's scream made all eyes turn towards the same point as her own, and Maggie's cheeks and ears began to burn, while uncle Glegg, a kind-looking, white-haired old gentleman, said:

'Heyday! what little gell's this—why, I don't know her. Is it some little gell you've picked up in the road, Kezia?'

'Why, she's gone and cut her hair herself,' said Mr. Tulliver in an under-tone to Mr. Deane, laughing with much enjoyment. 'Did you ever know such a little hussy as it is?'

'Why, little miss, you've made yourself look very

funny,' said uncle Pullet, and perhaps he never in his life made an observation which was felt to be so lacerating.

'Fie, for shame!' said aunt Glegg, in her loudest, severest tone of reproof. 'Little gells as cut their own hair should be whipped and fed on bread-and-water—not come and sit down with their aunts and uncles.'

'Ay, ay,' said uncle Glegg, meaning to give a playful turn to this denunciation, 'she must be sent to jail, I think, and they'll cut the rest of her hair off there, and make it all even.'

'She's more like a gypsy nor ever,' said aunt Pullet, in a pitying tone; 'it's very bad luck, sister, as the gell should be so brown—the boy's fair enough. I doubt it'll stand in her way i' life to be so brown.'

'She's a naughty child, as'll break her mother's heart,' said Mrs. Tulliver, with the tears in her eyes.

Maggie seemed to be listening to a chorus of reproach and derision. Her first flush came from anger, which gave her a transient power of defiance, and Tom thought she was braving it out, supported by the recent appearance of the pudding and custard. Under this impression, he whispered, 'O my! Maggie, I told you you'd catch it.' He meant to be friendly, but Maggie felt convinced that Tom was rejoicing in her ignominy. Her feeble power of defiance left her in an instant, her heart swelled, and, getting up from her chair, she ran to her father, hid her face on his shoulder, and burst out into loud sobbing.

'Come, come, my wench,' said her father soothingly, putting his arm round her, 'never mind; you was i' the right to cut it off if it plagued you; give over crying: father'll take your part.'

Delicious words of tenderness! Maggie never forgot any of these moments when her father 'took her part;' she kept them in her heart, and thought of them long years after, when everyone else said that her father had done very ill by his children.

'How your husband does spoil that child, Bessy!' said Mrs. Glegg, in a loud 'aside,' to Mrs. Tulliver. 'It'll be the ruin of her, if you don't take care. *My* father niver

brought his children up so, else we should ha' been a
different sort o' family to what we are.'

Mrs. Tulliver's domestic sorrows seemed at this moment
to have reached the point at which insensibility begins.
She took no notice of her sister's remark, but threw back her
cap-strings and dispensed the pudding, in mute resignation.

With the dessert there came entire deliverance for
Maggie, for the children were told they might have their
nuts and wine in the summer-house, since the day was so
mild, and they scampered out among the budding bushes
of the garden with the alacrity of small animals getting
from under a burning glass.

Mrs. Tulliver had her special reason for this permission:
now the dinner was despatched, and every one's mind
disengaged, it was the right moment to communicate Mr.
Tulliver's intention concerning Tom, and it would be as
well for Tom himself to be absent. The children were used
to hear themselves talked of as freely as if they were
birds, and could understand nothing, however they might
stretch their necks and listen; but on this occasion Mrs.
Tulliver manifested an unusual discretion, because she
had recently had evidence that the going to school to a
clergyman was a sore point with Tom, who looked at it
as very much on a par with going to school to a constable.
Mrs. Tulliver had a sighing sense that her husband would
do as he liked, whatever sister Glegg said, or sister Pullet
either, but at least they would not be able to say, if the
thing turned out ill, that Bessy had fallen in with her
husband's folly without letting her own friends know a
word about it.

'Mr. Tulliver,' she said, interrupting her husband in his
talk with Mr. Deane, 'it's time now to tell the children's
aunts and uncles what you're thinking of doing with Tom,
isn't it?'

'Very well,' said Mr. Tulliver rather sharply, 'I've no
objections to tell anybody what I mean to do with him.
I've settled'—he added, looking towards Mr. Glegg and
Mr. Deane—'I've settled to send him to a Mr. Stelling, a

parson, down at King's Lorton, there—an uncommon clever fellow, I understand—as'll put him up to most things.'

There was a rustling demonstration of surprise in the company, such as you may have observed in a country congregation when they hear an allusion to their week-day affairs from the pulpit. It was equally astonishing to the aunts and uncles to find a parson introduced into Mr. Tulliver's family arrangements. As for uncle Pullet, he could hardly have been more thoroughly obfuscated if Mr. Tulliver had said that he was going to send Tom to the Lord Chancellor: for uncle Pullet belonged to that extinct class of British yeomen who, dressed in good broadcloth, paid high rates and taxes, went to church, and ate a particularly good dinner on Sunday, without dreaming that the British constitution in Church and State had a traceable origin any more than the solar system and the fixed stars. It is melancholy, but true, that Mr. Pullet had the most confused idea of a bishop as a sort of a baronet, who might or might not be a clergyman; and as the rector of his own parish was a man of high family and fortune, the idea that a clergyman could be a schoolmaster was too remote from Mr. Pullet's experience to be readily conceivable. I know it is difficult for people in these instructed times to believe in uncle Pullet's ignorance; but let them reflect on the remarkable results of a great natural faculty under favouring circumstances. And uncle Pullet had a great natural faculty for ignorance. He was the first to give utterance to his astonishment.

'Why, what can you be going to send him to a parson for?' he said, with an amazed twinkling in his eyes, looking at Mr. Glegg and Mr. Deane, to see if they showed any signs of comprehension.

'Why, because the parsons are the best schoolmasters, by what I can make out,' said poor Mr. Tulliver, who, in the maze of this puzzling world, laid hold of any clue with great readiness and tenacity. 'Jacobs at th' academy's no parson, and he's done very bad by the boy; and I made up my mind, if I sent him to school again, it should be to somebody different to Jacobs. And this Mr. Stelling, by what I can make out, is the sort o' man I want. And I mean my boy to go to him at Midsummer,' he concluded in a tone of decision, tapping his snuff-box and taking a pinch.

'You'll have to pay a swinging half-yearly bill, then, eh, Tulliver? The clergymen have highish notions, in general,' said Mr. Deane, taking snuff vigorously, as he always did when wishing to maintain a neutral position.

'What! do you think the parson'll teach him to know a good sample o' wheat when he sees it, neighbour Tulliver?' said Mr. Glegg, who was fond of his jest; and, having retired from business, felt that it was not only allowable but becoming in him to take a playful view of things.

'Why, you see, I've got a plan i' my head about Tom,' said Mr. Tulliver, pausing after that statement and lifting up his glass.

'Well, if I may be allowed to speak, and it's seldom as I am,' said Mrs. Glegg, with a tone of bitter meaning, 'I should like to know what good is to come to the boy, by bringin' him up above his fortin.'

'Why,' said Mr. Tulliver, not looking at Mrs. Glegg, but at the male part of his audience, 'you see, I've made up my mind not to bring Tom up to my own business. I've had my thoughts about it all along, and I made up my mind by what I saw with Garnett and *his* son. I mean to put him to some business, as he can go into without capital, and I want to give him an eddication as he'll be even wi' the lawyers and folks, and put me up to a notion now an' then.'

Mrs. Glegg emitted a long sort of guttural sound with closed lips, that smiled in mingled pity and scorn.

'It 'ud be a fine deal better for some people,' she said after that introductory note, 'if they'd let the lawyers alone.'

'Is he at the head of a grammar school, then, this clergyman—such as that at Market Bewley?' said Mr. Deane.

'No—nothing o' that,' said Mr. Tulliver. 'He won't take more than two or three pupils—and so he'll have the more time to attend to 'em, you know.'

'Ah, and get his eddication done the sooner: they can't learn much at a time when there's so many of 'em,' said uncle Pullet, feeling that he was getting quite an insight into this difficult matter.

'But he'll want the more pay, I doubt,' said Mr. Glegg.

'Ay, ay, a cool hundred a year—that's all,' said Mr. Tulliver with some pride at his own spirited course. 'But then, you know, it's an investment; Tom's eddication 'ull be so much capital to him.'

'Ay, there's something in that,' said Mr. Glegg. 'Well, well, neighbour Tulliver, you may be right, you may be right:

> "When land is gone and money's spent,
> Then learning is most excellent."

I remember seeing those two lines wrote on a window at Buxton. But us that have got no learning had better keep our money, eh, neighbour Pullet?' Mr. Glegg rubbed his knees and looked very pleasant.

'Mr. Glegg, I wonder *at* you,' said his wife. 'It's very unbecoming in a man o' your age and belongings.'

'What's unbecoming, Mrs. G.?' said Mr. Glegg, winking pleasantly at the company. 'My new blue coat as I've got on?'

'I pity your weakness, Mr. Glegg. I say it's unbecoming to be making a joke when you see your own kin going headlongs to ruin.'

'If you mean me by that,' said Mr. Tulliver, considerably nettled, 'you needn't trouble yourself to fret about me. I can manage my own affairs without troubling other folks.'

'Bless me,' said Mr. Deane, judiciously introducing a new idea, 'why, now I come to think of it, somebody said Wakem was going to send his son—the deformed lad—to a clergyman, didn't they, Susan?' (appealing to his wife).

'I can give no account of it, I'm sure,' said Mrs. Deane,

closing her lips very tightly again. Mrs. Deane was not a woman to take part in a scene where missiles were flying.

'Well,' said Mr. Tulliver, speaking all the more cheerfully that Mrs. Glegg might see he didn't mind her, 'if Wakem thinks o' sending his son to a clergyman, depend on it I shall make no mistake i' sending Tom to one. Wakem's as big a scoundrel as Old Harry ever made, but he knows the length of every man's foot he's got to deal with. Ay, ay, tell me who's Wakem's butcher, and I'll tell you where to get your meat.'

'But lawyer Wakem's son's got a hump-back,' said Mrs. Pullet, who felt as if the whole business had a funereal aspect; 'it's more nat'ral to send *him* to a clergyman.'

'Yes,' said Mr. Glegg, interpreting Mrs. Pullet's observation with erroneous plausibility, 'you must consider that, neighbour Tulliver; Wakem's son isn't likely to follow any business. Wakem'll make a gentleman of him, poor fellow.'

'Mr. Glegg,' said Mrs. G. in a tone which implied that her indignation would fizz and ooze a little, though she was determined to keep it corked up, 'you'd far better hold your tongue. Mr. Tulliver doesn't want to know your opinion nor mine neither. There's folks in the world as know better than everybody else.'

'Why, I should think that's you, if we're to trust your own tale,' said Mr. Tulliver, beginning to boil up again.

'O, *I* say nothing,' said Mrs. Glegg sarcastically. 'My advice has never been asked, and I don't give it.'

'It'll be the first time, then,' said Mr. Tulliver. 'It's the only thing you're over-ready at giving.'

'I've been over-ready at lending, then, if I haven't been over-ready at giving,' said Mrs. Glegg. 'There's folk I've lent money to, as perhaps I shall repent o' lending money to kin.'

'Come, come, come,' said Mr. Glegg soothingly. But Mr. Tulliver was not to be hindered of his retort.

'You've got a bond for it, I reckon,' he said; 'and you've had your five per cent., kin or no kin.'

'Sister,' said Mrs. Tulliver pleadingly, 'drink your wine, and let me give you some almonds and raisins.'

'Bessy, I'm sorry for you,' said Mrs. Glegg, very much with the feeling of a cur that seizes the opportunity of diverting his bark towards the man who carries no stick. 'It's poor work talking o' almonds and raisins.'

'Lors, sister Glegg, don't be quarrelsome,' said Mrs. Pullet, beginning to cry a little. 'You may be struck with a fit, getting so red in the face after dinner, and we are but just out o' mourning, all of us—and all wi' gowns craped alike and just put by—it's very bad among sisters.'

'I should think it *is* bad,' said Mrs. Glegg. 'Things are come to a fine pass when one sister invites the other to her house o' purpose to quarrel with her and abuse her.'

'Softly, softly, Jane—be reasonable—be reasonable,' said Mr. Glegg.

But while he was speaking, Mr. Tulliver, who had by no means said enough to satisfy his anger, burst out again:

'Who wants to quarrel with you?' he said. 'It's you as can't let people alone, but must be gnawing at 'em for ever. *I* should never want to quarrel with any woman, if she kept her place.'

'My place, indeed!' said Mrs. Glegg, getting rather shrill. 'There's your betters, Mr. Tulliver, as are dead and in their grave, treated me with a different sort o' respect to what you do—*though* I've got a husband as'll sit by and see me abused by them as 'ud never ha' had the chance if there hadn't been them in our family as married worse than they might ha' done.'

'If you talk o' that,' said Mr. Tulliver, 'my family's as good as yours—and better, for it hasn't got a damned ill-tempered woman in it.'

'Well!' said Mrs. Glegg, rising from her chair, 'I don't know whether you think it's a fine thing to sit by and hear me swore at, Mr. Glegg; but I'm not going to stay a minute longer in this house. You can stay behind, and come home with the gig—and I'll walk home.'

'Dear heart, dear heart!' said Mr. Glegg in a melancholy tone, as he followed his wife out of the room.

'Mr. Tulliver, how could you talk so?' said Mrs. Tulliver, with the tears in her eyes.

'Let her go,' said Mr. Tulliver, too hot to be damped by
any amount of tears. 'Let her go, and the sooner the
better: she won't be trying to domineer over *me* again in
a hurry.'

'Sister Pullet,' said Mrs. Tulliver helplessly, 'do you
think it 'ud be any use for you to go after her and try to
pacify her?'

'Better not, better not,' said Mr. Deane. 'You'll make
it up another day.'

'Then, sisters, shall we go and look at the children?'
said Mrs. Tulliver, drying her eyes.

No proposition could have been more seasonable. Mr.
Tulliver felt very much as if the air had been cleared of
obtrusive flies now the women were out of the room. There
were few things he liked better than a chat with Mr. Deane,
whose close application to business allowed the pleasure
very rarely. Mr. Deane, he considered, was the 'knowing-
est' man of his acquaintance, and he had besides a ready
causticity of tongue that made an agreeable supplement to
Mr. Tulliver's own tendency that way, which had remained
in rather an inarticulate condition. And now the women
were gone, they could carry on their serious talk without
frivolous interruption. They could exchange their views
concerning the Duke of Wellington, whose conduct in the
Catholic Question had thrown such an entirely new light
on his character; and speak slightingly of his conduct at
the battle of Waterloo, which he would never have won if
there hadn't been a great many Englishmen at his back,
not to speak of Blucher and the Prussians, who, as Mr.
Tulliver had heard from a person of particular knowledge
in that matter, had come up in the very nick of time;
though here there was a slight dissidence, Mr. Deane re-
marking that he was not disposed to give much credit to
the Prussians, the build of their vessels, together with the
unsatisfactory character of transactions in Dantzic beer,
inclining him to form rather a low view of Prussian pluck
generally. Rather beaten on this ground, Mr. Tulliver proceeded to express his fears that the country could never
again be what it used to be; but Mr. Deane, attached to

a firm of which the returns were on the increase, naturally took a more lively view of the present; and had some details to give concerning the state of the imports, especially in hides and spelter, which soothed Mr. Tulliver's imagination by throwing into more distant perspective the period when the country would become utterly the prey of Papists and Radicals, and there would be no more chance for honest men.

Uncle Pullet sat by and listened with twinkling eyes to these high matters. He didn't understand politics himself—thought they were a natural gift—but by what he could make out, this Duke of Wellington was no better than he should be.

VIII

MR. TULLIVER SHOWS HIS WEAKER SIDE

'SUPPOSE sister Glegg should call her money in—it 'ud be very awkward for you to have to raise five hundred pound now,' said Mrs. Tulliver to her husband that evening, as she took a plaintive review of the day.

Mrs. Tulliver had lived thirteen years with her husband, yet she retained in all the freshness of her early married life a facility of saying things which drove him in the opposite direction to the one she desired. Some minds are wonderful for keeping their bloom in this way, as a patriarchal gold-fish apparently retains to the last its youthful illusion that it can swim in a straight line beyond the encircling glass. Mrs. Tulliver was an amiable fish of this kind, and after running her head against the same resisting medium for thirteen years, would go at it again to-day with un-dulled alacrity.

This observation of hers tended directly to convince Mr. Tulliver that it would not be at all awkward for him to raise five hundred pounds; and when Mrs. Tulliver became rather pressing to know *how* he would raise it without mortgaging the mill and the house which he had said he never *would* mortgage, since nowadays people were non so ready to lend money without security, Mr. Tulliver, getting warm, declared that Mrs. Glegg might do as she liked about calling in her money—he should pay it in, whether or not. He was not going to be beholden to his wife's sisters. When a man had married into a family where there was a whole litter of women, he might have plenty to put up with if he chose. But Mr. Tulliver did *not* choose.

Mrs. Tulliver cried a little in a trickling quiet way as she put on her nightcap; but presently sank into a comfortable sleep, lulled by the thought that she would talk everything over with her sister Pullet to-morrow, when she was to take the children to Garum Firs to tea. Not that she looked forward to any distinct issue from that talk; but it seemed impossible that past events should be so obstinate as to remain unmodified when they were complained against.

Her husband lay awake rather longer, for he too was thinking of a visit he would pay on the morrow; and his ideas on the subject were not of so vague and soothing a kind as those of his amiable partner.

Mr. Tulliver, when under the influence of a strong feeling, had a promptitude in action that may seem inconsistent with that painful sense of the complicated puzzling nature of human affairs under which his more dispassionate deliberations were conducted; but it is really not improbable that there was a direct relation between these apparently contradictory phenomena, since I have observed that for getting a strong impression that a skein is tangled, there is nothing like snatching hastily at a single thread. It was owing to this promptitude that Mr. Tulliver was on horseback soon after dinner the next day (he was not dyspeptic) on his way to Basset to see his sister Moss and her husband. For having made up his mind irrevocably that he would pay Mrs. Glegg her loan of five hundred pounds, it naturally occurred to him that he had a promissory note for three hundred pounds lent to his brother-in-law Moss, and if the said brother-in-law could manage to pay in the money within a given time it would go far to lessen the fallacious

air of inconvenience which Mr. Tulliver's spirited step
might have worn in the eyes of weak people who require to
know precisely *how* a thing is to be done before they are
strongly confident that it will be easy.

For Mr. Tulliver was in a position neither new nor
striking, but, like other everyday things, sure to have a
cumulative effect that will be felt in the long run: he was
held to be a much more substantial man than he really was.
And as we are all apt to believe what the world believes
about us, it was his habit to think of failure and ruin with
the same sort of remote pity with which a spare long-
necked man hears that his plethoric short-necked neighbour is stricken with apoplexy. He had been always used to
hear pleasant jokes about his advantages as a man who
worked his own mill, and owned a pretty bit of land; and
these jokes naturally kept up his sense that he was a man
of considerable substance. They gave a pleasant flavour
to his glass on a market-day, and if it had not been for the
recurrence of half-yearly payments, Mr. Tulliver would
really have forgotten that there was a mortgage of two
thousand pounds on his very desirable freehold. That was
not altogether his own fault, since one of the thousand
pounds was his sister's fortune, which he had to pay on her
marriage; and a man who has neighbours that *will* go to
law with him, is not likely to pay off his mortgages, especially if he enjoys the good opinion of acquaintances who
want to borrow a hundred pounds on security too lofty to
be represented by parchment. Our friend Mr. Tulliver had
a good-natured fibre in him, and did not like to give harsh
refusals even to a sister, who had not only come into the
world in that superfluous way characteristic of sisters,
creating a necessity for mortgages, but had quite thrown
herself away in marriage, and had crowned her mistakes by
having an eighth baby. On this point Mr. Tulliver was
conscious of being a little weak; but he apologised to himself by saying that poor Gritty had been a good-looking
wench before she married Moss—he would sometimes say
this even with a slight tremulousness in his voice. But this
morning he was in a mood more becoming a man of busi-

ness, and in the course of his ride along the Basset lanes, with their deep ruts, lying so far away from a market-town that the labour of drawing produce and manure was enough to take away the best part of the profits on such poor land as that parish was made of, he got up a due amount of irritation against Moss as a man without capital, who, if murrain and blight were abroad, was sure to have his share of them, and who, the more you tried to help him out of the mud, would sink the further in. It would do him good rather than harm, now, if he were obliged to raise this three hundred pounds: it would make him look about him better, and not act so foolishly about his wool this year as he did the last: in fact, Mr. Tulliver had been too easy with his brother-in-law, and because he had let the interest run on for two years, Moss was likely enough to think that he should never be troubled about the principal. But Mr. Tulliver was determined not to encourage such shuffling people any longer; and a ride along the Basset lanes was not likely to enervate a man's resolution by softening his temper. The deep-trodden hoof-marks, made in the muddiest days of winter, gave him a shake now and then which suggested a rash but stimulating snarl at the father of lawyers, who, whether by means of his hoof or otherwise, had doubtless something to do with this state of the roads; and the abundance of foul land and neglected fences that met his eye, though they made no part of his brother Moss's farm, strongly contributed to his dissatisfaction with that unlucky agriculturist. If this wasn't Moss's fallow, it might have been; Basset was all alike; it was a beggarly parish in Mr. Tulliver's opinion, and his opinion was certainly not groundless. Basset had a poor soil, poor roads, a poor non-resident landlord, a poor non-resident vicar, and rather less than half a curate, also poor. If any one strongly impressed with the power of the human mind to triumph over circumstances, will contend that the parishioners of Basset might nevertheless have been a very superior class of people, I have nothing to urge against that abstract proposition; I only know that, in point of fact, the Basset mind was in strict keeping with its circumstances.

The muddy lanes, green or clayey, that seemed to the un-accustomed eye to lead nowhere but into each other, did really lead, with patience, to a distant high-road; but there were many feet in Basset which they led more frequently to a centre of dissipation, spoken of formally as the 'Markis o' Granby,' but among intimates as 'Dickison's.' A large low room with a sanded floor, a cold scent of tobacco, modified by undetected beer-dregs, Mr. Dickison leaning against the doorpost with a melancholy pimpled face, look-ing as irrelevant to the daylight as a last night's guttered candle—all this may not seem a very seductive form of temptation; but the majority of men in Basset found it fatally alluring when encountered on their road towards four o'clock on a wintry afternoon; and if any wife in Basset wished to indicate that her husband was not a pleasure-seeking man, she could hardly do it more em-phatically than by saying that he didn't spend a shilling at Dickison's from one Whitsuntide to another. Mrs. Moss had said so of *her* husband more than once, when her brother was in a mood to find fault with him, as he certainly was to-day. And nothing could be less pacifying to Mr. Tulliver than the behaviour of the farmyard gate, which he no sooner attempted to push open with his riding-stick, than it acted as gates without the upper hinge are known to do, to the peril of shins, whether equine or human. He was about to get down and lead his horse through the damp dirt of the hollow farmyard, shadowed drearily by the large half-timbered buildings, up to the long line of tumbledown dwelling-house standing on a raised causeway; but the timely appearance of a cowboy saved him that frustration of a plan he had determined on—namely, not to get down from his horse during this visit. If a man means to be hard, let him keep in his saddle and speak from that height, above the level of pleading eyes, and with the command of a distant horizon. Mrs. Moss heard the sound of the horse's feet, and, when her brother rode up, was already outside the kitchen door, with a half-weary smile on her face, and a black-eyed baby in her arms. Mrs. Moss's face bore a faded resemblance to her brother's; baby's little fat hand, pressed against her cheek, seemed to show more strikingly that the cheek was faded.

'Brother, I'm glad to see you,' she said, in an affectionate tone. 'I didn't look for you to-day. How do you do?'

'Oh, ... pretty well, Mrs. Moss ... pretty well,' answered the brother, with cool deliberation, as if it were rather too forward of her to ask that question. She knew at once that her brother was not in a good humour: he never called her Mrs. Moss except when he was angry, and when they were in company. But she thought it was in the order of nature that people who were poorly off should be snubbed. Mrs. Moss did not take her stand on the equality of the human race: she was a patient, prolific, loving-hearted woman.

'Your husband isn't in the house, I suppose?' added Mr. Tulliver, after a grave pause, during which four children had run out, like chickens whose mother has been suddenly in eclipse behind the hencoop.

'No,' said Mrs. Moss, 'but he's only in the potato-field yonders. Georgy, run to the Far Close in a minute, and tell father your uncle's come. You'll get down, brother, won't you, and take something?'

'No, no; I can't get down. I must be going home again directly,' said Mr. Tulliver, looking at the distance.

'And how's Mrs. Tulliver and the children?' said Mrs. Moss humbly, not daring to press her invitation.

'Oh ... pretty well. Tom's going to a new school at Midsummer—a deal of expense to me. It's bad work for me, lying out o' my money.'

'I wish you'd be so good as let the children come and see their cousins some day. My little uns want to see their cousin Maggie, so as never was. And me her god-mother, and so fond of her—there's nobody 'ud make a bigger fuss with her, according to what they've got. And I know she likes to come, for she's a loving child, and how quick and clever she is, to be sure!'

If Mrs. Moss had been one of the most astute women in the world, instead of being one of the simplest, she could have thought of nothing more likely to propitiate her

brother than this praise of Maggie. He seldom found any
one volunteering praise of 'the little wench:' it was usually
left entirely to himself to insist on her merits. But Maggie
always appeared in the most amiable light at her aunt
Moss's: it was her Alsatia, where she was out of the reach
of law—if she upset anything, dirtied her shoes, or tore her
frock, these things were matters of course at her aunt
Moss's. In spite of himself, Mr. Tulliver's eyes got milder,
and he did not look away from his sister, as he said:

'Ay: she's fonder o' you than o' the other aunts, I
think. She takes after our family: not a bit of her mother's
in her.'

'Moss says she's just like what I used to be,' said Mrs.
Moss, 'though I was never so quick and fond o' the books.
But I think my Lizzy's like her—*she's* sharp. Come here,
Lizzy, my dear, and let your uncle see you: he hardly
knows you; you grow so fast.'

Lizzy, a black-eyed child of seven, looked very shy when
her mother drew her forward, for the small Mosses were
much in awe of their uncle from Dorlcote Mill. She was
inferior enough to Maggie in fire and strength of expression
to make the resemblance between the two entirely flattering to Mr. Tulliver's fatherly love.

'Ay, they're a bit alike,' he said, looking kindly at the
little figure in the soiled pinafore. 'They both take after
our mother. You've got enough o' gells, Gritty,' he added,
in a tone half compassionate, half reproachful.

'Four of 'em, bless 'em,' said Mrs. Moss, with a sigh,
stroking Lizzy's hair on each side of her forehead; 'as many
as there's boys. They've got a brother a-piece.'

'Ah, but they must turn out and fend for themselves,'
said Mr. Tulliver, feeling that his severity was relaxing, and
trying to brace it by throwing out a wholesome hint. 'They
mustn't look to hanging on their brothers.'

'No: but I hope their brothers 'ull love the poor things,
and remember they came o' one father and mother: the
lads 'ull never be the poorer for that,' said Mrs. Moss,
flashing out with hurried timidity, like a half-smothered
fire.

Mr. Tulliver gave his horse a little stroke on the flank, then checked it, and said angrily: 'Stand still with you!' much to the astonishment of that innocent animal.

'And the more there is of 'em, the more they must love one another,' Mrs. Moss went on, looking at her children with a didactic purpose. But she turned towards her brother again to say, 'Not but what I hope your boy'll allays be good to his sister, though there's but two of 'em, like you and me, brother.'

That arrow went straight to Mr. Tulliver's heart. He had not a rapid imagination, but the thought of Maggie was very near to him, and he was not long in seeing his relation to his own sister side by side with Tom's relation to Maggie. Would the little wench ever be poorly off, and Tom rather hard upon her?

'Ay, ay, Gritty,' said the miller, with a new softness in his tone; 'but I've allays done what I could for you,' he added, as if vindicating himself from a reproach.

'I'm not denying that, brother, and I'm noways ungrateful,' said poor Mrs. Moss, too fagged by toil and children to have strength left for any pride. 'But here's the father. What a while you've been, Moss!'

'While, do you call it?' said Mr. Moss, feeling out of breath and injured. 'I've been running all the way. Won't you 'light, Mr. Tulliver?'

'Well, I'll just get down and have a bit o' talk with you in the garden,' said Mr. Tulliver, thinking that he should be more likely to show a due spirit of resolve if his sister were not present.

He got down, and passed with Mr. Moss into the garden, towards an old yew-tree arbour, while his sister stood rapping her baby on the back, and looking wistfully after them.

Their entrance into the yew-tree arbour surprised several fowls that were recreating themselves by scratching deep holes in the dusty ground, and at once took flight with much pother and cackling. Mr. Tulliver sat down on the bench, and tapping the ground curiously here and there with his stick, as if he suspected some hollowness, opened the conversation by observing, with something like a snarl in his tone:

'Why, you've got wheat again in that Corner Close, I see: and never a bit o' dressing on it. You'll do no good with it this year.'

Mr. Moss, who, when he married Miss Tulliver, had been regarded as the buck of Basset, now wore a beard nearly a week old, and had the depressed, unexpectant air of a machine-horse. He answered in a patient-grumbling tone. 'Why, poor farmers like me must do as they can; they must leave it to them as have got money to play with, to put half as much into the ground as they mean to get out of it.'

'I don't know who should have money to play with, if it isn't them as can borrow money without paying interest,' said Mr. Tulliver, who wished to get into a slight quarrel; it was the most natural and easy introduction to calling in money.

'I know I'm behind with the interest,' said Mr. Moss, 'but I was so unlucky with the wool last year; and what with the Missis being laid up so, things have gone awk'arder nor usual.'

'Ay,' snarled Mr. Tulliver, 'there's folks as things 'ull allays go awk'ard with: empty sacks 'ull never stand upright.'

'Well, I don't know what fault you've got to find wi' me, Mr. Tulliver,' said Mr. Moss deprecatingly; 'I know there isn't a day-labourer works harder.'

'What's the use o' that,' said Mr. Tulliver sharply, 'when a man marries, and 's got no capital to work his farm but his wife's bit of fortin? I was against it from the first; but you'd neither of you listen to me. And I can't lie out o' my money any longer, for I've got to pay five hundred o' Mrs Glegg's, and there'll be Tom an expense to me—I should find myself short, even saying I'd got back all as is my own. You must look about and see how you can pay me the three hundred pound.'

'Well, if that's what you mean,' said Mr. Moss, looking blankly before him, 'we'd better be sold up, and ha' done with it; I must part wi' every head o' stock I've got, to pay you and the landlord too.'

Poor relations are undeniably irritating—their existence is so entirely uncalled for on our part, and they are almost always very faulty people. Mr. Tulliver had succeeded in getting quite as much irritated with Mr. Moss as he had desired, and he was able to say angrily, rising from his seat: 'Well, you must do as you can. *I* can't find money for everybody else as well as myself. I must look to my own business and my own family. I can't lie out o' my money any longer. You must raise it as quick as you can.'

Mr. Tulliver walked abruptly out of the arbour as he uttered the last sentence, and, without looking round at Mr. Moss, went on to the kitchen door, where the eldest boy was holding his horse, and his sister was waiting in a state of wondering alarm, which was not without its alleviations, for baby was making pleasant gurgling sounds, and performing a great deal of finger practice on the faded face. Mrs. Moss had eight children, but could never overcome her regret that the twins had not lived. Mr. Moss thought their removal was not without its consolations. 'Won't you come in, brother?' she said, looking anxiously at her husband, who was walking slowly up, while Mr. Tulliver had his foot already in the stirrup.

'No, no; good-bye,' said he, turning his horse's head and riding away.

No man could feel more resolute till he got outside the yard-gate, and a little way along the deep-rutted lane, but before he reached the next turning, which would take him out of sight of the dilapidated farm-buildings, he appeared to be smitten by some sudden thought. He checked his horse, and made it stand still in the same spot for two or three minutes, during which he turned his head from side to side in a melancholy way, as if he were looking at some painful object on more sides than one. Evidently, after his fit of promptitude, Mr. Tulliver was relapsing into the sense that this is a puzzling world. He turned his horse, and rode slowly back, giving vent to the climax of feeling which had determined this movement by saying aloud, as he struck his horse, 'Poor little wench! she'll have nobody but Tom belike, when I'm gone.'

Mr. Tulliver's return into the yard was descried b several young Mosses, who immediately ran in with th exciting news to their mother, so that Mrs. Moss was agai on the door-step when her brother rode up. She had bee crying, but was rocking baby to sleep in her arms now, an made no ostentatious show of sorrow as her brother looke at her, but merely said:

'The father's gone to the field again, if you want him brother.'

'No, Gritty, no,' said Mr. Tulliver, in a gentle tone 'Don't you fret—that's all—I'll make a shift without th money a bit—only you must be as clever and contriving a you can.'

Mrs. Moss's tears came again at this unexpected kind ness, and she could say nothing.

'Come, come!—the little wench shall come and see you I'll bring her and Tom some day before he goes to schoo You mustn't fret. . . . I'll allays be a good brother to you

'Thank you for that word, brother,' said Mrs. Moss drying her tears; then turning to Lizzy, she said, 'Run now and fetch the coloured egg for cousin Maggie.' Lizzy ra in, and quickly reappeared with a small paper parcel.

'It's boiled hard, brother, and coloured with thrums— very pretty; it was done o' purpose for Maggie. Will yo please to carry it in your pocket?'

'Ay, ay,' said Mr. Tulliver, putting it carefully in hi side-pocket. 'Good-bye.'

And so the respectable miller returned along the Basse lanes rather more puzzled than before as to ways an means, but still with the sense of a danger escaped. It ha come across his mind that if he were hard upon his sister it might somehow tend to make Tom hard upon Maggie a some distant day, when her father was no longer there t take her part; for simple people, like our friend Mr. Tulliver are apt to clothe unimpeachable feelings in erroneous ideas and this was his confused way of explaining to himself tha his love and anxiety for 'the little wench' had given hir a new sensibility towards his sister.

IX

TO GARUM FIRS

WHILE the possible troubles of Maggie's future were occupy-
ing her father's mind, she herself was tasting only the
bitterness of the present. Childhood has no forebodings;
but then, it is soothed by no memories of outlived sorrow.
The fact was, the day had begun ill with Maggie. The
pleasure of having Lucy to look at, and the prospect of the
afternoon visit to Garum Firs, where she would hear uncle
Pullet's musical box, had been marred as early as eleven
o'clock by the advent of the hairdresser from St. Ogg's, who
had spoken in the severest terms of the condition in which
he had found her hair, holding up one jagged lock after
another and saying, 'See here! tut—tut—tut!' in a tone of
mingled disgust and pity, which to Maggie's imagination
was equivalent to the strongest expression of public opinion. Mr. Rappit, the hairdresser, with his well-anointed
coronal locks tending wavily upward, like the simulated
pyramid of flame on a monumental urn, seemed to her at
that moment the most formidable of her contemporaries,
into whose street at St. Ogg's she would carefully refrain
from entering through the rest of her life.

Moreover, the preparation for a visit being always a
serious affair in the Dodson family, Martha was enjoined
to have Mrs. Tulliver's room ready an hour earlier than
usual, that the laying-out of the best clothes might not be
deferred till the last moment, as was sometimes the case in
families of lax views, where the ribbon-strings were never
rolled up, where there was little or no wrapping in silver
paper, and where the sense that the Sunday clothes could
be got at quite easily produced no shock to the mind.
Already, at twelve o'clock, Mrs. Tulliver had on her visiting
costume, with a protective apparatus of brown holland, as
if she had been a piece of satin furniture in danger of flies;
Maggie was frowning and twisting her shoulders, that she
might if possible shrink away from the prickliest of tuckers,

while her mother was remonstrating, 'Don't, Maggie, m
dear—don't make yourself so ugly!' and Tom's cheeks wer
looking particularly brilliant as a relief to his best blue suit
which he wore with becoming calmness; having, after
little wrangling, effected what was always the one point o
interest to him in his toilette—he had transferred all th
contents of his everyday pockets to those actually in wear

As for Lucy, she was just as pretty and neat as she ha
been yesterday; no accidents ever happened to her clothes
and she was never uncomfortable in them, so that sh
looked with wondering pity at Maggie pouting and writh
ing under the exasperating tucker. Maggie would certainl
have torn it off, if she had not been checked by the re
membrance of her recent humiliation about her hair: as i
was, she confined herself to fretting and twisting, and be
having peevishly about the card-houses which they wer
allowed to build till dinner, as a suitable amusement fo
boys and girls in their best clothes. Tom could build perfec
pyramids of houses; but Maggie's would never bear th
laying on of the roof: it was always so with the things tha
Maggie made; and Tom had deduced the conclusion that n
girls could ever make anything. But it happened tha
Lucy proved wonderfully clever at building: she handle
the cards so lightly, and moved so gently, that Tom con
descended to admire her houses as well as his own, the mor
readily because she had asked him to teach her. Maggie
too, would have admired Lucy's houses, and would hav
given up her own unsuccessful building to contemplat
them, without ill-temper, if her tucker had not made he
peevish and if Tom had not inconsiderately laughed whe
her houses fell, and told her she was 'a stupid.'

'Don't laugh at me, Tom!' she burst out angrily; 'I'n
not a stupid. I know a great many things you don't.'

'Oh, I daresay, Miss Spitfire! I'd never be such a cros
thing as you—making faces like that. Lucy doesn't do so
I like Lucy better than you: *I* wish Lucy was *my* sister.'

'Then it's very wicked and cruel of you to wish so,' sai
Maggie, starting up hurriedly from her place on the floor
and upsetting Tom's wonderful pagoda. She really did no

mean it, but the circumstantial evidence was against her,
and Tom turned white with anger, but said nothing: he
would have struck her, only he knew it was cowardly to
strike a girl, and Tom Tulliver was quite determined he
would never do anything cowardly.

Maggie stood in dismay and terror, while Tom got up
from the floor and walked away, pale, from the scattered ruins of his pagoda, and Lucy looked on mutely,
like a kitten pausing from its lapping.

'O Tom,' said Maggie at last, going half way towards
him, 'I didn't mean to knock it down—indeed, indeed I
didn't.'

Tom took no notice of her, but took, instead, two or
three hard peas out of his pocket, and shot them with his
thumb-nail against the window—vaguely at first, but presently with the distinct aim of hitting a superannuated
blue-bottle which was exposing its imbecility in the spring
sunshine, clearly against the views of Nature, who had provided Tom and the peas for the speedy destruction of this
weak individual.

Thus the morning had been made heavy to Maggie, and
Tom's persistent coldness to her all through their walk
spoiled the fresh air and sunshine for her. He called Lucy
to look at the half-built bird's nest without caring to show
it Maggie, and peeled a willow switch for Lucy and himself,
without offering one to Maggie. Lucy had said, 'Maggie,
shouldn't *you* like one?' but Tom was deaf.

Still the sight of the peacock opportunely spreading his
tail on the stackyard wall, just as they reached Garum Firs,
was enough to divert the mind temporarily from personal
grievances. And this was only the beginning of beautiful
sights at Garum Firs. All the farmyard life was wonderful
there—bantams, speckled and top-knotted; Friesland hens,
with their feathers all turned the wrong way; Guinea-fowls
that flew and screamed and dropped their pretty-spotted
feathers; pouter-pigeons and a tame magpie; nay, a goat,
and a wonderful brindled dog, half mastiff, half bull-dog, as
large as a lion. Then there were white railings and white
gates all about, and glittering weathercocks of various

design, and garden-walks paved with pebbles in beautifu
patterns—nothing was quite common at Garum Firs: an
Tom thought that the unusual size of the toads there wa
simply due to the general unusualness which characterize
uncle Pullet's possessions as a gentleman farmer. Toad
who paid rent were naturally leaner. As for the house, i
was not less remarkable; it had a receding centre, and tw
wings with battlemented turrets, and was covered wit
glittering white stucco.

Uncle Pullet had seen the expected party approachin
from the window, and made haste to unbar and unchai
the front door, kept always in this fortified condition fron
fear of tramps, who might be supposed to know of the glass
case of stuffed birds in the hall, and to contemplate rushin
in and carrying it away on their heads. Aunt Pullet, too
appeared at the doorway, and as soon as her sister wa
within hearing said, 'Stop the children, for God's sak
Bessy—don't let 'em come up the door-steps: Sally
bringing the old mat and the duster, to rub their shoes.'

Mrs. Pullet's front-door mats were by no means intende
to wipe shoes on: the very scraper had a deputy to do it
dirty work. Tom rebelled particularly against this shoe
wiping, which he always considered in the light of an in
dignity to his sex. He felt it as the beginning of the dis
agreeables incident to a visit at aunt Pullet's, where he ha
once been compelled to sit with towels wrapped round hi
boots; a fact which may serve to correct the too hast
conclusion that a visit to Garum Firs must have been
great treat to a young gentleman fond of animals—fond
that is, of throwing stones at them.

The next disagreeable was confined to his feminine com
panions: it was the mounting of the polished oak stair
which had very handsome carpets rolled up and laid by i
a spare bedroom, so that the ascent of these glossy step
might have served, in barbarous times, as a trial by orde
from which none but the most spotless virtue could hav
come off with unbroken limbs. Sophy's weakness abou
these polished stairs was always a subject of bitter remon
strance on Mrs. Glegg's part; but Mrs. Tulliver venture

n no comment, only thinking to herself it was a mercy
hen she and the children were safe on the landing.

'Mrs. Gray has sent home my new bonnet, Bessy,' said
Mrs. Pullet, in a pathetic tone, as Mrs. Tulliver adjusted
er cap.

'Has she, sister?' said Mrs. Tulliver, with an air of much
nterest. 'And how do you like it?'

'It's apt to make a mess with clothes, taking 'em out and
utting 'em in again,' said Mrs. Pullet, drawing a bunch of
eys from her pocket and looking at them earnestly, 'but
'ud be a pity for you to go away without seeing it.
here's no knowing what may happen.'

Mrs. Pullet shook her head slowly at this last serious con-
ideration, which determined her to single out a particular
ey.

'I'm afraid it'll be troublesome to you getting it out,
ister,' said Mrs. Tulliver,'but I *should* like to see what sort
f a crown she's made you.'

Mrs. Pullet rose with a melancholy air and unlocked one
ving of a very bright wardrobe, where you may have
astily supposed she would find the new bonnet. Not at all.
uch a supposition could only have arisen from a too super-
cial acquaintance with the habits of the Dodson family.
n this wardrobe Mrs. Pullet was seeking something small
nough to be hidden among layers of linen—it was a door-
ey.

'You must come with me into the best room,' said Mrs.
'ullet.

'May the children come too, sister?' inquired Mrs. Tul-
ver, who saw that Maggie and Lucy were looking rather
ager.

'Well,' said aunt Pullet reflectively, 'it'll perhaps be safer
or 'em to come—they'll be touching something if we leave
m behind.'

So they went in procession along the bright and slippery
orridor, dimly lighted by the semi-lunar top of the window
vhich rose above the closed shutter: it was really quite
olemn. Aunt Pullet paused and unlocked a door which
pened on something still more solemn than the passage: a

darkened room, in which the outer light, entering feebly
showed what looked like the corpses of furniture in white
shrouds. Everything that was not shrouded stood with its
legs upwards. Lucy laid hold of Maggie's frock, and
Maggie's heart beat rapidly.

Aunt Pullet half-opened the shutter and then unlocked
the wardrobe, with a melancholy deliberateness which was
quite in keeping with the funereal solemnity of the scene.
The delicious scent of rose-leaves that issued from the wardrobe, made the process of taking out sheet after sheet of
silver paper quite pleasant to assist at, though the sight of
the bonnet at last was an anticlimax to Maggie, who would
have preferred something more strikingly preternatural.
But few things could have been more impressive to Mrs.
Tulliver. She looked all round it in silence for some
moments, and then said emphatically: 'Well, sister, I'll
never speak against the full crowns again!'

It was a great concession, and Mrs. Pullet felt it: she felt
something was due to it.

'You'd like to see it on, sister?' she said sadly. 'I'll open
the shutter a bit further.'

'Well, if you don't mind taking off your cap, sister,' said
Mrs. Tulliver.

Mrs. Pullet took off her cap, displaying the brown silk
scalp with a jutting promontory of curls which was common to the more mature and judicious women of those
times, and, placing the bonnet on her head, turned slowly
round, like a draper's lay-figure, that Mrs. Tulliver might
miss no point of view.

'I've sometimes thought there's a loop too much of
ribbon on this left side, sister; what do you think?' said
Mrs. Pullet.

Mrs. Tulliver looked earnestly at the point indicated, and
turned her head on one side. 'Well, I think it's best as it is;
if you meddled with it, sister, you might repent.'

'That's true,' said aunt Pullet, taking off the bonnet and
looking at it contemplatively.

'How much might she charge you for that bonnet,
sister?' said Mrs. Tulliver, whose mind was actively en-

aged on the possibility of getting a humble imitation of his *chef-d'œuvre* made from a piece of silk she had at home.

Mrs. Pullet screwed up her mouth and shook her head, and then whispered, 'Pullet pays for it: he said I was to have the best bonnet at Garum Church, let the next best be whose it would.'

She began slowly to adjust the trimmings in preparation for returning it to its place in the wardrobe, and her thoughts seemed to have taken a melancholy turn, for she shook her head.

'Ah,' she said at last, 'I may never wear it twice, sister: who knows?'

'Don't talk o' that, sister,' answered Mrs. Tulliver. 'I hope you'll have your health this summer.'

'Ah! but there may come a death in the family, as there did soon after I had my green satin bonnet. Cousin Abbott may go, and we can't think o' wearing crape less nor half a year for him.'

'That *would* be unlucky,' said Mrs. Tulliver, entering thoroughly into the possibility of an inopportune decease. 'There's never so much pleasure i' wearing a bonnet the second year, especially when the crowns are so chancy—never two summers alike.'

'Ah, it's the way i' this world,' said Mrs. Pullet, returning the bonnet to the wardrobe and locking it up. She maintained a silence characterized by head-shaking, until they had all issued from the solemn chamber and were in her own room again. Then, beginning to cry, she said, 'Sister, if you should never see that bonnet again till I'm dead and gone, you'll remember I showed it you this day.'

Mrs. Tulliver felt that she ought to be affected, but she was a woman of sparse tears, stout and healthy—she couldn't cry so much as her sister Pullet did, and had often felt her deficiency at funerals. Her effort to bring tears into her eyes issued in an odd contraction of her face. Maggie, looking on attentively, felt that there was some painful mystery about her aunt's bonnet which she was considered too young to understand; indignantly conscious, all the while, that she could have understood that, as well a everything else, if she had been taken into confidence.

When they went down, uncle Pullet observed with som acumen, that he reckoned the missis had been showing he bonnet—that was what had made them so long up-stairs With Tom the interval had seemed still longer, for he ha been seated in irksome constraint on the edge of a sof directly opposite his uncle Pullet, who regarded him wit twinkling grey eyes, and occasionally addressed him a 'Young sir.'

'Well, young sir, what do you learn at school?' was standing question with uncle Pullet; whereupon Tom always looked sheepish, rubbed his hands across his face and answered, 'I don't know.' It was altogether so em barrassing to be seated *tête-à-tête* with uncle Pullet, tha Tom could not even look at the prints on the walls, or th fly-cages, or the wonderful flowerpots; he saw nothing bu his uncle's gaiters. Not that Tom was in awe of his uncle' mental superiority; indeed, he had made up his mind tha he didn't want to be a gentleman farmer, because h shouldn't like to be such a thin-legged silly fellow as hi uncle Pullet—a mollycoddle, in fact. A boy's sheepishnes is by no means a sign of overmastering reverence; and whil you are making encouraging advances to him under the ide that he is overwhelmed by a sense of your age and wisdom ten to one he is thinking you extremely queer. The onl consolation I can suggest to you is, that the Greek boy probably thought the same of Aristotle. It is only whe you have mastered a restive horse, or thrashed a drayman or have got a gun in your hand, that these shy juniors fee you to be a truly admirable and enviable character. A least, I am quite sure of Tom Tulliver's sentiments on thes points. In very tender years, when he still wore a lac border under his outdoor cap, he was often observed peepin through the bars of a gate and making minatory gesture with his small fore-finger while he scolded the sheep wit an inarticulate burr, intended to strike terror into thei astonished minds; indicating thus early that desire fo mastery over the inferior animals, wild and domestic, in

luding cockchafers, neighbours' dogs, and small sisters,
which in all ages has been an attribute of so much promise
for the fortunes of our race. Now Mr. Pullet never rode
anything taller than a low pony, and was the least predatory
of men, considering fire-arms dangerous, as apt to go off of
themselves by nobody's particular desire. So that Tom was
not without strong reasons when, in confidential talk with
a chum, he had described uncle Pullet as a nincompoop,
taking care at the same time to observe that he was a 'very
rich fellow.'

The only alleviating circumstance in a *tête-à-tête* with
uncle Pullet was that he kept a variety of lozenges and
peppermint drops about his person, and when at a loss for
conversation, he filled up the void by proposing a mutual
solace of this kind.

'Do you like peppermints, young sir?' required only a
tacit answer when it was accompanied by a presentation of
the article in question.

The appearance of the little girls suggested to uncle
Pullet the further solace of small sweet cakes, of which he
also kept a stock under lock and key for his own private
eating on wet days; but the three children had no sooner
got the tempting delicacy between their fingers, than aunt
Pullet desired them to abstain from eating it till the tray
and the plates came, since with those crisp cakes they would
make the floor 'all over' crumbs. Lucy didn't mind that
much, for the cake was so pretty, she thought it was rather
a pity to eat it; but Tom, watching his opportunity while
the elders were talking, hastily stowed it in his mouth at
two bites, and chewed it furtively. As for Maggie, becoming fascinated, as usual, by a print of Ulysses and Nausicaa,
which uncle Pullet had bought as a 'pretty Scripture thing,'
she presently let fall her cake, and in an unlucky movement
crushed it beneath her foot—a source of so much agitation
to aunt Pullet and conscious disgrace to Maggie, that she
began to despair of hearing the musical snuff-box to-day,
till, after some reflection, it occurred to her that Lucy was
in high favour enough to venture on asking for a tune. So
she whispered to Lucy, and Lucy, who always did what she

was desired to do, went up quietly to her uncle's knee, and blushing all over her neck while she fingered her necklace said: 'Will you please play us a tune, uncle?'

Lucy thought it was by reason of some exceptiona talent in uncle Pullet that the snuff-box played such beautiful tunes, and indeed the thing was viewed in tha light by the majority of his neighbours in Garum. Mr. Pu let had *bought* the box, to begin with, and he understoo winding it up, and knew which tune it was going to play beforehand; altogether, the possession of this unique 'piec of music' was a proof that Mr. Pullet's character was not o that entire nullity which might otherwise have been attri buted to it. But uncle Pullet, when entreated to exhibit hi accomplishment, never depreciated it by a too ready con sent. 'We'll see about it,' was the answer he always gave carefully abstaining from any sign of compliance till a suit able number of minutes had passed. Uncle Pullet had programme for all great social occasions, and in this way fenced himself in from much painful confusion and per plexing freedom of will.

Perhaps the suspense did heighten Maggie's enjoymen when the fairy tune began: for the first time she quite for got that she had a load on her mind—that Tom was angry with her; and by the time 'Hush, ye pretty warbling choir,' had been played, her face wore that bright look of happi ness, while she sat immovable with her hands clasped which sometimes comforted her mother with the sense tha Maggie could look pretty now and then, in spite of he brown skin. But when the magic music ceased, she jumpe up, and, running towards Tom, put her arm round his nec and said: 'O, Tom, isn't it pretty?'

Lest you should think it showed a revolting insensibility in Tom that he felt any new anger towards Maggie for thi uncalled-for and, to him, inexplicable caress, I must tel you that he had his glass of cowslip wine in his hand, and tha she jerked him so as to make him spill half of it. He mus have been an extreme milksop not to say angrily, 'Look there now!' especially when his resentment was sanctioned as it was, by general disapprobation of Maggie's behaviour.

'Why don't you sit still, Maggie?' her mother said peevishly.

'Little gells mustn't come to see me if they behave in that way,' said aunt Pullet.

'Why, you're too rough, little miss,' said uncle Pullet.

Poor Maggie sat down again, with the music all chased out of her soul, and the seven small demons all in again.

Mrs. Tulliver, foreseeing nothing but misbehaviour while the children remained in doors, took an early opportunity of suggesting that, now they were rested after their walk, they might go and play out of doors; and aunt Pullet gave permission, only enjoining them not to go off the paved walks in the garden, and if they wanted to see the poultry fed, to view them from a distance on the horse-block; a restriction which had been imposed ever since Tom had been found guilty of running after the peacock, with an illusory idea that fright would make one of its feathers drop off.

Mrs. Tulliver's thoughts had been temporarily diverted from the quarrel with Mrs. Glegg by millinery and maternal cares, but now the great theme of the bonnet was thrown into perspective, and the children were out of the way, yesterday's anxieties recurred.

'It weighs on my mind so as never was,' she said, by way of opening the subject, 'sister Glegg's leaving the house in that way. I'm sure I'd no wish t' offend a sister.'

'Ah,' said aunt Pullet, 'there's no accounting for what Jane 'ull do. I wouldn't speak of it out o' the family—if it wasn't to Dr. Turnbull; but it's my belief Jane lives too low. I've said so to Pullet often and often, and he knows it.'

'Why, you said so last Monday was a week, when we came away from drinking tea with 'em,' said Mr. Pullet, beginning to nurse his knee and shelter it with his pocket-handkerchief, as was his way when the conversation took an interesting turn.

'Very like I did,' said Mrs. Pullet, 'for you remember when I said things better than I can remember myself. He's got a wonderful memory, Pullet has,' she continued, looking pathetically at her sister. 'I should be poorly off if

he was to have a stroke, for he always remembers when I'v
got to take my doctor's stuff—and I'm taking three sort
now.'

'There's the "pills as before" every other night, and th
new drops at eleven and four, and the 'fervescing mixtur
"when agreeable,"' rehearsed Mr. Pullet, with a punctua
tion determined by a lozenge on his tongue.

'Ah, perhaps it 'ud be better for sister Glegg, if *she*'d g
to the doctor sometimes, instead o' chewing Turkey rhubar
whenever there's anything the matter with her,' said Mrs
Tulliver, who naturally saw the wide subject of medicin
chiefly in relation to Mrs. Glegg.

'It's dreadful to think on,' said aunt Pullet, raising he
hands and letting them fall again, 'people playing wit
their own insides in that way! And it's flying i' the face c
Providence; for what are the doctors for, if we aren't to cal
'em in? And when folks have got the money to pay for
doctor, it isn't respectable, as I've told Jane many a time
I'm ashamed of acquaintance knowing it.'

'Well, *we*'ve no call to be ashamed,' said Mr. Pullet, 'fo
Doctor Turnbull hasn't got such another patient as you i
this parish, now old Mrs. Sutton's gone.'

'Pullet keeps all my physic-bottles—did you know
Bessy?' said Mrs. Pullet. 'He won't have one sold. H
says it's nothing but right folks should see 'em when I'
gone. They fill two o' the long store-room shelves a'ready—
but,' she added, beginning to cry a little, 'it's well if the
ever fill three. I may go before I've made up the dozen c
these last sizes. The pill-boxes are in the closet in my roo
—you'll remember that, sister—but there's nothing t
show for the boluses, if it isn't the bills.'

'Don't talk o' your going, sister,' said Mrs. Tulliver: '
should have nobody to stand between me and sister Gleg
if you was gone. And there's nobody but you can get he
to make it up with Mr. Tulliver, for sister Deane's never c
my side, and if she was, it's not to be looked for as she ca
speak like them as have got an independent fortin.'

'Well, your husband *is* awk'ard, you know, Bessy,' sai
Mrs. Pullet, good-naturedly ready to use her deep depressio

a her sister's account as well as her own. 'He's never be-
aved quite so pretty to our family as he should do, and the
aildren take after him—the boy's very mischievous, and
ans away from his aunts and uncles, and the gell's rude and
rown. It's your bad-luck, and I'm sorry for you, Bessy;
r you was allays my favourite sister, and we allays liked
ae same patterns.'

'I know Tulliver's hasty, and says odd things,' said Mrs.
ulliver, wiping away one small tear from the corner of her
ve, 'but I'm sure he's never been the man, since he
arried me, to object to my making the friends o' my side
the family welcome to the house.'

'*I* don't want to make the worst of you, Bessy,' said Mrs.
ullet compassionately, 'for I doubt you'll have trouble
aough without that; and your husband's got that poor
ster and her children hanging on him, and so given to
wing, they say. I doubt he'll leave you poorly off when he
ies. Not as I'd have it said out o' the family.'

This view of her position was naturally far from cheering
Mrs. Tulliver. Her imagination was not easily acted on,
ut she could not help thinking that her case was a hard
ne, since it appeared that other people thought it hard.

'I'm sure, sister, I can't help myself,' she said, urged by
ae fear lest her anticipated misfortunes might be held re-
ibutive, to take a comprehensive review of her past con-
uct. 'There's no woman strives more for her children; and
m sure, at scouring time this Ladyday as I've had all the
ed-hangings taken down, I did as much as the two gells
ut together; and there's this last elder-flower wine I've
aade—beautiful! I allays offer it along with the sherry,
aough sister Glegg will have it I'm so extravagant; and as
r liking to have my clothes tidy, and not go a fright about
ae house, there's nobody in the parish can say anything
gainst me in respect o' backbiting and making mischief,
r I don't wish anybody any harm; and nobody loses by
ending me a pork-pie, for my pies are fit to show with the
est o' my neighbours'; and the linen's so in order, as if I
as to die to-morrow I shouldn't be ashamed. A woman
an do no more nor she can.'

'But it's all o' no use, you know, Bessy,' said Mrs. Pullet, holding her head on one side, and fixing her eyes pathetically on her sister, 'if your husband makes away with his money. Not but what if you was sold up, and other folks bought your furniture, it's a comfort to think as you've kept it well rubbed. And there's the linen, with your maiden mark on, might go all over the country. It 'ud be a sad pity for our family.' Mrs. Pullet shook her head slowly.

'But what can I do, sister?' said Mrs. Tulliver. 'Mr Tulliver's not a man to be dictated to—not if I was to go to the parson, and get by heart what I should tell my husband for the best. And I'm sure I don't pretend to know anything about putting out money and all that. I could never see into men's business as sister Glegg does.'

'Well, you're like me in that, Bessy,' said Mrs. Pullet, 'and I think it 'ud be a deal more becoming o' Jane if she'd have that pier-glass rubbed oftener—there was ever so many spots on it last week—instead o' dictating to folks as have more comings in than she ever had, and telling 'em what they've to do with their money. But Jane and me were allays contrary: she *would* have striped things, and I like spots. You like a spot, Bessy: we allays hung together i' that.'

'Yes, Sophy,' said Mrs. Tulliver, 'I remember our having a blue ground with a white spot both alike—I've got a bit in a bed-quilt now; and if you would but go and see sister Glegg, and persuade her to make it up with Tulliver, I should take it very kind of you. You was allays a good sister to me.'

'But the right thing 'ud be for Tulliver to go and make it up with her himself, and say he was sorry for speaking so rash. If he's borrowed money of her, he shouldn't be above that,' said Mrs. Pullet, whose partiality did not blind her to principles: she did not forget what was due to people of independent fortune.

'It's no use talking o' that,' said poor Mrs. Tulliver almost peevishly. 'If I was to go down on my bare knees on the gravel to Tulliver, he'd never humble himself.'

'Well, you can't expect me to persuade *Jane* to beg

pardon,' said Mrs. Pullet. 'Her temper's beyond everything; it's well if it doesn't carry her off her mind, though there never *was* any of our family went to a madhouse.'

'I'm not thinking of her begging pardon,' said Mrs. Tulliver. 'But if she'd just take no notice, and not call her money in; as it's not so much for one sister to ask of another; time 'ud mend things, and Tulliver 'ud forget all about it, and they'd be friends again.'

Mrs. Tulliver, you perceive, was not aware of her husband's irrevocable determination to pay in the five hundred pounds; at least such a determination exceeded her powers of belief.

'Well, Bessy,' said Mrs. Pullet mournfully, '*I* don't want to help you on to ruin. I won't be behindhand i' doing you a good turn, if it is to be done. And I don't like it said among acquaintance as we've got quarrels in the family. I shall tell Jane that; and I don't mind driving to Jane's to-morrow, if Pullet doesn't mind. What do you say, Mr. Pullet?'

'I've no objections,' said Mr. Pullet, who was perfectly contented with any course the quarrel might take, so that Mr. Tulliver did not apply to *him* for money. Mr. Pullet was nervous about his investments, and did not see how a man could have any security for his money unless he turned it into land.

After a little further discussion as to whether it would not be better for Mrs. Tulliver to accompany them on a visit to sister Glegg, Mrs. Pullet, observing that it was tea-time, turned to reach from a drawer a delicate damask napkin, which she pinned before her in the fashion of an apron. The door did, in fact, soon open, but instead of the tea-tray, Sally introduced an object so startling that both Mrs. Pullet and Mrs. Tulliver gave a scream, causing uncle Pullet to swallow his lozenge—for the fifth time in his life, as he afterwards noted.

X

MAGGIE BEHAVES WORSE THAN SHE EXPECTED

THE startling object which thus made an epoch for uncl
Pullet was no other than little Lucy, with one side of he
person, from her small foot to her bonnet-crown, wet an
discoloured with mud, holding out two tiny blackene
hands, and making a very piteous face. To account for thi
unprecedented apparition in aunt Pullet's parlour, we mus
return to the moment when the three children went to pla
out of doors, and the small demons who had taken posses
sion of Maggie's soul at an early period of the day had re
turned in all the greater force after a temporary absence
All the disagreeable recollections of the morning were thic
upon her, when Tom, whose displeasure towards her ha
been considerably refreshed by her foolish trick of causin
him to upset his cowslip wine, said, 'Here, Lucy, you com
along with me,' and walked off to the area where the toad
were, as if there were no Maggie in existence. Seeing thi
Maggie lingered at a distance, looking like a small Medus
with her snakes cropped. Lucy was naturally pleased tha
cousin Tom was so good to her, and it was very amusing t
see him tickling a fat toad with a piece of string when th
toad was safe down the area, with an iron grating over him
Still Lucy wished Maggie to enjoy the spectacle also
especially as she would doubtless find a name for the toad
and say what had been its past history; for Lucy had
delighted semi-belief in Maggie's stories about the liv
things they came upon by accident—how Mrs. Earwig ha
a wash at home, and one of her children had fallen into th
hot copper, for which reason she was running so fast t
fetch the doctor. Tom had a profound contempt for thi
nonsense of Maggie's, smashing the earwig at once as
superfluous yet easy means of proving the entire unrealit
of such a story; but Lucy, for the life of her, could not hel
fancying there was something in it, and at all event
thought it was very pretty make-believe. So now the desir

o know the history of a very portly toad, added to her
habitual affectionateness, made her run back to Maggie
and say, 'O, there is such a big, funny toad, Maggie! Do
come and see.'

Maggie said nothing, but turned away from her with a
deeper frown. As long as Tom seemed to prefer Lucy to
her, Lucy made part of his unkindness. Maggie would have
thought a little while ago that she could never be cross with
pretty little Lucy, any more than she could be cruel to a
little white mouse; but then, Tom had always been quite
indifferent to Lucy before, and it had been left to Maggie to
pet and make much of her. As it was, she was actually
beginning to think that she should like to make Lucy cry,
by slapping or pinching her, especially as it might vex Tom,
whom it was of no use to slap, even if she dared, because he
didn't mind it. And if Lucy hadn't been there, Maggie was
sure he would have got friends with her sooner.

Tickling a fat toad who is not highly sensitive, is an
amusement that it is possible to exhaust, and Tom by-
and-by began to look round for some other mode of passing
the time. But in so prim a garden, where they were not to
go off the paved walks, there was not a great choice of sport.
The only great pleasure such a restriction suggested was
the pleasure of breaking it, and Tom began to meditate an
insurrectionary visit to the pond, about a field's length
beyond the garden.

'I say, Lucy,' he began, nodding his head up and down
with great significance, as he coiled up his string again,
'what do you think I mean to do?'

'What, Tom?' said Lucy with curiosity.

'I mean to go to the pond, and look at the pike. You
may go with me if you like,' said the young sultan.

'O Tom, *dare* you?' said Lucy. 'Aunt said we mustn't
go out of the garden.'

'O, I shall go out at the other end of the garden,' said
Tom. 'Nobody'll see us. Besides, I don't care if they do—
I'll run off home.'

'But *I* couldn't run,' said Lucy, who had never before
been exposed to such severe temptation.

'O, never mind—they won't be cross with *you*,' said Tom. 'You say I took you.'

Tom walked along, and Lucy trotted by his side, timidly enjoying the rare treat of doing something naughty—excited also by the mention of that celebrity, the pike, about which she was quite uncertain whether it was a fish or a fowl. Maggie saw them leaving the garden, and could not resist the impulse to follow. Anger and jealousy can no more bear to lose sight of their objects than love, and that Tom and Lucy should do or see anything of which she was ignorant would have been an intolerable idea to Maggie. So she kept a few yards behind them, unobserved by Tom, who was presently absorbed in watching for the pike—a highly interesting monster; he was said to be so very old, so very large, and to have such a remarkable appetite. The pike, like other celebrities, did not show when he was watched for, but Tom caught sight of something in rapid movement in the water, which attracted him to another spot on the brink of the pond.

'Here, Lucy!' he said in a loud whisper, 'come here! take care! keep on the grass—don't step where the cows have been!' he added, pointing to a peninsula of dry grass, with trodden mud on each side of it; for Tom's contemptuous conception of a girl included the attribute of being unfit to walk in dirty places.

Lucy came carefully as she was bidden, and bent down to look at what seemed a golden arrow-head darting through the water. It was a water-snake, Tom told her, and Lucy at last could see the serpentine wave of its body, very much wondering that a snake could swim. Maggie had drawn nearer and nearer—she *must* see it too, though it was bitter to her like everything else, since Tom did not care about her seeing it. At last, she was close by Lucy, and Tom, who had been aware of her approach, but would not notice it till he was obliged, turned round and said:

'Now, get away, Maggie; there's no room for you on the grass here. Nobody asked *you* to come.'

There were passions at war in Maggie at that moment to

ave made a tragedy, if tragedies were made by passion
nly; but the essential τι μέγεθος which was present in the
assion was wanting to the action: the utmost Maggie
ould do, with a fierce thrust of her small brown arm, was
o push poor little pink and white Lucy into the cow-
rodden mud.

Then Tom could not restrain himself, and gave Maggie
wo smart slaps on the arm as he ran to pick up Lucy, who
ay crying helplessly. Maggie retreated to the roots of a
ree a few yards off, and looked on impenitently. Usually
er repentance came quickly after one rash deed, but now
Tom and Lucy had made her so miserable, she was glad to
poil their happiness—glad to make everybody uncomfort-
ble. Why should she be sorry? Tom was very slow to
orgive *her*, however sorry she might have been.

'I shall tell mother, you know, Miss Mag,' said Tom
oudly and emphatically, as soon as Lucy was up and ready
to walk away. It was not Tom's practice to 'tell,' but here
justice clearly demanded that Maggie should be visited with
the utmost punishment: not that Tom had learnt to put
his views in that abstract form; he never mentioned
'justice,' and had no idea that his desire to punish might be
called by that fine name. Lucy was too entirely absorbed
by the evil that had befallen her—the spoiling of her pretty
best clothes, and the discomfort of being wet and dirty—to
think much of the cause, which was entirely mysterious
to her. She could never have guessed what she had done to
make Maggie angry with her; but she felt that Maggie was
very unkind and disagreeable, and made no magnanimous
entreaties to Tom that he would not 'tell,' only running
along by his side and crying piteously, while Maggie sat on
the roots of the tree and looked after them with her small
Medusa face.

'Sally,' said Tom, when they reached the kitchen door,
and Sally looked at them in speechless amaze, with a piece
of bread-and-butter in her mouth and a toasting-fork in
her hand—'Sally, tell mother it was Maggie pushed Lucy
into the mud.'

'But Lors ha' massy, how did you get near such mud as

that?' said Sally, making a wry face, as she stooped down and examined the *corpus delicti*.

Tom's imagination had not been rapid and capacious enough to include this question among the foreseen consequences, but it was no sooner put than he foresaw whither it tended, and that Maggie would not be considered the only culprit in the case. He walked quietly away from the kitchen door, leaving Sally to that pleasure of guessing which active minds notoriously prefer to ready-made knowledge.

Sally, as you are aware, lost no time in presenting Lucy at the parlour door, for to have so dirty an object introduced into the house at Garum Firs was too great a weight to be sustained by a single mind.

'Goodness gracious!' aunt Pullet exclaimed, after preluding by an inarticulate scream; 'keep her at the door, Sally! Don't bring her off the oil-cloth, whatever you do.'

'Why, she's tumbled into some nasty mud,' said Mrs Tulliver, going up to Lucy to examine into the amount of damage to clothes for which she felt herself responsible to her sister Deane.

'If you please, 'um, it was Miss Maggie as pushed her in,' said Sally; 'Master Tom's been and said so, and they must ha' been to the pond, for it's only there they could ha' got into such dirt.'

'There it is, Bessy; it's what I've been telling you,' said Mrs. Pullet, in a tone of prophetic sadness: 'it's your children—there's no knowing what they'll come to.'

Mrs. Tulliver was mute, feeling herself a truly wretched mother. As usual, the thought pressed upon her that people would think she had done something wicked to deserve her maternal troubles, while Mrs. Pullet began to give elaborate directions to Sally how to guard the premises from serious injury in the course of removing the dirt. Meantime tea was to be brought in by the cook, and the two naughty children were to have theirs in an ignominious manner in the kitchen. Mrs. Tulliver went out to speak to these naughty children, supposing them to be close at hand; but it was not until after some search that she found Tom leaning with rather hardened careless air against the white paling of the poultry-yard, and lowering his piece of string on the other side as a means of exasperating the turkey-cock.

'Tom, you naughty boy, where's your sister?' said Mrs. Tulliver, in a distressed voice.

'I don't know,' said Tom; his eagerness for justice on Maggie had diminished since he had seen clearly that it could hardly be brought about without the injustice of some blame on his own conduct.

'Why, where did you leave her?' said his mother, looking round.

'Sitting under the tree against the pond,' said Tom, apparently indifferent to everything but the string and the turkey-cock.

'Then go and fetch her in this minute, you naughty boy. And how could you think o' going to the pond, and taking your sister where there was dirt? You know she'll do mischief, if there's mischief to be done.'

It was Mrs. Tulliver's way, if she blamed Tom, to refer his misdemeanour, somehow or other, to Maggie.

The idea of Maggie sitting alone by the pond, roused an habitual fear in Mrs. Tulliver's mind, and she mounted the horse-block to satisfy herself by a sight of that fatal child, while Tom walked—not very quickly—on his way towards her.

'They're such children for the water, mine are,' she said aloud, without reflecting that there was no one to hear her; 'they'll be brought in dead and drownded some day. I wish that river was far enough.'

But when she not only failed to discern Maggie, but presently saw Tom returning from the pool alone, this hovering fear entered and took complete possession of her, and she hurried to meet him.

'Maggie's nowhere about the pond, mother,' said Tom; 'she's gone away.'

You may conceive the terrified search for Maggie, and the difficulty of convincing her mother that she was not in the pond. Mrs. Pullet observed that the child might come to a worse end if she lived—there was no knowing; and

Mr. Pullet, confused and overwhelmed by this revolutionary aspect of things—the tea deferred and the poultry alarmed by the unusual running to and fro—took up his spud as an instrument of search, and reached down a key to unlock the goose-pen, as a likely place for Maggie to lie concealed in.

Tom, after a while, started the idea that Maggie was gone home (without thinking it necessary to state that it was what he should have done himself under the circumstances), and the suggestion was seized as a comfort by his mother.

'Sister, for goodness' sake let 'em put the horse in the carriage and take me home—we shall perhaps find her on the road. Lucy can't walk in her dirty clothes,' she said, looking at that innocent victim, who was wrapped up in a shawl, and sitting with naked feet on the sofa.

Aunt Pullet was quite willing to take the shortest means of restoring her premises to order and quiet, and it was not long before Mrs. Tulliver was in the chaise looking anxiously at the most distant point before her. What the father would say if Maggie was lost was a question that predominated over every other.

XI

MAGGIE TRIES TO RUN AWAY FROM HER SHADOW

Maggie's intentions, as usual, were on a larger scale than Tom had imagined. The resolution that gathered in her mind, after Tom and Lucy had walked away, was not so simple as that of going home. No! she would run away and go to the gypsies, and Tom should never see her any more. That was by no means a new idea to Maggie; she had been so often told she was like a gypsy, and 'half wild,' that when she was miserable it seemed to her the only way of escaping opprobrium, and being entirely in harmony with circumstances would be to live in a little brown tent on the commons: the gypsies, she considered, would gladly receive her, and pay her much respect on account of her superior knowledge. She had once mentioned her views on this point to Tom, and suggested that he should stain his

face brown, and they should run away together; but Tom
rejected the scheme with contempt, observing that gypsies
were thieves, and hardly got anything to eat, and had nothing to drive but a donkey. To-day, however, Maggie
thought her misery had reached a pitch at which gypsydom
was her only refuge, and she rose from her seat on the roots
of the tree with the sense that this was a great crisis in her
life; she would run straight away till she came to Dunlow
Common, where there would certainly be gypsies; and
cruel Tom, and the rest of her relations who found fault
with her, should never see her any more. She thought of
her father as she ran along, but she reconciled herself to the
idea of parting with him, by determining that she would
secretly send him a letter by a small gypsy, who would run
away without telling where she was, and just let him know
that she was well and happy, and always loved him very
much.

Maggie soon got out of breath with running, but by the
time Tom got to the pond again, she was at the distance of
three long fields, and was on the edge of the lane leading to
the high-road. She stopped to pant a little, reflecting that
running away was not a pleasant thing until one had got
quite to the common where the gypsies were, but her resolution had not abated: she presently passed through the gate
into the lane, not knowing where it would lead her, for it
was not this way that they came from Dorlcote Mill to
Garum Firs, and she felt all the safer for that, because
there was no chance of her being overtaken. But she was
soon aware, not without trembling, that there were two
men coming along the lane in front of her: she had not
thought of meeting strangers—she had been too much
occupied with the idea of her friends coming after her. The
formidable strangers were two shabby-looking men with
flushed faces, one of them carrying a bundle on a stick over
his shoulder: but to her surprise, while she was dreading
their disapprobation as a runaway, the man with the
bundle stopped, and in a half-whining, half-coaxing tone,
asked her if she had a copper to give a poor man. Maggie
had a sixpence in her pocket—her uncle Glegg's present—

which she immediately drew out and gave this poor man
with a polite smile, hoping he would feel very kindly to
wards her as a generous person. 'That's the only money
I've got,' she said apologetically. 'Thank you, little miss,'
said the man in a less respectful and grateful tone than
Maggie anticipated, and she even observed that he smiled
and winked at his companion. She walked on hurriedly,
but was aware that the two men were standing still, prob
ably to look after her, and she presently heard them laugh
ing loudly. Suddenly it occurred to her that they might
think she was an idiot: Tom had said that her cropped hair
made her look like an idiot, and it was too painful an idea
to be readily forgotten. Besides, she had no sleeves on—
only a cape and a bonnet. It was clear that she was not
likely to make a favourable impression on passengers, and
she thought she would turn into the fields again; but not
on the same side of the lane as before, lest they should still
be uncle Pullet's fields. She turned through the first gate
that was not locked, and felt a delightful sense of privacy
in creeping along by the hedgerows, after her recent
humiliating encounter. She was used to wandering about
the fields by herself, and was less timid there than on the
high-road. Sometimes she had to climb over high gates,
but that was a small evil; she was getting out of reach very
fast, and she should probably soon come within sight of
Dunlow Common, or at least of some other common, for
she had heard her father say that you couldn't go very far
without coming to a common. She hoped so, for she was
getting rather tired and hungry, and until she reached the
gypsies there was no definite prospect of bread-and-butter.
It was still broad daylight, for aunt Pullet, retaining the
early habits of the Dodson family, took tea at half-past
four by the sun, and at five by the kitchen clock; so
though it was nearly an hour since Maggie started, there
was no gathering gloom on the fields to remind her that the
night would come. Still, it seemed to her that she had been
walking a very great distance indeed, and it was really sur
prising that the common did not come within sight.
Hitherto she had been in the rich parish of Garum, where

ere was a great deal of pasture-land, and she had only
en one labourer at a distance. That was fortunate in
me respects, as labourers might be too ignorant to under-
and the propriety of her wanting to go to Dunlow Com-
on; yet it would have been better if she could have met
me one who would tell her the way without wanting to
now anything about her private business. At last, how-
ver, the green fields came to an end, and Maggie found her-
lf looking through the bars of a gate into a lane with a
ide margin of grass on each side of it. She had never seen
ich a wide lane before, and, without her knowing why, it
ave her the impression that the common could not be far
ff; perhaps it was because she saw a donkey with a log to
is foot feeding on the grassy margin, for she had seen a
onkey with that pitiable encumbrance on Dunlow Com-
on when she had been across it in her father's gig. She
rept through the bars of the gate and walked on with new
pirit, though not without haunting images of Apollyon,
nd a highwayman with a pistol, and a blinking dwarf in
ellow, with a mouth from ear to ear, and other miscel-
neous dangers. For poor little Maggie had at once the
midity of an active imagination and the daring that
omes from overmastering impulse. She had rushed into
e adventure of seeking her unknown kindred, the gypsies;
nd now she was in this strange lane, she hardly dared look
n one side of her, lest she should see the diabolical black-
mith in his leathern apron grinning at her with arms
kimbo. It was not without a leaping of the heart that she
aught sight of a small pair of bare legs sticking up, feet
ppermost, by the side of a hillock; they seemed something
ideously preternatural—a diabolical kind of fungus; for
e was too much agitated at the first glance to see the
agged clothes and the dark shaggy head attached to them.
t was a boy asleep, and Maggie trotted along faster and
ore lightly, lest she should wake him: it did not occur to
er that he was one of her friends the gypsies, who in all
robability would have very genial manners. But the fact
as so, for at the next bend in the lane, Maggie actually
w the little semicircular black tent with the blue smoke

rising before it, which was to be her refuge from all the
blighting obloquy that had pursued her in civilized life.
She even saw a tall female figure by the column of smoke—
doubtless the gypsy-mother, who provided the tea and
other groceries; it was astonishing to herself that she did
not feel more delighted. But it was startling to find the
gypsies in a lane, after all, and not on a common; indeed, it
was rather disappointing; for a mysterious illimitable common, where there were sand-pits to hide in, and one was
out of everybody's reach, had always made part of Maggie's
picture of gypsy life. She went on, however, and though
with some comfort that gypsies most likely knew nothing
about idiots, so there was no danger of their falling into the
mistake of setting her down at the first glance as an idiot.
It was plain she had attracted attention; for the tall figure
who proved to be a young woman with a baby on her arm
walked slowly to meet her. Maggie looked up in the new
face rather tremblingly as it approached, and was reassured
by the thought that her aunt Pullet and the rest were right
when they called her a gypsy, for this face, with the bright
dark eyes and the long hair, was really something like what
she used to see in the glass before she cut her hair off.

'My little lady, where are you going to?' the gypsy said,
in a tone of coaxing deference.

It was delightful, and just what Maggie expected; the
gypsies saw at once that she was a little lady, and were prepared to treat her accordingly.

'Not any farther,' said Maggie, feeling as if she were saying what she had rehearsed in a dream. 'I'm come to stay
with *you*, please.'

'That's pretty; come, then. Why, what a nice little lady
you are, to be sure,' said the gypsy, taking her by the hand.
Maggie thought her very agreeable, but wished she had not
been so dirty.

There was quite a group round the fire when they reached
it. An old gypsy woman was seated on the ground nursing
her knees, and occasionally poking a skewer into the round
kettle that sent forth an odorous steam: two small shock-
headed children were lying prone and resting on their

elbows something like small sphinxes; and a placid donkey was bending his head over a tall girl, who, lying on her back, was scratching his nose and indulging him with a bite of excellent stolen hay. The slanting sunlight fell kindly upon them, and the scene was really very pretty and comfortable, Maggie thought, only she hoped they would soon set out the tea-cups. Everything would be quite charming when she had taught the gypsies to use a washing-basin, and to feel an interest in books. It was a little confusing, though, that the young woman began to speak to the old one in a language which Maggie did not understand, while the tall girl, who was feeding the donkey, sat up and stared at her without offering any salutation. At last the old woman said:

'What, my pretty lady, are you come to stay with us? Sit ye down and tell us where ye come from.'

It was just like a story: Maggie liked to be called pretty lady and treated in this way. She sat down and said:

'I'm come from home because I'm unhappy, and I mean to be a gypsy. I'll live with you if you like, and I can teach you a great many things.'

'Such a clever little lady,' said the woman with the baby, sitting down by Maggie, and allowing baby to crawl; 'and such a pretty bonnet and frock,' she added, taking off Maggie's bonnet and looking at it while she made an observation to the old woman, in the unknown language. The tall girl snatched the bonnet and put it on her own head hind-foremost with a grin; but Maggie was determined not to show any weakness on this subject, as if she were susceptible about her bonnet.

'I don't want to wear a bonnet,' she said, 'I'd rather wear a red handkerchief, like yours' (looking at her friend by her side); 'my hair was quite long till yesterday, when I cut it off: but I daresay it will grow again very soon,' she added apologetically, thinking it probable the gypsies had a strong prejudice in favour of long hair. And Maggie had forgotten even her hunger at that moment in the desire to conciliate gypsy opinion.

'O what a nice little lady!—and rich, I'm sure,' said the

old woman. 'Didn't you live in a beautiful house a
home?'

'Yes, my home is pretty, and I'm very fond of the river
where we go fishing—but I'm often very unhappy. I shoul
have liked to bring my books with me, but I came away i
a hurry, you know. But I can tell you almost everythin
there is in my books, I've read them so many times—an
that will amuse you. And I can tell you something abou
Geography too—that's about the world we live in—ver
useful and interesting. Did you ever hear about Columbus ?

Maggie's eyes had begun to sparkle and her cheeks t
flush—she was really beginning to instruct the gypsies an
gaining great influence over them. The gypsies themselve
were not without amazement at this talk, though thei
attention was divided by the contents of Maggie's pocke
which the friend at her right hand had by this time emptie
without attracting her notice.

'Is that where you live, my little lady?' said the ol
woman, at the mention of Columbus.

'O no!' said Maggie, with some pity; 'Columbus was
very wonderful man, who found out half the world, an
they put chains on him and treated him very badly, yo
know—it's in my Catechism of Geography—but perhap
it's rather too long to tell before tea . . . *I want my tea so*

The last words burst from Maggie, in spite of hersel
with a sudden drop from patronising instruction to simpl
peevishness.

'Why, she's hungry, poor little lady,' said the younge
woman. 'Give her some o' the cold victual. You've bee
walking a good way, I'll be bound, my dear. Where's you
home?'

'It's Dorlcote Mill, a good way off,' said Maggie. 'M
father is Mr. Tulliver, but we mustn't let him know where
am, else he'll fetch me home again. Where does the quee
of the gypsies live?'

'What! do you want to go to her, my little lady?' sai
the younger woman. The tall girl meanwhile was con
stantly staring at Maggie and grinning. Her manners wer
certainly not agreeable.

'No,' said Maggie, 'I'm only thinking that if she isn't a very good queen you might be glad when she died, and you could choose another. If I was a queen, I'd be a very good queen, and kind to everybody.'

'Here's a bit o' nice victual, then,' said the old woman, handing to Maggie a lump of dry bread, which she had taken from a bag of scraps, and a piece of cold bacon.

'Thank you,' said Maggie, looking at the food without taking it; 'but will you give me some bread-and-butter and tea instead? I don't like bacon.'

'We've got no tea nor butter,' said the old woman with something like a scowl, as if she were getting tired of coaxing.

'O, a little bread and treacle would do,' said Maggie.

'We han't got no treacle,' said the old woman crossly, whereupon there followed a sharp dialogue between the two women in their unknown tongue, and one of the small sphinxes snatched at the bread-and-bacon, and began to eat it. At this moment the tall girl, who had gone a few yards off, came back, and said something which produced a strong effect. The old woman, seeming to forget Maggie's hunger, poked the skewer into the pot with new vigour, and the younger crept under the tent, and reached out some platters and spoons. Maggie trembled a little, and was afraid the tears would come into her eyes. Meanwhile the tall girl gave a shrill cry, and presently came running up the boy whom Maggie had passed as he was sleeping—a rough urchin about the age of Tom. He stared at Maggie, and there ensued much incomprehensible chattering. She felt very lonely, and was quite sure she should begin to cry before long: the gypsies didn't seem to mind her at all, and she felt quite weak among them. But the springing tears were checked by new terror, when two men came up, whose approach had been the cause of the sudden excitement. The elder of the two carried a bag, which he flung down, addressing the women in a loud and scolding tone, which they answered by a shower of treble sauciness; while a black cur ran barking up to Maggie, and threw her into a tremor that only found a new cause in the curses with which the younger man called the dog off. and gave him a rap with great stick he held in his hand.

Maggie felt that it was impossible she should ever b queen of these people, or even communicate to ther amusing and useful knowledge.

Both the men now seemed to be inquiring about Maggie for they looked at her, and the tone of the conversatio became of that pacific kind which implies curiosity on on side and the power of satisfying it on the other. At last th younger woman said in her previous deferential coaxin tone:

'This nice little lady's come to live with us: aren't yo glad?'

'Ay, very glad,' said the younger man, who was lookin at Maggie's silver thimble and other small matters that ha been taken from her pocket. He returned them all excep the thimble to the younger woman, with some observatio and she immediately restored them to Maggie's pocke while the men seated themselves, and began to attack th contents of the kettle—a stew of meat and potatoes— which had been taken off the fire and turned out into yellow platter.

Maggie began to think that Tom must be right about th gypsies—they must certainly be thieves, unless the ma meant to return her thimble by-and-by. She would wil ingly have given it to him, for she was not at all attache to her thimble; but the idea that she was among thieve prevented her from feeling any comfort in the revival c deference and attention towards her—all thieves, excep Robin Hood, were wicked people. The women saw she wa frightened.

'We've got nothing nice for a lady to eat,' said the ol woman, in her coaxing tone. 'And she's so hungry, swee little lady.'

'Here, my dear, try if you can eat a bit o' this,' said th younger woman, handing some of the stew on a brown dis with an iron spoon to Maggie, who, remembering that th old woman had seemed angry with her for not liking th bread-and-bacon, dared not refuse the stew, though fea

ad chased away her appetite. If her father would but come
y in the gig and take her up! Or even if Jack the Giant-
iller, or Mr. Greatheart, or St. George who slew the dragon
n the halfpennies, would happen to pass that way! But
Iaggie thought with a sinking heart that these heroes were
ever seen in the neighbourhood of St. Ogg's—nothing very
onderful ever came there.

Maggie Tulliver, you perceive, was by no means that
ell-trained, well-informed young person that a small
emale of eight or nine necessarily is in these days: she had
nly been to school a year at St. Ogg's, and had so few
ooks that she sometimes read the dictionary; so that in
ravelling over her small mind you would have found the
tost unexpected ignorance as well as unexpected know-
dge. She could have informed you that there was such a
ord as 'polygamy,' and being also acquainted with 'poly-
yllable,' she had deduced the conclusion that 'poly' meant
nany;' but she had had no idea that gypsies were not well
upplied with groceries, and her thoughts generally were
he oddest mixture of clear-eyed acumen and blind dreams.

Her ideas about the gypsies had undergone a rapid modi-
cation in the last five minutes. From having considered
hem very respectful companions, amenable to instruction,
he had begun to think that they meant perhaps to kill her
s soon as it was dark, and cut up her body for gradual
ooking: the suspicion crossed her that the fierce-eyed old
tan was in fact the devil, who might drop that transparent
isguise at any moment, and turn either into the grinning
lacksmith or else a fiery-eyed monster with dragon's wings.
t was no use trying to eat the stew, and yet the thing she
tost dreaded was to offend the gypsies, by betraying her
xtremely unfavourable opinion of them, and she won-
ered, with a keenness of interest that no theologian could
ave exceeded, whether, if the devil were really present, he
ould know her thoughts.

'What! you don't like the smell of it, my dear,' said the
oung woman, observing that Maggie did not even take a
poonful of the stew. 'Try a bit—come.'

'No, thank you,' said Maggie, summoning all her force

for a desperate effort, and trying to smile in a friendly wa;
'I haven't time, I think—it seems getting darker. I thin
I must go home now, and come again another day, an
then I can bring you a basket with some jam-tarts an
things.'

Maggie rose from her seat as she threw out this illusor
prospect, devoutly hoping that Apollyon was gullible; bu
her hope sank when the old gypsy-woman said, 'Stop a bi
stop a bit, little lady—we'll take you home, all safe, whe
we've done supper: you shall ride home, like a lady.'

Maggie sat down again, with little faith in this promis
though she presently saw the tall girl putting a bridle c
the donkey, and throwing a couple of bags on his back.

'Now, then, little missis,' said the younger man, risin
and leading the donkey forward, 'tell us where you live—
what's the name o' the place?'

'Dorlcote Mill is my home,' said Maggie eagerly. 'M
father is Mr. Tulliver—he lives there.'

'What! a big mill a little way this side o' St. Ogg's?'

'Yes,' said Maggie. 'Is it far off? I think I should lil
to walk there, if you please.'

'No, no, it'll be getting dark, we must make haste. An
the donkey'll carry you as nice as can be—you'll see.'

He lifted Maggie as he spoke, and set her on the donke
She felt relieved that it was not the old man who seemed
be going with her, but she had only a trembling hope th
she was really going home.

'Here's your pretty bonnet,' said the younger woma
putting that recently-despised but now welcome article
costume on Maggie's head; 'and you'll say we've been ver
good to you, won't you? and what a nice little lady we sai
you was.'

'O, yes, thank you,' said Maggie, 'I'm very muc
obliged to you. But I wish you'd go with me too.' Sh
thought anything was better than going with one of th
dreadful men alone: it would be more cheerful to
murdered by a larger party.

'Ah, you're fondest o' *me*, aren't you?' said the woma
'But I can't go—you'll go too fast for me.'

It now appeared that the man also was to be seated on the donkey, holding Maggie before him, and she was as incapable of remonstrating against this arrangement as the donkey himself, though no nightmare had ever seemed to her more horrible. When the woman had patted her on the back, and said 'Good-bye,' the donkey, at a strong hint from the man's stick, set off at a rapid walk along the lane towards the point Maggie had come from an hour ago, while the tall girl and the rough urchin, also furnished with sticks, obligingly escorted them for the first hundred yards, with much screaming and thwacking.

Not Leonore, in that preternatural midnight excursion with her phantom lover, was more terrified than poor Maggie in this entirely natural ride on a short-paced donkey, with a gypsy behind her, who considered that he was earning half-a-crown. The red light of the setting sun seemed to have a portentous meaning, with which the alarming bray of the second donkey with the log on its foot must surely have some connection. Two low thatched cottages—the only houses they passed in this lane—seemed to add to its dreariness: they had no windows to speak of, and the doors were closed: it was probable that they were inhabited by witches, and it was a relief to find that the donkey did not stop there.

At last—O, sight of joy!—this lane, the longest in the world, was coming to an end, was opening on a broad highroad, where there was actually a coach passing! And there was a finger-post at the corner: she had surely seen that finger-post before—'To St. Ogg's, 2 miles.' The gypsy really meant to take her home, then: he was probably a good man, after all, and might have been rather hurt at the thought that she didn't like coming with him alone. This idea became stronger as she felt more and more certain that he knew the road quite well, and she was considering how she might open a conversation with the injured gypsy, and not only gratify his feelings but efface the impression of her cowardice, when, as they reached the cross-road, Maggie caught sight of some one coming on a white-faced horse.

'O, stop, stop!' she cried out. 'There's my father! (father, father!'

The sudden joy was almost painful, and before her fathe reached her, she was sobbing. Great was Mr. Tulliver wonder, for he had made a round from Basset, and had n yet been home.

'Why, what's the meaning o' this?' he said, checking h horse, while Maggie slipped from the donkey and ran to h father's stirrup.

'The little miss lost herself, I reckon,' said the gypsy 'She'd come to our tent at the far end o' Dunlow Lan and I was bringing her where she said her home was. It a good way to come arter being on the tramp all day.'

'O, yes, father, he's been very good to bring me home said Maggie. 'A very kind, good man!'

'Here, then, my man,' said Mr. Tulliver, taking ou five shillings. 'It's the best day's work *you* ever did. couldn't afford to lose the little wench; here, lift her u before me.'

'Why, Maggie, how's this, how's this?' he said, as the rode along, while she laid her head against her father, an sobbed. 'How came you to be rambling about and lo yourself?'

'O, father,' sobbed Maggie, 'I ran away because I was unhappy—Tom was so angry with me. I couldn't bear it.'

'Pooh, pooh,' said Mr. Tulliver soothingly, 'you mustn think o' running away from father. What 'ud father c without his little wench?'

'O no, I never will again, father—never.'

Mr. Tulliver spoke his mind very strongly when I reached home that evening, and the effect was seen in th remarkable fact, that Maggie never heard one reproach fro her mother, or one taunt from Tom, about this fooli business of her running away to the gypsies. Maggie w rather awe-stricken by this unusual treatment, and som times thought that her conduct had been too wicked to alluded to.

XII

MR. AND MRS. GLEGG AT HOME

In order to see Mr. and Mrs. Glegg at home, we must enter the town of St. Ogg's—that venerable town with the red-fluted roofs and the broad warehouse gables, where the black ships unlade themselves of their burthens from the far north, and carry away, in exchange, the precious inland products, the well-crushed cheese and the soft fleeces, which my refined readers have doubtless become acquainted with through the medium of the best classic pastorals.

It is one of those old, old towns which impress one as a continuation and outgrowth of nature, as much as the nests of the bower-birds or the winding galleries of the white ants: a town which carries the traces of its long growth and history like a millennial tree, and has sprung up and developed in the same spot between the river and the low hill from the time when the Roman legions turned their backs on it from the camp on the hill-side, and the long-haired sea-kings came up the river and looked with fierce eager eyes at the fatness of the land. It is a town 'familiar with forgotten years.' The shadow of the Saxon hero-king still walks there fitfully, reviewing the scenes of his youth and lovetime, and is met by the gloomier shadow of the dreadful heathen Dane, who was stabbed in the midst of his warriors by the sword of an invisible avenger, and who rises on autumn evenings like a white mist from his tumulus on the hill, and hovers in the court of the old hall by the river-side—the spot where he was thus miraculously slain in the days before the old hall was built. It was the Normans who began to build that fine old hall, which is like the town, telling of the thoughts and hands of widely-sundered generations; but it is all so old that we look with loving pardon at its inconsistencies, and are well content that they who built the stone oriel, and they who built the Gothic façade and towers of finest small brickwork with the trefoil ornament, and the windows and battlements defined with stone, did

not sacrilegiously pull down the ancient half-timbere
body with its oak-roofed banqueting-hall.

But older even than this old hall is perhaps the bit of wal
now built into the belfry of the parish church, and said to
be a remnant of the original chapel dedicated to St. Ogg
the patron saint of this ancient town, of whose history I
possess several manuscript versions. I incline to the brief
est, since, if it should not be wholly true, it is at least likely
to contain the least falsehood. 'Ogg the son of Beorl,' say
my private hagiographer, 'was a boatman who gained a
scanty living by ferrying passengers across the river Floss
And it came to pass, one evening when the winds were high
that there sat moaning by the brink of the river a woman
with a child in her arms; and she was clad in rags, and had
a worn and weathered look, and she craved to be rowed
across the river. And the men thereabout questioned her
and said, "Wherefore dost thou desire to cross the river
Tarry till the morning, and take shelter here for the night
so shalt thou be wise, and not foolish." Still she went on to
mourn and crave. But Ogg the son of Beorl came up and
said, "I will ferry thee across: it is enough that thy heart
needs it." And he ferried her across. And it came to pass
when she stepped ashore, that her rags were turned into
robes of flowing white, and her face became bright with
exceeding beauty, and there was a glory around it, so that
she shed a light on the water like the moon in its brightness
And she said—"Ogg the son of Beorl, thou art blessed in
that thou didst not question and wrangle with the heart's
need, but wast smitten with pity, and didst straightway re
lieve the same. And from henceforth whoso steps into thy
boat shall be in no peril from the storm; and whenever it
puts forth to the rescue, it shall save the lives both of men
and beasts." And when the floods came, many were saved
by reason of that blessing on the boat. But when Ogg the
son of Beorl died, behold, in the parting of his soul, the boat
loosed itself from its moorings, and was floated with the
ebbing tide in great swiftness to the ocean, and was seen no
more. Yet it was witnessed in the floods of aftertime, that
at the coming on of eventide, Ogg the son of Beorl was

always seen with his boat upon the wide-spreading waters, and the Blessed Virgin sat in the prow, shedding a light around as of the moon in its brightness, so that the rowers in the gathering darkness took heart and pulled anew.'

This legend, one sees, reflects from a far-off time the visitation of the floods, which, even when they left human life untouched, were widely fatal to the helpless cattle, and swept as sudden death over all smaller living things. But the town knew worse troubles even than the floods—troubles of the civil wars, when it was a continual fighting-place, where first Puritans thanked God for the blood of the Loyalists, and then Loyalists thanked God for the blood of the Puritans. Many honest citizens lost all their possessions for conscience' sake in those times, and went forth beggared from their native town. Doubtless there are many houses standing now on which those honest citizens turned their backs in sorrow: quaint-gabled houses looking on the river, jammed between newer warehouses, and penetrated by surprising passages, which turn and turn at sharp angles till they lead you out on a muddy strand overflowed continually by the rushing tide. Everywhere the brick houses have a mellow look, and in Mrs. Glegg's day there was no incongruous new-fashioned smartness, no plate-glass in shop windows, no fresh stucco-facing or other fallacious attempt to make fine old red St. Ogg's wear the air of a town that sprang up yesterday. The shop windows were small and unpretending; for the farmers' wives and daughters who came to do their shopping on market-days were not to be withdrawn from their regular well-known shops; and the tradesmen had no wares intended for customers who would go on their way and be seen no more. Ah! even Mrs. Glegg's day seems far back in the past now, separated from us by changes that widen the years. War and the rumour of war had then died out from the minds of men, and if they were ever thought of by the farmers in drab great-coats, who shook the grain out of their sample-bags and buzzed over it in the full market-place, it was as a state of things that belonged to a past golden age, when prices were high. Surely the time was gone for ever when the broad river could bring up unwelcome ships: Russia was only the place where the linseed came from—the more the better—making grist for the great vertical millstones with their scythe-like arms, roaring and grinding and carefully sweeping as if an informing soul were in them. The Catholics, bad harvests, and the mysterious fluctuations of trade, were the three evils mankind had to fear: even the floods had not been great of late years. The mind of St. Ogg's did not look extensively before or after. It inherited a long past without thinking of it, and had no eyes for the spirits that walk the streets. Since the centuries when St. Ogg with his boat and the Virgin Mother at the prow had been seen on the wide water, so many memories had been left behind, and had gradually vanished like the receding hill-tops! And the present time was like the level plain where men lose their belief in volcanoes and earthquakes, thinking to-morrow will be as yesterday, and the giant forces that used to shake the earth are for ever laid to sleep. The days were gone when people could be greatly wrought upon by their faith, still less change it: the Catholics were formidable because they would lay hold of government and property, and burn men alive; not because any sane and honest parishioner of St. Ogg's could be brought to believe in the Pope. One aged person remembered how a rude multitude had been swayed when John Wesley preached in the cattle-market; but for a long while it had not been expected of preachers that they should shake the souls of men. An occasional burst of fervour, in Dissenting pulpits, on the subject of infant baptism, was the only symptom of a zeal unsuited to sober times when men had done with change. Protestantism sat at ease, unmindful of schisms, careless of proselytism: Dissent was an inheritance along with a superior pew and a business connection; and Churchmanship only wondered contemptuously at Dissent as a foolish habit that clung greatly to families in the grocery and chandlering lines, though not incompatible with prosperous wholesale dealing. But with the Catholic Question had come a slight wind of controversy to break the calm: the elderly rector had become occasionally historical and argumentative, and Mr. Spray, the Independent minister, had begun to preach political sermons, in which he distinguished with much subtlety between his fervent belief in the right of the Catholics to the franchise and his fervent belief in their eternal perdition. Most of Mr. Spray's hearers, however, were incapable of following his subtleties, and many old-fashioned Dissenters were much pained by his 'siding with the Catholics;' while others thought he had better let politics alone. Public spirit was not held in high esteem at St. Ogg's, and men who busied themselves with political questions were regarded with some suspicion, as dangerous characters: they were usually persons who had little or no business of their own to manage, or, if they had, were likely enough to become insolvent.

This was the general aspect of things at St. Ogg's in Mrs. Glegg's day, and at that particular period in her family history when she had had her quarrel with Mr. Tulliver. It was a time when ignorance was much more comfortable than at present, and was received with all the honours in very good society, without being obliged to dress itself in an elaborate costume of knowledge; a time when cheap periodicals were not, and when country surgeons never thought of asking their female patients if they were fond of reading, but simply took it for granted that they preferred gossip; a time when ladies in rich silk gowns wore large pockets, in which they carried a mutton-bone to secure them against cramp. Mrs. Glegg carried such a bone, which she had inherited from her grandmother with a brocaded gown that would stand up empty, like a suit of armour, and a silver-headed walking-stick; for the Dodson family had been respectable for many generations.

Mrs. Glegg had both a front and a back parlour in her excellent house at St. Ogg's, so that she had two points of view from which she could observe the weakness of her fellow-beings, and reinforce her thankfulness for her own exceptional strength of mind. From her front windows she could look down the Tofton Road, leading out of St. Ogg's, and note the growing tendency to 'gadding about' in the wives of men not retired from business, together with a practice of wearing woven cotton stockings, which opened a dreary prospect for the coming generation; and from her back windows she could look down the pleasant garden and orchard which stretched to the river, and observe the folly of Mr. Glegg in spending his time among 'them flowers and vegetables.' For Mr. Glegg, having retired from active business as a wool-stapler, for the purpose of enjoying himself through the rest of his life, had found this last occupation so much more severe than his business, that he had been driven into amateur hard labour as a dissipation, and habitually relaxed by doing the work of two ordinary gardeners. The economising of a gardener's wages might perhaps have induced Mrs. Glegg to wink at this folly, if it were possible for a healthy female mind even to simulate respect for a husband's hobby. But it is well known that this conjugal complacency belongs only to the weaker portion of the sex, who are scarcely alive to the responsibilities of a wife as a constituted check on her husband's pleasures, which are hardly ever of a rational or commendable kind.

Mr. Glegg on his side, too, had a double source of mental occupation, which gave every promise of being inexhaustible. On the one hand, he surprised himself by his discoveries in natural history, finding that his piece of garden-ground contained wonderful caterpillars, slugs, and insects, which, so far as he had heard, had never before attracted human observation; and he noticed remarkable coincidences between these zoological phenomena and the great events of that time,—as, for example, that before the burning of York Minster there had been mysterious serpentine marks on the leaves of the rose-trees, together with an unusual prevalence of slugs, which he had been puzzled to know the meaning of, until it flashed upon him with this melancholy conflagration. (Mr. Glegg had an unusual amount of mental activity, which, when disengaged from the wool business, naturally made itself a pathway in other directions.) And his second subject of meditation was the 'contrairiness' of the female mind, as typically exhibited in Mrs. Glegg. That a creature made—in a genealogical

sense—out of a man's rib, and in this particular case maintained in the highest respectability without any trouble
of her own, should be normally in a state of contradiction to the blandest propositions and even to the most
accommodating concessions, was a mystery in the scheme
of things to which he had often in vain sought a clue in
the early chapters of Genesis. Mr. Glegg had chosen the
eldest Miss Dodson as a handsome embodiment of female
prudence and thrift, and being himself of a money-getting,
money-keeping turn, had calculated on much conjugal
harmony. But in that curious compound, the feminine
character, it may easily happen that the flavour is unpleasant in spite of excellent ingredients; and a fine systematic
stinginess may be accompanied with a seasoning that quite
spoils its relish. Now, good Mr. Glegg himself was stingy
in the most amiable manner: his neighbours called him
'near,' which always means that the person in question
is a lovable skinflint. If you expressed a preference for
cheese-parings, Mr. Glegg would remember to save them
for you, with a good-natured delight in gratifying your
palate, and he was given to pet all animals which required
no appreciable keep. There was no humbug or hypocrisy
about Mr. Glegg; his eyes would have watered with true
feeling over the sale of a widow's furniture, which a five-
pound note from his side-pocket would have prevented;
but a donation of five pounds to a person 'in a small way
of life' would have seemed to him a mad kind of lavishness
rather than 'charity,' which had always presented itself to
him as a contribution of small aids, not a neutralising of
misfortune. And Mr. Glegg was just as fond of saving other
people's money as his own: he would have ridden as far
round to avoid a turnpike when his expenses were to be
paid for him, as when they were to come out of his own
pocket, and was quite zealous in trying to induce indifferent acquaintances to adopt a cheap substitute for blacking.
This inalienable habit of saving, as an end in itself, belonged
to the industrious men of business of a former generation,
who made their fortunes slowly, almost as the tracking of
the fox belongs to the harrier—it constituted them a 'race,'

which is nearly lost in these days of rapid money-getting, when lavishness comes close on the back of want. In old-fashioned times, an 'independence' was hardly ever made without a little miserliness as a condition, and you would have found that quality in every provincial district, combined with characters as various as the fruits from which we can extract acid. The true Harpagons were always marked and exceptional characters: not so the worthy tax-payers, who, having once pinched from real necessity, retained even in the midst of their comfortable retirement, with their wall-fruit and wine-bins, the habit of regarding life as an ingenious process of nibbling out one's livelihood without leaving any perceptible deficit, and who would have been as immediately prompted to give up a newly-taxed luxury when they had their clear five hundred a-year, as when they had only five hundred pounds of capital. Mr. Glegg was one of these men, found so impracticable by chancellors of the exchequer; and knowing this, you will be the better able to understand why he had not swerved from the conviction that he had made an eligible marriage, in spite of the too pungent seasoning that nature had given to the eldest Miss Dodson's virtues. A man with an affectionate disposition, who finds a wife to concur with his fundamental idea of life, easily comes to persuade himself that no other woman would have suited him so well, and does a little daily snapping and quarrelling without any sense of alienation. Mr. Glegg, being of a reflective turn, and no longer occupied with wool, had much wondering meditation on the peculiar constitution of the female mind as unfolded to him in his domestic life; and yet he thought Mrs. Glegg's household ways a model for her sex: it struck him as a pitiable irregularity in other women if they did not roll up their table-napkins with the same tightness and emphasis as Mrs. Glegg did, if their pastry had a less leathery consistence, and their damson cheese a less venerable hardness than hers; nay, even the peculiar combination of grocery and drug-like odours in Mrs. Glegg's private cupboard impressed him as the only right thing in the way of cupboard smells. I am not sure that he would not have longed for the quarrelling again, if it had ceased for an entire week; and it is certain that an acquiescent mild wife would have left his meditations comparatively jejune and barren of mischief.

Mr. Glegg's unmistakable kind-heartedness was shown in this, that it pained him more to see his wife at variance with others—even with Dolly, the servant—than to be in a state of cavil with her himself; and the quarrel between her and Mr. Tulliver vexed him so much that it quite nullified the pleasure he would otherwise have had in the state of his early cabbages, as he walked in his garden before breakfast the next morning. Still he went in to breakfast with some slight hope that, now Mrs. Glegg had 'slept upon it,' her anger might be subdued enough to give way to her usually strong sense of family decorum. She had been used to boast that there had never been any of those deadly quarrels among the Dodsons which had disgraced other families; that no Dodson had ever been 'cut off with a shilling,' and no cousin of the Dodsons disowned; as, indeed, why should they be? for they had no cousins who had not money out at use, or some houses of their own, at the very least.

There was one evening-cloud which had always disappeared from Mrs. Glegg's brow when she sat at the breakfast-table: it was her fuzzy front of curls; for as she occupied herself in household matters in the morning, it would have been a mere extravagance to put on anything so superfluous to the making of leathery pastry as a fuzzy curled front. By half-past ten decorum demanded the front: until then Mrs. Glegg could economize it, and society would never be any the wiser. But the absence of that cloud only left it more apparent that the cloud of severity remained; and Mr. Glegg, perceiving this, as he sat down to his milk-porridge, which it was his old frugal habit to stem his morning hunger with, prudently resolved to leave the first remark to Mrs. Glegg, lest, to so delicate an article as a lady's temper, the slightest touch should do mischief. People who seem to enjoy their ill-temper have a way of keeping it in fine condition by inflicting privations on

themselves. That was Mrs. Glegg's way: she made her tea
weaker than usual this morning, and declined butter. It
was a hard case that a vigorous mood for quarrelling, so
highly capable of using any opportunity, should not meet
with a single remark from Mr. Glegg on which to exercise
itself. But by-and-by it appeared that his silence would
answer the purpose, for he heard himself apostrophized at
last in that tone peculiar to the wife of one's bosom.

'Well, Mr. Glegg! it's a poor return I get for making you
the wife I've made you all these years. If this is the way
I'm to be treated, I'd better ha' known it before my poor
father died, and then, when I'd wanted a home, I should
ha' gone elsewhere—as the choice was offered me.'

Mr. Glegg paused from his porridge and looked up—not
with any new amazement, but simply with that quiet,
habitual wonder with which we regard constant mysteries.

'Why, Mrs. G., what have I done now?'

'Done now, Mr. Glegg? *done now?* . . . I'm sorry for you.'

Not seeing his way to any pertinent answer, Mr. Glegg
reverted to his porridge.

'There's husbands in the world,' continued Mrs. Glegg,
after a pause, 'as 'ud have known how to do something
different to siding with everybody else against their own
wives. Perhaps I'm wrong, and you can teach me better.
But I've allays heard as it's the husband's place to stand
by the wife, instead o' rejoicing and triumphing when folks
insult her.'

'Now, what call have you to say that?' said Mr. Glegg,
rather warmly, for though a kind man, he was not as meek
as Moses. 'When did I rejoice or triumph over you?'

'There's ways o' doing things worse than speaking out
plain, Mr. Glegg. I'd sooner you'd tell me to my face as
you make light of me, than try to make out as everybody's
in the right but me, and come to your breakfast in the
morning, as I've hardly slept an hour this night, and sulk
at me as if I was the dirt under your feet.'

'Sulk at you?' said Mr. Glegg, in a tone of angry facetious-
ness. 'You're like a tipsy man as thinks everybody's had
too much but himself.'

'Don't lower yourself with using coarse language to *me*, Mr. Glegg! It makes you look very small, though you can't see yourself,' said Mrs. Glegg, in a tone of energetic compassion. 'A man in your place should set an example, and talk more sensible.'

'Yes; but will you listen to sense?' retorted Mr. Glegg sharply. 'The best sense I can talk to you is what I said last night—as you're i' the wrong to think o' calling in your money, when it's safe enough if you'd let it alone, all because of a bit of a tiff, and I was in hopes you'd ha' altered your mind this morning. But if you'd like to call it in, don't do it in a hurry now, and breed more enmity in the family—but wait till there's a pretty mortgage to be had without any trouble. You'd have to set the lawyer to work now to find an investment, and make no end o' expense.'

Mrs. Glegg felt there was really something in this, but she tossed her head and emitted a guttural interjection to indicate that her silence was only an armistice, not a peace. And, in fact, hostilities soon broke out again.

'I'll thank you for my cup o' tea, now, Mrs. G.,' said Mr. Glegg, seeing that she did not proceed to give it him as usual, when he had finished his porridge. She lifted the teapot with a slight toss of the head, and said,

'I'm glad to hear you'll *thank* me, Mr. Glegg. It's little thanks *I* get for what I do for folks i' this world. Though there's never a woman o' *your* side o' the family, Mr. Glegg, as is fit to stand up with me, and I'd say it if I was on my dying bed. Not but what I've allays conducted myself civil to your kin, and there isn't one of 'em can say the contrary, though my equils they aren't, and nobody shall make me say it.'

'You'd better leave finding fault wi' my kin till you've left off quarrelling with your own, Mrs. G.,' said Mr. Glegg with angry sarcasm. 'I'll trouble you for the milk-jug.'

'That's as false a word as ever you spoke, Mr. Glegg,' said the lady, pouring out the milk with unusual profuseness, as much as to say, if he wanted milk he should have it with a vengeance. 'And you know it's false. I'm not the

woman to quarrel with my own kin: *you* may, for I've
known you to do it.'

'Why, what did you call it yesterday, then, leaving your
sister's house in a tantrum?'

'I'd no quarrel wi' my sister, Mr. Glegg, and it's false to
say it. Mr. Tulliver's none o' my blood, and it was him
quarrelled with me, and drove me out o' the house. But
perhaps you'd have had me stay and be swore at, Mr.
Glegg; perhaps you was vexed not to hear more abuse and
foul language poured out upo' your own wife. But, let me
tell you, it's *your* disgrace.'

'Did ever anybody hear the like i' this parish?' said Mr.
Glegg, getting hot. 'A woman with everything provided for
her, and allowed to keep her own money the same as if it
were settled on her, and with a gig new stuffed and lined at
no end o' expense, and provided for when I die beyond
anything she could expect . . . to go on i' this way, biting
and snapping like a mad dog! It's beyond everything, as
God A'mighty should ha' made women *so.*' (These last
words were uttered in a tone of sorrowful agitation. Mr.
Glegg pushed his tea from him, and tapped the table with
both his hands.)

'Well, Mr. Glegg! if those are your feelings, it's best they
should be known,' said Mrs. Glegg, taking off her napkin,
and folding it in an excited manner. 'But if you talk o' my
being provided for beyond what I could expect, I beg leave
to tell you as I'd a right to expect a many things as I don't
find. And as to my being like a mad dog, it's well if you're
not cried shame on by the county for your treatment of me,
for it's what I can't bear and I won't bear. . . .'

Here Mrs. Glegg's voice intimated that she was going to
cry, and, breaking off from speech, she rang the bell violently.

'Sally,' she said, rising from her chair, and speaking in
rather a choked voice, 'light a fire up-stairs, and put the
blinds down. Mr. Glegg, you'll please to order what you'd
like for dinner. I shall have gruel.'

Mrs. Glegg walked across the room to the small bookcase,
and took down Baxter's 'Saint's Everlasting Rest,' which
she carried with her up-stairs. It was the book she was

accustomed to lay open before her on special occasions: on wet Sunday mornings, or when she heard of a death in the family, or when, as in this case, her quarrel with Mr. Glegg had been set an octave higher than usual.

But Mrs. Glegg carried something else up-stairs with her, which, together with the 'Saint's Rest' and the gruel, may have had some influence in gradually calming her feelings, and making it possible for her to endure existence on the ground floor shortly before tea-time. This was, partly, Mr. Glegg's suggestion, that she would do well to let her five hundred lie still until a good investment turned up; and, further, his parenthetic hint at his handsome provision for her in case of his death. Mr. Glegg, like all men of his stamp, was extremely reticent about his will; and Mrs. Glegg, in her gloomier moments, had forebodings that, like other husbands of whom she had heard, he might cherish the mean project of heightening her grief at his death by leaving her poorly off, in which case she was firmly resolved that she would have scarcely any weeper on her bonnet, and would cry no more than if he had been a second husband. But if he had really shown her any testamentary tenderness, it would be affecting to think of him, poor man, when he was gone; and even his foolish fuss about the flowers and garden-stuff, and his insistence on the subject of snails, would be touching when it was once fairly at an end. To survive Mr. Glegg, and talk eulogistically of him as a man who might have his weaknesses, but who had done the right thing by her, notwithstanding his numerous poor relations—to have sums of interest coming in more frequently, and secrete it in various corners, baffling to the most ingenious of thieves (for, to Mrs. Glegg's mind, banks and strong-boxes would have nullified the pleasure of property—she might as well have taken her food in capsules)—finally, to be looked up to by her own family and the neighbourhood, so as no woman can ever hope to be who has not the præterite and present dignity comprised in being a 'widow well left'—all this made a flattering and conciliatory view of the future. So that when good Mr. Glegg, restored to good-humour by much hoeing, and moved by the sight of his wife's empty chair, with her knitting rolled up in the corner, went up-stairs to her, and observed that the bell had been tolling for poor Mr. Morton. Mrs. Glegg answered magnanimously, quite as if she had been an uninjured woman: 'Ah! then, there'll be a good business for somebody to take to.'

Baxter had been open at least eight hours by this time, for it was nearly five o'clock; and if people are to quarrel often, it follows as a corollary that their quarrels cannot be protracted beyond certain limits.

Mr. and Mrs. Glegg talked quite amicably about the Tullivers that evening. Mr. Glegg went the length of admitting that Tulliver was a sad man for getting into hot water, and was like enough to run through his property; and Mrs. Glegg, meeting this acknowledgment half-way, declared that it was beneath her to take notice of such a man's conduct, and that, for her sister's sake, she would let him keep the five hundred a while longer, for when she put it out on a mortgage she should only get four per cent.

XIII

MR. TULLIVER FURTHER ENTANGLES THE SKEIN OF LIFE

Owing to this new adjustment of Mrs. Glegg's thoughts, Mrs. Pullet found her task of mediation the next day surprisingly easy. Mrs. Glegg, indeed, checked her rather sharply for thinking it would be necessary to tell her eldest sister what was the right mode of behaviour in family matters. Mrs. Pullet's argument, that it would look ill in the neighbourhood if people should have it in their power to say that there was a quarrel in the family, was particularly offensive. If the family name never suffered except through Mrs. Glegg, Mrs. Pullet might lay her head on her pillow in perfect confidence.

'It's not to be expected, I suppose,' observed Mrs. Glegg, by way of winding up the subject, 'as I shall go to the mill again before Bessy comes to see me, or as I shall go and fall down o' my knees to Mr. Tulliver, and ask his pardon for showing him favours; but I shall bear no malice, and when Mr. Tulliver speaks civil to me, I'll speak civil to him. Nobody has any call to tell me what's becoming.'

Finding it unnecessary to plead for the Tullivers, it was natural that aunt Pullet should relax a little in her anxiety for them, and recur to the annoyance she had suffered yesterday from the offspring of that apparently ill-fated house. Mrs. Glegg heard a circumstantial narrative, to which Mr. Pullet's remarkable memory furnished some items; and while aunt Pullet pitied poor Bessy's bad-luck with her children, and expressed a half-formed project of paying for Maggie's being sent to a distant boarding-school, which would not prevent her being so brown, but might tend to subdue some other vices in her, aunt Glegg blamed Bessy for her weakness, and appealed to all witnesses who should be living when the Tulliver children had turned out ill, that she, Mrs. Glegg, had always said how it would be from the very first, observing that it was wonderful to herself how all her words came true.

'Then I may call and tell Bessie you'll bear no malice, and everything be as it was before?' Mrs. Pullet said, just before parting.

'Yes, you may, Sophy,' said Mrs. Glegg; 'you may tell Mr. Tulliver, and Bessie too, as I'm not going to behave ill because folks behave ill to me: I know it's my place, as the eldest, to set an example in every respect, and I do it. Nobody can say different of me, if they'll keep to the truth.'

Mrs. Glegg being in this state of satisfaction in her own lofty magnanimity, I leave you to judge what effect was produced on her by the reception of a short letter from Mr. Tulliver, that very evening, after Mrs. Pullet's departure, informing her that she needn't trouble her mind about her five hundred pounds, for it should be paid back to her in the course of the next month at farthest, together with the interest due thereon until the time of payment. And furthermore, that Mr. Tulliver had no wish to behave uncivilly to Mrs. Glegg, and she was welcome to his house whenever she liked to come, but he desired no favours from her, either for himself or his children.

It was poor Mrs. Tulliver who had hastened this catastrophe, entirely through that irrepressible hopefulness of hers which led her to expect that similar causes may at any time produce different results. It had very often occurred in her experience that Mr. Tulliver had done something because other people had said he was not able to do it, or had pitied him for his supposed inability, or in any other way piqued his pride; still, she thought to-day, if she told him when he came in to tea that sister Pullet was gone to try and make everything up with sister Glegg, so that he needn't think about paying in the money, it would give a cheerful effect to the meal. Mr. Tulliver had never slackened in his resolve to raise the money, but now he at once determined to write a letter to Mrs. Glegg which should cut off all possibility of mistake. Mrs. Pullet gone to beg and pray for *him* indeed! Mr. Tulliver did not willingly write a letter, and found the relation between spoken and written language, briefly known as spelling, one of the most puzzling things in this puzzling world. Nevertheless, like all fervid writing, the task was done in less time than usual, and if the spelling differed from Mrs. Glegg's—why she belonged, like himself, to a generation with whom spelling was a matter of private judgment.

Mrs. Glegg did not alter her will in consequence of this letter, and cut off the Tulliver children from their sixth and seventh share in her thousand pounds; for she had her principles. No one must be able to say of her when she was dead that she had not divided her money with perfect fairness among her own kin: in the matter of wills, personal qualities were subordinate to the great fundamental fact of blood; and to be determined in the distribution of your property by caprice, and not make your legacies bear a direct ratio to degrees of kinship, was a prospective disgrace that would have embittered her life. This had always been a principle in the Dodson family: it was one form of that sense of honour and rectitude which was a proud tradition in such families—a tradition which has been the salt of our provincial society.

But though the letter could not shake Mrs. Glegg's principles, it made the family breach much more difficult to mend; and as to the effect it produced on Mrs. Glegg's opinion of Mr. Tulliver—she begged to be understood from that time forth that she had nothing whatever to say about him: his state of mind, apparently, was too corrupt for her to contemplate it for a moment. It was not until the evening before Tom went to school, at the beginning of August, that Mrs. Glegg paid a visit to her sister Tulliver, sitting in her gig all the while, and showing her displeasure by markedly abstaining from all advice and criticism, for, as she observed to her sister Deane, 'Bessy must bear the consequence o' having such a husband, though I'm sorry for her,' and Mrs. Deane agreed that Bessie was pitiable.

That evening Tom observed to Maggie, 'O my! Maggie, aunt Glegg's beginning to come again; I'm glad I'm going to school. *You'll* catch it all now!'

Maggie was already so full of sorrow at the thought of Tom's going away from her, that this playful exultation of his seemed very unkind, and she cried herself to sleep that night.

Mr. Tulliver's prompt procedure entailed on him further promptitude in finding the convenient person who was desirous of lending five hundred pounds on bond. 'It must be no client of Wakem's,' he said to himself; and yet at the end of a fortnight it turned out to the contrary; not because Mr. Tulliver's will was feeble, but because external fact was stronger. Wakem's client was the only convenient person to be found. Mr. Tulliver had a destiny as well as Œdipus, and in this case he might plead, like Œdipus, that his deed was inflicted on him rather than committed by him.

BOOK SECOND

SCHOOL-TIME

I

TOM'S 'FIRST HALF'

TOM TULLIVER'S sufferings during the first quarter he was at King's Lorton, under the distinguished care of the Rev. Walter Stelling, were rather severe. At Mr. Jacobs' academy, life had not presented itself to him as a difficult problem: there were plenty of fellows to play with, and Tom being good at all active games—fighting especially—had that precedence among them which appeared to him inseparable from the personality of Tom Tulliver. Mr. Jacobs himself, familiarly known as Old Goggles, from his habit of wearing spectacles, imposed no painful awe; and if it was the property of snuffy old hypocrites like him to write like copperplate and surround their signatures with arabesques, to spell without forethought, and to spout 'My name is Norval' without bungling, Tom, for his part, was rather glad he was not in danger of those mean accomplishments. He was not going to be a snuffy schoolmaster—he; but a substantial man, like his father, who used to go hunting when he was younger, and rode a capital black mare—as pretty a bit of horse-flesh as ever you saw: Tom had heard what her points were a hundred times. *He* meant to go hunting too, and to be generally respected. When people were grown up, he considered, nobody inquired about their writing and spelling: when he was a man, he should be master of everything, and do just as he liked. It had been very difficult for him to reconcile himself to the idea that his school-time was to be prolonged, and that he was not to be brought up to his father's business, which he had always thought extremely pleasant, for it was nothing

ut riding about, giving orders, and going to market; and
e thought that a clergyman would give him a great many
Scripture lessons, and probably make him learn the Gospel
nd Epistle on a Sunday as well as the Collect. But in the
bsence of specific information, it was impossible for him
o imagine that school and a schoolmaster would be some-
hing entirely different from the academy of Mr. Jacobs.
So, not to be at a deficiency, in case of his finding genial
ompanions, he had taken care to carry with him a small
ox of percussion-caps; not that there was anything par-
icular to be done with them, but they would serve to
mpress strange boys with a sense of his familiarity with
guns. Thus poor Tom, though he saw very clearly through
Maggie's illusions, was not without illusions of his own,
which were to be cruelly dissipated by his enlarged ex-
erience at King's Lorton.

He had not been there a fortnight before it was evident
o him that life, complicated not only with the Latin
rammar but with a new standard of English pronuncia-
ion, was a very difficult business, made all the more
bscure by a thick mist of bashfulness. Tom, as you have
bserved, was never an exception among boys for ease of
ddress; but the difficulty of enunciating a monosyllable in
eply to Mr. or Mrs. Stelling was so great, that he even
readed to be asked at table whether he would have more
udding. As to the percussion-caps, he had almost resolved,
n the bitterness of his heart, that he would throw them into
  neighbouring pond: for not only was he the solitary
upil, but he began even to have a certain scepticism about
uns, and a general sense that his theory of life was under-
nined. For Mr. Stelling thought nothing of guns, or horses
ither, apparently; and yet it was impossible for Tom to
espise Mr. Stelling as he had despised Old Goggles. If
here were anything that was not thoroughly genuine about
Ir. Stelling, it lay quite beyond Tom's power to detect it:
t is only by a wide comparison of facts that the wisest full-
rown man can distinguish well-rolled barrels from mere
upernal thunder.

Mr. Stelling was a well-sized, broad-chested man, not yet

thirty, with flaxen hair standing erect, and large lightish grey eyes, which were always very wide open ; he had a sonorous bass voice, and an air of defiant self-confidence inclining to brazenness. He had entered on his career with great vigour, and intended to make a considerable impression on his fellow-men. The Rev. Walter Stelling was not a man who would remain among the 'inferior clergy' all his life. He had a true British determination to push his way in the world. As a schoolmaster, in the first place; for there were capital masterships of grammar-schools to be had, and Mr. Stelling meant to have one of them. But as a preacher also, for he meant always to preach in a striking manner, so as to have his congregation swelled by admirers from neighbouring parishes, and to produce a great sensation whenever he took occasional duty for a brother clergyman of minor gifts. The style of preaching he had chosen was the extemporaneous, which was held little short of the miraculous in rural parishes like King's Lorton. Some passages of Massillon and Bourdaloue, which he knew by heart, were really very effective when rolled out in Mr. Stelling's deepest tones; but as comparatively feeble appeals of his own were delivered in the same loud and impressive manner, they were often thought quite as striking by his hearers. Mr. Stelling's doctrine was of no particular school; if anything, it had a tinge of evangelicalism, for that was 'the telling thing' just then in the diocese to which King's Lorton belonged. In short, Mr. Stelling was a man who meant to rise in his profession, and to rise by merit clearly, since he had no interest beyond what might be promised by a problematic relationship to a great lawyer who had not yet become Lord Chancellor. A clergyman who has such vigorous intentions naturally gets a little into debt at starting; it is not to be expected that he will live in the meagre style of a man who means to be a poor curate all his life, and if the few hundreds Mr. Timpson advanced towards his daughter's fortune did not suffice for the purchase of handsome furniture, together with a stock of wine, a grand piano, and the laying-out of a superior flower-garden, it followed in the most rigorous manner, either that these

hings must be procured by some other means, or else that
he Rev. Mr. Stelling must go without them—which last
lternative would be an absurd procrastination of the fruits
f success, where success was certain. Mr. Stelling was so
road-chested and resolute that he felt equal to anything;
e would become celebrated by shaking the consciences of
is hearers, and he would by-and-by edit a Greek play, and
nvent several new readings. He had not yet selected the
lay, for having been married little more than two years,
is leisure time had been much occupied with attentions to
Mrs. Stelling; but he had told that fine woman what he
meant to do some day, and she felt great confidence in her
usband, as a man who understood everything of that sort.

But the immediate step to future success was to bring on
Tom Tulliver during this first half-year; for, by a singular
oincidence, there had been some negotiation concerning
nother pupil from the same neighbourhood, and it might
urther a decision in Mr. Stelling's favour, if it were under-
tood that young Tulliver, who, Mr. Stelling observed in
onjugal privacy, was rather a rough cub, had made pro-
igious progress in a short time. It was on this ground that
e was severe with Tom about his lessons: he was clearly
 boy whose powers would never be developed through the
medium of the Latin grammar, without the application of
ome sternness. Not that Mr. Stelling was a harsh-tempered
r unkind man—quite the contrary: he was jocose with
Tom at table, and corrected his provincialisms and his
eportment in the most playful manner; but poor Tom was
nly the more cowed and confused by this double novelty,
or he had never been used to jokes at all like Mr. Stelling's;
nd for the first time in his life he had a painful sense that
e was all wrong somehow. When Mr. Stelling said, as the
oast-beef was being uncovered, 'Now, Tulliver! which
would you rather decline, roast-beef or the Latin for it'—
Tom, to whom in his coolest moments a pun would have
een a hard nut, was thrown into a state of embarrassed
larm that made everything dim to him except the feeling
hat he would rather not have anything to do with Latin:
f course he answered, 'Roast-beef,' whereupon there

followed much laughter and some practical joking with the
plates, from which Tom gathered that he had in some
mysterious way refused beef, and, in fact, made himself
appear 'a silly.' If he could have seen a fellow-pupil under
go these painful operations and survive them in good
spirits, he might sooner have taken them as a matter of
course. But there are two expensive forms of education
either of which a parent may procure for his son by sending
him as solitary pupil to a clergyman: one is, the enjoyment
of the reverend gentleman's undivided neglect; the other
is, the endurance of the reverend gentleman's undivided
attention. It was the latter privilege for which Mr. Tulliver
paid a high price in Tom's initiatory months at King's
Lorton.

That respectable miller and maltster had left Tom be
hind, and driven homeward in a state of great mental satis
faction. He considered that it was a happy moment for
him when he had thought of asking Riley's advice about
a tutor for Tom. Mr. Stelling's eyes were so wide open, and
he talked in such an off-hand, matter-of-fact way—answer
ing every difficult slow remark of Mr. Tulliver's with, ' I see
my good sir, I see ;' 'To be sure, to be sure ;' 'You want
your son to be a man who will make his way in the world,'—
that Mr. Tulliver was delighted to find in him a clergyman
whose knowledge was so applicable to the everyday affairs
of this life. Except Counsellor Wylde, whom he had heard
at the last sessions, Mr. Tulliver thought the Rev. Mr. Stell
ing was the shrewdest fellow he had ever met with—not
unlike Wylde, in fact: he had the same way of sticking his
thumbs in the armholes of his waistcoat. Mr. Tulliver was
not by any means an exception in mistaking brazenness for
shrewdness: most laymen thought Stelling shrewd, and a
man of remarkable powers generally: it was chiefly by his
clerical brethren that he was considered rather a dull
fellow. But he told Mr. Tulliver several stories about
'Swing' and incendiarism, and asked his advice about
feeding pigs in so thoroughly secular and judicious a
manner, with so much polished glibness of tongue, that the
miller thought, here was the very thing he wanted for Tom.

He had no doubt this first-rate man was acquainted with every branch of information, and knew exactly what Tom must learn in order to become a match for the lawyers—which poor Mr. Tulliver himself did *not* know, and so was necessarily thrown for self-direction on this wide kind of inference. It is hardly fair to laugh at him, for I have known much more highly-instructed persons than he make inferences quite as wide, and not at all wiser.

As for Mrs. Tulliver—finding that Mrs. Stelling's views as to the airing of linen and the frequent recurrence of hunger in a growing boy, entirely coincided with her own; moreover, that Mrs. Stelling, though so young a woman, and only anticipating her second confinement, had gone through very nearly the same experience as herself with regard to the behaviour and fundamental character of the monthly nurse—she expressed great contentment to her husband, when they drove away, at leaving Tom with a woman who, in spite of her youth, seemed quite sensible and motherly, and asked advice as prettily as could be.

'They must be very well off, though,' said Mrs. Tulliver, 'for everything's as nice as can be all over the house, and that watered-silk she had on cost a pretty penny. Sister Pullet has got one like it.'

'Ah,' said Mr. Tulliver, 'he's got some income besides the curacy, I reckon. Perhaps her father allows 'em something. There's Tom 'ull be another hundred to him, and not much trouble either, by his own account: he says teaching comes natural to him. That's wonderful, now,' added Mr. Tulliver, turning his head on one side, and giving his horse a meditative tickling on the flank.

Perhaps it was because teaching came naturally to Mr. Stelling, that he set about it with that uniformity of method and independence of circumstances, which distinguish the actions of animals understood to be under the immediate teaching of nature. Mr. Broderip's amiable beaver, as that charming naturalist tells us, busied himself as earnestly in constructing a dam, in a room up three pair of stairs in London, as if he had been laying his foundation in a stream or lake in Upper Canada. It was 'Binny's'

function to build: the absence of water or of possibl
progeny was an accident for which he was not accountable
With the same unerring instinct Mr. Stelling set to work a
his natural method of instilling the Eton Grammar an
Euclid into the mind of Tom Tulliver. This, he considere
was the only basis of solid instruction: all other means o
education were mere charlatanism, and could produc
nothing better than smatterers. Fixed on this firm basi
a man might observe the display of various or special know
ledge made by irregularly educated people with a pityin,
smile: all that sort of thing was very well, but it was im
possible these people could form sound opinions. In hold
ing this conviction Mr. Stelling was not biassed, as som
tutors have been, by the excessive accuracy or extent of hi
own scholarship; and as to his views about Euclid, n
opinion could have been freer from personal partiality
Mr. Stelling was very far from being led astray by enthu
siasm, either religious or intellectual; on the other hand, h
had no secret belief that everything was humbug. H
thought religion was a very excellent thing, and Aristotl
a great authority, and deaneries and prebends useful insti
tutions, and Great Britain the providential bulwark o
Protestantism, and faith in the unseen a great support t
afflicted minds: he believed in all these things, as a Swis
hotel-keeper believes in the beauty of the scenery aroun
him, and in the pleasures it gives to artistic visitors. An
in the same way Mr. Stelling believed in his method o
education; he had no doubt that he was doing the very bes
thing for Mr. Tulliver's boy. Of course, when the mille
talked of 'mapping' and 'summing' in a vague and diffi
dent manner, Mr. Stelling had set his mind at rest by a
assurance that he understood what was wanted; for hov
was it possible the good man could form any reasonabl
judgment about the matter? Mr. Stelling's duty was t
teach the lad in the only right way—indeed, he knew n
other: he had not wasted his time in the acquirement o
anything abnormal.

He very soon set down poor Tom as a thoroughly stupi
lad, for though by hard labour he could get particular de

tensions into his brain, anything so abstract as the relation between cases and terminations could by no means get such lodgment there as to enable him to recognise a chance genitive or dative. This struck Mr. Stelling as something more than natural stupidity: he suspected obstinacy, or at any rate, indifference; and lectured Tom severely on his want of thorough application. 'You feel no interest in what you're doing, sir,' Mr. Stelling would say, and the reproach was painfully true. Tom had never found any difficulty in discerning a pointer from a setter, when once he had been told the distinction, and his perceptive powers were not at all deficient. I fancy they were quite as strong as those of the Rev. Mr. Stelling; for Tom could predict with accuracy what number of horses were cantering behind him, he could throw a stone right into the centre of a given ripple, he could guess to a fraction how many lengths of his stick it would take to reach across the playground, and could draw almost perfect squares on his slate without any measurement. But Mr. Stelling took no note of these things: he only observed that Tom's faculties failed him before the abstractions hideously symbolised to him in the pages of the Eton Grammar, and that he was in a state bordering on idiocy with regard to the demonstration that two given triangles must be equal—though he could discern with great promptitude and certainty the fact that they *were* equal. Whence Mr. Stelling concluded that Tom's brain being peculiarly impervious to etymology and demonstrations, was peculiarly in need of being ploughed and harrowed by these patent implements: it was his favourite metaphor, that the classics and geometry constituted that culture of the mind which prepared it for the reception of any subsequent crop. I say nothing against Mr. Stelling's theory: if we are to have one regimen for all minds, his seems to me as good as any other. I only know it turned out as uncomfortably for Tom Tulliver as if he had been plied with cheese in order to remedy a gastric weakness which prevented him from digesting it. It is astonishing what a different result one gets by changing the metaphor! Once call the brain an intellectual stomach, and one's ingenious conception of

the classics and geometry as ploughs and harrows seems t
settle nothing. But then it is open to some one else t
follow great authorities, and call the mind a sheet of whit
paper or a mirror, in which case one's knowledge of th
digestive process becomes quite irrelevant. It was doub
less an ingenious idea to call the camel the ship of th
desert, but it would hardly lead one far in training that use
ful beast. O Aristotle! if you had had the advantage o
being 'the freshest modern' instead of the greatest ancien
would you not have mingled your praise of metaphorica
speech, as a sign of high intelligence, with a lamentatio
that intelligence so rarely shows itself in speech withou
metaphor,—that we can so seldom declare what a thing i
except by saying it is something else?

Tom Tulliver, being abundant in no form of speech, di
not use any metaphor to declare his views as to the natur
of Latin: he never called it an instrument of torture; and
was not until he had got on some way in the next half-yea
and in the Delectus, that he was advanced enough to call
a 'bore' and 'beastly stuff.' At present, in relation to th
demand that he should learn Latin declensions and conjuga
tions, Tom was in a state of as blank unimaginativenes
concerning the cause and tendency of his sufferings, as
he had been an innocent shrew-mouse imprisoned in th
split trunk of an ash-tree in order to cure lameness in cattle
It is doubtless almost incredible to instructed minds of th
present day that a boy of twelve, not belonging strictly t
'the masses,' who are now understood to have the mono
poly of mental darkness, should have had no distinct ide
how there came to be such a thing as Latin on this earth
yet so it was with Tom. It would have taken a long whil
to make conceivable to him that there ever existed a peopl
who bought and sold sheep and oxen, and transacted th
everyday affairs of life, through the medium of this lan
guage, and still longer to make him understand why h
should be called upon to learn it, when its connection wit
those affairs had become entirely latent. So far as Tom ha
gained any acquaintance with the Romans at Mr. Jacob
academy, his knowledge was strictly correct, but it wen

no farther than the fact that they were 'in the New Testament;' and Mr. Stelling was not the man to enfeeble and emasculate his pupil's mind by simplifying and explaining, or to reduce the tonic effect of etymology by mixing it with smattering, extraneous information, such as is given to girls.

Yet, strange to say, under this vigorous treatment Tom became more like a girl than he had ever been in his life before. He had a large share of pride, which had hitherto found itself very comfortable in the world, despising Old Goggles, and reposing in the sense of unquestioned rights; but now this same pride met with nothing but bruises and crushings. Tom was too clear-sighted not to be aware that Mr. Stelling's standard of things was quite different, was certainly something higher in the eyes of the world than that of the people he had been living amongst, and that, brought in contact with it, he, Tom Tulliver, appeared uncouth and stupid: he was by no means indifferent to this, and his pride got into an uneasy condition which quite nullified his boyish self-satisfaction, and gave him something of the girl's susceptibility. He was of a very firm, not to say obstinate disposition, but there was no brute-like rebellion and recklessness in his nature: the human sensibilities predominated, and if it had occurred to him that he could enable himself to show some quickness at his lessons, and so acquire Mr. Stelling's approbation, by standing on one leg for an inconvenient length of time, or rapping his head moderately against the wall, or any voluntary action of that sort, he would certainly have tried it. But no— Tom had never heard that these measures would brighten the understanding, or strengthen the verbal memory; and he was not given to hypothesis and experiment. It did occur to him that he could perhaps get some help by praying for it; but as the prayers he said every evening were forms learned by heart, he rather shrank from the novelty and irregularity of introducing an extempore passage on a topic of petition for which he was not aware of any precedent. But one day when he had broken down, for the fifth time, in the supines of the third conjugation, and Mr.

Stelling, convinced that this must be carelessness, since it transcended the bounds of possible stupidity, had lectured him very seriously, pointing out that if he failed to seize the present golden opportunity of learning supines, he would have to regret it when he became a man,—Tom, more miserable than usual, determined to try his sole resource; and that evening, after his usual form of prayer for his parents and 'little sister' (he had begun to pray for Maggie when she was a baby), and that he might be able always to keep God's commandments, he added, in the same low whisper 'and please to make me always remember my Latin.' He paused a little to consider how he should pray about Euclid—whether he should ask to see what it meant, or whether there was any other mental state which would be more applicable to the case. But at last he added— 'And make Mr. Stelling say I shan't do Euclid any more. Amen.'

The fact that he got through his supines without mistake the next day, encouraged him to persevere in this appendix to his prayers, and neutralised any scepticism that might have arisen from Mr. Stelling's continued demand for Euclid. But his faith broke down under the apparent absence of all help when he got into the irregular verbs. It seemed clear that Tom's despair under the caprices of the present tense did not constitute a *nodus* worthy of interference, and since this was the climax of his difficulties, where was the use of praying for help any longer? He made up his mind to this conclusion in one of his dull, lonely evenings, which he spent in the study, preparing his lessons for the morrow. His eyes were apt to get dim over the page—though he hated crying, and was ashamed of it: he couldn't help thinking with some affection even of Spouncer, whom he used to fight and quarrel with; he would have felt at home with Spouncer, and in a condition of superiority. And then the mill, and the river, and Yap pricking up his ears, ready to obey the least sign when Tom said 'Hoigh!' would all come before him in a sort of calenture, when his fingers played absently in his pocket with his great knife and his coil of whip-cord and other relics of the past. Tom, as I said, had never been so much like a girl in his life before, and at that epoch of irregular verbs his spirit was further depressed by a new means of mental development, which had been thought of for him out of school hours. Mrs. Stelling had lately had her second baby, and as nothing could be more salutary for a boy than to feel himself useful, Mrs. Stelling considered she was doing Tom a service by setting him to watch the little cherub Laura while the nurse was occupied with the sickly baby. It was quite a pretty employment for Tom to take little Laura out in the sunniest hour of the autumn day—it would help to make him feel that Lorton Parsonage was a home for him, and that he was one of the family. The little cherub Laura, not being an accomplished walker at present, had a ribbon fastened round her waist, by which Tom held her as if she had been a little dog during the minutes in which she chose to walk; but as these were rare, he was for the most part carrying this fine child round and round the garden, within sight of Mrs. Stelling's window—according to orders. If anyone considers this unfair and even oppressive towards Tom, I beg him to consider that there are feminine virtues which are with difficulty combined, even if they are not incompatible. When the wife of a poor curate contrives, under all her disadvantages, to dress extremely well, and to have a style of coiffure which requires that her nurse shall occasionally officiate as lady's-maid,—when, moreover, her dinner-parties and her drawing-room show that effort at elegance and completeness of appointment to which ordinary women might imagine a large income necessary, it would be unreasonable to expect of her that she should employ a second nurse, or even act as a nurse herself. Mr. Stelling knew better: he saw that his wife did wonders already, and was proud of her: it was certainly not the best thing in the world for young Tulliver's gait to carry a heavy child, but he had plenty of exercise in long walks with himself, and next half-year Mr. Stelling would see about having a drilling-master. Among the many means whereby Mr. Stelling intended to be more fortunate than the bulk of his fellow-men, he had entirely given up that of having his

own way in his own house. What then? he had married 'a
kind a little soul as ever breathed,' according to Mr. Riley
who had been acquainted with Mrs. Stelling's blond ringlet
and smiling demeanour throughout her maiden life, and o
the strength of that knowledge would have been ready an
day to pronounce that whatever domestic differences migh
arise in her married life must be entirely Mr. Stelling's fault

If Tom had had a worse disposition, he would certainly
have hated the little cherub Laura, but he was too kind
hearted a lad for that—there was too much in him of th
fibre that turns to true manliness, and to protecting pity fo
the weak. I am afraid he hated Mrs. Stelling, and contracte
a lasting dislike to pale blond ringlets and broad plaits, a
directly associated with haughtiness of manner, and
frequent reference to other people's 'duty.' But he couldn'
help playing with little Laura, and liking to amuse her: h
even sacrificed his percussion-caps for her sake, in despai
of their ever serving a greater purpose—thinking the smal
flash and bang would delight her, and thereby drawing
down on himself a rebuke from Mrs. Stelling for teaching
her child to play with fire. Laura was a sort of playfellow—
and O how Tom longed for playfellows! In his secret heart
he yearned to have Maggie with him, and was almost ready
to dote on her exasperating acts of forgetfulness; though
when he was at home, he always represented it as a great
favour on his part to let Maggie trot by his side on his
pleasure excursions.

And before this dreary half-year was ended, Maggie
actually came. Mrs. Stelling had given a general invitation
for the little girl to come and stay with her brother: so
when Mr. Tulliver drove over to King's Lorton late in
October, Maggie came too, with the sense that she was
taking a great journey, and beginning to see the world. It
was Mr. Tulliver's first visit to see Tom, for the lad must
learn not to think too much about home.

'Well, my lad,' he said to Tom, when Mr. Stelling had
left the room to announce the arrival to his wife, and
Maggie had begun to kiss Tom freely, 'you look rarely
School agrees with you.'

Tom wished he had looked rather ill.

'I don't think I *am* well, father,' said Tom; 'I wish you'd ask Mr. Stelling not to let me do Euclid—it brings on the toothache, I think.'

(The toothache was the only malady to which Tom had ever been subject.)

'Euclid, my lad—why, what's that?' said Mr. Tulliver.

'O, I don't know: it's definitions, and axioms, and triangles, and things. It's a book I've got to learn in—there's no sense in it.'

'Go, go!' said Mr. Tulliver reprovingly, 'you mustn't say so. You must learn what your master tells you. He knows what it's right for you to learn.'

'*I'll* help you now, Tom,' said Maggie, with a little air of patronizing consolation. 'I'm come to stay ever so long, if Mrs. Stelling asks me. I've brought my box and my pinafores, haven't I, father?'

'*You* help me, you silly little thing!' said Tom, in such high spirits at this announcement that he quite enjoyed the idea of confounding Maggie by showing her a page of *my* lessons! Why, I learn Latin too! Girls never learn such things. They're too silly.'

'I know what Latin is very well,' said Maggie confidently. 'Latin's a language. There are Latin words in the Dictionary. There's bonus, a gift.'

'Now, you're just wrong there, Miss Maggie!' said Tom, secretly astonished. 'You think you're very wise! But "bonus" means "good," as it happens—bonus, bona, bonum.'

'Well, that's no reason why it shouldn't mean "gift,"' said Maggie stoutly. 'It may mean several things—almost every word does. There's "lawn,"—it means the grassplot, as well as the stuff pocket-handkerchiefs are made of.'

'Well done, little 'un,' said Mr. Tulliver, laughing, while Tom felt rather disgusted with Maggie's knowingness, though beyond measure cheerful at the thought that she was going to stay with him. Her conceit would soon be overawed by the actual inspection of his books.

Mrs. Stelling, in her pressing invitation, did not mention a longer time than a week for Maggie's stay; but Mr. Stelling, who took her between his knees, and asked her where she stole her dark eyes from, insisted that she must stay a fortnight. Maggie thought Mr. Stelling was a charming man, and Mr. Tulliver was quite proud to leave his little wench where she would have an opportunity of showing her cleverness to appreciating strangers. So it was agreed that she should not be fetched home till the end of the fortnight.

'Now, then, come with me into the study, Maggie,' said Tom, as their father drove away. 'What do you shake and toss your head now for, you silly?' he continued; for though her hair was now under a new dispensation, and was brushed smoothly behind her ears, she seemed still in imagination to be tossing it out of her eyes. 'It makes you look as if you were crazy.'

'O, I can't help it,' said Maggie impatiently. 'Don't tease me, Tom. Oh, what books!' she exclaimed, as she saw the bookcases in the study. 'How I should like to have as many books as that!'

'Why, you couldn't read one of 'em,' said Tom triumphantly. 'They're all Latin.'

'No, they aren't,' said Maggie. 'I can read the back of this . . . History of the Decline and Fall of the Roman Empire.'

'Well, what does that mean? *You* don't know,' said Tom, wagging his head.

'But I could soon find out,' said Maggie scornfully.

'Why, how?'

'I should look inside, and see what it was about.'

'You'd better not, Miss Maggie,' said Tom, seeing her hand on the volume. 'Mr. Stelling lets nobody touch his books without leave, and *I* shall catch it, if you take it out.'

'O, very well! Let me see all *your* books, then,' said Maggie, turning to throw her arms round Tom's neck, and rub his cheek with her small round nose.

Tom, in the gladness of his heart at having dear old

Maggie to dispute with and crow over again, seized her round the waist, and began to jump with her round the large library table. Away they jumped with more and more vigour, till Maggie's hair flew from behind her ears, and twirled about like an animated mop. But the revolutions round the table became more and more irregular in their sweep, till at last reaching Mr. Stelling's reading-stand, they sent it thundering down with its heavy lexicons to the floor. Happily it was the ground-floor, and the study was a one-storied wing to the house, so that the downfall made no alarming resonance, though Tom stood dizzy and aghast for a few minutes, dreading the appearance of Mr. or Mrs. Stelling.

'O, I say, Maggie,' said Tom at last, lifting up the stand, 'we must keep quiet here, you know. If we break anything, Mrs. Stelling'll make us cry peccavi.'

'What's that?' said Maggie.

'O, it's the Latin for a good scolding,' said Tom, not without some pride in his knowledge.

'Is she a cross woman?' said Maggie.

'I believe you!' said Tom, with an emphatic nod.

'I think all women are crosser than men,' said Maggie. 'Aunt Glegg's a great deal crosser than uncle Glegg, and mother scolds me more than father does.'

'Well, *you'll* be a woman some day,' said Tom, 'so *you* needn't talk.'

'But I shall be a *clever* woman,' said Maggie, with a toss.

'O, I dare say, and a nasty conceited thing. Everybody'll hate you.'

'But you oughtn't to hate me, Tom: it'll be very wicked of you, for I shall be your sister.'

'Yes, but if you're a nasty disagreeable thing, I *shall* hate you.'

'O but, Tom, you won't! I shan't be disagreeable. I shall be very good to you—and I shall be good to every-body. You won't hate me really, will you, Tom?'

'O, bother! never mind! Come, it's time for me to learn my lessons. See here! what I've got to do,' said Tom, drawing Maggie towards him and showing her his theorem, while she pushed her hair behind her ears, and prepared herself to prove her capability of helping him in Euclid. She began to read with full confidence in her own powers, but presently, becoming quite bewildered, her face flushed with irritation. It was unavoidable—she must confess her incompetency, and she was not fond of humiliation.

'It's nonsense!' she said, 'and very ugly stuff—nobody need want to make it out.'

'Ah, there now, Miss Maggie!' said Tom, drawing the book away, and wagging his head at her, 'you see you're not so clever as you thought you were.'

'O,' said Maggie, pouting, 'I dare say I could make it out, if I'd learned what goes before, as you have.'

'But that's what you just couldn't, Miss Wisdom,' said Tom. 'For it's all the harder when you know what goes before: for then you've got to say what definition 3. is, and what axiom V. is. But get along with you now: I must go on with this. Here's the Latin Grammar. See what you can make of that.'

Maggie found the Latin Grammar quite soothing after her mathematical mortification; for she delighted in new words, and quickly found that there was an English Key at the end, which would make her very wise about Latin, at slight expense. She presently made up her mind to skip the rules in the Syntax—the examples became so absorbing. These mysterious sentences, snatched from an unknown context,—like strange horns of beasts, and leaves of unknown plants, brought from some far-off region,—gave boundless scope to her imagination, and were all the more fascinating because they were in a peculiar tongue of their own, which she could learn to interpret. It was really very interesting—the Latin Grammar that Tom had said no girl could learn: and she was proud because she found it interesting. The most fragmentary examples were her favourites. *Mors omnibus est communis* would have been jejune only she liked to know the Latin; but the fortunate gentleman whom everyone congratulated because he had a son 'endowed with *such* a disposition' afforded her a great deal of pleasant conjecture, and she was quite lost in the 'thick grove penetrable by no star,' when Tom called out:

'Now, then, Magsie, give us the Grammar!'

'O, Tom, it's such a pretty book!' she said, as she jumped out of the large arm-chair to give it him; 'it's much prettier than the Dictionary. I could learn Latin very soon. I don't think it's at all hard.'

'O, I know what you've been doing,' said Tom; 'you've been reading the English at the end. Any donkey can do that.'

Tom seized the book and opened it with a determined and business-like air, as much as to say that he had a lesson to learn which no donkeys would find themselves equal to. Maggie, rather piqued, turned to the bookcases to amuse herself with puzzling out the titles.

Presently Tom called to her: 'Here, Magsie, come and hear if I can say this. Stand at that end of the table, where Mr. Stelling sits when he hears me.'

Maggie obeyed, and took the open book.

'Where do you begin, Tom?'

'O, I begin at '*Appellativa arborum*,' because I say all over again what I've been learning this week.'

Tom sailed along pretty well for three lines; and Maggie was beginning to forget her office of prompter in speculating as to what *mas* could mean, which came twice over, when he stuck fast at *Sunt etiam volucrum*.

'Don't tell me, Magsie; *Sunt etiam volucrum . . . Sunt etiam volucrum . . . ut ostrea, cetus . . .*'

'No,' said Maggie, opening her mouth and shaking her head.

'*Sunt etiam volucrum*,' said Tom, very slowly, as if the next words might be expected to come sooner when he gave them this strong hint that they were waited for.

'C, e, u,' said Maggie, getting impatient.

'O, I know—hold your tongue,' said Tom. '*Ceu passer, hirundo; Ferarum . . . ferarum . . .*' Tom took his pencil and made several hard dots with it on his book-cover . . . *ferarum . . .*'

'O dear, O dear, Tom,' said Maggie, 'what a time you are! *Ut* . . .'

'*Ut, ostrea* . . .'

'No, no,' said Maggie, '*ut, tigris* . . .'

'O yes, now I can do,' said Tom; 'it was *tigris, vulpes* I'd forgotten: *ut tigris, vulpes; et Piscium.*'

With some further stammering and repetition, Tom got through the next few lines.

'Now, then,' he said, 'the next is what I've just learnt for to-morrow. Give me hold of the book a minute.'

After some whispered gabbling, assisted by the beating of his fist on the table, Tom returned the book.

'*Mascula nomina in a,*' he began.

'No, Tom,' said Maggie, 'that doesn't come next. It's *Nomen non creskens genītivo.* . . .'

'*Creskens genittivo,*' exclaimed Tom, with a derisive laugh, for Tom had learned this omitted passage for his yesterday's lesson, and a young gentleman does not require an intimate or extensive acquaintance with Latin before he can feel the pitiable absurdity of a false quantity. '*Creskens genittivo!* What a little silly you are, Maggie!'

'Well, you needn't laugh, Tom, for you didn't remember it at all. I'm sure it's spelt so; how was I to know?'

'Phee-e-e-h! I told you girls couldn't learn Latin. It's *Nomen non crescens genitivo.*'

'Very well, then,' said Maggie, pouting. 'I can say that as well as you can. And you don't mind your stops. For you ought to stop twice as long at a semicolon as you do at a comma, and you make the longest stops where there ought to be no stop at all.'

'O, well, don't chatter. Let me go on.'

They were presently fetched to spend the rest of the evening in the drawing-room, and Maggie became so animated with Mr. Stelling, who, she felt sure, admired her cleverness, that Tom was rather amazed and alarmed at her audacity. But she was suddenly subdued by Mr. Stelling's alluding to a little girl of whom he had heard that she once ran away to the gypsies.

'What a very odd little girl that must be!' said Mrs.

Stelling, meaning to be playful—but a playfulness that turned on her supposed oddity was not at all to Maggie's taste. She feared that Mr. Stelling, after all, did not think much of her, and went to bed in rather low spirits. Mrs. Stelling, she felt, looked at her as if she thought her hair was very ugly because it hung down straight behind.

Nevertheless it was a very happy fortnight to Maggie, this visit to Tom. She was allowed to be in the study while he had his lessons, and in her various readings got very deep into the examples in the Latin Grammar. The astronomer who hated women generally, caused her so much puzzling speculation that she one day asked Mr. Stelling if all astronomers hated women, or whether it was only this particular astronomer. But, forestalling his answer, she said:

'I suppose it's all astronomers: because, you know, they live up in high towers, and if the women came there, they might talk and hinder them from looking at the stars.'

Mr. Stelling liked her prattle immensely, and they were on the best terms. She told Tom she should like to go to school to Mr. Stelling, as he did, and learn just the same things. She knew she could do Euclid, for she had looked into it again, and she saw what A B C meant: they were the names of the lines.

'I'm sure you couldn't do it, now,' said Tom; 'and I'll just ask Mr. Stelling if you could.'

'I don't mind,' said the little conceited minx. 'I'll ask him myself.'

'Mr. Stelling,' she said, that same evening when they were in the drawing-room, 'couldn't I do Euclid, and all Tom's lessons, if you were to teach me instead of him?'

'No; you couldn't,' said Tom indignantly. 'Girls can't do Euclid: can they, sir?'

'They can pick up a little of everything, I daresay,' said Mr. Stelling. 'They've a great deal of superficial cleverness; but they couldn't go far into anything. They're quick and shallow.'

Tom, delighted with this verdict, telegraphed his triumph

by wagging his head at Maggie behind Mr. Stelling's chair. As for Maggie, she had hardly ever been so mortified. She had been so proud to be called 'quick' all her little life, and now it appeared that this quickness was the brand of inferiority. It would have been better to be slow, like Tom.

'Ha, ha! Miss Maggie!' said Tom, when they were alone; 'you see it's not such a fine thing to be quick. You'll never go far into anything, you know.'

And Maggie was so oppressed by this dreadful destiny that she had no spirit for a retort.

But when this small apparatus of shallow quickness was fetched away in the gig by Luke, and the study was once more quite lonely for Tom, he missed her grievously. He had really been brighter, and had got through his lessons better, since she had been there; and she had asked Mr. Stelling so many questions about the Roman empire, and whether there really ever was a man who said, in Latin, 'I would not buy it for a farthing or a rotten nut,' or whether that had only been turned into Latin, that Tom had actually come to a dim understanding of the fact that there had once been people upon the earth who were so fortunate as to know Latin without learning it through the medium of the Eton Grammar. This luminous idea was a great addition to his historical acquirements during this half-year, which were otherwise confined to an epitomised history of the Jews.

But the dreary half-year *did* come to an end. How glad Tom was to see the last yellow leaves fluttering before the cold wind! The dark afternoons, and the first December snow, seemed to him far livelier than the August sunshine; and that he might make himself the surer about the flight of the days that were carrying him homeward, he stuck twenty-one sticks deep in a corner of the garden, when he was three weeks from the holidays, and pulled up one every day with a great wrench, throwing it to a distance with a vigour of will which would have carried it to limbo, if it had been in the nature of sticks to travel so far.

But it was worth purchasing, even at the heavy price of

the Latin Grammar—the happiness of seeing the bright light in the parlour at home, as the gig passed noiselessly over the snow-covered bridge: the happiness of passing from the cold air to the warmth and the kisses and the smiles of that familiar hearth, where the pattern of the rug and the grate and the fire-irons were 'first ideas' that it was no more possible to criticise than the solidity and extension of matter. There is no sense of ease like the ease we felt in those scenes where we were born, where objects became dear to us before we had known the labour of choice, and where the outer world seemed only an extension of our own personality: we accepted and loved it as we accepted our own sense of existence and our own limbs. Very common-place, even ugly, that furniture of our early home might look if it were put up to auction; an improved taste in upholstery scorns it; and is not the striving after something better and better in our surroundings, the grand characteristic that distinguishes man from the brute—or, to satisfy a scrupulous accuracy of definition, that distinguishes the British man from the foreign brute? But Heaven knows where that striving might lead us, if our affections had not a trick of twining round those old inferior things—if the loves and sanctities of our life had no deep immovable roots in memory. One's delight in an elderberry bush overhanging the confused leafage of a hedgerow bank, as a more gladdening sight than the finest cistus or fuchsia spreading itself on the softest undulating turf, is an entirely unjustifiable preference to a nursery-gardener, or to any of those severely regulated minds who are free from the weakness of any attachment that does not rest on a demonstrable superiority of qualities. And there is no better reason for preferring this elderberry bush than that it stirs an early memory—that it is no novelty in my life, speaking to me merely through my present sensibilities to form and colour, but the long companion of my existence, that wove itself into my joys when joys were vivid.

II

THE CHRISTMAS HOLIDAYS

FINE old Christmas, with the snowy hair and ruddy face, had done his duty that year in the noblest fashion, and had set off his rich gifts of warmth and colour with all the heightening contrast of frost and snow.

Snow lay on the croft and river-bank in undulations softer than the limbs of infancy; it lay with the neatliest finished border on every sloping roof, making the dark-red gables stand out with a new depth of colour; it weighed heavily on the laurels and fir-trees, till it fell from them with a shuddering sound; it clothed the rough turnip-field with whiteness, and made the sheep look like dark blotches; the gates were all blocked up with the sloping drifts, and here and there a disregarded four-footed beast stood as if petrified 'in unrecumbent sadness;' there was no gleam, no shadow, for the heavens, too, were one still, pale cloud— no sound or motion in anything but the dark river that flowed and moaned like an unresting sorrow. But old Christmas smiled as he laid this cruel-seeming spell on the out-door world, for he meant to light up home with new brightness, to deepen all the richness of indoor colour, and give a keener edge of delight to the warm fragrance of food: he meant to prepare a sweet imprisonment that would strengthen the primitive fellowship of kindred, and make the sunshine of familiar human faces as welcome as the hidden day-star. His kindness fell but hardly on the homeless—fell but hardly on the homes where the hearth was not very warm, and where the food had little fragrance; where the human faces had no sunshine in them, but rather the leaden, black-eyed gaze of unexpectant want. But the fine old season meant well; and if he has not learnt the secret how to bless men impartially, it is because his father Time, with ever-relenting purpose, still hides that secret in his own mighty, slow-beating heart.

And yet this Christmas day, in spite of Tom's fresh de-

light in home, was not, he thought, somehow or other.
quite so happy as it had always been before. The red
berries were just as abundant on the holly, and he and
Maggie had dressed all the windows and mantelpieces and
picture-frames on Christmas eve with as much taste as ever.
wedding the thick-set scarlet clusters with branches of the
black-berried ivy. There had been singing under the
windows after midnight—supernatural singing, Maggie
always felt, in spite of Tom's contemptuous insistence that
the singers were old Patch, the parish clerk, and the rest of
the church choir: she trembled with awe when their carol-
ing broke in upon her dreams, and the image of men in
fustian clothes was always thrust away by the vision of
angels resting on the parted cloud. The midnight chant had
helped as usual to lift the morning above the level of common days; and then there was the smell of hot toast and
ale from the kitchen, at the breakfast hour; the favourite
anthem, the green boughs, and the short sermon, gave the
appropriate festal character to the church-going; and aunt
and uncle Moss, with all their seven children, were looking
like so many reflectors of the bright parlour fire, when the
church-goers came back, stamping the snow from their feet.
The plum-pudding was of the same handsome roundness as
ever, and came in with the symbolic blue flames around it,
as if it had been heroically snatched from the nether fires
into which it had been thrown by dyspeptic Puritans; the
dessert was as splendid as ever, with its golden oranges,
brown nuts, and the crystalline light and dark of apple jelly
and damson cheese: in all these things Christmas was as it
had always been since Tom could remember; it was only
distinguished, if by anything, by superior sliding and snow-
balls.

Christmas was cheery, but not so Mr. Tulliver. He was
irate and defiant, and Tom, though he espoused his father's
quarrels and shared his father's sense of injury, was not
without some of the feeling that oppressed Maggie when Mr.
Tulliver got louder and more angry in narration and assertion with the increased leisure of dessert. The attention
that Tom might have concentrated on his nuts and wine was

distracted by a sense that there were rascally enemies in the world, and that the business of grown-up life could hardly be conducted without a good deal of quarrelling. Now Tom was not fond of quarrelling, unless it could soon be put an end to by a fair stand-up fight with an adversary whom he had every chance of thrashing; and his father's irritable talk made him uncomfortable, though he never accounted to himself for the feeling, or conceived the notion that his father was faulty in this respect.

The particular embodiment of the evil principle now exciting Mr. Tulliver's determined resistance was Mr. Pivart, who, having lands higher up the Ripple, was taking measures for their irrigation, which either were, or would be, or were bound to be (on the principle that water was water), an infringement on Mr. Tulliver's legitimate share of water-power. Dix, who had a mill on the stream, was a feeble auxiliary of Old Harry compared with Pivart. Dix had been brought to his senses by arbitration, and Wakem's advice had not carried *him* far; no: Dix, Mr. Tulliver considered, had been as good as nowhere in point of law; and in the intensity of his indignation against Pivart, his contempt for a baffled adversary like Dix began to wear the air of a friendly attachment. He had no male audience to-day except Mr. Moss, who knew nothing, as he said, of the 'natur' o' mills,' and could only assent to Mr. Tulliver's arguments on the *a priori* ground of family relationship and monetary obligation; but Mr. Tulliver did not talk with the futile intention of convincing his audience—he talked to relieve himself; while good Mr. Moss made strong efforts to keep his eyes wide open, in spite of the sleepiness which an unusually good dinner produced in his hard-worked frame. Mrs. Moss, more alive to the subject, and interested in everything that affected her brother, listened and put in a word as often as maternal preoccupations allowed.

'Why, Pivart's a new name hereabout, brother, isn't it?' she said: 'he didn't own the land in father's time, nor yours either, before I was married.'

'New name? Yes, I should think it *is* a new name,' said Mr. Tulliver, with angry emphasis. 'Dorlcote Mill's been in

our family a hundred year and better, and nobody ever
heard of a Pivart meddling with the river, till this fellow
came and bought Bincomb's farm out of hand, before anybody else could so much as say "snap". But I'll *Pivart*
him!' added Mr. Tulliver, lifting his glass with a sense that
he had defined his resolution in an unmistakable manner.

'You won't be forced to go to law with him, I hope,
brother?' said Mrs. Moss, with some anxiety.

'I don't know what I shall be forced to; but I know what
I shall force *him* to, with his dykes and erigations, if there's
any law to be brought to bear o' the right side. I know well
enough who's at the bottom of it; he's got Wakem to back
him and egg him on. I know Wakem tells him the law can't
touch him for it, but there's folks can handle the law besides Wakem. It takes a big raskil to beat him, but there's
bigger to be found, as know more o' th' ins and outs o' the
law, else how came Wakem to lose Brumley's suit for him?'

Mr. Tulliver was a strictly honest man, and proud of
being honest, but he considered that in law the ends of
justice could only be achieved by employing a stronger
knave to frustrate a weaker. Law was a sort of cock-fight,
in which it was the business of injured honesty to get a
game bird with the best pluck and the strongest spurs.

'Gore's no fool—you needn't tell me that,' he observed
presently, in a pugnacious tone, as if poor Gritty had been
urging that lawyer's capabilities; 'but, you see, he isn't up
to the law as Wakem is. And water's a very particular thing
—you can't pick it up with a pitch-fork. That's why it's
been nuts to Old Harry and the lawyers. It's plain enough
what's the rights and the wrongs of water, if you look at it
straightforrard; for a river's a river, and if you've got a
mill, you must have water to turn it; and it's no use telling
me, Pivart's erigation and nonsense won't stop my wheel;
I know what belongs to water better than that. Talk to
me o' what th' engineers say! I say it's common sense, as
Pivart's dykes must do me an injury. But if that's their
engineering, I'll put Tom to it by-and-by, and he shall see
if he can't find a bit more sense in th' engineering business
than what *that* comes to.'

Tom, looking round with some anxiety at this announcement of his prospects, unthinkingly withdrew a small rattle he was amusing Baby Moss with, whereupon she, being a baby that knew her own mind with remarkable clearness, instantaneously expressed her sentiments in a piercing yell, and was not to be appeased even by the restoration of the rattle, feeling apparently that the original wrong of having it taken from her remained in all its force. Mrs. Moss hurried away with her into another room, and expressed to Mrs. Tulliver, who accompanied her, the conviction that the dear child had good reasons for crying; implying that if it was supposed to be the rattle that baby clamoured for, she was a misunderstood baby. The thoroughly justifiable yell being quieted, Mrs. Moss looked at her sister-in-law and said:

'I'm sorry to see brother so put out about this water work.'

'It's your brother's way, Mrs. Moss; I'd never anything o' that sort before I was married,' said Mrs. Tulliver, with a half-implied reproach. She always spoke of her husband as 'your brother' to Mrs. Moss in any case when his line of conduct was not matter of pure admiration. Amiable Mrs. Tulliver, who was never angry in her life, had yet her mild share of that spirit without which she could hardly have been at once a Dodson and a woman. Being always on the defensive towards her own sisters, it was natural that she should be keenly conscious of her superiority, even as the weakest Dodson, over a husband's sister, who, besides being poorly off, and inclined to 'hang on' her brother, had the good-natured submissiveness of a large, easy-tempered, untidy, prolific woman, with affection enough in her not only for her own husband and abundant children, but for any number of collateral relations.

'I hope and pray he won't go to law,' said Mrs. Moss, 'for there's never any knowing where that'll end. And the right doesn't allays win. This Mr. Pivart's a rich man, by what I can make out, and the rich mostly get things their own way.'

'As to that,' said Mrs. Tulliver, stroking her dress down,

'I've seen what riches are in my own family; for my sisters have got husbands as can afford to do pretty much what they like. But I think sometimes I shall be drove off my head with the talk about this law and erigation; and my sisters lay all the fault to me, for they don't know what it is to marry a man like your brother—how should they? Sister Pullet has her own way from morning till night.'

'Well,' said Mrs. Moss, 'I don't think I should like my husband if he hadn't got any wits of his own, and I had to find head-piece for him. It's a deal easier to do what pleases one's husband, than to be puzzling what else one should do.'

'If people come to talk o' doing what pleases their husbands,' said Mrs. Tulliver, with a faint imitation of her sister Glegg, 'I'm sure your brother might have waited a long while before he'd have found a wife that 'ud have let him have his say in everything, as I do. It's nothing but law and erigation now, from when we first get up in the morning till we go to bed at night; and I never contradict him; I only say—"Well, Mr. Tulliver, do as you like; but whatever you do, don't go to law."'

Mrs. Tulliver, as we have seen, was not without influence over her husband. No woman is; she can always incline him to do either what she wishes, or the reverse; and on the composite impulses that were threatening to hurry Mr. Tulliver into 'law,' Mrs. Tulliver's monotonous pleading had doubtless its share of force; it might even be comparable to that proverbial feather which has the credit or discredit of breaking the camel's back; though, on a strictly impartial view, the blame ought rather to lie with the previous weight of feathers which had already placed the back in such imminent peril, that an otherwise innocent feather could not settle on it without mischief. Not that Mrs. Tulliver's feeble beseeching could have had this feather's weight in virtue of her single personality; but whenever she departed from entire assent to her husband, he saw in her the representative of the Dodson family; and it was a guiding principle with Mr. Tulliver, to let the Dodsons know that they were not to domineer over *him*, or—more specifically—that a male Tulliver was far more than equal

to four female Dodsons, even though one of them was Mrs.
Glegg.

But not even a direct argument from that typical Dodson female herself against his going to law, could have
heightened his disposition towards it so much as the mere
thought of Wakem, continually freshened by the sight of
the too able attorney on market days. Wakem, to his
certain knowledge, was (metaphorically speaking) at the
bottom of Pivart's irrigation: Wakem had tried to make
Dix stand out, and go to law about the dam: it was un-
questionably Wakem who had caused Mr. Tulliver to lose
the suit about the right of road and the bridge that made
a thoroughfare of his land for every vagabond who preferred an opportunity of damaging private property to
walking like an honest man along the high-road: all lawyers
were more or less rascals, but Wakem's rascality was of that
peculiarly aggravated kind which placed itself in opposition
to that form of right embodied in Mr. Tulliver's interests
and opinions. And as an extra touch of bitterness, the injured miller had recently, in borrowing the five hundred
pounds, been obliged to carry a little business to Wakem's
office on his own account. A hook-nosed glib fellow! as cool
as a cucumber—always looking so sure of his game! And it
was vexatious that Lawyer Gore was not more like him,
but was a bald, round-featured man, with bland manners
and fat hands; a game-cock that you would be rash to bet
upon against Wakem. Gore was a sly fellow; his weakness
did not lie on the side of scrupulosity; but the largest
amount of winking, however significant, is not equivalent
to seeing through a stone wall; and confident as Mr. Tulliver
was in his principle that water was water, and in the direct
inference that Pivart had not a leg to stand on in this affair
of irrigation, he had an uncomfortable suspicion that
Wakem had more law to show against this (rationally) irre-
fragable inference, than Gore could show for it. But then,
if they went to law, there was a chance for Mr. Tulliver to
employ Counsellor Wylde on his side, instead of having that
admirable bully against him; and the prospect of seeing a
witness of Wakem's made to perspire and become con-

founded, as Mr. Tulliver's witness had once been, was alluring to the love of retributive justice.

Much rumination had Mr. Tulliver on these puzzling subjects during his rides on the gray horse—much turning of the head from side to side, as the scales dipped alternately; but the probable result was still out of sight, only to be reached through much hot argument and iteration in domestic and social life. That initial stage of the dispute which consisted in the narration of the case and the enforcement of Mr. Tulliver's views concerning it throughout the entire circle of his connections would necessarily take time, and at the beginning of February, when Tom was going to school again, there were scarcely any new items to be detected in his father's statement of the case against Pivart, or any more specific indication of the measures he was bent on taking against that rash contravener of the principle that water was water. Iteration, like friction, is likely to generate heat instead of progress, and Mr. Tulliver's heat was certainly more and more palpable. If there had been no new evidence on any other point, there had been new evidence that Pivart was as 'thick as mud' with Wakem.

'Father,' said Tom, one evening near the end of the holidays, 'uncle Glegg says Lawyer Wakem *is* going to send his son to Mr. Stelling. It isn't true—what they said about his going to be sent to France. You won't like me to go to school with Wakem's son, shall you?'

'It's no matter for that, my boy,' said Mr. Tulliver; 'don't you learn anything bad of him, that's all. The lad's a poor deformed creatur', and takes after his mother in the face: I think there isn't much of his father in him. It's a sign Wakem thinks high o' Mr. Stelling, as he sends his son to him, and Wakem knows meal from bran.'

Mr. Tulliver in his heart was rather proud of the fact that his son was to have the same advantages as Wakem's: but Tom was not at all easy on the point; it would have been much clearer if the lawyer's son had not been deformed, for then Tom would have had the prospect of pitching into him with all that freedom which is derived from a high moral sanction.

III

THE NEW SCHOOLFELLOW

It was a cold, wet January day on which Tom went back to school; a day quite in keeping with this severe phase of his destiny. If he had not carried in his pocket a parcel of sugar-candy and a small Dutch doll for little Laura, there would have been no ray of expected pleasure to enliven the general gloom. But he liked to think how Laura would put out her lips and her tiny hands for the bits of sugar-candy; and, to give the greater keenness to these pleasures of imagination, he took out the parcel, made a small hole in the paper, and bit off a crystal or two, which had so solacing an effect under the confined prospect and damp odours of the gig-umbrella, that he repeated the process more than once on his way.

'Well, Tulliver, we're glad to see you again,' said Mr. Stelling heartily. 'Take off your wrappings and come into the study till dinner. You'll find a bright fire there, and a new companion.'

Tom felt in an uncomfortable flutter as he took off his woollen comforter and other wrappings. He had seen Philip Wakem at St. Ogg's, but had always turned his eyes away from him as quickly as possible. He would have disliked having a deformed boy for his companion, even if Philip had not been the son of a bad man. And Tom did not see how a bad man's son could be very good. His own father was a good man, and he would readily have fought anyone who said the contrary. He was in a state of mingled embarrassment and defiance as he followed Mr. Stelling to the study.

'Here is a new companion for you to shake hands with, Tulliver,' said the gentleman on entering the study— 'Master Philip Wakem. I shall leave you to make acquaintance by yourselves. You already know something of each other, I imagine; for you are neighbours at home.'

Tom looked confused and awkward, while Philip rose

and glanced at him timidly. Tom did not like to go up and put out his hand, and he was not prepared to say, 'How do you do?' on so short a notice.

Mr. Stelling wisely turned away, and closed the door behind him: boys' shyness only wears off in the absence of their elders.

Philip was at once too proud and too timid to walk towards Tom. He thought, or rather felt, that Tom had an aversion to looking at him: everyone, almost, disliked looking at him; and his deformity was more conspicuous when he walked. So they remained without shaking hands or even speaking, while Tom went to the fire and warmed himself, every now and then casting furtive glances at Philip, who seemed to be drawing absently first one object and then another on a piece of paper he had before him. He had seated himself again, and as he drew, was thinking what he could say to Tom, and trying to overcome his own repugnance to making the first advances.

Tom began to look oftener and longer at Philip's face, for he could see it without noticing the hump, and it was really not a disagreeable face—very old-looking, Tom thought. He wondered how much older Philip was than himself. An anatomist—even a mere physiognomist—would have seen that the deformity of Philip's spine was not a congenital hump, but the result of an accident in infancy; but you do not expect from Tom any acquaintance with such distinctions: to him, Philip was simply a humpback. He had a vague notion that the deformity of Wakem's son had some relation to the lawyer's rascality, of which he had so often heard his father talk with hot emphasis; and he felt, too, a half-admitted fear of him as probably a spiteful fellow, who, not being able to fight you, had cunning ways of doing you a mischief by the sly. There was a hump-backed tailor in the neighbourhood of Mr. Jacobs' academy, who was considered a very unamiable character, and was much hooted after by public-spirited boys solely on the ground of his unsatisfactory moral qualities; so that Tom was not without a basis of fact to go upon. Still, no face could be more unlike that ugly tailor's than this melancholy boy's face; the brown hair round it waved and curled at the ends like a girl's: Tom thought that truly pitiable. This Wakem was a pale, puny fellow, and it was quite clear he would not be able to play at anything worth speaking of: but he handled his pencil in an enviable manner, and was apparently making one thing after another without any trouble. What was he drawing? Tom was quite warm now, and wanted something new to be going forward. It was certainly more agreeable to have an ill-natured humpback as a companion than to stand looking out of the study window at the rain, and kicking his foot against the washboard in solitude; something would happen every day—'a quarrel or something;' and Tom thought he should rather like to show Philip that he had better not try his spiteful tricks on *him*. He suddenly walked across the hearth, and looked over Philip's paper.

'Why, that's a donkey with panniers—and a spaniel and partridges in the corn!' he exclaimed, his tongue being completely loosed by surprise and admiration. 'O my buttons! I wish I could draw like that. I'm to learn drawing this half—I wonder if I shall learn to make dogs and donkeys!'

'O, you can do them without learning,' said Philip; 'I never learned drawing.'

'Never learned?' said Tom in amazement. 'Why, when I make dogs and horses, and those things, the heads and the legs won't come right; though I can see how they ought to be very well. I can make houses, and all sorts of chimneys—chimneys going all down the wall, and windows in the roof, and all that. But I dare say I could do dogs and horses if I was to try more,' he added, reflecting that Philip might falsely suppose that he was going to 'knock under,' if he were too frank about the imperfection of his accomplishments.

'O yes,' said Philip, 'it's very easy. You've only to look well at things, and draw them over and over again. What you do wrong once, you can alter the next time.'

'But haven't you been taught *anything*?' said Tom, beginning to have a puzzled suspicion that Philip's crooked

back might be the source of remarkable faculties. 'I
thought you'd been to school a long while.'

'Yes,' said Philip, smiling, 'I've been taught Latin, and
Greek, and mathematics,—and writing, and such things.'

'O, but I say, you don't like Latin, though, do you?'
said Tom, lowering his voice confidentially.

'Pretty well; I don't care much about it,' said Philip.

'Ah, but perhaps you haven't got into the *Propria quæ
maribus*,' said Tom, nodding his head sideways, as much as
to say, 'that was the test: it was easy talking till you came
to *that*.'

Philip felt some bitter complacency in the promising
stupidity of this well-made active-looking boy; but made
polite by his own extreme sensitiveness, as well as by his
desire to conciliate, he checked his inclination to laugh,
and said quietly:

'I've done with the grammar; I don't learn that any more.'

'Then you won't have the same lessons as I shall?' said
Tom, with a sense of disappointment.

'No; but I daresay I can help you. I shall be very glad
to help you if I can.'

Tom did not say 'Thank you,' for he was quite absorbed
in the thought that Wakem's son did not seem so spiteful
a fellow as might have been expected.

'I say,' he said presently, 'do you love your father?'

'Yes,' said Philip, colouring deeply; 'don't you love
yours?'

'O yes. . . . I only wanted to know,' said Tom, rather
ashamed of himself, now he saw Philip colouring and looking
uncomfortable. He found much difficulty in adjusting his
attitude of mind towards the son of Lawyer Wakem, and it
had occurred to him that if Philip disliked his father, that
fact might go some way towards clearing up his perplexity.

'Shall you learn drawing now?' he said, by way of
changing the subject.

'No,' said Philip. 'My father wishes me to give all my
time to other things now.'

'What! Latin, and Euclid, and those things?' said Tom.

'Yes,' said Philip, who had left off using his pencil, and

was resting his head on one hand, while Tom was leaning forward on both elbows, and looking with increasing admiration at the dog and the donkey.

'And you don't mind that?' said Tom, with strong curiosity.

'No: I like to know what everybody else knows. I can study what I like by-and-by.'

'I can't think why anybody should learn Latin,' said Tom. 'It's no good.'

'It's part of the education of a gentleman,' said Philip. 'All gentlemen learn the same things.'

'What! do you think Sir John Crake, the master of the harriers, knows Latin?' said Tom, who had often thought he should like to resemble Sir John Crake.

'He learnt it when he was a boy, of course,' said Philip. 'But I daresay he's forgotten it.'

'O, well, I can do that, then,' said Tom, not with any epigrammatic intention, but with serious satisfaction at the idea that, as far as Latin was concerned, there was no hindrance to his resembling Sir John Crake. 'Only you're obliged to remember it while you're at school, else you've got to learn ever so many lines of "Speaker." Mr. Stelling's very particular—did you know? He'll have you up ten times if you say "nam" for "jam" ... he won't let you go a letter wrong, *I* can tell you.'

'O, I don't mind,' said Philip, unable to choke a laugh; 'I can remember things easily. And there are some lessons I'm very fond of. I'm very fond of Greek history and everything about the Greeks. I should like to have been a Greek and fought the Persians, and then have come home and have written tragedies, or else have been listened to by everybody for my wisdom, like Socrates, and have died a grand death.' (Philip, you perceive, was not without a wish to impress the well-made barbarian with a sense of his mental superiority.)

'Why, were the Greeks great fighters?' said Tom, who saw a vista in this direction. 'Is there anything like David, and Goliath, and Samson, in the Greek history? Those are the only bits I like in the history of the Jews.'

'O, there are very fine stories of that sort about the Greeks—about the heroes of early times who killed the wild beasts, as Samson did. And in the *Odyssey*—that's a beautiful poem—there's a more wonderful giant than Goliath—Polypheme, who had only one eye in the middle of his forehead; and Ulysses, a little fellow, but very wise and cunning, got a red-hot pine-tree and stuck it into this one eye, and made him roar like a thousand bulls.'

'O, what fun!' said Tom, jumping away from the table, and stamping first with one leg and then the other. 'I say, can you tell me all about those stories? Because I shan't learn Greek you know. . . . Shall I?' he added, pausing in his stamping with a sudden alarm, lest the contrary might be possible. 'Does every gentleman learn Greek? . . . Will Mr. Stelling make me begin with it, do you think?'

'No, I should think not—very likely not,' said Philip. 'But you may read those stories without knowing Greek. I've got them in English.'

'O, but I don't like reading; I'd sooner have you tell them me. But only the fighting ones, you know. My sister Maggie is always wanting to tell me stories—but they're stupid things. Girls' stories always are. Can you tell a good many fighting stories?'

'O yes,' said Philip; 'lots of them, besides the Greek stories. I can tell you about Richard Cœur-de-Lion and Saladin, and about William Wallace, and Robert Bruce, and James Douglas—I know no end.'

'You're older than I am, aren't you?' said Tom.

'Why, how old are *you*? I'm fifteen.'

'I'm only going in fourteen,' said Tom. 'But I thrashed all the fellows at Jacobs'—that's where I was before I came here. And I beat 'em all at bandy and climbing. And I wish Mr. Stelling would let us go fishing. *I* could show you how to fish. You *could* fish, couldn't you? It's only standing, and sitting still, you know.'

Tom, in his turn, wished to make the balance dip in his favour. This hunchback must not suppose that his acquaintance with fighting stories put him on a par with an actual fighting hero, like Tom Tulliver. Philip winced under this allusion to his unfitness for active sports, and he answered almost peevishly:

'I can't bear fishing. I think people look like fools sitting watching a line hour after hour—or else throwing and throwing, and catching nothing.'

'Ah, but you wouldn't say they looked like fools when they landed a big pike, I can tell you,' said Tom, who had never caught anything that was 'big' in his life, but whose imagination was on the stretch with indignant zeal for the honour of sport. Wakem's son, it was plain, had his disagreeable points, and must be kept in due check. Happily for the harmony of this first interview, they were now called to dinner, and Philip was not allowed to develop farther his unsound views on the subject of fishing. But Tom said to himself, that was just what he should have expected from a hunchback.

IV

'THE YOUNG IDEA'

THE alternations of feeling in that first dialogue between Tom and Philip continued to mark their intercourse even after many weeks of schoolboy intimacy. Tom never quite lost the feeling that Philip, being the son of a 'rascal,' was his natural enemy, never thoroughly overcame his repulsion to Philip's deformity: he was a boy who adhered tenaciously to impressions once received: as with all minds in which mere perception predominates over thought and emotion, the external remained to him rigidly what it was in the first instance. But then, it was impossible not to like Philip's company when he was in a good humour; he could help one so well in one's Latin exercises, which Tom regarded as a kind of puzzle that could only be found out by a lucky chance; and he could tell such wonderful fighting stories about Hal of the Wynd, for example, and other heroes who were especial favourites with Tom, because they laid about them with heavy strokes. He had small opinion of Saladin, whose scimitar could cut a cushion in

wo in an instant: who wanted to cut cushions? That was
stupid story, and he didn't care to hear it again. But when
:obert Bruce, on the black pony, rose in his stirrups, and,
fting his good battle-axe, cracked at once the helmet and
1e skull of the too-hasty knight at Bannockburn, then
om felt all the exaltation of sympathy, and if he had had
cocoa-nut at hand, he would have cracked it at once with
1e poker. Philip in his happier moods indulged Tom to
1e top of his bent, heightening the crash and bang and
ary of every fight with all the artillery of epithets and
miles at his command. But he was not always in a good
umour or happy mood. The slight spurt of peevish sus-
-ptibility which had escaped him in their first interview,
'as a symptom of a perpetually-recurring mental ailment
-half of it nervous irritability, half of it the heart-bitter-
ss produced by the sense of his deformity. In these fits
f susceptibility every glance seemed to him to be charged
ther with offensive pity or with ill-repressed disgust—at
1e very least it was an indifferent glance, and Philip felt
difference as a child of the south feels the chill air of a
orthern spring. Poor Tom's blundering patronage when
1ey were out of doors together would sometimes make him
1rn upon the well-meaning lad quite savagely; and his
yes, usually sad and quiet, would flash with anything but
layful lightning. No wonder Tom retained his suspicions
f the humpback.

But Philip's self-taught skill in drawing was another link
etween them; for Tom found, to his disgust, that his new
rawing-master gave him no dogs and donkeys to draw,
it brooks and rustic bridges and ruins, all with a general
oftness of black-lead surface, indicating that nature, if
1ything, was rather satiny; and as Tom's feeling for the
cturesque in landscape was at present quite latent, it is
ot surprising that Mr. Goodrich's productions seemed to
im an uninteresting form of art. Mr. Tulliver, having a
ague intention that Tom should be put to some business
hich included the drawing out of plans and maps, had
mplained to Mr. Riley, when he saw him at Mudport,
1at Tom seemed to be learning nothing of that sort;

whereupon that obliging adviser had suggested that Tom should have drawing-lessons. Mr. Tulliver must not mind paying extra for drawing: let Tom be made a good draughtsman, and he would be able to turn his pencil to any purpose. So it was ordered that Tom should have drawing lessons; and whom should Mr. Stelling have selected as a master if not Mr. Goodrich, who was considered quite at the head of his profession within a circuit of twelve miles round King's Lorton? By which means Tom learned to make an extremely fine point to his pencil, and to represent landscape with a 'broad generality,' which, doubtless from a narrow tendency in his mind to details, he thought extremely dull.

All this, you remember, happened in those dark ages when there were no schools of design—before schoolmasters were invariably men of scrupulous integrity, and before the clergy were all men of enlarged minds and varied culture. In those less-favoured days, it is no fable that there were other clergymen besides Mr. Stelling who had narrow intellects and large wants, and whose income, by a logical confusion to which Fortune, being a female as well as blindfold, is peculiarly liable, was proportioned not to their wants but to their intellect—with which income has clearly no inherent relation. The problem these gentlemen had to solve was to readjust the proportion between their wants and their income; and since wants are not easily starved to death, the simpler method appeared to be—to raise their income. There was but one way of doing this; any of those low callings in which men are obliged to do good work at a low price were forbidden to clergymen: was it their fault if their only resource was to turn out very poor work at a high price? Besides, how should Mr. Stelling be expected to know that education was a delicate and difficult business? any more than an animal endowed with a power of boring a hole through a rock should be expected to have wide views of excavation. Mr. Stelling's faculties had been early trained to boring in a straight line, and he had no faculty to spare. But among Tom's contemporaries, whose fathers cast their sons on clerical instruction to find them ignorant after many days, there were many far less lucky than Tom Tulliver. Education was almost entirely a matter of luck—usually of ill-luck—in those distant days. The state of mind in which you take a billiard-cue or a dice-box in your hand is one of sober certainty compared with that of old-fashioned fathers, like Mr. Tulliver, when they selected a school or a tutor for their sons. Excellent men, who had been forced all their lives to spell on an impromptu-phonetic system, and having carried on a successful business in spite of this disadvantage, had acquired money enough to give their sons a better start in life than they had had themselves, must necessarily take their chance as to the conscience and the competence of the schoolmaster whose circular fell in their way, and appeared to promise so much more than they would ever have thought of asking for, including the return of linen, fork, and spoon. It was happy for them if some ambitious draper of their acquaintance had not brought up his son to the Church, and if that young gentleman, at the age of four-and-twenty, had not closed his college dissipations by an imprudent marriage: otherwise, these innocent fathers, desirous of doing the best for their offspring, could only escape the draper's son by happening to be on the foundation of a grammar-school as yet unvisited by commissioners, where two or three boys could have, all to themselves, the advantages of a large and lofty building, together with a head master, toothless, dim-eyed, and deaf, whose erudite indistinctness and inattention were engrossed by them at the rate of three hundred pounds a-head—a ripe scholar, doubtless, when first appointed; but all ripeness beneath the sun has a further stage less esteemed in the market.

Tom Tulliver, then, compared with many other British youths of his time who have since had to scramble through life with some fragments of more or less relevant knowledge, and a great deal of strictly relevant ignorance, was not so very unlucky. Mr. Stelling was a broad-chested healthy man, with the bearing of a gentleman, a conviction that a growing boy required a sufficiency of beef and a certain hearty kindness in him that made him like to see

Tom looking well and enjoying his dinner; not a man of refined conscience, or with any deep sense of the infinite issues belonging to everyday duties; not quite competent to his high offices; but incompetent gentlemen must live, and without private fortune it is difficult to see how they could all live genteelly if they had nothing to do with education or government. Besides, it was the fault of Tom's mental constitution that his faculties could not be nourished on the sort of knowledge Mr. Stelling had to communicate. A boy born with a deficient power of apprehending signs and abstractions must suffer the penalty of his congenital deficiency, just as if he had been born with one leg shorter than the other. A method of education sanctioned by the long practice of our venerable ancestors was not to give way before the exceptional dulness of a boy who was merely living at the time then present. And Mr. Stelling was convinced that a boy so stupid at signs and abstractions must be stupid at everything else, even if that reverend gentleman could have taught him everything else. It was the practice of our venerable ancestors to apply that ingenious instrument the thumb-screw, and to tighten and tighten it in order to elicit non-existent facts; they had a fixed opinion to begin with, that the facts were existent, and what had they to do but to tighten the thumb-screw? In like manner, Mr. Stelling had a fixed opinion that all boys with any capacity could learn what it was the only regular thing to teach: if they were slow, the thumb-screw must be tightened—the exercises must be insisted on with increased severity, and a page of Virgil be awarded as a penalty, to encourage and stimulate a too languid inclination to Latin verse.

The thumb-screw was a little relaxed, however, during this second half-year. Philip was so advanced in his studies, and so apt, that Mr. Stelling could obtain credit by his facility, which required little help, much more easily than by the troublesome process of overcoming Tom's dulness. Gentlemen with broad chests and ambitious intentions do sometimes disappoint their friends by failing to carry the world before them. Perhaps it is, that high achievements emand some other unusual qualification besides an unsual desire for higher prizes; perhaps it is that these stalart gentlemen are rather indolent, their *divinæ particulum uræ* being obstructed from soaring by a too hearty appete. Some reason or other there was why Mr. Stelling derred the execution of many spirited projects—why he id not begin the editing of his Greek play, or any other ork of scholarship in his leisure hours, but, after turning he key of his private study with much resolution, sat down o one of Theodore Hook's novels. Tom was gradually llowed to shuffle through his lessons with less rigour, and aving Philip to help him, he was able to make some show f having applied his mind in a confused and blundering ay, without being cross-examined into a betrayal that his aind had been entirely neutral in the matter. He thought chool much more bearable under this modification of rcumstances; and he went on contentedly enough, picking up a promiscuous education chiefly from things that ere not intended as education at all. What was understood to be his education, was simply the practice of reading, writing, and spelling, carried on by an elaborate appliance of unintelligible ideas, and by much failure in the ffort to learn by rote.

Nevertheless, there was a visible improvement in Tom nder this training; perhaps because he was not a boy in he abstract, existing solely to illustrate the evils of a misaken education, but a boy made of flesh and blood, with ispositions not entirely at the mercy of circumstances.

There was a great improvement in his bearing, for exmple, and some credit on this score was due to Mr. Poulter, he village schoolmaster, who being an old Peninsular oldier, was employed to drill Tom—a source of high autual pleasure. Mr. Poulter, who was understood by the ompany at the Black Swan to have once struck terror to he hearts of the French, was no longer personally formidble. He had rather a shrunken appearance, and was remulous in the mornings, not from age, but from the xtreme perversity of the King's Lorton boys, which nothag but gin could enable him to sustain with any firmness.

Still, he carried himself with martial erectness, had his clothes scrupulously brushed, and his trousers tightly strapped; and on the Wednesday and Saturday afternoons when he came to Tom, he was always inspired with gin and old memories, which gave him an exceptionally spirited air as of a superannuated charger who hears the drum. The drilling-lessons were always protracted by episodes of war-like narrative, much more interesting to Tom than Philip's stories out of the *Iliad*; for there were no cannon in the *Iliad*, and, besides, Tom had felt some disgust on learning that Hector and Achilles might possibly never have existed. But the Duke of Wellington was really alive, and Bony had not been long dead—therefore Mr. Poulter's reminiscences of the Peninsular War were removed from all suspicion of being mythical. Mr. Poulter, it appeared, had been a conspicuous figure at Talavera, and had contributed not a little to the peculiar terror with which his regiment of infantry was regarded by the enemy. On afternoons, when his memory was more stimulated than usual, he remembered that the Duke of Wellington had (in strict privacy, lest jealousies should be awakened) expressed his esteem for that fine fellow Poulter. The very surgeon who attended him in the hospital after he had received his gunshot wound, had been profoundly impressed with the superiority of Mr. Poulter's flesh: no other flesh would have healed in anything like the same time. On less personal matters connected with the important warfare in which he had been engaged, Mr. Poulter was more reticent, only taking care not to give the weight of his authority to any loose notions concerning military history. Anyone who pretended to a knowledge of what occurred at the siege of Badajos, was especially an object of silent pity to Mr. Poulter; he wished that prating person had been run down, and had the breath trampled out of him at the first go-off, as he himself had—he might talk about the siege of Badajos then! Tom did not escape irritating his drilling-master occasionally, by his curiosity concerning other military matters than Mr. Poulter's personal experience.

'And General Wolfe, Mr. Poulter? wasn't he a wonderful

fighter?' said Tom, who held the notion that all the martial heroes commemorated on the public-house signs were engaged in the war with Bony.

'Not at all!' said Mr. Poulter contemptuously. 'Nothing o' the sort! . . . Heads up!' he added, in a tone of stern command, which delighted Tom, and made him feel as if he were a regiment in his own person.

'No, no!' Mr. Poulter would continue, on coming to a pause in his discipline. 'They'd better not talk to me about General Wolfe. He did nothing but die of his wound; that's a poor haction, I consider. Any other man 'ud have died o' the wounds I've had. . . . One of my sword-cuts 'ud ha' killed a fellow like General Wolfe.'

'Mr. Poulter,' Tom would say, at any allusion to the sword, 'I wish you'd bring your sword and do the sword-exercise!'

For a long while Mr. Poulter only shook his head in a significant manner at this request, and smiled patronisingly, as Jupiter may have done when Semele urged her too ambitious request. But one afternoon, when a sudden shower of heavy rain had detained Mr. Poulter twenty minutes longer than usual at the Black Swan, the sword was brought —just for Tom to look at.

'And this is the real sword you fought with in all the battles, Mr. Poulter?' said Tom, handling the hilt. 'Has it ever cut a Frenchman's head off?'

'Head off? Ah! and would, if he'd had three heads.'

'But you had a gun and bayonet besides?' said Tom. '*I* should like the gun and bayonet best, because you could shoot 'em first and spear 'em after. Bang! Ps-s-s-s!' Tom gave the requisite pantomime to indicate the double enjoyment of pulling the trigger and thrusting the spear.

'Ah, but the sword's the thing when you come to close fighting,' said Mr. Poulter, involuntarily falling in with Tom's enthusiasm, and drawing the sword so suddenly that Tom leaped back with much agility.

'O but, Mr. Poulter, if you're going to do the exercise,' said Tom, a little conscious that he had not stood his ground as became an Englishman, 'let me go and call Philip. He'll like to see you, you know.'

'What! the humpbacked lad?' said Mr. Poulter contemptuously. 'What's the use of *his* looking on?'

'O but he knows a great deal about fighting,' said Tom, 'and how they used to fight with bows and arrows, and battle-axes.'

'Let him come then. I'll show him something different from his bows and arrows,' said Mr. Poulter, coughing, and drawing himself up, while he gave a little preliminary play to his wrist.

Tom ran in to Philip, who was enjoying his afternoon's holiday at the piano, in the drawing-room, picking out tunes for himself and singing them. He was supremely happy, perched like an amorphous bundle on the high stool, with his head thrown back, his eyes fixed on the opposite cornice, and his lips wide open, sending forth, with all his might, impromptu syllables to a tune of Arne's, which had hit his fancy.

'Come, Philip,' said Tom, bursting in; 'don't stay roaring "la la" there—come and see old Poulter do his sword-exercise in the carriage-house!'

The jar of this interruption—the discord of Tom's tones coming across the notes to which Philip was vibrating in soul and body, would have been enough to unhinge his temper, even if there had been no question of Poulter the drilling-master; and Tom, in the hurry of seizing something to say to prevent Mr. Poulter from thinking he was afraid of the sword when he sprang away from it, had alighted on this proposition to fetch Philip—though he knew well enough that Philip hated to hear him mention his drilling-lessons. Tom would never have done so inconsiderate a thing except under the severe stress of his personal pride.

Philip shuddered visibly as he paused from his music. Then turning red, he said, with violent passion:

'Get away, you lumbering idiot! Don't come bellowing at me—you're not fit to speak to anything but a cart-horse!'

It was not the first time Philip had been made angry by him, but Tom had never before been assailed with verbal missiles that he understood so well.

'I'm fit to speak to something better than you—you poor-spirited imp!' said Tom, lighting up immediately at Philip's fire. 'You know I won't hit you, because you're no better than a girl. But I'm an honest man's son, and your father's a rogue—everybody says so!'

Tom flung out of the room, and slammed the door after him, made strangely heedless by his anger; for to slam doors within the hearing of Mrs. Stelling, who was probably not far off, was an offence only to be wiped out by twenty lines of Virgil. In fact, that lady did presently descend from her room, in double wonder at the noise and the subsequent cessation of Philip's music. She found him sitting in a heap on the hassock, and crying bitterly.

'What's the matter, Wakem? What was that noise about? Who slammed the door?'

Philip looked up, and hastily dried his eyes. 'It was Tulliver who came in . . . to ask me to go out with him.'

'And what are you in trouble about?' said Mrs. Stelling.

Philip was not her favourite of the two pupils; he was less obliging than Tom, who was made useful in many ways. Still his father paid more than Mr. Tulliver did, and she meant him to feel that she behaved exceedingly well to him. Philip, however, met her advances towards a good understanding very much as a caressed mollusc meets an invitation to show himself out of his shell. Mrs. Stelling was not a loving, tender-hearted woman: she was a woman whose skirt sat well, who adjusted her waist and patted her curls with a preoccupied air when she inquired after your welfare. These things, doubtless, represent a great social power, but it is not the power of love—and no other power could win Philip from his personal reserve.

He said, in answer to her question, 'My toothache came on, and made me hysterical again.'

This had been the fact once, and Philip was glad of the recollection—it was like an inspiration to enable him to excuse his crying. He had to accept eau-de-cologne, and to refuse creosote in consequence; but that was easy.

Meanwhile Tom, who had for the first time sent a poisoned

arrow into Philip's heart, had returned to the carriage house, where he found Mr. Poulter, with a fixed and earnest eye, wasting the perfections of his sword-exercise on probably observant but inappreciative rats. But Mr. Poulter was a host in himself; that is to say, he admired himself more than a whole army of spectators could have admired him. He took no notice of Tom's return, being too entirely absorbed in the cut and thrust—the solemn one, two, three, four; and Tom, not without a slight feeling of alarm at Mr. Poulter's fixed eye and hungry-looking sword, which seemed impatient for something else to cut besides the air, admired the performance from as great a distance as possible. It was not until Mr. Poulter paused and wiped the perspiration from his forehead, that Tom felt the full charm of the sword-exercise, and wished it to be repeated.

'Mr. Poulter,' said Tom, when the sword was being finally sheathed, 'I wish you'd lend me your sword a little while to keep.'

'No, no, young gentleman,' said Mr. Poulter, shaking his head decidedly, 'you might do yourself some mischief with it.'

'No, I'm sure I wouldn't—I'm sure I'd take care and not hurt myself. I shouldn't take it out of the sheath much, but I could ground arms with it, and all that.'

'No, no, it won't do, I tell you; it won't do,' said Mr. Poulter, preparing to depart. 'What 'ud Mr. Stelling say to me?'

'O, I say, do, Mr. Poulter! I'd give you my five-shilling piece if you'd let me keep the sword a week. Look here!' said Tom, reaching out the attractively large round of silver. The young dog calculated the effect as well as if he had been a philosopher.

'Well,' said Mr. Poulter, with still deeper gravity, 'you must keep it out of sight, you know.'

'O yes, I'll keep it under the bed,' said Tom eagerly, 'or else at the bottom of my large box.'

'And let me see, now, whether you can draw it out of the sheath without hurting yourself.'

That process having been gone through more than once,

Mr. Poulter felt that he had acted with scrupulous conscientiousness, and said, 'Well, now, Master Tulliver, if I take the crown-piece, it is to make sure as you'll do no mischief with the sword.'

'O no, indeed, Mr. Poulter,' said Tom, delightedly handing him the crown-piece, and grasping the sword, which, he thought, might have been lighter with advantage.

'But if Mr. Stelling catches you carrying it in?' said Mr. Poulter, pocketing the crown-piece provisionally while he raised this new doubt.

'O, he always keeps in his up-stairs study on Saturday afternoons,' said Tom, who disliked anything sneaking, but was not disinclined to a little stratagem in a worthy cause. So he carried off the sword in triumph, mixed with dread—dread that he might encounter Mr. or Mrs. Stelling—to his bedroom, where, after some consideration, he hid it in the closet behind some hanging clothes. That night he fell asleep in the thought that he would astonish Maggie with it when she came; tie it round his waist with his red comforter, and make her believe that the sword was his own, and that he was going to be a soldier. There was nobody but Maggie who would be silly enough to believe him, or whom he dared allow to know that he had a sword; and Maggie was really coming next week to see Tom, before she went to a boarding-school with Lucy.

If you think a lad of thirteen would not have been so childish, you must be an exceptionally wise man, who, although you are devoted to a civil calling, requiring you to look bland rather than formidable, yet never, since you had a beard, threw yourself into a martial attitude, and frowned before the looking-glass. It is doubtful whether our soldiers would be maintained if there were not pacific people at home who like to fancy themselves soldiers. War, like other dramatic spectacles, might possibly cease for want of a 'public.'

V

MAGGIE'S SECOND VISIT

THIS last breach between the two lads was not readily
mended, and for some time they spoke to each other no
more than was necessary. Their natural antipathy of
temperament made resentment an easy passage to hatred,
and in Philip the transition seemed to have begun: there
was no malignity in his disposition, but there was a susceptibility that made him peculiarly liable to a strong sense
of repulsion. The ox—we may venture to assert it on the
authority of a great classic—is not given to use his teeth as
an instrument of attack; and Tom was an excellent bovine
lad, who ran at questionable objects in a truly ingenious
bovine manner; but he had blundered on Philip's tenderest
point, and had caused him as much acute pain as if he had
studied the means with the nicest precision and the most
envenomed spite. Tom saw no reason why they should not
make up this quarrel as they had done many others, by
behaving as if nothing had happened; for though he had
never before said to Philip that his father was a rogue, this
idea had so habitually made a part of his feeling as to the
relation between himself and his dubious schoolfellow,
whom he could neither like nor dislike, that the mere utterance did not make such an epoch to him as it did to Philip.
And he had a right to say so when Philip hectored over
him, and called him names. But perceiving that his first
advances toward amity were not met, he relapsed into his
least favourable disposition towards Philip, and resolved
never to appeal to him either about drawing or exercises
again. They were only so far civil to each other as was
necessary to prevent their state of feud from being observed by Mr. Stelling, who would have 'put down' such
nonsense with great vigour.

When Maggie came, however, she could not help looking
with growing interest at the new schoolfellow, although he
was the son of that wicked Lawyer Wakem, who made her

father so angry. She had arrived in the middle of school-hours, and had sat by while Philip went through his lessons with Mr. Stelling. Tom, some weeks ago, had sent her word that Philip knew no end of stories—not stupid stories like hers; and she was convinced now from her own observation that he must be very clever: she hoped he would think *her* rather clever too, when she came to talk to him. Maggie, moreover, had rather a tenderness for deformed things; she preferred the wry-necked lambs, because it seemed to her that the lambs which were quite strong and well made wouldn't mind so much about being petted: and she was especially fond of petting objects that would think it very delightful to be petted by her. She loved Tom very dearly, but she often wished that he *cared* more about her loving him.

'I think Philip Wakem seems a nice boy, Tom,' she said, when they went out of the study together into the garden, to pass the interval before dinner. 'He couldn't choose his father, you know: and I've read of very bad men who had good sons, as well as good parents who had bad children. And if Philip is good, I think we ought to be the more sorry for him because his father is not a good man. *You* like him, don't you?'

'O, he's a queer fellow,' said Tom curtly, 'and he's as sulky as can be with me, because I told him his father was a rogue. And I'd a right to tell him so, for it was true—and *he* began it, with calling me names. But you stop here by yourself a bit, Magsie, will you? I've got something I want to do up-stairs.'

'Can't I go, too?' said Maggie, who, in this first day of meeting again, loved Tom's shadow.

'No, it's something I'll tell you about by-and-by, not yet,' said Tom, skipping away.

In the afternoon the boys were at their books in the study, preparing the morrow's lessons, that they might have a holiday in the evening in honour of Maggie's arrival. Tom was hanging over his Latin grammar, moving his lips inaudibly like a strict but impatient Catholic repeating his tale of paternosters; and Philip, at the other end of the

room, was busy with two volumes, with a look of contented
diligence that excited Maggie's curiosity; he did not look at
all as if he were learning a lesson. She sat on a low stool at
nearly a right angle with the two boys, watching first one
and then the other; and Philip, looking off his book once
towards the fireplace, caught the pair of questioning dark
eyes fixed upon him. He thought this sister of Tulliver's
seemed a nice little thing, quite unlike her brother; he
wished *he* had a little sister. What was it, he wondered,
that made Maggie's dark eyes remind him of the stories
about princesses being turned into animals? . . . I think it
was that her eyes were full of unsatisfied intelligence, and
unsatisfied, beseeching affection.

'I say, Magsie,' said Tom at last, shutting his books and
putting them away with the energy and decision of a perfect master in the art of leaving off, 'I've done my lessons
now. Come up-stairs with me.'

'What is it?' said Maggie, when they were outside the
door, a slight suspicion crossing her mind as she remembered
Tom's preliminary visit up-stairs. 'It isn't a trick you're
going to play me, now?'

'No, no, Maggie,' said Tom, in his most coaxing tone;
'it's something you'll like *ever so*.'

He put his arm round her neck, and she put hers round his
waist, and, twined together in this way, they went up-
stairs.

'I say, Magsie, you must not tell anybody, you know,'
said Tom, 'else I shall get fifty lines.'

'Is it alive?' said Maggie, whose imagination had settled
for the moment on the idea that Tom kept a ferret clandes-
tinely.

'O, I shan't tell you,' said he. 'Now you go into that
corner and hide your face, while I reach it out,' he added,
as he locked the bedroom door behind them. 'I'll tell you
when to turn round. You mustn't squeal out, you know.'

'O, but if you frighten me, I shall,' said Maggie, beginning to look rather serious.

'You won't be frightened, you silly thing,' said Tom.
'Go and hide your face, and mind you don't peep.'

'Of course I shan't peep,' said Maggie disdainfully; and she buried her face in the pillow like a person of strict honour.

But Tom looked round warily as he walked to the closet; then he stepped into the narrow space, and almost closed the door. Maggie kept her face buried without the aid of principle, for in that dream-suggestive attitude she had soon forgotten where she was, and her thoughts were busy with the poor deformed boy, who was so clever, when Tom called out, 'Now then, Magsie!'

Nothing but long meditation and preconcerted arrangement of effects could have enabled Tom to present so striking a figure as he did to Maggie when she looked up. Dissatisfied with the pacific aspect of a face which had no more than the faintest hint of flaxen eyebrow, together with a pair of amiable blue-grey eyes and round pink cheeks that refused to look formidable, let him frown as he would before the looking-glass—(Philip had once told him of a man who had a horse-shoe frown, and Tom had tried with all his frowning-might to make a horse-shoe on his forehead)—he had had recourse to that unfailing source of the terrible, burnt cork, and had made himself a pair of black eyebrows that met in a satisfactory manner over his nose, and were matched by a less carefully adjusted blackness about the chin. He had wound a red handkerchief round his cloth cap to give it the air of a turban, and his red comforter across his breast as a scarf—an amount of red which, with the tremendous frown on his brow, and the decision with which he grasped the sword, as he held it with its point resting on the ground, would suffice to convey an approximate idea of his fierce and bloodthirsty disposition.

Maggie looked bewildered for a moment, and Tom enjoyed that moment keenly; but in the next, she laughed, clapped her hands together, and said, 'O Tom, you've made yourself like Bluebeard at the show.'

It was clear she had not been struck with the presence of the sword—it was not unsheathed. Her frivolous mind required a more direct appeal to its sense of the terrible, and

Tom prepared for his master-stroke. Frowning with a double amount of intention, if not of corrugation, he (carefully) drew the sword from its sheath and pointed it at Maggie.

'O Tom, please don't,' exclaimed Maggie, in a tone of suppressed dread, shrinking away from him into the opposite corner. 'I *shall* scream—I'm sure I shall! O don't. I wish I'd never come up-stairs!'

The corners of Tom's mouth showed an inclination to a smile of complacency that was immediately checked as inconsistent with the severity of a great warrior. Slowly he let down the scabbard on the floor, lest it should make too much noise, and then said sternly—

'I'm the Duke of Wellington! March!' stamping forward with the right leg a little bent, and the sword still pointing towards Maggie, who, trembling, and with tear-filled eyes, got upon the bed, as the only means of widening the space between them.

Tom, happy in this spectator of his military performances, even though the spectator was only Maggie, proceeded, with the utmost exertion of his force, to such an exhibition of the cut and thrust as would necessarily be expected of the Duke of Wellington.

'Tom, I *will not* bear it—I *will* scream,' said Maggie, at the first movement of the sword. 'You'll hurt yourself; you'll cut your head off!'

'One—two,' said Tom resolutely, though at 'two' his wrist trembled a little. 'Three,' came more slowly, and with it the sword swung downwards, and Maggie gave a loud shriek. The sword had fallen, and with its edge on Tom's foot, and in a moment after, he had fallen too. Maggie leaped from the bed, still shrieking, and immediately there was a rush of footsteps towards the room. Mr. Stelling, from his up-stairs study, was the first to enter. He found both the children on the floor. Tom had fainted, and Maggie was shaking him by the collar of his jacket, screaming, with wild eyes. She thought he was dead, poor child! and yet she shook him, as if that would bring him back to life. In another minute she was sobbing with joy because

Tom had opened his eyes: she couldn't sorrow yet that he had hurt his foot—it seemed as if all happiness lay in his being alive.

VI

A LOVE SCENE

Poor Tom bore his severe pain heroically, and was resolute in not 'telling' of Mr. Poulter more than was unavoidable: the five-shilling piece remained a secret even to Maggie. But there was a terrible dread weighing on his mind—so terrible that he dared not even ask the question which might bring the fatal 'yes'—he dared not ask the surgeon or Mr. Stelling, 'Shall I be lame, sir?' He mastered himself so as not to cry out at the pain, but when his foot had been dressed, and he was left alone with Maggie seated by his bedside, the children sobbed together with their heads laid on the same pillow. Tom was thinking of himself walking about on crutches, like the wheelwright's son; and Maggie, who did not guess what was in his mind, sobbed for company. It had not occurred to the surgeon or to Mr. Stelling to anticipate this dread in Tom's mind, and to reassure him by hopeful words. But Philip watched the surgeon out of the house, and waylaid Mr. Stelling to ask the very question that Tom had not dared to ask for himself.

'I beg your pardon, sir,—but does Mr. Askern say Tulliver will be lame?'

'O no, O no,' said Mr. Stelling, 'not permanently, only for a little while.'

'Did he tell Tulliver so, sir, do you think?'

'No: nothing was said to him on the subject.'

'Then may I go and tell him, sir?'

'Yes, to be sure: now you mention it, I daresay he may be troubling about that. Go to his bedroom, but be very quiet at present.'

It had been Philip's first thought when he heard of the accident—'Will Tulliver be lame? It will be very hard for him if he is'—and Tom's hitherto unforgiven offences were washed out by that pity. Philip felt that they were no longer in a state of repulsion, but were being drawn into a common current of suffering and sad privation. His imagination did not dwell on the outward calamity and its future effect on Tom's life, but it made vividly present to him the probable state of Tom's feeling. Philip had only lived fourteen years, but those years had, most of them, been steeped in the sense of a lot irremediably hard.

'Mr. Askern says you'll soon be all right again, Tulliver, did you know?' he said, rather timidly, as he stepped gently up to Tom's bed. 'I've just been to ask Mr. Stelling, and he says you'll walk as well as ever again, by-and-by.'

Tom looked up with that momentary stopping of the breath which comes with a sudden joy; then he gave a long sigh, and turned his blue-grey eyes straight on Philip's face, as he had not done for a fortnight or more. As for Maggie, this intimation of a possibility she had not thought of before, affected her as a new trouble; the bare idea of Tom's being always lame overpowered the assurance that such a misfortune was not likely to befall him, and she clung to him and cried afresh.

'Don't be a little silly, Magsie,' said Tom tenderly, feeling very brave now. 'I shall soon get well.'

'Good-bye, Tulliver,' said Philip, putting out his small delicate hand, which Tom clasped immediately with his more substantial fingers.

'I say,' said Tom, 'ask Mr. Stelling to let you come and sit with me sometimes, till I get up again, Wakem—and tell me about Robert Bruce, you know.'

After that, Philip spent all his time out of school-hours with Tom and Maggie. Tom liked to hear fighting stories as much as ever, but he insisted strongly on the fact that those great fighters, who did so many wonderful things and came off unhurt, wore excellent armour from head to foot, which made fighting easy work, he considered. He should not have hurt his foot if he had had an iron shoe on. He listened with great interest to a new story of Philip's about a man who had a very bad wound in his foot, and cried out so dreadfully with the pain that his friends could bear with him no longer, but put him ashore on a desert island, with nothing but some wonderful poisoned arrows to kill animals with for food.

'I didn't roar out a bit, you know,' Tom said, 'and I daresay my foot was as bad as his. It's cowardly to roar.'

But Maggie would have it that when anything hurt you very much, it was quite permissible to cry out, and it was cruel of people not to bear it. She wanted to know if Philoctetes had a sister, and why *she* didn't go with him on the desert island and take care of him.

One day, soon after Philip had told this story, he and Maggie were in the study alone together while Tom's foot was being dressed. Philip was at his books, and Maggie, after sauntering idly round the room, not caring to do anything in particular, because she would soon go to Tom again, went and leaned on the table near Philip to see what he was doing, for they were quite old friends now, and perfectly at home with each other.

'What are you reading about in Greek?' she said. 'It's poetry—I can see that, because the lines are so short.'

'It's about Philoctetes—the lame man I was telling you of yesterday,' he answered, resting his head on his hand, and looking at her, as if he were not at all sorry to be interrupted. Maggie, in her absent way, continued to lean forward, resting on her arms and moving her feet about, while her dark eyes got more and more fixed and vacant, as if she had quite forgotten Philip and his book.

'Maggie,' said Philip, after a minute or two, still leaning on his elbow and looking at her, 'if you had had a brother like me, do you think you should have loved him as well as Tom?'

Maggie started a little on being roused from her reverie, and said, 'What?' Philip repeated his question.

'O yes, better,' she answered immediately. 'No, not better; because I don't think I *could* love you better than Tom. But I should be so sorry—*so sorry* for you.'

Philip coloured: he had meant to imply, would she love him as well in spite of his deformity, and yet when she alluded to it so plainly, he winced under her pity. Maggie, young as she was, felt her mistake. Hitherto she had in-stinctively behaved as if she were quite unconscious of Philip's deformity: her own keen sensitiveness and experience under family criticism sufficed to teach her this as well as if she had been directed by the most finished breeding.

'But you are so very clever, Philip, and you can play and sing,' she added quickly. 'I wish you *were* my brother. I'm very fond of you. And you would stay at home with me when Tom went out, and you would teach me every-thing—wouldn't you? Greek and everything?'

'But you'll go away soon, and go to school, Maggie,' said Philip, 'and then you'll forget all about me, and not care for me any more. And then I shall see you when you're grown up, and you'll hardly take any notice of me.'

'O no, I shan't forget you, I'm sure,' said Maggie, shaking her head very seriously. 'I never forget anything, and I think about everybody when I'm away from them. I think about poor Yap—he's got a lump in his throat, and Luke says he'll die. Only don't you tell Tom, because it will vex him so. You never saw Yap: he's a queer little dog—no-body cares about him but Tom and me.'

'Do you care as much about me as you do about Yap, Maggie?' said Philip, smiling rather sadly.

'O yes, I should think so,' said Maggie, laughing.

'I'm very fond of *you*, Maggie; I shall never forget *you*,' said Philip, 'and when I'm very unhappy, I shall always think of you, and wish I had a sister with dark eyes, just like yours.'

'Why do you like my eyes?' said Maggie, well pleased. She had never heard any one but her father speak of her eyes as if they had merit.

'I don't know,' said Philip. 'They're not like any other eyes. They seem trying to speak—trying to speak kindly. I don't like other people to look at me much, but I like you to look at me, Maggie.'

'Why, I think you're fonder of me than Tom is,' said Maggie, rather sorrowfully. Then, wondering how she could convince Philip that she could like him just as well, although he was crooked, she said:

'Should you like me to kiss you, as I do Tom? I will if you like.'

'Yes, very much: nobody kisses me.'

Maggie put her arm round his neck and kissed him quite earnestly.

'There now,' she said, 'I shall always remember you, and kiss you when I see you again, if it's ever so long. But I'll go now, because I think Mr. Askern's done with Tom's foot.'

When their father came the second time, Maggie said to him, 'O father, Philip Wakem is so very good to Tom—he is such a clever boy, and I *do* love him. And you love him too, Tom, don't you! *Say* you love him,' she added entreatingly.

Tom coloured a little as he looked at his father, and said, 'I shan't be friends with him when I leave school, father; but we've made it up now, since my foot has been bad, and he's taught me to play at draughts, and I can beat him.'

'Well, well,' said Mr. Tulliver, 'if he's good to you, try and make him amends, and be good to *him*. He's a poor crooked creatur', and takes after his dead mother. But don't you be getting too thick with him—he's got his father's blood in him too. Ay, ay, the grey colt may chance to kick like his black sire.'

The jarring natures of the two boys effected what Mr. Tulliver's admonition alone might have failed to effect: in spite of Philip's new kindness, and Tom's answering regard in this time of his trouble, they never became close friends. When Maggie was gone, and when Tom by-and-by began to walk about as usual, the friendly warmth that had been kindled by pity and gratitude died out by degrees, and left them in their old relation to each other. Philip was often peevish and contemptuous; and Tom's more specific and kindly impressions gradually melted into the old background of suspicion and dislike towards him as a queer fellow, a humpback, and the son of a rogue. If boys and men are to be welded together in the glow of transient feeling, they must be made of metal that will mix, else they inevitably fall asunder when the heat dies out.

VII

THE GOLDEN GATES ARE PASSED

So Tom went on even to the fifth half-year—till he was
turned sixteen—at King's Lorton, while Maggie was growing with a rapidity which her aunts considered highly
reprehensible, at Miss Firniss's boarding-school in the
ancient town of Laceham on the Floss, with cousin Lucy
for her companion. In her early letters to Tom she had
always sent her love to Philip, and asked many questions
about him, which were answered by brief sentences about
Tom's toothache, and a turf-house which he was helping to
build in the garden, with other items of that kind. She was
pained to hear Tom say in the holidays that Philip was as
queer as ever again, and often cross: they were no longer
very good friends, she perceived; and when she reminded
Tom that he ought always to love Philip for being so good
to him when his foot was bad, he answered, 'Well, it isn't
my fault: *I* don't do anything to him.' She hardly ever saw
Philip during the remainder of their school-life; in the Midsummer holidays he was always away at the seaside, and at
Christmas she could only meet him at long intervals in the
streets of St. Ogg's. When they did meet, she remembered
her promise to kiss him, but, as a young lady who had been
at a boarding-school, she knew now that such a greeting
was out of the question, and Philip would not expect it.
The promise was void, like so many other sweet, illusory
promises of our childhood; void as promises made in Eden
before the seasons were divided, and when the starry
blossoms grew side by side with the ripening peach—impossible to be fulfilled when the golden gates had been
passed.

But when their father was actually engaged in the long-
threatened lawsuit, and Wakem, as the agent at once of
Pivart and Old Harry, was acting against him, even Maggie
felt, with some sadness, that they were not likely ever to
have any intimacy with Philip again: the very name of

Wakem made her father angry, and she had once heard him say, that if that crook-backed son lived to inherit his father's ill-gotten gains, there would be a curse upon him. 'Have as little to do with him at school as you can, my lad,' he said to Tom; and the command was obeyed the more easily because Mr. Stelling by this time had two additional pupils; for though this gentleman's rise in the world was not of that meteor-like rapidity which the admirers of his extemporaneous eloquence had expected for a preacher whose voice demanded so wide a sphere, he had yet enough of growing prosperity to enable him to increase his expenditure in continued disproportion to his income.

As for Tom's school course, it went on with mill-like monotony, his mind continuing to move with a slow, half-stifled pulse in a medium of uninteresting or unintelligible ideas. But each vacation he brought home larger and larger drawings with the satiny rendering of landscape, and water-colours in vivid greens, together with manuscript books full of exercises and problems, in which the hand-writing was all the finer because he gave his whole mind to it. Each vacation he brought home a new book or two, indicating his progress through different stages of history, Christian doctrine, and Latin literature; and that passage was not entirely without result, besides the possession of the books. Tom's ear and tongue had become accustomed to a great many words and phrases which are understood to be signs of an educated condition; and though he had never really applied his mind to any one of his lessons, the lessons had left a deposit of vague, fragmentary, ineffectual notions. Mr. Tulliver, seeing signs of acquirement beyond the reach of his own criticism, thought it was probably all right with Tom's education: he observed, indeed, that there were no maps, and not enough 'summing;' but he made no formal complaint to Mr. Stelling. It was a puzzling business, this schooling; and if he took Tom away, where could he send him with better effect?

By the time Tom had reached his last quarter at King's Lorton, the years had made striking changes in him since the day we saw him returning from Mr. Jacobs' academy.

He was a tall youth now, carrying himself without the least awkwardness, and speaking without more shyness than was a becoming symptom of blended diffidence and pride: he wore his tail-coat and his stand-up collars, and watched the down on his lip with eager impatience, looking every day at his virgin razor, with which he had provided himself in the last holidays. Philip had already left—at the autumn quarter—that he might go to the south for the winter, for the sake of his health; and this change helped to give Tom the unsettled, exultant feeling that usually belongs to the last months before leaving school. This quarter, too, there was some hope of his father's lawsuit being decided: *that* made the prospect of home more entirely pleasurable. For Tom, who had gathered his view of the case from his father's conversation, had no doubt that Pivart would be beaten.

Tom had not heard anything from home for some weeks —a fact which did not surprise him, for his father and mother were not apt to manifest their affection in unnecessary letters—when, to his great surprise, on the morning of a dark cold day near the end of November, he was told, soon after entering the study at nine o'clock, that his sister was in the drawing-room. It was Mrs. Stelling who had come into the study to tell him, and she left him to enter the drawing-room alone.

Maggie, too, was tall now, with braided and coiled hair: she was almost as tall as Tom, though she was only thirteen; and she really looked older than he did at that moment. She had thrown off her bonnet, her heavy braids were pushed back from her forehead, as if it would not bear that extra load, and her young face had a strangely worn look, as her eyes turned anxiously towards the door. When Tom entered she did not speak, but only went up to him, put her arms round his neck, and kissed him earnestly. He was used to various moods of hers, and felt no alarm at the unusual seriousness of her greeting.

'Why, how is it you're come so early this cold morning, Maggie? Did you come in the gig?' said Tom, as she backed towards the sofa, and drew him to her side.

'No, I came by the coach. I've walked from the turn-pike.'

'But how is it you're not at school? The holidays have not begun yet?'

'Father wanted me at home,' said Maggie, with a slight trembling of the lip. 'I came home three or four days ago.'

'Isn't my father well?' said Tom rather anxiously.

'Not quite,' said Maggie. 'He's very unhappy, Tom. The lawsuit is ended, and I came to tell you, because I thought it would be better for you to know it before you came home, and I didn't like only to send you a letter.'

'My father hasn't lost?' said Tom hastily, springing from the sofa, and standing before Maggie with his hands suddenly thrust in his pockets.

'Yes, dear Tom,' said Maggie, looking up at him with trembling.

Tom was silent a minute or two, with his eyes fixed on the floor. Then he said:

'My father will have to pay a good deal of money, then?'

'Yes,' said Maggie rather faintly.

'Well, it can't be helped,' said Tom bravely, not translating the loss of a large sum of money into any tangible results. 'But my father's very much vexed, I daresay?' he added, looking at Maggie, and thinking that her agitated face was only part of her girlish way of taking things.

'Yes,' said Maggie, again faintly. Then, urged to fuller speech by Tom's freedom from apprehension, she said loudly and rapidly, as if the words *would* burst from her, 'O Tom, he will lose the mill and the land, and everything; he will have nothing left.'

Tom's eyes flashed out one look of surprise at her, before he turned pale, and trembled visibly. He said nothing, but sat down on the sofa again, looking vaguely out of the opposite window.

Anxiety about the future had never entered Tom's mind. His father had always ridden a good horse, kept a good house, and had the cheerful, confident air of a man who has plenty of property to fall back upon. Tom had never dreamed that his father would 'fail;' *that* was a form of misfortune which he had always heard spoken of as a deep disgrace, and disgrace was an idea that he could not associate with any of his relations, least of all with his father. A proud sense of family respectability was part of the very air Tom had been born and brought up in. He knew there were people in St. Ogg's who made a show without money to support it, and he had always heard such people spoken of by his friends with contempt and reprobation. He had a strong belief, which was a life-long habit, and required no definite evidence to rest on, that his father could spend a great deal of money if he chose; and since his education at Mr. Stelling's had given him a more expensive view of life, he had often thought that when he got older he would make a figure in the world, with his horse and dogs and saddle, and other accoutrements of a fine young man, and show himself equal to any of his contemporaries at St. Ogg's, who might consider themselves a grade above him in society, because their fathers were professional men, or had large oil-mills. As to the prognostics and headshaking of his aunts and uncles, they had never produced the least effect on him, except to make him think that aunts and uncles were disagreeable society: he had heard them find fault in much the same way as long as he could remember. His father knew better than they did.

The down had come on Tom's lip, yet his thoughts and expectations had been hitherto only the reproduction, in changed forms, of the boyish dreams in which he had lived three years ago. He was awakened now with a violent shock.

Maggie was frightened at Tom's pale, trembling silence. There was something else to tell him—something worse. She threw her arms round him at last, and said, with a half sob—

'O Tom—dear, dear Tom, don't fret too much—try and bear it well.'

Tom turned his cheek passively to meet her entreating kisses, and there gathered a moisture in his eyes, which he just rubbed away with his hand. The action seemed to rouse him, for he shook himself and said, 'I shall go home with you, Maggie. Didn't my father say I was to go?'

'No, Tom, father didn't wish it,' said Maggie, her anxiety about *his* feeling helping her to master her agitation. What *would* he do when she told him all? 'But mother wants you to come—poor mother!—she cries so. O Tom, it's so dreadful at home.'

Maggie's lips grew whiter, and she began to tremble almost as Tom had done. The two poor things clung closer to each other—both trembling—the one at an unshapen fear, the other at the image of a terrible certainty. When Maggie spoke, it was hardly above a whisper.

'And . . . and . . . poor father . . . !'

Maggie could not utter it. But the suspense was intolerable to Tom. A vague idea of going to prison, as a consequence of debt, was the shape his fears had begun to take.

'Where's my father?' he said impatiently. '*Tell* me, Maggie.'

'He's at home,' said Maggie, finding it easier to reply to that question. 'But,' she added, after a pause, 'not himself. . . . He fell off his horse. . . . He has known nobody but me ever since. . . . He seems to have lost his senses. . . . O, father, father . . .'

With these last words, Maggie's sobs burst forth with the more violence for the previous struggle against them. Tom felt that pressure of the heart which forbids tears: he had no distinct vision of their troubles as Maggie had, who had been at home; he only felt the crushing weight of what seemed unmitigated misfortune. He tightened his arm almost convulsively round Maggie as she sobbed, but his face looked rigid and tearless—his eyes blank—as if a black curtain of cloud had suddenly fallen on his path.

But Maggie soon checked herself abruptly: a single thought had acted on her like a startling sound.

'We must set out, Tom—we must not stay—father will miss me—we must be at the turnpike at ten to meet the coach.' She said this with hasty decision, rubbing her eyes, and rising to seize her bonnet.

Tom at once felt the same impulse, and rose too. 'Wait a minute, Maggie,' he said. 'I must speak to Mr. Stelling, and then we'll go.'

He thought he must go to the study where the pupils were, but on his way he met Mr. Stelling, who had heard from his wife that Maggie appeared to be in trouble when she asked for her brother; and, now that he thought the brother and sister had been alone long enough, was coming to inquire and offer his sympathy.

'Please, sir, I must go home,' Tom said abruptly, as he met Mr. Stelling in the passage. 'I must go back with my sister directly. My father's lost his lawsuit—he's lost all his property—and he's very ill.'

Mr. Stelling felt like a kind-hearted man; he foresaw a probable money loss for himself, but this had no appreciable share in his feeling, while he looked with grave pity at the brother and sister for whom youth and sorrow had begun together. When he knew how Maggie had come, and how eager she was to get home again, he hurried their departure, only whispering something to Mrs. Stelling, who had followed him, and who immediately left the room.

Tom and Maggie were standing on the door-step, ready to set out, when Mrs. Stelling came with a little basket, which she hung on Maggie's arms, saying, 'Do remember to eat something on the way, dear.' Maggie's heart went out towards this woman whom she had never liked, and she kissed her silently. It was the first sign within the poor child of that new sense which is the gift of sorrow—that susceptibility to the bare offices of humanity which raises them into a bond of loving fellowship, as to haggard men among the icebergs the mere presence of an ordinary comrade stirs the deep fountains of affection.

Mr. Stelling put his hand on Tom's shoulder and said, 'God bless you, my boy: let me know how you get on.' Then he pressed Maggie's hand; but there were no audible good-byes. Tom had so often thought how joyful he should be the day he left school 'for good!' And now his school years seemed like a holiday that had come to an end.

The two slight youthful figures soon grew indistinct on

the distant road—were soon lost behind the projecting hedgerow.

They had gone forth together into their new life of sorrow, and they would never more see the sunshine undimmed by remembered cares. They had entered the thorny wilderness, and the golden gates of their childhood had for ever closed behind them.

BOOK THIRD

THE DOWNFALL

I

WHAT HAD HAPPENED AT HOME

When Mr. Tulliver first knew the fact that the lawsuit was decided against him, and that Pivart and Wakem were triumphant, everyone who happened to observe him at the time thought that, for so confident and hot-tempered a man, he bore the blow remarkably well. He thought so himself: he thought he was going to show that if Wakem or anybody else considered him crushed, they would find themselves mistaken. He could not refuse to see that the costs of this protracted suit would take more than he possessed to pay them; but he appeared to himself to be full of expedients by which he could ward off any results but such as were tolerable, and could avoid the appearance of breaking down in the world. All the obstinacy and defiance of his nature, driven out of their old channel, found a vent for themselves in the immediate formation of plans by which he would meet his difficulties, and remain Mr. Tulliver of Dorlcote Mill in spite of them. There was such a rush of projects in his brain, that it was no wonder his face was flushed when he came away from his talk with his attorney, Mr. Gore, and mounted his horse to ride home from Lindum. There was Furley, who held the mortgage on the land—a reasonable fellow, who would see his own interest, Mr. Tulliver was convinced, and who would be glad not only to purchase the whole estate, including the mill and homestead, but would accept Mr. Tulliver as tenant, and be willing to advance money to be repaid with high interest out of the profits of the business, which would be made over to him, Mr. Tulliver only taking enough barely to maintain himself and his family. Who would neglect such a profitable investment? Certainly not Furley, for Mr. Tulliver had determined that Furley should meet his plans with the utmost alacrity; and there are men whose brains have not yet been dangerously heated by the loss of a lawsuit, who are apt to see in their own interest or desires a motive for other men's actions. There was no doubt (in the miller's mind) that Furley would do just what was desirable; and if he did—why, things would not be so very much worse. Mr. Tulliver and his family must live more meagrely and humbly, but it would only be till the profits of the business had paid off Furley's advances, and that might be while Mr. Tulliver had still a good many years of life before him. It was clear that the cost of the suit could be paid without his being obliged to turn out of his old place, and look like a ruined man. It was certainly an awkward moment in his affairs. There was that suretyship for poor Riley, who had died suddenly last April, and left his friend saddled with a debt of two hundred and fifty pounds —a fact which had helped to make Mr. Tulliver's banking book less pleasant reading than a man might desire towards Christmas. Well! he had never been one of those poor-spirited sneaks who would refuse to give a helping hand to a fellow-traveller in this puzzling world. The really vexatious business was the fact that some months ago the creditor who had lent him the five hundred pounds to repay Mrs. Glegg, had become uneasy about his money (set on by Wakem, of course), and Mr. Tulliver, still confident that he should gain his suit, and finding it eminently inconvenient to raise the said sum until that desirable issue had taken place, had rashly acceded to the demand that he should give a bill of sale on his household furniture, and some other effects, as security in lieu of the bond. It was all one, he had said to himself: he should soon pay off the money, and there was no harm in giving that security any more than another. But now the consequences of this bill of sale occurred to him in a new light, and he remembered that the time was close at hand, when it would be enforced unless the money were repaid. Two months ago he would have declared stoutly that he would never be beholden to his wife's friends; but now he told himself as stoutly that it was nothing but right and natural that Bessy should go to the Pullets and explain the thing to them: they would hardly let Bessy's furniture be sold, and it might be security to Pullet if he advanced the money—there would, after all, be no gift or favour in the matter. Mr. Tulliver would never have asked for anything from so poor-spirited a fellow for himself, but Bessy might do so if she liked.

It is precisely the proudest and most obstinate men who are the most liable to shift their position and contradict themselves in this sudden manner: everything is easier to them than to face the simple fact that they have been thoroughly defeated, and must begin life anew. And Mr. Tulliver, you perceive, though nothing more than a superior miller and maltster, was as proud and obstinate as if he had been a very lofty personage, in whom such dispositions might be a source of that conspicuous, far-echoing tragedy, which sweeps the stage in regal robes and makes the dullest chronicler sublime. The pride and obstinacy of millers, and other insignificant people, whom you pass unnoticingly on the road every day, have their tragedy too; but it is of that unwept, hidden sort, that goes on from generation to generation, and leaves no record—such tragedy, perhaps, as lies in the conflicts of young souls, hungry for joy, under a lot made suddenly hard to them, under the dreariness of a home where the morning brings no promise with it, and where the unexpectant discontent of worn and disappointed parents weighs on the children like a damp, thick air, in which all the functions of life are depressed; or such tragedy as lies in the slow or sudden death that follows on a bruised passion, though it may be a death that finds only a parish funeral. There are certain animals to which tenacity of position is a law of life—they can never flourish again, after a single wrench: and there are certain human beings to whom predominance is a law of life—they can only sustain humiliation so long as they can refuse to believe in it, and, in their own conception, predominate still.

Mr. Tulliver was still predominating in his own imagination as he approached St. Ogg's, through which he had to pass on his way homeward. But what was it that suggested to him, as he saw the Laceham coach entering the town, to follow it to the coach-office, and get the clerk there to write a letter, requiring Maggie to come home the very next day? Mr. Tulliver's own hand shook too much under his excitement for him to write himself, and he wanted the letter to be given to the coachman to deliver at Miss Firniss's school in the morning. There was a craving which he would not account for to himself, to have Maggie near him—without delay—she must come back by the coach to-morrow.

To Mrs. Tulliver, when he got home, he would admit no difficulties, and scolded down her burst of grief on hearing that the lawsuit was lost, by angry assertions that there was nothing to grieve about. He said nothing to her that night about the bill of sale, and the application to Mrs. Pullet, for he had kept her in ignorance of the nature of that transaction, and had explained the necessity for taking an inventory of the goods as a matter connected with his will. The possession of a wife conspicuously one's inferior in intellect, is, like other high privileges, attended with a few inconveniences, and, among the rest, with the occasional necessity for using a little deception.

The next day Mr. Tulliver was again on horseback in the afternoon, on his way to Mr. Gore's office at St. Ogg's. Gore was to have seen Furley in the morning, and to have sounded him in relation to Mr. Tulliver's affairs. But he had not gone half-way when he met a clerk from Mr. Gore's office, who was bringing a letter to Mr. Tulliver. Mr. Gore had been prevented by a sudden call of business from waiting at his office to see Mr. Tulliver, according to appointment, but would be at his office at eleven to-morrow morning, and meanwhile had sent some important information by letter.

'O!' said Mr. Tulliver, taking the letter, but not opening it. 'Then tell Gore I'll see him to-morrow at eleven;' and he turned his horse.

The clerk, struck with Mr. Tulliver's glistening, excited glance, looked after him for a few moments, and then rode away. The reading of a letter was not the affair of an instant to Mr. Tulliver; he took in the sense of a statement very slowly through the medium of written or even printed characters; so he had put the letter in his pocket, thinking he would open it in his arm-chair at home. But by-and-by it occurred to him that there might be something in the letter Mrs. Tulliver must not know about, and if so, it would be better to keep it out of her sight altogether. He stopped his horse, took out the letter, and read it. It was only a short letter; the substance was, that Mr. Gore had ascertained, on secret but sure authority, that Furley had been lately much straitened for money, and had parted with his securities—among the rest, the mortgage on Mr. Tulliver's property, which he had transferred to——Wakem.

In half an hour after this, Mr. Tulliver's own waggoner found him lying by the roadside insensible, with an open letter near him, and his grey horse snuffing uneasily about him.

When Maggie reached home that evening, in obedience to her father's call, he was no longer insensible. About an hour before, he had become conscious, and after vague, vacant looks around him, had muttered something about 'a letter,' which he presently repeated impatiently. At the instance of Mr. Turnbull, the medical man, Gore's letter was brought and laid on the bed, and the previous impatience seemed to be allayed. The stricken man lay for some time with his eyes fixed on the letter, as if he were trying to knit up his thoughts by its help. But presently a new wave of memory seemed to have come and swept the other away; he turned his eyes from the letter to the door, and after looking uneasily, as if striving to see something his eyes were too dim for, he said, 'The little wench.'

He repeated the words impatiently from time to time, appearing entirely unconscious of everything except this one importunate want, and giving no sign of knowing his wife or any one else; and poor Mrs. Tulliver, her feeble faculties almost paralysed by this sudden accumulation of troubles, went backwards and forwards to the gate to see if the Laceham coach were coming, though it was not yet time.

But it came at last, and set down the poor anxious girl, no longer the 'little wench,' except to her father's fond memory.

'O mother, what is the matter?' Maggie said, with pale lips, as her mother came towards her crying. She didn't think her father was ill, because the letter had come at his dictation from the office at St. Ogg's.

But Mr. Turnbull came now to meet her: a medical man is the good angel of the troubled house, and Maggie ran towards the kind old friend, whom she remembered as long as she could remember anything, with a trembling, questioning look.

'Don't alarm yourself too much, my dear,' he said, taking her hand. 'Your father has had a sudden attack, and has not quite recovered his memory. But he has been asking for you, and it will do him good to see you. Keep as quiet as you can; take off your things, and come up-stairs with me.'

Maggie obeyed, with that terrible beating of the heart which makes existence seem simply a painful pulsation. The very quietness with which Mr. Turnbull spoke had frightened her susceptible imagination. Her father's eyes were still turned uneasily towards the door when she entered and met the strange, yearning, helpless look that had been seeking her in vain. With a sudden flash and movement, he raised himself in the bed—she rushed towards him, and clasped him with agonised kisses.

Poor child! it was very early for her to know one of those supreme moments in life when all we have hoped or delighted in, all we can dread or endure, falls away from our regard as insignificant—is lost, like a trivial memory, in that simple, primitive love which knits us to the beings who have been nearest to us, in their times of helplessness or of anguish.

But that flash of recognition had been too great a strain on the father's bruised, enfeebled powers. He sank back again in renewed insensibility and rigidity, which lasted for many hours, and was only broken by a flickering return of consciousness, in which he took passively everything that was given to him, and seemed to have a sort of infantine satisfaction in Maggie's near presence—such satisfaction as a baby has when it is returned to the nurse's lap.

Mrs. Tulliver sent for her sisters, and there was much wailing and lifting up of hands below stairs: both uncles and aunts saw that the ruin of Bessy and her family was as complete as they had ever foreboded it, and there was a general family sense that a judgment had fallen on Mr. Tulliver, which it would be an impiety to counteract by too much kindness. But Maggie heard little of this, scarcely ever leaving her father's bedside, where she sat opposite him with her hand on his. Mrs. Tulliver wanted to have Tom fetched home, and seemed to be thinking more of her boy even than of her husband; but the aunts and uncles opposed this. Tom was better at school, since Mr. Turnbull said there was no immediate danger, he believed. But at the end of the second day, when Maggie had become more accustomed to her father's fits of insensibility, and to the expectation that he would revive from them, the thought of Tom had become urgent with *her* too; and when her mother sate crying at night and saying, 'My poor lad . . . it's nothing but right he should come home;' Maggie said, 'Let me go for him, and tell him, mother: I'll go to-morrow morning if father doesn't know me and want me. It would be so hard for Tom to come home and not know anything about it beforehand.'

And the next morning Maggie went, as we have seen. Sitting on the coach on their way home, the brother and sister talked to each other in sad, interrupted whispers.

'They say Mr. Wakem has got a mortgage or something on the land, Tom,' said Maggie. 'It was the letter with that news in it that made father ill, they think.'

'I believe that scoundrel's been planning all along to ruin my father,' said Tom, leaping from the vaguest impressions to a definite conclusion. 'I'll make him feel for it when I'm a man. Mind you never speak to Philip again.'

'O, Tom!' said Maggie, in a tone of sad remonstrance; But she had no spirit to dispute anything then, still less to vex Tom by opposing him.

II

MRS. TULLIVER'S TERAPHIM, OR HOUSEHOLD GODS

WHEN the coach set down Tom and Maggie, it was five hours since she had started from home, and she was thinking with some trembling that her father had perhaps missed her, and asked for 'the little wench' in vain. She thought of no other change that might have happened.

She hurried along the gravel-walk and entered the house before Tom; but in the entrance she was startled by a strong smell of tobacco. The parlour door was ajar—that was where the smell came from. It was very strange: could any visitor be smoking at a time like this? Was her mother there? If so, she must be told that Tom was come. Maggie, after this pause of surprise, was only in the act of opening the door when Tom came up, and they both looked into the parlour together. There was a coarse, dingy man, of whose face Tom had some vague recollection, sitting in his father's chair, smoking, with a jug and glass beside him.

The truth flashed on Tom's mind in an instant. To 'have the bailiff in the house,' and 'to be sold up,' were phrases which he had been used to, even as a little boy: they were part of the disgrace and misery of 'failing,' of losing all one's money, and being ruined—sinking into the condition of poor working people. It seemed only natural that this should happen, since his father had lost all his property, and he thought of no more special cause for this particular form of misfortune than the loss of the lawsuit. But the immediate presence of this disgrace was so much keener an experience to Tom than the worst form of apprehension, that he felt at this moment as if his real trouble had only just begun: it was a touch on the irritated nerve compared with its spontaneous dull aching.

'How do you do, sir?' said the man, taking the pipe out of his mouth, with rough, embarrassed civility. The two young startled faces made him a little uncomfortable.

But Tom turned away hastily without speaking: the

sight was too hateful. Maggie had not understood the appearance of this stranger as Tom had. She followed him, whispering, 'Who can it be, Tom?—what is the matter?' Then, with a sudden undefined dread lest this stranger might have something to do with a change in her father, she rushed up-stairs, checking herself at the bedroom door to throw off her bonnet, and enter on tiptoe. All was silent there: her father was lying, heedless of everything around him, with his eyes closed as when she had left him. A servant was there, but not her mother.

'Where's my mother?' she whispered. The servant did not know.

Maggie hastened out, and said to Tom, 'Father is lying quiet: let us go and look for my mother. I wonder where she is.'

Mrs. Tulliver was not down-stairs—not in any of the bedrooms. There was but one room below the attic which Maggie had left unsearched: it was the store-room, where her mother kept all her linen and all the precious 'best things' that were only unwrapped and brought out on special occasions. Tom, preceding Maggie as they returned along the passage, opened the door of this room, and immediately said 'Mother!'

Mrs. Tulliver was seated there with all her laid-up treasures. One of the linen-chests was open: the silver tea-pot was unwrapped from its many folds of paper, and the best china was laid out on the top of the closed linen-chest; spoons and skewers and ladles were spread in rows on the shelves; and the poor woman was shaking her head and weeping, with a bitter tension of the mouth, over the mark, 'Elizabeth Dodson,' on the corner of some table-cloths she held in her lap.

She dropped them, and started up as Tom spoke.

'O my boy, my boy!' she said, clasping him round the neck. 'To think as I should live to see this day! We're ruined . . . everything's going to be sold up . . . to think as your father should ha' married me to bring me to this! We've got nothing . . . we shall be beggars . . . we must go to the workhouse. . . .'

She kissed him, then seated herself again, and took another table-cloth on her lap, unfolding it a little way to look at the pattern, while the children stood by in mute wretchedness—their minds quite filled for the moment with the words 'beggars' and 'workhouse.'

'To think o' these clothes as I spun myself,' she went on, lifting things out and turning them over with an excitement all the more strange and piteous because the stout blond woman was usually so passive: if she had been ruffled before, it was at the surface merely: 'and Job Haxey wove 'em, and brought the piece home on his back, as I remember standing at the door and seeing him come, before I ever thought o' marrying your father! And the pattern as I chose myself—and bleached so beautiful, and I marked 'em so as nobody ever saw such marking—they must cut the cloth to get it out, for it's a particular stitch. And they're all to be sold—and go into strange people's houses, and perhaps be cut with the knives, and wore out before I'm dead. You'll never have one of 'em, my boy,' she said, looking up at Tom with her eyes full of tears, 'and I meant 'em for you. I wanted you to have all o' this pattern. Maggie could have had the large check—it never shows so well when the dishes are on it.'

Tom was touched to the quick, but there was an angry reaction immediately. His face flushed as he said:

'But will my aunts let them be sold, mother? Do they know about it? They'll never let your linen go, will they? Haven't you sent to them?'

'Yes, I sent Luke directly they'd put the bailies in, and your aunt Pullet's been—and, O dear, O dear, she cries so, and says your father's disgraced my family and made it the talk o' the country; and she'll buy the spotted cloths for herself, because she's never had so many as she wanted o' that pattern, and they shan't go to strangers, but she's got more checks a'ready nor she can do with.' (Here Mrs. Tulliver began to lay back the table-cloths in the chest, folding and stroking them automatically.) 'And your uncle Glegg's been too, and he says things must be bought in for us to lie down on, but he must talk to your aunt; and they're all coming to consult. . . . But I know they'll none of 'em take my chany,' she added, turning towards the cups and saucers—'for they all found fault with 'em when I bought 'em, 'cause o' the small gold sprig all over 'em, between the flowers. But there's none of 'em got better chany, not even your aunt Pullet herself,—and I bought it wi' my own money as I'd saved ever since I was turned fifteen; and the silver teapot, too—your father never paid for 'em. And to think as he should ha' married me, and brought me to this.'

Mrs. Tulliver burst out crying afresh, and she sobbed with her handkerchief at her eyes a few moments, but then removing it, she said in a deprecating way, still half-sobbing, as if she were called upon to speak before she could command her voice:

'And I *did* say to him times and times, "Whativer you do, don't go to law"—and what more could I do? I've had to sit by while my own fortin's been spent, and what should ha' been my children's, too. You'll have niver a penny, my boy . . . but it isn't your poor mother's fault.'

She put out one arm towards Tom, looking up at him piteously with her helpless, childish blue eyes. The poor lad went to her and kissed her, and she clung to him. For the first time Tom thought of his father with some reproach. His natural inclination to blame, hitherto kept entirely in abeyance towards his father by the predisposition to think him always right, simply on the ground that he was Tom Tulliver's father—was turned into this new channel by his mother's plaints, and with his indignation against Wakem there began to mingle some indignation of another sort. Perhaps his father might have helped bringing them all down in the world, and making people talk of them with contempt; but no one should talk long of Tom Tulliver with contempt. The natural strength and firmness of his nature was beginning to assert itself, urged by the double stimulus of resentment against his aunts, and the sense that he must behave like a man and take care of his mother.

'Don't fret, mother,' he said tenderly. 'I shall soon be able to get money: I'll get a situation of some sort.'

'Bless you, my boy!' said Mrs. Tulliver, a little soothed. Then, looking round sadly, 'But I shouldn't ha' minded so much if we could ha' kept the things wi' my name on 'em.'

Maggie had witnessed this scene with gathering anger. The implied reproaches against her father—her father, who was lying there in a sort of living death—neutralized all her pity for griefs about table-cloths and china; and her anger on her father's account was heightened by some egoistic resentment of Tom's silent concurrence with her mother in shutting her out from the common calamity. She had become almost indifferent to her mother's habitual depreciation of her, but she was keenly alive to any sanction of it, however passive, that she might suspect in Tom. Poor Maggie was by no means made up of unalloyed devotedness, but put forth large claims for herself where she loved strongly. She burst out at last in an agitated, almost violent tone, 'Mother, how can you talk so? as if you cared only for things with *your* name on, and not for what has my father's name too—and to care about anything but dear father himself!—when he's lying there, and may never speak to us again. Tom, you ought to say so too—you ought not to let anyone find fault with my father.'

Maggie, almost choked with mingled grief and anger, left the room, and took her old place on her father's bed. Her heart went out to him with a stronger movement than ever, at the thought that people would blame him. Maggie hated blame: she had been blamed all her life, and nothing had come of it but evil tempers. Her father had always defended and excused her, and her loving remembrance of his tenderness was a force within her that would enable her to do or bear anything for his sake.

Tom was a little shocked at Maggie's outburst—telling *him* as well as his mother what it was right to do! She ought to have learned better than have those hectoring, assuming manners, by this time. But he presently went into his father's room, and the sight there touched him in a way that effaced the slighter impressions of the previous hour. When Maggie saw how he was moved, she went to him and put her arm round his neck as he sat by the bed, and the two children forgot everything else in the sense that they had one father and one sorrow.

III

THE FAMILY COUNCIL

It was at eleven o'clock the next morning that the aunts and uncles came to hold their consultation. The fire was lighted in the large parlour, and poor Mrs. Tulliver, with a confused impression that it was a great occasion, like a funeral, unbagged the bell-rope tassels, and unpinned the curtains, adjusting them in proper folds—looking round and shaking her head sadly at the polished tops and legs of the tables, which sister Pullet herself could not accuse of insufficient brightness.

Mr. Deane was not coming—he was away on business; but Mrs. Deane appeared punctually in that handsome new gig with the head to it, and the livery-servant driving it, which had thrown so clear a light on several traits in her character to some of her female friends in St. Ogg's. Mr. Deane had been advancing in the world as rapidly as Mr. Tulliver had been going down in it; and in Mrs. Deane's house the Dodson linen and plate were beginning to hold quite a subordinate position, as a mere supplement to the handsomer articles of the same kind, purchased in recent years: a change which had caused an occasional coolness in the sisterly intercourse between her and Mrs. Glegg, who felt that Susan was getting 'like the rest,' and there would soon be little of the true Dodson spirit surviving except in herself, and, it might be hoped, in those nephews who supported the Dodson name on the family land, far away in the Wolds. People who live at a distance are naturally less faulty than those immediately under our own eyes; and it seems superfluous, when we consider the remote geographical position of the Ethiopians, and how very little the

Greeks had to do with them, to inquire further why Homer calls them 'blameless.'

Mrs. Deane was the first to arrive; and when she had taken her seat in the large parlour, Mrs. Tulliver came down to her with her comely face a little distorted, nearly as it would have been if she had been crying: she was not a woman who could shed abundant tears, except in moments when the prospect of losing her furniture became unusually vivid, but she felt how unfitting it was to be quite calm under present circumstances.

'O sister, what a world this is!' she exclaimed as she entered; 'what trouble, O dear!'

Mrs. Deane was a thin-lipped woman, who made small well-considered speeches on peculiar occasions, repeating them afterwards to her husband, and asking him if she had not spoken very properly.

'Yes, sister,' she said deliberately, 'this is a changing world, and we don't know to-day what may happen to-morrow. But it's right to be prepared for all things, and if trouble's sent, to remember as it isn't sent without a cause. I'm very sorry for you as a sister, and if the doctor orders jelly for Mr. Tulliver, I hope you'll let me know: I'll send it willingly. For it is but right he should have proper attendance while he's ill.'

'Thank you, Susan,' said Mrs. Tulliver, rather faintly, withdrawing her fat hand from her sister's thin one. 'But there's been no talk o' jelly yet.' Then after a moment's pause she added, 'There's a dozen o' cut jelly-glasses upstairs. . . . I shall niver put jelly into 'em no more.'

Her voice was rather agitated as she uttered the last words, but the sound of wheels diverted her thoughts. Mr. and Mrs. Glegg were come, and were almost immediately followed by Mr. and Mrs. Pullet.

Mrs. Pullet entered crying, as a compendious mode, at all times, of expressing what were her views of life in general, and what, in brief, were the opinions she held concerning the particular case before her.

Mrs. Glegg had on her fuzziest front, and garments which appeared to have had a recent resurrection from rather a creasy form of burial; a costume selected with the high moral purpose of instilling perfect humility into Bessy and her children.

'Mrs. G., won't you come nearer the fire?' said her husband, unwilling to take the more comfortable seat without offering it to her.

'You see I've seated myself here, Mr. Glegg,' returned this superior woman; '*you* can roast yourself, if you like.'

'Well,' said Mr. Glegg, seating himself good-humouredly, 'and how's the poor man up-stairs?'

'Dr. Turnbull thought him a deal better this morning,' said Mrs. Tulliver; 'he took more notice, and spoke to me; but he's never known Tom yet—looks at the poor lad as if he was a stranger, though he said something once about Tom and the pony. The doctor says his memory has gone a long way back, and he doesn't know Tom because he's thinking of him when he was little. Eh dear, eh dear!'

'I doubt it's the water got on his brain,' said aunt Pullet, turning round from adjusting her cap in a melancholy way at the pier-glass. 'It's much if he ever gets up again; and if he does, he'll most like be childish, as Mr. Carr was, poor man! They fed him with a spoon as if he'd been a baby for three year. He'd quite lost the use of his limbs; but then he'd got a bath chair, and somebody to draw him; and that's what you won't have, I doubt, Bessy.'

'Sister Pullet,' said Mrs. Glegg severely, 'if I understand right, we've come together this morning to advise and consult about what's to be done in this disgrace as has fallen upon the family, and not to talk o' people as don't belong to us. Mr. Carr was none of our blood, nor noways connected with us, as I've ever heared.'

'Sister Glegg,' said Mrs. Pullet in a pleading tone, drawing on her gloves again, and stroking the fingers in an agitated manner, 'if you've got anything disrespectful to say o' Mr. Carr, I do beg of you as you won't say it to me. *I* know what he was,' she added, with a sigh; 'his breath was short to that degree as you could hear him two rooms off.'

'Sophy!' said Mrs. Glegg with indignant disgust, 'you *do*

talk o' people's complaints till it's quite undecent. But I say again, as I said before, I didn't come away from home to talk about acquaintance, whether they'd short breath or long. If we aren't come together for one to hear what the other 'ull do to save a sister and her children from the parish, *I* shall go back. *One* can't act without the other, I suppose; it isn't to be expected as *I* should do everything.'

'Well, Jane,' said Mrs. Pullet, 'I don't see as you've been so very forrard at doing. So far as I know, this is the first time as here you've been, since it's been known as the bailiff's in the house; and I was here yesterday, and looked at all Bessy's linen and things, and I told her I'd buy in the spotted table-cloths. I couldn't speak fairer; for as for the teapot as she doesn't want to go out o' the family, it stands to sense I can't do with two silver teapots, not if it *hadn't* a straight spout—but the spotted damask I was allays fond on.'

'I wish it could be managed so as my teapot and chany and the best castors needn't be put up for sale,' said poor Mrs. Tulliver beseechingly, 'and the sugar-tongs, the first things ever I bought.'

'But that can't be helped, you know,' said Mr. Glegg. 'If one o' the family chooses to buy 'em in, they can, but one thing must be bid for as well as another.'

'And it isn't to be looked for,' said uncle Pullet, with unwonted independence of idea, 'as your own family should pay more for things nor they'll fetch. They may go for an old song by auction.'

'O dear, O dear,' said Mrs. Tulliver, 'to think o' my chany being sold i' that way—and I bought it when I was married, just as you did yours, Jane and Sophy; and I know you didn't like mine because o' the sprig, but I was fond of it; and there's never been a bit broke, for I've washed it myself—and there's the tulips on the cups, and the roses, as anybody might go and look at 'em for pleasure. You wouldn't like *your* chany to go for an old song and be broke to pieces, though yours has got no colour in it, Jane—it's all white and flutted, and didn't cost so much as mine. And there's the castors—sister Deane, I can't think but you'd like to have the castors, for I've heard you say they're pretty.'

'Well, I've no objection to buy some of the best things,' said Mrs. Deane, rather loftily; 'we can do with extra things in our house.'

'Best things!' exclaimed Mrs. Glegg with severity, which had gathered intensity from her long silence. 'It drives me past patience to hear you all talking o' best things, and buying in this, that, and the other, such as silver and chany. You must bring your mind to your circumstances, Bessy, and not be thinking o' silver and chany; but whether you shall get so much as a flock bed to lie on, and a blanket to cover you, and a stool to sit on. You must remember, if you get 'em, it'll be because your friends have bought 'em for you, for you're dependent upon *them* for everything; for your husband lies there helpless, and hasn't got a penny i' the world to call his own. And it's for your own good I say this, for it's right you should feel what your state is, and what disgrace your husband's brought on your own family, as you've got to look to for everything—and be humble in your mind.'

Mrs. Glegg paused, for speaking with much energy for the good of others is naturally exhausting. Mrs. Tulliver, always borne down by the family predominance of sister Jane, who had made her wear the yoke of a younger sister in very tender years, said pleadingly:

'I'm sure, sister, I've never asked anybody to do anything, only buy things as it 'ud be a pleasure to 'em to have, so as they mightn't go and be spoiled i' strange houses. I never asked anybody to buy the things in for me and my children; though there's the linen I spun, and I thought when Tom was born—I thought one o' the first things when he was lying i' the cradle, as all the things I'd bought wi' my own money, and been so careful of, 'ud go to him. But I've said nothing as I wanted my sisters to pay their money for me. What my husband has done for *his* sister's unknown, and we should ha' been better off this day if it hadn't been as he's lent money and never asked for it again.'

'Come, come,' said Mr. Glegg kindly, 'don't let us make

things too dark. What's done can't be undone. We shall make a shift among us to buy what's sufficient for you; though, as Mrs. G. says, they must be useful, plain things. We mustn't be thinking o' what's unnecessary. A table, and a chair or two, and kitchen things, and a good bed, and suchlike. Why, I've seen the day when I shouldn't ha' known myself if I'd lain on sacking i'stead o' the floor. We get a deal of useless things about us, only because we've got the money to spend.'

'Mr. Glegg,' said Mrs. G., 'if you'll be kind enough to let me speak, i'stead o' taking the words out o' my mouth—I was going to say, Bessy, as it's fine talking for you to say as you've never asked us to buy anything for you; let me tell you, you *ought* to have asked us. Pray, how are you to be purvided for, if your own family don't help you? You must go to the parish, if they didn't. And you ought to know that, and keep it in mind, and ask us humble to do what we can for you, i'stead o' saying, and making a boast, as you've never asked us for anything.'

'You talked o' the Mosses, and what Mr. Tulliver's done for 'em,' said uncle Pullet, who became unusually suggestive where advances of money were concerned. 'Haven't *they* been anear you? They ought to do something, as well as other folks; and if he's lent 'em money, they ought to be made to pay it back.'

'Yes, to be sure,' said Mrs. Deane; 'I've been thinking so. How is it Mr. and Mrs. Moss aren't here to meet us? It is but right they should do their share.'

'O dear!' said Mrs. Tulliver, 'I never sent 'em word about Mr. Tulliver, and they live so back'ard among the lanes at Basset, they niver hear anything only when Mr. Moss comes to market. But I niver gave 'em a thought. I wonder Maggie didn't, though, for she was allays so fond of her aunt Moss.'

'Why don't your children come in, Bessy?' said Mrs. Pullet, at the mention of Maggie. 'They should hear what their aunts and uncles have got to say: and Maggie—when it's me as have paid for half her schooling, she ought to think more of her aunt Pullet than of aunt Mosses. I may go off sudden when I get home to-day—there's no telling.'

'If I'd had *my* way,' said Mrs. Glegg, 'the children 'ud ha' been in the room from the first. It's time they knew who they've to look to, and it's right as *somebody* should talk to 'em, and let 'em know their condition i' life, and what they're come down to, and make 'em feel as they've got to suffer for their father's faults.'

'Well, I'll go and fetch 'em, sister,' said Mrs. Tulliver resignedly. She was quite crushed now, and thought of the treasures in the store-room with no other feeling than blank despair.

She went up-stairs to fetch Tom and Maggie, who were both in their father's room, and was on her way down again, when the sight of the store-room door suggested a new thought to her. She went towards it, and left the children to go down by themselves.

The aunts and uncles appeared to have been in warm discussion when the brother and sister entered—both with shrinking reluctance; for though Tom, with a practical sagacity which had been roused into activity by the strong stimulus of the new emotions he had undergone since yesterday, had been turning over in his mind a plan which he meant to propose to one of his aunts or uncles, he felt by no means amicably towards them, and dreaded meeting them all at once as he would have dreaded a large dose of concentrated physic, which was but just endurable in small draughts. As for Maggie, she was peculiarly depressed this morning: she had been called up after brief rest, at three o'clock, and had that strange dreamy weariness which comes from watching in a sick-room through the chill hours of early twilight and breaking day—in which the outside daylight life seems to have no importance, and to be a mere margin to the hours in the darkened chamber. Their entrance interrupted the conversation. The shaking of hands was a melancholy and silent ceremony, till uncle Pullet observed, as Tom approached him:

'Well, young sir, we've been talking as we should want

your pen and ink; you can write rarely now, after all your schooling, I should think.'

'Ay, ay,' said uncle Glegg, with admonition which he meant to be kind, 'we must look to see the good of all this schooling, as your father's sunk so much money in, now:

> "When land is gone and money's spent,
>   Then learning is most excellent."

Now's the time, Tom, to let us see the good o' your learning. Let us see whether you can do better than I can, as have made my fortin without it. But I began wi' doing with little, you see: I could live on a basin o' porridge and a crust o' bread-and-cheese. But I doubt high living and high learning 'ull make it harder for you, young man, nor it was for me.'

'But he must do it,' interposed aunt Glegg energetically, 'whether it's hard or no. He hasn't got to consider what's hard; he must consider as he isn't to trusten to his friends to keep him in idleness and luxury: he's got to bear the fruits of his father's misconduct, and bring his mind to fare hard and to work hard. And he must be humble and grateful to his aunts and uncles for what they're doing for his mother and father, as must be turned out into the streets and go to the workhouse if they didn't help 'em. And his sister, too,' continued Mrs. Glegg, looking severely at Maggie, who had sat down on the sofa by her aunt Deane, drawn to her by the sense that she was Lucy's mother, 'she must make up her mind to be humble and work; for there'll be no servants to wait on her any more—she must remember that. She must do the work o' the house, and she must respect and love her aunts as have done so much for her, and saved their money to leave to their nepheys and nieces.'

Tom was still standing before the table in the centre of the group. There was a heightened colour in his face, and he was very far from looking humbled, but he was preparing to say, in a respectful tone, something he had previously meditated, when the door opened and his mother re-entered.

Poor Mrs. Tulliver had in her hands a small tray, on

which she had placed her silver teapot, a specimen teacup and saucer, the castors, and sugar-tongs.

'See here, sister,' she said, looking at Mrs. Deane, as she set the tray on the table, 'I thought, perhaps, if you looked at the teapot again—it's a good while since you saw it— you might like the pattern better: it makes beautiful tea, and there's a stand and everything: you might use it for every day, or else lay it by for Lucy when she goes to housekeeping. I should be so loth for 'em to buy it at the Golden Lion,' said the poor woman, her heart swelling, and the tears coming, 'my teapot as I bought when I was married, and to think of its being scratched, and set before the travellers and folks, and my letters on it—see here. E. D.—and everybody to see 'em.'

'Ah, dear, dear!' said aunt Pullet, shaking her head with deep sadness, 'it's very bad—to think o' the family initials going about everywhere—it niver was so before: you're a very unlucky sister, Bessy. But what's the use o' buying the teapot, when there's the linen and spoons and everything to go, and some of 'em with your full name—and when it's got that straight spout, too.'

'As to disgrace o' the family,' said Mrs. Glegg, 'that can't be helped wi' buying teapots. The disgrace is, for one o' the family to ha' married a man as has brought her to beggary. The disgrace is, as they're to be sold up. We can't hinder the country from knowing that.'

Maggie had started up from the sofa at the allusion to her father, but Tom saw her action and flushed face in time to prevent her from speaking. 'Be quiet, Maggie,' he said authoritatively, pushing her aside. It was a remarkable manifestation of self-command and practical judgment in a lad of fifteen, that when his aunt Glegg ceased, he began to speak in a quiet and respectful manner, though with a good deal of trembling in his voice; for his mother's words had cut him to the quick.

'Then, aunt,' he said, looking straight at Mrs. Glegg, 'if you think it's a disgrace to the family that we should be sold up, wouldn't it be better to prevent it altogether? And if you and my aunt Pullet,' he continued, looking at the latter, 'think of leaving any money to me and Maggie, wouldn't it be better to give it now, and pay the debt we're going to be sold up for, and save my mother from parting with her furniture?'

There was silence for a few moments, for every one, including Maggie, was astonished at Tom's sudden manliness of tone. Uncle Glegg was the first to speak.

'Ay, ay, young man—come now! You show some notion o' things. But there's the interest, you must remember; your aunts get five per cent. on their money, and they'd lose that if they advanced it—you haven't thought o' that.'

'I could work and pay that every year,' said Tom promptly. 'I'd do anything to save my mother from parting with her things.'

'Well done!' said uncle Glegg admiringly. He had been drawing Tom out, rather than reflecting on the practicability of his proposal. But he had produced the unfortunate result of irritating his wife.

'Yes, Mr. Glegg!' said that lady with angry sarcasm. 'It's pleasant work for you to be giving my money away, as you've pretended to leave at my own disposal. And my money, as was my own father's gift, and not yours, Mr. Glegg; and I've saved it, and added to it myself, and had more to put out almost every year, and it's to go and be sunk in other folks' furniture, and encourage 'em in luxury and extravagance as they've no means of supporting; and I'm to alter my will, or have a codicil made, and leave two or three hundred less behind me when I die—me as have allays done right and been careful, and the eldest o' the family; and my money's to go and be squandered on them as have had the same chance as me, only they've been wicked and wasteful. Sister Pullet, *you* may do as you like, and you may let your husband rob you back again o' the money he's given you, but that isn't *my* sperrit.'

'La, Jane, how fiery you are!' said Mrs. Pullet. 'I'm sure you'll have the blood in your head, and have to be cupped. I'm sorry for Bessie and her children—I'm sure I think of 'em o' nights dreadful, for I sleep very bad wi'

this new medicine: but it's no use for me to think o' doing
anything, if you won't meet me half-way.'

'Why, there's this to be considered,' said Mr. Glegg.
'It's no use to pay off this debt and save the furniture,
when there's all the law debts behind, as 'ud take every
shilling, and more than could be made out o' land and
stock, for I've made that out from Lawyer Gore. We'd
need save our money to keep the poor man with, instead
o' spending it on furniture as he can neither eat nor drink.
You *will* be so hasty, Jane, as if I didn't know what was
reasonable.'

'Then speak accordingly, Mr. Glegg!' said his wife, with
slow, loud emphasis, bending her head towards him sig-
nificantly.

Tom's countenance had fallen during this conversation,
and his lip quivered; but he was determined not to give
way. He would behave like a man. Maggie, on the contrary,
after her momentary delight in Tom's speech, had relapsed
into her state of trembling indignation. Her mother had
been standing close by Tom's side, and had been clinging
to his arm ever since he had last spoken: Maggie suddenly
started up and stood in front of them, her eyes flashing like
the eyes of a young lioness.

'Why do you come, then,' she burst out, 'talking and
interfering with us and scolding us, if you don't mean to do
anything to help my poor mother—your own sister—if
you've no feeling for her when she's in trouble, and won't
part with anything, though you would never miss it, to
save her from pain? Keep away from us then, and don't
come to find fault with my father—he was better than any
of you—he was kind—he would have helped *you*, if you
had been in trouble. Tom and I don't ever want to have
any of your money, if you won't help my mother. We'd
rather not have it! we'll do without you.'

Maggie, having hurled her defiance at aunts and uncles
in this way, stood still, with her large dark eyes glaring at
them, as if she were ready to await all consequences.

Mrs. Tulliver was frightened; there was something portentous in this mad outbreak; she did not see how life could

go on after it. Tom was vexed; it was no *use* to talk so. The aunts were silent with surprise for some moments. At length, in a case of aberration such as this, comment presented itself as more expedient than any answer.

'You haven't seen the end o' your trouble wi' that child, Bessy,' said Mrs. Pullet; 'she's beyond everything for boldness and unthankfulness. It's dreadful. I might ha' let alone paying for her schooling, for she's worse nor ever.'

'It's no more than what I've allays said,' followed Mrs. Glegg. 'Other folks may be surprised, but I'm not. I've said over and over again—years ago I've said—"Mark my words; that child 'ull come to no good: there isn't a bit of our family in her." And as for her having so much schooling, I never thought well o' that. I'd my reasons when I said *I* wouldn't pay anything towards it.'

'Come, come,' said Mr. Glegg, 'let's waste no more time in talking—let's go to business. Tom now, get the pen and ink——'

While Mr. Glegg was speaking, a tall dark figure was seen hurrying past the window.

'Why, there's Mrs. Moss,' said Mrs. Tulliver. 'The bad news must ha' reached her, then;' and she went out to open the door, Maggie eagerly following her.

'That's fortunate,' said Mrs. Glegg. 'She can agree to the list o' things to be bought in. It's but right she should do her share when it's her own brother.'

Mrs. Moss was in too much agitation to resist Mrs. Tulliver's movement, as she drew her into the parlour automatically, without reflecting that it was hardly kind to take her among so many persons in the first painful moment of arrival. The tall, worn, dark-haired woman was a strong contrast to the Dodson sisters as she entered in her shabby dress, with her shawl and bonnet looking as if they had been hastily huddled on, and with that entire absence of self-consciousness which belongs to keenly-felt trouble. Maggie was clinging to her arm; and Mrs. Moss seemed to notice no one else except Tom, whom she went straight up to and took by the hand.

'O my dear children,' she burst out, 'you've no call

to think well o' me; I'm a poor aunt to you, for I'm one o' them as take all and give nothing. How's my poor brother?'

'Mr. Turnbull thinks he'll get better,' said Maggie. 'Sit down, aunt Gritty. Don't fret.'

'O my sweet child, I feel torn i' two,' said Mrs. Moss, allowing Maggie to lead her to the sofa, but still not seeming to notice the presence of the rest. 'We've three hundred pounds o' my brother's money, and now he wants it, and you all want it, poor things!—and yet we must be sold up to pay it, and there's my poor children—eight of 'em, and the little un of all can't speak plain. And I feel as if I was a robber. But I'm sure I'd no thought as my brother. . . .'

The poor woman was interrupted by a rising sob.

'Three hundred pounds! O dear, dear,' said Mrs. Tulliver, who, when she had said that her husband had done 'unknown' things for his sister, had not had any particular sum in her mind, and felt a wife's irritation at having been kept in the dark.

'What madness, to be sure!' said Mrs. Glegg. 'A man with a family! He'd no right to lend his money i' that way; and without security, I'll be bound, if the truth was known.'

Mrs. Glegg's voice had arrested Mrs. Moss's attention, and, looking up, she said:

'Yes, there *was* security: my husband gave a note for it. We're not that sort o' people, neither of us, as 'ud rob my brother's children; and we looked to paying back the money, when the times got a bit better.'

'Well, but now,' said Mr. Glegg gently, 'hasn't your husband no way o' raising this money? Because it 'ud be a little fortin, like, for these folks, if we can do without Tulliver's being made a bankrupt. Your husband's got stock: it is but right he should raise the money, as it seems to me—not but what I'm sorry for you, Mrs. Moss.'

'O sir, you don't know what bad luck my husband's had with his stock. The farm's suffering so as never was for want o' stock; and we've sold all the wheat, and we're behind with our rent . . . not but what we'd like to do what's right, and I'd sit up and work half the night, if it 'ud be any good . . . but there's them poor children . . . four of 'em such little uns. . . .'

'Don't cry so, aunt—don't fret,' whispered Maggie, who had kept hold of Mrs. Moss's hand.

'Did Mr. Tulliver let you have the money all at once?' said Mrs. Tulliver, still lost in the conception of things which had been 'going on' without her knowledge.

'No; at twice,' said Mrs. Moss, rubbing her eyes and making an effort to restrain her tears. 'The last was after my bad illness, four years ago, as everything went wrong, and there was a new note made then. What with illness and bad luck, I've been nothing but cumber all my life.'

'Yes, Mrs. Moss,' said Mrs. Glegg, with decision. 'Yours is a very unlucky family; the more's the pity for *my* sister.'

'I set off in the cart as soon as ever I heard o' what had happened,' said Mrs. Moss, looking at Mrs. Tulliver. 'I should never ha' stayed away all this while, if you'd thought well to let me know. And it isn't as I'm thinking all about ourselves, and nothing about my brother—only the money was so on my mind, I couldn't help speaking about it. And my husband and me desire to do the right thing, sir,' she added, looking at Mr. Glegg, 'and we'll make shift and pay the money, come what will, if that's all my brother's got to trust to. We've been used to trouble, and don't look for much else. It's only the thought o' my poor children pulls me i' two.'

'Why, there's this to be thought on, Mrs. Moss,' said Mr. Glegg, 'and it's right to warn you; if Tulliver's made a bankrupt, and he's got a note-of-hand of your husband's for three hundred pounds, you'll be obliged to pay it: the assignees 'ull come on you for it.'

'O dear, O dear!' said Mrs. Tulliver, thinking of the bankruptcy, and not of Mrs. Moss's concern in it. Poor Mrs. Moss herself listened in trembling submission, while Maggie looked with bewildered distress at Tom to see if *he* showed any signs of understanding this trouble, and caring about poor aunt Moss. Tom was only looking thoughtful, with his eyes on the table-cloth.

'And if he isn't made bankrupt,' continued Mr. Glegg, 'as I said before, three hundred pounds 'ud be a little fortin for him, poor man. We don't know but what he may be partly helpless, if he ever gets up again. I'm very sorry if it goes hard with you, Mrs. Moss—but my opinion is, looking at it one way, it'll be right for you to raise the money; and looking at it th' other way, you'll be obliged to pay it. You won't think ill o' me for speaking the truth.'

'Uncle,' said Tom, looking up suddenly from his meditative view of the table-cloth, 'I don't think it would be right for my aunt Moss to pay the money, if it would be against my father's will for her to pay it; would it?'

Mr. Glegg looked surprised for a moment or two before he said, 'Why, no, perhaps not, Tom; but then he'd ha' destroyed the note, you know. We must look for the note. What makes you think it 'ud be against his will?'

'Why,' said Tom, colouring, but trying to speak firmly, in spite of a boyish tremor, 'I remember quite well, before I went to school to Mr. Stelling, my father said to me one night, when we were sitting by the fire together, and no one else was in the room . . .'

Tom hesitated a little, and then went on:

'He said something to me about Maggie, and then he said, "I've always been good to my sister, though she married against my will—and I've lent Moss money; but I shall never think of distressing him to pay it: I'd rather lose it. My children must not mind being the poorer for that." And now my father's ill, and not able to speak for himself, I shouldn't like anything to be done contrary to what he said to me.'

'Well, but then, my boy,' said uncle Glegg, whose good feeling led him to enter into Tom's wish, but who could not at once shake off his habitual abhorrence of such recklessness as destroying securities, or alienating anything important enough to make an appreciable difference in a man's property, 'we should have to make away wi' the note, you know, if we're to guard against what may happen, supposing your father's made bankrupt . . .'

'Mr. Glegg,' interrupted his wife severely, 'mind what

you're saying. You're putting yourself very forrard in other folks's business. If you speak rash, don't say it was my fault.'

'That's such a thing as I never heared of before,' said uncle Pullet, who had been making haste with his lozenge in order to express his amazement; 'making away with a note! I should think anybody could set the constable on you for it.'

'Well, but,' said Mrs. Tulliver, 'if the note's worth all that money, why can't we pay it away, and save my things from going away? We've no call to meddle with your uncle and aunt Moss, Tom, if you think your father 'ud be angry when he gets well.'

Mrs. Tulliver had not studied the question of exchange, and was straining her mind after original ideas on the subject.

'Pooh, pooh, pooh! you women don't understand these things,' said uncle Glegg. 'There's no way o' making it safe for Mr. and Mrs. Moss but destroying the note.'

'Then I hope you'll help me to do it, uncle,' said Tom earnestly. 'If my father shouldn't get well, I should be very unhappy to think anything had been done against his will, that I could hinder. And I'm sure he meant me to remember what he said that evening. I ought to obey my father's wish about his property.'

Even Mrs. Glegg could not withhold her approval from Tom's words: she felt that the Dodson blood was certainly speaking in him, though, if his father had been a Dodson, there would never have been this wicked alienation of money. Maggie would hardly have restrained herself from leaping on Tom's neck, if her aunt Moss had not prevented her by herself rising and taking Tom's hand, while she said, with rather a choked voice:

'You'll never be the poorer for this, my dear boy, if there's a God above; and if the money's wanted for your father, Moss and me 'ull pay it, the same as if there was ever such security. We'll do as we'd be done by; for if my children have got no other luck, they've got an honest father and mother.'

'Well,' said Mr. Glegg, who had been meditating after Tom's words, 'we shouldn't be doing any wrong by the creditors, supposing your father *was* bankrupt. I've been thinking o' that, for I've been a creditor myself, and seen no end o' cheating. If he meant to give your aunt the money before ever he got into this sad work o' lawing, it's the same as if he'd made away with the note himself; for he'd made up his mind to be that much poorer. But there's a deal o' things to be considered, young man,' Mr. Glegg added, looking admonishingly at Tom, 'when you come to money business, and you may be taking one man's dinner away to make another man's breakfast. You don't understand that, I doubt?'

'Yes, I do,' said Tom decidedly. 'I know if I owe money to one man, I've no right to give it to another. But if my father had made up his mind to give my aunt the money before he was in debt, he had a right to do it.'

'Well done, young man! I didn't think you'd been so sharp,' said uncle Glegg, with much candour. 'But perhaps your father *did* make away with the note. Let us go and see if we can find it in the chest.'

'It's in my father's room. Let us go too, aunt Gritty,' whispered Maggie.

IV

A VANISHING GLEAM

Mr. TULLIVER, even between the fits of spasmodic rigidity which had recurred at intervals ever since he had been found fallen from his horse, was usually in so apathetic a condition that the exits and entrances into his room were not felt to be of great importance. He had lain so still, with his eyes closed, all this morning, that Maggie told her aunt Moss she must not expect her father to take any notice of them.

They entered very quietly, and Mrs. Moss took her seat near the head of the bed, while Maggie sat in her old place on the bed, and put her hand on her father's, without causing any change in his face.

Mr. Glegg and Tom had also entered, treading softly, and were busy selecting the key of the old oak chest from the bunch which Tom had brought from his father's bureau. They succeeded in opening the chest—which stood opposite the foot of Mr. Tulliver's bed—and propping the lid with the iron holder, without much noise.

'There's a tin box,' whispered Mr. Glegg; 'he'd most like put a small thing like a note in there. Lift it out, Tom; but I'll just lift up these deeds—they're the deeds o' the house and mill, I suppose—and see what there is under 'em.'

Mr. Glegg had lifted out the parchments, and had fortunately drawn back a little when the iron holder gave way, and the heavy lid fell with a loud bang, that resounded over the house.

Perhaps there was something in that sound more than the mere fact of the strong vibration that produced the instantaneous effects on the frame of the prostrate man, and for the time completely shook off the obstruction of paralysis. The chest had belonged to his father and his father's father, and it had always been rather a solemn business to visit it. All long-known objects, even a mere window fastening or a particular door-latch, have sounds which are a sort of recognized voice to us—a voice that will thrill and awaken, when it has been used to touch deep-lying fibres. In the same moment when all the eyes in the room were turned upon him, he started up and looked at the chest, the parchments in Mr. Glegg's hand, and Tom holding the tin box, with a glance of perfect consciousness and recognition.

'What are you going to do with those deeds?' he said, in his ordinary tone of sharp questioning whenever he was irritated. 'Come here, Tom. What do you do, going to my chest?'

Tom obeyed, with some trembling: it was the first time his father had recognized him. But instead of saying anything more to him, his father continued to look with a growing distinctness of suspicion at Mr. Glegg and the deeds.

'What's been happening, then?' he said sharply. 'What are you meddling with my deeds for? Is Wakem laying hold of everything?... Why don't you tell me what you've been a-doing?' he added impatiently, as Mr. Glegg advanced to the foot of the bed before speaking.

'No, no, friend Tulliver,' said Mr. Glegg, in a soothing tone. 'Nobody's getting hold of anything as yet. We only came to look and see what was in the chest. You've been ill, you know, and we've had to look after things a bit. But let's hope you'll soon get well enough to attend to everything yourself.'

Mr. Tulliver looked round him meditatively—at Tom, at Mr. Glegg, and at Maggie; then suddenly appearing aware that someone was seated by his side at the head of the bed, he turned sharply round and saw his sister.

'Eh, Gritty!' he said, in the half-sad, affectionate tone in which he had been wont to speak to her. 'What! you're there, are you? How could you manage to leave the children?'

'O, brother!' said good Mrs. Moss, too impulsive to be prudent, 'I'm thankful I'm come now to see you yourself again—I thought you'd never know us any more.'

'What! have I had a stroke?' said Mr. Tulliver anxiously, looking at Mr. Glegg.

'A fall from your horse—shook you a bit—that's all, I think,' said Mr. Glegg. 'But you'll soon get over it, let's hope.'

Mr. Tulliver fixed his eyes on the bed-clothes, and remained silent for two or three minutes. A new shadow came over his face. He looked up at Maggie first, and said in a lower tone, 'You got the letter, then, my wench?'

'Yes, father,' she said, kissing him with a full heart. She felt as if her father were come back to her from the dead, and her yearning to show him how she had always loved him could be fulfilled.

'Where's your mother?' he said, so preoccupied that he received the kiss as passively as some quiet animal might have received it.

'She's down-stairs with my aunts, father: shall I fetch her?'

'Ay, ay: poor Bessy!' and his eyes turned towards Tom as Maggie left the room.

'You'll have to take care of 'em both if I die, you know, Tom. You'll be badly off, I doubt. But you must see and pay everybody. And mind—there's fifty pound o' Luke's as I put into the business—he gave it me a bit at a time, and he's got nothing to show for it. You must pay him first thing.'

Uncle Glegg involuntarily shook his head, and looked more concerned than ever, but Tom said firmly:

'Yes, father. And haven't you a note from my uncle Moss for three hundred pounds? We came to look for that. What do you wish to be done about it, father?'

'Ah! I'm glad you thought o' that, my lad,' said Mr. Tulliver. 'I allays meant to be easy about that money, because o' your aunt. You mustn't mind losing the money, if they can't pay it—and it's like enough they can't. The note's in that box, mind! I allays meant to be good to you, Gritty,' said Mr. Tulliver, turning to his sister; 'but, you know, you aggravated me when you would have Moss.'

At this moment Maggie re-entered with her mother, who came in much agitated by the news that her husband was quite himself again.

'Well, Bessy,' he said, as she kissed him, 'you must forgive me if you're worse off than you ever expected to be. But it's the fault o' the law—it's none o' mine,' he added angrily. 'It's the fault o' raskills! Tom—you mind this: if ever you've got the chance, you make Wakem smart. If you don't, you're a good-for-nothing son. You might horse-whip him—but he'd set the law on you—the law's made to take care o' raskills.'

Mr. Tulliver was getting excited, and an alarming flush was on his face. Mr. Glegg wanted to say something soothing, but he was prevented by Mr. Tulliver's speaking again to his wife. 'They'll make a shift to pay everything, Bessy,' he said, 'and yet leave you your furniture; and your sisters'll do something for you . . . and Tom'll grow up . . . though what he's to be I don't know. . . . I've done what I could.

. . . I've given him a eddication . . . and there's the little wench, she'll get married . . . but it's a poor tale. . . .'

The sanative effect of the strong vibration was exhausted, and with the last words the poor man fell again, rigid and insensible. Though this was only a recurrence of what had happened before, it struck all present as if it had been death, not only from its contrast with the completeness of the revival, but because his words had all had reference to the possibility that his death was near. But with poor Tulliver death was not to be a leap: it was to be a long descent under thickening shadows.

Mr. Turnbull was sent for; but when he heard what had passed, he said this complete restoration, though only temporary, was a hopeful sign, proving that there was no permanent lesion to prevent ultimate recovery.

Among the threads of the past which the stricken man had gathered up, he had omitted the bill of sale; the flash of memory had only lit up prominent ideas, and he sank into forgetfulness again with half his humiliation unlearned.

But Tom was clear upon two points—that his uncle Moss's note must be destroyed, and that Luke's money must be paid, if in no other way, out of his own and Maggie's money now in the savings bank. There were subjects, you perceive, on which Tom was much quicker than on the niceties of classical construction, or the relations of a mathematical demonstration.

V

TOM APPLIES HIS KNIFE TO THE OYSTER

THE next day, at ten o'clock, Tom was on his way to St. Ogg's, to see his uncle Deane, who was to come home last night, his aunt had said; and Tom had made up his mind that his uncle Deane was the right person to ask for advice about getting some employment. He was in a great way of business; he had not the narrow notions of uncle Glegg; and he had risen in the world on a scale of advancement which accorded with Tom's ambition.

It was a dark, chill, misty morning, likely to end in rain
—one of those mornings when even happy people take
refuge in their hopes. And Tom was very unhappy: he felt
the humiliation as well as the prospective hardships of his
lot with all the keenness of a proud nature; and with all
his resolute dutifulness towards his father there mingled an
irrepressible indignation against him which gave misfortune
the less endurable aspect of a wrong. Since these were the
consequences of going to law, his father was really blamable, as his aunts and uncles had always said he was; and
it was a significant indication of Tom's character, that
though he thought his aunts ought to do something more for
his mother, he felt nothing like Maggie's violent resentment against them for showing no eager tenderness and
generosity. There were no impulses in Tom that led him to
expect what did not present itself to him as a right to be
demanded. Why should people give away their money
plentifully to those who had not taken care of their own
money? Tom saw some justice in severity; and all the
more, because he had confidence in himself that he should
never deserve that just severity. It was very hard upon
him that he should be put at this disadvantage in life by
his father's want of prudence; but he was not going to
complain and to find fault with people because they did
not make everything easy for him. He would ask no one
to help him, more than to give him work and pay him for it.
Poor Tom was not without his hopes to take refuge in
under the chill damp imprisonment of the December fog
which seemed only like a part of his home troubles. At sixteen, the mind that has the strongest affinity for fact cannot
escape illusion and self-flattery; and Tom, in sketching his
future, had no other guide in arranging his facts than the
suggestions of his own brave self-reliance. Both Mr. Glegg
and Mr. Deane, he knew, had been very poor once: he did
not want to save money slowly and retire on a moderate
fortune like his uncle Glegg, but he would be like his
uncle Deane—get a situation in some great house of business and rise fast. He had scarcely seen anything of his
uncle Deane for the last three years—the two families had

been getting wider apart; but for this very reason Tom was
the more hopeful about applying to him. His uncle Glegg,
he felt sure, would never encourage any spirited project,
but he had a vague imposing idea of the resources at his
uncle Deane's command. He had heard his father say, long
ago, how Deane had made himself so valuable to Guest &
Co. that they were glad enough to offer him a share in the
business: that was what Tom resolved *he* would do. It
was intolerable to think of being poor and looked down
upon all one's life. He would provide for his mother and
sister, and make every one say that he was a man of high
character. He leaped over the years in this way, and in
the haste of strong purpose and strong desire, did not
see how they would be made up of slow days, hours, and
minutes.

By the time he had crossed the stone bridge over the
Floss and was entering St. Ogg's he was thinking that he
would buy his father's mill and land again when he was
rich enough, and improve the house and live there: he
should prefer it to any smarter, newer place, and he could
keep as many horses and dogs as he liked.

Walking along the street with a firm, rapid step, at this
point in his reverie he was startled by some one who had
crossed without his notice, and who said to him in a rough,
familiar voice:

'Why, Master Tom, how's your father this morning?'
It was a publican of St. Ogg's—one of his father's
customers.

Tom disliked being spoken to just then; but he said
civilly, 'He's still very ill, thank you.'

'Ay, it's been a sore chance for you, young man, hasn't
it?—this lawsuit turning out against him,' said the publican, with a confused beery idea of being good-natured.

Tom reddened and passed on: he would have felt it like
the handling of a bruise, even if there had been the most
polite and delicate reference to his position.

'That's Tulliver's son,' said the publican to a grocer
standing on the adjacent doorstep.

'Ah!' said the grocer, 'I thought I knew his features.

He takes after his mother's family: she was a Dodson. He's a fine, straight youth: what's he been brought up to?'

'Oh! to turn up his nose at his father's customers, and be a fine gentleman—not much else, I think.'

Tom, roused from his dream of the future to a thorough consciousness of the present, made all the greater haste to reach the warehouse offices of Guest & Co., where he expected to find his uncle Deane. But this was Mr. Deane's morning at the bank, a clerk told him, with some contempt for his ignorance: Mr. Deane was not to be found in River Street on a Thursday morning.

At the bank Tom was admitted into the private room where his uncle was, immediately after sending in his name. Mr. Deane was auditing accounts; but he looked up as Tom entered, and, putting out his hand, said, 'Well, Tom, nothing fresh the matter at home, I hope? How's your father?'

'Much the same, thank you, uncle,' said Tom, feeling nervous. 'But I want to speak to you, please, when you're at liberty.'

'Sit down, sit down,' said Mr. Deane, relapsing into his accounts, in which he and the managing-clerk remained so absorbed for the next half-hour that Tom began to wonder whether he should have to sit in this way till the bank closed—there seemed so little tendency towards a conclusion in the quiet monotonous procedure of these sleek, prosperous men of business. Would his uncle give him a place in the bank? it would be very dull, prosy work, he thought, writing there for ever to the loud ticking of a timepiece. He preferred some other way of getting rich. But at last there was a change: his uncle took a pen and wrote something with a flourish at the end.

'You'll just step up to Torry's now, Mr. Spence, will you?' said Mr. Deane, and the clock suddenly became less loud and deliberate in Tom's ears.

'Well, Tom,' said Mr. Deane, when they were alone, turning his substantial person a little in his chair, and taking out his snuff-box, 'what's the business, my boy—what's the business?' Mr. Deane, who had heard from his wife what had passed the day before, thought Tom was come to appeal to him for some means of averting the sale.

'I hope you'll excuse me for troubling you, uncle,' said Tom, colouring, but speaking in a tone which, though tremulous, had a certain proud independence in it; 'but I thought you were the best person to advise me what to do.'

'Ah!' said Mr. Deane, reserving his pinch of snuff, and looking at Tom with new attention, 'let us hear.'

'I want to get a situation, uncle, so that I may earn some money,' said Tom, who never fell into circumlocution.

'A situation?' said Mr. Deane, and then took his pinch of snuff with elaborate justice to each nostril. Tom thought snuff-taking a most provoking habit.

'Why, let me see, how old are you?' said Mr. Deane, as he threw himself backward again.

'Sixteen—I mean, I'm going in seventeen,' said Tom, hoping his uncle noticed how much beard he had.

'Let me see—your father had some notion of making you an engineer, I think?'

'But I don't think I could get any money at that for a long while, could I?'

'That's true; but people don't get much money at anything, my boy, when they're only sixteen. You've had a good deal of schooling, however: I suppose you're pretty well up in accounts, eh? You understand book-keeping?'

'No,' said Tom, rather falteringly. 'I was in Practice. But Mr. Stelling says I write a good hand, uncle. That's my writing,' added Tom, laying on the table a copy of the list he had made yesterday.

'Ah! that's good, that's good. But, you see, the best hand in the world'll not get you a better place than a copying-clerk's, if you know nothing of book-keeping—nothing of accounts. And a copying-clerk's a cheap article. But what have you been learning at school, then?'

Mr. Deane had not occupied himself with methods of education, and had no precise conception of what went forward in expensive schools.

'We learned Latin,' said Tom, pausing a little between each item, as if he were turning over the books in his school-desk to assist his memory—'a good deal of Latin; and the last year I did Themes, one week in Latin and one in English; and Greek and Roman History; and Euclid; and I began Algebra, but I left it off again; and we had one day every week for Arithmetic. Then I used to have drawing-lessons; and there were several other books we either read or learned out of, English Poetry, and Horæ Paulinæ, and Blair's Rhetoric, the last half.'

Mr. Deane tapped his snuff-box again, and screwed up his mouth: he felt in the position of many estimable persons when they had read the New Tariff, and found how many commodities were imported of which they knew nothing: like a cautious man of business, he was not going to speak rashly of a raw material in which he had had no experience. But the presumption was, that if it had been good for anything, so successful a man as himself would hardly have been ignorant of it. About Latin he had an opinion, and thought that in case of another war, since people would no longer wear hair-powder, it would be well to put a tax upon Latin, as a luxury much run upon by the higher classes, and not telling at all on the ship-owning department. But, for what he knew, the Horæ Paulinæ might be something less neutral. On the whole, this list of acquirements gave him a sort of repulsion towards poor Tom.

'Well,' he said, at last, in rather a cold, sardonic tone, 'you've had three years at these things—you must be pretty strong in 'em. Hadn't you better take up some line where they'll come in handy?'

Tom coloured, and burst out, with new energy:

'I'd rather not have any employment of that sort, uncle. I don't like Latin and those things. I don't know what I could do with them unless I went as usher in a school; and I don't know them well enough for that: besides, I would as soon carry a pair of panniers. I don't want to be that sort of person. I should like to enter into some business where I can get on—a manly business, where I should have to look after things, and get credit for what I did. And I shall want to keep my mother and sister.'

'Ah, young gentleman,' said Mr. Deane, with that tendency to repress youthful hopes which stout and successful men of fifty find one of their easiest duties, 'that's sooner said than done—sooner said than done.'

'But didn't *you* get on in that way, uncle?' said Tom, a little irritated that Mr. Deane did not enter more rapidly into his views. 'I mean, didn't you rise from one place to another through your abilities and good conduct?'

'Ay, ay, sir,' said Mr. Deane, spreading himself in his chair a little, and entering with great readiness into a retrospect of his own career. 'But I'll tell you how I got on. It wasn't by getting astride a stick, and thinking it would turn into a horse if I sat on it long enough. I kept my eyes and ears open, sir, and I wasn't too fond of my own back, and I made my master's interests my own. Why, with only looking into what went on in the mill, I found out how there was a waste of five hundred a-year that might be hindered. Why, sir, I hadn't more schooling to begin with than a charity boy; but I saw pretty soon that I couldn't get on far without mastering accounts, and I learned 'em between working hours, after I had been unlading. Look here.' Mr. Deane opened a book, and pointed to the page. 'I write a good hand enough, and I'll match anybody at all sorts of reckoning by the head, and I got it all by hard work, and paid for it out of my own earnings—often out of my own dinner and supper. And I looked into the nature of all the things we had to do with in the business, and picked up knowledge as I went about my work, and turned it over in my head. Why, I'm no mechanic—I never pretended to be—but I've thought of a thing or two that the mechanics never thought of, and it's made a fine difference in our returns. And there isn't an article shipped or unshipped at our wharf but I know the quality of it. If I got places, sir, it was because I made myself fit for 'em. If you want to slip into a round hole, you must make a ball of yourself—that's where it is.'

Mr. Deane tapped his box again. He had been led on by pure enthusiasm in his subject, and had really forgotten what bearing this retrospective survey had on his listener.

He had found occasion for saying the same thing more than once before, and was not distinctly aware that he had not his port-wine before him.

'Well, uncle,' said Tom, with a slight complaint in his tone, 'that's what I should like to do. Can't *I* get on in the same way?'

'In the same way?' said Mr. Deane, eyeing Tom with quiet deliberation. 'There go two or three questions to that, Master Tom. That depends on what sort of material you are, to begin with, and whether you've been put into the right mill. But I'll tell you what it is. Your poor father went the wrong way to work in giving you an education. It wasn't my business, and I didn't interfere: but it is as I thought it would be. You've had a sort of learning that's all very well for a young fellow like our Mr. Stephen Guest, who'll have nothing to do but sign cheques all his life, and may as well have Latin inside his head as any other sort of stuffing.'

'But, uncle,' said Tom earnestly, 'I don't see why the Latin need hinder me from getting on in business. I shall soon forget it all: it makes no difference to me. I had to do my lessons at school; but I always thought they'd never be of any use to me afterwards—I didn't care about them.'

'Ay, ay, that's all very well,' said Mr. Deane; 'but it doesn't alter what I was going to say. Your Latin and rigmarole may soon dry off you, but you'll be but a bare stick after that. Besides, it's whitened your hands and taken the rough work out of you. And what do you know? Why, you know nothing about book-keeping, to begin with, and not so much of reckoning as a common shopman. You'll have to begin at a low round of the ladder, let me tell you, if you mean to get on in life. It's no use forgetting the education your father's been paying for, if you don't give yourself a new un.'

Tom bit his lips hard; he felt as if the tears were rising, and he would rather die than let them.

'You want me to help you to a situation,' Mr. Deane went on; 'well, I've no fault to find with that. I'm willing to do something for you. But you youngsters now-a-days think you're to begin with living well and working easy: you've no notion of running afoot before you get on horseback. Now, you must remember what you are—you're a lad of sixteen, trained to nothing particular. There's heaps of your sort, like so many pebbles, made to fit in nowhere. Well, you might be apprenticed to some business—a chemist's and druggist's perhaps: your Latin might come in a bit there. . . .'

Tom was going to speak, but Mr. Deane put up his hand and said:

'Stop! hear what I've got to say. You don't want to be a 'prentice—I know, I know—you want to make more haste —and you don't want to stand behind a counter. But if you're a copying-clerk, you'll have to stand behind a desk, and stare at your ink and paper all day: there isn't much out-look there, and you won't be much wiser at the end of the year than at the beginning. The world isn't made of pen, ink, and paper, and if you're to get on in the world, young man, you must know what the world's made of. Now the best chance for you 'ud be to have a place on a wharf, or in a warehouse, where you'd learn the smell of things—but you wouldn't like that, I'll be bound; you'd have to stand cold and wet, and be shouldered about by rough fellows. You're too fine a gentleman for that.'

Mr. Deane paused and looked hard at Tom, who certainly felt some inward struggle before he could reply.

'I would rather do what will be best for me in the end, sir: I would put up with what was disagreeable.'

'That's well, if you can carry it out. But you must remember it isn't only laying hold of a rope—you must go on pulling. It's the mistake you lads make that have got nothing either in your brains or your pocket, to think you've got a better start in the world if you stick yourselves in a place where you can keep your coats clean, and have the shop-wenches take you for fine gentlemen. That wasn't the way *I* started, young man: when I was sixteen, my jacket smelt of tar, and I wasn't afraid of handling cheeses. That's the reason I can wear good broadcloth

now, and have my legs under the same table with the heads
of the best firms in St. Ogg's.'

Uncle Deane tapped his box, and seemed to expand a
little under his waistcoat and gold chain, as he squared his
shoulders in the chair.

'Is there any place at liberty that you know of now,
uncle, that I should do for? I should like to set to work at
once,' said Tom, with a slight tremor in his voice.

'Stop a bit, stop a bit; we mustn't be in too great a
hurry. You must bear in mind, if I put you in a place
you're a bit young for, because you happen to be my
nephew, I shall be responsible for you. And there's no
better reason, you know, than your being my nephew;
because it remains to be seen whether you're good for anything.'

'I hope I should never do you any discredit, uncle,' said
Tom, hurt, as all boys are at the statement of the unpleasant
truth that people feel no ground for trusting them. 'I care
about my own credit too much for that.'

'Well done, Tom, well done! That's the right spirit, and
I never refuse to help anybody if they've a mind to do
themselves justice. There's a young man of two-and-
twenty I've got my eye on now. I shall do what I can for
that young man—he's got some pith in him. But then,
you see, he's made good use of his time—a first-rate calcu-
lator—can tell you the cubic contents of anything in no
time, and put me up the other day to a new market for
Swedish bark; he's uncommonly knowing in manufactures,
that young fellow.'

'I'd better set about learning book-keeping, hadn't I,
uncle?' said Tom, anxious to prove his readiness to exert
himself.

'Yes, yes, you can't do amiss there. But . . . ah, Spence,
you're back again. Well, Tom, there's nothing more to be
said just now, I think, and I must go to business again.
Good-bye. Remember me to your mother.'

Mr. Deane put out his hand, with an air of friendly dis-
missal, and Tom had not courage to ask another question,
specially in the presence of Mr. Spence. So he went out

again into the cold damp air. He had to call at his uncle Glegg's about the money in the savings bank, and by the time he set out again, the mist had thickened, and he could not see very far before him; but going along River Street again, he was startled, when he was within two yards of the projecting side of a shop-window, by the words 'Dorlcote Mill' in large letters on a hand-bill, placed as if on purpose to stare at him. It was the catalogue of the sale to take place the next week—it was a reason for hurrying faster out of the town.

Poor Tom formed no visions of the distant future as he made his way homeward; he only felt that the present was very hard. It seemed a wrong towards him that his uncle Deane had no confidence in him—did not see at once that he should acquit himself well, which Tom himself was as certain of as of the daylight. Apparently he, Tom Tulliver, was likely to be held of small account in the world, and for the first time he felt a sinking of heart under the sense that he really was very ignorant, and could do very little. Who was that enviable young man, that could tell the cubic contents of things in no time, and make suggestions about Swedish bark? Swedish bark! Tom had been used to be so entirely satisfied with himself in spite of his breaking down in a demonstration, and construing *nunc illas promite vires*, as 'now promise those men;' but now he suddenly felt at a disadvantage, because he knew less than someone else knew. There must be a world of things connected with that Swedish bark, which, if he only knew them, might have helped him to get on. It would have been much easier to make a figure with a spirited horse and a new saddle.

Two hours ago, as Tom was walking to St. Ogg's, he saw the distant future before him, as he might have seen a tempting stretch of smooth sandy beach beyond a belt of flinty shingles; he was on the grassy bank then, and thought the shingles might soon be passed. But now his feet were on the sharp stones; the belt of shingles had widened, and the stretch of sand had dwindled into narrowness.

'What did my uncle Deane say, Tom?' said Maggie, putting her arm through Tom's as he was warming himself rather drearily by the kitchen fire. 'Did he say he would give you a situation?'

'No, he didn't say that. He didn't quite promise me anything; he seemed to think I couldn't have a very good situation. I'm too young.'

'But didn't he speak kindly, Tom?'

'Kindly? Pooh! what's the use of talking about that? I wouldn't care about his speaking kindly, if I could get a situation. But it's such a nuisance and bother—I've been at school all this while learning Latin and things—not a bit of good to me—and now my uncle says, I must set about learning book-keeping and calculation, and those things. He seems to make out I'm good for nothing.'

Tom's mouth twitched with a bitter expression as he looked at the fire.

'O what a pity we haven't got Dominie Sampson,' said Maggie, who couldn't help mingling some gaiety with their sadness. 'If he had taught me book-keeping by double entry and after the Italian method, as he did Lucy Bertram, I could teach you, Tom.'

'*You* teach! Yes, I daresay. That's always the tone you take,' said Tom.

'Dear Tom! I was only joking,' said Maggie, putting her cheek against his coat-sleeve.

'But it's always the same, Maggie,' said Tom, with the little frown he put on when he was about to be justifiably severe. 'You're always setting yourself up above me and everyone else, and I've wanted to tell you about it several times. You ought not to have spoken as you did to my uncles and aunts—you should leave it to me to take care of my mother and you, and not put yourself forward. You think you know better than anyone, but you're almost always wrong. I can judge much better than you can.'

Poor Tom! he had just come from being lectured and made to feel his inferiority: the reaction of his strong, self-asserting nature must take place somehow; and here was a case in which he could justly show himself dominant. Maggie's cheek flushed and her lip quivered with conflicting resentment and affection, and a certain awe as well as admiration of Tom's firmer and more effective character. She did not answer immediately; very angry words rose to her lips, but they were driven back again, and she said at last:

'You often think I'm conceited, Tom, when I don't mean what I say at all in that way. I don't mean to put myself above you—I know you behaved better than I did yesterday. But you are always so harsh to me, Tom.'

With the last words the resentment was rising again.

'No, I'm not harsh,' said Tom, with severe decision. 'I'm always kind to you; and so I shall be: I shall always take care of you. But you must mind what I say.'

Their mother came in now, and Maggie rushed away, that her burst of tears, which she felt must come, might not happen till she was safe up-stairs. They were very bitter tears: everybody in the world seemed so hard and unkind to Maggie: there was no indulgence, no fondness, such as she imagined when she fashioned the world afresh in her own thoughts. In books there were people who were always agreeable or tender, and delighted to do things that made one happy, and who did not show their kindness by finding fault. The world outside the books was not a happy one, Maggie felt: it seemed to be a world where people behaved the best to those they did not pretend to love, and that did not belong to them. And if life had no love in it, what else was there for Maggie? Nothing but poverty and the companionship of her mother's narrow griefs—perhaps of her father's heart-cutting childish dependence. There is no hopelessness so sad as that of early youth, when the soul is made up of wants, and has no long memories, no super added life in the life of others; though we who look on think lightly of such premature despair, as if our vision of the future lightened the blind sufferer's present.

Maggie in her brown frock, with her eyes reddened and her heavy hair pushed back, looking from the bed where her father lay, to the dull walls of this sad chamber which was the centre of her world, was a creature full of eager passionate longings for all that was beautiful and glad; thirsty for all knowledge; with an ear straining after dreamy music that died away and would not come near to her; with a blind, unconscious yearning for something that would link together the wonderful impressions of this mysterious life, and give her soul a sense of home in it.

No wonder, when there is this contrast between the outward and the inward, that painful collisions come of it.

VI

TENDING TO REFUTE THE POPULAR PREJUDICE AGAINST THE PRESENT OF A POCKET-KNIFE

In that dark time of December, the sale of the household furniture lasted beyond the middle of the second day. Mr. Tulliver, who had begun, in his intervals of consciousness, to manifest an irritability which often appeared to have as a direct effect the recurrence of spasmodic rigidity and insensibility, had lain in this living death throughout the critical hours when the noise of the sale came nearest to his chamber. Mr. Turnbull had decided that it would be a less risk to let him remain where he was, than to move him to Luke's cottage—a plan which the good Luke had proposed to Mrs. Tulliver, thinking it would be very bad if the master were 'to waken up' at the noise of the sale; and the wife and children had sat imprisoned in the silent chamber, watching the large prostrate figure on the bed, and trembling lest the blank face should suddenly show some response to the sounds which fell on their own ears with such obstinate, painful repetition.

But it was over at last—that time of importunate certainty and eye-straining suspense. The sharp sound of a voice, almost as metallic as the rap that followed it, had ceased; the tramping of footsteps on the gravel had died out. Mrs. Tulliver's blond face seemed aged ten years by the last thirty hours: the poor woman's mind had been busy divining when her favourite things were being knocked down by the terrible hammer; her heart had been fluttering at the thought that first one thing and then another had

gone to be identified as hers in the hateful publicity of the
Golden Lion; and all the while she had to sit and make no
sign of this inward agitation. Such things bring lines in
well-rounded faces, and broaden the streaks of white among
the hairs that once looked as if they had been dipped in
pure sunshine. Already, at three o'clock, Kezia, the good-
hearted, bad-tempered housemaid, who regarded all
people that came to the sale as her personal enemies, the
dirt on whose feet was of a peculiarly vile quality, had begun to scrub and swill with an energy much assisted by a
continual low muttering against 'folks as came to buy up
other folks's things,' and made light of 'scrazing' the tops of
mahogany tables over which better folks than themselves
had had to—suffer a waste of tissue through evaporation.
She was not scrubbing indiscriminately, for there would be
further dirt of the same atrocious kind made by people who
had still to fetch away their purchases: but she was bent on
bringing the parlour, where that 'pipe-smoking pig' the
bailiff had sat, to such an appearance of scant comfort as
could be given to it by cleanliness, and the few articles of
furniture bought in for the family. Her mistress and the
young folks should have their tea in it that night, Kezia was
determined.

It was between five and six o'clock, near the usual tea-
time, when she came up-stairs and said that Master Tom
was wanted. The person who wanted him was in the
kitchen, and in the first moments, by the imperfect fire and
candle-light, Tom had not even an indefinite sense of any
acquaintance with the rather broad-set but active figure,
perhaps two years older than himself, that looked at him
with a pair of blue eyes set in a disc of freckles, and pulled
some curly red locks with a strong intention of respect. A
low-crowned oilskin-covered hat, and a certain shiny deposit
of dirt on the rest of the costume, as of tablets prepared for
writing upon, suggested a calling that had to do with boats;
but this did not help Tom's memory.

'Sarvant, Mister Tom,' said he of the red locks, with a
smile which seemed to break through a self-imposed air of
melancholy. 'You don't know me again, I doubt,' he went

on, as Tom continued to look at him inquiringly; 'but I'd like to talk to you by yourself a bit, please.'

'There's a fire in the parlour, Master Tom,' said Kezia, who objected to leaving the kitchen in the crisis of toasting.

'Come this way, then,' said Tom, wondering if this young fellow belonged to Guest & Co.'s Wharf; for his imagination ran continually towards that particular spot, and uncle Deane might any time be sending for him to say that there was a situation at liberty.

The bright fire in the parlour was the only light that showed the few chairs, the bureau, the carpetless floor, and the one table—no, not the *one* table: there was a second table, in a corner, with a large Bible and a few other books upon it. It was this new strange bareness that Tom felt first, before he thought of looking again at the face which was also lit up by the fire, and which stole a half-shy, questioning glance at him as the entirely strange voice said—

'Why! you don't remember Bob, then, as you gen the pocket-knife to, Tom?'

The rough-handled pocket-knife was taken out in the same moment, and the largest blade opened by way of irresistible demonstration.

'What! Bob Jakin?' said Tom—not with any cordial delight, for he felt a little ashamed of that early intimacy symbolized by the pocket-knife, and was not at all sure that Bob's motives for recalling it were entirely admirable.

'Ay, ay, Bob Jakin—if Jakin it must be, 'cause there's so many Bobs—as you went arter the squerrils with, that day as I plumped right down from the bough, and bruised my shins a good un—but I got the squerril tight for all that, an' a scratter it was. An' this littlish blade's broke, you see, but I wouldn't hev a new un put in, 'cause they might be cheatin' me an' givin' me another knife istid, for there isn't such a blade i' the country—it's got used to my hand, like. An' there was niver nobody else gen me nothin' but what I got by my own sharpness, only you, Mr. Tom; if it wasn't Bill Fawks as gen me the terrier pup istid o' drowndin' it, an' I had to jaw him a good 'un afore he'd give it me.'

Bob spoke with a sharp and rather treble volubility, and got through his long speech with surprising despatch, giving the blade of his knife an affectionate rub on his sleeve when he had finished.

'Well, Bob,' said Tom, with a slight air of patronage, the foregoing reminiscences having disposed him to be as friendly as was becoming, though there was no part of his acquaintance with Bob that he remembered better than the cause of their parting quarrel; 'is there anything I can do for you?'

'Why, no, Mr. Tom,' answered Bob, shutting up his knife with a click and returning it to his pocket, where he seemed to be feeling for something else. 'I shouldn't ha' come back upon you now ye're i' trouble, an' folks say as the master, as I used to frighten the birds for, an' he flogged me a bit for fun when he catched me eatin' the turnip, as they say he'll niver lift up his yead no more—I shouldn't ha' come now to ax you to gi' me another knife, 'cause you gen me one afore. If a chap gives me one black eye, that's enough for me: I shan't ax him for another afore I sarve him out; an' a good turn's worth as much as a bad un, anyhow. I shall niver grow down'ards again, Mr. Tom, an' you war the little chap as I liked the best when *I* war a little chap, for all you leathered me, and wouldn't look at me again. There's Dick Brumby, there, I could leather him as much as I'd a mind; but lors! you get tired o' leatherin' a chap when you can niver make him see what you want him to shy at. I'n seen chaps as 'ud stand starin' at a bough till their eyes shot out, afore they'd see as a bird's tail warn't a leaf. It's poor work goin' wi' such raff— but you war allays a rare 'un at shying, Mr. Tom, an' I could trusten to you for droppin' down wi' your stick in the nick o' time at a runnin' rat, or a stoat, or that, when I war a-beatin' the bushes.'

Bob had drawn out a dirty canvas bag, and would perhaps not have paused just then if Maggie had not entered the room and darted a look of surprise and curiosity at him, whereupon he pulled his red locks again with due respect. But the next moment the sense of the altered room came upon Maggie with a force that overpowered the thought of Bob's presence. Her eyes had immediately glanced from him to the place where the bookcase had hung; there was nothing now but the oblong unfaded space on the wall, and below it the small table with the Bible and a few other books.

'O Tom,' she burst out, clasping her hands, 'where are the books? I thought my uncle Glegg said he would buy them—didn't he?—are those all they've left us?'

'I suppose so,' said Tom, with a sort of desperate indifference. 'Why should they buy many books when they bought so little furniture?'

'O but, Tom,' said Maggie, her eyes filling with tears, as she rushed up to the table to see what books had been rescued. 'Our dear old Pilgrim's Progress that you coloured with your little paints; and that picture of Pilgrim with a mantle on, looking just like a turtle—O dear!' Maggie went on, half sobbing as she turned over the few books. 'I thought we should never part with that while we lived—everything is going away from us—the end of our lives will have nothing in it like the beginning!'

Maggie turned away from the table and threw herself into a chair, with the big tears ready to roll down her cheeks—quite blinded to the presence of Bob, who was looking at her with the pursuant gaze of an intelligent dumb animal, with perceptions more perfect than his comprehension.

'Well, Bob,' said Tom, feeling that the subject of the books was unseasonable, 'I suppose you just came to see me because we're in trouble? That was very good-natured of you.'

'I'll tell you how it is, Master Tom,' said Bob, beginning to untwist his canvas bag. 'You see, I'n been with a barge this two 'ear—that's how I'n been gettin' my livin'—if it wasn't when I was tentin' the furnace, between whiles, at Torry's mill. But a fortni't ago I'd a rare bit o' luck—I allays thought I was a lucky chap, for I never set a trap but what I catched something; but this wasn't a trap, it was a fire i' Torry's mill, an' I doused it, else it 'ud ha' set th' oil alight, an' the genelman gen me ten suvreigns—he gen me 'em himself last week. An' he said first, I was a sperrited chap—but I knowed that afore—but then he outs wi' the ten suvreigns, an' that war summat new. Here they are—all but one!' Here Bob emptied the canvas bag on the table. 'An' when I'd got 'em, my head was all of a boil like a kettle o' broth, thinkin' what sort o' life I should take to—for there war a many trades I'd thought on; for as for the barge, I'm clean tired out wi't, for it pulls the days out till they're as long as pigs' chitterlings. An' I thought first I'd ha' ferrets an' dogs, an' be a rat-catcher; an' then I thought as I should like a bigger way o' life, as I didn't know so well; for I'n seen to the bottom o' rat-catching; an' I thought, an' thought, till at last I settled I'd be a packman, for they're knowin' fellers, the packmen are—an' I'd carry the lightest things I could i' my pack—an' there'd be a use for a feller's tongue, as is no use neither wi' rats nor barges. An' I should go about the country far an' wide, an' come round the women wi' my tongue, an' get my dinner hot at the public—lors! it 'ud be a lovely life!'

Bob paused, and then said, with defiant decision, as if resolutely turning his back on that paradisaic picture:

'But I don't mind about it—not a chip! An' I'n changed one o' the suvreigns to buy my mother a goose for dinner, an' I'n bought a blue plush wescoat, an' a sealskin cap—for if I meant to be a packman, I'd do it respectable. But I don't mind about it—not a chip! My yead isn't a turnip, an' I shall p'r'aps have a chance o' dousing another fire afore long. I'm a lucky chap. So I'll thank you to take the nine suvreigns, Mr. Tom, and set yoursen up with 'em somehow—if it's true as the master's broke. They mayn't go fur enough—but they'll help.'

Tom was touched keenly enough to forget his pride and suspicion.

'You're a very kind fellow, Bob,' he said, colouring, with that little diffident tremor in his voice, which gave a certain charm even to Tom's pride and severity, 'and I shan't forget you again, though I didn't know you this evening. But I can't take the nine sovereigns: I should be taking your little fortune from you, and they wouldn't do me much good either.'

'Wouldn't they, Mr. Tom?' said Bob regretfully. 'Now don't say so 'cause you think I want 'em. I aren't a poor chap. My mother gets a good penn'orth wi' picking feathers an' things; an' if she eats nothin' but bread-an'-water, it runs to fat. An' I'm such a lucky chap: an' I doubt you aren't quite so lucky, Mr. Tom—th' old master isn't, anyhow—an' so you might take a slice o' my luck, an' no harm done. Lors! I found a leg o' pork i' the river one day: it had tumbled out o' one o' them round-sterned Dutchmen, I'll be bound. Come, think better on it, Mr. Tom, for old 'quintance sake—else I shall think you bear me a grudge.'

Bob pushed the sovereigns forward, but before Tom could speak, Maggie, clasping her hands, and looking penitently at Bob, said:

'O, I'm so sorry, Bob—I never thought you were so good. Why, I think you're the kindest person in the world!'

Bob had not been aware of the injurious opinion for which Maggie was performing an inward act of penitence, but he smiled with pleasure at this handsome eulogy— especially from a young lass, who, as he informed his mother that evening, had 'such uncommon eyes, they looked somehow as they made him feel nohow.'

'No, indeed, Bob, I can't take them,' said Tom; 'but don't think I feel your kindness less because I say no. I don't want to take anything from anybody, but to work my own way. And those sovereigns wouldn't help me much— they wouldn't, really—if I were to take them. Let me shake hands with you instead.'

Tom put out his pink palm, and Bob was not slow to place his hard, grimy hand within it.

'Let me put the sovereigns in the bag again,' said Maggie; 'and you'll come and see us when you've bought your pack, Bob.'

'It's like as if I'd come out o' make-believe, o' purpose to show 'em you,' said Bob, with an air of discontent, as Maggie gave him the bag again, 'a-taking 'em back i' this way. I *am* a bit of a Do, you know; but it isn't that sort o' Do; it's on'y when a feller's a big rogue, or a big flat, I like to let him in a bit, that's all.'

'Now, don't you be up to any tricks, Bob,' said Tom, 'else you'll get transported some day.'

'No, no; not me, Mr. Tom,' said Bob, with an air of cheerful confidence. 'There's no law again' flea-bites. If I wasn't to take a fool in now and then, he'd niver get any wiser. But, lors! hev a suvreign to buy you and Miss summat, on'y for a token—just to match my pocket-knife.'

While Bob was speaking he laid down the sovereign, and resolutely twisted up his bag again. Tom pushed back the gold, and said, 'No, indeed, Bob; thank you heartily; but I can't take it.' And Maggie, taking it between her fingers, held it up to Bob, and said, more persuasively:

'Not now—but perhaps another time. If ever Tom or my father wants help that you can give, we'll let you know —won't we, Tom? That's what you would like—to have us always depend on you as a friend that we can go to— isn't it, Bob?'

'Yes, Miss, and thank you,' said Bob, reluctantly taking the money; 'that's what I'd like—anything as you like. An' I wish you good-bye, Miss, and good-luck, Mr. Tom, and thank you for shaking hands wi' me, *though* you wouldn't take the money.'

Kezia's entrance, with very black looks, to inquire if she shouldn't bring in the tea now, or whether the toast was to get hardened to a brick, was a seasonable check on Bob's flux of words, and hastened his parting bow.

VII

HOW A HEN TAKES TO STRATAGEM

THE days passed, and Mr. Tulliver showed, at least to the eyes of the medical man, stronger and stronger symptoms of a gradual return to his normal condition: the paralytic obstruction was, little by little, losing its tenacity, and the mind was rising from under it with fitful struggles, like a living creature making its way from under a great snowdrift, that slides and slides again, and shuts up the newly-made opening.

Time would have seemed to creep to the watchers by the bed, if it had only been measured by the doubtful distant hope which kept count of the moments within the chamber; but it was measured for them by a fast-approaching dread which made the nights come too quickly. While Mr. Tulliver was slowly becoming himself again, his lot was hastening towards its moment of most palpable change. The taxing-masters had done their work like any respectable gunsmith conscientiously preparing the musket, that, duly pointed by a brave arm, will spoil a life or two. Allocaturs, filing of bills in Chancery, decrees of sale, are legal chain-shot or bomb-shells that can never hit a solitary mark, but must fall with widespread shattering. So deeply inherent is it in this life of ours that men have to suffer for each other's sins, so inevitably diffusive is human suffering, that even justice makes its victims, and we can conceive no retribution that does not spread beyond its mark in pulsations of unmerited pain.

By the beginning of the second week in January the bills were out advertising the sale, under a decree of Chancery, of Mr. Tulliver's farming and other stock, to be followed by a sale of the mill and land, held in the proper after-dinner hour at the Golden Lion. The miller himself, un-aware of the lapse of time, fancied himself still in that first stage of his misfortunes when expedients might be thought of; and often in his conscious hours talked in a feeble, dis-jointed manner, of plans he would carry out when he 'got well.' The wife and children were not without hope of an issue that would at least save Mr. Tulliver from leaving the old spot, and seeking an entirely strange life. For uncle Deane had been induced to interest himself in this stage of the business. It would not, he acknowledged, be a bad speculation for Guest & Co. to buy Dorlcote Mill, and carry on the business, which was a good one, and might be in-creased by the addition of steam-power; in which case Tulliver might be retained as manager. Still Mr. Deane would say nothing decided about the matter: the fact that

Wakem held the mortgage on the land might put it into his head to bid for the whole estate, and further, to outbid the cautious firm of Guest & Co., who did not carry on business on sentimental grounds. Mr. Deane was obliged to tell Mrs. Tulliver something to that effect, when he rode over to the mill to inspect the books in company with Mrs. Glegg: for she had observed that 'if Guest & Co. would only think about it, Mr. Tulliver's father and grandfather had been carrying on Dorlcote Mill long before the oil-mill of that firm had been so much as thought of.' Mr. Deane, in reply, doubted whether that was precisely the relation between the two mills which would determine their value as investments. As for uncle Glegg, the thing lay quite beyond his imagination; the good-natured man felt sincere pity for the Tulliver family, but his money was all locked up in excellent mortgages, and he could run no risk; that would be unfair to his own relatives; but he had made up his mind that Tulliver should have some new flannel waistcoats which he had himself renounced in favour of a more elastic commodity, and that he would buy Mrs. Tulliver a pound of tea now and then; it would be a journey which his benevolence delighted in beforehand, to carry the tea, and see her pleasure on being assured it was the best black.

Still, it was clear that Mr. Deane was kindly disposed towards the Tullivers. One day he had brought Lucy, who was come home for the Christmas holidays, and the little blond angel-head had pressed itself against Maggie's darker cheek with many kisses and some tears. These fair slim daughters keep up a tender spot in the heart of many a respectable partner in a respectable firm, and perhaps Lucy's anxious pitying questions about her poor cousins helped to make uncle Deane more prompt in finding Tom a temporary place in the warehouse, and in putting him in the way of getting evening lessons in book-keeping and calculation.

That might have cheered the lad and fed his hopes a little, if there had not come at the same time the much-dreaded blow of finding that his father must be a bankrupt, after all; at least, the creditors must be asked to take less than their due, which to Tom's untechnical mind was the same thing as bankruptcy. His father must not only be said to have 'lost his property,' but to have 'failed'—the word that carried the worst obloquy to Tom's mind. For when the defendant's claim for costs had been satisfied, there would remain the friendly bill of Mr. Gore, and the deficiency at the bank, as well as the other debts, which would make the assets shrink into unequivocal disproportion: 'not more than ten or twelve shillings in the pound,' predicted Mr. Deane, in a decided tone, tightening his lips; and the words fell on Tom like a scalding liquid, leaving a continual smart.

He was sadly in want of something to keep up his spirits a little in the unpleasant newness of his position—suddenly transported from the easy carpeted ennui of study-hours at Mr. Stelling's, and the busy idleness of castle-building in a 'last-half' at school, to the companionship of sacks and hides, and bawling men thundering down heavy weights at his elbow. The first step towards getting on in the world was a chill, dusty, noisy affair, and implied going without one's tea in order to stay in St. Ogg's and have an evening lesson from a one-armed elderly clerk, in a room smelling strongly of bad tobacco. Tom's young pink-and-white face had its colours very much deadened by the time he took off his hat at home, and sat down with keen hunger to his supper. No wonder he was a little cross if his mother or Maggie spoke to him.

But all this while Mrs. Tulliver was brooding over a scheme by which she, and no one else, would avert the result most to be dreaded, and prevent Wakem from entertaining the purpose of bidding for the mill. Imagine a truly respectable and amiable hen, by some portentous anomaly, taking to reflection and inventing combinations by which she might prevail on Hodge not to wring her neck, or send her and her chicks to market: the result could hardly be other than much cackling and fluttering. Mrs. Tulliver, seeing that everything had gone wrong, had begun to think that she had been too passive in life; and that, if she had applied her mind to business, and taken a strong resolution now and

then, it would have been all the better for her and her
family. Nobody, it appeared, had thought of going to
speak to Wakem on this business of the mill; and yet, Mrs.
Tulliver reflected, it would have been quite the shortest
method of securing the right end. It would have been of no
use, to be sure, for Mr. Tulliver to go—even if he had been
able and willing—for he had been 'going to law against
Wakem' and abusing him for the last ten years; Wakem
was always likely to have a spite against him. And now
that Mrs. Tulliver had come to the conclusion that her
husband was very much in the wrong to bring her into
this trouble, she was inclined to think that his opinion of
Wakem was wrong too. To be sure, Wakem had 'put the
bailies in the house, and sold them up;' but she supposed
he did that to please the man that lent Mr. Tulliver the
money, for a lawyer had more folks to please than one, and
he wasn't likely to put Mr. Tulliver, who had gone to law
with him, above everybody else in the world. The attorney
might be a very reasonable man—why not? He had
married a Miss Clint, and at the time Mrs. Tulliver had
heard of that marriage, the summer when she wore her blue
satin spencer, and had not yet any thoughts of Mr. Tulliver,
she knew no harm of Wakem. And certainly towards herself—whom he knew to have been a Miss Dodson—it was
out of all possibility that he could entertain anything but
goodwill, when it was once brought home to his observation
that she, for her part, had never wanted to go to law, and
indeed was at present disposed to take Mr. Wakem's view
of all subjects rather than her husband's. In fact, if that
attorney saw a respectable matron like herself disposed 'to
give him good words,' why shouldn't he listen to her repre-
sentations? For she would put the matter clearly before
him, which had never been done yet. And he would never
go and bid for the mill on purpose to spite her, an innocent
woman, who thought it likely enough that she had danced
with him in their youth at Squire Darleigh's, for at those
big dances she had often and often danced with young men
whose names she had forgotten.

Mrs. Tulliver hid these reasonings in her own bosom; for

when she had thrown out a hint to Mr. Deane and Mr. Glegg, that she wouldn't mind going to speak to Wakem herself, they had said, 'No, no, no,' and 'Pooh, pooh,' and 'Let Wakem alone,' in the tone of men who were not likely to give a candid attention to a more definite exposition of her project; still less dared she mention the plan to Tom and Maggie, for 'the children were always so against everything their mother said;' and Tom, she observed, was almost as much set against Wakem as his father was. But this unusual concentration of thought naturally gave Mrs. Tulliver an unusual power of device and determination; and a day or two before the sale, to be held at the Golden Lion, when there was no longer any time to be lost, she carried out her plan by a stratagem. There were pickles in question—a large stock of pickles and ketchup which Mrs. Tulliver possessed, and which Mr. Hyndmarsh the grocer would certainly purchase if she could transact the business in a personal interview, so she would walk with Tom to St. Ogg's that morning: and when Tom urged that she might let the pickles be, at present—he didn't like her to go about just yet—she appeared so hurt at this conduct in her son, contradicting her about pickles which she had made after the family receipts inherited from his own grandmother, who had died when his mother was a little girl, that he gave way, and they walked together until she turned towards Danish Street, where Mr. Hyndmarsh retailed his grocery, not far from the offices of Mr. Wakem.

That gentleman was not yet come to his office: would Mrs. Tulliver sit down by the fire in his private room and wait for him? She had not long to wait before the punctual attorney entered, knitting his brow with an examining glance at the stout blond woman who rose, curtsying deferentially:—a tallish man, with an aquiline nose and abundant iron-grey hair. You have never seen Mr. Wakem before, and are possibly wondering whether he was really as eminent a rascal, and as crafty, bitter an enemy of honest humanity in general, and of Mr. Tulliver in particular, as he is represented to be in that eidolon or portrait of him which we have seen to exist in the miller's mind.

It is clear that the irascible miller was a man to interpret any chance-shot that grazed him as an attempt on his own life, and was liable to entanglements in this puzzling world, which, due consideration had to his own infallibility, required the hypothesis of a very active diabolical agency to explain them. It is still possible to believe that the attorney was not more guilty towards him than an ingenious machine, which performs its work with much regularity, is guilty towards the rash man who, venturing too near it, is caught up by some fly-wheel or other, and suddenly converted into unexpected mince-meat.

But it is really impossible to decide this question by a glance at his person: the lines and lights of the human countenance are like other symbols—not always easy to read without a key. On an *a priori* view of Wakem's aquiline nose, which offended Mr. Tulliver, there was not more rascality than in the shape of his stiff shirt-collar, though this too, along with his nose, might have become fraught with damnatory meaning when once the rascality was ascertained.

'Mrs. Tulliver, I think?' said Mr. Wakem.

'Yes, sir. Miss Elizabeth Dodson as was.'

'Pray be seated. You have some business with me?'

'Well, sir, yes,' said Mrs. Tulliver, beginning to feel alarmed at her own courage, now she was really in presence of the formidable man, and reflecting that she had not settled with herself how she should begin. Mr. Wakem felt in his waistcoat pockets, and looked at her in silence.

'I hope, sir,' she began at last—'I hope, sir, you're not a-thinkin' as *I* bear you any ill-will because o' my husband's losing his lawsuit, and the bailies being put in, and the linen being sold—O dear! . . . for I wasn't brought up in that way. I'm sure you remember my father sir, for he was close friends with Squire Darleigh, and we allays went to the dances there—the Miss Dodsons—nobody could be more looked on—and justly, for there was four of us, and you're quite aware as Mrs. Glegg and Mrs. Deane are my sisters. And as for going to law, and losing money, and having sales before you're dead, I never saw anything o' that before

I was married, nor for a long while after. And I'm not to be answerable for my bad luck i' marrying out o' my own family into one where the goings-on was different. And as for being drawn in t' abuse you as other folks abuse you, sir, *that* I niver was, and nobody can say it of me.'

Mrs. Tulliver shook her head a little, and looked at the hem of her pocket-handkerchief.

'I've no doubt of what you say, Mrs. Tulliver,' said Mr. Wakem, with cold politeness. 'But you have some question to ask me?'

'Well, sir, yes. But that's what I've said to myself—I've said you'd have some nat'ral feeling; and as for my husband, as hasn't been himself for this two months, I'm not a-defending him, in no way, for being so hot about th' erigation—not but what there's worse men, for he never wronged nobody of a shilling nor a penny, not willingly—and as for his fieriness and lawing, what could I do? And him struck as if it was with death when he got the letter as said you'd the hold upo' the land. But I can't believe but what you'll behave as a gentleman.'

'What does all this mean, Mrs. Tulliver?' said Mr. Wakem rather sharply. 'What do you want to ask me?'

'Why, sir, if you'll be so good,' said Mrs. Tulliver, starting a little, and speaking more hurriedly, 'if you'll be so good not to buy the mill an' the land—the land wouldn't so much matter, only my husband 'ull be like mad at your having it.'

Something like a new thought flashed across Mr. Wakem's face as he said, 'Who told you I meant to buy it?'

'Why, sir, it's none o' my inventing; and I should never ha' thought of it, for my husband, as ought to know about the law, he allays used to say as lawyers had never no call to buy anything—either lands or houses—for they allays got 'em into their hands other ways. An' I should think that 'ud be the way with you, sir; and I niver said as you'd be the man to do contrairy to that.'

'Ah, well, who was it that *did* say so?' said Wakem, opening his desk, and moving things about, with the accompaniment of an almost inaudible whistle.

'Why, sir, it was Mr. Glegg and Mr. Deane, as have all

the management: and Mr. Deane thinks as Guest & Co. 'ud buy the mill and let Mr. Tulliver work it for 'em, if you didn't bid for it and raise the price. And it 'ud be such a thing for my husband to stay where he is, if he could get his living: for it was his father's before him, the mill was, and his grandfather built it, though I wasn't fond o' the noise of it, when first I was married, for there was no mills in our family—not the Dodsons'—and if I'd known as the mills had so much to do with the law, it wouldn't have been me as 'ud have been the first Dodson to marry one; but I went into it blindfold, that I did, erigation and everything.'

'What! Guest & Co. will keep the mill in their own hands, I suppose, and pay your husband wages?'

'O dear, sir, it's hard to think of,' said poor Mrs. Tulliver, a little tear making its way, 'as my husband should take wage. But it 'ud look more like what used to be, to stay at the mill than to go anywhere else: and if you'll only think— if you was to bid for the mill and buy it, my husband might be struck worse than he was before, and niver get better again as he's getting now.'

'Well, but if I bought the mill, and allowed your husband to act as my manager in the same way, how then?' said Mr. Wakem.

'O sir, I doubt he could niver be got to do it, not if the very mill stood still to beg and pray of him. For your name's like poison to him, it's so as never was; and he looks upon it as you've been the ruin of him all along, ever since you set the law on him about the road through the meadow—that's eight year ago, and he's been going on ever since—as I've allays told him he was wrong. . . .'

'He's a pig-headed, foul-mouthed fool!' burst out Mr. Wakem, forgetting himself.

'O dear, sir!' said Mrs. Tulliver, frightened at a result so different from the one she had fixed her mind on; 'I wouldn't wish to contradict you, but it's like enough he's changed his mind with this illness—he's forgot a many things he used to talk about. And you wouldn't like to have a corpse on your mind, if he was to die; and they *do* say as it's allays unlucky when Dorlcote Mill changes hands, and the water might all run away, and *then* . . . not as I'm wishing you any ill-luck, sir, for I forgot to tell you as I remember your wedding as if it was yesterday—Mrs. Wakem was a Miss Clint, I know *that*—and my boy, as there isn't a nicer, handsomer, straighter boy nowhere, went to school with your son. . . .'

Mr. Wakem rose, opened the door, and called to one of his clerks.

'You must excuse me for interrupting you, Mrs. Tulliver; I have business that must be attended to; and I think there is nothing more necessary to be said.'

'But if you *would* bear it in mind, sir,' said Mrs. Tulliver, rising, 'and not run against me and my children; and I'm not denying Mr. Tulliver's been in the wrong, but he's been punished enough, and there's worse men, for it's been giving to other folks has been his fault. He's done nobody any harm but himself and his family—the more's the pity —and I go and look at the bare shelves every day, and think where all my things used to stand.'

'Yes, yes, I'll bear it in mind,' said Mr. Wakem hastily, looking towards the open door.

'And if you'd please not to say as I've been to speak to you, for my son 'ud be very angry with me for demeaning myself, I know he would, and I've trouble enough without being scolded by my children.'

Poor Mrs. Tulliver's voice trembled a little, and she could make no answer to the attorney's 'good morning,' but curt-sied and walked out in silence.

'Which day is it that Dorlcote Mill is to be sold? Where's the bill?' said Mr. Wakem to his clerk when they were alone.

'Next Friday is the day: Friday, at six o'clock.'

'Oh! just run to Winship's the auctioneer, and see if he's at home. I have some business for him: ask him to come up.'

Although, when Mr. Wakem entered his office that morning, he had had no intention of purchasing Dorlcote Mill, his mind was already made up: Mrs. Tulliver had suggested to him several determining motives, and his mental glance was very rapid: he was one of those men who can be prompt without being rash, because their motives run in fixed tracks, and they have no need to reconcile conflicting aims.

To suppose that Wakem had the same sort of inveterate hatred towards Tulliver, that Tulliver had towards him, would be like supposing that a pike and a roach can look at each other from a similar point of view. The roach necessarily abhors the mode in which the pike gets his living, and the pike is likely to think nothing further even of the most indignant roach than that he is excellent good eating; it could only be when the roach choked him that the pike could entertain a strong personal animosity. If Mr. Tulliver had ever seriously injured or thwarted the attorney, Wakem would not have refused him the distinction of being a special object of his vindictiveness. But when Mr. Tulliver called Wakem a rascal at the market dinner-table, the attorney's clients were not a whit inclined to withdraw their business from him; and if, when Wakem himself happened to be present, some jocose cattle-feeder, stimulated by opportunity and brandy, made a thrust at him by alluding to old ladies' wills, he maintained perfect *sang froid*, and knew quite well that the majority of substantial men then present were perfectly contented with the fact that 'Wakem was Wakem;' that is to say, a man who always knew the stepping-stones that would carry him through very muddy bits of practice. A man who had made a large fortune, had a handsome house among the trees at Tofton, and decidedly the finest stock of port-wine in the neighbourhood of St. Ogg's, was likely to feel himself on a level with public opinion. And I am not sure that even honest Mr. Tulliver himself, with his general view of law as a cockpit, might not, under opposite circumstances, have seen a fine appropriateness in the truth that 'Wakem was Wakem;' since I have understood from persons versed in history, that mankind is not disposed to look narrowly into the conduct of great victors when their victory is on the right side. Tulliver, then, could be no obstruction to Wakem; on the contrary, he was a poor devil whom the lawyer had defeated several times—a hot-tempered fellow, who would always give you a handle against him. Wakem's conscience was not uneasy because he had used a few tricks against the miller: why should he hate that unsuccessful plaintiff—that pitiable, furious bull entangled in the meshes of a net?

Still, among the various excesses to which human nature is subject, moralists have never numbered that of being too fond of the people who openly revile us. The successful Yellow candidate for the borough of Old Topping, perhaps, feels no pursuant meditative hatred toward the Blue editor who consoles his subscribers with vituperative rhetoric against Yellow men who sell their country, and are the demons of private life; but he might not be sorry, if law and opportunity favoured, to kick that Blue editor to a deeper shade of his favourite colour. Prosperous men take a little vengeance now and then, as they take a diversion, when it comes easily in their way, and is no hindrance to business; and such small unimpassioned revenges have an enormous effect in life, running through all degrees of pleasant infliction, blocking the fit men out of places, and blackening characters in unpremeditated talk. Still more, to see people who have been only insignificantly offensive to us, reduced in life and humiliated without any special efforts of ours, is apt to have a soothing, flattering influence: Providence, or some other prince of this world, it appears, has undertaken the task of retribution for us; and really, by an agreeable constitution of things, our enemies some-how *don't* prosper.

Wakem was not without this parenthetic vindictiveness towards the uncomplimentary miller; and now Mrs. Tulliver had put the notion into his head, it presented itself to him as a pleasure to do the very thing that would cause Mr. Tulliver the most deadly mortification,—and a pleasure of a complex kind, not made up of crude malice, but mingling with it the relish of self-approbation. To see an enemy humiliated gives a certain contentment, but this is jejune compared with the highly blent satisfaction of seeing him humiliated by your benevolent action or concession on his behalf. That is a sort of revenge which falls into the scale of virtue, and Wakem was not without an intention of keeping that scale respectably filled. He had once had the pleasure of putting an old enemy of his into one of the St. Ogg's alms-houses, to the rebuilding of which he had given a large subscription; and here was an opportunity of providing for another by making him his own servant. Such things give a completeness to prosperity, and contribute elements of agreeable consciousness that are not dreamed of by that short-sighted, over-heated vindictiveness which goes out of its way to wreak itself in direct injury. And Tulliver, with his rough tongue filed by a sense of obligation, would make a better servant than any chance-fellow who was cap-in-hand for a situation. Tulliver was known to be a man of proud honesty, and Wakem was too acute not to believe in the existence of honesty. He was given to observing individuals, not to judging of them according to maxims, and no one knew better than he that all men were not like himself. Besides, he intended to overlook the whole business of land and mill pretty closely: he was fond of these practical rural matters. But there were good reasons for purchasing Dorlcote Mill, quite apart from any benevolent vengeance on the miller. It was really a capital investment; besides, Guest & Co. were going to bid for it. Mr. Guest and Mr. Wakem were on friendly dining terms, and the attorney liked to predominate over a ship-owner and mill-owner who was a little too loud in the town affairs as well as in his table-talk. For Wakem was not a mere man of business: he was considered a pleasant fellow in the upper circles of St. Ogg's—chatted amusingly over his port-wine, did a little amateur farming, and had certainly been an excellent husband and father: at church, when he went there, he sat under the handsomest of mural monuments erected to the memory of his wife. Most men would have married again under his circumstances, but he was said to be more tender to his deformed son than most men were to their best-shapen offspring. Not that Mr. Wakem had not other sons besides Philip; but towards them he held only a chiaroscuro parentage, and provided for them in a grade of

ife duly beneath his own. In this fact, indeed, there lay
the clenching motive to the purchase of Dorlcote Mill. While
Mrs. Tulliver was talking, it had occurred to the rapid-
minded lawyer, among all the other circumstances of the
case, that this purchase would, in a few years to come,
furnish a highly suitable position for a certain favourite lad
whom he meant to bring on in the world.

These were the mental conditions on which Mrs. Tulliver
had undertaken to act persuasively, and had failed: a fact
which may receive some illustration from the remark of a
great philosopher, that fly-fishers fail in preparing their bait
so as to make it alluring in the right quarter, for want of a
due acquaintance with the subjectivity of fishes.

VIII

DAYLIGHT ON THE WRECK

It was a clear frosty January day on which Mr. Tulliver
first came down-stairs: the bright sun on the chestnut
boughs and the roofs opposite his window had made him
impatiently declare that he would be caged up no longer:
he thought everywhere would be more cheery under this
sunshine than his bedroom; for he knew nothing of the
bareness below, which made the flood of sunshine importunate, as if it had an unfeeling pleasure in showing the
empty places, and the marks where well-known objects
once had been. The impression on his mind that it was but
yesterday when he received the letter from Mr. Gore was so
continually implied in his talk, and the attempts to convey
to him the idea that many weeks had passed and much had
happened since then, had been so soon swept away by recurrent forgetfulness, that even Mr. Turnbull had begun to
despair of preparing him to meet the facts by previous
knowledge. The full sense of the present could only be im-
parted gradually by new experience—not by mere words,
which must remain weaker than the impressions left by
the *old* experience. This resolution to come down-stairs
was heard with trembling by the wife and children. Mrs.

Tulliver said Tom must not go to St. Ogg's at the usual hour —he must wait and see his father down-stairs: and Tom complied, though with an intense inward shrinking from the painful scene. The hearts of all three had been more deeply dejected than ever during the last few days. For Guest & Co. had not bought the mill: both mill and land had been knocked down to Wakem, who had been over the premises, and had laid before Mr. Deane and Mr. Glegg, in Mrs. Tulliver's presence, his willingness to employ Mr. Tulliver, in case of his recovery, as a manager of the business. This proposition had occasioned much family debating. Uncles and aunts were almost unanimously of opinion that such an offer ought not to be rejected when there was nothing in the way but a feeling in Mr. Tulliver's mind, which, as neither aunts nor uncles shared it, was regarded as entirely unreasonable and childish—indeed, as a transferring towards Wakem of that indignation and hatred which Mr. Tulliver ought properly to have directed against himself for his general quarrelsomeness, and his special exhibition of it in going to law. Here was an opportunity for Mr. Tulliver to provide for his wife and daughter without any assistance from his wife's relations, and without that too evident descent into pauperism which makes it annoying to respectable people to meet the degraded member of the family by the wayside. Mr. Tulliver, Mrs. Glegg considered, must be made to feel, when he came to his right mind, that he could never humble himself enough; for *that* had come which she had always foreseen would come of his insolence in time past 'to them as were the best friends he'd got to look to.' Mr. Glegg and Mr. Deane were less stern in their views, but they both of them thought Tulliver had done enough harm by his hot-tempered crotchets, and ought to put them out of the question when a livelihood was offered him: Wakem showed a right feeling about the matter—*he* had no grudge against Tulliver. Tom had protested against entertaining the proposition: he shouldn't like his father to be under Wakem: he thought it would look mean-spirited; but his mother's main distress was the utter impossibility of ever 'turning Mr. Tulliver

round about Wakem,' or getting him to hear reason—no,
they would all have to go and live in a pigsty on purpose to
spite Wakem, who spoke 'so as nobody could be fairer.'
Indeed, Mrs. Tulliver's mind was reduced to such confusion
by living in this strange medium of unaccountable sorrow,
against which she continually appealed by asking, 'O dear,
what *have* I done to deserve worse than other women?' that
Maggie began to suspect her poor mother's wits were quite
going.

'Tom,' she said, when they were out of their father's
room together, 'we *must* try to make father understand a
little of what has happened before he goes down-stairs. But
we must get my mother away. She will say something that
will do harm. Ask Kezia to fetch her down, and keep her
engaged with something in the kitchen.'

Kezia was equal to the task. Having declared her intention of staying till the master could get about again,
'wage or no wage,' she had found a certain recompense in
keeping a strong hand over her mistress, scolding her for
'moithering' herself, and going about all day without
changing her cap, and looking as if she was 'mushed.'
Altogether, this time of trouble was rather a Saturnalian
time to Kezia: she could scold her betters with unreproved
freedom. On this particular occasion there were drying
clothes to be fetched in: she wished to know if one pair of
hands could do everything in-doors and out, and observed
that *she* should have thought it would be good for Mrs.
Tulliver to put on her bonnet, and get a breath of fresh air
by doing that needful piece of work. Poor Mrs. Tulliver
went submissively down-stairs: to be ordered about by
a servant was the last remnant of her household dignities—
she would soon have no servant to scold her.

Mr. Tulliver was resting in his chair a little after the
fatigue of dressing, and Maggie and Tom were seated near
him, when Luke entered to ask if he should help master
down-stairs.

'Ay, ay, Luke, stop a bit, sit down,' said Mr. Tulliver,
pointing his stick towards a chair, and looking at him with
that pursuant gaze which convalescent persons often have

for those who have tended them, reminding one of an infant
gazing about after its nurse. For Luke had been a constant
night-watcher by his master's bed.

'How's the water now, eh, Luke?' said Mr. Tulliver.
'Dix hasn't been choking you up again, eh?'

'No, sir, it's all right.'

'Ay, I thought not: he won't be in a hurry at that again,
now Riley's been to settle him. That was what I said to
Riley yesterday . . . I said. . . .'

Mr. Tulliver leaned forward, resting his elbows on the
arm-chair, and looking on the ground as if in search of
something—striving after vanishing images like a man
struggling against a doze. Maggie looked at Tom in mute
distress—their father's mind was so far off the present,
which would by-and-by thrust itself on his wandering
consciousness! Tom was almost ready to rush away, with
that impatience of painful emotion which makes one
of the differences between youth and maiden, man and
woman.

'Father,' said Maggie, laying her hand on his, 'don't you
remember that Mr. Riley is dead?'

'Dead?' said Mr. Tulliver sharply, looking in her face
with a strange, examining glance.

'Yes, he died of apoplexy nearly a year ago; I remember
hearing you say you had to pay money for him; and he left
his daughters badly off—one of them is under-teacher at
Miss Firniss's, where I've been to school, you know. . . .'

'Ah?' said her father doubtfully, still looking in her face.
But as soon as Tom began to speak he turned to look at
him with the same inquiring glances, as if he were rather
surprised at the presence of these two young people. Whenever his mind was wandering in the far past, he fell into this
oblivion of their actual faces: they were not those of the lad
and the little wench who belonged to that past.

'It's a long while since you had the dispute with Dix,
father,' said Tom. 'I remember your talking about it three
years ago, before I went to school at Mr. Stelling's. I've
been at school there three years; don't you remember?'

Mr. Tulliver threw himself backward again, losing th

childlike outward glance under a rush of new ideas, which diverted him from external impressions.

'Ay, ay,' he said, after a minute or two, 'I've paid a deal o' money . . . I was determined my son should have a good eddication: I'd none myself, and I've felt the miss of it. And he'll want no other fortin: that's what I say . . . if Wakem was to get the better of me again. . . .'

The thought of Wakem roused new vibrations, and after a moment's pause he began to look at the coat he had on, and to feel in his side-pocket. Then he turned to Tom, and said, in his old sharp way, 'Where have they put Gore's letter?'

It was close at hand in a drawer, for he had often asked for it before.

'You know what there is in the letter, father?' said Tom, as he gave it to him.

'To be sure I do,' said Mr. Tulliver, rather angrily. 'What o' that? If Furley can't take to the property, somebody else can: there's plenty o' people in the world besides Furley. But it's hindering—my not being well—go and tell 'em to get the horse in the gig, Luke: I can get down to St. Ogg's well enough—Gore's expecting me.'

'No, dear father!' Maggie burst out entreatingly, 'it's a very long while since all that: you've been ill a great many weeks—more than two months—everything is changed.'

Mr. Tulliver looked at them all three alternately with a startled gaze: the idea that much had happened of which he knew nothing had often transiently arrested him before, but it came upon him now with entire novelty.

'Yes, father,' said Tom, in answer to the gaze. 'You needn't trouble your mind about business until you are quite well: everything is settled about that for the present —about the mill and the land and the debts.'

'What's settled, then?' said his father angrily.

'Don't you take on too much about it, sir,' said Luke. 'You'd ha' paid iverybody if you could—that's what I said to Master Tom—I said you'd ha' paid iverybody if you could.'

Good Luke felt, after the manner of contented hard-working men whose lives have been spent in servitude, that sense of natural fitness in rank which made his master's downfall a tragedy to him. He was urged, in his slow way, to say something that would express his share in the family sorrow, and these words, which he had used over and over again to Tom when he wanted to decline the full payment of his fifty pounds out of the children's money, were the most ready to his tongue. They were just the words to lay the most painful hold on his master's bewildered mind.

'Paid everybody?' he said, with vehement agitation, his face flushing, and his eye lighting up. 'Why . . . what . . . have they made me a *bankrupt*?'

'O father, dear father!' said Maggie, who thought that terrible word really represented the fact; 'bear it well—because we love you—your children will always love you. Tom will pay them all; he says he will when he's a man.'

She felt her father beginning to tremble—his voice trembled too, as he said, after a few moments:

'Ay, my little wench, but I shall never live twice o'er.'

'But perhaps you will live to see me pay everybody, father,' said Tom, speaking with a great effort.

'Ah, my lad,' said Mr. Tulliver, shaking his head slowly, 'but what's broke can never be whole again: it 'ud be your doing, not mine.' Then, looking up at him, 'You're only sixteen—it's an up-hill fight for you—but you mustn't throw it at your father; the raskills have been too many for him. I've given you a good eddication—that'll start you.'

Something in his throat half-choked the last words; the flush which had alarmed his children because it had so often preceded a recurrence of paralysis, had subsided, and his face looked pale and tremulous. Tom said nothing: he was still struggling against his inclination to rush away. His father remained quiet a minute or two, but his mind did not seem to be wandering again.

'Have they sold me up, then?' he said, more calmly, as if he were possessed simply by the desire to know what had happened.

'Everything is sold, father; but we don't know all about the mill and the land yet,' said Tom, anxious to ward off any question leading to the fact that Wakem was the purchaser.

'You must not be surprised to see the room look very bare down-stairs, father,' said Maggie; 'but there's your chair and the bureau—*they're* not gone.'

'Let us go—help me down, Luke—I'll go and see everything,' said Mr. Tulliver, leaning on his stick, and stretching out his other hand towards Luke.

'Ay, sir,' said Luke, as he gave his arm to his master, 'you'll make up your mind to 't a bit better when you've seen iverything: you'll get used to 't. That's what my mother says about her shortness o' breath—she says she's made friends wi't now, though she fought again' it sore when it fust come on.'

Maggie ran on before to see that all was right in the dreary parlour, where the fire, dulled by the frosty sunshine, seemed part of the general shabbiness. She turned her father's chair, and pushed aside the table to make an easy way for him, and then stood with a beating heart to see him enter and look round for the first time. Tom advanced before him, carrying the leg-rest, and stood beside Maggie on the hearth. Of those two young hearts Tom's suffered the most unmixed pain, for Maggie, with all her keen susceptibility, yet felt as if the sorrow made larger room for her love to flow in, and gave breathing-space to her passionate nature. No true boy feels that: he would rather go and slay the Nemean lion, or perform any round of heroic labours, than endure perpetual appeals to his pity, for evils over which he can make no conquest.

Mr. Tulliver paused just inside the door, resting on Luke, and looking round him at all the bare places, which for him were filled with the shadows of departed objects—the daily companions of his life. His faculties seemed to be renewing their strength from getting a footing on this demonstration of the senses.

'Ah!' he said slowly, moving towards his chair, 'they've sold me up . . . they've sold me up.'

Then seating himself and laying down his stick, while Luke left the room, he looked round again.

'They've left the big Bible,' he said. 'It's got everything in—when I was born and married—bring it me, Tom.'

The quarto Bible was laid open before him at the fly-leaf, and while he was reading with slowly-travelling eyes, Mrs. Tulliver entered the room, but stood in mute surprise to find her husband down already, and with the great Bible before him.

'Ah,' he said, looking at a spot where his finger rested, 'my mother was Margaret Beaton—she died when she was forty-seven: hers wasn't a long-lived family—we're our mother's children—Gritty and me are—we shall go to our last bed before long.'

He seemed to be pausing over the record of his sister's birth and marriage, as if it were suggesting new thoughts to him: then he suddenly looked up at Tom, and said, in a sharp tone of alarm:

'They haven't come upo' Moss for the money as I lent him, have they?'

'No, father,' said Tom; 'the note was burnt.'

Mr. Tulliver turned his eyes on the page again, and presently said:

'Ah ... Elizabeth Dodson ... it's eighteen year since I married her.'

'Come next Ladyday,' said Mrs. Tulliver, going up to his side and looking at the page.

Her husband fixed his eyes earnestly on her face.

'Poor Bessy,' he said, 'you was a pretty lass then—everybody said so—and I used to think you kept your good looks rarely. But you're sorely aged ... don't you bear me ill-will ... I meant to do well by you ... we promised one another for better or for worse. ...'

'But I never thought it 'ud be so for worse as this,' said poor Mrs. Tulliver, with the strange scared look that had come over her of late; 'and my poor father gave me away ... and to come on so all at once. ...'

'O mother,' said Maggie, 'don't talk in that way.'

'No, I know you won't let your poor mother speak ...

that's been the way all my life ... your father never minded
what I said ... it 'ud have been o' no use for me to beg and
pray ... and it 'ud be no use now, not if I was to go down
o' my hands and knees. ...'

'Don't say so, Bessy,' said Mr. Tulliver, whose pride, in
these first moments of humiliation, was in abeyance to the
sense of some justice in his wife's reproach. 'If there's anything left as I could do to make you amends, I wouldn't say
you nay.'

'Then we might stay here and get a living, and I might
keep among my own sisters ... and me been such a good
wife to you, and never crossed you from week's end to
week's end ... and they all say so ... they say it 'ud
be nothing but right ... only you're so turned against
Wakem.'

'Mother,' said Tom severely, 'this is not the time to talk
about that.'

'Let her be,' said Mr. Tulliver. 'Say what you mean,
Bessy.'

'Why, now the mill and the land's all Wakem's, and he's
got everything in his hands, and what's the use o' setting
your face against him?—when he says you may stay here,
and speaks as fair as can be, and says you may manage the
business, and have thirty shilling a-week, and a horse to
ride about to market? And where have we got to put our
heads? We must go into one o' the cottages in the village
... and me and my children brought down to that ... and
all because you must set your mind against folks till there's
no turning you.'

Mr. Tulliver had sunk back in his chair trembling.

'You may do as you like wi' me, Bessy,' he said, in a low
voice; 'I've been the bringing of you to poverty ... this
world's too many for me ... I'm nought but a bankrupt—
it's no use standing up for anything now.'

'Father,' said Tom, 'I don't agree with my mother or my
uncles, and I don't think you ought to submit to be under
Wakem. I get a pound a-week now, and you can find
something else to do when you get well.'

'Say no more, Tom, say no more: I've had enough for

this day. Give me a kiss, Bessy, and let us bear one another no ill-will: we shall never be young again. . . . This world's been too many for me.'

IX

AN ITEM ADDED TO THE FAMILY REGISTER

THAT first moment of renunciation and submission was followed by days of violent struggle in the miller's mind, as the gradual access of bodily strength brought with it increasing ability to embrace in one view all the conflicting conditions under which he found himself. Feeble limbs easily resign themselves to be tethered, and when we are subdued by sickness it seems possible to us to fulfil pledges which the old vigour comes back and breaks. There were times when poor Tulliver thought the fulfilment of his promise to Bessy was something quite too hard for human nature: he had promised her without knowing what she was going to say—she might as well have asked him to carry a ton weight on his back. But again, there were many feelings arguing on her side, besides the sense that life had been made hard to her by having married him. He saw a possibility, by much pinching, of saving money out of his salary towards paying a second dividend to his creditors, and it would not be easy elsewhere to get a situation such as he could fill. He had led an easy life, ordering much and working little, and had no aptitude for any new business. He must perhaps take to day-labour, and his wife must have help from her sisters—a prospect doubly bitter to him, now they had let all Bessy's precious things be sold, probably because they liked to set her against him, by making her feel that he had brought her to that pass. He listened to their admonitory talk, when they came to urge on him what he was bound to do for poor Bessy's sake, with averted eyes, that every now and then flashed on them furtively when their backs were turned. Nothing but the dread of needing their help could have made it an easier alternative to take their advice.

But the strongest influence of all was the love of the old premises where he had run about when he was a boy, just as Tom had done after him. The Tullivers had lived on this spot for generations, and he had sat listening on a low stool on winter evenings while his father talked of the old half-timbered mill that had been there before the last great floods which damaged it so that his grandfather pulled it down and built the new one. It was when he got able to walk about and look at all the old objects, that he felt the strain of this clinging affection for the old home as part of his life, part of himself. He couldn't bear to think of himself living on any other spot than this, where he knew the sound of every gate and door, and felt that the shape and colour of every roof and weather-stain and broken hillock was good, because his growing senses had been fed on them. Our instructed vagrancy, which has hardly time to linger by the hedgerows, but runs away early to the tropics, and is at home with palms and banyans,—which is nourished on books of travel, and stretches the theatre of its imagination to the Zambesi,—can hardly get a dim notion of what an old-fashioned man like Tulliver felt for this spot, where all his memories centred, and where life seemed like a familiar smooth-handled tool that the fingers clutch with loving ease. And just now he was living in that freshened memory of the far-off time which comes to us in the passive hours of recovery from sickness.

'Ay, Luke,' he said, one afternoon, as he stood looking over the orchard gate, 'I remember the day they planted those apple-trees. My father was a huge man for planting—it was like a merrymaking to him to get a cart full o' young trees—and I used to stand i' the cold with him, and follow him about like a dog.'

Then he turned round, and, leaning against the gate-post, looked at the opposite buildings.

'The old mill 'ud miss me, I think, Luke. There's a story as when the mill changes hands, the river's angry—I've heard my father say it many a time. There's no telling whether there mayn't be summat *in* the story, for this is a puzzling world, and Old Harry's got a finger in it—it's been too many for me, I know.'

'Ay, sir,' said Luke, with soothing sympathy, 'what wi' the rust on the wheat, an' the firin' o' the ricks an' that, as I've seen in my time—things often looks comical: there's the bacon fat wi' our last pig runs away like butter—it leaves nought but a scratchin'.'

'It's just as if it was yesterday, now,' Mr. Tulliver went on, 'when my father began the malting. I remember, the day they finished the malt-house, I thought summat great was to come of it; for we'd a plum-pudding that day and a bit of a feast, and I said to my mother—she was a fine dark-eyed woman, my mother was—the little wench 'ull be as like her as two peas.'—Here Mr. Tulliver put his stick between his legs, and took out his snuff-box, for the greater enjoyment of this anecdote, which dropped from him in fragments, as if he every other moment lost narration in vision. 'I was a little chap no higher much than my mother's knee—she was sore fond of us children, Gritty and me—and so I said to her, "Mother," I said, "shall we have plum-pudding *every* day because o' the malt-house?" She used to tell me o' that till her dying day. She was but a young woman when she died, my mother was. But it's forty good year since they finished the malt-house, and it isn't many days out of 'em all, as I haven't looked out into the yard there, the first thing in the morning—all weathers, from year's end to year's end. I should go off my head in a new place. I should be like as if I'd lost my way. It's all hard, whichever way I look at it—the harness 'ull gall me—but it 'ud be summat to draw along the old road, instead of a new un.'

'Ay, sir,' said Luke, 'you'd be a deal better here nor in some new place. I can't abide new places mysen: things is allays awk'ard—narrow-wheeled waggins, belike, and the stiles all another sort, an' oatcake i' some places, tow'rt th' head o' the Floss, there. It's poor work, changing your country-side.'

'But I doubt, Luke, they'll be for getting rid o' Ben, and making you do with a lad—and I must help a bit wi' the mill. You'll have a worse place.'

'Ne'er mind, sir,' said Luke, 'I shan't plague mysen. I'n been wi' you twenty year, an' you can't get twenty year wi' whistlin' for 'em, no more nor you can make the trees grow: you mun wait till God A'mighty sends 'em. I can't abide new victual nor new faces, *I* can't—you niver know but what they'll gripe you.'

The walk was finished in silence after this, for Luke had disburthened himself of thoughts to an extent that left his conversational resources quite barren, and Mr. Tulliver had relapsed from his recollections into a painful meditation on the choice of hardships before him. Maggie noticed that he was unusually absent that evening at tea; and afterwards he sat leaning forward in his chair, looking at the ground, moving his lips, and shaking his head from time to time. Then he looked hard at Mrs. Tulliver, who was knitting opposite him, then at Maggie, who, as she bent over her sewing, was intensely conscious of some drama going forward in her father's mind. Suddenly he took up the poker and broke the large coal fiercely.

'Dear heart, Mr. Tulliver, what can you be thinking of?' said his wife, looking up in alarm: 'it's very wasteful, breaking the coal, and we've got hardly any large coal left, and I don't know where the rest is to come from.'

'I don't think you're quite so well to-night, are you, father?' said Maggie; 'you seem uneasy.'

'Why, how is it Tom doesn't come?' said Mr. Tulliver impatiently.

'Dear heart! is it time? I must go and get his supper,' said Mrs. Tulliver, laying down her knitting, and leaving the room.

'It's nigh upon half-past eight,' said Mr. Tulliver. 'He'll be here soon. Go, go and get the big Bible, and open it at the beginning, where everything's set down. And get the pen and ink.'

Maggie obeyed, wondering: but her father gave no further orders, and only sat listening for Tom's foot-fall on the gravel, apparently irritated by the wind, which had risen, and was roaring so as to drown all other sounds. There was a strange light in his eyes that rather frightened Maggie: *she* began to wish that Tom would come, too.

'There he is, then,' said Mr. Tulliver, in an excited way, when the knock came at last. Maggie went to open the door, but her mother came out of the kitchen hurriedly, saying, 'Stop a bit, Maggie: I'll open it.'

Mrs. Tulliver had begun to be a little frightened at her boy, but she was jealous of every office others did for him.

'Your supper's ready by the kitchen-fire, my boy,' she said, as he took off his hat and coat. 'You shall have it by yourself, just as you like, and I won't speak to you.'

'I think my father wants Tom, mother,' said Maggie; 'he must come into the parlour first.'

Tom entered with his usual saddened evening face, but his eyes fell immediately on the open Bible and the ink-stand, and he glanced with a look of anxious surprise at his father, who was saying:

'Come, come, you're late—I want you.'

'Is there anything the matter, father?' said Tom.

'You sit down—all of you,' said Mr. Tulliver peremptorily. 'And, Tom, sit down here; I've got something for you to write i' the Bible.'

They all three sat down, looking at him. He began to speak slowly, looking first at his wife.

'I've made up my mind, Bessy, and I'll be as good as my word to you. There'll be the same grave made for us to lie down in, and we mustn't be bearing one another ill-will. I'll stop in the old place, and I'll serve under Wakem—and I'll serve him like an honest man: there's no Tulliver but what's honest, mind that, Tom'—here his voice rose. 'they'll have it to throw up against me as I paid a dividend —but it wasn't my fault—it was because there's raskills in the world. They've been too many for me, and I must give in. I'll put my neck in harness—for you've a right to say as I've brought you into trouble, Bessy—and I'll serve him as honest as if he was no raskill: I'm an honest man, though I shall never hold my head up no more—I'm a tree as is broke —a tree as is broke.'

He paused, and looked on the ground. Then suddenly raising his head, he said, in a louder yet deeper tone:

'But I won't forgive him! I know what they say—he never meant me any harm—that's the way Old Harry props up the raskills—he's been at the bottom of everything—but he's a fine gentleman—I know, I know. I shouldn't ha' gone to law, they say. But who made it so as there was no arbitratin', and no justice to be got? It signifies nothing to him—I know that; he's one o' them fine gentlemen as get money by doing business for poorer folks, and when he's made beggars of 'em he'll give 'em charity. I won't forgive him! I wish he might be punished with shame till his own son 'ud like to forget him. I wish he may do summat as they'd make him work at the treadmill! But he won't—he's too big a raskill to let the law lay hold on him. And you mind this, Tom—you never forgive him, neither, if you mean to be my son. There'll maybe come a time when you may make him feel—it'll never come to me —'n got my head under the yoke. Now write—write it i' the Bible.'

'O father, what?' said Maggie, sinking down by his knee, pale and trembling. 'It's wicked to curse and bear malice.'

'It isn't wicked, I tell you,' said her father fiercely. 'It's wicked as the raskills should prosper—it's the devil's doing. Do as I tell you, Tom. Write.'

'What am I to write, father?' said Tom, with gloomy submission.

'Write as your father, Edward Tulliver, took service under John Wakem, the man as had helped to ruin him, because I'd promised my wife to make her what amends I could for her trouble, and because I wanted to die in th' old place, where I was born and my father was born. Put that i' the right words—you know how—and then write, as I don't forgive Wakem, for all that; and for all I'll serve him honest, I wish evil may befall him. Write that.'

There was a dead silence as Tom's pen moved along the paper: Mrs. Tulliver looked scared, and Maggie trembled like a leaf.

'Now let me hear what you've wrote,' said Mr. Tulliver. Tom read aloud, slowly.

'Now write—write as you'll remember what Wakem's done to your father, and you'll make him and his feel it, if ever the day comes. And sign your name Thomas Tulliver.'

'O no, father, dear father!' said Maggie, almost choked with fear. 'You shouldn't make Tom write that.'

'Be quiet, Maggie!' said Tom. 'I *shall* write it.'

BOOK FOURTH

THE VALLEY OF HUMILIATION

A VARIATION OF PROTESTANTISM UNKNOWN TO BOSSUET

JOURNEYING down the Rhône on a summer's day, you have perhaps felt the sunshine made dreary by those ruined villages which stud the banks in certain parts of its course, telling how the swift river once rose, like an angry, destroying god, sweeping down the feeble generations whose breath is in their nostrils, and making their dwellings a desolation. Strange contrast, you may have thought, between the effect produced on us by these dismal remnants of commonplace houses, which in their best days were but the sign of a sordid life, belonging in all its details to our own vulgar era; and the effect produced by those ruins on the castled Rhine, which have crumbled and mellowed into such harmony with the green and rocky steeps, that they seem to have a natural fitness, like the mountain-pine: nay, even in the day when they were built they must have had this fitness, as if they had been raised by an earth-born race, who had inherited from their mighty parent a sublime instinct of form. And that was a day of romance! If those robber-barons were somewhat grim and drunken ogres, they had a certain grandeur of the wild beast in them— they were forest boars with tusks, tearing and rending, not the ordinary domestic grunter; they represented the demon forces for ever in collision with beauty, virtue, and the gentle uses of life; they made a fine contrast in the picture with the wandering minstrel, the soft-lipped princess, the pious recluse, and the timid Israelite. That was a time of colour, when the sunlight fell on glancing steel and floating banners; a time of adventure and fierce struggle—nay, of living, religious art and religious enthusiasm; for were not cathedrals built in those days, and did not great emperors leave their Western palaces to die before the infidel strongholds in the sacred East? Therefore it is that these Rhine castles thrill me with a sense of poetry: they belong to the grand historic life of humanity, and raise up for me the vision of an epoch. But these dead-tinted, hollow-eyed, angular skeletons of villages on the Rhône oppress me with the feeling that human life—very much of it—is a narrow, ugly, grovelling existence, which even calamity does not elevate, but rather tends to exhibit in all its bare vulgarity of conception; and I have a cruel conviction that the lives these ruins are the traces of, were part of a gross sum of obscure vitality, that will be swept into the same oblivion with the generations of ants and beavers.

Perhaps something akin to this oppressive feeling may have weighed upon you in watching this old-fashioned family life on the banks of the Floss, which even sorrow hardly suffices to lift above the level of the tragi-comic. It is a sordid life, you say, this of the Tullivers and Dodsons—irradiated by no sublime principles, no romantic visions, no active, self-renouncing faith—moved by none of those wild, uncontrollable passions which create the dark shadows of misery and crime—without that primitive rough simplicity of wants, that hard submissive ill-paid toil, that childlike spelling-out of what nature has written, which gives its poetry to peasant life. Here, one has conventional worldly notions and habits without instruction and without polish —surely the most prosaic form of human life: proud respectability in a gig of unfashionable build: worldliness without side-dishes. Observing these people narrowly, even when the iron hand of misfortune has shaken them from their unquestioning hold on the world, one sees little trace of religion, still less of a distinctively Christian creed. Their belief in the Unseen, so far as it manifests itself at all, seems to be rather of a pagan kind; their moral notions, though held with strong tenacity, seem to have no standard beyond hereditary custom. You could not live among such people;

you are stifled for want of an outlet towards something beautiful, great, or noble; you are irritated with these dull men and women, as a kind of population out of keeping with the earth on which they live—with this rich plain where the great river flows for ever onward, and links the small pulse of the old English town with the beatings of the world's mighty heart. A vigorous superstition, that lashes its gods or lashes its own back, seems to be more congruous with the mystery of the human lot, than the mental condition of these emmet-like Dodsons and Tullivers.

I share with you this sense of oppressive narrowness; but it is necessary that we should feel it, if we care to understand how it acted on the lives of Tom and Maggie—how it has acted on young natures in many generations, that in the onward tendency of human things have risen above the mental level of the generation before them, to which they have been nevertheless tied by the strongest fibres of their hearts. The suffering, whether of martyr or victim, which belongs to every historical advance of mankind, is represented in this way in every town, and by hundreds of obscure hearths; and we need not shrink from this comparison of small things with great; for does not science tell us that its highest striving is after the ascertainment of a unity which shall bind the smallest things with the greatest? In natural science, I have understood, there is nothing petty to the mind that has a large vision of relations, and to which every single object suggests a vast sum of conditions. It is surely the same with the observation of human life.

Certainly the religious and moral ideas of the Dodsons and Tullivers were of too specific a kind to be arrived at deductively, from the statement that they were part of the Protestant population of Great Britain. Their theory of life had its core of soundness, as all theories must have on which decent and prosperous families have been reared and have flourished: but it had the very slightest tincture of theology. If, in the maiden days of the Dodson sisters, their Bibles opened more easily at some parts than others, it was because of dried tulip-petals, which had been distributed quite impartially, without preference for the historical, devotional, or doctrinal. Their religion was of a simple, semi-pagan kind, but there was no heresy in it—if heresy properly means choice—for they didn't know there was any other religion, except that of chapel-goers, which appeared to run in families, like asthma. How *should* they know? The vicar of their pleasant rural parish was not a controversialist, but a good hand at whist, and one who had a joke always ready for a blooming female parishioner. The religion of the Dodsons consisted in revering whatever was customary and respectable: it was necessary to be baptized, else one could not be buried in the churchyard, and to take the sacrament before death as a security against more dimly understood perils; but it was of equal necessity to have the proper pall-bearers and well-cured hams at one's funeral, and to leave an unimpeachable will. A Dodson would not be taxed with the omission of anything that was becoming, or that belonged to that eternal fitness of things which was plainly indicated in the practice of the most substantial parishioners, and in the family traditions—such as, obedience to parents, faithfulness to kindred, industry, rigid honesty, thrift, the thorough scouring of wooden and copper utensils, the hoarding of coins likely to disappear from the currency, the production of first-rate commodities for the market, and the general preference for whatever was home-made. The Dodsons were a very proud race, and their pride lay in the utter frustration of all desire to tax them with a breach of traditional duty or propriety. A wholesome pride in many respects, since it identified honour with perfect integrity, thoroughness of work, and faithfulness to admitted rules: and society owes some worthy qualities in many of her members to mothers of the Dodson class, who made their butter and their fromenty well, and would have felt disgraced to make it otherwise. To be honest and poor was never a Dodson motto, still less to seem rich though being poor; rather, the family badge was to be honest and rich; and not only rich, but richer than was supposed. To live respected, and have the proper bearers at your funeral, was an achievement of the ends of existence that would be entirely nullified if, on the reading of your will, you sank in the opinion of your fellow-men, either by turning out to be poorer than they expected, or by leaving your money in a capricious manner, without strict regard to degrees of kin. The right thing must always be done towards kindred. The right thing was to correct them severely, if they were other than a credit to the family, but still not to alienate from them the smallest rightful share in the family shoe-buckles and other property. A conspicuous quality in the Dodson character was its genuineness: its vices and virtues alike were phases of a proud, honest egoism, which had a hearty dislike to whatever made against its own credit and interest, and would be frankly hard of speech to inconvenient 'kin,' but would never forsake or ignore them—would not let them want bread, but only require them to eat it with bitter herbs.

The same sort of traditional belief ran in the Tulliver veins, but it was carried in richer blood, having elements of generous imprudence, warm affection, and hot-tempered rashness. Mr. Tulliver's grandfather had been heard to say that he was descended from one Ralph Tulliver, a wonderfully clever fellow, who had ruined himself. It is likely enough that the clever Ralph was a high liver, rode spirited horses, and was very decidedly of his own opinion. On the other hand, nobody had ever heard of a Dodson who had ruined himself: it was not the way of that family.

If such were the views of life on which the Dodsons and Tullivers had been reared in the praiseworthy past of Pitt and high prices, you will infer from what you already know concerning the state of society in St. Ogg's, that there had been no highly modifying influence to act on them in their maturer life. It was still possible, even in that later time of anti-Catholic preaching, for people to hold many pagan ideas, and believe themselves good church-people notwithstanding; so we need hardly feel any surprise at the fact that Mr. Tulliver, though a regular church-goer, recorded his vindictiveness on the fly-leaf of his Bible. It was not that any harm could be said concerning the vicar of that charming rural parish to which Dorlcote Mill belonged: he was a man of excellent family, an irreproachable bachelor, of elegant pursuits,—had taken honours, and held a fellowship. Mr. Tulliver regarded him with dutiful respect, as he did everything else belonging to the church-service; but he considered that church was one thing and common-sense another, and he wanted nobody to tell *him* what common-sense was. Certain seeds which are required to find a nidus for themselves under unfavourable circumstances, have been supplied by nature with an apparatus of hooks, so that they will get a hold on very unreceptive surfaces. The spiritual seed which had been scattered over Mr. Tulliver had apparently been destitute of any corresponding provision, and had slipped off to the winds again, from a total absence of hooks.

II

THE TORN NEST IS PIERCED BY THE THORNS

THERE is something sustaining in the very agitation that accompanies the first shocks of trouble, just as an acute pain is often a stimulus, and produces an excitement which is transient strength. It is in the slow, changed life that follows—in the time when sorrow has become stale, and has no longer an emotive intensity that counteracts its pain—in the time when day follows day in dull unexpectant sameness, and trial is a dreary routine;—it is then that despair threatens; it is then that the peremptory hunger of the soul is felt, and eye and ear are strained after some unlearned secret of our existence, which shall give to endurance the nature of satisfaction.

This time of utmost need was come to Maggie, with her short span of thirteen years. To the usual precocity of the girl, she added that early experience of struggle, of conflict between the inward impulse and outward fact, which is the lot of every imaginative and passionate nature; and the years since she hammered the nails into her wooden Fetish among the worm-eaten shelves of the attic, had been filled with so eager a life in the triple world of Reality, Books, and Waking Dreams, that Maggie was strangely old for her years in everything except in her entire want of that prudence and self-command which were the qualities that made Tom manly in the midst of his intellectual boyishness. And now her lot was beginning to have a still, sad monotony, which threw her more than ever on her inward self. Her father was able to attend to business again, his affairs were settled, and he was acting as Wakem's manager on the old spot. Tom went to and fro every morning and evening, and became more and more silent in the short intervals at home: what was there to say? One day was like another, and Tom's interest in life, driven back and crushed on every other side, was concentrating itself into the one channel of ambitious resistance to misfortune. The peculiarities of his father and mother were very irksome to him, now they were laid bare of all the softening accompaniments of an easy prosperous home; for Tom had very clear prosaic eyes, not apt to be dimmed by mists of feeling or imagination. Poor Mrs. Tulliver, it seemed, would never recover her old self— her placid household activity: how could she? The objects among which her mind had moved complacently were all gone—all the little hopes, and schemes, and speculations, all the pleasant little cares about her treasures which had made the world quite comprehensible to her for a quarter of a century, since she had made her first purchase of the sugar-tongs, had been suddenly snatched away from her, and she remained bewildered in this empty life. Why that should have happened to her which had not happened to other women, remained an insoluble question by which she expressed her perpetual ruminating comparison of the past with the present. It was piteous to see the comely woman getting thinner and more worn under a bodily as well as mental restlessness, which made her often wander about the empty house after her work was done, until Maggie, becoming alarmed about her, would seek her, and bring her down by telling her how it vexed Tom that she was injuring her health by never sitting down and resting herself. Yet amidst this helpless imbecility there was a touching trait of humble self-devoting maternity, which made

Maggie feel tenderly towards her poor mother amidst all the little wearing griefs caused by her mental feebleness. She would let Maggie do none of the work that was heaviest and most soiling to the hands, and was quite peevish when Maggie attempted to relieve her from her grate-brushing and scouring: 'Let it alone, my dear; your hands 'ull get as hard as hard,' she would say: 'it's your mother's place to do that. I can't do the sewing—my eyes fail me.' And she would still brush and carefully tend Maggie's hair, which she had become reconciled to, in spite of its refusal to curl, now it was so long and massy. Maggie was not her pet child, and, in general, would have been much better if she had been quite different; yet the womanly heart, so bruised in its small personal desires, found a future to rest on in the life of this young thing, and the mother pleased herself with wearing out her own hands to save the hands that had so much more life in them.

But the constant presence of her mother's regretful bewilderment was less painful to Maggie than that of her father's sullen incommunicative depression. As long as the paralysis was upon him, and it seemed as if he might always be in a childlike condition of dependence—as long as he was still only half-awakened to his trouble, Maggie had felt the strong tide of pitying love almost as an inspiration, a new power, that would make the most difficult life easy for his sake; but now, instead of childlike dependence there had come a taciturn hard concentration of purpose, in strange contrast with his old vehement communicativeness and high spirit; and this lasted from day to day, and from week to week, the dull eye never brightening with any eagerness or any joy. It is something cruelly incomprehensible to youthful natures, this sombre sameness in middle-aged and elderly people, whose life has resulted in disappointment and discontent, to whose faces a smile becomes so strange that the sad lines all about the lips and brow seem to take no notice of it, and it hurries away again for want of a welcome. 'Why will they not kindle up and be glad sometimes?' thinks young elasticity. 'It would be so easy if they only liked to do it.' And these leaden clouds that never part are apt to create impatience even in the filial affection that streams forth in nothing but tenderness and pity in the time of more obvious affliction.

Mr. Tulliver lingered nowhere away from home: he hurried away from market, he refused all invitations to stay and chat, as in old times, in the houses where he called on business. He could not be reconciled with his lot: there was no attitude in which his pride did not feel its bruises; and in all behaviour towards him, whether kind or cold, he detected an allusion to the change in his circumstances. Even the days on which Wakem came to ride round the land and inquire into the business, were not so black to him as those market-days on which he had met several creditors who had accepted a composition from him. To save something towards the repayment of those creditors, was the object towards which he was now bending all his thoughts and efforts; and under the influence of this all-compelling demand of his nature, the somewhat profuse man, who hated to be stinted or to stint any one else in his own house, was gradually metamorphosed into the keen-eyed grudger of morsels. Mrs. Tulliver could not economise enough to satisfy him, in their food and firing; and he would eat nothing himself but what was of the coarsest quality. Tom, though depressed and strongly repelled by his father's sullenness, and the dreariness of home, entered thoroughly into his father's feelings about paying the creditors; and the poor lad brought his first quarter's money, with a delicious sense of achievement, and gave it to his father to put into the tin box which held the savings. The little store of sovereigns in the tin box seemed to be the only sight that brought a faint gleam of pleasure into the miller's eyes—faint and transient, for it was soon dispelled by the thought that the time would be long—perhaps longer than his life—before the narrow savings could remove the hateful incubus of debt. A deficit of more than five hundred pounds with the accumulating interest, seemed a deep pit to fill with the savings from thirty shillings a-week, even when Tom's probable savings were to be added. On this one point there was entire community of feeling in the four widely different beings who sat round the dying fire of sticks, which made a cheap warmth for them on the verge of bed-time. Mrs. Tulliver carried the proud integrity of the Dodsons in her blood, and had been brought up to think that to wrong people of their money, which was another phrase for debt, was a sort of moral pillory: it would have been wickedness, to her mind, to have run counter to her husband's desire to 'do the right thing,' and retrieve his name. She had a confused dreamy notion that, if the creditors were all paid, her plate and linen ought to come back to her; but she had an inbred perception that while people owed money they were unable to pay, they couldn't rightly call anything their own. She murmured a little that Mr. Tulliver so peremptorily refused to receive anything in repayment from Mr. and Mrs. Moss; but to all his requirements of household economy she was submissive to the point of denying herself the cheapest indulgences of mere flavour: her only rebellion was to smuggle into the kitchen something that would make rather a better supper than usual for Tom.

These narrow notions about debt, held by the old-fashioned Tullivers, may perhaps excite a smile on the faces of many readers in these days of wide commercial views and wide philosophy, according to which everything rights itself without any trouble of ours: the fact that my tradesman is out of pocket by me, is to be looked at through the serene certainty that somebody else's tradesman is in pocket by somebody else; and since there must be bad debts in the world, why, it is mere egoism not to like that we in particular should make them instead of our fellow-citizens. I am telling the history of very simple people, who had never had any illuminating doubts as to personal integrity and honour.

Under all this grim melancholy and narrowing concentration of desire, Mr. Tulliver retained the feeling towards his 'little wench' which made her presence a need to him, though it would not suffice to cheer him. She was still the desire of his eyes; but the sweet spring of fatherly love was now mingled with bitterness, like everything else. When

Maggie laid down her work at night, it was her habit to get a low stool and sit by her father's knee, leaning her cheek against it. How she wished he would stroke her head, or give some sign that he was soothed by the sense that he had a daughter who loved him! But now she got no answer to her little caresses, either from her father or from Tom—the two idols of her life. Tom was weary and abstracted in the short intervals when he was at home, and her father was bitterly preoccupied with the thought that the girl was growing up—was shooting up into a woman; and how was she to do well in life? She had a poor chance for marrying, down in the world as they were. And he hated the thought of her marrying poorly, as her aunt Gritty had done: *that* would be a thing to make him turn in his grave—the little wench so pulled down by children and toil, as her aunt Moss was. When uncultured minds, confined to a narrow range of personal experience, are under the pressure of continued misfortune, their inward life is apt to become a perpetually repeated round of sad and bitter thoughts: the same words, the same scenes are revolved over and over again, the same mood accompanies them—the end of the year finds them as much what they were at the beginning as if they were machines set to a recurrent series of movements.

The sameness of the days was broken by few visitors. Uncles and aunts paid only short visits now: of course, they could not stay to meals, and the constraint caused by Mr. Tulliver's savage silence, which seemed to add to the hollow resonance of the bare uncarpeted room when the aunts were talking, heightened the unpleasantness of these family visits on all sides, and tended to make them rare. As for other acquaintances—there is a chill air surrounding those who are down in the world, and people are glad to get away from them, as from a cold room: human beings, mere men and women, without furniture, without anything to offer you, who have ceased to count as anybody, present an embarrassing negation of reasons for wishing to see them, or of subjects on which to converse with them. At that distant day there was a dreary isolation in the civilized Christian society of these realms for families that had dropped below their original level, unless they belonged to a sectarian church, which gets some warmth of brotherhood by walling in the sacred fire.

III

A VOICE FROM THE PAST

ONE afternoon, when the chestnuts were coming into flower, Maggie had brought her chair outside the front door, and was seated there with a book on her knees. Her dark eyes had wandered from the book, but they did not seem to be enjoying the sunshine which pierced the screen of jasmine on the projecting porch at her right, and threw leafy shadows on her pale round cheek; they seemed rather to be searching for something that was not disclosed by the sunshine. It had been a more miserable day than usual: her father, after a visit of Wakem's, had had a paroxysm of rage, in which for some trifling fault he had beaten the boy who served in the mill. Once before, since his illness, he had had a similar paroxysm, in which he had beaten his horse, and the scene had left a lasting terror in Maggie's mind. The thought had risen, that some time or other he might beat her mother if she happened to speak in her feeble way at the wrong moment. The keenest of all dread with her was, lest her father should add to his present misfortune the wretchedness of doing something irretrievably disgraceful. The battered school-book of Tom's which she held on her knees could give her no fortitude under the pressure of that dread, and again and again her eyes had filled with tears, as they wandered vaguely, seeing neither the chestnut-trees nor the distant horizon, but only future scenes of home-sorrow.

Suddenly she was roused by the sound of the opening gate and of footsteps on the gravel. It was not Tom who was entering, but a man in a seal-skin cap and a blue plush waistcoat, carrying a pack on his back, and followed closely by a bull-terrier of brindled coat and defiant aspect.

'O Bob, it's you!' said Maggie, starting up with a smile

of pleased recognition, for there had been no abundance of kind acts to efface the recollection of Bob's generosity; 'I'm so glad to see you.'

'Thank you, Miss,' said Bob, lifting his cap and showing a delighted face, but immediately relieving himself of some accompanying embarrassment by looking down at his dog, and saying in a tone of disgust, 'Get out wi' you, you thunderin' sawney!'

'My brother is not at home yet, Bob,' said Maggie; 'he is always at St. Ogg's in the daytime.'

'Well, Miss,' said Bob, 'I should be glad to see Mr. Tom —but that isn't just what I'm come for—look here!'

Bob was in the act of depositing his pack on the door-step, and with it a row of small books fastened together with string. Apparently, however, they were not the object to which he wished to call Maggie's attention, but rather something which he had carried under his arm, wrapped in a red handkerchief.

'See here!' he said again, laying the red parcel on the others and unfolding it; 'you won't think I'm a-makin' too free, Miss, I hope, but I lighted on these books, and I thought they might make up to you a bit for them as you've lost; for I heared you speak o' picturs—an' as for picturs, *look* here!'

The opening of the red handkerchief had disclosed a superannuated 'Keepsake' and six or seven numbers of a 'Portrait Gallery,' in royal octavo; and the emphatic request to look referred to a portrait of George the Fourth in all the majesty of his depressed cranium and voluminous neckcloth.

'There's all sorts o' genelmen here,' Bob went on, turning over the leaves with some excitement, 'wi' all sorts o' noses —an' some bald an' some wi' wigs—Parlament genelmen, I reckon. An' here,' he added, opening the 'Keepsake,' '*here's* ladies for you, some wi' curly hair and some wi' smooth, an' some a-smiling wi' their heads o' one side, an' some as if they was going' to cry—look here—a-sittin' on the ground out o' door, dressed like the ladies I'n seen get out o' the carriages at the balls in th' Old Hall there. My eyes, I wonder what the chaps wear as go a-courtin' em! I sot up till the clock was gone twelve last night a-lookin' at 'em—I did—till they stared at me out o' the picturs as if they'd know when I spoke to 'em. But, lors! I shouldn't know what to say to 'em. They'll be more fittin' company for you, Miss; and the man at the book-stall, he said they banged iverything for picturs—he said they was a fust-rate article.'

'And you've bought them for me, Bob?' said Maggie, deeply touched by this simple kindness. 'How very, very good of you! But I'm afraid you gave a great deal of money for them.'

'Not me!' said Bob. 'I'd ha' gev three times the money if they'll make up to you a bit for them as was sold away from you, Miss. For I'n niver forgot how you looked when you fretted about the books bein' gone—it's stuck by me as if it was a pictur hingin' before me. An' when I see'd the book open upo' the stall, wi' the lady lookin' out of it wi' eyes a bit like your'n when you was frettin'—you'll excuse my takin' the liberty, Miss—I thought I'd make free to buy it for you, an' then I bought the books full o' genelmen to match—an' then'—here Bob took up the small stringed packet of books—'I thought you might like a bit more print as well as the picturs, an' I got these for a say-so—they're cram-full o' print, an' I thought they'd do no harm comin' along wi' these bettermost books. An' I hope you won't say me nay, an' tell me as you won't have 'em, like Mr. Tom did wi' the suvreigns.'

'No, indeed, Bob,' said Maggie, 'I'm very thankful to you for thinking of me, and being so good to me and Tom. I don't think anyone ever did such a kind thing for me before. I haven't many friends who care for me.'

'Hev a dog, Miss!—they're better friends nor any Christian,' said Bob, laying down his pack again, which he had taken up with the intention of hurrying away; for he felt considerable shyness in talking to a young lass like Maggie, though, as he usually said of himself, 'his tongue overrun him' when he began to speak. 'I can't give you Mumps, 'cause he'd break his heart to go away from me—eh,

Mumps, what do you say, you riff-raff?'—(Mumps declined to express himself more diffusely than by a single affirmative movement of his tail.) 'But I'd get you a pup, Miss, an' welcome.'

'No, thank you, Bob. We have a yard dog, and I mayn't keep a dog of my own.'

'Eh, that's a pity: else there's a pup—if you didn't mind about it not being thoroughbred: its mother acts in the Punch show—an uncommon sensable bitch—she means more sense wi' her bark nor half the chaps can put into their talk from breakfast to sundown. There's one chap carries pots,—a poor low trade as any on the road,—he says, "Why, Toby's nought but a mongrel—there's nought to look at in her." But I says to him, "Why, what are you yoursen but a mongrel? There wasn't much pickin' o' *your* feyther an' mother, to look at you." Not but what I like a bit o' breed myself, but I can't abide to see one cur grinnin' at another. I wish you good-evenin', Miss,' added Bob, abruptly taking up his pack again under the consciousness that his tongue was acting in an undisciplined manner.

'Won't you come in the evening some time, and see my brother, Bob?' said Maggie.

'Yes, Miss, thank you—another time. You'll give my duty to him, if you please. Eh, he's a fine growed chap, Mr. Tom is; he took to growin' i' the legs, an' *I* didn't.'

The pack was down again, now—the hook of the stick having somehow gone wrong.

'You don't call Mumps a cur, I suppose?' said Maggie, divining that any interest she showed in Mumps would be gratifying to his master.

'No, Miss, a fine way off that,' said Bob, with a pitying smile; 'Mumps is as fine a cross as you'll see anywhere along the Floss, an' I'n been up it wi' the barge times enow. Why, the gentry stops to look at him; but you won't catch Mumps a-looking at the gentry much—he minds his own business, he does.'

The expression of Mumps's face, which seemed to be tolerating the superfluous existence of objects in general, was strongly confirmatory of this high praise.

'He looks dreadfully surly,' said Maggie. 'Would he let me pat him?'

'Ay, that would he, and thank you. He knows his company, Mumps does. He isn't a dog as 'ull be caught wi' gingerbread: he'd smell a thief a good deal stronger nor the gingerbread—he would. Lors, I talk to him by th' hour together, when I'm walking i' lone places, and if I'n done a bit o' mischief, I allays tell him. I'n got no secrets but what Mumps knows 'em. He knows about my big thumb, he does.'

'Your big thumb—what's that, Bob?' said Maggie.

'That's what it is, Miss,' said Bob quickly, exhibiting a singularly broad specimen of that difference between the man and the monkey. 'It tells i' measuring out the flannel, you see. I carry flannel, 'cause it's light for my pack, an' it's dear stuff, you see, so a big thumb tells. I clap my thumb at the end o' the yard and cut o' the hither side of it, and the old women aren't up to 't.'

'But, Bob,' said Maggie, looking serious, 'that's cheating: I don't like to hear you say that.'

'Don't you, Miss?' said Bob regretfully. 'Then I'm sorry I said it. But I'm so used to talking to Mumps, an' he doesn't mind a bit o' cheating, when it's them skinflint women, as haggle an' haggle, an' 'ud like to get their flannel for nothing, an' 'ud niver ask theirselves how I got my dinner out on't. I niver cheat anybody as doesn't want to cheat me, Miss—lors, I'm a honest chap, I am; only I must hev a bit o' sport, an' now I don't go wi' the ferrets, I'n got no varmint to come over but them haggling women. I wish you good-evening, Miss.'

'Good-bye, Bob. Thank you very much for bringing me the books. And come again to see Tom.'

'Yes, Miss,' said Bob, moving on a few steps; then turning half round, he said, 'I'll leave off that trick wi' my big thumb, if you don't think well on me for it, Miss—but it 'ud be a pity, it would. I couldn't find another trick so good—an' what 'ud be the use o' havin' a big thumb? It might as well ha' been narrow.'

Maggie, thus exalted into Bob's directing Madonna,

laughed in spite of herself; at which her worshipper's blue eyes twinkled too, and under these favouring auspices he touched his cap and walked away.

The days of chivalry are not gone, notwithstanding Burke's grand dirge over them: they live still in that far-off worship paid by many a youth and man to the woman of whom he never dreams that he shall touch so much as her little finger or the hem of her robe. Bob, with the pack on his back, had as respectful an adoration for this dark-eyed maiden as if he had been a knight in armour calling aloud on her name as he pricked on to the fight.

That gleam of merriment soon died away from Maggie's face, and perhaps only made the returning gloom deeper by contrast. She was too dispirited even to like answering questions about Bob's present of books, and she carried them away to her bedroom, laying them down there and seating herself on her one stool, without caring to look at them just yet. She leaned her cheek against the window-frame, and thought that the light-hearted Bob had a lot much happier than hers.

Maggie's sense of loneliness, and utter privation of joy, had deepened with the brightness of advancing spring. All the favourite out-door nooks about home, which seemed to have done their part with her parents in nurturing and cherishing her, were now mixed up with the home-sadness, and gathered no smile from the sunshine. Every affection, every delight the poor child had had, was like an aching nerve to her. There was no music for her any more—no piano, no harmonized voices, no delicious stringed instruments, with their passionate cries of imprisoned spirits sending a strange vibration through her frame. And of all her school-life there was nothing left her now but her little collection of school-books, which she turned over with a sickening sense that she knew them all, and they were all barren of comfort. Even at school she had often wished for books with *more* in them: everything she learned there seemed like the ends of long threads that snapped immediately. And now—without the indirect charm of school-emulation—Télémaque was mere bran; so were the hard dry questions on Christian doctrine: there was no flavour in them—no strength. Sometimes Maggie thought she could have been contented with absorbing fancies; if she could have had all Scott's novels and all Byron's poems!—then, perhaps, she might have found happiness enough to dull her sensibility to her actual daily life. And yet . . . they were hardly what she wanted. She could make dream-worlds of her own—but no dream-world would satisfy her now. She wanted some explanation of this hard, real life: the unhappy-looking father, seated at the dull breakfast-table; the childish, bewildered mother; the little sordid tasks that filled the hours, or the more oppressive emptiness of weary, joyless leisure; the need of some tender, demonstrative love; the cruel sense that Tom didn't mind what she thought or felt, and that they were no longer playfellows together; the privation of all pleasant things that had come to *her* more than to others: she wanted some key that would enable her to understand, and, in understanding, endure, the heavy weight that had fallen on her young heart. If she had been taught 'real learning and wisdom, such as great men knew,' she thought she should have held the secrets of life; if she had only books, that she might learn for herself what wise men knew! Saints and martyrs had never interested Maggie so much as sages and poets. She knew little of saints and martyrs, and had gathered, as a general result of her teaching, that they were a temporary provision against the spread of Catholicism, and had all died at Smithfield.

In one of these meditations it occurred to her that she had forgotten Tom's school-books, which had been sent home in his trunk. But she found the stock unaccountably shrunk down to the few old ones which had been well thumbed—the Latin Dictionary and Grammar, a Delectus, a torn Eutropius, the well-worn Virgil, Aldrich's Logic, and the exasperating Euclid. Still, Latin, Euclid, and Logic would surely be a considerable step in masculine wisdom—in that knowledge which made men contented, and even glad to live. Not that the yearning for effectual wisdom was quite unmixed: a certain mirage would now and then rise on the desert of the future, in which she seemed to see herself honoured for her surprising attainments. And so the poor child, with her soul's hunger and her illusions of self-flattery, began to nibble at this thick-rinded fruit of the tree of knowledge, filling her vacant hours with Latin, geometry, and the forms of the syllogism, and feeling a gleam of triumph now and then that her understanding was quite equal to these peculiarly masculine studies. For a week or two she went on resolutely enough, though with an occasional sinking of heart, as if she had set out toward the Promised Land alone, and found it a thirsty, trackless, uncertain journey. In the severity of her early resolution, she would take Aldrich out into the fields, and then look off her book towards the sky, where the lark was twinkling, or to the reeds and bushes by the river, from which the waterfowl rustled forth on its anxious, awkward flight—with a startled sense that the relation between Aldrich and this living world was extremely remote for her. The discouragement deepened as the days went on, and the eager heart gained faster and faster on the patient mind. Somehow, when she sat at the window with her book, her eyes *would* fix themselves blankly on the out-door sunshine; then they would fill with tears, and sometimes, if her mother was not in the room, the studies would all end in sobbing. She rebelled against her lot, she fainted under its loneliness, and fits even of anger and hatred towards her father and mother, who were so unlike what she would have them to be—towards Tom, who checked her, and met her thought or feeling always by some thwarting difference—would flow out over her affections and conscience like a lava stream, and frighten her with a sense that it was not difficult for her to become a demon. Then her brain would be busy with wild romances of a flight from home in search of something less sordid and dreary: she would go to some great man— Walter Scott, perhaps—and tell him how wretched and how clever she was, and he would surely do something for her. But, in the middle of her vision, her father would perhaps enter the room for the evening, and, surprised that she sat still without noticing him, would say complainingly, 'Come, am I to fetch my slippers myself?' The voice pierced through Maggie like a sword: there was another sadness besides her own, and she had been thinking of turning her back on it and forsaking it.

This afternoon, the sight of Bob's cheerful freckled face had given her discontent a new direction. She thought it was part of the hardship of her life that there was laid upon her the burthen of larger wants than others seemed to feel —that she had to endure this wide hopeless yearning for that something, whatever it was, that was greatest and best on this earth. She wished she could have been like Bob, with his easily satisfied ignorance, or like Tom, who had something to do on which he could fix his mind with a steady purpose, and disregard everything else. Poor child! as she leaned her head against the window-frame, with her hands clasped tighter and tighter, and her foot beating the ground, she was as lonely in her trouble as if she had been the only girl in the civilized world of that day who had come out of her school-life with a soul untrained for inevitable struggles—with no other part of her inherited share in the hard-won treasures of thought, which generations of painful toil have laid up for the race of men, than shreds and patches of feeble literature and false history—with much futile information about Saxon and other kings of doubtful example—but unhappily quite without that knowledge of the irreversible laws within and without her, which, governing the habits, becomes morality, and, developing the feelings of submission and dependence, becomes religion:—as lonely in her trouble as if every other girl besides herself had been cherished and watched over by elder minds, not forgetful of their own early time, when need was keen and impulse strong.

At last Maggie's eyes glanced down on the books that lay on the window-shelf, and she half forsook her reverie to turn over listlessly the leaves of the 'Portrait Gallery,' but she soon pushed this aside to examine the little row of books tied together with string. 'Beauties of the Spectator,' 'Rasselas,' 'Economy of Human Life,' 'Gregory's Letters' —she knew the sort of matter that was inside all these: the 'Christian Year'—that seemed to be a hymn-book, and she laid it down again; but *Thomas à Kempis?*—the name had come across her in her reading, and she felt the satisfaction, which every one knows, of getting some ideas to attach to a name that strays solitary in the memory. She took up the little, old, clumsy book with some curiosity: it had the corners turned down in many places, and some hand, now for ever quiet, had made at certain passages strong pen-and-ink marks, long since browned by time. Maggie turned from leaf to leaf, and read where the quiet hand pointed ... 'Know that the love of thyself doth hurt thee more than anything in the world.... If thou seekest this or that, and wouldst be here or there to enjoy thy own will and pleasure, thou shalt never be quiet nor free from care: for in everything somewhat will be wanting, and in every place there will be some that will cross thee.... Both above and below, which way soever thou dost turn thee, everywhere thou shalt find the Cross: and everywhere of necessity thou must have patience, if thou wilt have inward peace, and enjoy an everlasting crown.... If thou desire to mount unto this height, thou must set out courageously, and lay the axe to the root, that thou mayest pluck up and destroy that hidden inordinate inclination to thyself, and unto all private and earthly good. On this sin, that a man inordinately loveth himself, almost all dependeth, whatsoever is thoroughly to be overcome; which evil being once overcome and subdued, there will presently ensue great peace and tranquillity.... It is but little thou sufferest in comparison of them that have suffered so much, were so strongly tempted, so grievously afflicted, so many ways tried and exercised. Thou oughtest therefore to call to mind the more heavy sufferings of others, that thou mayest the easier bear thy little adversities. And if they seem not little unto thee, beware lest thy impatience be the cause thereof. ... Blessed are those ears that receive the whispers of the divine voice, and listen not to the whisperings of the world. Blessed are those ears which hearken not unto the voice which soundeth outwardly, but unto the Truth, which teacheth inwardly. ...'

A strange thrill of awe passed through Maggie while she

read, as if she had been wakened in the night by a strain of solemn music, telling of beings whose souls had been astir while hers was in stupor. She went on from one brown mark to another, where the quiet hand seemed to point, hardly conscious that she was reading—seeming rather to listen while a low voice said:

'Why dost thou here gaze about, since this is not the place of thy rest? In heaven ought to be thy dwelling, and all earthly things are to be looked on as they forward thy journey thither. All things pass away, and thou together with them. Beware thou cleave not unto them, lest thou be entangled and perish. . . . If a man should give all his substance, yet it is as nothing. And if he should do great penances, yet are they but little. And if he should attain to all knowledge, he is yet far off. And if he should be of great virtue, and very fervent devotion, yet is there much wanting; to wit, one thing, which is most necessary for him. What is that? That having left all, he leave himself, and go wholly out of himself, and retain nothing of self-love. . . . I have often said unto thee, and now again I say the same, Forsake thyself, resign thyself, and thou shalt enjoy much inward peace. . . . Then shall all vain imaginations, evil perturbations, and superfluous cares fly away; then shall immoderate fear leave thee, and inordinate love shall die.'

Maggie drew a long breath and pushed her heavy hair back, as if to see a sudden vision more clearly. Here, then, was a secret of life that would enable her to renounce all other secrets—here was a sublime height to be reached without the help of outward things—here was insight, and strength, and conquest, to be won by means entirely within her own soul, where a supreme Teacher was waiting to be heard. It flashed through her like the suddenly apprehended solution of a problem, that all the miseries of her young life had come from fixing her heart on her own pleasure, as if that were the central necessity of the universe; and for the first time she saw the possibility of shifting the position from which she looked at the gratification of her own desires—of taking her stand out of herself, and looking at her own life as an insignificant part of a divinely-guided whole. She read on and on in the old book, devouring eagerly the dialogues with the invisible Teacher, the pattern of sorrow, the source of all strength; returning to it after she had been called away, and reading till the sun went down behind the willows. With all the hurry of an imagination that could never rest in the present, she sat in the deepening twilight forming plans of self-humiliation and entire devotedness; and, in the ardour of first discovery, renunciation seemed to her the entrance into that satisfaction which she had so long been craving in vain. She had not perceived—how could she until she had lived longer?—the inmost truth of the old monk's outpourings, that renunciation remains sorrow, though a sorrow borne willingly. Maggie was still panting for happiness, and was in ecstasy because she had found the key to it. She knew nothing of doctrines and systems—of mysticism or quietism; but this voice out of the far-off middle ages was the direct communication of a human soul's belief and experience, and came to Maggie as an unquestioned message.

I suppose that is the reason why the small old-fashioned book, for which you need only pay sixpence at a book-stall, works miracles to this day, turning bitter waters into sweetness; while expensive sermons and treatises, newly issued, leave all things as they were before. It was written down by a hand that waited for the heart's prompting: it is the chronicle of a solitary, hidden anguish, struggle, trust and triumph—not written on velvet cushions to teach endurance to those who are treading with bleeding feet on the stones. And so it remains to all time a lasting record of human needs and human consolations: the voice of a brother who, ages ago, felt and suffered and renounced—in the cloister, perhaps, with serge gown and tonsured head, with much chanting and long fasts, and with a fashion of speech different from ours—but under the same silent far-off heavens, and with the same passionate desires, the same strivings, the same failures, the same weariness.

In writing the history of unfashionable families, one is apt to fall into a tone of emphasis which is very far from being the tone of good society, where principles and beliefs are not only of an extremely moderate kind, but are always presupposed, no subjects being eligible but such as can be touched with a light and graceful irony. But then, good society has its claret and its velvet-carpets, its dinner-engagements six weeks deep, its opera, and its faëry ballrooms; rides off its ennui on thoroughbred horses, lounges at the club, has to keep clear of crinoline vortices, gets its science done by Faraday, and its religion by the superior clergy who are to be met in the best houses: how should it have time or need for belief and emphasis? But good society, floated on gossamer wings of light irony, is of very expensive production; requiring nothing less than a wide and arduous national life condensed in unfragrant deafening factories, cramping itself in mines, sweating at furnaces, grinding, hammering, weaving under more or less oppression of carbonic acid—or else, spread over sheepwalks, and scattered in lonely houses and huts on the clayey or chalky corn-lands, where the rainy days look dreary. This wide national life is based entirely on emphasis—the emphasis of want, which urges it into all the activities necessary for the maintenance of good society and light irony: it spends its heavy years often in a chill, uncarpeted fashion, amidst family discord unsoftened by long corridors. Under such circumstances, there are many among its myriads of souls who have absolutely needed an emphatic belief: life in this unpleasurable shape demanding some solution even to unspeculative minds; just as you inquire into the stuffing of your couch when anything galls you there, whereas eider-down and perfect French springs excite no question. Some have an emphatic belief in alcohol, and seek their *ekstasis* or outside standing-ground in gin; but the rest require something that good society calls 'enthusiasm,' something that will present motives in an entire absence of high prizes, something that will give patience and feed human love when the limbs ache with weariness, and human looks are hard upon us—something, clearly, that lies outside personal desires, that includes resignation for ourselves and active love for what is not ourselves. Now and then, that sort of enthusiasm finds a far-echoing voice that comes from an experience springing out of the deepest need. And it was by being brought within the long lingering vibrations of such a voice that Maggie, with her girl's face and unnoted sorrows, found an effort and a hope that helped her through years of loneliness, making out a faith for herself without the aid of established authorities and appointed guides—for they were not at hand, and her need was pressing. From what you know of her, you will not be surprised that she threw some exaggeration and wilfulness, some pride and impetuosity, even into her self-renunciation: her own life was still a drama for her, in which she demanded of herself that her part should be played with intensity. And so it came to pass that she often lost the spirit of humility by being excessive in the outward act; she often strove after too high a flight, and came down with her poor little half-fledged wings dabbled in the mud. For example, she not only determined to work at plain sewing, that she might contribute something towards the fund in the tin box, but she went, in the first instance, in her zeal of self-mortification, to ask for it at a linen-shop in St. Ogg's, instead of getting it in a more quiet and indirect way; and could see nothing but what was entirely wrong and unkind, nay, persecuting, in Tom's reproof of her for this unnecessary act. 'I don't like *my* sister to do such things,' said Tom; '*I'll* take care that the debts are paid, without your lowering yourself in that way.' Surely there was some tenderness and bravery mingled with the worldliness and self-assertion of that little speech; but Maggie held it as dross, overlooking the grains of gold, and took Tom's rebuke as one of her outward crosses. Tom was very hard to her, she used to think, in her long night-watchings—to her who had always loved him so; and then she strove to be contented with that hardness, and to require nothing. That is the path we all like when we set out on our abandonment of egoism—the path of martyrdom and endurance, where the palm-branches grow, rather than the steep highway of tolerance, just allowance, and self-blame, where there are no leafy honours to be gathered and worn.

The old books, Virgil, Euclid, and Aldrich—that wrinkled fruit of the tree of knowledge—had been all laid by; for Maggie had turned her back on the vain ambition to share the thoughts of the wise. In her first ardour she flung away the books with a sort of triumph that she had risen above the need of them; and if they had been her own, she would have burned them, believing that she would never repent. She read so eagerly and constantly in her three books, the Bible, Thomas à Kempis, and the 'Christian Year' (no longer rejected as a 'hymn-book'), that they filled her mind with a continual stream of rhythmic memories; and she was too ardently learning to see all nature and life in the light of her new faith, to need any other material for her mind to work on, as she sat with her well-plied needle, making shirts and other complicated stitchings, falsely called 'plain'—by no means plain to Maggie, since wristband and sleeve and the like had a capability of being sewed in wrong side outwards in moments of mental wandering.

Hanging diligently over her sewing, Maggie was a sight any one might have been pleased to look at. That new inward life of hers, notwithstanding some volcanic upheavings of imprisoned passions, yet shone out in her face with a tender soft light that mingled itself as added loveliness with the gradually enriched colour and outline of her blossoming youth. Her mother felt the change in her with a sort of puzzled wonder that Maggie should be 'growing up so good'; it was amazing that this once 'contrary' child was become so submissive, so backward to assert her own will. Maggie used to look up from her work and find her mother's eyes fixed upon her: they were watching and waiting for the large young glance, as if her elder frame got some needful warmth from it. The mother was getting fond of her tall, brown girl, the only bit of furniture now on which she could bestow her anxiety and pride; and Maggie, in spite of her own ascetic wish to have no personal adornment, was obliged to give way to her mother about her hair, and submit to have the abundant black locks plaited into a coronet on the summit of her head, after the pitiable fashion of those antiquated times.

'Let your mother have that bit o' pleasure, my dear,' said Mrs. Tulliver; 'I'd trouble enough with your hair once.'

So Maggie, glad of anything that would soothe her mother, and cheer their long day together, consented to the vain decoration, and showed a queenly head above her old frocks—steadily refusing, however, to look at herself in the glass. Mrs. Tulliver liked to call the father's attention to Maggie's hair and other unexpected virtues, but he had a brusque reply to give.

'I knew well enough what she'd be, before now—it's nothing new to me. But it's a pity she isn't made o' commoner stuff—she'll be thrown away, I doubt: there'll be nobody to marry her as is fit for her.'

And Maggie's graces of mind and body fed his gloom. He sat patiently enough while she read him a chapter, or said something timidly when they were alone together about trouble being turned into a blessing. He took it all as part of his daughter's goodness, which made his misfortunes the sadder to him because they damaged her chance in life. In a mind charged with an eager purpose and an unsatisfied vindictiveness, there is no room for new feelings: Mr. Tulliver did not want spiritual consolation—he wanted to shake off the degradation of debt, and to have his revenge.

BOOK FIFTH

WHEAT AND TARES

I

IN THE RED DEEPS

THE family sitting-room was a long room with a window at each end; one looking towards the croft and along the Ripple to the banks of the Floss, the other into the mill-yard. Maggie was sitting with her work against the latter window when she saw Mr. Wakem entering the yard, as usual, on his fine black horse; but not alone, as usual. Someone was with him—a figure in a cloak, on a handsome pony. Maggie had hardly time to feel that it was Philip come back, before they were in front of the window, and he was raising his hat to her; while his father, catching the movement by a side-glance, looked sharply round at them both.

Maggie hurried away from the window and carried her work up-stairs; for Mr. Wakem sometimes came in and inspected the books, and Maggie felt that the meeting with Philip would be robbed of all pleasure in the presence of the two fathers. Some day, perhaps, she should see him when they could just shake hands, and she could tell him that she remembered his goodness to Tom, and the things he had said to her in the old days, though they could never be friends any more. It was not at all agitating to Maggie to see Philip again: she retained her childish gratitude and pity towards him, and remembered his cleverness; and in the early weeks of her loneliness she had continually recalled the image of him among the people who had been kind to her in life; often wishing she had him for a brother and a teacher, as they had fancied it might have been, in their talk together. But that sort of wishing had been banished along with other dreams that savoured of seeking her own will; and she thought, besides, that Philip might be altered by his life abroad—he might have become worldly, and really not care about her saying anything to him now. And yet, his face was wonderfully little altered—it was only a larger, more manly copy of the pale small-featured boy's face, with the grey eyes and the boyish waving brown hair: there was the old deformity to awaken the old pity: and after all her meditations, Maggie felt that she really *should* like to say a few words to him. He might still be melancholy, as he always used to be, and like her to look at him kindly. She wondered if he remembered how he used to like her eyes; with that thought Maggie glanced towards the square looking-glass which was condemned to hang with its face towards the wall, and she half-started from her seat to reach it down; but she checked herself and snatched up her work, trying to repress the rising wishes by forcing her memory to recall snatches of hymns, until she saw Philip and his father returning along the road, and she could go down again.

It was far on in June now, and Maggie was inclined to lengthen the daily walk which was her one indulgence; but this day and the following she was so busy with work which must be finished that she never went beyond the gate, and satisfied her need of the open air by sitting out of doors. One of her frequent walks, when she was not obliged to go to St. Ogg's, was to a spot that lay beyond what was called the 'Hill'—an insignificant rise of ground crowned by trees, lying along the side of the road which ran by the gates of Dorlcote Mill. Insignificant I call it, because in height it was hardly more than a bank: but there may come moments when Nature makes a mere bank a means towards a fateful result, and that is why I ask you to imagine this high bank crowned with trees, making an uneven wall for some quarter of a mile along the left side of Dorlcote Mill and the pleasant fields behind it, bounded by the murmuring Ripple. Just where this line of bank sloped down again to the level, a by-road turned off and led to the other side of the rise, where it was broken into very capricious hollows

and mounds by the working of an exhausted stone-quarry
—so long exhausted that both mounds and hollows were
now clothed with brambles and trees, and here and there
by a stretch of grass which a few sheep kept close-nibbled.
In her childish days Maggie held this place, called the Red
Deeps, in very great awe, and needed all her confidence in
Tom's bravery to reconcile her to an excursion thither—
visions of robbers and fierce animals haunting every hollow.
But now it had the charm for her which any broken ground,
any mimic rock and ravine, have for the eyes that rest
habitually on the level; especially in summer, when she
could sit on a grassy hollow under the shadow of a branch-
ing ash, stooping aslant from the steep above her, and
listen to the hum of insects, like tiniest bells on the garment
of Silence, or see the sunlight piercing the distant boughs,
as if to chase and drive home the truant heavenly blue of
the wild hyacinths. In this June time, too, the dog-roses
were in their glory, and that was an additional reason why
Maggie should direct her walk to the Red Deeps, rather
than to any other spot, on the first day she was free to
wander at her will—a pleasure she loved so well, that sometimes, in her ardours of renunciation, she thought she ought
to deny herself the frequent indulgence in it.

You may see her now, as she walks down the favourite
turning, and enters the Deeps by a narrow path through a
group of Scotch firs—her tall figure and old lavender gown
visible through an hereditary black silk shawl of some wide-
meshed net-like material; and now she is sure of being
unseen, she takes off her bonnet and ties it over her arm.
One would certainly suppose her to be farther on in life
than her seventeenth year—perhaps because of the slow
resigned sadness of the glance, from which all search and
unrest seem to have departed, perhaps because her broad-
chested figure has the mould of early womanhood. Youth
and health have withstood well the involuntary and
voluntary hardships of her lot, and the nights in which she
has lain on the hard floor for a penance have left no obvious
trace; the eyes are liquid, the brown cheek is firm and
rounded, the full lips are red. With her dark colouring and

jet crown surmounting her tall figure, she seems to have a sort of kinship with the grand Scotch firs, at which she is looking up as if she loved them well. Yet one has a sense of uneasiness in looking at her—a sense of opposing elements, of which a fierce collision is imminent: surely there is a hushed expression, such as one often sees in older faces under borderless caps, out of keeping with the resistant youth, which one expects to flash out in a sudden, passionate glance, that will dissipate all the quietude, like a damp fire leaping out again when all seemed safe.

But Maggie herself was not uneasy at this moment. She was calmly enjoying the free air, while she looked up at the old fir-trees, and thought that those broken ends of branches were the records of past storms, which had only made the red stems soar higher. But while her eyes were still turned upward, she became conscious of a moving shadow cast by the evening sun on the grassy path before her, and looked down with a startled gesture to see Philip Wakem, who first raised his hat, and then, blushing deeply, came forward to her and put out his hand. Maggie, too, coloured with surprise, which soon gave way to pleasure. She put out her hand and looked down at the deformed figure before her with frank eyes, filled for the moment with nothing but the memory of her child's feelings—a memory that was always strong in her. She was the first to speak.

'You startled me,' she said, smiling faintly. 'I never meet anyone here. How came you to be walking here? Did you come to meet *me*?'

It was impossible not to perceive that Maggie felt herself a child again.

'Yes, I did,' said Philip, still embarrassed: 'I wished to see you very much. I watched a long while yesterday on the bank near your house to see if you would come out, but you never came. Then I watched again to-day, and when I saw the way you took, I kept you in sight and came down the bank, behind there. I hope you will not be displeased with me.'

'No,' said Maggie, with simple seriousness, walking on, as if she meant Philip to accompany her, 'I'm very glad you came, for I wished very much to have an opportunity of speaking to you. I've never forgotten how good you were long ago to Tom, and me too; but I was not sure that you would remember us so well. Tom and I have had a great deal of trouble since then, and I think *that* makes one think more of what happened before the trouble came.'

'I can't believe that you have thought of me so much as I have thought of you,' said Philip timidly. 'Do you know, when I was away, I made a picture of you as you looked that morning in the study when you said you would not forget me.'

Philip drew a large miniature-case from his pocket, and opened it. Maggie saw her old self leaning on a table, with her black locks hanging down behind her ears, looking into space with strange, dreamy eyes. It was a water-colour sketch, of real merit as a portrait.

'O dear,' said Maggie, smiling, and flushed with pleasure, 'what a queer little girl I was! I remember myself with my hair in that way, in that pink frock. I really *was* like a gypsy. I daresay I am now,' she added, after a little pause; 'am I like what you expected me to be?'

The words might have been those of a coquette, but the full bright glance Maggie turned on Philip was not that of a coquette. She really did hope he liked her face as it was now, but it was simply the rising again of her innate delight in admiration and love. Philip met her eyes and looked at her in silence for a long moment, before he said quietly, 'No, Maggie.'

The light died out a little from Maggie's face, and there was a slight trembling of the lip. Her eyelids fell lower, but she did not turn away her head, and Philip continued to look at her. Then he said slowly:

'You are very much more beautiful than I thought you would be.'

'Am I?' said Maggie, the pleasure returning in a deeper flush. She turned her face away from him and took some steps, looking straight before her in silence, as if she were adjusting her consciousness to this new idea. Girls are so accustomed to think of dress as the main ground of vanity, that, in abstaining from the looking-glass, Maggie had thought more of abandoning all care for adornment than of renouncing the contemplation of her face. Comparing herself with elegant, wealthy young ladies, it had not occurred to her that she could produce any effect with her person. Philip seemed to like the silence well. He walked by her side, watching her face, as if that sight left no room for any other wish. They had passed from among the fir-trees, and had now come to a green hollow almost surrounded by an amphitheatre of the pale pink dog-roses. But as the light about them had brightened, Maggie's face had lost its glow. She stood still when they were in the hollows, and, looking at Philip again, she said, in a serious, sad voice:

'I wish we could have been friends—I mean, if it would have been good and right for us. But that is the trial I have to bear in everything: I may not keep anything I used to love when I was little. The old books went; and Tom is different—and my father. It is like death. I must part with everything I cared for when I was a child. And I must part with you: we must never take any notice of each other again. That was what I wanted to speak to you for. I wanted to let you know that Tom and I can't do as we like about such things, and that if I behave as if I had forgotten all about you, it is not out of envy or pride—or—or any bad feeling.'

Maggie spoke with more and more sorrowful gentleness as she went on, and her eyes began to fill with tears. The deepening expression of pain on Philip's face gave him a stronger resemblance to his boyish self, and made the deformity appeal more strongly to her pity.

'I know—I see all that you mean,' he said, in a voice that had become feebler from discouragement: 'I know what there is to keep us apart on both sides. But it is not right, Maggie—don't you be angry with me, I am so used to call you Maggie in my thoughts—it is not right to sacrifice everything to other people's unreasonable feelings. I would give up a great deal for *my* father; but I would not give up a friendship or—or an attachment of any sort, in obedience to any wish of his that I didn't recognise as right.'

'I don't know,' said Maggie musingly. 'Often, when I have been angry and discontented, it has seemed to me that I was not bound to give up anything; and I have gone on thinking till it has seemed to me that I could think away all my duty. But no good has ever come of that—it was an evil state of mind. I'm quite sure that whatever I might do, I should wish in the end that I had gone without anything for myself, rather than have made my father's life harder to him.'

'But would it make his life harder if we were to see each other sometimes?' said Philip. He was going to say something else, but checked himself.

'O, I'm sure he wouldn't like it. Don't ask me why, or anything about it,' said Maggie, in a distressed tone. 'My father feels so strongly about some things. He is not at all happy.'

'No more am I,' said Philip impetuously: 'I am not happy.'

'Why?' said Maggie gently. 'At least—I ought not to ask—but I'm very, very sorry.'

Philip turned to walk on, as if he had not patience to stand still any longer, and they went out of the hollow winding amongst the trees and bushes in silence. After that last word of Philip's, Maggie could not bear to insist immediately on their parting.

'I've been a great deal happier,' she said at last timidly, 'since I have given up thinking about what is easy and pleasant, and being discontented because I couldn't have my own will. Our life is determined for us—and it makes the mind very free when we give up wishing, and only think of bearing what is laid upon us, and doing what is given us to do.'

'But I can't give up wishing,' said Philip impatiently. 'It seems to me we can never give up longing and wishing while we are thoroughly alive. There are certain things we feel to be beautiful and good, and we *must* hunger after them. How can we ever be satisfied without them until our feelings are deadened? I delight in fine pictures—I long to be able to paint such. I strive and strive, and can't produce what I want. That is pain to me, and always *will* be pain, until my faculties lose their keenness, like aged eyes. Then there are many other things I long for'—here Philip hesitated a little, and then said—'things that other men have, and that will always be denied me. My life will have nothing great or beautiful in it; I would rather not have lived.'

'O, Philip,' said Maggie, 'I wish you didn't feel so.' But her heart began to beat with something of Philip's discontent.

'Well, then,' said he, turning quickly round and fixing his grey eyes entreatingly on her face, 'I should be contented to live, if you would let me see you sometimes.' Then, checked by a fear which her face suggested, he looked away again, and said, more calmly, 'I have no friend to whom I can tell everything—no one who cares enough about me; and if I could only see you now and then, and you would let me talk to you a little, and show me that you cared for me—and that we may always be friends in heart, and help each other—then I might come to be glad of life.'

'But how can I see you, Philip?' said Maggie falteringly. (Could she really do him good? It would be very hard to say 'good-bye' this day, and not speak to him again. Here was a new interest to vary the days—it was so much easier to renounce the interest before it came.)

'If you would let me see you here sometimes—walk with you here—I would be contented if it were only once or twice in a month. *That* could injure no one's happiness, and it would sweeten my life. Besides,' Philip went on, with all the inventive astuteness of love at one-and-twenty, 'if there is any enmity between those who belong to us, we ought all the more to try and quench it by our friendship—I mean, that by our influence on both sides we might bring about a healing of the wounds that have been made in the past, if I could know everything about them. And I don't believe there is any enmity in my own father's mind: I think he has proved the contrary.'

Maggie shook her head slowly, and was silent, under conflicting thoughts. It seemed to her inclination, that to see Philip now and then, and keep up the bond of friendship with him, was something not only innocent, but good: perhaps she might really help him to find contentment as she had found it. The voice that said this made sweet music to Maggie; but athwart it there came an urgent monotonous warning from another voice which she had been learning to obey: the warning that such interviews implied secrecy—implied doing something she would dread to be discovered in—something that, if discovered, must cause anger and pain; and that the admission of anything so near doubleness would act as a spiritual blight. Yet the music would swell out again, like chimes borne onward by a recurrent breeze, persuading her that the wrong lay all in the faults and weaknesses of others, and that there was such a thing as futile sacrifice for one to the injury of another. It was very cruel for Philip that he should be shrunk from, because of an unjustifiable vindictiveness towards his father—poor Philip, whom some people would shrink from only because he was deformed. The idea that he might become her lover, or that her meeting him could cause disapproval in that light, had not occurred to her; and Philip saw the absence of this idea clearly enough—saw it with a certain pang, although it made her consent to his request the less unlikely. There was bitterness to him in the perception that Maggie was almost as frank and unconstrained towards him as when she was a child.

'I can't say either yes or no,' she said at last, turning round and walking towards the way she had come; 'I must wait, lest I should decide wrongly. I must seek for guidance.'

'May I come again, then—to-morrow—or the next day—or next week?'

'I think I had better write,' said Maggie, faltering again. 'I have to go to St. Ogg's sometimes, and I can put the letter in the post.'

'O no,' said Philip eagerly; 'that would not be so well. My father might see the letter—and—he has not any enmity, I believe, but he views things differently from me: he thinks a great deal about wealth and position. Pray let me come here once more. *Tell* me when it shall be; or if

you can't tell me, I will come as often as I can till I do
see you.'

'I think it must be so, then,' said Maggie, 'for I can't be
quite certain of coming here any particular evening.'

Maggie felt a great relief in adjourning the decision. She
was free now to enjoy the minutes of companionship; she
almost thought she might linger a little; the next time they
met she should have to pain Philip by telling him her determination.

'I can't help thinking,' she said, looking smilingly at him,
after a few moments of silence, 'how strange it is that we
should have met and talked to each other, just as if it had
been only yesterday when we parted at Lorton. And yet
we must both be very much altered in those five years—I
think it is five years. How was it you seemed to have a sort
of feeling that I was the same Maggie?—I was not quite so
sure that you would be the same: I know you are so clever,
and you must have seen and learnt so much to fill your
mind: I was not quite sure you would care about me now.'

'I have never had any doubt that you would be the same
whenever I might see you,' said Philip. 'I mean, the same in
everything that made me like you better than anyone else.
I don't want to explain that: I don't think any of the
strongest effects our natures are susceptible of can ever be
explained. We can neither detect the process by which they
are arrived at, nor the mode in which they act on us. The
greatest of painters only once painted a mysteriously divine
child; he couldn't have told how he did it, and we can't
tell why we feel it to be divine. I think there are stores laid
up in our human nature that our understandings can make
no complete inventory of. Certain strains of music affect
me so strangely—I can never hear them without their
changing my whole attitude of mind for a time, and if the
effect would last, I might be capable of heroisms.'

'Ah! I know what you mean about music—*I* feel so,' said
Maggie, clasping her hands with her old impetuosity. 'At
least' she added, in a saddened tone, 'I used to feel so when
I had any music: I never have any now except the organ at
church.'

'And you long for it, Maggie?' said Philip, looking at her with affectionate pity. 'Ah, you can have very little that is beautiful in your life. Have you many books? You were so fond of them when you were a little girl.'

They were come back to the hollow, round which the dog-roses grew, and they both paused under the charm of the faëry evening light, reflected from the pale pink clusters.

'No, I have given up books,' said Maggie quietly, 'except a very, very few.'

Philip had already taken from his pocket a small volume, and was looking at the back, as he said:

'Ah, this is the second volume, I see, else you might have liked to take it home with you. I put it in my pocket because I am studying a scene for a picture.'

Maggie had looked at the back too, and saw the title: it revived an old impression with overmastering force.

'"The Pirate,"' she said, taking the book from Philip's hands. 'O, I began that once; I read to where Minna is walking with Cleveland, and I could never get to read the rest. I went on with it in my own head, and I made several endings; but they were all unhappy. I could never make a happy ending out of that beginning. Poor Minna! I wonder what is the real end. For a long while I couldn't get my mind away from the Shetland Isles—I used to feel the wind blowing on me from the rough sea.'

Maggie spoke rapidly, with glistening eyes.

'Take that volume home with you, Maggie,' said Philip, watching her with delight. 'I don't want it now. I shall make a picture of you instead—you, among the Scotch firs and the slanting shadows.'

Maggie had not heard a word he had said: she was absorbed in a page at which she had opened. But suddenly she closed the book, and gave it back to Philip, shaking her head with a backward movement, as if to say 'avaunt' to floating visions.

'Do keep it, Maggie,' said Philip entreatingly; 'it will give you pleasure.'

'No, thank you,' said Maggie, putting it aside with her

hand and walking on. 'It would make me in love with this world again, as I used to be—it would make me long to see and know many things—it would make me long for a full life.'

'But you will not always be shut up in your present lot: why should you starve your mind in that way? It is narrow asceticism—I don't like to see you persisting in it, Maggie. Poetry and art and knowledge are sacred and pure.'

'But not for me—not for me,' said Maggie, walking more hurriedly. 'Because I should want too much. I must wait —this life will not last long.'

'Don't hurry away from me without saying "good-bye," Maggie,' said Philip, as they reached the group of Scotch firs, and she continued still to walk along without speaking. 'I must not go any farther, I think, must I?'

'O no, I forgot; good-bye,' said Maggie, pausing, and putting out her hand to him. The action brought her feeling back in a strong current to Philip; and after they had stood looking at each other in silence for a few moments, with their hands clasped, she said, withdrawing her hand:

'I'm very grateful to you for thinking of me all those years. It is very sweet to have people love us. What a wonderful, beautiful thing it seems that God should have made your heart so that you could care about a queer little girl whom you only knew for a few weeks! I remember saying to you, that I thought you cared for me more than Tom did.'

'Ah, Maggie,' said Philip, almost fretfully, 'you would never love me so well as you love your brother.'

'Perhaps not,' said Maggie simply; 'but then, you know, the first thing I ever remember in my life is standing with Tom by the side of the Floss, while he held my hand: everything before that is dark to me. But I shall never forget you—though we must keep apart.'

'Don't say so, Maggie,' said Philip. 'If I kept that little girl in my mind for five years, didn't I earn some part in her? She ought not to take herself quite away from me.'

'Not if I were free,' said Maggie; 'but I am not—I must

submit.' She hesitated a moment, and then added: 'And I wanted to say to you, that you had better not take more notice of my brother than just bowing to him. He once told me not to speak to you again, and he doesn't change his mind. . . . O dear, the sun is set. I am too long away. Good-bye.' She gave him her hand once more.

'I shall come here as often as I can, till I see you again, Maggie. Have some feeling for *me* as well as for others.'

'Yes, yes, I have,' said Maggie, hurrying away, and quickly disappearing behind the last fir-tree; though Philip's gaze after her remained immovable for minutes as if he saw her still.

Maggie went home, with an inward conflict already begun; Philip went home to do nothing but remember and hope. You can hardly help blaming him severely. He was four or five years older than Maggie, and had a full consciousness of his feeling towards her to aid him in foreseeing the character his contemplated interviews with her would bear in the opinion of a third person. But you must not suppose that he was capable of a gross selfishness, or that he could have been satisfied without persuading himself that he was seeking to infuse some happiness into Maggie's life—seeking this even more than any direct ends for himself. He could give her sympathy—he could give her help. There was not the slightest promise of love towards him in her manner; it was nothing more than the sweet girlish tenderness she had shown him when she was twelve: perhaps she would never love him—perhaps no woman ever *could* love him: well, then, he would endure that; he should at least have the happiness of seeing her—of feeling some nearness to her. And he clutched passionately the possibility that she *might* love him: perhaps the feeling would grow, if she could come to associate him with that watchful tenderness which her nature would be so keenly alive to. If any woman could love him, surely Maggie was that woman: there was such wealth of love in her, and there was no one to claim it all. Then—the pity of it, that a mind like hers should be withering in its very youth, like a young forest-tree, for want of the light and space it was formed to flourish in! Could he not hinder that by persuading her out of her system of privation? He would be her guardian angel: he would do anything, bear anything, for her sake—except not seeing her.

II

AUNT GLEGG LEARNS THE BREADTH OF BOB'S THUMB

WHILE Maggie's life-struggles had lain almost entirely within her own soul, one shadowy army fighting another, and the slain shadows for ever rising again, Tom was engaged in a dustier, noisier warfare, grappling with more substantial obstacles, and gaining more definite conquests. So it has been since the days of Hecuba, and of Hector, Tamer of horses: inside the gates, the women with streaming hair and uplifted hands offering prayers, watching the world's combat from afar, filling their long, empty days with memories and fears: outside, the men, in fierce struggle with things divine and human, quenching memory in the stronger light of purpose, losing the sense of dread and even of wounds in the hurrying ardour of action.

From what you have seen of Tom, I think he is not a youth of whom you would prophesy failure in anything he had thoroughly wished: the wagers are likely to be on his side, notwithstanding his small success in the classics. For Tom had never desired success in this field of enterprise; and for getting a fine flourishing growth of stupidity there is nothing like pouring out on a mind a good amount of subjects on which it feels no interest. But now Tom's strong will bound together his integrity, his pride, his family regrets, and his personal ambition, and made them one force, concentrating his efforts and surmounting discouragements. His uncle Deane, who watched him closely, soon began to conceive hopes of him, and to be rather proud that he had brought into the employment of the firm a nephew who appeared to be made of such good commercial stuff. The real kindness of placing him in the warehouse first was soon evident to Tom, in the hints his uncle began to throw out, that after a time he might perhaps be trusted to travel at certain seasons, and buy in for the firm various vulgar commodities with which I need not shock refined ears in this place; and it was doubtless with a view to this result that Mr. Deane, when he expected to take his wine alone, would tell Tom to step in and sit with him an hour, and would pass that hour in much lecturing and catechising concerning articles of export and import, with an occasional excursus of more indirect utility on the relative advantages to the merchants of St. Ogg's of having goods brought in their own and in foreign bottoms—a subject on which Mr. Deane, as a shipowner, naturally threw off a few sparks when he got warmed with talk and wine. Already, in the second year, Tom's salary was raised; but all, except the price of his dinner and clothes, went home into the tin box; and he shunned comradeship, lest it should lead him into expenses in spite of himself. Not that Tom was moulded on the spooney type of the Industrious Apprentice; he had a very strong appetite for pleasure—would have liked to be a Tamer of horses, and to make a distinguished figure in all neighbouring eyes, dispensing treats and benefits to others with well-judged liberality, and being pronounced one of the finest young fellows of those parts; nay, he determined to achieve these things sooner or later; but his practical shrewdness told him that the means to such achievements could only lie for him in present abstinence and self-denial; there were certain milestones to be passed, and one of the first was the payment of his father's debts. Having made up his mind on that point, he strode along without swerving, contracting some rather saturnine sternness, as a young man is likely to do who has a premature call upon him for self-reliance. Tom felt intensely that common cause with his father which springs from family pride, and was bent on being irreproachable as a son: but his growing experience caused him to pass much silent criticism on the rashness and imprudence of his father's past conduct: their dispositions were not in sympathy, and Tom's face showed little radiance during his few home hours. Maggie had an awe of him, against which she struggled as something unfair to her consciousness of wider thoughts and deeper motives; but it was of no use to struggle. A character at unity with itself—that performs what it intends, subdues every counteracting impulse, and has no visions beyond the distinctly possible—is strong by its very negations.

You may imagine that Tom's more and more obvious unlikeness to his father was well fitted to conciliate the maternal aunts and uncles; and Mr. Deane's favourable reports and predictions to Mr. Glegg concerning Tom's qualifications for business, began to be discussed amongst them with various acceptance. He was likely, it appeared, to do the family credit, without causing it any expense and trouble. Mrs. Pullet had always thought it strange if Tom's excellent complexion, so entirely that of the Dodsons, did not argue a certainty that he would turn out well, his juvenile errors of running down the peacock, and general disrespect to his aunts, only indicating a tinge of Tulliver blood which he had doubtless outgrown. Mr. Glegg, who had contracted a cautious liking for Tom ever since his spirited and sensible behaviour when the execution was in the house, was now warming into a resolution to further his prospects actively—some time, when an opportunity offered of doing so in a prudent manner, without ultimate loss; but Mrs. Glegg observed that she was not given to speak without book, as some people were; that those who said least were most likely to find their words made good; and that when the right moment came, it would be seen who could do something better than talk. Uncle Pullet, after silent meditation for a period of several lozenges, came distinctly to the conclusion, that when a young man was likely to do well, it was better not to meddle with him.

Tom, meanwhile, had shown no disposition to rely on anyone but himself, though, with a natural sensitiveness towards all indications of favourable opinion, he was glad to see his uncle Glegg look in on him sometimes in a friendly way during business hours, and glad to be invited to dine at his house, though he usually preferred declining on the ground that he was not sure of being punctual. But about a year ago, something had occurred which induced Tom to test his uncle Glegg's friendly disposition.

Bob Jakin, who rarely returned from one of his rounds without seeing Tom and Maggie, awaited him on the bridge as he was coming home from St. Ogg's one evening, that they might have a little private talk. He took the liberty of asking if Mr. Tom had ever thought of making money by trading a bit on his own account. Trading, how? Tom wished to know. Why, by sending out a bit of a cargo to foreign ports; because Bob had a particular friend who had offered to do a little business for him in that way in Laceham goods, and would be glad to serve Mr. Tom on the same footing. Tom was interested at once, and begged for full explanation; wondering he had not thought of this plan before. He was so well pleased with the prospect of a speculation that might change the slow process of addition into multiplication, that he at once determined to mention the matter to his father, and get his consent to appropriate some of the savings in the tin box to the purchase of a small cargo. He would rather not have consulted his father, but he had just paid his last quarter's money into the tin box, and there was no other resource. All the savings were there; for Mr. Tulliver would not consent to put the money out at interest lest he should lose it. Since he had speculated in the purchase of some corn, and had lost by it, he could not be easy without keeping the money under his eye.

Tom approached the subject carefully, as he was seated on the hearth with his father that evening, and Mr. Tulliver listened, leaning forward in his arm-chair and looking up in Tom's face with a sceptical glance. His first impulse was to give a positive refusal, but he was in some awe of Tom's wishes, and since he had had the sense of being an 'unlucky' father, he had lost some of his old peremptoriness and determination to be master. He took the key of the bureau from his pocket, got out the key of the large chest, and fetched down the tin box—slowly, as if he were trying to defer the moment of a painful parting. Then he seated himself against the table, and opened the box with that little padlock-key which he fingered in his waistcoat pocket in all

vacant moments. There they were, the dingy bank-notes
and the bright sovereigns, and he counted them out on the
table—only a hundred and sixteen pounds in two years,
after all the pinching.

'How much do you want, then?' he said, speaking as if
the words burnt his lips.

'Suppose I begin with the thirty-six pounds, father?'
said Tom.

Mr. Tulliver separated this sum from the rest, and keeping his hand over it, said:

'It's as much as I can save out o' my pay in a year.'

'Yes, father: it is such slow work—saving out of the little
money we get. And in this way we might double our
savings.'

'Ay, my lad,' said the father, keeping his hand on the
money, 'but you might lose it—you might lose a year o' my
life—and I haven't got many.'

Tom was silent.

'And you know I wouldn't pay a dividend with the first
hundred, because I wanted to see it all in a lump—and
when I see it, I'm sure on't. If you trust to luck, it's sure to
be against me. It's Old Harry's got the luck in his hands;
and if I lose one year, I shall never pick it up again—death
'ull o'ertake me.'

Mr. Tulliver's voice trembled, and Tom was silent for a
few minutes before he said:

'I'll give it up, father, since you object to it so strongly.'

But, unwilling to abandon the scheme altogether, he determined to ask his uncle Glegg to venture twenty pounds,
on condition of receiving five per cent. of the profits. That
was really a very small thing to ask. So when Bob called
the next day at the wharf to know the decision, Tom proposed that they should go together to his uncle Glegg's to
open the business; for his diffident pride clung to him, and
made him feel that Bob's tongue would relieve him from
some embarrassment.

Mr. Glegg, at the pleasant hour of four in the afternoon
of a hot August day, was naturally counting his wall-fruit
to assure himself that the sum total had not varied since

yesterday. To him entered Tom, in what appeared to Mr. Glegg very questionable companionship: that of a man with a pack on his back—for Bob was equipped for a new journey—and of a huge brindled bull-terrier, who walked with a slow swaying movement from side to side, and glanced from under his eyelids with a surly indifference which might after all be a cover to the most offensive designs. Mr. Glegg's spectacles, which had been assisting him in counting the fruit, made these suspicious details alarmingly evident to him.

'Heigh! heigh! keep that dog back, will you?' he shouted, snatching up a stake and holding it before him as a shield when the visitors were within three yards of him.

'Get out wi' you, Mumps,' said Bob, with a kick. 'He's as quiet as a lamb, sir,'—an observation which Mumps corroborated by a low growl as he retreated behind his master's legs.

'Why, what ever does this mean, Tom?' said Mr. Glegg. 'Have you brought information about the scoundrels as cut my trees?' If Bob came in the character of 'information,' Mr. Glegg saw reasons for tolerating some irregularity.

'No, sir,' said Tom: 'I came to speak to you about a little matter of business of my own.'

'Ay—well; but what has this dog got to do with it?' said the old gentleman, getting mild again.

'It's my dog, sir,' said the ready Bob. 'An' it's me as put Mr. Tom up to the bit o' business; for Mr. Tom's been a friend o' mine iver since I was a little chap: fust thing iver I did was frightenin' the birds for th' old master. An' if a bit o' luck turns up, I'm allays thinkin' if I can let Mr. Tom have a pull at it. An' it's a downright roarin' shame, as when he's got the chance o' making a bit o' money wi' sending goods out—ten or twelve per zent. clear, when freight an' commission's paid—as he shouldn't lay hold o' the chance for want o' money. An' when there's the Laceham goods—lors! they're made o' purpose for folks as want to send out a little carguy; light, an' take up no room—you may pack twenty pound so as you can't see the passill: an' they're manifacturs as please fools, so I reckon they aren't like to want a market. An' I'd go to Laceham an' buy in the goods for Mr. Tom along wi' my own. An' there's the shupercargo o' the bit of a vessel as is goin' to take 'em out. I know him partic'lar; he's a solid man, an' got a family i' the town here. Salt, his name is—an' a briny chap he is too—an' if you don't believe me, I can take you to him.'

Uncle Glegg stood open-mouthed with astonishment at this unembarrassed loquacity, with which his understanding could hardly keep pace. He looked at Bob, first over his spectacles, then through them, then over them again; while Tom, doubtful of his uncle's impression, began to wish he had not brought this singular Aaron or mouthpiece: Bob's talk appeared less seemly, now some one besides himself was listening to it.

'You seem to be a knowing fellow,' said Mr. Glegg, at last.

'Ay, sir, you say true,' returned Bob, nodding his head aside; 'I think my head's all alive inside like an old cheese, for I'm so full o' plans, one knocks another over. If I hadn't Mumps to talk to, I should get top-heavy an' tumble in a fit. I suppose it's because I niver went to school much. That's what I jaw my old mother for. I says, "You should ha' sent me to school a bit more," I says—"an' then I could ha' read i' the books like fun, an' kep' my head cool an' empty." Lors, she's fine an' comfor'ble now, my old mother is: she ates her baked meat and taters as often as she likes. For I'm gettin' so full o' money, I must hev a wife to spend it for me. But it's botherin', a wife is—and Mumps mightn't like her.'

Uncle Glegg, who regarded himself as a jocose man since he had retired from business, was beginning to find Bob amusing, but he had still a disapproving observation to make, which kept his face serious.

'Ah,' he said, 'I should think you're at a loss for ways o' spending your money, else you wouldn't keep that big dog, to eat as much as two Christians. It's shameful—shameful!' But he spoke more in sorrow than in anger, and quickly added:

'But, come now, let's hear more about this business, Tom. I suppose you want a little sum to make a venture with. But where's all your own money? You don't spend it all—eh?'

'No, sir,' said Tom, colouring; 'but my father is unwilling to risk it, and I don't like to press him. If I could get twenty or thirty pounds to begin with, I could pay five per cent. for it, and then I could gradually make a little capital of my own, and do without a loan.'

'Ay ... ay,' said Mr. Glegg, in an approving tone; 'that's not a bad notion, and I won't say as I wouldn't be your man. But it 'ull be as well for me to see this Salt as you talk on. And then ... here's this friend o' yours offers to buy the goods for you. Perhaps you've got somebody to stand surety for you if the money's put into your hands?' added the cautious old gentleman, looking over his spectacles at Bob.

'I don't think that's necessary, uncle,' said Tom. 'At least, I mean it would not be necessary for me, because I know Bob well; but perhaps it would be right for you to have some security.'

'You get your percentage out o' the purchase, I suppose?' said Mr. Glegg, looking at Bob.

'No, sir,' said Bob, rather indignantly; 'I didn't offer to get an apple for Mr. Tom, o' purpose to hev a bite out of it myself. When I play folks tricks there'll be more fun in 'em nor that.'

'Well, but it's nothing but right you should have a small percentage,' said Mr. Glegg. 'I've no opinion o' transactions where folks do things for nothing. It allays looks bad.'

'Well, then,' said Bob, whose keenness saw at once what was implied, 'I'll tell you what I get by't, an' it's money in my pocket in the end:—I make myself look big, wi' makin' a bigger purchase. That's what I'm thinking on. Lors! I'm a 'cute chap—I am.'

'Mr. Glegg, Mr. Glegg,' said a severe voice from the open parlour window, 'pray are you coming in to tea?—or are you going to stand talking with packmen till you get murdered in the open daylight?'

'Murdered?' said Mr. Glegg; 'what's the woman talking of? Here's your nephey Tom come about a bit o' business.'

'Murdered—yes—it isn't many 'sizes ago since a packman murdered a young woman in a lone place, and stole her thimble, and threw her body into a ditch.'

'Nay, nay,' said Mr. Glegg soothingly, 'you're thinking o' the man wi' no legs, as drove a dog-cart.'

'Well, it's the same thing, Mr. Glegg—only you're fond o' contradicting what I say; and if my nephey's come about business, it 'ud be more fitting if you'd bring him into the house, and let his aunt know about it, instead o' whispering in corners, in that plotting, undermining way.'

'Well, well,' said Mr. Glegg, 'we'll come in now.'

'You needn't stay here,' said the lady to Bob, in a loud voice, adapted to the moral not the physical distance between them. 'We don't want anything. I don't deal wi' packmen. Mind you shut the gate after you.'

'Stop a bit; not so fast,' said Mr. Glegg: 'I haven't done with this young man yet. Come in, Tom; come in,' he added, stepping in at the French window.

'Mr. Glegg,' said Mrs. G., in a fatal tone, 'if you're going to let that man and his dog in on my carpet, before my very face, be so good as to let me know. A wife's got a right to ask that, I hope.'

'Don't you be uneasy, mum,' said Bob, touching his cap. He saw at once that Mrs. Glegg was a bit of game worth running down, and longed to be at the sport; 'we'll stay out upo' the gravel here—Mumps and me will. Mumps knows his company—he does. I might hish at him by th' hour together, before he'd fly at a real gentlewoman like you. It's wonderful how he knows which is the good-looking ladies—and 's partic'lar fond of 'em when they've good shapes. Lors!' added Bob, laying down his pack on the gravel, 'it's a thousand pities such a lady as you shouldn't deal with a packman, i'stead o' goin' into these new-fangled shops, where there's half-a-dozen fine gents wi' their chins propped up wi' a stiff stock, a-looking like bottles wi' ornamental stoppers, an' all got to get their dinner out of a bit o' calico: it stan's to reason you must pay three times the price you pay a packman, as is the nat'ral way o' gettin' goods—an' pays no rent, and isn't forced to throttle himself till the lies are squeezed out on him, whether he will or no. But lors! mum, you know what it is better nor I do—*you* can see through them shopmen, I'll be bound.'

'Yes, I reckon I can, and through the packmen too,' observed Mrs. Glegg, intending to imply that Bob's flattery had produced no effect on *her*; while her husband, standing behind her with his hands in his pockets and legs apart, winked and smiled with conjugal delight at the probability of his wife's being circumvented.

'Ay, to be sure, mum,' said Bob. 'Why, you must ha' dealt wi' no end o' packmen when you war a young lass—before the master here had the luck to set eyes on you. I know where you lived, I do—seen th' house many a time—close upon Squire Darleigh's—a stone house wi' steps. . . .'

'Ah, that it had,' said Mrs. Glegg, pouring out the tea. 'You know something o' my family then . . . are you akin to that packman with a squint in his eye, as used to bring th' Irish linen?'

'Look you there now!' said Bob evasively. 'Didn't I know as you'd remember the best bargains you've made in your life was made wi' packmen? Why, you see, even a squintin' packman's better nor a shopman as can see straight. Lors! if I'd had the luck to call at the stone house wi' my pack, as lies here,'—stooping and thumping the bundle emphatically with his fist,—'an' th' handsome young lasses all stannin' out on the stone steps, it 'ud ha' been summat like openin' a pack—that would. It's on'y the poor houses now as a packman calls on, if it isn't for the sake o' the sarvant-maids. They're paltry times—these are. Why, mum, look at the printed cottons now, an' what they was when you wore 'em—why, you wouldn't put such a thing on now, I can see. It must be first-rate quality—the manifactur as you'd buy—summat as 'ud wear as well as your own faitures.'

'Yes, better quality nor any you're like to carry: you've got nothing first-rate but brazenness, I'll be bound,' said Mrs. Glegg, with a triumphant sense of her insurmountable sagacity. 'Mr. Glegg, are you going ever to sit down to your tea? Tom, there's a cup for you.'

'You speak true there, mum,' said Bob. 'My pack isn't for ladies like you. The time's gone by for that. Bargains picked up dirt cheap! A bit o' damage here an' there, as can be cut out, or else never seen i' the wearin'; but not fit to offer to rich folks as can pay for the look o' things as nobody sees. I'm not the man as 'ud offer t' open my pack to *you*, mum: no, no; I'm a imperent chap, as you say— these times makes folks imperent—but I'm not up to the mark o' that.'

'Why, what goods do you carry in your pack?' said Mrs. Glegg. 'Fine-coloured things, I suppose—shawls an' that?'

'All sorts, mum, all sorts,' said Bob, thumping his bundle; 'but let us say no more about that, if *you* please. I'm here upo' Mr. Tom's business, an' I'm not the man to take up the time wi' my own.'

'And pray, what *is* this business as is to be kept from me?' said Mrs. Glegg, who, solicited by a double curiosity, was obliged to let the one-half wait.

'A little plan o' nephey Tom's here,' said good-natured Mr. Glegg; 'and not altogether a bad un, I think. A little plan for making money: that's the right sort o' plan for young folks as have got their fortin to make, eh, Jane?'

'But I hope it isn't a plan where he expects iverything to be done for him by his friends: that's what the young folks think of mostly nowadays. And pray, what has this packman got to do wi' what goes on in our family? Can't you speak for yourself, Tom, and let your aunt know things, as a nephey should?'

'This is Bob Jakin, aunt,' said Tom, bridling the irritation that aunt Glegg's voice always produced. 'I've known him ever since we were little boys. He's a very good fellow, and always ready to do me a kindness. And he has had some experience in sending goods out—a small part of a cargo as a private speculation; and he thinks, if I could begin to do a little in the same way, I might make some money. A large interest is got in that way.'

'Large int'rest?' said aunt Glegg, with eagerness; 'and what do you call large int'rest?'

'Ten or twelve per cent., Bob says, after expenses are paid.'

'Then why wasn't I let to know o' such things before, Mr. Glegg?' said Mrs. Glegg, turning to her husband, with a deep grating tone of reproach. 'Haven't you allays told me as there was no getting more nor five per cent.?'

'Pooh, pooh, nonsense, my good woman,' said Mr. Glegg. 'You couldn't go into trade, could you? You can't get more than five per cent. with security.'

'But I can turn a bit o' money for you, an' welcome, mum,' said Bob, 'if you'd like to risk it—not as there's any risk to speak on. But if you'd a mind to lend a bit o' money to Mr. Tom, he'd pay you six or seven per zent., an' get a trifle for himself as well; an' a good-natur'd lady like you 'ud like the feel o' the money better if your nephey took part on it.'

'What do you say, Mrs. G.?' said Mr. Glegg. 'I've a notion, when I've made a bit more inquiry, as I shall perhaps start Tom here with a bit of a nest-egg—he'll pay me int'rest, you know—an' if you've got some little sums lyin' idle twisted up in a stockin' toe, or that. . . .'

'Mr. Glegg, it's beyond iverything! You'll go and give information to the tramps next, as they may come and rob me.'

'Well, well, as I was sayin', if you like to join me wi' twenty pounds, you can—I'll make it fifty. That'll be a pretty good nest-egg—eh, Tom?'

'You're not counting on me, Mr. Glegg, I hope,' said his wife. 'You could do fine things wi' my money, I don't doubt.'

'Very well,' said Mr. Glegg rather snappishly, 'then we'll do without you. I shall go with you to see this Salt,' he added, turning to Bob.

'And now, I suppose, you'll go all the other way, Mr. Glegg,' said Mrs. G., 'and want to shut me out o' my own nephey's business. I never said I wouldn't put money into it—I don't say as it shall be twenty pounds, though you're so ready to say it for me—but he'll see some day as his aunt's in the right not to risk the money she's saved for him till it's proved as it won't be lost.'

'Ay, that's a pleasant sort o' risk, that is,' said Mr. Glegg, indiscreetly winking at Tom, who couldn't avoid smiling. But Bob stemmed the injured lady's outburst.

'Ay, mum,' he said admiringly, 'you know what's what —you do. An' it's nothing but fair. *You* see how the first bit of a job answers, an' then you'll come down handsome. Lors, it's a fine thing to hev good kin. I got my bit of a nest-egg, as the master calls it, all by my own sharpness— ten suvreigns it was—wi' dousing the fire at Torry's mill, an' it's growed an' growed by a bit an' a bit, till I'n got a matter o' thirty pound to lay out, besides makin' my mother comfor'ble. I should get more, on'y I'm such a soft wi' the women—I can't help lettin' 'em hev such good bargains. There's this bundle, now' (thumping it lustily), 'any other chap 'ud make a pretty penny out on it. But me! . . . lors, I shall sell 'em for pretty near what I paid for 'em.'

'Have you got a bit of good net, now?' said Mrs. Glegg, in a patronising tone, moving from the tea-table, and folding her napkin.

'Eh, mum, not what you'd think it worth your while to look at. I'd scorn to show it you. It 'ud be an insult to you.'

'But let me see,' said Mrs. Glegg, still patronising. 'If they're damaged goods, they're like enough to be a bit the better quality.'

'No, mum. I know my place,' said Bob, lifting up his pack and shouldering it. 'I'm not going t' expose the low-ness o' my trade to a lady like you. Packs is come down i' the world: it 'ud cut you to th' heart to see the difference. I'm at your sarvice, sir, when you've a mind to go and see Salt.'

'All in good time,' said Mr. Glegg, really unwilling to cut short the dialogue. 'Are you wanted at the wharf, Tom?'

'No, sir; I left Stowe in my place.'

'Come, put down your pack, and let me see,' said Mrs.

Glegg, drawing a chair to the window, and seating herself with much dignity.

'Don't you ask it, mum,' said Bob entreatingly.

'Make no more words,' said Mrs. Glegg severely, 'but do as I tell you.'

'Eh, mum, I'm loth—that I am,' said Bob, slowly depositing his pack on the step, and beginning to untie it with unwilling fingers. 'But what you order shall be done' (much fumbling in pauses between the sentences). 'It's not as you'll buy a single thing on me . . . I'd be sorry for you to do it . . . for think o' them poor women up i' the villages there, as niver stir a hundred yards from home . . . it 'ud be a pity for anybody to buy up their bargains. Lors, it's as good as a junketing to 'em when they see me wi' my pack . . . an' I shall niver pick up such bargains for 'em again. Least ways, I've no time now, for I'm off to Laceham. See here, now,' Bob went on, becoming rapid again, and holding up a scarlet woollen kerchief with an embroidered wreath in the corner; 'here's a thing to make a lass's mouth water, an' on'y two shillin'—an' why? Why, 'cause there's a bit of a moth-hole i' this plain end. Lors, I think the moths an' the mildew was sent by Providence o' purpose to cheapen the goods a bit for the good-lookin' women as han't got much money. If it hadn't been for the moths, now, every hankicher on 'em 'ud ha' gone to the rich handsome ladies, like you, mum, at five shillin' apiece—not a farthin' less; but what does the moth do? Why, it nibbles off three shillin' o' the price i' no time, an' then a packman like me can carry't to the poor lasses as live under the dark thack, to make a bit of a blaze for 'em. Lors, it's as good as a fire, to look at such a hankicher!'

Bob held it at a distance for admiration, but Mrs. Glegg said sharply:

'Yes, but nobody wants a fire this time o' year. Put these coloured things by—let me look at your nets, if you've got 'em.'

'Eh, mum, I told you how it 'ud be,' said Bob, flinging aside the coloured things with an air of desperation. 'I knowed it 'ud turn again' you to look at such paltry articles

as I carry. Here's a piece o' figured muslin now—what's
the use o' you lookin' at it? You might as well look at poor
folks's victual, mum—it 'ud on'y take away your appetite.
There's a yard i' the middle on't as the pattern's all missed
—lors, why it's a muslin as the Princess Victoree might ha'
wore—but,' added Bob, flinging it behind him on to the
turf, as if to save Mrs. Glegg's eyes, 'it'll be bought up by
the huckster's wife at Fibb's End—that's where *it*'ll go—
ten shillin' for the whole lot—ten yards, countin' the
damaged un—five-an'-twenty shillin' 'ud ha' been the price
—not a penny less. But I'll say no more, mum; it's nothing to you—a piece o' muslin like that; you can afford to
pay three times the money for a thing as isn't half so good.
It's nets *you* talked on; well, I've got a piece as 'ull serve
you to make fun on. . . .'

'Bring me that muslin,' said Mrs. Glegg: 'it's a buff—
I'm partial to buff.'

'Eh, but a *damaged* thing,' said Bob, in a tone of deprecating disgust. 'You'd do nothing with it, mum—you'd
give it to the cook, I know you would—an' it 'ud be a pity
—she'd look too much like a lady in it—it's unbecoming
for servants.'

'Fetch it, and let me see you measure it,' said Mrs. Glegg
authoritatively.

Bob obeyed with ostentatious reluctance.

'See what there is over measure!' he said, holding forth
the extra half-yard, while Mrs. Glegg was busy examining
the damaged yard, and throwing her head back to see how
far the fault would be lost on a distant view.

'I'll give you six shilling for it,' she said, throwing it
down with the air of a person who mentions an ultimatum.

'Didn't I tell you now, mum, as it 'ud hurt your feelings
to look at my pack? That damaged bit's turned your
stomach now—I see it has,' said Bob, wrapping the muslin
up with the utmost quickness, and apparently about to
fasten up his pack. 'You're used to seein' a different sort o'
article carried by packmen, when you lived at the stone
house. Packs is come down i' the world: I told you that:
my goods are for common folks. Mrs. Pepper 'ull give me

ten shillin' for that muslin, an' be sorry as I didn't ask her more. Such articles answer i' the wearin'—they keep their colour till the threads melt away i' the wash-tub, an' that won't be while *I*'m a young un.'

'Well, seven shilling,' said Mrs. Glegg.

'Put it out o' your mind, mum, now do,' said Bob. 'Here's a bit o' net, then, for you to look at before I tie up my pack; just for you to see what my trade's come to: spotted and sprigged, you see, beautiful, but yallow—'s been lyin' by an' got the wrong colour. I could niver ha' bought such net, if it hadn't been yallow. Lors, it's took me a deal o' study to know the vally o' such articles; when I begun to carry a pack, I was as ignirant as a pig—net or calico was all the same to me. I thought them things the most vally as was the thickest. I was took in dreadful—for I'm a straightforrard chap—up to no tricks, mum. I can on'y say my nose is my own, for if I went beyond, I should lose myself pretty quick. An' I gev five-an'-eightpence for that piece o' net—if I was to tell y' anything else I should be tellin' you fibs: an' five-an'-eightpence I shall ask for it— not a penny more—for it's a woman's article, an' I like to 'commodate the women. Five-an'-eightpence for six yards —as cheap as if it was only the dirt on it as was paid for.'

'I don't mind having three yards of it,' said Mrs. Glegg.

'Why, there's but six altogether,' said Bob. 'No, mum, it isn't worth your while; you can go to the shop to-morrow an' get the same pattern ready whitened. It's on'y three times the money—what's that to a lady like you?' He gave an emphatic tie to his bundle.

'Come, lay me out that muslin,' said Mrs. Glegg. 'Here's eight shilling for it.'

'You *will* be jokin', mum,' said Bob, looking up with a laughing face; 'I see'd you was a pleasant lady when I fust come to the winder.'

'Well, put it me out,' said Mrs. Glegg peremptorily.

'But if I let you have it for ten shillin', mum, you'll be so good as not tell nobody. I should be a laughin'-stock— the trade 'ud hoot me, if they knowed it. I'm obliged to make believe as I ask more nor I do for my goods, else

they'd find out I was a flat. I'm glad you don't insist upo'
buyin' the net, for then I should ha' lost my two best bargains for Mrs. Pepper o' Fibb's End—an' she's a rare
customer.'

'Let me look at the net again,' said Mrs. Glegg, yearning after the cheap spots and sprigs, now they were
vanishing.

'Well, I can't deny *you*, mum,' said Bob, handing it out.
'Eh! see what a pattern now! Real Laceham goods. Now,
this is the sort o' article I'm recommendin' Mr. Tom to send
out. Lors, it's a fine thing for anybody as has got a bit
o' money—these Laceham goods 'ud make it breed like
maggits. If I was a lady wi' a bit o' money!—why, I know
one as put thirty pound into them goods—a lady wi' a cork
leg; but as sharp—you wouldn't catch *her* runnin' her head
into a sack: *she*'d see her way clear out o' anything afore
she'd be in a hurry to start. Well, she let out thirty pound
to a young man in the drapering line, and he laid it out i'
Laceham goods, an' a shupercargo o' my acquinetance (not
Salt) took 'em out, an' she got her eight per zent. Just go off
—an' now you can't hold her but she must be sendin' out
carguies wi' every ship, till she's gettin' as rich as a Jew.
Bucks her name is—she doesn't live i' this town. Now then,
mum, if you'll please to give me the net. . . .'

'Here's fifteen shilling, then, for the two,' said Mrs.
Glegg. 'But it's a shameful price.'

'Nay, mum, you'll niver say that when you're upo' your
knees i' church i' five years' time. I'm makin' you a present o' th' articles—I am, indeed. That eightpence shaves
off my profit as clean as a razor. Now then, sir,' continued
Bob, shouldering his pack, 'if you please, I'll be glad to go
and see about makin' Mr. Tom's fortin. Eh, I wish I'd got
another twenty pound to lay out for *my*sen: I shouldn't stay
to say my Catechism afore I knowed what to do wi't.'

'Stop a bit, Mr. Glegg,' said the lady, as her husband
took his hat, 'you never *will* give me the chance o' speaking. You'll go away now, and finish everything about this
business, and come back and tell me it's too late for me to
speak. As if I wasn't my nephey's own aunt, and th' head

o' the family on his mother's side! and laid by guineas, all full weight, for him—as he'll know who to respect when I'm laid in my coffin.'

'Well, Mrs. G., say what you mean,' said Mr. G. hastily.

'Well, then, I desire as nothing may be done without my knowing. I don't say as I shan't venture twenty pounds, if you make out as everything's right and safe. And if I do, Tom,' concluded Mrs. Glegg, turning impressively to her nephew, 'I hope you'll allays bear it in mind and be grateful for such an aunt. I mean you to pay me interest, you know—I don't approve o' giving; we niver looked for that in *my* family.'

'Thank you, aunt,' said Tom, rather proudly. 'I prefer having the money only lent to me.'

'Very well: that's the Dodson sperrit,' said Mrs. Glegg, rising to get her knitting with the sense that any further remark after this would be bathos.

Salt—that eminently 'briny chap'—having been discovered in a cloud of tobacco-smoke at the Anchor Tavern, Mr. Glegg commenced inquiries which turned out satisfactorily enough to warrant the advance of the 'nest-egg,' to which aunt Glegg contributed twenty pounds; and in this modest beginning you see the ground of a fact which might otherwise surprise you—namely, Tom's accumulation of a fund, unknown to his father, that promised in no very long time to meet the more tardy process of saving, and quite cover the deficit. When once his attention had been turned to this source of gain, Tom determined to make the most of it, and lost no opportunity of obtaining information and extending his small enterprises. In not telling his father, he was influenced by that strange mixture of opposite feelings which often gives equal truth to those who blame an action and those who admire it: partly, it was that disinclination to confidence which is seen between near kindred—that family repulsion which spoils the most sacred relations of our lives; partly, it was the desire to surprise his father with a great joy. He did not see that it would have been better to soothe the interval with a new hope, and prevent the delirium of a too sudden elation.

At the time of Maggie's first meeting with Philip, Tom had already nearly a hundred and fifty pounds of his own capital; and while they were walking by the evening light in the Red Deeps, he, by the same evening light, was riding into Laceham, proud of being on his first journey on behalf of Guest & Co., and revolving in his mind all the chances that by the end of another year he should have doubled his gains, lifted off the obloquy of debt from his father's name, and perhaps—for he should be twenty-one—have got a new start for himself, on a higher platform of employment. Did he not deserve it? He was quite sure that he did.

III

THE WAVERING BALANCE

I SAID that Maggie went home that evening from the Red Deeps with a mental conflict already begun. You have seen clearly enough, in her interview with Philip, what that conflict was. Here suddenly was an opening in the rocky wall which shut in the narrow valley of humiliation, where all her prospect was the remote unfathomed sky; and some of the memory-haunting earthly delights were no longer out of her reach. She might have books, converse, affection— she might hear tidings of the world from which her mind had not yet lost its sense of exile; and it would be a kindness to Philip too, who was pitiable—clearly not happy; and perhaps here was an opportunity indicated for making her mind more worthy of its highest service—perhaps the noblest, completest devoutness could hardly exist without some width of knowledge: *must* she always live in this resigned imprisonment? It was so blameless, so good a thing that there should be friendship between her and Philip; the motives that forbade it were so unreasonable— so unchristian! But the severe monotonous warning came again and again—that she was losing the simplicity and clearness of her life by admitting a ground of concealment, and that, by forsaking the simple rule of renunciation, she was throwing herself under the seductive guidance of illimitable wants. She thought she had won strength to obey the warning before she allowed herself the next week to turn her steps in the evening to the Red Deeps. But while she was resolved to say an affectionate farewell to Philip, how she looked forward to that evening walk in the still, fleckered shade of the hollows, away from all that was harsh and unlovely; to the affectionate admiring looks that would meet her; to the sense of comradeship that childish memories would give to wiser, older talk; to the certainty that Philip would care to hear everything she said, which no one else cared for! It was a half-hour that it would be very hard to turn her back upon, with the sense that there would be no other like it. Yet she said what she meant to say; she looked firm as well as sad.

'Philip, I have made up my mind—it is right that we should give each other up, in everything but memory. I could not see you without concealment—stay, I know what you are going to say—it is other people's wrong feelings that make concealment necessary; but concealment is bad, however it may be caused. I feel that it would be bad for me, for us both. And then, if our secret were discovered, there would be nothing but misery—dreadful anger; and then we must part after all, and it would be harder, when we were used to seeing each other.'

Philip's face had flushed, and there was a momentary eagerness of expression, as if he had been about to resist this decision with all his might. But he controlled himself, and said, with assumed calmness, 'Well, Maggie, if we must part, let us try and forget it for one half-hour: let us talk together a little while—for the last time.'

He took her hand, and Maggie felt no reason to withdraw it: his quietness made her all the more sure she had given him great pain, and she wanted to show him how unwillingly she had given it. They walked together hand in hand in silence.

'Let us sit down in the hollow,' said Philip, 'where we stood the last time. See how the dog-roses have strewed the ground, and spread their opal petals over it!'

They sat at the roots of the slanting ash.

'I've begun my picture of you among the Scotch firs, Maggie,' said Philip, 'so you must let me study your face a little, while you stay—since I am not to see it again. Please, turn your head this way.'

This was said in an entreating voice, and it would have been very hard of Maggie to refuse. The full lustrous face, with the bright black coronet, looked down like that of a divinity well pleased to be worshipped, on the pale-hued, small-featured face that was turned up to it.

'I shall be sitting for my second portrait then,' she said, smiling. 'Will it be larger than the other?'

'O yes, much larger. It is an oil-painting. You will look like a tall Hamadryad, dark and strong and noble, just issued from one of the fir-trees, when the stems are casting their afternoon shadows on the grass.'

'You seem to think more of painting than of anything now, Philip?'

'Perhaps I do,' said Philip rather sadly; 'but I think of too many things—sow all sorts of seeds, and get no great harvest from any one of them. I'm cursed with suscepti- bility in every direction, and effective faculty in none. I care for painting and music; I care for classic literature, and mediæval literature, and modern literature: I flutter all ways, and fly in none.'

'But surely that is a happiness to have so many tastes— to enjoy so many beautiful things—when they are within your reach,' said Maggie musingly. 'It always seemed to me a sort of clever stupidity only to have one sort of talent —almost like a carrier-pigeon.'

'It might be a happiness to have many tastes if I were like other men,' said Philip bitterly. 'I might get some power and distinction by mere mediocrity, as they do; at least I should get those middling satisfactions which make men contented to do without great ones. I might think society at St. Ogg's agreeable then. But nothing could make life worth the purchase-money of pain to me, but some faculty that would lift me above the dead level of provincial existence. Yes—there is one thing: a passion answers as well as a faculty.'

Maggie did not hear the last words: she was struggling against the consciousness that Philip's words had set her own discontent vibrating again as it used to do.

'I understand what you mean,' she said, 'though I know so much less than you do. I used to think I could never bear life if it kept on being the same every day, and I must always be doing things of no consequence, and never know anything greater. But, dear Philip, I think we are only like children, that someone who is wiser is taking care of. Is it not right to resign ourselves entirely, whatever may be denied us? I have found great peace in that for the last two or three years—even joy in subduing my own will.'

'Yes, Maggie,' said Philip vehemently; 'and you are shutting yourself up in a narrow self-delusive fanaticism, which is only a way of escaping pain by starving into dulness all the highest powers of your nature. Joy and peace are not resignation: resignation is the willing endurance of a pain that is not allayed—that you don't expect to be allayed. Stupefaction is not resignation: and it is stupefaction to remain in ignorance—to shut up all the avenues by which the life of your fellow-men might become known to you. I am not resigned: I am not sure that life is long enough to learn that lesson. *You* are not resigned: you are only trying to stupefy yourself.'

Maggie's lips trembled; she felt there was some truth in what Philip said, and yet there was a deeper consciousness that, for any immediate application it had to her conduct, it was no better than falsity. Her double impression corresponded to the double impulse of the speaker. Philip seriously believed what he said, but he said it with vehemence because it made an argument against the resolution that opposed his wishes. But Maggie's face, made more child-like by the gathering tears, touched him with a tenderer, less egoistic feeling. He took her hand and said gently:

'Don't let us think of such things in this short half-hour, Maggie. Let us only care about being together. . . . We shall be friends in spite of separation. . . . We shall always think of each other. I shall be glad to live as long as you are alive, because I shall think there may always come a time when I can—when you will let me help you in some way.'

'What a dear, good brother you would have been, Philip,' said Maggie, smiling through the haze of tears. 'I think you would have made as much fuss about me, and been as pleased for me to love you, as would have satisfied even me. You would have loved me well enough to bear with me, and forgive me everything. That was what I always longed that Tom should do. I was never satisfied with a *little* of anything. That is why it is better for me to do without earthly happiness altogether. . . . I never felt that I had enough music—I wanted more instruments playing together—I wanted voices to be fuller and deeper. Do you ever sing now, Philip?' she added abruptly, as if she had forgotten what went before.

'Yes,' he said, 'every day, almost. But my voice is only middling—like everything else in me.'

'O sing me something—just one song. I *may* listen to that before I go—something you used to sing at Lorton on a Saturday afternoon, when we had the drawing-room all to ourselves, and I put my apron over my head to listen.'

'*I* know,' said Philip, and Maggie buried her face in her hands, while he sang *sotto voce*, 'Love in her eyes sits playing;' and then said, 'That's it, isn't it?'

'O no, I won't stay,' said Maggie, starting up. 'It will only haunt me. Let us walk, Philip. I must go home.'

She moved away, so that he was obliged to rise and follow her.

'Maggie,' he said, in a tone of remonstrance, 'don't persist in this wilful, senseless privation. It makes me wretched to see you benumbing and cramping your nature in this way. You were so full of life when you were a child: I thought you would be a brilliant woman—all wit and bright imagination. And it flashes out in your face still, until you draw that veil of dull quiescence over it.'

'Why do you speak so bitterly to me, Philip?' said Maggie.

'Because I foresee it will not end well: you can never carry on this self-torture.'

'I shall have strength given me,' said Maggie tremulously.

'No, you will not, Maggie: no one has strength given to do what is unnatural. It is mere cowardice to seek safety in negations. No character becomes strong in that way. You will be thrown into the world some day, and then every rational satisfaction of your nature that you deny now, will assault you like a savage appetite.'

Maggie started and paused, looking at Philip with alarm in her face.

'Philip, how dare you shake me in this way? You are a tempter.'

'No, I am not; but love gives insight, Maggie, and insight often gives foreboding. *Listen* to me—*let* me supply you with books; do let me see you sometimes—be your brother and teacher, as you said at Lorton. It is less wrong that you should see me than that you should be committing this long suicide.'

Maggie felt unable to speak. She shook her head and walked on in silence, till they came to the end of the Scotch firs, and she put out her hand in sign of parting.

'Do you banish me from this place for ever, then, Maggie? Surely I may come and walk in it sometimes? If I meet you by chance, there is no concealment in that?'

It is the moment when our resolution seems about to become irrevocable—when the fatal iron gates are about to close upon us—that tests our strength. Then, after hours of clear reasoning and firm conviction, we snatch at any sophistry that will nullify our long struggles, and bring us the defeat that we love better than victory.

Maggie felt her heart leap at this subterfuge of Philip's, and there passed over her face that almost imperceptible shock which accompanies any relief. He saw it, and they parted in silence.

Philip's sense of the situation was too complete for him not to be visited with glancing fears lest he had been intervening too presumptuously in the action of Maggie's conscience—perhaps for a selfish end. But no!—he persuaded himself his end was not selfish. He had little hope that Maggie would ever return the strong feeling he had for her;

and it must be better for Maggie's future life, when these petty family obstacles to her freedom had disappeared, that the present should not be entirely sacrificed, and that she should have some opportunity of culture—some interchange with a mind above the vulgar level of those she was now condemned to live with. If we only look far enough off for the consequence of our actions, we can always find some point in the combination of results by which those actions can be justified: by adopting the point of view of a Providence who arranges results, or of a philosopher who traces them, we shall find it possible to obtain perfect complacency in choosing to do what is most agreeable to us in the present moment. And it was in this way that Philip justified his subtle efforts to overcome Maggie's true prompting against a concealment that would introduce doubleness into her own mind, and might cause new misery to those who had the primary natural claim on her. But there was a surplus of passion in him that made him half independent of justifying motives. His longing to see Maggie, and make an element in her life, had in it some of that savage impulse to snatch an offered joy, which springs from a life in which the mental and bodily constitution have made pain predominate. He had not his full share in the common good of men: he could not even pass muster with the insignificant, but must be singled out for pity, and excepted from what was a matter of course with others. Even to Maggie he was an exception: it was clear that the thought of his being her lover had never entered her mind.

Do not think too hardly of Philip. Ugly and deformed people have great need of unusual virtues, because they are likely to be extremely uncomfortable without them: but the theory that unusual virtues spring by a direct consequence out of personal disadvantages, as animals get thicker wool in severe climates, is perhaps a little overstrained. The temptations of beauty are much dwelt upon, but I fancy they only bear the same relation to those of ugliness, as the temptation to excess at a feast, where the delights are varied for eye and ear as well as palate, bears to the temptations that assail the desperation of hunger.

Does not the Hunger Tower stand as the type of the utmost trial to what is human in us?

Philip had never been soothed by that mother's love which flows out to us in the greater abundance because our need is greater, which clings to us the more tenderly because we are the less likely to be winners in the game of life; and the sense of his father's affection and indulgence towards him was marred by the keener perception of his father's faults. Kept aloof from all practical life as Philip had been, and by nature half feminine in sensitiveness, he had some of the woman's intolerant repulsion towards worldliness and the deliberate pursuit of sensual enjoyment; and this one strong natural tie in his life—his relation as a son—was like an aching limb to him. Perhaps there is inevitably something morbid in a human being who is in any way unfavourably excepted from ordinary conditions, until the good force has had time to triumph; and it has rarely had time for that at two-and-twenty. That force was present in Philip in much strength, but the sun himself looks feeble through the morning mists.

IV

ANOTHER LOVE SCENE

EARLY in the following April, nearly a year after that dubious parting you have just witnessed, you may, if you like, again see Maggie entering the Red Deeps through the group of Scotch firs. But it is early afternoon and not evening, and the edge of sharpness in the spring air makes her draw her large shawl close about her and trip along rather quickly; though she looks round, as usual, that she may take in the sight of her beloved trees. There is a more eager, inquiring look in her eyes than there was last June, and a smile is hovering about her lips, as if some playful speech were awaiting the right hearer. The hearer was not long in appearing.

'Take back your *Corinne*,' said Maggie, drawing a book from under her shawl. 'You were right in telling me she would do me no good; but you were wrong in thinking I should wish to be like her.'

'Wouldn't you really like to be a tenth Muse, then, Maggie?' said Philip, looking up in her face as we look at a first parting in the clouds that promises us a bright heaven once more.

'Not at all,' said Maggie, laughing. 'The Muses were uncomfortable goddesses, I think—obliged always to carry rolls and musical instruments about with them. If I carried a harp in this climate, you know, I must have a green baize cover for it—and I should be sure to leave it behind me by mistake.'

'You agree with me in not liking Corinne, then?'

'I didn't finish the book,' said Maggie. 'As soon as I came to the blond-haired young lady reading in the park, I shut it up, and determined to read no further. I foresaw that that light-complexioned girl would win away all the love from Corinne and make her miserable. I'm determined to read no more books where the blond-haired women carry away all the happiness. I should begin to have a prejudice against them. If you could give me some story, now, where the dark woman triumphs, it would restore the balance. I want to avenge Rebecca and Flora MacIvor, and Minna and all the rest of the dark unhappy ones. Since you are my tutor, you ought to preserve my mind from prejudices— you are always arguing against prejudices.'

'Well, perhaps you will avenge the dark women in your own person, and carry away all the love from your cousin Lucy. She is sure to have some handsome young man of St. Ogg's at her feet now: and you have only to shine upon him—your fair little cousin will be quite quenched in your beams.'

'Philip, that is not pretty of you, to apply my nonsense to anything real,' said Maggie, looking hurt. 'As if I, with my old gowns and want of all accomplishments, could be a rival of dear little Lucy, who knows and does all sorts of charming things, and is ten times prettier than I am—even if I were odious and base enough to wish to be her rival. Besides, I never go to aunt Deane's when anyone is there:

it is only because dear Lucy is good, and loves me, that she comes to see me, and will have me go to see her sometimes.'

'Maggie,' said Philip, with surprise, 'it is not like you to take playfulness literally. You must have been in St. Ogg's this morning, and brought away a slight infection of dulness.'

'Well,' said Maggie, smiling, 'if you meant that for a joke, it was a poor one; but I thought it was a very good reproof. I thought you wanted to remind me that I am vain, and wish everyone to admire me most. But it isn't for that, that I'm jealous for the dark women—not because I'm dark myself. It's because I always care the most about the un-happy people: if the blond girl were forsaken, I should like *her* best. I always take the side of the rejected lover in the stories.'

'Then you would never have the heart to reject one yourself—should you, Maggie?' said Philip, flushing a little.

'I don't know,' said Maggie hesitatingly. Then with a bright smile—'I think perhaps I could if he were very con-ceited; and yet, if he got extremely humiliated afterwards, I should relent.'

'I've often wondered, Maggie,' Philip said, with some effort, 'whether you wouldn't really be more likely to love a man that other women were not likely to love.'

'That would depend on what they didn't like him for,' said Maggie, laughing. 'He might be very disagreeable. He might look at me through an eye-glass stuck in his eye, making a hideous face, as young Torry does. I should think other women are not fond of that; but I never felt any pity for young Torry. I've never any pity for conceited people, because I think they carry their comfort about with them.'

'But suppose, Maggie—suppose it was a man who was not conceited—who felt he had nothing to be conceited about—who had been marked from childhood for a peculiar kind of suffering—and to whom you were the day-star of his life—who loved you, worshipped you, so entirely that he felt it happiness enough for him if you would let him see you at rare moments. . . .'

Philip paused with a pang of dread lest his confession

should cut short this very happiness—a pang of the same dread that had kept his love mute through long months. A rush of self-consciousness told him that he was besotted to have said all this. Maggie's manner this morning had been as unconstrained and indifferent as ever.

But she was not looking indifferent now. Struck with the unusual emotion in Philip's tone, she had turned quickly to look at him, and as he went on speaking, a great change came over her face—a flush and slight spasm of the features such as we see in people who hear some news that will require them to re-adjust their conceptions of the past. She was quite silent, and, walking on towards the trunk of a fallen tree, she sat down, as if she had no strength to spare for her muscles. She was trembling.

'Maggie,' said Philip, getting more and more alarmed in every fresh moment of silence, 'I was a fool to say it—forget that I've said it. I shall be contented if things can be as they were.'

The distress with which he spoke urged Maggie to say something. 'I am so surprised, Philip—I had not thought of it.' And the effort to say this brought the tears down too.

'Has it made you hate me, Maggie?' said Philip impetuously. 'Do you think I'm a presumptuous fool?'

'O Philip!' said Maggie, 'how can you think I have such feelings?—as if I were not grateful for *any* love. But . . . but I had never thought of your being my lover. It seemed so far off—like a dream—only like one of the stories one imagines—that I should ever have a lover.'

'Then can you bear to think of me as your lover, Maggie?' said Philip, seating himself by her, and taking her hand, in the elation of a sudden hope. '*Do* you love me?'

Maggie turned rather pale: this direct question seemed not easy to answer. But her eyes met Philip's, which were in this moment liquid and beautiful with beseeching love. She spoke with hesitation, yet with sweet, simple, girlish tenderness.

'I think I could hardly love anyone better: there is nothing but what I love you for.' She paused a little while, and then added, 'But it will be better for us not to say any more about it—won't it, dear Philip? You know we couldn't even be friends, if our friendship were discovered. I have never felt that I was right in giving way about seeing you—though it has been so precious to me in some ways; and now the fear comes upon me strongly again, that it will lead to evil.'

'But no evil has come, Maggie: and if you had been guided by that fear before, you would only have lived through another dreary benumbing year, instead of re-viving into your real self.'

Maggie shook her head. 'It has been very sweet, I know —all the talking together, and the books, and the feeling that I had the walk to look forward to, when I could tell you the thoughts that had come into my head while I was away from you. But it has made me restless: it has made me think a great deal about the world; and I have impatient thoughts again—I get weary of my home—and then it cuts me to the heart afterwards, that I should ever have felt weary of my father and mother. I think what you call being benumbed was better—better for me—for then my selfish desires were benumbed.'

Philip had risen again, and was walking backwards and forwards impatiently.

'No, Maggie, you have wrong ideas of self-conquest, as I've often told you. What you call self-conquest—blinding and deafening yourself to all but one train of impressions— is only the culture of monomania in a nature like yours.'

He had spoken with some irritation, but now he sat down by her again, and took her hand.

'Don't think of the past now, Maggie; think only of our love. If you can really cling to me with all your heart, every obstacle will be overcome in time: we need only wait. I can live on hope. Look at me, Maggie; tell me again, it is possible for you to love me. Don't look away from me to that cloven tree; it is a bad omen.'

She turned her large dark glance upon him with a sad smile.

'Come, Maggie, say one kind word, or else you were better to me at Lorton. You asked me if I should like you to kiss me—don't you remember?—and you promised to kiss me when you met me again. You never kept the promise.'

The recollection of that childish time came as a sweet relief to Maggie. It made the present moment less strange to her. She kissed him almost as simply and quietly as she had done when she was twelve years old. Philip's eyes flashed with delight, but his next words were words of discontent.

'You don't seem happy enough, Maggie: you are forcing yourself to say you love me, out of pity.'

'No, Philip,' said Maggie, shaking her head, in her old childish way; 'I'm telling you the truth. It is all new and strange to me; but I don't think I could love anyone better than I love you. I should like always to live with you—to make you happy. I have always been happy when I have been with you. There is only one thing I will not do for your sake: I will never do anything to wound my father. You must never ask that from me.'

'No, Maggie: I will ask nothing—I will bear everything —I'll wait another year only for a kiss, if you will only give me the first place in your heart.'

'No,' said Maggie, smiling, 'I won't make you wait so long as that.' But then, looking serious again, she added, as she rose from her seat:

'But what would your own father say, Philip? O, it is quite impossible we can ever be more than friends—brother and sister in secret, as we have been. Let us give up thinking of everything else.'

'No, Maggie, I can't give you up—unless you are deceiving me—unless you really only care for me as if I were your brother. Tell me the truth.'

'Indeed, I do, Philip. What happiness have I ever had so great as being with you?—since I was a little girl—the days Tom was good to me. And your mind is a sort of world to me: you can tell me all I want to know. I think I should never be tired of being with you.'

They were walking hand in hand, looking at each other; Maggie, indeed, was hurrying along, for she felt it time to be gone. But the sense that their parting was near, made her more anxious lest she should have unintentionally left some painful impression on Philip's mind. It was one of those dangerous moments when speech is at once sincere and deceptive—when feeling, rising high above its average depth, leaves flood-marks which are never reached again.

They stopped to part among the Scotch firs.

'Then my life will be filled with hope, Maggie—and I shall be happier than other men, in spite of all? We *do* belong to each other—for always—whether we are apart or together?'

'Yes, Philip: I should like never to part: I should like to make your life very happy.'

'I am waiting for something else—I wonder whether it will come.'

Maggie smiled, with glistening tears, and then stooped her tall head to kiss the pale face that was full of pleading, timid love—like a woman's.

She had a moment of real happiness then—a moment of belief that, if there were sacrifice in this love, it was all the richer and more satisfying.

She turned away and hurried home, feeling that in the hour since she had trodden this road before, a new era had begun for her. The tissue of vague dreams must now get narrower and narrower, and all the threads of thought and emotion be gradually absorbed in the woof of her actual daily life.

V

THE CLOVEN TREE

SECRETS are rarely betrayed or discovered according to any programme our fear has sketched out. Fear is almost always haunted by terrible dramatic scenes, which recur in spite of the best-argued probabilities against them; and during a year that Maggie had had the burthen of concealment on her mind, the possibility of discovery had continually presented itself under the form of a sudden meeting with her father or Tom when she was walking with Philip in the Red Deeps. She was aware that this was not one of the most likely events; but it was the scene that most completely symbolised her inward dread. Those slight indirect suggestions which are dependent on apparently trivial coincidences and incalculable states of mind, are the favourite machinery of Fact, but are not the stuff in which imagination is apt to work.

Certainly one of the persons about whom Maggie's fears were farthest from troubling themselves was her aunt Pullet, on whom, seeing that she did not live in St. Ogg's, and was neither sharp-eyed nor sharp-tempered, it would surely have been quite whimsical of them to fix rather than on aunt Glegg. And yet the channel of fatality—the pathway of the lightning—was no other than aunt Pullet. She did not live at St. Ogg's, but the road from Garum Firs lay by the Red Deeps, at the end opposite that by which Maggie entered.

The day after Maggie's last meeting with Philip, being a Sunday on which Mr. Pullet was bound to appear in funeral hat-band and scarf at St. Ogg's church, Mrs. Pullet made this the occasion of dining with sister Glegg, and taking tea with poor sister Tulliver. Sunday was the one day in the week on which Tom was at home in the afternoon; and to-day the brighter spirits he had been in of late had flowed over in unusually cheerful open chat with his father, and in the invitation, 'Come, Magsie, you come too!' when he strolled out with his mother in the garden to see the advancing cherry-blossoms. He had been better pleased with Maggie since she had been less odd and ascetic; he was even getting rather proud of her: several persons had remarked in his hearing that his sister was a very fine girl. To-day there was a peculiar brightness in her face, due in reality to an undercurrent of excitement, which had as much doubt and pain as pleasure in it; but it might pass for a sign of happiness.

'You look very well, my dear,' said aunt Pullet, shaking her head sadly, as they sat round the tea-table. 'I niver thought your girl 'ud be so good-looking, Bessy. But you must wear pink, my dear: that blue thing as your aunt Glegg gave you turns you into a crowflower. Jane never *was* tasty. Why don't you wear that gown o' mine?'

'It is so pretty and so smart, aunt. I think it's too showy for me—at least, for my other clothes, that I must wear with it.'

'To be sure, it 'ud be unbecoming if it wasn't well known you've got them belonging to you as can afford to give you such things when they've done with 'em themselves. It stands to reason I must give my own niece clothes now and then—such things as *I* buy every year, and never wear anything out. And as for Lucy, there's no giving to her, for she's got everything o' the choicest: sister Deane may well hold her head up, though she looks dreadful yellow, poor thing—I doubt this liver complaint 'ull carry her off. That's what this new vicar, this Dr. Kenn, said in the funeral sermon to-day.'

'Ah, he's a wonderful preacher, by all account—isn't he, Sophy?' said Mrs. Tulliver.

'Why, Lucy had got a collar on this blessed day,' continued Mrs. Pullet, with her eyes fixed in a ruminating manner, 'as I don't say I haven't got as good, but I must look out my best to match it.'

'Miss Lucy's called the bell o' St. Ogg's, they say: that's a cur'ous word,' observed Mr. Pullet, on whom the mysteries of etymology sometimes fell with an oppressive weight.

'Pooh!' said Mr. Tulliver, jealous for Maggie, 'she's a small thing, not much of a figure. But fine feathers make fine birds. I see nothing so much to admire in those diminutive women; they look silly by the side o' the men—out o' proportion. When I chose my wife, I chose her the right size—neither too little nor too big.'

The poor wife, with her withered beauty, smiled complacently.

'But the men aren't *all* big,' said uncle Pullet, not without some self-reference; 'a young fellow may be good-looking and yet not be a six-foot, like Master Tom here.'

'Ah, it's poor talking about littleness and bigness,—anybody may think it's a mercy they're straight,' said aunt

Pullet. 'There's that mismade son o' Lawyer Wakem's—I saw him at church to-day. Dear, dear! to think o' the property he's like to have; and they say he's very queer and lonely—doesn't like much company. I shouldn't wonder if he goes out of his mind; for we never come along the road but he's a-scrambling out o' the trees and brambles at the Red Deeps.'

This wide statement, by which Mrs. Pullet represented the fact that she had twice seen Philip at the spot indicated, produced an effect on Maggie which was all the stronger because Tom sate opposite her, and she was intensely anxious to look indifferent. At Philip's name she had blushed, and the blush deepened every instant from consciousness, until the mention of the Red Deeps made her feel as if the whole secret were betrayed, and she dared not even hold her teaspoon lest she should show how she trembled. She sat with her hands clasped under the table, not daring to look round. Happily, her father was seated on the same side with herself, beyond her uncle Pullet, and could not see her face without stooping forward. Her mother's voice brought the first relief—turning the conversation; for Mrs. Tulliver was always alarmed when the name of Wakem was mentioned in her husband's presence. Gradually Maggie recovered composure enough to look up; her eyes met Tom's, but he turned away his head immediately; and she went to bed that night wondering if he had gathered any suspicion from her confusion. Perhaps not: perhaps he would think it was only her alarm at her aunt's mention of Wakem before her father: that was the interpretation her mother had put on it. To her father Wakem was like a disfiguring disease, of which he was obliged to endure the consciousness, but was exasperated to have the existence recognised by others; and no amount of sensitiveness in her about her father could be surprising, Maggie thought.

But Tom was too keen-sighted to rest satisfied with such an interpretation: he had seen clearly enough that there was something distinct from anxiety about her father in Maggie's excessive confusion. In trying to recall all the details that could give shape to his suspicions, he remembered only lately hearing his mother scold Maggie for walking in the Red Deeps when the ground was wet, and bringing home shoes clogged with red soil: still Tom, retaining all his old repulsion for Philip's deformity, shrank from attributing to his sister the probability of feeling more than a friendly interest in such an unfortunate exception to the common run of men. Tom's was a nature which had a sort of superstitious repugnance to everything exceptional. A love for a deformed man would be odious in any woman—in a sister intolerable. But if she had been carrying on any kind of intercourse whatever with Philip, a stop must be put to it at once: she was disobeying her father's strongest feelings and her brother's express commands, besides compromising herself by secret meetings. He left home the next morning in that watchful state of mind which turns the most ordinary course of things into pregnant coincidences.

That afternoon, about half-past three o'clock, Tom was standing on the wharf, talking with Bob Jakin about the probability of the good ship *Adelaide* coming in, in a day or two, with results highly important to both of them.

'Eh,' said Bob parenthetically, as he looked over the fields on the other side of the river, 'there goes that crooked young Wakem. I know him or his shadder as far off as I can see 'em: I'm allays lighting on him o' that side the river.'

A sudden thought seemed to have darted through Tom's mind. 'I must go, Bob,' he said, 'I've something to attend to,' hurrying off to the warehouse, where he left notice for someone to take his place—he was called away home on peremptory business.

The swiftest pace and the shortest road took him to the gate, and he was pausing to open it deliberately, that he might walk into the house with an appearance of perfect composure, when Maggie came out at the front door in bonnet and shawl. His conjecture was fulfilled, and he waited for her at the gate. She started violently when she saw him.

'Tom, how is it you are come home? Is there anything the matter?' Maggie spoke in a low tremulous voice.

'I'm come to walk with you to the Red Deeps and meet Philip Wakem,' said Tom, the central fold in his brow, which had become habitual with him, deepening as he spoke.

Maggie stood helpless—pale and cold. By some means, then, Tom knew everything. At last she said, 'I'm not going,' and turned round.

'Yes, you are; but I want to speak to you first. Where is my father?'

'Out on horseback.'

'And my mother?'

'In the yard, I think, with the poultry.'

'I can go in, then, without her seeing me?'

They walked in together, and Tom, entering the parlour, said to Maggie, 'Come in here.'

She obeyed, and he closed the door behind her.

'Now, Maggie, tell me this instant everything that has passed between you and Philip Wakem.'

'Does my father know anything?' said Maggie, still trembling.

'No,' said Tom indignantly. 'But he *shall* know, if you attempt to use deceit towards me any further.'

'I don't wish to use deceit,' said Maggie, flushing into resentment at hearing this word applied to her conduct.

'Tell me the whole truth then.'

'Perhaps you know it.'

'Never mind whether I know it or not. Tell me exactly what has happened, or my father shall know everything.'

'I tell it for my father's sake, then.'

'Yes, it becomes you to profess affection for your father, when you have despised his strongest feelings.'

'You never do wrong, Tom,' said Maggie tauntingly.

'Not if I know it,' answered Tom, with proud sincerity. 'But I have nothing to say to you, beyond this: tell me what has passed between you and Philip Wakem. When did you first meet him in the Red Deeps?'

'A year ago,' said Maggie quietly. Tom's severity gave her a certain fund of defiance, and kept her sense of error in abeyance. 'You need ask me no more questions. We have been friendly a year. We have met and walked together often. He has lent me books.'

'Is that all?' said Tom, looking straight at her with his frown.

Maggie paused a moment; then, determined to make an end of Tom's right to accuse her of deceit, she said haughtily:

'No, not quite all. On Saturday he told me that he loved me. I didn't think of it before then—I had only thought of him as an old friend.'

'And you *encouraged* him?' said Tom, with an expression of disgust.

'I told him that I loved him too.'

Tom was silent a few moments, looking on the ground and frowning, with his hands in his pockets. At last, he looked up, and said coldly:

'Now, then, Maggie, there are but two courses for you to take; either you vow solemnly to me, with your hand on my father's Bible, that you will never have another meeting or speak another word in private with Philip Wakem, or you refuse, and I tell my father everything; and this month, when by my exertions he might be made happy once more, you will cause him the blow of knowing that you are a disobedient, deceitful daughter, who throws away her own respectability by clandestine meetings with the son of a man that has helped to ruin her father. Choose!' Tom ended with cold decision, going up to the large Bible, drawing it forward, and opening it at the fly-leaf, where the writing was.

It was a crushing alternative to Maggie.

'Tom,' she said, urged out of pride into pleading, 'don't ask me that. I will promise you to give up all intercourse with Philip, if you will let me see him once, or even only write to him and explain everything—to give it up as long as it would ever cause any pain to my father . . . I feel something for Philip too. *He* is not happy.'

'I don't wish to hear anything of your feelings; I have said exactly what I mean: choose—and quickly, lest my mother should come in.'

'If I give you my word, that will be as strong a bond to me as if I laid my hand on the Bible. I don't require that to bind me.'

'Do what *I* require,' said Tom. 'I can't trust you, Maggie. There is no consistency in you. Put your hand on this Bible, and say, "I renounce all private speech and intercourse with Philip Wakem from this time forth." Else you will bring shame on us all, and grief on my father; and what is the use of my exerting myself and giving up everything else for the sake of paying my father's debts, if you are to bring madness and vexation on him, just when he might be easy and hold up his head once more?'

'O Tom—*will* the debts be paid soon?' said Maggie, clasping her hands, with a sudden flash of joy across her wretchedness.

'If things turn out as I expect,' said Tom. 'But,' he added, his voice trembling with indignation, 'while I have been contriving and working that my father may have some peace of mind before he dies—working for the respectability of our family—you have done all you can to destroy both.'

Maggie felt a deep movement of compunction: for the moment, her mind ceased to contend against what she felt to be cruel and unreasonable, and in her self-blame she justified her brother.

'Tom,' she said in a low voice, 'it was wrong of me—but I was so lonely—and I was sorry for Philip. And I think enmity and hatred are wicked.'

'Nonsense!' said Tom. 'Your duty was clear enough. Say no more; but promise, in the words I told you.'

'I *must* speak to Philip once more.'

'You will go with me now and speak to him.'

'I give you my word not to meet him or write to him again without your knowledge. That is the only thing I will say. I will put my hand on the Bible if you like.'

'Say it, then.'

Maggie laid her hand on the page of manuscript and repeated the promise. Tom closed the book, and said, 'Now, let us go.'

Not a word was spoken as they walked along. Maggie was suffering in anticipation of what Philip was about to suffer, and dreading the galling words that would fall on him from Tom's lips; but she felt it was in vain to attempt anything but submission. Tom had his terrible clutch on her conscience and her deepest dread: she writhed under the demonstrable truth of the character he had given to her conduct, and yet her whole soul rebelled against it as unfair from its incompleteness. He, meanwhile, felt the impetus of his indignation diverted towards Philip. He did not know how much of an old boyish repulsion and of mere personal pride and animosity was concerned in the bitter severity of the words by which he meant to do the duty of a son and a brother. Tom was not given to inquire subtly into his own motives, any more than into other matters of an intangible kind; he was quite sure that his own motives as well as actions were good, else he would have had nothing to do with them.

Maggie's only hope was that something might, for the first time, have prevented Philip from coming. Then there would be delay—then she might get Tom's permission to write to him. Her heart beat with double violence when they got under the Scotch firs. It was the last moment of suspense, she thought; Philip always met her soon after she got beyond them. But they passed across the more open green space, and entered the narrow bushy path by the mound. Another turning, and they came so close upon him that both Tom and Philip stopped suddenly within a yard of each other. There was a moment's silence, in which Philip darted a look of inquiry at Maggie's face. He saw an answer there, in the pale parted lips, and the terrified tension of the large eyes. Her imagination, always rushing extravagantly beyond an immediate impression, saw her tall strong brother grasping the feeble Philip bodily, crushing him and trampling on him.

'Do you call this acting the part of a man and a gentleman, sir?' Tom said, in a voice of harsh scorn, as soon as Philip's eyes were turned on him again.

'What do you mean?' answered Philip haughtily.

'Mean? Stand farther from me, lest I should lay hands on you, and I'll tell you what I mean. I mean, taking advantage of a young girl's foolishness and ignorance to get her to have secret meetings with you. I mean, daring to trifle with the respectability of a family that has a good and honest name to support.'

'I deny that,' interrupted Philip impetuously. 'I could never trifle with anything that affected your sister's happiness. She is dearer to me than she is to you; I honour her more than you can ever honour her; I would give up my life to her.'

'Don't talk high-flown nonsense to me, sir! Do you mean to pretend that you didn't know it would be injurious to her to meet you here week after week? Do you pretend you had any right to make professions of love to her, even if you had been a fit husband for her, when neither her father nor your father would ever consent to a marriage between you? And *you*—*you* to try and worm yourself into the affections of a handsome girl who is not eighteen, and has been shut out from the world by her father's misfortunes! That's your crooked notion of honour, is it? I call it base treachery—I call it taking advantage of circumstances to win what's too good for you—what you'd never get by fair means.'

'It is manly of you to talk in this way to *me*,' said Philip bitterly, his whole frame shaken by violent emotions. 'Giants have an immemorial right to stupidity and insolent abuse. You are incapable even of understanding what I feel for your sister. I feel so much for her that I could even desire to be at friendship with *you*.'

'I should be very sorry to understand your feelings,' said Tom, with scorching contempt. 'What I wish is that you should understand *me*—that I shall take care of *my* sister, and that if you dare to make the least attempt to come near her, or to write to her, or to keep the slightest hold on her mind, your puny, miserable body, that ought to have put some modesty into your mind, shall not protect you. I'll thrash you—I'll hold you up to public scorn. Who wouldn't laugh at the idea of *your* turning lover to a fine girl?'

'Tom, I will not bear it—I will listen no longer,' Maggie burst out, in a convulsed voice.

'Stay, Maggie!' said Philip, making a strong effort to speak. Then, looking at Tom, 'You have dragged your sister here, I suppose, that she may stand by while you threaten and insult me. These naturally seemed to you the right means to influence me. But you are mistaken. Let your sister speak. If she says she is bound to give me up, I shall abide by her wishes to the slightest word.'

'It was for my father's sake, Philip,' said Maggie imploringly. 'Tom threatens to tell my father—and he couldn't bear it: I have promised, I have vowed solemnly, that we will not have any intercourse without my brother's knowledge.'

'It is enough, Maggie. *I* shall not change; but I wish you to hold yourself entirely free. But trust me—remember that I can never seek for anything but good to what belongs to you.'

'Yes,' said Tom, exasperated by this attitude of Philip's, 'you can talk of seeking good for her and what belongs to her now: did you seek her good before?'

'I did—at some risk, perhaps. But I wished her to have a friend for life—who would cherish her, who would do her more justice than a coarse and narrow-minded brother, that she has always lavished her affections on.'

'Yes, my way of befriending her is different from yours; and I'll tell you what is my way. I'll save her from disobeying and disgracing her father: I'll save her from throwing herself away on you—from making herself a laughing-stock—from being flouted by a man like *your* father, because she's not good enough for his son. You know well enough what sort of justice and cherishing you were preparing for her. I'm not to be imposed upon by fine words: I can see what actions mean. Come away, Maggie.'

He seized Maggie's right wrist as he spoke, and she put out her left hand. Philip clasped it an instant, with one eager look, and then hurried away.

Tom and Maggie walked on in silence for some yards. He was still holding her wrist tightly, as if he were compelling a culprit from the scene of action. At last Maggie, with a violent snatch, drew her hand away, and her pent-up, long-gathered irritation burst into utterance.

'Don't suppose that I think you are right, Tom, or that I bow to your will. I despise the feelings you have shown in speaking to Philip: I detest your insulting unmanly allusions to his deformity. You have been reproaching other people all your life—you have been always sure you yourself are right; it is because you have not a mind large enough to see that there is anything better than your own conduct and your own petty aims.'

'Certainly,' said Tom coolly. 'I don't see that your conduct is better, or your aims either. If your conduct, and Philip Wakem's conduct, has been right, why are you ashamed of its being known? Answer me that. I know what I have aimed at in my conduct, and I've succeeded: pray, what good has your conduct brought to you or anyone else?'

'I don't want to defend myself,' said Maggie, still with vehemence: 'I know I've been wrong—often, continually. But yet, sometimes when I have done wrong, it has been because I have feelings that you would be the better for, if you had them. If *you* were in fault ever—if you had done anything very wrong, I should be sorry for the pain it brought you; I should not want punishment to be heaped on you. But you have always enjoyed punishing me—you have always been hard and cruel to me: even when I was a little girl, and always loved you better than anyone else in the world, you would let me go crying to bed without forgiving me. You have no pity: you have no sense of your own imperfection and your own sins. It is a sin to be hard; it is not fitting for a mortal—for a Christian. You are nothing but a Pharisee. You thank God for nothing but your own virtues—you think they are great enough to win you everything else. You have not even a vision of feelings by the side of which your shining virtues are mere darkness!'

'Well,' said Tom, with cold scorn, 'if your feelings are so much better than mine, let me see you show them in some

other way than by conduct that's likely to disgrace us all—
than by ridiculous flights first into one extreme and then
into another. Pray, how have you shown your love, that
you talk of, either to me or my father? By disobeying
and deceiving us. I have a different way of showing my
affection.'

'Because you are a man, Tom, and have power, and can
do something in the world.'

'Then, if you can do nothing, submit to those that can.'

'So I *will* submit to what I acknowledge and feel to be
right. I will submit even to what is unreasonable from my
father, but I will not submit to it from you. You boast of
your virtues as if they purchased you a right to be cruel and
unmanly as you've been to-day. Don't suppose I would
give up Philip Wakem in obedience to you. The deformity
you insult would make me cling to him and care for him the
more.'

'Very well—that is your view of things,' said Tom, more
coldly than ever; 'you need say no more to show me what
a wide distance there is between us. Let us remember that
in future, and be silent.'

Tom went back to St. Ogg's, to fulfil an appointment
with his uncle Deane, and receive directions about a journey
on which he was to set out the next morning.

Maggie went up to her own room to pour out all that indignant remonstrance, against which Tom's mind was close
barred, in bitter tears. Then, when the first burst of unsatisfied anger was gone by, came the recollection of that
quiet time before the pleasure which had ended in to-day's
misery had perturbed the clearness and simplicity of her
life. She used to think in that time that she had made great
conquests, and won a lasting stand on serene heights above
worldly temptations and conflict. And here she was down
again in the thick of a hot strife with her own and others'
passions. Life was not so short, then, and perfect rest was
not so near as she had dreamed when she was two years
younger. There was more struggle for her—perhaps more
falling. If she had felt that she was entirely wrong, and that
Tom had been entirely right, she could sooner have re-

covered more inward harmony; but now her penitence and submission were constantly obstructed by resentment that would present itself to her no otherwise than as a just indignation. Her heart bled for Philip: she went on recalling the insults that had been flung at him with so vivid a conception of what he had felt under them, that it was almost like a sharp bodily pain to her, making her beat the floor with her foot, and tighten her fingers on her palm.

And yet, how was it that she was now and then conscious of a certain dim background of relief in the forced separation from Philip? Surely it was only because the sense of a deliverance from concealment was welcome at any cost.

VI

THE HARD-WON TRIUMPH

THREE weeks later, when Dorlcote Mill was at its prettiest moment in all the year—the great chestnuts in blossom, and the grass all deep and daisied—Tom Tulliver came home to it earlier than usual in the evening, and as he passed over the bridge, he looked with the old deep-rooted affection at the respectable red brick house, which always seemed cheerful and inviting outside, let the rooms be as bare and the hearts as sad as they might, inside. There is a very pleasant light in Tom's blue-grey eyes as he glances at the house-windows: that fold in his brow never disappears, but it is not unbecoming; it seems to imply a strength of will that may possibly be without harshness, when the eyes and mouth have their gentlest expression. His firm step becomes quicker, and the corners of his mouth rebel against the compression which is meant to forbid a smile.

The eyes in the parlour were not turned towards the bridge just then, and the group there was sitting in unexpectant silence—Mr. Tulliver in his arm-chair, tired with a long ride, and ruminating with a worn look, fixed chiefly on Maggie, who was bending over her sewing while her mother was making the tea.

They all looked up with surprise when they heard the well-known foot.

'Why, what's up now, Tom?' said his father. 'You're a bit earlier than usual.'

'O, there was nothing more for me to do, so I came away. Well, mother!'

Tom went up to his mother and kissed her, a sign of unusual good-humour with him. Hardly a word or look had passed between him and Maggie in all the three weeks; but his usual incommunicativeness at home prevented this from being noticeable to their parents.

'Father,' said Tom, when they had finished tea, 'do you know exactly how much money there is in the tin box?'

'Only a hundred and ninety-three pound,' said Mr. Tulliver. 'You've brought less o' late—but young fellows like to have their own way with their money. Though I didn't do as I liked before *I* was of age.' He spoke with rather timid discontent.

'Are you quite sure that's the sum, father?' said Tom: 'I wish you would take the trouble to fetch the tin box down. I think you have perhaps made a mistake.'

'How should I make a mistake?' said his father sharply. 'I've counted it often enough; but I can fetch it, if you won't believe me.'

It was always an incident Mr. Tulliver liked, in his gloomy life, to fetch the tin box and count the money.

'Don't go out of the room, mother,' said Tom, as he saw her moving when his father was gone up-stairs.

'And isn't Maggie to go?' said Mrs. Tulliver; 'because somebody must take away the things.'

'Just as she likes,' said Tom indifferently.

That was a cutting word to Maggie. Her heart had leaped with the sudden conviction that Tom was going to tell their father the debts could be paid—and Tom would have let her be absent when that news was told! But she carried away the tray, and came back immediately. The feeling of injury on her own behalf could not predominate at that moment.

Tom drew to the corner of the table near his father when

the tin box was set down and opened, and the red evening light falling on them made conspicuous the worn, sour gloom of the dark-eyed father and the suppressed joy in the face of the fair-complexioned son. The mother and Maggie sat at the other end of the table, the one in blank patience, the other in palpitating expectation.

Mr. Tulliver counted out the money, setting it in order on the table, and then said, glancing sharply at Tom:

'There now! you see I was right enough.'

He paused, looking at the money with bitter despondency.

'There's more nor three hundred wanting—it'll be a fine while before *I* can save that. Losing that forty-two pound wi' the corn was a sore job. This world's been too many for me. It's took four year to lay *this* by—it's much if I'm above ground for another four year. . . . I must trusten to you to pay 'em,' he went on, with a trembling voice, 'if you keep i' the same mind now you're coming o' age. . . . But you're like enough to bury me first.'

He looked up in Tom's face with a querulous desire for some assurance.

'No, father,' said Tom, speaking with energetic decision, though there was tremor discernible in his voice too, 'you will live to see the debts all paid. You shall pay them with your own hand.'

His tone implied something more than mere hopefulness or resolution. A slight electric shock seemed to pass through Mr. Tulliver, and he kept his eyes fixed on Tom with a look of eager inquiry, while Maggie, unable to restrain herself, rushed to her father's side and knelt down by him. Tom was silent a little while before he went on.

'A good while ago, my uncle Glegg lent me a little money to trade with, and that has answered. I have three hundred and twenty pounds in the bank.'

His mother's arms were round his neck as soon as the last words were uttered, and she said, half-crying:

'O, my boy, I knew you'd make iverything right again, when you got a man.'

But his father was silent: the flood of emotion hemmed

in all power of speech. Both Tom and Maggie were struck
with fear lest the shock of joy might even be fatal. But the
blessed relief of tears came. The broad chest heaved, the
muscles of the face gave way, and the grey-haired man
burst into loud sobs. The fit of weeping gradually subsided,
and he sat quiet, recovering the regularity of his breathing.
At last he looked up at his wife and said, in a gentle tone:

'Bessy, you must come and kiss me now—the lad has
made you amends. You'll see a bit o' comfort again, belike.'

When she had kissed him, and he had held her hand a
minute, his thought went back to the money.

'I wish you'd brought me the money to look at, Tom,' he
said, fingering the sovereigns on the table; 'I should ha' felt
surer.'

'You shall see it to-morrow, father,' said Tom. 'My uncle
Deane has appointed the creditors to meet to-morrow at
the Golden Lion, and he has ordered a dinner for them at
two o'clock. My uncle Glegg and he will both be there. It
was advertised in the *Messenger* on Saturday.'

'Then Wakem knows on't!' said Mr. Tulliver, his eye
kindling with triumphant fire. 'Ah!' he went on, with a
long-drawn guttural enunciation, taking out his snuff-box,
the only luxury he had left himself, and tapping it with
something of his old air of defiance—'I'll get from under
his thumb now—though I *must* leave th' old mill. I thought
I could ha' held out to die here—but I can't. . . . We've
got a glass o' nothing in the house, have we, Bessy?'

'Yes,' said Mrs. Tulliver, drawing out her much-reduced
bunch of keys, 'there's some brandy sister Deane brought
me when I was ill.'

'Get it me, then, get it me. I feel a bit weak.'

'Tom, my lad,' he said, in a stronger voice, when he had
taken some brandy-and-water, 'you shall make a speech to
'em. I'll tell 'em it's you as got the best part o' the money.
They'll see I'm honest at last, and ha' got an honest son.
Ah! Wakem 'ud be fine and glad to have a son like mine—a
fine straight fellow—i'stead o' that poor crooked creatur!
You'll prosper i' the world, my lad; you'll maybe see the

day when Wakem and his son 'ull be a round or two below you. You'll like enough be ta'en into partnership, as your uncle Deane was before you—you're in the right way for't; and then there's nothing to hinder your getting rich. . . . And if ever you're rich enough—mind this—try and get th' old mill again.'

Mr. Tulliver threw himself back in his chair: his mind, which had so long been the home of nothing but bitter discontent and foreboding, suddenly filled, by the magic of joy, with visions of good fortune. But some subtle influence prevented him from foreseeing the good fortune as happening to himself.

'Shake hands wi' me, my lad,' he said, suddenly putting out his hand. 'It's a great thing when a man can be proud as he's got a good son. I've had *that* luck.'

Tom never lived to taste another moment so delicious as that; and Maggie couldn't help forgetting her own grievances. Tom *was* good; and in the sweet humility that springs in us all in moments of true admiration and gratitude, she felt that the faults he had to pardon in her had never been redeemed, as his faults were. She felt no jealousy this evening that, for the first time, she seemed to be thrown into the background in her father's mind.

There was much more talk before bed-time. Mr. Tulliver naturally wanted to hear all the particulars of Tom's trading adventures, and he listened with growing excitement and delight. He was curious to know what had been said on every occasion—if possible, what had been thought: and Bob Jakin's part in the business threw him into peculiar outbursts of sympathy with the triumphant knowingness of that remarkable packman. Bob's juvenile history, so far as it had come under Mr. Tulliver's knowledge, was recalled with that sense of astonishing promise it displayed, which is observable in all reminiscences of the childhood of great men.

It was well that there was this interest of narrative to keep under the vague but fierce sense of triumph over Wakem, which would otherwise have been the channel his joy would have rushed into with dangerous force. Even as it was, that feeling from time to time gave threats of its ultimate mastery, in sudden bursts of irrelevant exclamation.

It was long before Mr. Tulliver got to sleep that night, and the sleep, when it came, was filled with vivid dreams. At half-past five o'clock in the morning, when Mrs. Tulliver was already rising, he alarmed her by starting up with a sort of smothered shout, and looking round in a bewildered way at the walls of the bedroom.

'What's the matter, Mr. Tulliver?' said his wife. He looked at her, still with a puzzled expression, and said at last:

'Ah!—I was dreaming . . . did I make a noise? . . . I thought I'd got hold of him.'

VII

A DAY OF RECKONING

Mr. Tulliver was an essentially sober man—able to take his glass and not averse to it, but never exceeding the bounds of moderation. He had naturally an active Hotspur temperament, which did not crave liquid fire to set it a-glow; his impetuosity was usually equal to an exciting occasion without any such reinforcements; and his desire for the brandy-and-water implied that the too sudden joy had fallen with a dangerous shock on a frame depressed by four years of gloom and unaccustomed hard fare. But that first doubtful tottering moment passed, he seemed to gather strength with his gathering excitement; and the next day, when he was seated at table with his creditors, his eye kindling and his cheek flushed with the consciousness that he was about to make an honourable figure once more, he looked more like the proud, confident, warmhearted and warm-tempered Tulliver of old times, than might have seemed possible to anyone who had met him a week before, riding along as had been his wont for the last four years since the sense of failure and debt had been upon him—with his head hanging down, casting brief, unwilling looks on those who forced themselves on his notice.

He made his speech, asserting his honest principles with his old confident eagerness, alluding to the rascals and the luck that had been against him, but that he had triumphed over, to some extent, by hard efforts and the aid of a good son; and winding up with the story of how Tom had got the best part of the needful money. But the streak of irritation and hostile triumph seemed to melt for a little while into purer fatherly pride and pleasure, when, Tom's health having been proposed, and uncle Deane having taken occasion to say a few words of eulogy on his general character and conduct, Tom himself got up and made the single speech of his life. It could hardly have been briefer: he thanked the gentlemen for the honour they had done him. He was glad that he had been able to help his father in proving his integrity and regaining his honest name; and, for his own part, he hoped he should never undo that work and disgrace that name. But the applause that followed was so great, and Tom looked so gentlemanly as well as tall and straight, that Mr. Tulliver remarked in an explanatory manner, to his friends on his right and left, that he had spent a deal of money on his son's education.

The party broke up in very sober fashion at five o'clock. Tom remained in St. Ogg's to attend to some business, and Mr. Tulliver mounted his horse to go home, and describe the memorable things that had been said and done, to 'poor Bessy and the little wench.' The air of excitement that hung about him was but faintly due to good cheer or any stimulus but the potent wine of triumphant joy. He did not choose any back street to-day, but rode slowly, with uplifted head and free glances, along the principal street all the way to the bridge. Why did he not happen to meet Wakem? The want of that coincidence vexed him, and set his mind at work in an irritating way. Perhaps Wakem was gone out of town to-day on purpose to avoid seeing or hearing anything of an honourable action, which might well cause him some unpleasant twinges. If Wakem were to meet him then, Mr. Tulliver would look straight at him, and the rascal would perhaps be forsaken a little by his cool domineering impudence. He would know by-and-by that an honest man was not going to serve *him* any longer, and lend his honesty to fill a pocket already over-full of dishonest gains. Perhaps the luck was beginning to turn; perhaps the devil didn't always hold the best cards in this world.

Simmering in this way, Mr. Tulliver approached the yard-gates of Dorlcote Mill, near enough to see a well-known figure coming out of them on a fine black horse. They met about fifty yards from the gates, between the great chestnuts and elms and the high bank.

'Tulliver,' said Wakem abruptly, in a haughtier tone than usual, 'what a fool's trick you did—spreading those hard lumps on that Far Close. I told you how it would be; but you men never learn to farm with any method.'

'Oh!' said Tulliver, suddenly boiling up. 'Get somebody else to farm for you, then, as'll ask *you* to teach him.'

'You have been drinking, I suppose,' said Wakem, really believing that this was the meaning of Tulliver's flushed face and sparkling eyes.

'No, I've not been drinking,' said Tulliver; 'I want no drinking to help me make up my mind as I'll serve no longer under a scoundrel.'

'Very well! you may leave my premises to-morrow, then: hold your insolent tongue and let me pass.' (Tulliver was backing his horse across the road to hem Wakem in.)

'No, I *shan't* let you pass,' said Tulliver, getting fiercer. 'I shall tell you what I think of you first. You're too big a raskill to get hanged—you're. . . .'

'Let me pass, you ignorant brute, or I'll ride over you.'

Mr. Tulliver, spurring his horse and raising his whip, made a rush forward, and Wakem's horse, rearing and staggering backward, threw his rider from the saddle and sent him sideways on the ground. Wakem had had the presence of mind to loose the bridle at once, and as the horse only staggered a few paces and then stood still, he might have risen and remounted without more inconvenience than a bruise and a shake. But before he could rise, Tulliver was off his horse too. The sight of the long-hated predominant man down and in his power, threw him

into a frenzy of triumphant vengeance, which seemed to
give him preternatural agility and strength. He rushed on
Wakem, who was in the act of trying to recover his feet,
grasped him by the left arm so as to press Wakem's whole
weight on the right arm, which rested on the ground, and
flogged him fiercely across the back with his riding-whip.
Wakem shouted for help, but no help came, until a woman's
scream was heard, and the cry of 'Father, father!'

Suddenly, Wakem felt, something had arrested Mr.
Tulliver's arm; for the flogging ceased, and the grasp on
his own arm was relaxed.

'Get away with you—go!' said Tulliver angrily. But it
was not to Wakem that he spoke. Slowly the lawyer rose,
and, as he turned his head, saw that Tulliver's arms were
being held by a girl—rather by the fear of hurting the girl
that clung to him with all her young might.

'O Luke—mother—come and help Mr. Wakem!' Maggie
cried, as she heard the longed-for footsteps.

'Help me on to that low horse,' said Wakem to Luke,
'then I shall perhaps manage: though—confound it—I
think this arm is sprained.'

With some difficulty, Wakem was heaved on to Tulliver's
horse. Then he turned toward the miller and said, with
white rage, 'You'll suffer for this, sir. Your daughter is a
witness that you've assaulted me.'

'I don't care,' said Mr. Tulliver, in a thick, fierce voice;
'go and show your back, and tell 'em I've thrashed you.
Tell 'em I've made things a bit more even i' the world.'

'Ride my horse home with me,' said Wakem to Luke.
'By the Tofton Ferry—not through the town.'

'Father, come in!' said Maggie imploringly. Then, seeing
that Wakem had ridden off, and that no further violence
was possible, she slackened her hold and burst into hysteric
sobs, while poor Mrs. Tulliver stood by in silence, quivering
with fear. But Maggie became conscious that as she was
slackening her hold, her father was beginning to grasp her
and lean on her. The surprise checked her sobs.

'I feel ill—faintish,' he said. 'Help me in, Bessy—I'm
giddy—I've a pain i' the head.'

He walked in slowly, propped by his wife and daughter, and tottered into his arm-chair. The almost purple flush had given way to paleness, and his hand was cold.

'Hadn't we better send for the doctor?' said Mrs. Tulliver.

He seemed to be too faint and suffering to hear her; but presently, when she said to Maggie, 'Go and see for somebody to fetch the doctor,' he looked up at her with full comprehension, and said, 'Doctor? no—no doctor. It's my head—that's all. Help me to bed.'

Sad ending to the day that had risen on them all like a beginning of better times! But mingled seed must bear a mingled crop.

In half an hour after his father had lain down Tom came home. Bob Jakin was with him—come to congratulate 'the old master,' not without some excusable pride that he had had his share in bringing about Mr. Tom's good-luck; and Tom had thought his father would like nothing better, as a finish to the day, than a talk with Bob. But now Tom could only spend the evening in gloomy expectation of the unpleasant consequences that must follow on this mad outbreak of his father's long-smothered hate. After the painful news had been told, he sat in silence: he had not spirit or inclination to tell his mother and sister anything about the dinner—they hardly cared to ask it. Apparently the mingled thread in the web of their life was so curiously twisted together, that there could be no joy without a sorrow coming close upon it. Tom was dejected by the thought that his exemplary effort must always be baffled by the wrong-doing of others: Maggie was living through, over and over again, the agony of the moment in which she had rushed to throw herself on her father's arm—with a vague, shuddering foreboding of wretched scenes to come. Not one of the three felt any particular alarm about Mr. Tulliver's health: the symptoms did not recall his former dangerous attack, and it seemed only a necessary consequence that his violent passion and effort of strength, after many hours of unusual excitement, should have made him feel ill. Rest would probably cure him.

Tom, tired out by his active day, fell asleep soon, and slept soundly: it seemed to him as if he had only just come to bed, when he waked to see his mother standing by him in the grey light of early morning.

'My boy, you must get up this minute: I've sent for the doctor, and your father wants you and Maggie to come to him.'

'Is he worse, mother?'

'He's been very ill all night with his head, but he doesn't say it's worse—he only said sudden, "Bessy, fetch the boy and girl. Tell 'em to make haste."'

Maggie and Tom threw on their clothes hastily in the chill grey light, and reached their father's room almost at the same moment. He was watching for them with an expression of pain on his brow, but with sharpened anxious consciousness in his eyes. Mrs. Tulliver stood at the foot of the bed, frightened and trembling, looking worn and aged from disturbed rest. Maggie was at the bedside first, but her father's glance was towards Tom, who came and stood next to her.

'Tom, my lad, it's come upon me as I shan't get up again. . . . This world's been too many for me, my lad, but you've done what you could to make things a bit even. Shake hands wi' me again, my lad, before I go away from you.'

The father and son clasped hands and looked at each other an instant. Then Tom said, trying to speak firmly:

'Have you any wish, father—that I can fulfil, when. . . .'

'Ay, my lad . . . you'll try and get the old mill back.'

'Yes, father.'

'And there's your mother—you'll try and make her amends, all you can, for my bad luck . . . and there's the little wench. . . .'

The father turned his eyes on Maggie with a still more eager look, while she, with a bursting heart, sank on her knees, to be closer to the dear, time-worn face which had been present with her through long years, as the sign of her deepest love and hardest trial.

'You must take care of her, Tom . . . don't you fret, my wench . . . there'll come somebody as'll love you and take your part . . . and you must be good to her, my lad. I was good to *my* sister. Kiss me, Maggie. . . . Come, Bessy. . . . You'll manage to pay for a brick grave, Tom, so as your mother and me can lie together.'

He looked away from them all when he had said this, and lay silent for some minutes, while they stood watching him, not daring to move. The morning light was growing clearer for them, and they could see the heaviness gathering in his face, and the dulness in his eyes. But at last he looked towards Tom and said:

'I had my turn—I beat him. That was nothing but fair. I never wanted anything but what was fair.'

'But, father, dear father,' said Maggie, an unspeakable anxiety predominating over her grief, 'you forgive him— you forgive everyone now?'

He did not move his eyes to look at her, but he said:

'No, my wench. I don't forgive him. . . . What's forgiving to do? I can't love a raskill. . . .'

His voice had become thicker; but he wanted to say more, and moved his lips again and again, struggling in vain to speak. At length the words forced their way.

'Does God forgive raskills? . . . but if He does, He won't be hard wi' me.'

His hands moved uneasily, as if he wanted them to remove some obstruction that weighed upon him. Two or three times there fell from him some broken words:

'This world's . . . too many . . . honest man . . . puzzling. . . .'

Soon they merged into mere mutterings; the eyes had ceased to discern; and then came the final silence.

But not of death. For an hour or more the chest heaved, the loud hard breathing continued, getting gradually slower, as the cold dews gathered on the brow.

At last there was total stillness, and poor Tulliver's dimly-lighted soul had for ever ceased to be vexed with the painful riddle of this world.

Help was come now: Luke and his wife were there, and

Mr. Turnbull had arrived, too late for everything but to say, 'This is death.'

Tom and Maggie went down-stairs together into the room where their father's place was empty. Their eyes turned to the same spot, and Maggie spoke:

'Tom, forgive me—let us always love each other;' and they clung and wept together.

BOOK SIXTH

THE GREAT TEMPTATION

I

A DUET IN PARADISE

THE well-furnished drawing-room, with the open grand piano, and the pleasant outlook down a sloping garden to a boat-house by the side of the Floss, is Mr. Deane's. The neat little lady in mourning, whose light-brown ringlets are falling over the coloured embroidery with which her fingers are busy, is of course Lucy Deane; and the fine young man who is leaning down from his chair to snap the scissors in the extremely abbreviated face of the 'King Charles' lying on the young lady's feet, is no other than Mr. Stephen Guest, whose diamond ring, attar of roses, and air of nonchalant leisure, at twelve o'clock in the day, are the graceful and odoriferous result of the largest oil-mill and the most extensive wharf in St. Ogg's. There is an apparent triviality in the action with the scissors, but your discernment perceives at once that there is a design in it which makes it eminently worthy of a large-headed, long-limbed young man; for you see that Lucy wants the scissors, and is compelled, reluctant as she may be, to shake her ringlets back, raise her soft hazel eyes, smile playfully down on the face that is so very nearly on a level with her knee, and, holding out her little shell-pink palm, to say:

'My scissors, please, if you can renounce the great pleasure of persecuting my poor Minny.'

The foolish scissors have slipped too far over the knuckles, it seems, and Hercules holds out his entrapped fingers hopelessly.

'Confound the scissors! The oval lies the wrong way. Please, draw them off for me.'

'Draw them off with your other hand,' says Miss Lucy roguishly.

'O, but that's my left hand: I'm not left-handed.' Lucy laughs, and the scissors are drawn off with gentle touches from tiny tips, which naturally dispose Mr. Stephen for a repetition *da capo*. Accordingly, he watches for the release of the scissors, that he may get them into his possession again.

'No, no,' said Lucy, sticking them in her band, 'you shall not have my scissors again—you have strained them already. Now don't set Minny growling again. Sit up and behave properly, and then I will tell you some news.'

'What is that?' said Stephen, throwing himself back and hanging his right arm over the corner of his chair. He might have been sitting for his portrait, which would have represented a rather striking young man of five-and-twenty, with a square forehead, short dark-brown hair standing erect, with a slight wave at the end, like a thick crop of corn, and a half-ardent, half-sarcastic glance from under his well-marked horizontal eyebrows. 'Is it very important news?'

'Yes—very. Guess.'

'You are going to change Minny's diet, and give him three ratafias soaked in a dessert-spoonful of cream daily?'

'Quite wrong.'

'Well, then, Dr. Kenn has been preaching against buckram, and you ladies have all been sending him a round-robin, saying—"This is a hard doctrine; who can bear it?"'

'For shame!' said Lucy, adjusting her little mouth gravely. 'It is rather dull of you not to guess my news, because it is about something I mentioned to you not very long ago.'

'But you have mentioned many things to me not long ago. Does your feminine tyranny require that when you say the thing you mean is one of several things, I should know it immediately by that mark?'

'Yes, I know you think I am silly.'

'I think you are perfectly charming.'

'And my silliness is part of my charm?'

'I didn't say *that*.'

'But I know you like women to be rather insipid. Philip Wakem betrayed you: he said so one day when you were not here.'

'O, I know Phil is fierce on that point; he makes it quite a personal matter. I think he must be love-sick for some unknown lady—some exalted Beatrice whom he met abroad.'

'By the by!' said Lucy, pausing in her work, 'it has just occurred to me that I have never found out whether my cousin Maggie would object to see Philip, as her brother does. Tom will not enter a room where Philip is, if he knows it: perhaps Maggie may be the same, and then we shan't be able to sing our glees—shall we?'

'What! is your cousin coming to stay with you?' said Stephen, with a look of slight annoyance.

'Yes; that was my news, which you have forgotten. She's going to leave her situation, where she has been nearly two years, poor thing—ever since her father's death; and she will stay with me a month or two—many months, I hope.'

'And am I bound to be pleased at that news?'

'O no, not at all,' said Lucy, with a little air of pique. '*I* am pleased, but that, of course, is no reason why *you* should be pleased. There is no girl in the world I love so well as my cousin Maggie.'

'And you will be inseparable, I suppose, when she comes. There will be no possibility of a *tête-à-tête* with you any more, unless you can find an admirer for her, who will pair off with her occasionally. What is the ground of dislike to Philip? He might have been a resource.'

'It is a family quarrel with Philip's father. There were very painful circumstances, I believe. I never quite understood them, or knew them all. My uncle Tulliver was unfortunate and lost all his property, and I think he considered Mr. Wakem was somehow the cause of it. Mr. Wakem bought Dorlcote Mill, my uncle's old place, where he always lived. You must remember my uncle Tulliver, don't you?'

'No,' said Stephen, with rather supercilious indifference. 'I've always known the name, and I daresay I knew the

man by sight, apart from his name. I know half the names
and faces in the neighbourhood in that detached, disjointed
way.'

'He was a very hot-tempered man. I remember, when I
was a little girl, and used to go to see my cousins, he often
frightened me by talking as if he were angry. Papa told me
there was a dreadful quarrel, the very day before my
uncle's death, between him and Mr. Wakem, but it was
hushed up. That was when you were in London. Papa
says my uncle was quite mistaken in many ways: his mind
had become embittered. But Tom and Maggie must naturally feel it very painful to be reminded of these things. They
have had so much—so very much trouble. Maggie was at
school with me six years ago, when she was fetched away
because of her father's misfortunes, and she has hardly had
any pleasure since, I think. She has been in a dreary situation in a school since uncle's death, because she is determined to be independent, and not live with aunt Pullet;
and I could hardly wish her to come to me then, because
dear mamma was ill, and everything was so sad. That is
why I want her to come to me now, and have a long, long
holiday.'

'Very sweet and angelic of you,' said Stephen, looking at
her with an admiring smile; 'and all the more so if she has
the conversational qualities of her mother.'

'Poor aunty! You are cruel to ridicule her. She is very
valuable to *me*, I know. She manages the house beautifully
—much better than any stranger would—and she was a
great comfort to me in mamma's illness.'

'Yes, but in point of companionship, one would prefer
that she should be represented by her brandy-cherries and
cream cakes. I think with a shudder that her daughter will
always be present in person, and have no agreeable proxies
of that kind—a fat, blond girl, with round blue eyes, who
will stare at us silently.'

'O yes!' exclaimed Lucy, laughing wickedly and clapping
her hands, 'that is just my cousin Maggie. You must have
seen her!'

'No, indeed: I'm only guessing what Mrs. Tulliver's

daughter must be; and then if she is to banish Philip, our only apology for a tenor, that will be an additional bore.'

'But I hope that may not be. I think I will ask you to call on Philip and tell him Maggie is coming to-morrow. He is quite aware of Tom's feeling, and always keeps out of his way; so he will understand, if you tell him, that I asked you to warn him not to come until I write and ask him.'

'I think you had better write a pretty note for me to take: Phil is so sensitive, you know the least thing might frighten him off coming at all, and we had hard work to get him. I can never induce him to come to the Park: he doesn't like my sisters, I think. It is only your faëry touch that can lay his ruffled feathers.'

Stephen mastered the little hand that was straying towards a table, and touched it lightly with his lips. Little Lucy felt very proud and happy. She and Stephen were in that stage of courtship which makes the most exquisite moment of youth, the freshest blossom-time of passion—when each is sure of the other's love, but no formal declaration has been made, and all its mutual divination, exalting the most trivial word, the lightest gesture, into thrills delicate and delicious as wafted jasmine scent. The explicitness of an engagement wears off this finest edge of susceptibility: it is jasmine gathered and presented in a large bouquet.

'But it is really odd that you should have hit so exactly on Maggie's appearance and manners,' said the cunning Lucy, moving to reach her desk, 'because she might have been like her brother, you know; and Tom has not round eyes; and he is as far as possible from staring at people.'

'O, I suppose he is like the father: he seems to be as proud as Lucifer. Not a brilliant companion, though, I should think.'

'I like Tom. He gave me my Minny when I lost Lolo; and papa is very fond of him: he says Tom has excellent principles. It was through him that his father was able to pay all his debts before he died.'

'Oh, ah; I've heard about that. I heard your father and mine talking about it a little while ago, after dinner, in one of their interminable discussions about business. They think of doing something for young Tulliver: he saved them from a considerable loss by riding home in some marvellous way, like Turpin, to bring them news about the stoppage of a bank, or something of that sort. But I was rather drowsy at the time.'

Stephen rose from his seat, and sauntered to the piano, humming in falsetto, 'Graceful Consort,' as he turned over the volume of 'The Creation,' which stood open on the desk.

'Come and sing this,' he said, when he saw Lucy rising.

'What! "Graceful Consort?" I don't think it suits your voice.'

'Never mind; it exactly suits my feeling, which, Philip will have it, is the grand element of good singing. I notice men with indifferent voices are usually of that opinion.'

'Philip burst into one of his invectives against "The Creation" the other day,' said Lucy, seating herself at the piano. 'He says it has a sort of sugared complacency and flattering make-believe in it, as if it were written for the birthday fête of a German Grand-Duke.'

'O pooh! He is the fallen Adam with a soured temper. We are Adam and Eve unfallen, in paradise. Now, then— the recitative, for the sake of the moral. You will sing the whole duty of woman—"And from obedience grows my pride and happiness."'

'O no, I shall not respect an Adam who drags the *tempo*, as you will,' said Lucy, beginning to play the duet.

Surely the only courtship unshaken by doubts and fears, must be that in which the lovers can sing together. The sense of mutual fitness that springs from the two deep notes fulfilling expectation just at the right moment between the notes of the silvery soprano, from the perfect accord of descending thirds and fifths, from the preconcerted loving chase of a fugue, is likely enough to supersede any immediate demand for less impassioned forms of agreement. The contralto will not care to catechise the bass: the tenor will foresee no embarrassing dearth of remark in evenings spent with the lovely soprano. In the provinces, too, where music was so scarce in that remote time, how could the

musical people avoid falling in love with each other? Even
political principle must have been in danger of relaxation
under such circumstances; and the violin, faithful to
rotten boroughs, must have been tempted to fraternise in
a demoralising way with a reforming violoncello. In this
case, the linnet-throated soprano, and the full-toned bass,
singing:

> '*With thee delight is ever new,*
> *With thee is life incessant bliss,*'

believed what they sang all the more *because* they sang it.

'Now for Raphael's great song,' said Lucy, when they
had finished the duet. 'You do the "heavy beasts" to per-
fection.'

'That sounds complimentary,' said Stephen, looking at
his watch. 'By Jove, it's nearly half-past one. Well, I can
just sing this.'

Stephen delivered with admirable ease the deep notes
representing the tread of the heavy beasts: but when a
singer has an audience of two, there is room for divided
sentiments. Minny's mistress was charmed; but Minny,
who had intrenched himself, trembling, in his basket as
soon as the music began, found this thunder so little to his
taste that he leaped out and scampered under the remotest
chiffonnière, as the most eligible place in which a small dog
could await the crack of doom.

'Adieu, "graceful consort,"' said Stephen, buttoning his
coat across when he had done singing, and smiling down from
his tall height, with the air of rather a patronising lover, at
the little lady on the music-stool. 'My bliss is not incessant,
for I must gallop home. I promised to be there at lunch.'

'You will not be able to call on Philip, then? It is of no
consequence: I have said everything in my note.'

'You will be engaged with your cousin to-morrow, I
suppose?'

'Yes, we are going to have a little family-party. My
cousin Tom will dine with us; and poor aunty will have her
two children together for the first time. It will be very
pretty; I think a great deal about it.'

'But I may come the next day?'

'O yes! Come and be introduced to my cousin Maggie—though you can hardly be said not to have seen her, you have described her so well.'

'Good-bye, then.' And there was that slight pressure of the hands, and momentary meeting of the eyes, which will often leave a little lady with a slight flush and smile on her face that do not subside immediately when the door is closed, and with an inclination to walk up and down the room rather than to seat herself quietly at her embroidery, or other rational and improving occupation. At least this was the effect on Lucy; and you will not, I hope, consider it an indication of vanity predominating over more tender impulses, that she just glanced in the chimney-glass as her walk brought her near it. The desire to know that one has not looked an absolute fright during a few hours of conversation, may be construed as lying within the bonds of a laudable benevolent consideration for others. And Lucy had so much of this benevolence in her nature that I am inclined to think her small egoisms were impregnated with it, just as there are people not altogether unknown to you, whose small benevolences have a predominant and somewhat rank odour of egoism. Even now, that she is walking up and down with a little triumphant flutter of her girlish heart at the sense that she is loved by the person of chief consequence in her small world, you may see in her hazel eyes an ever-present sunny benignity, in which the momentary harmless flashes of personal vanity are quite lost; and if she is happy in thinking of her lover, it is because the thought of him mingles readily with all the gentle affections and good-natured offices with which she fills her peaceful days. Even now, her mind, with that instantaneous alternation which makes two currents of feeling or imagination seem simultaneous, is glancing continually from Stephen to the preparations she has only half finished in Maggie's room. Cousin Maggie should be treated as well as the grandest lady-visitor—nay, better, for she should have Lucy's best prints and drawings in her bedroom, and the very finest bouquet of spring flowers on her table.

Maggie would enjoy all that—she was so fond of pretty things! And there was poor aunt Tulliver, that no one made any account of—she was to be surprised with the present of a cap of superlative quality, and to have her health drunk in a gratifying manner, for which Lucy was going to lay a plot with her father this evening. Clearly, she had not time to indulge in long reveries about her own happy love-affairs. With this thought she walked towards the door, but paused there.

'What's the matter, then, Minny?' she said, stooping in answer to some whimpering of that small quadruped, and lifting his glossy head against her pink cheek. 'Did you think I was going without you? Come, then, let us go and see Sinbad.'

Sinbad was Lucy's chestnut horse, that she always fed with her own hand when he was turned out in the paddock. She was fond of feeding dependent creatures, and knew the private tastes of all the animals about the house, delighting in the little rippling sounds of her canaries when their beaks were busy with fresh seed, and in the small nibbling pleasures of certain animals which, lest she should appear too trivial, I will here call 'the more familiar rodents.'

Was not Stephen Guest right in his decided opinion that this slim maiden of eighteen was quite the sort of wife a man would not be likely to repent of marrying?—a woman who was loving and thoughtful for other women, not giving them Judas-kisses with eyes askance on their welcome defects, but with real care and vision for their half-hidden pains and mortifications, with long ruminating enjoyment of little pleasures prepared for them? Perhaps the emphasis of his admiration did not fall precisely on this rarest quality in her—perhaps he approved his own choice of her chiefly because she did not strike him as a remarkable rarity. A man likes his wife to be pretty: well, Lucy was pretty, but not to a maddening extent. A man likes his wife to be accomplished, gentle, affectionate, and not stupid; and Lucy had all these qualifications. Stephen was not surprised to find himself in love with her, and was conscious of excellent judgment in preferring her to Miss Leyburn, the daughter of the county member, although Lucy was only the daughter of his father's subordinate partner; besides, he had had to defy and overcome a slight unwillingness and disappointment in his father and sisters—a circumstance which gives a young man an agreeable consciousness of his own dignity. Stephen was aware that he had sense and independence enough to choose the wife who was likely to make him happy, unbiassed by any indirect considerations. He meant to choose Lucy: she was a little darling, and exactly the sort of woman he had always most admired.

II

FIRST IMPRESSIONS

'He is very clever, Maggie,' said Lucy. She was kneeling on a footstool at Maggie's feet, after placing that dark lady in the large crimson-velvet chair. 'I feel sure you will like him. I hope you will.'

'I shall be very difficult to please,' said Maggie, smiling, and holding up one of Lucy's long curls, that the sunlight might shine through it. 'A gentleman who thinks he is good enough for Lucy must expect to be sharply criticised.'

'Indeed, he's a great deal too good for me. And sometimes, when he is away, I almost think it can't really be that he loves me. But I can never doubt it when he is with me—though I couldn't bear anyone but you to know that I feel in that way, Maggie.'

'Oh, then, if I disapprove of him you can give him up, since you are not engaged,' said Maggie with playful gravity.

'I would rather not be engaged. When people are engaged, they begin to think of being married soon,' said Lucy, too thoroughly preoccupied to notice Maggie's joke; 'and I should like everything to go on for a long while just as it is. Sometimes I am quite frightened lest Stephen should say that he has spoken to papa; and from something that fell from papa the other day, I feel sure he and Mr. Guest are expecting that. And Stephen's sisters are very civil to me now. At first, I think they didn't like his paying me attention; and that was natural. It *does* seem out of keeping that I should ever live in a great place like the Park House—such a little insignificant thing as I am.'

'But people are not expected to be large in proportion to the houses they live in, like snails,' said Maggie, laughing. 'Pray, are Mr. Guest's sisters giantesses?'

'O no; and not handsome—that is, not very,' said Lucy, half-penitent at this uncharitable remark.

'But *he* is—at least he is generally considered very handsome.'

'Though you are unable to share that opinion?'

'O, I don't know,' said Lucy, blushing pink over brow and neck. 'It is a bad plan to raise expectation; you will perhaps be disappointed. But I have prepared a charming surprise for *him*; I shall have a glorious laugh against him. I shall not tell you what it is, though.'

Lucy rose from her knees and went to a little distance, holding her pretty head on one side, as if she had been arranging Maggie for a portrait, and wished to judge of the general effect.

'Stand up a moment, Maggie.'

'What is your pleasure now?' said Maggie, smiling languidly as she rose from her chair and looked down on her slight, aërial cousin, whose figure was quite subordinate to her faultless drapery of silk and crape.

Lucy kept her contemplative attitude a moment or two in silence, and then said:

'I can't think what witchery it is in you, Maggie, that makes you look best in shabby clothes; though you really must have a new dress now. But do you know, last night I was trying to fancy you in a handsome fashionable dress, and do what I would, that old limp merino would come back as the only right thing for you. I wonder if Marie Antoinette looked all the grander when her gown was darned at the elbows. Now, if *I* were to put anything shabby on, I should be quite unnoticeable—I should be a mere rag.'

'O, quite,' said Maggie, with mock gravity. 'You would be liable to be swept out of the room with the cobwebs and carpet-dust, and to find yourself under the grate, like Cinderella. Mayn't I sit down now?'

'Yes, now you may,' said Lucy, laughing. Then, with an air of serious reflection, unfastening her large jet brooch, 'But you must change brooches, Maggie; that little butterfly looks silly on you!'

'But won't that mar the charming effect of my consistent shabbiness?' said Maggie, seating herself submissively, while Lucy knelt again and unfastened the contemptible butterfly. 'I wish my mother were of your opinion, for she was fretting last night because this is my best frock. I've been saving my money to pay for some lessons: I shall never get a better situation without more accomplishments.'

Maggie gave a little sigh.

'Now, don't put on that sad look again,' said Lucy, pinning the large brooch below Maggie's fine throat. 'You're forgetting that you've left that dreary schoolroom behind you, and have no little girls' clothes to mend.'

'Yes,' said Maggie. 'It is with me as I used to think it would be with the poor uneasy white bear I saw at the show. I thought he must have got so stupid with the habit of turning backwards and forwards in that narrow space, that he would keep doing it if they set him free. One gets a bad habit of being unhappy.'

'But I shall put you under a discipline of pleasure that will make you lose that bad habit,' said Lucy, sticking the black butterfly absently in her own collar, while her eyes met Maggie's affectionately.

'You dear, tiny thing,' said Maggie, in one of her bursts of loving admiration, 'you enjoy other people's happiness so much, I believe you would do without any of your own. I wish I were like you.'

'I've never been tried in that way,' said Lucy. 'I've always been so happy. I don't know whether I could bear much trouble; I never had any but poor mamma's death. You *have* been tried, Maggie; and I'm sure you feel for other people quite as much as I do.'

'No, Lucy,' said Maggie, shaking her head slowly, 'I don't

enjoy their happiness as you do—else I should be more contented. I do feel for them when they are in trouble; I don't think I could ever bear to make any one unhappy; and yet I often hate myself, because I get angry sometimes at the sight of happy people. I think I get worse as I get older—more selfish. That seems very dreadful.'

'Now, Maggie!' said Lucy in a tone of remonstrance, 'I don't believe a word of that. It is all a gloomy fancy—just because you are depressed by a dull, wearisome life.'

'Well, perhaps it is,' said Maggie, resolutely clearing away the clouds from her face with a bright smile, and throwing herself backward in her chair. 'Perhaps it comes from the school diet—watery rice-pudding spiced with Pinnock. Let us hope it will give way before my mother's custards and this charming Geoffrey Crayon.'

Maggie took up the 'Sketch Book,' which lay by her on the table.

'Do I look fit to be seen with this little brooch?' said Lucy, going to survey the effect in the chimney-glass.

'O no, Mr. Guest will be obliged to go out of the room again if he sees you in it. Pray make haste and put another on.'

Lucy hurried out of the room, but Maggie did not take the opportunity of opening her book: she let it fall on her knees, while her eyes wandered to the window, where she could see the sunshine falling on the rich clumps of spring flowers and on the long hedge of laurels—and beyond, the silvery breadth of the dear old Floss, that at this distance seemed to be sleeping in a morning holiday. The sweet fresh garden-scent came through the open window, and the birds were busy flitting and alighting, gurgling and singing. Yet Maggie's eyes began to fill with tears. The sight of the old scenes had made the rush of memories so painful, that even yesterday she had only been able to rejoice in her mother's restored comfort and Tom's brotherly friendliness as we rejoice in good news of friends at a distance, rather than in the presence of a happiness which we share. Memory and imagination urged upon her a sense of privation too keen to let her taste what was offered in the transient present:

her future, she thought, was likely to be worse than her past, for after her years of contented renunciation, she had slipped back into desire and longing: she found joyless days of distasteful occupation harder and harder—she found the image of the intense and varied life she yearned for, and despaired of, becoming more and more importunate. The sound of the opening door roused her, and, hastily wiping away her tears, she began to turn over the leaves of her book.

'There is one pleasure, I know, Maggie, that your deepest dismalness will never resist,' said Lucy, beginning to speak as soon as she entered the room. 'That is music, and I mean you to have quite a riotous feast of it. I mean you to get up your playing again, which used to be so much better than mine, when we were at Laceham.'

'You would have laughed to see me playing the little girls' tunes over and over to them, when I took them to practice,' said Maggie, 'just for the sake of fingering the dear keys again. But I don't know whether I could play anything more difficult now than "Begone, dull care!"'

'I know what a wild state of joy you used to be in when the glee-men came round,' said Lucy, taking up her embroidery, 'and we might have all those old glees that you used to love so, if I were certain that you don't feel exactly as Tom does about some things.'

'I should have thought there was nothing you might be more certain of,' said Maggie, smiling.

'I ought rather to have said, one particular thing. Because if you feel just as he does about that, we shall want our third voice. St. Ogg's is so miserably provided with musical gentlemen. There are really only Stephen and Philip Wakem who have any knowledge of music, so as to be able to sing a part.'

Lucy had looked up from her work as she uttered the last sentence, and saw that there was a change in Maggie's face.

'Does it hurt you to hear the name mentioned, Maggie? If it does, I will not speak of him again. I know Tom will not see him if he can avoid it.'

'I don't feel at all as Tom does on that subject,' said

Maggie, rising and going to the window as if she wanted to see more of the landscape. 'I've always liked Philip Wakem ever since I was a little girl, and saw him at Lorton. He was so good when Tom hurt his foot.'

'O, I'm so glad!' said Lucy. 'Then you won't mind his coming sometimes, and we can have much more music than we could without him. I'm very fond of poor Philip, only I wish he were not so morbid about his deformity. I suppose it *is* his deformity that makes him so sad—and sometimes bitter. It is certainly very piteous to see his poor little crooked body and pale face among great strong people.'

'But, Lucy,' said Maggie, trying to arrest the prattling stream. . . .

'Ah, there is the door-bell. That must be Stephen,' Lucy went on, not noticing Maggie's faint effort to speak. 'One of the things I most admire in Stephen is, that he makes a greater friend of Philip than any one.'

It was too late for Maggie to speak now: the drawing-room door was opening, and Minny was already growling in a small way at the entrance of a tall gentleman, who went up to Lucy and took her hand with a half-polite, half-tender glance and tone of inquiry, which seemed to indicate that he was unconscious of any other presence.

'Let me introduce you to my cousin, Miss Tulliver,' said Lucy, turning with wicked enjoyment towards Maggie, who now approached from the farther window. 'This is Mr. Stephen Guest.'

For one instant Stephen could not conceal his astonishment at the sight of this tall dark-eyed nymph with her jet-black coronet of hair; the next, Maggie felt herself, for the first time in her life, receiving the tribute of a very deep blush and a very deep bow from a person towards whom she herself was conscious of timidity. This new experience was very agreeable to her—so agreeable, that it almost effaced her previous emotion about Philip. There was a new brightness in her eyes, and a very becoming flush on her cheek, as she seated herself.

'I hope you perceive what a striking likeness you drew the day before yesterday,' said Lucy, with a pretty laugh of triumph. She enjoyed her lover's confusion—the advantage was usually on his side.

'This designing cousin of yours quite deceived me, Miss Tulliver,' said Stephen, seating himself by Lucy, and stooping to play with Minny—only looking at Maggie furtively. 'She said you had light hair and blue eyes.'

'Nay, it was you who said so,' remonstrated Lucy. 'I only refrained from destroying your confidence in your own second-sight.'

'I wish I could always err in the same way,' said Stephen, 'and find reality so much more beautiful than my preconceptions.'

'Now you have proved yourself equal to the occasion,' said Maggie, 'and said what it was incumbent on you to say under the circumstances.'

She flashed a slightly defiant look at him: it was clear to her that he had been drawing a satirical portrait of her beforehand. Lucy had said he was inclined to be satirical, and Maggie had mentally supplied the addition—'and rather conceited.'

'An alarming amount of devil there,' was Stephen's first thought. The second, when she had bent over her work, was, 'I wish she would look at me again.' The next was to answer:

'I suppose all phrases of mere compliment have their turn to be true. A man is occasionally grateful when he says "thank you." It's rather hard upon him that he must use the same words with which all the world declines a disagreeable invitation—don't you think so, Miss Tulliver?'

'No,' said Maggie, looking at him with her direct glance; 'if we use common words on a great occasion, they are the more striking, because they are felt at once to have a particular meaning, like old banners, or everyday clothes, hung up in a sacred place.'

'Then my compliment ought to be eloquent,' said Stephen, really not quite knowing what he said while Maggie looked at him, 'seeing that the words were so far beneath the occasion.'

'No compliment can be eloquent, except as an expression of indifference,' said Maggie, blushing a little.

Lucy was rather alarmed: she thought Stephen and Maggie were not going to like each other. She had always feared lest Maggie should appear too odd and clever to please that critical gentleman. 'Why, dear Maggie,' she interposed, 'you have always pretended that you are too fond of being admired; and now, I think, you are angry because some one ventures to admire you.'

'Not at all,' said Maggie; 'I like too well to feel that I am admired, but compliments never make me feel that.'

'I will never pay you a compliment again, Miss Tulliver,' said Stephen.

'Thank you; that will be a proof of respect.'

Poor Maggie! She was so unused to society that she could take nothing as a matter of course, and had never in her life spoken from the lips merely, so that she must necessarily appear absurd to more experienced ladies, from the excessive feeling she was apt to throw into very trivial incidents. But she was even conscious herself of a little absurdity in this instance. It was true she had a theoretic objection to compliments, and had once said impatiently to Philip, that she didn't see why women were to be told with a simper that they were beautiful, any more than old men were to be told that they were venerable: still, to be so irritated by a common practice in the case of a stranger like Mr. Stephen Guest, and to care about his having spoken slightingly of her before he had seen her, was certainly unreasonable, and as soon as she was silent she began to be ashamed of herself. It did not occur to her that her irritation was due to the pleasanter emotion which preceded it, just as when we are satisfied with a sense of glowing warmth, an innocent drop of cold water may fall upon us as a sudden smart.

Stephen was too well-bred not to seem unaware that the previous conversation could have been felt embarrassing, and at once began to talk of impersonal matters, asking Lucy if she knew when the bazaar was at length to take place, so that there might be some hope of seeing her rain the influence of her eyes on objects more grateful than those worsted flowers that were growing under her fingers.

'Some day next month, I believe,' said Lucy. 'But your sisters are doing more for it than I am: they are to have the largest stall.'

'Ah, yes; but they carry on their manufactures in their own sitting-room, where I don't intrude on them. I see you are not addicted to the fashionable vice of fancy-work, Miss Tulliver,' said Stephen, looking at Maggie's plain hemming.

'No,' said Maggie, 'I can do nothing more difficult or more elegant than shirt-making.'

'And your plain sewing is so beautiful, Maggie,' said Lucy, 'that I think I shall beg a few specimens of you to show as fancy-work. Your exquisite sewing is quite a mystery to me—you used to dislike that sort of work so much in old days.'

'It is a mystery easily explained, dear,' said Maggie, looking up quietly. 'Plain sewing was the only thing I could get money by; so I was obliged to try and do it well.'

Lucy, good and simple as she was, could not help blushing a little: she did not quite like that Stephen should know that—Maggie need not have mentioned it. Perhaps there was some pride in the confession: the pride of poverty that will not be ashamed of itself. But if Maggie had been the queen of coquettes she could hardly have invented a means of giving greater piquancy to her beauty in Stephen's eyes: I am not sure that the quiet admission of plain sewing and poverty would have done alone, but assisted by the beauty, they made Maggie more unlike other women even than she had seemed at first.

'But I can knit, Lucy,' Maggie went on, 'if that will be of any use for your bazaar.'

'O yes, of infinite use. I shall set you to work with scarlet wool to-morrow. But my sister is the most enviable person,' continued Lucy, turning to Stephen, 'to have the talent of modelling. She is doing a wonderful bust of Dr. Kenn entirely from memory.'

'Why, if she can remember to put the eyes very near

together, and the corners of the mouth very far apart, the likeness can hardly fail to be striking in St. Ogg's.'

'Now that is very wicked of you,' said Lucy, looking rather hurt. 'I didn't think you would speak disrespectfully of Dr. Kenn.'

'I say anything disrespectful of Dr. Kenn? Heaven forbid! But I am not bound to respect a libellous bust of him. I think Kenn one of the finest fellows in the world. I don't care much about the tall candlesticks he has put on the communion-table, and I shouldn't like to spoil my temper by getting up to early prayers every morning. But he's the only man I ever knew personally who seems to me to have anything of the real apostle in him—a man who has eight hundred a-year, and is contented with deal furniture and boiled beef because he gives away two-thirds of his income. That was a very fine thing of him—taking into his house that poor lad Grattan who shot his mother by accident. He sacrifices more time than a less busy man could spare, to save the poor fellow from getting into a morbid state of mind about it. He takes the lad out with him constantly, I see.'

'That is beautiful,' said Maggie, who had let her work fall, and was listening with keen interest. 'I never knew anyone who did such things.'

'And one admires that sort of action in Kenn all the more,' said Stephen, 'because his manners in general are rather cold and severe. There's nothing sugary and maudlin about him.'

'O, I think he's a perfect character!' said Lucy, with pretty enthusiasm.

'No; there I can't agree with you,' said Stephen, shaking his head with sarcastic gravity.

'Now, what fault can you point out in him?'

'He's an Anglican.'

'Well, those are the right views, I think,' said Lucy gravely.

'That settles the question in the abstract,' said Stephen, 'but not from a parliamentary point of view. He has set the Dissenters and the Church people by the ears; and a rising senator like myself, of whose services the country is very much in need, will find it inconvenient when he puts up for the honour of representing St. Ogg's in Parliament.'

'Do you really think of that?' said Lucy, her eyes brightening with a proud pleasure that made her neglect the argumentative interests of Anglicanism.

'Decidedly—whenever old Mr. Leyburn's public spirit and gout induce him to give way. My father's heart is set on it; and gifts like mine, you know'—here Stephen drew himself up, and rubbed his large white hands over his hair with playful self-admiration—'gifts like mine involve great responsibilities. Don't you think so, Miss Tulliver?'

'Yes,' said Maggie, smiling, but not looking up; 'so much fluency and self-possession should not be wasted entirely on private occasions.'

'Ah, I see how much penetration you have,' said Stephen. 'You have discovered already that I am talkative and impudent. Now superficial people never discern that—owing to my manner, I suppose.'

'She doesn't look at me when I talk of myself,' he thought, while his listeners were laughing. 'I must try other subjects.'

Did Lucy intend to be present at the meeting of the Book Club next week? was the next question. Then followed the recommendation to choose Southey's 'Life of Cowper,' unless she were inclined to be philosophical, and startle the ladies of St. Ogg's by voting for one of the Bridgewater Treatises. Of course Lucy wished to know what these alarmingly learned books were; and as it is always pleasant to improve the minds of ladies by talking to them at ease on subjects of which they know nothing, Stephen became quite brilliant in an account of Buckland's Treatise, which he had just been reading. He was rewarded by seeing Maggie let her work fall, and gradually get so absorbed in his wonderful geological story that she sat looking at him, leaning forward with crossed arms, and with an entire absence of self-consciousness, as if he had been the snuffiest of old professors, and she a downy-lipped alumnus. He was so fascinated by this clear, large gaze, that at last he forgot to look away from it occasionally towards Lucy; but she, sweet child, was only rejoicing that Stephen was proving to Maggie how clever he was, and that they would certainly be good friends after all.

'I will bring you the book, shall I, Miss Tulliver?' said Stephen, when he found the stream of his recollections running rather shallow. 'There are many illustrations in it that you will like to see.'

'O, thank you,' said Maggie, blushing with returning self-consciousness at this direct address, and taking up her work again.

'No, no,' Lucy interposed. 'I must forbid your plunging Maggie in books. I shall never get her away from them; and I want her to have delicious do-nothing days, filled with boating, and chatting, and riding, and driving: that is the holiday she needs.'

'Apropos!' said Stephen, looking at his watch. 'Shall we go out for a row on the river now? The tide will suit for us to go the Tofton way, and we can walk back.'

That was a delightful proposition to Maggie, for it was years since she had been on the river. When she was gone to put on her bonnet, Lucy lingered to give an order to the servant, and took the opportunity of telling Stephen that Maggie had no objection to seeing Philip, so that it was a pity she had sent that note the day before yesterday. But she would write another to-morrow and invite him.

'I'll call and beat him up to-morrow,' said Stephen, 'and bring him with me in the evening, shall I? My sisters will want to call on you when I tell them your cousin is with you. I must leave the field clear for them in the morning.'

'O yes, pray bring him,' said Lucy. 'And you *will* like Maggie, shan't you?' she added, in a beseeching tone. 'Isn't she a dear, noble-looking creature?'

'Too tall,' said Stephen, smiling down upon her, 'and a little too fiery. She is not my type of woman, you know.'

Gentlemen, you are aware, are apt to impart these imprudent confidences to ladies concerning their unfavourable opinion of sister fair ones. That is why so many women have the advantage of knowing that they are secretly repulsive to men who have self-denyingly made ardent love to them. And hardly anything could be more distinctively characteristic of Lucy, than that she both implicitly believed what Stephen said, and was determined that Maggie should not know it. But you, who have a higher logic than the verbal to guide you, have already foreseen, as the direct sequence to that unfavourable opinion of Stephen's, that he walked down to the boat-house calculating, by the aid of a vivid imagination, that Maggie must give him her hand at least twice in consequence of this pleasant boating plan, and that a gentleman who wishes ladies to look at him is advantageously situated when he is rowing them in a boat. What then? Had he fallen in love with this surprising daughter of Mrs. Tulliver at first sight? Certainly not. Such passions are never heard of in real life. Besides, he was in love already, and half engaged to the dearest little creature in the world; and he was not a man to make a fool of himself in any way. But when one is five-and-twenty, one has not chalk-stones at one's finger-ends that the touch of a handsome girl should be entirely indifferent. It was perfectly natural and safe to admire beauty and enjoy looking at it—at least under such circumstances as the present. And there was really something very interesting about this girl, with her poverty and troubles: it was gratifying to see the friendship between the two cousins. Generally, Stephen admitted, he was not fond of women who had any peculiarity of character—but here the peculiarity seemed really of a superior kind; and provided one is not obliged to marry such women, why, they certainly make a variety in social intercourse.

Maggie did not fulfil Stephen's hope by looking at him during the first quarter of an hour: her eyes were too full of the old banks that she knew so well. She felt lonely, cut off from Philip—the only person who had ever seemed to love her devotedly, as she had always longed to be loved. But presently the rhythmic movement of the oars attracted her, and she thought she should like to learn how to row. This roused her from her reverie, and she asked if she might take an oar. It appeared that she required much teaching, and she became ambitious. The exercise brought the warm blood into her cheeks, and made her inclined to take her lesson merrily.

'I shall not be satisfied until I can manage both oars, and row you and Lucy,' she said, looking very bright as she stepped out of the boat. Maggie, we know, was apt to forget the thing she was doing, and she had chosen an inopportune moment for her remark: her foot slipped, but happily Mr. Stephen Guest held her hand, and kept her up with a firm grasp.

'You have not hurt yourself at all, I hope?' he said, bending to look in her face with anxiety. It was very charming to be taken care of in that kind graceful manner by some one taller and stronger than one's self. Maggie had never felt just in the same way before.

When they reached home again, they found uncle and aunt Pullet seated with Mrs. Tulliver in the drawing-room, and Stephen hurried away, asking leave to come again in the evening.

'And pray bring with you the volume of Purcell that you took away,' said Lucy. 'I want Maggie to hear your best songs.'

Aunt Pullet, under the certainty that Maggie would be invited to go out with Lucy, probably to Park House, was much shocked at the shabbiness of her clothes, which, when witnessed by the higher society of St. Ogg's, would be a discredit to the family that demanded a strong and prompt remedy; and the consultation as to what would be most suitable to this end from among the superfluities of Mrs. Pullet's wardrobe, was one that Lucy as well as Mrs. Tulliver entered into with some zeal. Maggie must really have an evening dress as soon as possible, and she was about the same height as aunt Pullet.

'But she's so much broader across the shoulders than I am—it's very ill-convenient,' said Mrs. Pullet, 'else she might wear that beautiful black brocade o' mine without any alteration; and her arms are beyond everything,' added Mrs. Pullet, sorrowfully, as she lifted Maggie's large round arm. 'She'd never get my sleeves on.'

'O never mind that, aunt: pray send us the dress,' said Lucy. 'I don't mean Maggie to have long sleeves, and I have abundance of black lace for trimming. Her arms will look beautiful.'

'Maggie's arms *are* a pretty shape,' said Mrs. Tulliver. 'They're like mine used to be—only mine was never brown: I wish she had *our* family skin.'

'Nonsense, aunty!' said Lucy, patting her aunt Tulliver's shoulder, 'you don't understand those things. A painter would think Maggie's complexion beautiful.'

'May be, my dear,' said Mrs. Tulliver submissively. 'You know better than I do. Only when I was young a brown skin wasn't thought well on among respectable folks.'

'No,' said uncle Pullet, who took intense interest in the ladies' conversation as he sucked his lozenges. 'Though there was a song about the "Nut-brown Maid," too; I think she was crazy—crazy Kate—but I can't justly remember.'

'O dear, dear!' said Maggie, laughing but impatient; 'I think that will be the end of *my* brown skin, if it is always to be talked about so much.'

III

CONFIDENTIAL MOMENTS

WHEN Maggie went up to her bedroom that night, it appeared that she was not at all inclined to undress. She set down her candle on the first table that presented itself, and began to walk up and down her room, which was a large one, with a firm, regular, and rather rapid step, which showed that the exercise was the instinctive vent of strong excitement. Her eyes and cheeks had an almost feverish brilliancy; her head was thrown backward, and her hands were clasped with the palms outward, and with that tension of the arms which is apt to accompany mental absorption.

Had anything remarkable happened?

Nothing that you are not likely to consider in the highest degree unimportant. She had been hearing some fine music sung by a fine bass voice—but then it was sung in a provincial, amateur fashion, such as would have left a critical ear much to desire. And she was conscious of having been looked at a great deal, in rather a furtive manner, from beneath a pair of well-marked horizontal eye-brows, with a glance that seemed somehow to have caught the vibratory influence of the voice. Such things could have had no perceptible effect on a thoroughly well-educated young lady, with a perfectly balanced mind, who had had all the advantages of fortune, training, and refined society. But if Maggie had been that young lady, you would probably have known nothing about her: her life would have had so few vicissitudes that it could hardly have been written; for the happiest women, like the happiest nations, have no history.

In poor Maggie's highly-strung, hungry nature—just come away from a third-rate schoolroom, with all its jarring sounds and petty round of tasks—these apparently trivial causes had the effect of rousing and exalting her imagination in a way that was mysterious to herself. It was not that she thought distinctly of Mr. Stephen Guest, or dwelt on the indications that he looked at her with admiration; it was rather that she felt the half-remote presence of a world of love and beauty and delight, made up of vague, mingled images from all the poetry and romance she had ever read, or had ever woven in her dreamy reveries. Her mind glanced back once or twice to the time when she had courted privation, when she had thought all longing, all impatience was subdued; but that condition seemed irrecoverably gone, and she recoiled from the remembrance of it. No prayer, no striving now, would bring back that negative peace: the battle of her life, it seemed, was not to be decided in that short and easy way—by perfect renunciation at the very threshold of her youth. The music was vibrating in her still—Purcell's music, with its wild passion and fancy—and she could not stay in the recollection of that bare, lonely past. She was in her brighter aërial world again, when a little tap came at the door: of course it was her cousin, who entered in ample white dressing-gown.

'Why, Maggie, you naughty child, haven't you begun to undress?' said Lucy, in astonishment. 'I promised not to come and talk to you, because I thought you must be tired. But here you are, looking as if you were ready to dress for a ball. Come, come, get on your dressing-gown, and unplait your hair.'

'Well, *you* are not very forward,' retorted Maggie, hastily reaching her own pink cotton gown, and looking at Lucy's light-brown hair, brushed back in curly disorder.

'O, I have not much to do. I shall sit down and talk to you till I see you are really on the way to bed.'

While Maggie stood and unplaited her long black hair over her pink drapery, Lucy sat down near the toilette-table, watching her with affectionate eyes, and head a little aside, like a pretty spaniel. If it appears to you at all incredible that young ladies should be led on to talk confidentially in a situation of this kind, I will beg you to remember that human life furnishes many exceptional cases.

'You really *have* enjoyed the music to-night, haven't you, Maggie?'

'O yes, that is what prevents me from feeling sleepy. I think I should have no other mortal wants, if I could always have plenty of music. It seems to infuse strength into my limbs, and ideas into my brain. Life seems to go on without effort, when I am filled with music. At other times one is conscious of carrying a weight.'

'And Stephen has a splendid voice, hasn't he?'

'Well, perhaps we are neither of us judges of that,' said Maggie, laughing, as she seated herself and tossed her long hair back. 'You are not impartial, and *I* think any barrel-organ splendid.'

'But tell me what you think of him, now. Tell me exactly —good and bad too.'

'O, I think you should humiliate him a little. A lover should not be so much at ease, and so self-confident. He ought to tremble more.'

'Nonsense, Maggie! As if anyone could tremble at me! You think he is conceited—I see that. But you don't dislike him, do you?'

'Dislike him! No. Am I in the habit of seeing such charming people, that I should be very difficult to please? Besides, how could I dislike anyone that promised to make you happy, you dear thing!' Maggie pinched Lucy's dimpled chin.

'We shall have more music to-morrow evening,' said Lucy, looking happy already, 'for Stephen will bring Philip Wakem with him.'

'O Lucy, I can't see him,' said Maggie, turning pale. 'At least, I could not see him without Tom's leave.'

'Is Tom such a tyrant as that?' said Lucy, surprised. 'I'll take the responsibility, then—tell him it was my fault.'

'But, dear,' said Maggie falteringly, 'I promised Tom very solemnly—before my father's death—I promised him I would not speak to Philip without his knowledge and consent. And I have a great dread of opening the subject with Tom—of getting into a quarrel with him again.'

'But I never heard of anything so strange and unreasonable. What harm can poor Philip have done? May I speak to Tom about it?'

'O no, pray don't, dear,' said Maggie. 'I'll go to him myself to-morrow, and tell him that you wish Philip to come. I've thought before of asking him to absolve me from my promise, but I've not had the courage to determine on it.'

They were both silent for some moments, and then Lucy said:

'Maggie, you have secrets from me, and I have none from you.'

Maggie looked meditatively away from Lucy. Then she turned to her and said, 'I *should* like to tell you about Philip. But, Lucy, you must not betray that you know it to anyone—least of all to Philip himself, or to Mr. Stephen Guest.'

The narrative lasted long, for Maggie had never before known the relief of such an outpouring: she had never be-

fore told Lucy anything of her inmost life; and the sweet
face bent towards her with sympathetic interest, and the
little hand pressing hers, encouraged her to speak on. On
two points only she was not expansive. She did not betray
fully what still rankled in her mind as Tom's great offence—
the insults he had heaped on Philip. Angry as the remembrance still made her, she could not bear that anyone
else should know it all—both for Tom's sake and Philip's.
And she could not bear to tell Lucy of the last scene between her father and Wakem, though it was this scene
which she had ever since felt to be a new barrier between
herself and Philip. She merely said, she saw now that Tom
was, on the whole, right in regarding any prospect of love
and marriage between her and Philip as put out of the
question by the relation of the two families. Of course
Philip's father would never consent.

'There, Lucy, you have had my story,' said Maggie,
smiling, with the tears in her eyes. 'You see I am like Sir
Andrew Aguecheek—*I* was adored once.'

'Ah, now I see how it is you know Shakespeare and
everything, and have learned so much since you left school;
which always seemed to me witchcraft before—part of
your general uncanniness,' said Lucy.

She mused a little with her eyes downward, and then
added, looking at Maggie, 'It is very beautiful that you
should love Philip: I never thought such a happiness would
befall him. And in my opinion, you ought not to give him
up. There are obstacles now; but they may be done away
with in time.'

Maggie shook her head.

'Yes, yes,' persisted Lucy; 'I can't help being hopeful
about it. There is something romantic in it—out of the
common way—just what everything that happens to you
ought to be. And Philip will adore you like a husband in a
fairy tale. O, I shall puzzle my small brain to contrive
some plot that will bring everybody into the right mind, so
that you may marry Philip, when I marry—somebody else.
Wouldn't that be a pretty ending to all my poor, poor
Maggie's troubles?'

Maggie tried to smile, but shivered, as if she felt a sudden chill.

'Ah, dear, you are cold,' said Lucy. 'You must go to bed; and so must I. I dare not think what time it is.'

They kissed each other, and Lucy went away—possessed of a confidence which had a strong influence over her subsequent impressions. Maggie had been thoroughly sincere: her nature had never found it easy to be otherwise. But confidences are sometimes blinding even when they are sincere.

IV

BROTHER AND SISTER

Maggie was obliged to go to Tom's lodgings in the middle of the day, when he would be coming in to dinner, else she would not have found him at home. He was not lodging with entire strangers. Our friend Bob Jakin had, with Mumps's tacit consent, taken not only a wife about eight months ago, but also one of those queer old houses pierced with surprising passages, by the water-side, where, as he observed, his wife and mother could keep themselves out of mischief by letting out two 'pleasure-boats,' in which he had invested some of his savings, and by taking in a lodger for the parlour and spare bedroom. Under these circumstances, what could be better for the interests of all parties, sanitary considerations apart, than that the lodger should be Mr. Tom?

It was Bob's wife who opened the door to Maggie. She was a tiny woman, with the general physiognomy of a Dutch doll, looking, in comparison with Bob's mother, who filled up the passage in the rear, very much like one of those human figures which the artist finds conveniently standing near a colossal statue to show the proportions. The tiny woman curtsied and looked up at Maggie with some awe as soon as she had opened the door; but the words, 'Is my brother at home?' which Maggie uttered smilingly, made her turn round with sudden excitement, and say:

Eh, mother, mother—tell Bob!—it's Miss Maggie! Come in, Miss, for goodness do,' she went on, opening a side door, and endeavouring to flatten her person against the wall to make the utmost space for the visitor.

Sad recollections crowded on Maggie as she entered the small parlour, which was now all that poor Tom had to call by the name of 'home'—that name which had once, so many years ago, meant for both of them the same sum of dear familiar objects. But everything was not strange to her in this new room: the first thing her eyes dwelt on was the large old Bible, and the sight was not likely to disperse the old memories. She stood without speaking.

'If you please to take the privilege o' sitting down, Miss,' said Mrs. Jakin, rubbing her apron over a perfectly clean chair, and then lifting up the corner of that garment and holding it to her face with an air of embarrassment, as she looked wonderingly at Maggie.

'Bob is at home, then?' said Maggie, recovering herself, and smiling at the bashful Dutch doll.

'Yes, Miss; but I think he must be washing and dressing himself—I'll go and see,' said Mrs. Jakin, disappearing.

But she presently came back walking with new courage a little way behind her husband, who showed the brilliancy of his blue eyes and regular white teeth in the doorway, bowing respectfully.

'How do you do, Bob?' said Maggie, coming forward and putting out her hand to him; 'I always meant to pay your wife a visit, and I shall come another day on purpose for that, if she will let me. But I was obliged to come to-day, to speak to my brother.'

'He'll be in before long, Miss. He's doin' finely, Mr. Tom is: he'll be one o' the first men hereabouts—you'll see that.'

'Well, Bob, I'm sure he'll be indebted to you, whatever he becomes: he said so himself only the other night, when he was talking of you.'

'Eh, Miss, that's his way o' takin' it. But I think the more on't when he says a thing, because his tongue doesn't overshoot him as mine does. Lors! I'm no better nor a titled bottle, I arn't—I can't stop mysen when once I begin. But you look rarely, Miss—it does me good to see you. What do you say now, Prissy?'—here Bob turned to his wife. 'Isn't it all come true as I said? Though there isn't many sorts o' goods as I can't over-praise when I set my tongue to't.'

Mrs. Bob's small nose seemed to be following the example of her eyes in turning up reverentially towards Maggie, but she was able now to smile and curtsy, and say, 'I'd looked forrard like aenything to seein' you, Miss, for my husband's tongue's been runnin' on you, like as if he was light-headed, iver since first he come a-courtin' on me.'

'Well, well,' said Bob, looking rather silly. 'Go an' see after the taters, else Mr. Tom 'ull have to wait for 'em.'

'I hope Mumps is friendly with Mrs. Jakin, Bob,' said Maggie, smiling. 'I remember you used to say, he wouldn't like your marrying.'

'Eh, Miss,' said Bob, grinning, 'he made up his mind to't when he see'd what a little un she was. He pretends not to see her mostly, or else to think as she isn't full-growed. But about Mr. Tom, Miss,' said Bob, speaking lower and looking serious, 'he's as close as a iron biler, he is; but I'm a 'cutish chap, an' when I've left off carrying my pack, an' am at a loose end, I've got more brains nor I know what to do wi', an' I'm forced to busy mysel' wi' other folks's insides. An' it worrets me as Mr. Tom 'ull sit by himself so glumpish, a-knittin' his brow, an' a-lookin' at the fire of a night. He should be a bit livelier now—a fine young fellow like him. My wife says, when she goes in sometimes, an' he takes no notice of her, he sits lookin' into the fire, and frownin' as if he was watchin' folks at work in it.'

'He thinks so much about business,' said Maggie.

'Ay,' said Bob, speaking lower; 'but do you think it's nothin' else, Miss? He's close, Mr. Tom is; but I'm a 'cute chap, I am, an' I thought tow'rt last Christmas as I'd found out a soft place in him. It was about a little black spaniel—a rare bit o' breed—as he made a fuss to get. But since then summat's come over him, as he's set his teeth again' things more nor iver, for all he's had such good-luck. An' I wanted to tell *you*, Miss, 'cause I thought you might work it out of him a bit, now you're come. He's a deal too lonely, and doesn't go into company enough.'

'I'm afraid I have very little power over him, Bob,' said Maggie, a good deal moved by Bob's suggestion. It was a totally new idea to her mind, that Tom could have his love troubles. Poor fellow!—and in love with Lucy too! But it was perhaps a mere fancy of Bob's too officious brain. The present of the dog meant nothing more than cousinship and gratitude. But Bob had already said, 'Here's Mr. Tom,' and the outer door was opening.

'There's no time to spare, Tom,' said Maggie, as soon as Bob had left the room. 'I must tell you at once what I came about, else I shall be hindering you from taking your dinner.'

Tom stood with his back against the chimney-piece, and Maggie was seated opposite the light. He noticed that she was tremulous, and he had a presentiment of the subject she was going to speak about. The presentiment made his voice colder and harder as he said, 'What is it?'

This tone roused a spirit of resistance in Maggie, and she put her request in quite a different form from the one she had predetermined on. She rose from her seat, and, looking straight at Tom, said:

'I want you to absolve me from my promise about Philip Wakem. Or rather, I promised you not to see him without telling you. I am come to tell you that I wish to see him.'

'Very well,' said Tom, still more coldly.

But Maggie had hardly finished speaking in that chill, defiant manner, before she repented, and felt the dread of alienation from her brother.

'Not for myself, dear Tom. Don't be angry. I shouldn't have asked it, only that Philip, you know, is a friend of Lucy's, and she wishes him to come—has invited him to come this evening; and I told her I couldn't see him without telling you. I shall only see him in the presence of other people. There will never be anything secret between us again.'

Tom looked away from Maggie, knitting his brow more

strongly for a little while. Then he turned to her and said, slowly and emphatically:

'You know what is my feeling on that subject, Maggie. There is no need for my repeating anything I said a year ago. While my father was living, I felt bound to use the utmost power over you, to prevent you from disgracing him as well as yourself, and all of us. But now I must leave you to your own choice. You wish to be independent—you told me so after my father's death. My opinion is not changed. If you think of Philip Wakem as a lover again, you must give up me.'

'I don't wish it, dear Tom—at least as things are: I see that it would lead to misery. But I shall soon go away to another situation, and I should like to be friends with him again while I am here. Lucy wishes it.'

The severity of Tom's face relaxed a little.

'I shouldn't mind your seeing him occasionally at my uncle's—I don't want you to make a fuss on the subject. But I have no confidence in you, Maggie. You would be led away to do anything.'

That was a cruel word. Maggie's lip began to tremble.

'Why will you say that, Tom? It is very hard of you. Have I not done and borne everything as well as I could? And I have kept my word to you—when—when. . . . My life has not been a happy one, any more than yours.'

She was obliged to be childish—the tears would come. When Maggie was not angry, she was as dependent on kind or cold words as the daisy on the sunshine or the cloud: the need of being loved would always subdue her, as, in old days, it subdued her in the worm-eaten attic. The brother's goodness came uppermost at this appeal, but it could only show itself in Tom's fashion. He put his hand gently on her arm, and said, in the tone of a kind pedagogue:

'Now listen to me, Maggie. I'll tell you what I mean. You're always in extremes—you have no judgment and self-command; and yet you think you know best, and will not submit to be guided. You know I didn't wish you to take a situation. My aunt Pullet was willing to give you a good home, and you might have lived respectably amongst your relations, until I could have provided a home for you with my mother. And that is what I should like to do. I wished my sister to be a lady, and I would always have taken care of you, as my father desired, until you were well married. But your ideas and mine never accord, and you will not give way. Yet you might have sense enough to see that a brother, who goes out into the world and mixes with men, necessarily knows better what is right and respectable for his sister than she can know herself. You think I am not kind; but my kindness can only be directed by what I believe to be good for you.'

'Yes—I know—dear Tom,' said Maggie, still half-sobbing, but trying to control her tears. 'I know you would do a great deal for me: I know how you work, and don't spare yourself. I am grateful to you. But, indeed, you can't quite judge for me—our natures are very different. You don't know how differently things affect me from what they do you.'

'Yes, I *do* know: I know it too well. I know how differently you must feel about all that affects our family, and your own dignity as a young woman, before you could think of receiving secret addresses from Philip Wakem. If it was not disgusting to me in every other way, I should object to my sister's name being associated for a moment with that of a young man whose father must hate the very thought of us all, and would spurn you. With anyone but you, I should think it quite certain that what you witnessed just before my father's death would secure you from ever thinking again of Philip Wakem as a lover. But I don't feel certain of it with you—I never feel certain about anything with *you*. At one time you take pleasure in a sort of perverse self-denial, and at another you have not resolution to resist a thing that you know to be wrong.'

There was a terrible cutting truth in Tom's words—that hard rind of truth which is discerned by unimaginative, unsympathetic minds. Maggie always writhed under this judgment of Tom's: she rebelled and was humiliated in the same moment: it seemed as if he held a glass before her to show her her own folly and weakness—as if he were a prophetic voice predicting her future fallings—and yet, all the while, she judged him in return: she said inwardly that he was narrow and unjust, that he was below feeling those mental needs which were often the source of the wrong-doing or absurdity that made her life a planless riddle to him.

She did not answer directly: her heart was too full, and she sat down, leaning her arm on the table. It was no use trying to make Tom feel that she was near to him. He always repelled her. Her feeling under his words was complicated by the allusion to the last scene between her father and Wakem; and at length that painful, solemn memory surmounted the immediate grievance. No! She did not think of such things with frivolous indifference, and Tom must not accuse her of that. She looked up at him with a grave, earnest gaze, and said:

'I can't make you think better of me, Tom, by anything I can say. But I am not so shut out from all your feelings as you believe me to be. I see as well as you do, that from our position with regard to Philip's father—not on other grounds—it would be unreasonable—it would be wrong for us to entertain the idea of marriage; and I have given up thinking of him as a lover. . . . I am telling you the truth, and you have no right to disbelieve me: I have kept my word to you, and you have never detected me in a falsehood. I should not only not encourage, I should carefully avoid, any intercourse with Philip on any other footing than that of quiet friendship. You may think that I am unable to keep my resolutions; but at least you ought not to treat me with hard contempt on the ground of faults that I have not committed yet.'

'Well, Maggie,' said Tom, softening under this appeal, 'I don't want to overstrain matters. I think, all things considered, it will be best for you to see Philip Wakem, if Lucy wishes him to come to the house. I believe what you say—at least you believe it yourself, I know: I can only warn you. I wish to be as good a brother to you as you will let me.'

There was a little tremor in Tom's voice as he uttered the

last words, and Maggie's ready affection came back with as sudden a glow as when they were children, and bit their cake together as a sacrament of conciliation. She rose and laid her hand on Tom's shoulder.

'Dear Tom, I know you mean to be good. I know you have had a great deal to bear, and have done a great deal. I should like to be a comfort to you—not to vex you. You don't think I'm altogether naughty, now, do you?'

Tom smiled at the eager face: his smiles were very pleasant to see when they did come, for the grey eyes could be tender underneath the frown.

'No, Maggie.'

'I may turn out better than you expect.'

'I hope you will.'

'And may I come some day and make tea for you, and see this extremely small wife of Bob's again?'

'Yes; but trot away now, for I've no more time to spare.' said Tom, looking at his watch.

'Not to give me a kiss?'

Tom bent to kiss her cheek, and then said:

'There! Be a good girl. I've got a great deal to think of to-day. I'm going to have a long consultation with my uncle Deane this afternoon.'

'You'll come to aunt Glegg's to-morrow? We're going all to dine early, that we may go there to tea. You *must* come: Lucy told me to say so.'

'O pooh! I've plenty else to do,' said Tom, pulling his bell violently, and bringing down the small bell-rope.

'I'm frightened—I shall run away,' said Maggie, making a laughing retreat; while Tom, with masculine philosophy, flung the bell-rope to the farther end of the room—not very far either: a touch of human experience which I flatter myself will come home to the bosoms of not a few substantial or distinguished men who were once at an early stage of their rise in the world, and were cherishing very large hopes in very small lodgings.

V

SHOWING THAT TOM HAD OPENED THE OYSTER

'And now we've settled this Newcastle business, Tom,' said Mr. Deane, that same afternoon, as they were seated in the private room at the Bank together, 'there's another matter I want to talk to you about. Since you're likely to have rather a smoky, unpleasant time of it at Newcastle for the next few weeks, you'll want a good prospect of some sort to keep up your spirits.'

Tom waited less nervously than he had done on a former occasion in this apartment, while his uncle took out his snuff-box and gratified each nostril with deliberate impartiality.

'You see, Tom,' said Mr. Deane, at last, throwing himself backward, 'the world goes on at a smarter pace now than it did when I was a young fellow. Why, sir, forty years ago, when I was much such a strapping youngster as you, a man expected to pull between the shafts the best part of his life, before he got the whip in his hand. The looms went slowish, and fashions didn't alter quite so fast: I'd a best suit that lasted me six years. Everything was on a lower scale, sir— in point of expenditure, I mean. It's this steam, you see, that has made the difference: it drives on every wheel double pace, and the wheel of fortune along with 'em, as our Mr. Stephen Guest said at the anniversary dinner (he hits these things off wonderfully, considering he's seen nothing of business). I don't find fault with the change, as some people do. Trade, sir, opens a man's eyes; and if the population is to get thicker upon the ground, as it's doing, the world must use its wits at inventions of one sort or other. I know I've done my share as an ordinary man of business. Somebody has said it's a fine thing to make two ears of corn grow where only one grew before; but, sir, it's a fine thing, too, to further the exchange of commodities, and bring the grains of corn to the mouths that are hungry. And that's our line of business; and I consider it as honourable a position as a man can hold, to be connected with it.'

Tom knew that the affair his uncle had to speak of was not urgent ; Mr. Deane was too shrewd and practical a man to allow either his reminiscences or his snuff to impede the progress of trade. Indeed, for the last month or two, there had been hints thrown out to Tom which enabled him to guess that he was going to hear some proposition for his own benefit. With the beginning of the last speech he had stretched out his legs, thrust his hands in his pockets, and prepared himself for some introductory diffuseness, tending to show that Mr. Deane had succeeded by his own merit, and that what he had to say to young men in general was, that if they didn't succeed too, it was because of their own demerit. He was rather surprised, then, when his uncle put a direct question to him.

'Let me see—it's going on for seven years now since you applied to me for a situation—eh, Tom ?'

'Yes, sir : I'm three-and-twenty now,' said Tom.

'Ah—it's as well not to say that, though : for you'd pass for a good deal older, and age tells well in business. I remember your coming very well : I remember I saw there was some pluck in you, and that was what made me give you encouragement. And I'm happy to say, I was right— I'm not often deceived. I was naturally a little shy at pushing my nephew, but I'm happy to say you've done me credit, sir ; and if I'd had a son o' my own, I shouldn't have been sorry to see him like you.'

Mr. Deane tapped his box and opened it again, repeating in a tone of some feeling—'No, I shouldn't have been sorry to see him like you.'

'I'm very glad I've given you satisfaction, sir ; I've done my best,' said Tom, in his proud, independent way.

'Yes, Tom, you've given me satisfaction. I don't speak of your conduct as a son ; though that weighs with me in my opinion of you. But what I have to do with, as a partner in our firm, is the qualities you've shown as a man o' business. Ours is a fine business—a splendid concern, sir— and there's no reason why it shouldn't go on growing :

there's a growing capital, and growing outlets for it; but there's another thing that's wanted for the prosperity of every concern, large or small, and that's men to conduct it —men of the right habits; none o' your flashy fellows, but such as are to be depended on. Now this is what Mr. Guest and I see clear enough. Three years ago, we took Gell into the concern: we gave him a share in the oil-mill. And why? Why, because Gell was a fellow whose services were worth a premium. So it will always be, sir. So it was with me. And though Gell is pretty near ten years older than you, there are other points in your favour.'

Tom was getting a little nervous as Mr. Deane went on speaking; he was conscious of something he had in his mind to say, which might not be agreeable to his uncle, simply because it was a new suggestion rather than an acceptance of the proposition he foresaw.

'It stands to reason,' Mr. Deane went on, when he had finished his new pinch, 'that your being my nephew weighs in your favour; but I don't deny that if you'd been no relation of mine at all, your conduct in that affair of Pelley's bank would have led Mr. Guest and myself to make some acknowledgement of the service you've been to us; and, backed by your general conduct and business ability, it has made us determine on giving you a share in the business—a share which we shall be glad to increase as the years go on. We think that'll be better, on all grounds, than raising your salary. It'll give you more importance, and prepare you better for taking some of the anxiety off my shoulders by-and-by. I'm equal to a good deal o' work at present, thank God; but I'm getting older—there's no denying that. I told Mr. Guest I would open the subject to you; and when you come back from this northern business, we can go into particulars. This is a great stride for a young fellow of three-and-twenty, but I'm bound to say you've deserved it.'

'I'm very grateful to Mr. Guest and you, sir; of course I feel the most indebted to *you*, who first took me into the business, and have taken a good deal of pains with me since.'

Tom spoke with a slight tremor, and paused after he had said this.

'Yes, yes,' said Mr. Deane. 'I don't spare pains when I see they'll be of any use. I gave myself some trouble with Gell—else he wouldn't have been what he is.'

'But there's one thing I should like to mention to you, uncle. I've never spoken to you of it before. If you remember, at the time my father's property was sold, there was some thought of your firm buying the Mill: I know you thought it would be a very good investment, especially if steam were applied.'

'To be sure, to be sure. But Wakem outbid us—he'd made up his mind to that. He's rather fond of carrying everything over other people's heads.'

'Perhaps it's of no use my mentioning it at present,' Tom went on, 'but I wish you to know what I have in my mind about the Mill. I've a strong feeling about it. It was my father's dying wish that I should try and get it back again whenever I could: it was in his family for five generations. I promised my father; and besides that, I'm attached to the place. I shall never like any other so well. And if it should ever suit your views to buy it for the firm, I should have a better chance of fulfilling my father's wish. I shouldn't have liked to mention the thing to you, only you've been kind enough to say my services have been of some value. And I'd give up a much greater chance in life for the sake of having the Mill again—I mean, having it in my own hands, and gradually working off the price.'

Mr. Deane had listened attentively, and now looked thoughtful.

'I see, I see,' he said after a while; 'the thing would be possible, if there were any chance of Wakem's parting with the property. But that I *don't* see. He's put that young Jetsome in the place; and he had his reasons when he bought it, I'll be bound.'

'He's a loose fish, that young Jetsome,' said Tom. 'He's taking to drinking, and they say he's letting the business go down. Luke told me about it—our old miller. He says, he shan't stay unless there's an alteration. I was thinking, if things went on in that way, Wakem might be more willing to part with the Mill. Luke says he's getting very sour about the way things are going on.'

'Well, I'll turn it over, Tom. I must inquire into the matter, and go into it with Mr. Guest. But, you see, it's rather striking out a new branch, and putting you to that, instead of keeping you where you are, which was what we'd wanted.'

'I should be able to manage more than the Mill when things were once set properly going, sir. I want to have plenty of work. There's nothing else I care about much.'

There was something rather sad in that speech from a young man of three-and-twenty, even in uncle Deane's business-loving ears.

'Pooh, pooh! you'll be having a wife to care about one of these days, if you get on at this pace in the world. But as to this Mill, we mustn't reckon on our chickens too early. However, I promise you to bear it in mind, and when you come back we'll talk of it again. I am going to dinner now. Come and breakfast with us to-morrow morning, and say good-bye to your mother and sister before you start.'

VI

ILLUSTRATING THE LAWS OF ATTRACTION

It is evident to you now, that Maggie had arrived at a moment in her life which must be considered by all prudent persons as a great opportunity for a young woman. Launched into the higher society of St. Ogg's, with a striking person, which had the advantage of being quite unfamiliar to the majority of beholders, and with such moderate assistance of costume as you have seen foreshadowed in Lucy's anxious colloquy with aunt Pullet, Maggie was certainly at a new starting-point in life. At Lucy's first evening-party, young Torry fatigued his facial muscles more than usual in order that 'the dark-eyed girl there, in the corner,' might see him in all the additional style conferred by his eye-glass; and several young ladies went home intending to have short sleeves with black lace, and to plait their hair in a broad coronet at the back of their head—'That cousin of Miss Deane's looked so very well.' In fact, poor Maggie, with all her inward consciousness of a painful past and her presentiment of a troublous future, was on the way to become an object of some envy—a topic of discussion in the newly-established billiard-room, and between fair friends who had no secrets from each other on the subject of trimmings. The Miss Guests, who associated chiefly on terms of condescension with the families of St. Ogg's, and were the glass of fashion there, took some exception to Maggie's manners. She had a way of not assenting at once to the observations current in good society, and of saying that she didn't know whether those observations were true or not, which gave her an air of *gaucherie*, and impeded the even flow of conversation; but it is a fact capable of an amiable interpretation, that ladies are not the worst disposed towards a new acquaintance of their own sex because she has points of inferiority. And Maggie was so entirely without those pretty airs of coquetry which had the traditional reputation of driving gentlemen to despair, that she won some feminine pity for being so ineffective in spite of her beauty. She had not had many advantages, poor thing! and it must be admitted there was no pretension about her: her abruptness and unevenness of manner were plainly the result of her secluded and lowly circumstances. It was only a wonder that there was no tinge of vulgarity about her, considering what the rest of poor Lucy's relations were: an allusion which always made the Miss Guests shudder a little. It was not agreeable to think of any connection by marriage with such people as the Gleggs and the Pullets; but it was of no use to contradict Stephen, when once he had set his mind on anything, and certainly there was no possible objection to Lucy in herself —no one could help liking her. She would naturally desire that the Miss Guests should behave kindly to this cousin of whom she was so fond, and Stephen would make a great fuss if they were deficient in civility. Under these circumstances the invitations to Park House were not wanting;

and elsewhere, also, Miss Deane was too popular and too distinguished a member of society in St. Ogg's for any attention towards her to be neglected.

Thus Maggie was introduced for the first time to the young lady's life, and knew what it was to get up in the morning without any imperative reason for doing one thing more than another. This new sense of leisure and unchecked enjoyment amidst the soft-breathing airs and garden-scents of advancing spring—amidst the new abundance of music, and lingering strolls in the sunshine, and the delicious dreaminess of gliding on the river—could hardly be without some intoxicating effect on her, after her years of privation; and even in the first week Maggie began to be less haunted by her sad memories and anticipations. Life was certainly very pleasant just now: it was becoming very pleasant to dress in the evening, and to feel that she was one of the beautiful things of this spring-time. And there were admiring eyes always awaiting her now; she was no longer an unheeded person, liable to be chid, from whom attention was continually claimed, and on whom no one felt bound to confer any. It was pleasant, too, when Stephen and Lucy were gone out riding, to sit down at the piano alone, and find that the old fitness between her fingers and the keys remained, and revived, like a sympathetic kinship not to be worn out by separation—to get the tunes she had heard the evening before, and repeat them again and again until she had found out a way of producing them so as to make them a more pregnant, passionate language to her. The mere concord of octaves was a delight to Maggie, and she would often take up a book of studies rather than any melody, that she might taste more keenly by abstraction the more primitive sensation of intervals. Not that her enjoyment of music was of the kind that indicates a great specific talent; it was rather that her sensibility to the supreme excitement of music was only one form of that passionate sensibility which belonged to her whole nature, and made her faults and virtues all merge in each other—made her affections sometimes an impatient demand, but also prevented her vanity from taking the form of mere feminine coquetry and device, and gave it the poetry of ambition. But you have known Maggie a long while, and need to be told, not her characteristics, but her history, which is a thing hardly to be predicted even from the completest knowledge of characteristics. For the tragedy of our lives is not created entirely from within. 'Character,' says Novalis, in one of his questionable aphorisms—'character is destiny.' But not the whole of our destiny. Hamlet, Prince of Denmark, was speculative and irresolute, and we have a great tragedy in consequence. But if his father had lived to a good old age, and his uncle had died an early death, we can conceive Hamlet's having married Ophelia, and got through life with a reputation of sanity, notwithstanding many soliloquies, and some moody sarcasms towards the fair daughter of Polonius, to say nothing of the frankest incivility to his father-in-law.

Maggie's destiny, then, is at present hidden, and we must wait for it to reveal itself like the course of an unmapped river; we only know that the river is full and rapid, and that for all rivers there is the same final home. Under the charm of her new pleasures, Maggie herself was ceasing to think, with her eager prefiguring imagination, of her future lot; and her anxiety about her first interview with Philip was losing its predominance: perhaps, unconsciously to herself, she was not sorry that the interview had been deferred.

For Philip had not come the evening he was expected, and Mr. Stephen Guest brought word that he was gone to the coast—probably, he thought, on a sketching expedition; but it was not certain when he would return. It was just like Philip—to go off in that way without telling anyone. It was not until the twelfth day that he returned, to find both Lucy's notes awaiting him: he had left before he knew of Maggie's arrival.

Perhaps one had need be nineteen again to be quite convinced of the feelings that were crowded for Maggie into those twelve days—of the length to which they were stretched for her by the novelty of her experience in them, and the varying attitudes of her mind. The early days of an acquaintance almost always have this importance for us, and fill up a larger space in our memory than longer subsequent periods, which have been less filled with discovery and new impressions. There were not many hours in those ten days in which Mr. Stephen Guest was not seated by Lucy's side, or standing near her at the piano, or accompanying her on some out-door excursion: his attentions were clearly becoming more assiduous; and that was what everyone had expected. Lucy was very happy: all the happier because Stephen's society seemed to have become much more interesting and amusing since Maggie had been there. Playful discussions—sometimes serious ones—were going forward, in which both Stephen and Maggie revealed themselves, to the admiration of the gentle unobtrusive Lucy; and it more than once crossed her mind what a charming quartet they should have through life when Maggie married Philip. Is it an inexplicable thing that a girl should enjoy her lover's society the more for the presence of a third person, and be without the slightest spasm of jealousy that the third person had the conversation habitually directed to her? Not when that girl is as tranquil-hearted as Lucy, thoroughly possessed with a belief that she knows the state of her companions' affections, and not prone to the feelings which shake such a belief in the absence of positive evidence against it. Besides, it was Lucy by whom Stephen sat, to whom he gave his arm, to whom he appealed as the person sure to agree with him; and every day there was the same tender politeness towards her, the same consciousness of her wants and care to supply them. Was there really the same?—it seemed to Lucy that there was more; and it was no wonder that the real significance of the change escaped her. It was a subtle act of conscience in Stephen that even he himself was not aware of. His personal attentions to Maggie were comparatively slight, and there had even sprung up an apparent distance between them, that prevented the renewal of that faint resemblance to gallantry into which he had fallen the first day in the boat. If Stephen came in when Lucy was out of the room—if Lucy left them together, they never spoke to each other: Stephen, perhaps, seemed to be examining books on music, and Maggie bent her head assiduously over her work. Each was oppressively conscious of the other's presence, even to the finger-ends. Yet each looked and longed for the same thing to happen the next day. Neither of them had begun to reflect on the matter, or silently to ask, 'To what does all this tend?' Maggie only felt that life was revealing something quite new to her; and she was absorbed in the direct, immediate experience, without any energy left for taking account of it and reasoning about it. Stephen wilfully abstained from self-questioning, and would not admit to himself that he felt an influence which was to have any determining effect on his conduct. And when Lucy came into the room again, they were once more unconstrained: Maggie could contradict Stephen and laugh at him, and he could recommend to her consideration the example of that most charming heroine, Miss Sophia Western, who had a great 'respect for the understandings of men.' Maggie could look at Stephen—which, for some reason or other, she always avoided when they were alone; and he could even ask her to play his accompaniment for him, since Lucy's fingers were so busy with that bazaar-work; and lecture her on hurrying the *tempo*, which was certainly Maggie's weak point.

One day—it was the day of Philip's return—Lucy had formed a sudden engagement to spend the evening with Mrs. Kenn, whose delicate state of health, threatening to become confirmed illness through an attack of bronchitis, obliged her to resign her functions at the coming bazaar into the hands of other ladies, of whom she wished Lucy to be one. The engagement had been formed in Stephen's presence, and he had heard Lucy promise to dine early and call at six o'clock for Miss Torry, who brought Mrs. Kenn's request.

'Here is another of the moral results of this idiotic bazaar,' Stephen burst forth, as soon as Miss Torry had left the room—'taking young ladies from the duties of the domestic hearth into scenes of dissipation among urn-rugs and embroidered reticules! I should like to know what is the proper function of women, if it is not to make reasons for husbands to stay at home, and still stronger reasons for bachelors to go out. If this goes on much longer, the bonds of society will be dissolved.'

'Well, it will not go on much longer,' said Lucy, laughing, 'for the bazaar is to take place on Monday week.'

'Thank Heaven!' said Stephen. 'Kenn himself said the other day, that he didn't like this plan of making vanity do the work of charity; but just as the British public is not reasonable enough to bear direct taxation, so St. Ogg's has not got force of motive enough to build and endow schools without calling in the force of folly.'

'Did he say so?' said little Lucy, her hazel eyes opening wide with anxiety. 'I never heard him say anything of that kind: I thought he approved of what we were doing.'

'I'm sure he approves *you*,' said Stephen, smiling at her affectionately: 'your conduct in going out to-night looks vicious, I own, but I know there is benevolence at the bottom of it.'

'O, you think too well of me,' said Lucy, shaking her head, with a pretty blush, and there the subject ended. But it was tacitly understood that Stephen would not come in the evening, and on the strength of that tacit understanding he made his morning visit the longer, not saying good-bye until after four.

Maggie was seated in the drawing-room alone, shortly after dinner, with Minny on her lap, having left her uncle to his wine and his nap, and her mother to the compromise between knitting and nodding, which, when there was no company, she always carried on in the dining-room till tea-time. Maggie was stooping to caress the tiny silken pet, and comforting him for his mistress's absence, when the sound of a footstep on the gravel made her look up, and she saw Mr. Stephen Guest walking up the garden, as if he had come straight from the river. It was very unusual to see him so soon after dinner! He often complained that their dinner-hour was late at Park House. Nevertheless, there he was, in his black dress: he had evidently been home, and must have come again by the river. Maggie felt her cheeks glowing and her heart beating: it was natural she should be nervous, for she was not accustomed to receive visitors alone. He had seen her look up through the open window, and raised his hat as he walked towards it, to enter that way instead of by the door. He blushed too, and certainly looked as foolish as a young man of some wit and self-possession can be expected to look, as he walked in with a roll of music in his hand, and said, with an air of hesitating improvisation:

'You are surprised to see me again, Miss Tulliver—I ought to apologise for coming upon you by surprise, but I wanted to come into the town, and I got our man to row me; so I thought I would bring these things from the "Maid of Artois" for your cousin: I forgot them this morning. Will you give them to her?'

'Yes,' said Maggie, who had risen confusedly with Minny in her arms, and now, not quite knowing what else to do, sat down again.

Stephen laid down his hat, with the music, which rolled on the floor, and sat down in the chair close by her. He had never done so before, and both he and Maggie were quite aware that it was an entirely new position.

'Well, you pampered minion!' said Stephen, leaning to pull the long curly ears that drooped over Maggie's arm. It was not a suggestive remark, and as the speaker did not follow it up by further development, it naturally left the conversation at a standstill. It seemed to Stephen like some action in a dream, that he was obliged to do, and wonder at himself all the while—to go on stroking Minny's head. Yet it was very pleasant: he only wished he dared look at Maggie, and that she would look at him—let him have one long look into those deep strange eyes of hers, and then he would be satisfied, and quite reasonable after that. He thought it was becoming a sort of monomania with him to want that long look from Maggie; and he was racking his invention continually to find out some means by which he could have it without its appearing singular and entailing subsequent embarrassment. As for Maggie, she had no distinct thought—only the sense of a presence like that of a closely-hovering, broad-winged bird in the darkness, for she was unable to look up, and saw nothing but Minny's black wavy coat.

But this must end some time—perhaps it ended very soon, and only *seemed* long, as a minute's dream does. Stephen at last sat upright sideways in his chair, leaning one hand and arm over the back and looking at Maggie. What should he say?

'We shall have a splendid sunset, I think; shan't you go out and see it?'

'I don't know,' said Maggie. Then, courageously raising her eyes and looking out of the window, 'If I'm not playing cribbage with my uncle.'

A pause: during which Minny is stroked again, but has sufficient insight not to be grateful for it—to growl rather.

'Do you like sitting alone?'

A rather arch look came over Maggie's face, and, just glancing at Stephen, she said, 'Would it be quite civil to say "yes"?'

'It *was* rather a dangerous question for an intruder to ask,' said Stephen, delighted with that glance, and getting determined to stay for another. 'But you will have more than half an hour to yourself after I am gone,' he added, taking out his watch. 'I know Mr. Deane never comes in till half-past seven.'

Another pause, during which Maggie looked steadily out of the window, till by a great effort she moved her head to look down at Minny's back again, and said:

'I wish Lucy had not been obliged to go out. We lose our music.'

'We shall have a new voice to-morrow night,' said Stephen. 'Will you tell your cousin that our friend Philip Wakem is come back? I saw him as I went home.'

Maggie gave a little start—it seemed hardly more than a vibration that passed from head to foot in an instant. But the new images summoned by Philip's name, dispersed half the oppressive spell she had been under. She rose from her chair with a sudden resolution, and, laying Minny on his cushion, went to reach Lucy's large work-basket from its corner. Stephen was vexed and disappointed: he thought, perhaps Maggie didn't like the name of Wakem to be mentioned to her in that abrupt way—for he now recalled what Lucy had told him of the family quarrel. It was of no use to stay any longer. Maggie was seating herself at the table with her work, and looking chill and proud: and he —he looked like a simpleton for having come. A gratuitous, entirely superfluous visit of that sort was sure to make a man disagreeable and ridiculous. Of course it was palpable to Maggie's thinking, that he had dined hastily in his own room for the sake of setting off again and finding her alone.

A boyish state of mind for an accomplished young gentleman of five-and-twenty, not without legal knowledge! But a reference to history, perhaps, may make it not incredible.

At this moment Maggie's ball of knitting-wool rolled along the ground, and she started up to reach it. Stephen rose too, and, picking up the ball, met her with a vexed complaining look that gave his eyes quite a new expression to Maggie, whose own eyes met them as he presented the ball to her.

'Good-bye,' said Stephen, in a tone that had the same beseeching discontent as his eyes. He dared not put out his hand—he thrust both hands into his tail-pockets as he spoke. Maggie thought she had perhaps been rude.

'Won't you stay?' she said timidly, not looking away, for that would have seemed rude again.

'No, thank you,' said Stephen, looking still into the half-unwilling, half-fascinated eyes, as a thirsty man looks towards the track of the distant brook. 'The boat is waiting for me. . . . You'll tell your cousin?'

'Yes.'

'That I brought the music, I mean?'

'Yes.'

'And that Philip is come back.'

'Yes.' (Maggie did not notice Philip's name this time.)

'Won't you come out a little way into the garden?' said Stephen, in a still gentler tone, but the next moment he was vexed that she did not say 'No,' for she moved away now towards the open window, and he was obliged to take his hat and walk by her side. But he thought of something to make him amends.

'Do take my arm,' he said, in a low tone, as if it were a secret.

There is something strangely winning to most women in that offer of the firm arm: the help is not wanted physically at that moment, but the sense of help—the presence of strength that is outside them and yet theirs—meets a continual want of the imagination. Either on that ground or some other, Maggie took the arm. And they walked together round the grass plot and under the drooping green of the laburnums, in the same dreamy state as they had been in a quarter of an hour before; only that Stephen had had the look he longed for, without yet perceiving in himself the symptoms of returning reasonableness, and Maggie had darting thoughts across the dimness:—how came she to be there?—why had she come out? Not a word was spoken. If it had been, each would have been less intensely conscious of the other.

'Take care of this step,' said Stephen, at last.

'O, I will go in now,' said Maggie, feeling that the step had come like a rescue. 'Good evening.'

In an instant she had withdrawn her arm, and was running back to the house. She did not reflect that this sudden action would only add to the embarrassing recollections of the last half-hour. She had no thought left for that. She only threw herself into the low arm-chair, and burst into tears.

'O Philip, Philip, I wish we were together again—so quietly—in the Red Deeps.'

Stephen looked after her a moment, then went on to the boat, and was soon landed at the wharf. He spent the evening in the billiard-room, smoking one cigar after another, and losing 'lives' at pool. But he would not leave off. He was determined not to think—not to admit any more distinct remembrance than was urged upon him by the perpetual presence of Maggie. He was looking at her, and she was on his arm.

But there came the necessity of walking home in the cool starlight, and with it the necessity of cursing his own folly, and bitterly determining that he would never trust himself alone with Maggie again. It was all madness: he was in love, thoroughly attached to Lucy, and engaged—engaged as strongly as an honourable man need be. He wished he had never seen this Maggie Tulliver, to be thrown into a fever by her in this way: she would make a sweet, strange, troublesome, adorable wife to some man or other, but he would never have chosen her himself. Did she feel as he did? He hoped she did—not. He ought not to have gone. He would master himself in future. He would make himself disagreeable to her—quarrel with her perhaps. Quarrel with her? Was it possible to quarrel with a creature who had such eyes—defying and deprecating, contradicting and clinging, imperious and beseeching—full of delicious opposites. To see such a creature subdued by love for one would be a lot worth having—to another man.

There was a muttered exclamation which ended this inward soliloquy, as Stephen threw away the end of his last cigar, and, thrusting his hands into his pockets, stalked along at a quieter pace through the shrubbery. It was not of a benedictory kind.

VII

PHILIP RE-ENTERS

THE next morning was very wet: the sort of morning on which male neighbours who have no imperative occupation at home are likely to pay their fair friends an illimitable visit. The rain, which has been endurable enough for the walk or ride one way, is sure to become so heavy, and at the same time so certain to clear up by-and-by, that nothing but an open quarrel can abbreviate the visit: latent detestation will not do at all. And if people happen to be lovers, what can be so delightful, in England, as a rainy morning? English sunshine is dubious; bonnets are never quite secure; and if you sit down on the grass, it may lead to catarrhs. But the rain is to be depended on. You gallop through it in a mackintosh, and presently find yourself in the seat you like best—a little above or a little below the one on which your goddess sits (it is the same thing to the metaphysical mind, and that is the reason why women are at once worshipped and looked down upon), with a satisfactory confidence that there will be no lady-callers.

'Stephen will come earlier this morning, I know,' said Lucy: 'he always does when it's rainy.'

Maggie made no answer. She was angry with Stephen: she began to think she should dislike him; and if it had not been for the rain, she would have gone to her aunt Glegg this morning, and so have avoided him altogether. As it was, she must find some reason for remaining out of the room with her mother.

But Stephen did not come earlier, and there was another visitor—a nearer neighbour—who preceded him. When Philip entered the room, he was going merely to bow to Maggie, feeling that their acquaintance was a secret which he was bound not to betray; but when she advanced towards him and put out her hand, he guessed at once that Lucy had been taken into her confidence. It was a moment of some agitation to both, though Philip had spent many hours in preparing for it; but like all persons who have passed through life with little expectation of sympathy, he seldom lost his self-control, and shrank with the most sensitive pride from any noticeable betrayal of emotion. A little extra paleness, a little tension of the nostril when he spoke, and the voice pitched in rather a higher key, that to strangers would seem expressive of cold indifference, were all the signs Philip usually gave of an inward drama that was not without its fierceness. But Maggie, who had little more power of concealing the impressions made upon her than if she had been constructed of musical strings, felt her eyes getting larger with tears as they took each other's hands in silence. They were not painful tears: they had rather something of the same origin as the tears women and children shed when they have found some protection to cling to, and look back on the threatened danger. For

Philip, who a little while ago was associated continually in Maggie's mind with the sense that Tom might reproach her with some justice, had now, in this short space, become a sort of outward conscience to her, that she might fly to for rescue and strength. Her tranquil, tender affection for Philip, with its root deep down in her childhood, and its memories of long quiet talk confirming by distinct successive impressions the first instinctive bias—the fact that in him the appeal was more strongly to her pity and womanly devotedness than to her vanity or other egoistic excitability of her nature, seemed now to make a sort of sacred place, a sanctuary where she could find refuge from an alluring influence which the best part of herself must resist, which must bring horrible tumult within, wretchedness without. This new sense of her relation to Philip nullified the anxious scruples she would otherwise have felt, lest she should overstep the limit of intercourse with him that Tom would sanction; and she put out her hand to him, and felt the tears in her eyes without any consciousness of an inward check. The scene was just what Lucy expected, and her kind heart delighted in bringing Philip and Maggie together again; though, even with all *her* regard for Philip, she could not resist the impression that her cousin Tom had some excuse for feeling shocked at the physical incongruity between the two—a prosaic person like cousin Tom, who didn't like poetry and fairy tales. But she began to speak as soon as possible, to set them at ease.

'This was very good and virtuous of you,' she said, in her pretty treble, like the low conversational notes of little birds, 'to come so soon after your arrival. And as it is, I think I will pardon you for running away in an inopportune manner, and giving your friends no notice. Come and sit down here,' she went on, placing the chair that would suit him best, 'and you shall find yourself treated mercifully.'

'You will never govern well, Miss Deane,' said Philip as he seated himself, 'because no one will ever believe in your severity. People will always encourage themselves in misdemeanours by the certainty that you will be indulgent.'

Lucy gave some playful contradiction, but Philip did not

hear what it was, for he had naturally turned towards Maggie, and she was looking at him with that open, affectionate scrutiny, which we give to a friend from whom we have been long separated. What a moment their parting had been! And Philip felt as if he were only in the morrow of it. He felt this so keenly—with such intense, detailed remembrance—with such passionate revival of all that had been said and looked in their last conversation—that with that jealousy and distrust which in diffident natures is almost inevitably linked with a strong feeling, he thought he read in Maggie's glance and manner the evidence of a change. The very fact that he feared and half expected it, would be sure to make this thought rush in, in the absence of positive proof to the contrary.

'I am having a great holiday, am I not?' said Maggie. 'Lucy is like a fairy godmother: she has turned me from a drudge into a princess in no time. I do nothing but indulge myself all day long, and she always finds out what I want before I know it myself.'

'I'm sure she is the happier for having you, then,' said Philip. 'You must be better than a whole menagerie of pets to her. And you look well—you are benefiting by the change.'

Artificial conversation of this sort went on a little while, till Lucy, determined to put an end to it, exclaimed, with a good imitation of annoyance, that she had forgotten something, and was quickly out of the room.

In a moment Maggie and Philip leaned forward, and the hands were clasped again, with a look of sad contentment like that of friends who meet in the memory of recent sorrow.

'I told my brother I wished to see you, Philip—I asked him to release me from my promise, and he consented.'

Maggie, in her impulsiveness, wanted Philip to know at once the position they must hold towards each other; but she checked herself. The things that had happened since he had spoken of his love for her were so painful that she shrank from being the first to allude to them. It seemed almost like an injury towards Philip even to mention her brother—

her brother who had insulted him. But he was thinking too entirely of her to be sensitive on any other point at that moment.

'Then we can at least be friends, Maggie? There is nothing to hinder that now?'

'Will not your father object?' said Maggie, withdrawing her hand.

'I should not give you up on any ground but your own wish, Maggie,' said Philip, colouring. 'There are points on which I should always resist my father, as I used to tell you. *That* is one.'

'Then there is nothing to hinder our being friends, Philip —seeing each other and talking to each other while I am here: I shall soon go away again. I mean to go very soon— to a new situation.'

'Is that inevitable, Maggie?'

'Yes: I must not stay here long. It would unfit me for the life I must begin again at last. I can't live in dependence—I can't live with my brother—though he is very good to me. He would like to provide for me; but that would be intolerable to me.'

Philip was silent a few moments, and then said, in that high, feeble voice which with him indicated the resolute suppression of emotion:

'Is there no other alternative, Maggie? Is that life, away from those who love you, the only one you will allow yourself to look forward to?'

'Yes, Philip,' she said, looking at him pleadingly, as if she entreated him to believe that she was compelled to this course. 'At least, as things are; I don't know what may be in years to come. But I begin to think there can never come much happiness to me from loving: I have always had so much pain mingled with it. I wish I could make myself a world outside it, as men do.'

'Now, you are returning to your old thought in a new form, Maggie—the thought I used to combat,' said Philip, with a slight tinge of bitterness. 'You want to find out a mode of renunciation that will be an escape from pain. I tell you again, there is no such escape possible except by perverting or mutilating one's nature. What would become of me, if I tried to escape from pain? Scorn and cynicism would be my only opium; unless I could fall into some kind of conceited madness, and fancy myself a favourite of Heaven because I am not a favourite with men.'

The bitterness had taken on some impetuosity as Philip went on speaking: the words were evidently an outlet for some immediate feeling of his own, as well as an answer to Maggie. There was a pain pressing on him at that moment. He shrank with proud delicacy from the faintest allusion to the words of love—of plighted love—that had passed between them. It would have seemed to him like reminding Maggie of a promise; it would have had for him something of the baseness of compulsion. He could not dwell on the fact that he himself had not changed; for that too would have had the air of an appeal. His love for Maggie was stamped, even more than the rest of his experience, with the exaggerated sense that he was an exception—that she, that everyone, saw him in the light of an exception.

But Maggie was conscience-stricken.

'Yes, Philip,' she said, with her childish contrition when he used to chide her, 'you are right, I know. I do always think too much of my own feelings, and not enough of others'—not enough of yours. I had need have you always to find fault with me and teach me: so many things have come true that you used to tell me.'

Maggie was resting her elbow on the table, leaning her head on her hand and looking at Philip with half-penitent dependent affection, as she said this; while he was returning her gaze with an expression that, to her consciousness, gradually became less vague—became charged with a specific recollection. Had his mind flown back to something that *she* now remembered?—something about a lover of Lucy's? It was a thought that made her shudder: it gave new definiteness to her present position, and to the tendency of what had happened the evening before. She moved her arm from the table, urged to change her position by that positive physical oppression at the heart that sometimes accompanies a sudden mental pang.

'What is the matter, Maggie? Has something happened?' Philip said, in inexpressible anxiety—his imagination being only too ready to weave everything that was fatal to them both.

'No—nothing,' said Maggie, rousing her latent will. Philip must not have that odious thought in his mind: she would banish it from her own. 'Nothing,' she repeated, 'except in my own mind. You used to say I should feel the effect of my starved life, as you called it, and I do. I am too eager in my enjoyment of music and all luxuries, now they are come to me.'

She took up her work and occupied herself resolutely, while Philip watched her, really in doubt whether she had anything more than this general allusion in her mind. It was quite in Maggie's character to be agitated by vague self-reproach. But soon there came a violent well-known ring at the doorbell resounding through the house.

'O what a startling announcement!' said Maggie, quite mistress of herself, though not without some inward flutter. 'I wonder where Lucy is.'

Lucy had not been deaf to the signal, and after an interval long enough for a few solicitous but not hurried inquiries, she herself ushered Stephen in.

'Well, old fellow,' he said, going straight up to Philip and shaking him heartily by the hand, bowing to Maggie in passing, 'it's glorious to have you back again; only I wish you'd conduct yourself a little less like a sparrow with a residence on the house-top, and not go in and out constantly without letting the servants know. This is about the twentieth time I've had to scamper up those countless stairs to that painting-room of yours, all to no purpose, because your people thought you were at home. Such incidents embitter friendship.'

'I've so few visitors—it seems hardly worth while to leave notice of my exit and entrances,' said Philip, feeling rather oppressed just then by Stephen's bright strong presence and strong voice.

'Are you quite well this morning, Miss Tulliver?' said

Stephen, turning to Maggie with stiff politeness, and putting out his hand with the air of fulfilling a social duty.

Maggie gave the tips of her fingers, and said, 'Quite well, thank you,' in a tone of proud indifference. Philip's eyes were watching them keenly; but Lucy was used to seeing variations in their manner to each other, and only thought with regret that there was some natural antipathy which every now and then surmounted their mutual goodwill. 'Maggie is not the sort of woman Stephen admires, and she is irritated by something in him which she interprets as conceit,' was the silent observation that accounted for everything to guileless Lucy. Stephen and Maggie had no sooner completed this studied greeting than each felt hurt by the other's coldness. And Stephen, while rattling on in questions to Philip about his recent sketching expedition, was thinking all the more about Maggie because he was not drawing her into the conversation as he had invariably done before. 'Maggie and Philip are not looking happy,' thought Lucy: 'this first interview has been saddening to them.'

'I think we people who have not been galloping,' she said to Stephen, 'are all a little damped by the rain. Let us have some music. We ought to take advantage of having Philip and you together. Give us the duet in "Masaniello:" Maggie has not heard that, and I know it will suit her.'

'Come, then,' said Stephen, going towards the piano, and giving a foretaste of the tune in his deep 'brum-brum,' very pleasant to hear.

'You, please, Philip—you play the accompaniment,' said Lucy, 'and then I can go on with my work. You *will* like to play, shan't you?' she added, with a pretty inquiring look, anxious, as usual, lest she should have proposed what was not pleasant to another; but with yearnings towards her unfinished embroidery.

Philip had brightened at the proposition, for there is no feeling, perhaps, except the extremes of fear and grief, that does not find relief in music—that does not make a man sing or play the better; and Philip had an abundance of pent-up feeling at this moment, as complex as any trio or quartet that was ever meant to express love and jealousy, and resignation and fierce suspicion, all at the same time.

'O yes,' he said, seating himself at the piano, 'it is a way of eking out one's imperfect life and being three people at once—to sing and make the piano sing, and hear them both all the while—or else to sing and paint.'

'Ah, there you are an enviable fellow. I can do nothing with my hands,' said Stephen. 'That has generally been observed in men of great administrative capacity, I believe. A tendency to predominance of the reflective powers in me! —haven't you observed that, Miss Tulliver?'

Stephen had fallen by mistake into his habit of playful appeal to Maggie, and she could not repress the answering flush and epigram.

'I *have* observed a tendency to predominance,' she said, smiling; and Philip at that moment devoutly hoped that she found the tendency disagreeable.

'Come, come,' said Lucy; 'music, music! We will discuss each other's qualities another time.'

Maggie always tried in vain to go on with her work when music began. She tried harder than ever to-day; for the thought that Stephen knew how much she cared for his singing was one that no longer roused a merely playful resistance; and she knew, too, that it was his habit always to stand so that he could look at her. But it was of no use: she soon threw her work down, and all her intentions were lost in the vague state of emotion produced by the inspiring duet—emotion that seemed to make her at once strong and weak: strong for all enjoyment, weak for all resistance. When the strain passed into the minor, she half-started from her seat with the sudden thrill of that change. Poor Maggie! She looked very beautiful when her soul was being played on in this way by the inexorable power of sound. You might have seen the slightest perceptible quivering through her whole frame as she leaned a little forward, clasping her hands as if to steady herself; while her eyes dilated and brightened into that wide-open, childish expression of wondering delight, which always came back in her happiest moments. Lucy, who at other times had always been at the piano when Maggie was looking in this way, could not resist the impulse to steal up to her and kiss her. Philip, too, caught a glimpse of her now and then round the open book on the desk, and felt that he had never before seen her under so strong an influence.

'More, more!' said Lucy, when the duet had been encored. 'Something spirited again. Maggie always says she likes a great rush of sound.'

'It must be "Let us take the road," then,' said Stephen —'so suitable for a wet morning. But are you prepared to abandon the most sacred duties of life, and come and sing with us ?'

'O yes,' said Lucy, laughing. 'If you will look out the "Beggar's Opera" from the large canterbury. It has a dingy cover.'

'That is a great clue, considering there are about a score covers here of rival dinginess,' said Stephen, drawing out the canterbury.

'O, play something the while, Philip,' said Lucy, noticing that his fingers were wandering over the keys. 'What is that you are falling into ?—something delicious that I don't know.'

'Don't you know that ?' said Philip, bringing out the tune more definitely. 'It's from the "Somnambula"— "Ah! perchè non posso odiarti." I don't know the opera, but it appears the tenor is telling the heroine that he shall always love her though she may forsake him. You've heard me sing it to the English words, "I love thee still."'

It was not quite unintentionally that Philip had wandered into this song, which might be an indirect expression to Maggie of what he could not prevail on himself to say to her directly. Her ears had been open to what he was saying, and when he began to sing, she understood the plaintive passion of the music. That pleading tenor had no very fine qualities as a voice, but it was not quite new to her: it had sung to her by snatches, in a subdued way, among the grassy walks and hollows, and underneath the leaning ash-tree in the Red Deeps. There seemed to be some reproach in the words—did Philip mean that? She wished she had assured him more distinctly in their conversation that she desired not to renew the hope of love between them, *only* because it clashed with her inevitable circumstances. She was touched, not thrilled by the song: it suggested distinct memories and thoughts, and brought quiet regret in the place of excitement.

'That's the way with you tenors,' said Stephen, who was waiting with music in his hand while Philip finished the song. 'You demoralize the fair sex by warbling your sentimental love and constancy under all sorts of vile treatment. Nothing short of having your heads served up in a dish like that mediæval tenor or troubadour, would prevent you from expressing your entire resignation. I must administer an antidote, while Miss Deane prepares to tear herself away from her bobbins.'

Stephen rolled out, with saucy energy:

> *Shall I, wasting in despair,*
> *Die because a woman's fair?*

and seemed to make all the air in the room alive with a new influence. Lucy, always proud of what Stephen did, went towards the piano with laughing, admiring looks at him; and Maggie, in spite of her resistance to the spirit of the song and to the singer, was taken hold of and shaken by the invisible influence—was borne along by a wave too strong for her.

But, angrily resolved not to betray herself, she seized her work, and went on making false stitches and pricking her fingers with much perseverance, not looking up or taking notice of what was going forward, until all the three voices united in 'Let us take the road.'

I am afraid there would have been a subtle, stealing gratification in her mind if she had known how entirely this saucy, defiant Stephen was occupied with her: how he was passing rapidly from a determination to treat her with ostentatious indifference to an irritating desire for some sign of inclination from her—some interchange of subdued word or look with her. It was not long before he found an opportunity, when they had passed to the music of 'The

Tempest.' Maggie, feeling the need of a footstool, was walking across the room to get one, when Stephen, who was not singing just then, and was conscious of all her movements, guessed her want, and flew to anticipate her, lifting the footstool with an entreating look at her, which made it impossible not to return a glance of gratitude. And then, to have the footstool placed carefully by a too self-confident personage—not *any* self-confident personage, but one in particular, who suddenly looks humble and anxious, and lingers, bending still, to ask if there is not some draught in that position between the window and the fireplace, and if he may not be allowed to move the work-table for her— these things will summon a little of the too-ready, traitorous tenderness into a woman's eyes, compelled as she is in her girlish time to learn her life-lessons in very trivial language. And to Maggie such things had not been everyday incidents, but were a new element in her life, and found her keen appetite for homage quite fresh. That tone of gentle solicitude obliged her to look at the face that was bent towards her, and to say, 'No, thank you;' and nothing could prevent that mutual glance from being delicious to both, as it had been the evening before.

It was but an ordinary act of politeness in Stephen; it had hardly taken two minutes; and Lucy, who was singing, scarcely noticed it. But to Philip's mind, filled already with a vague anxiety that was likely to find a definite ground for itself in any trivial incident, this sudden eagerness in Stephen, and the change in Maggie's face, which was plainly reflecting a beam from his, seemed so strong a contrast with the previous overwrought signs of indifference, as to be charged with painful meaning. Stephen's voice, pouring in again, jarred upon his nervous susceptibility as if it had been the clang of sheet-iron, and he felt inclined to make the piano shriek in utter discord. He had really seen no communicable ground for suspecting any unusual feeling between Stephen and Maggie: his own reason told him so, and he wanted to go home at once that he might reflect coolly on these false images, till he had convinced himself of their nullity. But then, again, he wanted to stay as long as Stephen stayed—always to be present when Stephen was present with Maggie. It seemed to poor Philip so natural, nay, inevitable, that any man who was near Maggie should fall in love with her! There was no promise of happiness for her if she were beguiled into loving Stephen Guest; and this thought emboldened Philip to view his own love for her in the light of a less unequal offering. He was beginning to play very falsely under this deafening inward tumult, and Lucy was looking at him in astonishment, when Mrs. Tulliver's entrance to summon them to lunch came as an excuse for abruptly breaking off the music.

'Ah, Mr. Philip,' said Mr. Deane, when they entered the dining-room, 'I've not seen you for a long while. Your father's not at home, I think, is he? I went after him to the office the other day, and they said he was out of town.'

'He's been to Mudport on business for several days,' said Philip; 'but he's come back now.'

'As fond of his farming hobby as ever, eh?'

'I believe so,' said Philip, rather wondering at this sudden interest in his father's pursuits.

'Ah!' said Mr. Deane, 'he's got some land in his own hands on this side the river as well as the other, I think?'

'Yes, he has.'

'Ah!' continued Mr. Deane, as he dispensed the pigeon-pie; 'he must find farming a heavy item—an expensive hobby. I never had a hobby myself—never would give in to that. And the worst of all hobbies are those that people think they can get money at. They shoot their money down like corn out of a sack then.'

Lucy felt a little nervous under her father's apparently gratuitous criticism of Mr. Wakem's expenditure. But it ceased there, and Mr. Deane became unusually silent and meditative during his luncheon. Lucy, accustomed to watch all indications in her father, and having reasons, which had recently become strong, for an extra interest in what referred to the Wakems, felt an unusual curiosity to know what had prompted her father's questions. His subsequent silence made her suspect there had been some special reason for them in his mind.

With this idea in her head, she resorted to her usual plan when she wanted to tell or ask her father anything particular: she found a reason for her aunt Tulliver to leave the dining-room after dinner, and seated herself on a small stool at her father's knee. Mr. Deane, under those circumstances, considered that he tasted some of the most agreeable moments his merits had purchased him in life, notwithstanding that Lucy, disliking to have her hair powdered with snuff, usually began by mastering his snuff-box on such occasions.

'You don't want to go to sleep yet, papa, *do* you?' she said, as she brought up her stool and opened the large fingers that clutched the snuff-box.

'Not yet,' said Mr. Deane, glancing at the reward of merit in the decanter. 'But what do *you* want?' he added, pinching the dimpled chin fondly. 'To coax some more sovereigns out of my pocket for your bazaar? Eh?'

'No, I have no base motives at all to-day. I only want to talk, not to beg. I want to know what made you ask Philip Wakem about his father's farming to-day, papa? It seemed rather odd, because you never hardly say anything to him about his father; and why should you care about Mr. Wakem's losing money by his hobby?'

'Something to do with business,' said Mr. Deane, waving his hands, as if to repel intrusion into that mystery.

'But, papa, you always say Mr. Wakem has brought Philip up like a girl: how came you to think you should get any business knowledge out of him? Those abrupt questions sounded rather oddly. Philip thought them queer.'

'Nonsense, child!' said Mr. Deane, willing to justify his social demeanour, with which he had taken some pains in his upward progress. 'There's a report that Wakem's mill and farm on the other side of the river—Dorlcote Mill, your uncle Tulliver's, you know—isn't answering so well as it did. I wanted to see if your friend Philip would let anything out about his father's being tired of farming.'

'Why? Would you buy the mill, papa, if he would part with it?' said Lucy eagerly. 'O, tell me everything—here, you shall have your snuff-box if you'll tell me. Because

Maggie says all their hearts are set on Tom's getting back the mill some time. It was one of the last things her father said to Tom, that he must get back the mill.'

'Hush, you little puss,' said Mr. Deane, availing himself of the restored snuff-box. 'You must not say a word about this thing—do you hear? There's very little chance of their getting the mill, or of anybody's getting it out of Wakem's hands. And if he knew that we wanted it with a view to the Tullivers getting it again, he'd be the less likely to part with it. It's natural, after what happened. He behaved well enough to Tulliver before; but a horsewhipping is not likely to be paid for with sugar-plums.'

'Now, papa,' said Lucy, with a little air of solemnity, 'will you trust me? You must not ask me all my reasons for what I'm going to say—but I have very strong reasons. And I'm very cautious—I am, indeed.'

'Well, let us hear.'

'Why, I believe, if you will let me take Philip Wakem into our confidence—let me tell him all about your wish to buy, and what it's for—that my cousins wish to have it, and why they wish to have it—I believe Philip would help to bring it about. I know he would desire to do it.'

'I don't see how that can be, child,' said Mr. Deane, looking puzzled. 'Why should *he* care?'—then, with a sudden penetrating look at his daughter, 'You don't think the poor lad's fond of you, and so you can make him do what you like?' (Mr. Deane felt quite safe about his daughter's affections.)

'No, papa; he cares very little about me—not so much as I care about him. But I have a reason for being quite sure of what I say. Don't you ask me. And if you ever guess, don't tell me. Only give me leave to do as I think fit about it.'

Lucy rose from her stool to seat herself on her father's knee, and kissed him with that last request.

'Are you sure you won't do mischief, now?' he said, looking at her with delight.

'Yes, papa, quite sure. I'm very wise; I've got all your business talents. Didn't you admire my accompt-book, now, when I showed it you?'

'Well, well, if this youngster will keep his counsel, there won't be much harm done. And to tell the truth, I think there's not much chance for us any other way. Now, let me go off to sleep.'

VIII

WAKEM IN A NEW LIGHT

Before three days had passed after the conversation you have just overheard between Lucy and her father, she had contrived to have a private interview with Philip during a visit of Maggie's to her aunt Glegg. For a day and a night Philip turned over in his mind with restless agitation all that Lucy had told him in that interview, till he had thoroughly resolved on a course of action. He thought he saw before him now a possibility of altering his position with respect to Maggie, and removing at least one obstacle between them. He laid his plan and calculated all his moves with the fervid deliberation of a chess-player in the days of his first ardour, and was amazed himself at his sudden genius as a tactician. His plan was as bold as it was thoroughly calculated. Having watched for a moment when his father had nothing more urgent on his hands than the newspaper, he went behind him, laid a hand on his shoulder, and said:

'Father, will you come into my sanctum, and look at my new sketches? I've arranged them now.'

'I'm getting terribly stiff in the joints, Phil, for climbing those stairs of yours,' said Wakem, looking kindly at his son as he laid down his paper. 'But come along, then.'

'This is a nice place for you, isn't it, Phil?—a capital light that from the roof, eh?' was, as usual, the first thing he said on entering the painting-room. He liked to remind himself and his son too that his fatherly indulgence had provided the accommodation. He had been a good father. Emily would have nothing to reproach him with there, if she came back again from her grave.

'Come, come,' he said, putting his double eye-glass over

his nose, and seating himself to take a general view while he rested, 'you've got a famous show here. Upon my word, I don't see that your things aren't as good as that London artist's—what's his name—that Leyburn gave so much money for.'

Philip shook his head and smiled. He had seated himself on his painting-stool, and had taken a lead pencil in his hand, with which he was making strong marks to counteract the sense of tremulousness. He watched his father get up, and walk slowly round, good-naturedly dwelling on the pictures much longer than his amount of genuine taste for landscape would have prompted, till he stopped before a stand on which two pictures were placed—one much larger than the other—the smaller one in a leather case.

'Bless me! what have you here?' said Wakem, startled by a sudden transition from landscape to portrait. 'I thought you'd left off figures. Who are these?'

'They are the same person,' said Philip, with calm promptness, 'at different ages.'

'And what person?' said Wakem, sharply fixing his eyes with a growing look of suspicion on the larger picture.

'Miss Tulliver. The small one is something like what she was when I was at school with her brother at King's Lorton: the larger one is not quite so good a likeness of what she was when I came from abroad.'

Wakem turned round fiercely, with a flushed face, letting his eye-glass fall, and looking at his son with a savage expression for a moment, as if he was ready to strike that daring feebleness from the stool. But he threw himself into the arm-chair again, and thrust his hands into his trouser-pockets, still looking angrily at his son, however. Philip did not return the look, but sat quietly watching the point of his pencil.

'And do you mean to say, then, that you have had any acquaintance with her since you came from abroad?' said Wakem, at last, with that vain effort which rage always makes to throw as much punishment as it desires to inflict into words and tones, since blows are forbidden.

'Yes: I saw a great deal of her for a whole year before her

father's death. We met often in that thicket—the Red Deeps—near Dorlcote Mill. I love her dearly: I shall never love any other woman. I have thought of her ever since she was a little girl.'

'Go on, sir!—and you have corresponded with her all this while?'

'No. I never told her I loved her till just before we parted, and she promised her brother not to see me again or to correspond with me. I am not sure that she loves me, or would consent to marry me. But if she would consent— if she *did* love me well enough—I should marry her.'

'And this is the return you make me for all the indulgences I've heaped on you?' said Wakem, getting white, and beginning to tremble under an enraged sense of impotence before Philip's calm defiance and concentration of purpose.

'No, father,' said Philip, looking up at him for the first time. 'I don't regard it as a return. You have been an indulgent father to me; but I have always felt that it was because you had an affectionate wish to give me as much happiness as my unfortunate lot would admit of—not that it was a debt you expected me to pay by sacrificing all my chances of happiness to satisfy feelings of yours, which I can never share.'

'I think most sons would share their father's feelings in this case,' said Wakem bitterly. 'The girl's father was an ignorant mad brute, who was within an inch of murdering me. The whole town knows it. And the brother is just as insolent, only in a cooler way. He forbade her seeing you, you say; he'll break every bone in your body, for your greater happiness, if you don't take care. But you seem to have made up your mind: you have counted the consequences, I suppose. Of course you are independent of me: you can marry this girl to-morrow, if you like: you are a man of five-and-twenty—you can go your way, and I can go mine. We need have no more to do with each other.'

Wakem rose and walked towards the door, but something held him back, and instead of leaving the room, he walked up and down it. Philip was slow to reply, and when he spoke, his tone had a more incisive quietness and clearness than ever.

'No: I can't marry Miss Tulliver, even if she would have me—if I have only my own resources to maintain her with. I have been brought up to no profession. I can't offer her poverty as well as deformity.'

'Ah, *there* is a reason for your clinging to me, doubtless,' said Wakem, still bitterly, though Philip's last words had given him a pang: they had stirred a feeling which had been a habit for a quarter of a century. He threw himself into the chair again.

'I expected all this,' said Philip. 'I know these scenes are often happening between father and son. If I were like other men of my age, I might answer your angry words by still angrier—we might part—I should marry the woman I love, and have a chance of being as happy as the rest. But if it will be a satisfaction to you to annihilate the very object of everything you've done for me, you have an advantage over most fathers: you can completely deprive me of the only thing that would make my life worth having.'

Philip paused, but his father was silent.

'You know best what satisfaction you would have, beyond that of gratifying a ridiculous rancour worthy only of wandering savages.'

'Ridiculous rancour!' Wakem burst out. 'What do you mean? Damn it! is a man to be horsewhipped by a boor and love him for it? Besides, there's that cold, proud devil of a son, who said a word to me I shall not forget when we had the settling. He would be as pleasant a mark for a bullet as I know—if he were worth the expense.'

'I don't mean your resentment towards them,' said Philip, who had his reasons for some sympathy with this view of Tom, 'though a feeling of revenge is not worth much, that you should care to keep it. I mean your extending the enmity to a helpless girl, who has too much sense and goodness to share their narrow prejudices. *She* has never entered into the family quarrels.'

'What does that signify? We don't ask what a woman does—we ask whom she belongs to. It's altogether a degrading thing to you—to think of marrying old Tulliver's daughter.'

For the first time in the dialogue, Philip lost some of his self-control, and coloured with anger.

'Miss Tulliver,' he said, with bitter incisiveness, 'has the only grounds of rank that anything but vulgar folly can suppose to belong to the middle class: she is thoroughly refined, and her friends, whatever else they may be, are respected for irreproachable honour and integrity. All St. Ogg's, I fancy, would pronounce her to be more than my equal.'

Wakem darted a glance of fierce question at his son; but Philip was not looking at him, and with a certain penitent consciousness went on, in a few moments, as if in amplification of his last words:

'Find a single person in St. Ogg's who will not tell you that a beautiful creature like her would be throwing herself away on a pitiable object like me.'

'Not she!' said Wakem, rising again, and forgetting everything else in a burst of resentful pride, half fatherly, half personal. 'It would be a deuced fine match for her. It's all stuff about an accidental deformity, when a girl's really attached to a man.'

'But girls are not apt to get attached under those circumstances,' said Philip.

'Well, then,' said Wakem, rather brutally, trying to recover his previous position, 'if she doesn't care for you, you might have spared yourself the trouble of talking to me about her—and you might have spared me the trouble of refusing my consent to what was never likely to happen.'

Wakem strode to the door, and, without looking round again, banged it after him.

Philip was not without confidence that his father would be ultimately wrought upon as he had expected by what had passed; but the scene had jarred upon his nerves, which were as sensitive as a woman's. He determined not to go down to dinner: he couldn't meet his father again that day. It was Wakem's habit, when he had no company at home, to go out in the evening—often as early as half-past seven;

and as it was far on in the afternoon now, Philip locked up his room and went out for a long ramble, thinking he would not return until his father was out of the house again. He got into a boat, and went down the river to a favourite village, where he dined, and lingered till it was late enough for him to return. He had never had any sort of quarrel with his father before, and had a sickening fear that this contest, just begun, might go on for weeks—and what might not happen in that time? He would not allow himself to define what that involuntary question meant. But if he could once be in the position of Maggie's accepted, acknowledged lover, there would be less room for vague dread. He went up to his painting-room again, and threw himself, with a sense of fatigue, into the arm-chair, looking round absently at the views of water and rock that were ranged around, till he fell into a doze, in which he fancied Maggie was slipping down a glistening, green, slimy channel of a waterfall, and he was looking on helpless, till he was awakened by what seemed a sudden, awful crash.

It was the opening of the door, and he could hardly have dozed more than a few moments, for there was no perceptible change in the evening light. It was his father who entered; and when Philip moved to vacate the chair for him, he said:

'Sit still. I'd rather walk about.'

He stalked up and down the room once or twice, and then, standing opposite Philip with his hand thrust in his side-pockets, he said, as if continuing a conversation that had not been broken off:

'But this girl seems to have been fond of you, Phil, else she wouldn't have met you in that way.'

Philip's heart was beating rapidly, and a transient flush passed over his face like a gleam. It was not quite easy to speak at once.

'She liked me at King's Lorton, when she was a little girl, because I used to sit with her brother a great deal when he had hurt his foot. She had kept that in her memory, and thought of me as a friend of a long while ago. She didn't think of me as a lover, when she met me.'

'Well, but you made love to her at last. What did she say then?' said Wakem, walking about again.

'She said she *did* love me then.'

'Confound it, then, what else do you want? Is she a jilt?'

'She was very young then,' said Philip hesitatingly. 'I'm afraid she hardly knew what she felt. I'm afraid our long separation, and the idea that events must always divide us, may have made a difference.'

'But she's in the town. I've seen her at church. Haven't you spoken to her since you came back?'

'Yes, at Mr. Deane's. But I couldn't renew my proposals to her on several grounds. One obstacle would be removed if you would give your consent—if you would be willing to think of her as a daughter-in-law.'

Wakem was silent a little while, pausing before Maggie's picture.

'She's not the sort of woman your mother was, though, Phil,' he said at last. 'I saw her at church—she's handsomer than this—deuced fine eyes and fine figure, I saw; but rather dangerous and unmanageable, eh?'

'She's very tender and affectionate; and so simple—without the airs and petty contrivances other women have.'

'Ah?' said Wakem. Then looking round at his son: 'But your mother looked gentler: she had that brown wavy hair and grey eyes, like yours. You can't remember her very well. It was a thousand pities I'd no likeness of her.'

'Then, shouldn't you be glad for me to have the same sort of happiness, father—to sweeten my life for me? There can never be another tie so strong to you as that which began eight-and-twenty years ago, when you married my mother, and you have been tightening it ever since.'

'Ah, Phil—you're the only fellow that knows the best of me,' said Wakem, giving his hand to his son. 'We must keep together if we can. And now, what am I to do? You must come down-stairs and tell me. Am I to go and call on this dark-eyed damsel?'

The barrier once thrown down in this way, Philip could talk freely to his father of their entire relation with the Tullivers—of the desire to get the mill and land back into the family—and of its transfer to Guest & Co. as an intermediate step. He could venture now to be persuasive and urgent, and his father yielded with more readiness than he had calculated on.

'*I* don't care about the mill,' he said at last, with a sort of angry compliance. 'I've had an infernal deal of bother lately about the mill. Let them pay me for my improvements, that's all. But there's one thing you needn't ask me. I shall have no direct transactions with young Tulliver. If you like to swallow him, for his sister's sake, you may; but I've no sauce that will make him go down.'

I leave you to imagine the agreeable feelings with which Philip went to Mr. Deane the next day, to say that Mr. Wakem was ready to open the negotiations, and Lucy's pretty triumph as she appealed to her father whether she had not proved her great business abilities. Mr. Deane was rather puzzled, and suspected that there had been something 'going on' among the young people to which he wanted a clue. But to men of Mr. Deane's stamp, what goes on among the young people is as extraneous to the real business of life as what goes on among the birds and butterflies—until it can be shown to have a malign bearing on monetary affairs. And in this case the bearing appeared to be entirely propitious.

IX

CHARITY IN FULL DRESS

THE culmination of Maggie's career as an admired member of society in St. Ogg's was certainly the day of the bazaar, when her simple, noble beauty, clad in a white muslin of some soft-floating kind, which I suspect must have come from the stores of aunt Pullet's wardrobe, appeared with marked distinction among the more adorned and conventional women around her. We perhaps never detect how much of our social demeanour is made up of artificial airs, until we see a person who is at once beautiful and simple: without the beauty, we are apt to call simplicity awkwardness.

The Miss Guests were much too well-bred to have any of the grimaces and affected tones that belong to pretentious vulgarity; but their stall being next to the one where Maggie sat, it seemed newly obvious to-day that Miss Guest held her chin too high, and that Miss Laura spoke and moved continually with a view to effect.

All well-drest St. Ogg's and its neighbourhood were there; and it would have been worth while to come, even from a distance, to see the fine old hall, with its open roof and carved oaken rafters, and great oaken folding doors, and light shed down from a height on the many-coloured show beneath: a very quaint place, with broad faded stripes painted on the walls, and here and there a show of heraldic animals of a bristly, long-snouted character, the cherished emblems of a noble family once the seigniors of this now civic hall. A grand arch, cut in the upper wall at one end, surmounted an oaken orchestra, with an open room behind it, where hothouse plants and stalls for refreshments were disposed: an agreeable resort for gentlemen, disposed to loiter, and yet to exchange the occasional crush down below for a more commodious point of view. In fact, the perfect fitness of this ancient building for an admirable modern purpose, that made charity truly elegant, and led through vanity up to the supply of a deficit, was so striking that hardly a person entered the room without exchanging the remark more than once. Near the great arch over the orchestra was the stone oriel with painted glass, which was one of the venerable inconsistencies of the old hall; and it was close by this that Lucy had her stall, for the convenience of certain large plain articles which she had taken charge of for Mrs. Kenn. Maggie had begged to sit at the open end of the stall, and to have the sale of these articles rather than of bead-mats and other elaborate products, of which she had but a dim understanding. But it soon appeared that the gentlemen's dressing-gowns, which were among her commodities, were objects of such general attention and inquiry, and excited so troublesome a curiosity as to their lining and comparative merits, together with a determination to test them by trying on, as to make her post a very conspicuous one. The ladies who had commodities of their own to sell, and did not want dressing-gowns, saw at once the frivolity and bad taste of this masculine preference for goods which any tailor could furnish; and it is possible that the emphatic notice of various kinds which was drawn towards Miss Tulliver on this public occasion, threw a very strong and unmistakeable light on her subsequent conduct in many minds then present. Not that anger, on account of spurned beauty, can dwell in the celestial breasts of charitable ladies, but rather, that the errors of persons who have once been much admired necessarily take a deeper tinge from the mere force of contrast; and also, that to-day Maggie's conspicuous position, for the first time, made evident certain characteristics which were subsequently felt to have an explanatory bearing. There was something rather bold in Miss Tulliver's direct gaze, and something undefinably coarse in the style of her beauty, which placed her, in the opinion of all feminine judges, far below her cousin Miss Deane; for the ladies of St. Ogg's had now completely ceded to Lucy their hypothetic claims on the admiration of Mr. Stephen Guest.

As for dear little Lucy herself, her late benevolent triumph about the Mill, and all the affectionate projects she was cherishing for Maggie and Philip, helped to give her the highest spirits to-day, and she felt nothing but pleasure in the evidence of Maggie's attractiveness. It is true, she was looking very charming herself, and Stephen was paying her the utmost attention on this public occasion; jealously buying up the articles he had seen under her fingers in the process of making, and gaily helping her to cajole the male customers into the purchase of the most effeminate futilities. He chose to lay aside his hat and wear a scarlet fez of her embroidering; but by superficial observers this was necessarily liable to be interpreted less as a compliment to Lucy than as a mark of coxcombry. 'Guest is a great coxcomb,' young Torry observed; 'but then he is a privileged person in St. Ogg's—he carries all before him: if another fellow did such things, everybody would say he made a fool of himself.'

And Stephen purchased absolutely nothing from Maggie, until Lucy said, in rather a vexed undertone:

'See, now; all the things of Maggie's knitting will be gone, and you will not have bought one. There are those deliciously soft warm things for the wrists—do buy them.'

'Oh, no,' said Stephen, 'they must be intended for imaginative persons, who can chill themselves on this warm day by thinking of the frosty Caucasus. Stern reason is my forte, you know. You must get Philip to buy those. By the way, why doesn't he come?'

'He never likes going where there are many people, though I enjoined him to come. He said he would buy up any of my goods that the rest of the world rejected. But now, do go and buy something of Maggie.'

'No, no—see—she has got a customer: there is old Wakem himself just coming up.'

Lucy's eyes turned with anxious interest towards Maggie, to see how she went through this first interview, since a sadly memorable time, with a man towards whom she must have so strange a mixture of feelings; but she was pleased to notice that Wakem had tact enough to enter at once into talk about the bazaar wares, and appear interested in purchasing, smiling now and then kindly at Maggie, and not calling on her to speak much, as if he observed that she was rather pale and tremulous.

'Why, Wakem is making himself particularly amiable to your cousin,' said Stephen in an under-tone to Lucy; 'is it pure magnanimity? you talked of a family quarrel.'

'O, that will soon be quite healed, I hope,' said Lucy, becoming a little indiscreet in her satisfaction, and speaking with an air of significance. But Stephen did not appear to notice this, and as some lady purchasers came up, he lounged on towards Maggie's end, handling trifles and standing aloof until Wakem, who had taken out his purse, had finished his transactions.

'My son came with me,' he overheard Wakem saying, 'but he has vanished into some other part of the building, and has left all these charitable gallantries to me. I hope you'll reproach him for his shabby conduct.'

She returned his smile and bow without speaking, and he turned away, only then observing Stephen, and nodding to him. Maggie, conscious that Stephen was still there, busied herself with counting money, and avoided looking up. She had been well pleased that he had devoted himself to Lucy to-day, and had not come near her. They had begun the morning with an indifferent salutation, and both had rejoiced in being aloof from each other, like a patient who has actually done without his opium, in spite of former failures in resolution. And during the last few days they had even been making up their minds to failures, looking to the outward events that must soon come to separate them, as a reason for dispensing with self-conquest in detail.

Stephen moved step by step as if he were being unwillingly dragged, until he had got round the open end of the stall, and was half hidden by a screen of draperies. Maggie went on counting her money till she suddenly heard a deep gentle voice saying:

'Aren't you very tired? Do let me bring you something—some fruit or jelly—mayn't I?'

The unexpected tones shook her like a sudden accidental vibration of a harp close by her.

'O no, thank you,' she said faintly, and only half-looking up for an instant.

'You look so pale,' Stephen insisted, in a more entreating tone. 'I'm sure you're exhausted. I must disobey you, and bring something.'

'No, indeed, I couldn't take it.'

'Are you angry with me? What have I done? *Do* look at me.'

'Pray go away,' said Maggie, looking at him helplessly, her eyes glancing immediately from him to the opposite corner of the orchestra, which was half hidden by the folds of the old faded green curtain.

Maggie had no sooner uttered this entreaty than she was wretched at the admission it implied; but Stephen turned away at once, and, following her upward glance, he saw Philip Wakem seated in the half-hidden corner, so that he could command little more than that angle of the hall in which Maggie sat. An entirely new thought occurred to Stephen, and, linking itself with what he had observed of Wakem's manner, and with Lucy's reply to his observation, it convinced him that there had been some former relation between Philip and Maggie beyond that childish one of which he had heard. More than one impulse made him immediately leave the hall and go upstairs to the refreshment-room, where, walking up to Philip, he sat down behind him, and put his hand on his shoulder.

'Are you studying for a portrait, Phil,' he said, 'or for a sketch of that oriel window? By George! it makes a capital bit from this dark corner, with the curtain just marking it off.'

'I have been studying expression,' said Philip curtly.

'What! Miss Tulliver's? It's rather of the savage-moody order to-day, I think—something of the fallen princess serving behind a counter. Her cousin sent me to her with a civil offer to get her some refreshment, but I have been snubbed, as usual. There's a natural antipathy between us, I suppose: I have seldom the honour to please her.'

'What a hypocrite you are!' said Philip, flushing angrily.

'What! because experience must have told me that I'm universally pleasing? I admit the law, but there's some disturbing force here.'

'I am going,' said Philip, rising abruptly.

'So am I—to get a breath of fresh air; this place gets oppressive. I think I have done suit and service long enough.'

The two friends walked downstairs together without speaking. Philip turned through the outer door into the courtyard, but Stephen, saying, 'O, by-the-by, I must call in here,' went on along the passage to one of the rooms at the other end of the building, which were appropriated to the town library. He had the room all to himself, and a man requires nothing less than this, when he wants to dash his cap on the table, throw himself astride a chair, and stare at a high brick wall with a frown which would not have been beneath the occasion if he had been slaying 'the giant Python.' The conduct that issues from a moral conflict has often so close a resemblance to vice, that the distinction escapes all outward judgments, founded on a mere comparison of actions. It is clear to you, I hope, that Stephen was not a hypocrite—capable of deliberate doubleness for a selfish end; and yet his fluctuations between the indulgence of a feeling and the systematic concealment of it, might have made a good case in support of Philip's accusation.

Meanwhile, Maggie sat at her stall cold and trembling, with that painful sensation in the eyes which comes from resolutely repressed tears. Was her life to be always like this?—always bringing some new source of inward strife? She heard confusedly the busy indifferent voices around her, and wished her mind could flow into that easy, babbling current. It was at this moment that Dr. Kenn, who had quite lately come into the hall, and was now walking down the middle with his hands behind him, taking a general view, fixed his eyes on Maggie for the first time, and was struck with the expression of pain on her beautiful face. She was sitting quite still, for the stream of customers had lessened at this late hour in the afternoon: the gentlemen had chiefly chosen the middle of the day, and Maggie's stall was looking rather bare. This, with her absent, pained expression, finished the contrast between her and her companions, who were all bright, eager, and busy. He was strongly arrested. Her face had naturally drawn his attention as a new and striking one at church, and he had been introduced to her during a short call on business at Mr. Deane's, but he had never spoken more than three words to her. He walked towards her now, and Maggie, perceiving someone approaching, roused herself to look up and be prepared to speak. She felt a childlike, instinctive relief from the sense of uneasiness in this exertion, when she saw it was Dr. Kenn's face that was looking at her: that plain, middle-aged face, with a grave, penetrating kindness in it, seeming to tell of a human being who had reached a firm, safe strand, but was looking with helpful pity towards the strugglers still tossed by the waves, had an effect on Maggie at this moment which was afterwards remembered by her as if it had been a promise. The middle-aged, who have lived through their strongest emotions, but are yet in the time when memory is still half passionate and not merely contemplative, should surely be a sort of natural priesthood, whom life has disciplined and consecrated to be the refuge and rescue of early stumblers and victims of self-despair. Most of us, at some moment in our young lives, would have welcomed a priest of that natural order in any sort of canonicals or uncanonicals, but had to scramble upwards into all the difficulties of nineteen entirely without such aid, as Maggie did.

'You find your office rather a fatiguing one, I fear, Miss Tulliver?' said Dr. Kenn.

'It is, rather,' said Maggie simply, not being accustomed to simper amiable denials of obvious facts.

'But I can tell Mrs. Kenn that you have disposed of her goods very quickly,' he added; 'she will be very much obliged to you.'

'O, I have done nothing: the gentlemen came very fast to buy the dressing-gowns and embroidered waistcoats, but I think any of the other ladies would have sold more: I didn't know what to say about them.'

Dr. Kenn smiled. 'I hope I'm going to have you as a permanent parishioner now, Miss Tulliver—am I? You have been at a distance from us hitherto.'

'I have been a teacher in a school, and I'm going into another situation of the same kind very soon.'

'Ah? I was hoping you would remain among your friends, who are all in this neighbourhood, I believe.'

'O, *I must go*,' said Maggie earnestly, looking at Dr. Kenn with an expression of reliance, as if she had told him her history in those three words. It was one of those moments of implicit revelation which will sometimes happen even between people who meet quite transiently—on a mile's journey, perhaps, or when resting by the wayside. There is always this possibility of a word or look from a stranger to keep alive the sense of human brotherhood.

Dr. Kenn's ear and eye took in all the signs that this brief confidence of Maggie's was charged with meaning.

'I understand,' he said; 'you feel it right to go. But that will not prevent our meeting again, I hope: it will not prevent my knowing you better, if I can be of any service to you.'

He put out his hand and pressed hers kindly before he turned away.

'She has some trouble or other at heart,' he thought. 'Poor child! she looks as if she might turn out to be one of

> "The souls by nature pitched too high,
> By suffering plunged too low."

There's something wonderfully honest in those beautiful eyes.'

It may be surprising that Maggie, among whose many imperfections an excessive delight in admiration and acknowledged supremacy were not absent now, any more than when she was instructing the gypsies with a view towards achieving a royal position among them, was not more elated on a day when she had had the tribute of so many looks and smiles, together with that satisfactory consciousness which had necessarily come from being taken before Lucy's cheval-glass, and made to look at the full length of her tall beauty, crowned by the night of her massy hair. Maggie had smiled at herself then, and for the moment had forgotten everything in the sense of her own beauty. If that state of mind could have lasted, her choice would have been to have Stephen Guest at her feet, offering her a life filled with all luxuries, with daily incense of adoration near and distant, and with all possibilities of culture at her command. But there were things in her stronger than vanity—passion, and affection, and long deep memories of early discipline and effort, of early claims on her love and pity; and the stream of vanity was soon swept along and mingled imperceptibly with that wider current which was at its highest force to-day, under the double urgency of the events and inward impulses brought by the last week.

Philip had not spoken to her himself about the removal of obstacles between them on his father's side—he shrank from that; but he had told everything to Lucy, with the hope that Maggie, being informed through her, might give him some encouraging sign that their being brought thus much nearer to each other was a happiness to her. The rush of conflicting feelings was too great for Maggie to say much when Lucy, with a face breathing playful joy, like one of Correggio's cherubs, poured forth her triumphant revelation; and Lucy could hardly be surprised that she could do little more than cry with gladness at the thought of her father's wish being fulfilled, and of Tom's getting the Mill again in reward for all his hard striving. The details of preparation for the bazaar had then come to usurp Lucy's attention for the next few days, and nothing had been said by the cousins on subjects that were likely to rouse deeper feelings. Philip had been to the house more than once, but Maggie had had no private conversation with him, and thus she had been left to fight her inward battle without interference.

But when the bazaar was fairly ended, and the cousins were alone again, resting together at home, Lucy said:

'You must give up going to stay with your aunt Moss the day after to-morrow, Maggie: write a note to her, and tell her you have put it off at my request, and I'll send the man with it. She won't be displeased; you'll have plenty of time to go by-and-by; and I don't want you to go out of the way just now.'

'Yes, indeed I must go, dear, I can't put it off. I wouldn't leave aunt Gritty out for the world. And I shall have very little time, for I'm going away to a new situation on the 25th of June.'

'Maggie!' said Lucy, almost white with astonishment.

'I didn't tell you, dear,' said Maggie, making a great effort to command herself, 'because you've been so busy. But some time ago I wrote to our old governess, Miss Firniss, to ask her to let me know if she met with any situation that I could fill, and the other day I had a letter from her telling me that I could take three orphan pupils of hers to the coast during the holidays, and then make trial of a situation with her as teacher. I wrote yesterday to accept the offer.'

Lucy felt so hurt that for some moments she was unable to speak.

'Maggie,' she said at last, 'how could you be so unkind to me—not to tell me—to take *such* a step—and now!' She hesitated a little, and then added—'And Philip? I thought everything was going to be so happy. O Maggie— what is the reason? Give it up; let me write. There is nothing now to keep you and Philip apart.'

'Yes,' said Maggie faintly. 'There is Tom's feeling. He said I must give him up if I married Philip. And I know he would not change—at least not for a long while—unless something happened to soften him.'

'But I will talk to him: he's coming back this week. And this good news about the Mill will soften him. And I'll talk to him about Philip. Tom's always very compliant to me: I don't think he's so obstinate.'

'But I must go,' said Maggie, in a distressed voice. 'I must leave some time to pass. Don't press me to stay, dear Lucy.'

Lucy was silent for two or three minutes, looking away and ruminating. At length she knelt down by her cousin, and, looking up in her face with anxious seriousness, said:

'Maggie, is it that you don't love Philip well enough to marry him?—tell me—trust me.'

Maggie held Lucy's hands tightly in silence a little while. Her own hands were quite cold. But when she spoke, her voice was quite clear and distinct.

'Yes, Lucy, I would choose to marry him. I think it would be the best and highest lot for me—to make his life happy. He loved me first. No one else could be quite what he is to me. But I can't divide myself from my brother for life. I must go away, and wait. Pray, don't speak to me again about it.'

Lucy obeyed in pain and wonder. The next word she said was:

'Well, dear Maggie, at least you will go to the dance at Park House to-morrow, and have some music and brightness, before you go to pay these dull, dutiful visits. Ah! here come aunty and the tea.'

X

THE SPELL SEEMS BROKEN

THE suite of rooms opening into each other at Park House looked duly brilliant with lights and flowers and the personal splendours of sixteen couples, with attendant parents and guardians. The focus of brilliancy was the long drawing-room, where the dancing went forward, under the inspiration of the grand piano; the library, into which it opened at one end, had the more sober illumination of maturity, with caps and cards; and at the other end, the pretty sitting-room with a conservatory attached, was left as an occasional cool retreat. Lucy, who had laid aside her black for the first time, and had her pretty slimness set off by an abundant dress of white crape, was the acknowledged queen of the occasion; for this was one of the Miss Guests' thoroughly condescending parties, including no member of any aristocracy higher than that of St. Ogg's, and stretching to the extreme limits of commercial and professional gentility.

Maggie at first refused to dance, saying that she had forgotten all the figures—it was so many years since she had danced at school; and she was glad to have that excuse, for it is ill dancing with a heavy heart. But at length the music wrought in her young limbs, and the longing came; even though it was the horrible young Torry, who walked up a second time to try and persuade her. She warned him that she could not dance anything but a country-dance; but he, of course, was willing to wait for that high felicity, meaning only to be complimentary when he assured her at several intervals that it was a 'great bore' that she couldn't waltz—he would have liked so much to waltz with her. But at last it was the turn of the good old-fashioned dance which has the least of vanity and the most of merriment in it, and Maggie quite forgot her troublous life in a childlike enjoyment of that half-rustic rhythm which seems to banish pretentious etiquette. She felt quite charitably towards young Torry, as his hand bore her along and held her up in the dance; her eyes and cheeks had that fire of young joy in them which will flame out if it can find the least breath to fan it; and her simple black dress, with its bit of black lace, seemed like the dim setting of a jewel.

Stephen had not yet asked her to dance—had not yet paid her more than a passing civility. Since yesterday, that inward vision of her which perpetually made part of his consciousness, had been half-screened by the image of Philip Wakem, which came across it like a blot: there was some attachment between her and Philip; at least there was an attachment on his side, which made her feel in some bondage. Here then, Stephen told himself, was another claim of honour which called on him to resist the attraction that was continually threatening to overpower him. He told himself so; and yet he had once or twice felt a certain savage resistance, and at another moment a shuddering repugnance, to this intrusion of Philip's image, which almost made it a new incitement to rush towards Maggie and claim her for himself. Nevertheless he had done what he meant to do this evening: he had kept aloof from her; he had hardly looked at her; and he had been gaily assiduous to Lucy. But now his eyes were devouring Maggie: he felt inclined to kick young Torry out of the dance, and take his place. Then he wanted the dance to end that he might get rid of his partner. The possibility that he too should dance with Maggie, and have her hand in his so long, was beginning to possess him like a thirst. But even now their hands were meeting in the dance—were meeting still to the very end of it, though they were far off each other.

Stephen hardly knew what happened, or in what automatic way he got through the duties of politeness in the interval, until he was free and saw Maggie seated alone again; at the farther end of the room. He made his way towards her round the couples that were forming for the waltz, and when Maggie became conscious that she was the person he sought, she felt, in spite of all the thoughts that had gone before, a glowing gladness at heart. Her eyes and cheeks were still brightened with her childlike enthusiasm in the dance: her whole frame was set to joy and tenderness; even the coming pain could not seem bitter—she was ready to welcome it as a part of life, for life at this moment seemed a keen vibrating consciousness poised above pleasure or pain. This one, this last night, she might expand unrestrainedly in the warmth of the present, without those chill eating thoughts of the past and the future.

'They're going to waltz again,' said Stephen, bending to speak to her, with that glance and tone of subdued tenderness which young dreams create to themselves in the summer woods when low cooing voices fill the air. Such glances and tones bring the breath of poetry with them into a room that is half-stifling with glaring gas and hard flirtation.

'They are going to waltz again: it is rather dizzy work to look on, and the room is very warm. Shall we walk about a little?'

He took her hand and placed it within his arm, and they walked on into the sitting-room, where the tables were strewn with engravings for the accommodation of visitors who would not want to look at them. But no visitors were here at this moment. They passed on into the conservatory.

'How strange and unreal the trees and flowers look with the lights among them,' said Maggie, in a low voice. 'They look as if they belonged to an enchanted land, and would never fade away:—I could fancy they were all made of jewels.'

She was looking at the tier of geraniums as she spoke, and Stephen made no answer: but he was looking at her—and does not a supreme poet blend light and sound into one, calling darkness mute, and light eloquent? Something strangely powerful there was in the light of Stephen's long gaze, for it made Maggie's face turn towards it and look upward at it—slowly, like a flower at the ascending brightness. And they walked unsteadily on, without feeling that they were walking—without feeling anything but that long grave mutual gaze which has the solemnity belonging to all deep human passion. The hovering thought that they must and would renounce each other made this moment of mute confession more intense in its rapture.

But they had reached the end of the conservatory, and were obliged to pause and turn. The change of movement brought a new consciousness to Maggie: she blushed deeply, turned away her head, and drew her arm from Stephen's, going up to some flowers to smell them. Stephen stood motionless, and still pale.

'O, may I get this rose?' said Maggie, making a great effort to say something, and dissipate the burning sense of irretrievable confession. 'I think I am quite wicked with roses—I like to gather them and smell them till they have no scent left.'

Stephen was mute; he was incapable of putting a sentence together, and Maggie bent her arm a little upward towards the large half-opened rose that had attracted her. Who has not felt the beauty of a woman's arm?—the unspeakable suggestions of tenderness that lie in the dimpled elbow, and all the varied gently-lessening curves down to the delicate wrist, with its tiniest, almost imperceptible nicks in the firm softness. A woman's arm touched the soul of a great sculptor two thousand years ago, so that he wrought an image of it for the Parthenon which moves us still as it clasps lovingly the time-worn marble of a headless trunk. Maggie's was such an arm as that—and it had the warm tints of life.

A mad impulse seized on Stephen; he darted towards the arm, and showered kisses on it, clasping the wrist.

But the next moment Maggie snatched it from him, and glared at him like a wounded war-goddess, quivering with rage and humiliation.

'How dare you?'—she spoke in a deeply-shaken, half-smothered voice. 'What right have I given you to insult me?'

She darted from him into the adjoining room, and threw herself on the sofa, panting and trembling.

A horrible punishment was come upon her for the sin of allowing a moment's happiness that was treachery to Lucy, to Philip—to her own better soul. That momentary happiness had been smitten with a blight—a leprosy: Stephen thought more lightly of *her* than he did of Lucy.

As for Stephen, he leaned back against the framework of the conservatory, dizzy with the conflict of passions—love, rage, and confused despair: despair at his want of self-mastery, and despair that he had offended Maggie.

The last feeling surmounted every other: to be by her side again and entreat forgiveness was the only thing that had the force of a motive for him, and she had not been seated for more than a few minutes when he came and stood humbly before her. But Maggie's bitter rage was unspent.

'Leave me to myself, if you please,' she said, with impetuous haughtiness, 'and for the future avoid me.'

Stephen turned away, and walked backwards and forwards at the end of the room. There was the dire necessity of going back into the dancing-room again, and he was beginning to be conscious of that. They had been absent so short a time, that when he went in again the waltz was not ended.

Maggie, too, was not long before she re-entered. All the pride of her nature was stung into activity: the hateful weakness which had dragged her within reach of this wound to her self-respect, had at least wrought its own cure. The thoughts and temptations of the last month should all be flung away into an unvisited chamber of memory: there was nothing to allure her now; duty would be easy, and all the old calm purposes would reign peacefully once more. She re-entered the drawing-room still with some excited brightness in her face, but with a sense of proud self-command that defied anything to agitate her. She refused to dance again, but she talked quite readily and calmly with everyone who addressed her. And when they got home that night, she kissed Lucy with a free heart, almost exulting in this scorching moment, which had delivered her from the possibility of another word or look that would have the stamp of treachery towards that gentle, unsuspicious sister.

The next morning Maggie did not set off to Basset quite so soon as she had expected. Her mother was to accompany her in the carriage, and household business could not be despatched hastily by Mrs. Tulliver. So Maggie, who had been in a hurry to prepare herself, had to sit waiting, equipped for the drive, in the garden. Lucy was busy in the house wrapping up some bazaar presents for the younger ones at Basset, and when there was a loud ring at the door-bell, Maggie felt some alarm lest Lucy should bring out Stephen to her: it was sure to be Stephen.

But presently the visitor came out into the garden alone, and seated himself by her on the garden-chair. It was not Stephen.

'We can just catch the tips of the Scotch firs, Maggie, from this seat,' said Philip.

They had taken each other's hands in silence, but Maggie had looked at him with a more complete revival of the old childlike affectionate smile than he had seen before, and he felt encouraged.

'Yes,' she said, 'I often look at them, and wish I could see the low sunlight on the stems again. But I have never been that way but once—to the churchyard, with my mother.'

'I have been there—I go there—continually,' said Philip. 'I have nothing but the past to live upon.'

A keen remembrance and keen pity impelled Maggie to put her hand in Philip's. They had so often walked hand-in-hand!

'I remember all the spots,' she said—'just where you told me of particular things—beautiful stories that I had never heard of before.'

'You will go there again soon—won't you, Maggie?' said Philip, getting timid. 'The Mill will soon be your brother's home again.'

'Yes; but I shall not be there,' said Maggie. 'I shall only hear of that happiness. I am going away again—Lucy has not told you, perhaps?'

'Then the future will never join on to the past again, Maggie? That book is quite closed?'

The grey eyes that had so often looked up at her with entreating worship, looked up at her now, with a last struggling ray of hope in them, and Maggie met them with her large sincere gaze.

'That book never will be closed, Philip,' she said, with

grave sadness; 'I desire no future that will break the ties of the past. But the tie to my brother is one of the strongest. I can do nothing willingly that will divide me always from him.'

'Is that the only reason that would keep us apart for ever, Maggie?' said Philip, with a desperate determination to have a definite answer.

'The only reason,' said Maggie, with calm decision.

And she believed it. At that moment she felt as if the enchanted cup had been dashed to the ground. The reactionary excitement that gave her a proud self-mastery had not subsided, and she looked at the future with a sense of calm choice.

They sat hand-in-hand without looking at each other or speaking for a few minutes: in Maggie's mind the first scenes of love and parting were more present than the actual moment, and she was looking at Philip in the Red Deeps.

Philip felt that he ought to have been thoroughly happy in that answer of hers: she was as open and transparent as a rock-pool. Why was he not thoroughly happy? Jealousy is never satisfied with anything short of an omniscience that would detect the subtlest fold of the heart.

XI

IN THE LANE

MAGGIE had been four days at her aunt Moss's, giving the early June sunshine quite a new brightness in the care-dimmed eyes of that affectionate woman, and making an epoch for her cousins great and small, who were learning her words and actions by heart, as if she had been a transient avatar of perfect wisdom and beauty.

She was standing on the causeway with her aunt and a group of cousins feeding the chickens, at that quiet moment in the life of the farmyard before the afternoon milking-time. The great buildings round the hollow yard were as dreary and tumble-down as ever, but over the old garden-wall the straggling rose-bushes were beginning to toss their summer weight, and the grey wood and old bricks of the house, on its higher level, had a look of sleepy age in the broad afternoon sunlight, that suited the quiescent time. Maggie, with her bonnet over her arm, was smiling down at the hatch of small fluffy chickens, when her aunt exclaimed:

'Goodness me! who is that gentleman coming in at the gate?'

It was a gentleman on a tall bay horse; and the flanks and neck of the horse were streaked black with fast riding. Maggie felt a beating at head and heart—horrible as the sudden leaping to life of a savage enemy who had feigned death.

'Who is it, my dear?' said Mrs. Moss, seeing in Maggie's face the evidence that she knew.

'It is Mr. Stephen Guest,' said Maggie rather faintly. 'My cousin Lucy's—— a gentleman who is very intimate at my cousin's.'

Stephen was already close to them, had jumped off his horse, and now raised his hat as he advanced.

'Hold the horse, Willy,' said Mrs. Moss to the twelve-year-old boy.

'No, thank you,' said Stephen, pulling at the horse's impatiently tossing head. 'I must be going again immediately. I have a message to deliver to you, Miss Tulliver—on private business. May I take the liberty of asking you to walk a few yards with me?'

He had a half-jaded, half-irritated look, such as a man gets when he has been dogged by some care or annoyance that makes his bed and his dinner of little use to him. He spoke almost abruptly, as if his errand were too pressing for him to trouble himself about what would be thought by Mrs. Moss of his visit and request. Good Mrs. Moss, rather nervous in the presence of this apparently haughty gentleman, was inwardly wondering whether she would be doing right or wrong to invite him again to leave his horse and walk in, when Maggie, feeling all the embarrassment of the situation, and unable to say anything, put on her bonnet, and turned to walk towards the gate.

Stephen turned too, and walked by her side, leading his horse.

Not a word was spoken till they were out in the lane, and had walked four or five yards, when Maggie, who had been looking straight before her all the while, turned again to walk back, saying, with haughty resentment:

'There is no need for me to go any farther. I don't know whether you consider it gentlemanly and delicate conduct to place me in a position that forced me to come out with you—or whether you wished to insult me still further by thrusting an interview upon me in this way.'

'Of course you are angry with me for coming,' said Stephen bitterly. 'Of course it is of no consequence what a man has to suffer—it is only your woman's dignity that you care about.'

Maggie gave a slight start, such as might have come from the slightest possible electric shock.

'As if it were not enough that I'm entangled in this way—that I'm mad with love for you—that I resist the strongest passion a man can feel, because I try to be true to other claims—but you must treat me as if I were a coarse brute, who would willingly offend you. And when, if I had my own choice, I should ask you to take my hand, and my fortune, and my whole life, and do what you liked with them! I know I forgot myself. I took an unwarrantable liberty. I hate myself for having done it. But I repented immediately—I've been repenting ever since. You ought not to think it unpardonable: a man who loves with his whole soul, as I do you, is liable to be mastered by his feelings for a moment; but you know—you must believe—that the worst pain I could have is to have pained you—that I would give the world to recall the error.'

Maggie dared not speak—dared not turn her head. The strength that had come from resentment was all gone, and her lips were quivering visibly. She could not trust herself to utter the full forgiveness that rose in answer to that confession.

They were come nearly in front of the gate again, and she paused, trembling.

'You must not say these things—I must not hear them,' she said, looking down in misery, as Stephen came in front of her, to prevent her from going farther towards the gate. 'I'm very sorry for any pain you have to go through; but it is of no use to speak.'

'Yes, it *is* of use,' said Stephen impetuously. 'It would be of use if you would treat me with some sort of pity and consideration, instead of doing me vile injustice in your mind. I could bear everything more quietly if I knew you didn't hate me for an insolent coxcomb. Look at me—see what a hunted devil I am: I've been riding thirty miles every day to get away from the thought of you.'

Maggie did not—dared not look. She had already seen the harassed face. But she said gently:

'I don't think any evil of you.'

'Then, dearest, look at me,' said Stephen, in deepest, tenderest tones of entreaty. 'Don't go away from me yet. Give me a moment's happiness—make me feel you've forgiven me.'

'Yes, I do forgive you,' said Maggie, shaken by those tones, and all the more frightened at herself. 'But pray let me go in again. Pray go away.'

A great tear fell from under her lowered eyelids.

'I can't go away from you—I can't leave you,' said Stephen, with still more passionate pleading. 'I shall come back again if you send me away with this coldness—I can't answer for myself. But if you will go with me only a little way, I can live on that. You see plainly enough that your anger has only made me ten times more unreasonable.'

Maggie turned. But Tancred, the bay horse, began to make such spirited remonstrances against this frequent change of direction, that Stephen, catching sight of Willy Moss peeping through the gate, called out, 'Here! just come and hold my horse for five minutes.'

'O no,' said Maggie hurriedly, 'my aunt will think it so strange.'

'Never mind,' Stephen answered impatiently; 'they don't know the people at St. Ogg's. Lead him up and down just here, for five minutes,' he added to Willy, who was now

close to them; and then he turned to Maggie's side, and
they walked on. It was clear that she *must* go on now.

'Take my arm,' said Stephen entreatingly; and she took
it, feeling all the while as if she were sliding downwards in
a nightmare.

'There is no end to this misery,' she began, struggling to
repel the influence by speech. 'It is wicked—base—ever
allowing a word or look that Lucy—that others might not
have seen. Think of Lucy.'

'I do think of her—bless her. If I didn't——' Stephen
had laid his hand on Maggie's that rested on his arm, and
they both felt it difficult to speak.

'And I have other ties,' Maggie went on at last, with a
desperate effort,—'even if Lucy did not exist.'

'You are engaged to Philip Wakem?' said Stephen
hastily. 'Is it so?'

'I consider myself engaged to him—I don't mean to
marry anyone else.'

Stephen was silent again until they had turned out of the
sun into a side lane, all grassy and sheltered. Then he burst
out impetuously:

'It is unnatural—it is horrible. Maggie, if you loved me
as I love you, we should throw everything else to the winds
for the sake of belonging to each other. We should break
all these mistaken ties that were made in blindness, and
determine to marry each other.'

'I would rather die than fall into that temptation,' said
Maggie, with deep, slow distinctness—all the gathered
spiritual force of painful years coming to her aid in this
extremity. She drew her arm from his as she spoke.

'Tell me, then, that you don't care for me,' he said,
almost violently. 'Tell me that you love someone else
better.'

It darted through Maggie's mind that here was a mode
of releasing herself from outward struggle—to tell Stephen
that her whole heart was Philip's. But her lips would not
utter that, and she was silent.

'If you do love me, dearest,' said Stephen gently, taking
up her hand again and laying it within his arm, 'it is better

—it is right that we should marry each other. We can't help the pain it will give. It is come upon us without our seeking: it is natural—it has taken hold of me in spite of every effort I have made to resist it. God knows, I've been trying to be faithful to tacit engagements, and I've only made things worse—I'd better have given way at first.'

Maggie was silent. If it were *not* wrong—if she were once convinced of that, and need no longer beat and struggle against this current, soft and strong as the summer stream!

'Say "yes," dearest,' said Stephen, leaning to look entreatingly in her face. 'What could we care about in the whole world beside, if we belonged to each other?'

Her breath was on his face—his lips were very near hers—but there was a great dread dwelling in his love for her.

Her lips and eyelids quivered; she opened her eyes full on his for an instant, like a lovely wild animal timid and struggling under caresses, and then turned sharp round towards home again.

'And after all,' he went on in an impatient tone, trying to defeat his own scruples as well as hers, 'I am breaking no positive engagement: if Lucy's affections had been withdrawn from me and given to someone else, I should have felt no right to assert a claim on her. If you are not absolutely pledged to Philip, we are neither of us bound.'

'You don't believe that—it is not your real feeling,' said Maggie earnestly. 'You feel, as I do, that the real tie lies in the feelings and expectations we have raised in other minds. Else all pledges might be broken, when there was no outward penalty. There would be no such thing as faithfulness.'

Stephen was silent: he could not pursue that argument; the opposite conviction had wrought in him too strongly through his previous time of struggle. But it soon presented itself in a new form.

'The pledge *can't* be fulfilled,' he said, with impetuous insistence. 'It is unnatural: we can only pretend to give ourselves to anyone else. There is wrong in that too—there may be misery in it for *them* as well as for us. Maggie, you must see that—you do see that.'

He was looking eagerly at her face for the least sign of compliance; his large, firm, gentle grasp was on her hand. She was silent for a few moments, with her eyes fixed on the ground; then she drew a deep breath, and said, looking up at him with solemn sadness:

'O it is difficult—life is very difficult! It seems right to me sometimes that we should follow our strongest feeling; —but then, such feelings continually come across the ties that all our former life has made for us—the ties that have made others dependent on us—and would cut them in two. If life were quite easy and simple, as it might have been in paradise, and we could always see that one being first towards whom . . . I mean, if life did not make duties for us before love comes, love would be a sign that two people ought to belong to each other. But I see—I feel it is not so now: there are things we must renounce in life; some of us must resign love. Many things are difficult and dark to me; but I see one thing quite clearly—that I must not, cannot, seek my own happiness by sacrificing others. Love is natural; but surely pity and faithfulness and memory are natural too. And they would live in me still, and punish me if I did not obey them. I should be haunted by the suffering I had caused. Our love would be poisoned. Don't urge me; help me—help me, *because* I love you.'

Maggie had become more and more earnest as she went on; her face had become flushed, and her eyes fuller and fuller of appealing love. Stephen had the fibre of nobleness in him that vibrated to her appeal: but in the same moment —how could it be otherwise?—that pleading beauty gained new power over him.

'Dearest,' he said, in scarcely more than a whisper, while his arm stole round her, 'I'll do, I'll bear anything you wish. But—one kiss—one—the last—before we part.'

One kiss—and then a long look—until Maggie said tremulously, 'Let me go—let us make haste back.'

She hurried along, and not another word was spoken. Stephen stood still and beckoned when they came within sight of Willy and the horse, and Maggie went on through the gate. Mrs. Moss was standing alone at the door of the old porch: she had sent all the cousins in, with kind thoughtfulness. It might be a joyful thing that Maggie had a rich and handsome lover, but she would naturally feel embarrassed at coming in again:—and it might *not* be joyful. In either case, Mrs. Moss waited anxiously to receive Maggie by herself. The speaking face told plainly enough that, if there was joy, it was of a very agitating, dubious sort.

'Sit down here a bit, my dear.' She drew Maggie into the porch, and sat down on the bench by her:—there was no privacy in the house.

'O aunt Gritty, I'm very wretched. I wish I could have died when I was fifteen. It seemed so easy to give things up then—it is so hard now.'

The poor child threw her arms round her aunt's neck, and fell into long, deep sobs.

XII

A FAMILY PARTY

MAGGIE left her good aunt Gritty at the end of the week, and went to Garum Firs to pay her visit to aunt Pullet according to agreement. In the meantime very unexpected things had happened, and there was to be a family party at Garum to discuss and celebrate a change in the fortunes of the Tullivers, which was likely finally to carry away the shadow of their demerits like the last limb of an eclipse, and cause their hitherto obscured virtues to shine forth in full-rounded splendour. It is pleasant to know that a new ministry just come into office are not the only fellow-men who enjoy a period of high appreciation and full-blown eulogy: in many respectable families throughout this realm, relatives becoming creditable meet with a similar cordiality of recognition, which, in its fine freedom from the coercion of any antecedents, suggests the hopeful possibility that we may some day without any notice find ourselves in full millennium, with cockatrices who have ceased to bite, and wolves that no longer show their teeth with any but the blandest intentions.

Lucy came so early as to have the start even of aunt Glegg; for she longed to have some undisturbed talk with Maggie about the wonderful news. It seemed—did it not? said Lucy, with her prettiest air of wisdom—as if everything, even other people's misfortunes (poor creatures!) were conspiring now to make poor dear aunt Tulliver, and cousin Tom, and naughty Maggie too, if she were not obstinately bent on the contrary, as happy as they deserved to be after all their troubles. To think that the very day— the *very day*—after Tom had come back from Newcastle, that unfortunate young Jetsome, whom Mr. Wakem had placed at the Mill, had been pitched off his horse in a drunken fit, and was lying at St. Ogg's in a dangerous state, so that Wakem had signified his wish that the new purchasers should enter on the premises at once! It was very dreadful for that unhappy young man, but it did seem as if the misfortune had happened then, rather than at any other time, in order that cousin Tom might all the sooner have the fit reward of his exemplary conduct—papa thought so very highly of him. Aunt Tulliver must certainly go to the Mill now, and keep house for Tom: that was rather a loss to Lucy in the matter of household comfort; but then, to think of poor aunty being in her old place again, and gradually getting comforts about her there!

On this last point Lucy had her cunning projects, and when she and Maggie had made their dangerous way down the bright stairs into the handsome parlour, where the very sunbeams seemed cleaner than elsewhere, she directed her manœuvres, as any other great tactician would have done, against the weaker side of the enemy.

'Aunt Pullet,' she said, seating herself on the sofa, and caressingly adjusting that lady's floating cap-string, 'I want you to make up your mind what linen and things you will give Tom towards housekeeping; because you're always so generous—you give such nice things, you know; and if you set the example, aunt Glegg will follow.'

'That she never can, my dear,' said Mrs. Pullet, with

unusual vigour, 'for she hasn't got the linen to follow suit wi' mine, I can tell you. She'd niver the taste, not if she'd spend the money. Big checks and live things, like stags and foxes, all her table-linen is—not a spot nor a diamont among 'em. But it's poor work, dividing one's linen before one dies—I niver thought to ha' done that, Bessy,' Mrs. Pullet continued, shaking her head and looking at her sister Tulliver, 'when you and me chose the double diamont, the first flax iver we'd spun—and the Lord knows where yours is gone.'

'I'd no choice, I'm sure, sister,' said poor Mrs. Tulliver, accustomed to consider herself in the light of an accused person. 'I'm sure it was no wish o' mine, iver, as I should lie awake o' nights thinking o' my best bleached linen all over the country.'

'Take a peppermint, Mrs. Tulliver,' said uncle Pullet, feeling that he was offering a cheap and wholesome form of comfort, which he was recommending by example.

'O but, aunt Pullet,' said Lucy, 'you've so much beautiful linen. And suppose you had had daughters! Then you must have divided it, when they were married.'

'Well, I don't say as I won't do it,' said Mrs. Pullet, 'for now Tom's so lucky, it's nothing but right his friends should look on him and help him. There's the table-cloths I bought at your sale, Bessy; it was nothing but good natur' o' me to buy 'em, for they've been lying in the chest ever since. But I'm not going to give Maggie any more o' my Indy muslin and things, if she's to go into service again, when she might stay and keep me company, and do my sewing for me, if she wasn't wanted at her brother's.'

'Going into service,' was the expression by which the Dodson mind represented to itself the position of teacher or governess, and Maggie's return to that menial condition, now circumstances offered her more eligible prospects, was likely to be a sore point with all her relatives, besides Lucy. Maggie in her crude form, with her hair down her back, and altogether in a state of dubious promise, was a most undesirable niece; but now she was capable of being at once ornamental and useful. The subject was revived in aunt and uncle Glegg's presence, over the tea and muffins.

'Hegh, hegh!' said Mr. Glegg, good-naturedly patting Maggie on the back, 'nonsense, nonsense! Don't let us hear of you taking a place again, Maggie. Why, you must ha' picked up half-a-dozen sweethearts at the bazaar: isn't there one of 'em the right sort of article? Come, now?'

'Mr. Glegg,' said his wife, with that shade of increased politeness in her severity which she always put on with her crisper fronts, 'you'll excuse me, but you're far too light for a man of your years. It's respect and duty to her aunts, and the rest of her kin as are so good to her, should have kept my niece from fixing about going away again without consulting us—not sweethearts, if I'm to use such a word, though it was never heard in *my* family.'

'Why, what did they call us, when we went to see 'em, then, eh, neighbour Pullet? They thought us sweet enough then,' said Mr. Glegg, winking pleasantly, while Mr. Pullet, at the suggestion of sweetness, took a little more sugar.

'Mr. Glegg,' said Mrs. G., 'if you're going to be undelicate, let me know.'

'La, Jane, your husband's only joking,' said Mrs. Pullet; 'let him joke while he's got health and strength. There's poor Mr. Tilt got his mouth drawn all o' one side, and couldn't laugh if he was to try.'

'I'll trouble you for the muffineer, then, Mr. Glegg,' said Mrs. G., 'if I may be so bold to interrupt your joking. Though it's other people must see the joke in a niece's putting a slight on her mother's eldest sister, as is the head o' the family; and only coming in and out on short visits, all the time she's been in the town, and then settling to go away without my knowledge—as I'd laid caps out on purpose for her to make 'em up for me,—and me as have divided my money so equal——'

'Sister,' Mrs. Tulliver broke in anxiously, 'I'm sure Maggie never thought o' going away without staying at your house as well as the others. Not as it's my wish she should go away at all—but quite contrary. I'm sure I'm innocent. I've said over and over again, "My dear, you've no call to go away." But there's ten days or a fortnight Maggie'll have before she's fixed to go: she can stay at your house just as well, and I'll step in when I can, and so will Lucy.'

'Bessy,' said Mrs. Glegg, 'if you'd exercise a little more thought, you might know I should hardly think it was worth while to unpin a bed, and go to all that trouble now, just at the end o' the time, when our house isn't above a quarter of an hour's walk from Mr. Deane's. She can come the first thing in the morning, and go back the last at night, and be thankful she's got a good aunt so close to her to come and sit with. I know *I* should, when I was her age.'

'La, Jane,' said Mrs. Pullet, 'it 'ud do your beds good to have somebody to sleep in 'em. There's that striped room smells dreadful mouldy, and the glass mildewed like anything. I'm sure I thought I should be struck with death when you took me in.'

'O, there is Tom!' exclaimed Lucy, clapping her hands. 'He's come on Sindbad, as I told him. I was afraid he was not going to keep his promise.'

Maggie jumped up to kiss Tom as he entered, with strong feeling, at this first meeting since the prospect of returning to the Mill had been opened to him; and she kept his hand, leading him to the chair by her side. To have no cloud between herself and Tom was still a perpetual yearning in her, that had its root deeper than all change. He smiled at her very kindly this evening, and said, 'Well, Magsie, how's aunt Moss?'

'Come, come, sir,' said Mr. Glegg, putting out his hand. 'Why, you're such a big man, you carry all before you, it seems. You're come into your luck a good deal earlier than us old folks did—but I wish you joy, I wish you joy. You'll get the Mill all for your own again, some day, I'll be bound. You won't stop half-way up the hill.'

'But I hope he'll bear in mind as it's his mother's family as he owes it to,' said Mrs. Glegg. 'If he hadn't had them to take after, he'd ha' been poorly off. There was never any failures, nor lawing, nor wastefulness in our family—nor dying without wills——'

'No, nor sudden deaths,' said aunt Pullet; 'allays the doctor called in. But Tom had the Dodson skin: I said that from the first. And I don't know what *you* mean to do, sister Glegg, but I mean to give him a table-cloth of all my three biggest sizes but one, besides sheets. I don't say what more I shall do; but *that* I shall do, and if I should die to-morrow, Mr. Pullet, you'll bear it in mind—though you'll be blundering with the keys, and never remember as that on the third shelf o' the left-hand wardrobe, behind the night-caps with the broad ties—not the narrow-frilled uns—is the key o' the drawer in the Blue Room, where the key o' the Blue Closet is. You'll make a mistake, and I shall niver be worthy to know it. You've a memory for my pills and draughts, wonderful—I'll allays say that of you—but you're lost among the keys.' This gloomy prospect of the confusion that would ensue on her decease, was very affecting to Mrs. Pullet.

'You carry it too far, Sophy—that locking in and out,' said Mrs. Glegg, in a tone of some disgust at this folly. 'You go beyond your own family. There's nobody can say I don't lock up; but I do what's reasonable, and no more. And as for the linen, I shall look out what's serviceable, to make a present of to my nephew: I've got cloth as has never been whittened, better worth having than other people's fine holland; and I hope he'll lie down in it and think of his aunt.'

Tom thanked Mrs. Glegg, but evaded any promise to meditate nightly on her virtues; and Mr. Glegg effected a diversion for him by asking about Mr. Deane's intentions concerning steam.

Lucy had had her far-sighted views in begging Tom to come on Sindbad. It appeared, when it was time to go home, that the man-servant was to ride the horse, and cousin Tom was to drive home his mother and Lucy. 'You must sit by yourself, aunty,' said that contriving young lady, 'because I must sit by Tom; I've a great deal to say to him.'

In the eagerness of her affectionate anxiety for Maggie, Lucy could not persuade herself to defer a conversation about her with Tom, who, she thought, with such a cup of joy before him as this rapid fulfilment of his wish about the Mill, must become pliant and flexible. Her nature supplied her with no key to Tom's; and she was puzzled as well as pained to notice the unpleasant change on his countenance when she gave him the history of the way in which Philip had used his influence with his father. She had counted on this revelation as a great stroke of policy, which was to turn Tom's heart towards Philip at once, and, besides that, prove that the elder Wakem was ready to receive Maggie with all the honours of a daughter-in-law. Nothing was wanted, then, but for dear Tom, who always had that pleasant smile when he looked at cousin Lucy, to turn completely round, say the opposite of what he had always said before, and declare that he, for his part, was delighted that all the old grievances should be healed, and that Maggie should have Philip with all suitable despatch: in cousin Lucy's opinion nothing could be easier.

But to minds strongly marked by the positive and negative qualities that create severity--strength of will, conscious rectitude of purpose, narrowness of imagination and intellect, great power of self-control, and a disposition to exert control over others—prejudices come as the natural food of tendencies which can get no sustenance out of that complex, fragmentary, doubt-provoking knowledge which we call truth. Let a prejudice be bequeathed, carried in the air, adopted by hearsay, caught in through the eye—however it may come, these minds will give it a habitation: it is something to assert strongly and bravely, something to fill up the void of spontaneous ideas, something to impose on others with the authority of conscious right: it is at once a staff and a baton. Every prejudice that will answer these purposes is self-evident. Our good upright Tom Tulliver's mind was of this class: his inward criticism of his father's faults did not prevent him from adopting his father's prejudice; it was a prejudice against a man of lax principle and lax life, and it was a meeting-point for all the disappointed feelings of family and personal pride. Other feelings added their force to produce Tom's bitter repugnance to Philip, and to Maggie's union with him; and notwithstanding Lucy's power over her strong-willed cousin, she got nothing but a cold refusal ever to sanction such a marriage: 'but of course Maggie could do as she liked—she had declared her determination to be independent. For Tom's part, he held himself bound by his duty to his father's memory, and by every manly feeling, never to consent to any relation with the Wakems.'

Thus, all that Lucy had effected by her zealous mediation was to fill Tom's mind with the expectation that Maggie's perverse resolve to go into a situation again would presently metamorphose itself, as her resolves were apt to do, into something equally perverse, but entirely different —a marriage with Philip Wakem.

XIII

BORNE ALONG BY THE TIDE

IN less than a week Maggie was at St. Ogg's again,—outwardly in much the same position as when her visit there had just begun. It was easy for her to fill her mornings apart from Lucy without any obvious effort; for she had her promised visits to pay to her aunt Glegg, and it was natural that she should give her mother more than usual of her companionship in these last weeks, especially as there were preparations to be thought of for Tom's housekeeping. But Lucy would hear of no pretext for her remaining away in the evenings: she must always come from aunt Glegg's before dinner—'else what shall I have of you?' said Lucy, with a tearful pout that could not be resisted. And Mr. Stephen Guest had unaccountably taken to dining at Mr. Deane's as often as possible, instead of avoiding that, as he used to do. At first he began his mornings with a resolution that he would not dine there—not even go in the evening, till Maggie was away. He had even devised a plan of starting off on a journey in this agreeable June weather: the headaches which he had constantly been alleging as a ground for stupidity and silence were a sufficient ostensible motive. But the journey was not taken, and by the fourth morning no distinct resolution was formed about the evenings: they were only foreseen as times when Maggie would still be present for a little while—when one more touch, one more glance, might be snatched. For, why not? There was nothing to conceal between them: they knew—they had confessed their love, and they had renounced each other: they were going to part. Honour and conscience were going to divide them: Maggie, with that appeal from her inmost soul, had decided it; but surely they might cast a lingering look at each other across the gulf, before they turned away never to look again till that strange light had for ever faded out of their eyes.

Maggie, all this time, moved about with a quiescence and even torpor of manner, so contrasted with her usual fitful brightness and ardour, that Lucy would have had to seek some other cause for such a change, if she had not been convinced that the position in which Maggie stood between Philip and her brother, and the prospect of her self-imposed wearisome banishment, were quite enough to account for a large amount of depression. But under this torpor there was a fierce battle of emotion, such as Maggie in all her life of struggle had never known or foreboded: it seemed to her as if all the worst evil in her had lain in ambush till now, and had suddenly started up full-armed, with hideous, overpowering strength! There were moments in which a cruel selfishness seemed to be getting possession of her: why should not Lucy—why should not Philip suffer? *She* had had to suffer through many years of her life; and who had renounced anything for her? And when something like that fulness of existence—love, wealth, ease, refinement, all that her nature craved—was brought within her reach, why was she to forego it, that another might have it—another, who perhaps needed it less? But amidst all this new passionate tumult there were the old voices making themselves heard with rising power, till, from time to time, the tumult seemed quelled. *Was* that existence which tempted her the full existence she dreamed? Where, then, would be all the memories of early striving—all the deep pity for another's pain, which had been nurtured in her through years of affection and hardship—all the divine presentiment of something higher than mere personal enjoyment, which had made the sacredness of life? She might as well hope to enjoy walking by maiming her feet, as hope to enjoy an existence in which she set out by maiming the faith and sympathy that were the best organs of her soul. And then, if pain were so hard to *her*, what was it to others?—'Ah, God! preserve me from inflicting—give me strength to bear it.'—How had she sunk into this struggle with a temptation that she would once have thought herself as secure from, as from deliberate crime? When was that first hateful moment in which she had been conscious of a feeling that clashed with her truth, affection, and gratitude, and had not shaken it from her with horror, as if it had been a loathsome thing?—And yet, since this strange, sweet, subduing influence did not, should not, conquer her—since it was to remain simply her own suffering . . . her mind was meeting Stephen's in that thought of his, that they might still snatch moments of mute confession before the parting came. For was not he suffering too? She saw it daily—saw it in the sickened look of fatigue with which, as soon as he was not compelled to exert himself, he relapsed into indifference towards everything but the possibility of watching her. Could she refuse sometimes to answer that beseeching look which she felt to be following her like a low murmur of love and pain? She refused it less and less, till at last the evening for them both was sometimes made of a moment's mutual gaze: they thought of it till it came, and when it had come, they thought of nothing else. One other thing Stephen seemed now and then to care for, and that was, to sing: it was a way of speaking to Maggie. Perhaps he was not distinctly conscious that he was impelled to it by a secret longing—running counter to all his self-confessed resolves—to deepen the hold he had on her. Watch your own speech, and notice how it is guided by your less conscious purposes, and you will understand that contradiction in Stephen.

Philip Wakem was a less frequent visitor, but he came

occasionally in the evening, and it happened that he was there when Lucy said, as they sat out on the lawn, near sunset:

'Now Maggie's tale of visits to aunt Glegg is completed, I mean that we shall go out boating every day until she goes. She has not had half enough boating because of these tiresome visits, and she likes it better than anything. Don't you, Maggie?'

'Better than any sort of locomotion, I hope you mean,' said Philip, smiling at Maggie, who was lolling backward in a low garden-chair, 'else she will be selling her soul to that ghostly boatman who haunts the Floss—only for the sake of being drifted in a boat for ever.'

'Should you like to be her boatman?' said Lucy. 'Because, if you would, you can come with us and take an oar. If the Floss were but a quiet lake instead of a river, we should be independent of any gentleman, for Maggie can row splendidly. As it is, we are reduced to ask services of knights and squires, who do not seem to offer them with great alacrity.'

She looked playful reproach at Stephen, who was sauntering up and down, and was just singing in pianissimo falsetto:

'*The thirst that from the soul doth rise,*
Doth ask a drink divine.'

He took no notice, but still kept aloof: he had done so frequently during Philip's recent visits.

'You don't seem inclined for boating,' said Lucy, when he came to sit down by her on the bench. 'Doesn't rowing suit you now?'

'O, I hate a large party in a boat,' he said, almost irritably. 'I'll come when you have no one else.'

Lucy coloured, feeling that Philip would be hurt: it was quite a new thing for Stephen to speak in that way; but he had certainly not been well of late. Philip coloured too, but less from a feeling of personal offence than from a vague suspicion that Stephen's moodiness had some relation to Maggie, who had started up from her chair as he spoke, and had walked towards the hedge of laurels to look at the descending sunlight on the river.

'As Miss Deane didn't know she was excluding others by inviting me,' said Philip, 'I am bound to resign.'

'No, indeed, you shall not,' said Lucy, much vexed. 'I particularly wish for your company to-morrow. The tide will suit at half-past ten: it will be a delicious time for a couple of hours to row to Luckreth and walk back, before the sun gets too hot. And how can you object to four people in a boat?' she added, looking at Stephen.

'I don't object to the people, but the number,' said Stephen, who had recovered himself, and was rather ashamed of his rudeness. 'If I voted for a fourth at all, of course it would be you, Phil. But we won't divide the pleasure of escorting the ladies; we'll take it alternately. I'll go the next day.'

This incident had the effect of drawing Philip's attention with freshened solicitude towards Stephen and Maggie; but when they re-entered the house, music was proposed, and Mrs. Tulliver and Mr. Deane being occupied with cribbage, Maggie sat apart near the table where the books and work were placed—doing nothing, however, but listening abstractedly to the music. Stephen presently turned to a duet which he insisted that Lucy and Philip should sing: he had often done the same thing before; but this evening Philip thought he divined some double intention in every word and look of Stephen's, and watched him keenly—angry with himself all the while for this clinging suspicion. For had not Maggie virtually denied any ground for his doubts on her side? and she was truth itself: it was impossible not to believe her word and glance when they had last spoken together in the garden. Stephen might be strongly fascinated by her (what was more natural?), but Philip felt himself rather base for intruding on what must be his friend's painful secret. Still, he watched. Stephen, moving away from the piano, sauntered slowly towards the table near which Maggie sat, and turned over the newspapers, apparently in mere idleness. Then he seated himself with his back to the piano, dragging a newspaper under his elbow, and thrusting his hand through his hair, as if he had been attracted by some bit of local news in the *Laceham Courier*. He was in reality looking at Maggie, who had not taken the slightest notice of his approach. She had always additional strength of resistance when Philip was present, just as we can restrain our speech better in a spot that we feel to be hallowed. But at last she heard the word 'dearest' uttered in the softest tone of pained entreaty, like that of a patient who asks for something that ought to have been given without asking. She had never heard that word since the moments in the lane at Basset, when it had come from Stephen again and again, almost as involuntarily as if it had been an inarticulate cry. Philip could hear no word, but he had moved to the opposite side of the piano, and could see Maggie start and blush, raise her eyes an instant towards Stephen's face, but immediately look apprehensively towards himself. It was not evident to her that Philip had observed her; but a pang of shame, under the sense of this concealment, made her move from her chair and walk to her mother's side to watch the game at cribbage.

Philip went home soon after in a state of hideous doubt mingled with wretched certainty. It was impossible for him now to resist the conviction that there was some mutual consciousness between Stephen and Maggie; and for half the night his irritable, susceptible nerves were pressed upon almost to frenzy by that one wretched fact: he could attempt no explanation that would reconcile it with her words and actions. When, at last, the need for belief in Maggie rose to its habitual predominance, he was not long in imagining the truth:—she was struggling, she was banishing herself—this was the clue to all he had seen since his return. But athwart that belief there came other possibilities that would not be driven out of sight. His imagination wrought out the whole story: Stephen was madly in love with her; he must have told her so; she had rejected him, and was hurrying away. But would he give her up, knowing—Philip felt the fact with heart-crushing despair—that she was made half helpless by her feeling towards him?

When the morning came, Philip was too ill to think of keeping his engagement to go in the boat. In his present agitation he could decide on nothing: he could only alternate between contradictory intentions. First, he thought he must have an interview with Maggie, and entreat her to confide in him; then again, he distrusted his own interference. Had he not been thrusting himself on Maggie all along? She had uttered words long ago in her young ignorance; it was enough to make her hate him that these should be continually present with her as a bond. And had he any right to ask her for a revelation of feelings which she had evidently intended to withhold from him? He would not trust himself to see her, till he had assured himself that he could act from pure anxiety for her, and not from egoistic irritation. He wrote a brief note to Stephen, and sent it early by the servant, saying that he was not well enough to fulfil his engagement to Miss Deane. Would Stephen take his excuse, and fill his place?

Lucy had arranged a charming plan, which had made her quite content with Stephen's refusal to go in the boat. She discovered that her father was to drive to Lindum this morning at ten: Lindum was the very place she wanted to go to, to make purchases—important purchases, which must by no means be put off to another opportunity; and aunt Tulliver must go too, because she was concerned in some of the purchases.

'You will have your row in the boat just the same, you know,' she said to Maggie when they went out of the breakfast-room and up-stairs together; 'Philip will be here at half-past ten, and it is a delicious morning. Now, don't say a word against it, you dear dolorous thing. What is the use of my being a fairy godmother, if you set your face against all the wonders I work for you? Don't think of awful cousin Tom: you may disobey him a little.'

Maggie did not persist in objecting. She was almost glad of the plan; for perhaps it would bring her some strength and calmness to be alone with Philip again: it was like revisiting the scene of a quieter life, in which the very struggles were repose, compared with the daily tumult of the present. She prepared herself for the boat, and at half-past ten sat waiting in the drawing-room.

The ring of the door-bell was punctual, and she was thinking with half-sad, affectionate pleasure of the surprise Philip would have in finding that he was to be with her alone, when she distinguished a firm rapid step across the hall, that was certainly not Philip's: the door opened, and Stephen Guest entered.

In the first moment they were both too much agitated to speak; for Stephen had learned from the servant that the others were gone out. Maggie had started up and sat down again, with her heart beating violently; and Stephen, throwing down his cap and gloves, came and sat by her in silence. She thought Philip would be coming soon; and with great effort—for she trembled visibly—she rose to go to a distant chair.

'He is not coming,' said Stephen, in a low tone. '*I* am going in the boat.'

'O, we can't go,' said Maggie, sinking into her chair again. 'Lucy did not expect—she would be hurt. Why is not Philip come?'

'He is not well; he asked me to come instead.'

'Lucy is gone to Lindum,' said Maggie, taking off her bonnet, with hurried, trembling fingers. 'We must not go.'

'Very well,' said Stephen dreamily, looking at her, as he rested his arm on the back of his chair. 'Then we'll stay here.'

He was looking into her deep, deep eyes—far-off and mysterious as the starlit blackness, and yet very near, and timidly loving. Maggie sat perfectly still—perhaps for moments, perhaps for minutes—until the helpless trembling had ceased, and there was a warm glow on her cheek.

'The man is waiting—he has taken the cushions,' she said. 'Will you go and tell him?'

'What shall I tell him?' said Stephen, almost in a whisper.

He was looking at the lips now.

Maggie made no answer.

'Let us go,' Stephen murmured entreatingly, rising, and

taking her hand to raise her too. 'We shall not be long together.'

And they went. Maggie felt that she was being led down the garden among the roses, being helped with firm tender care into the boat, having the cushion and cloak arranged for her feet, and her parasol opened for her (which she had forgotten)—all by this stronger presence that seemed to bear her along without any act of her own will, like the added self which comes with the sudden exalting influence of a strong tonic—and she felt nothing else. Memory was excluded.

They glided rapidly along, Stephen rowing, helped by the backward-flowing tide, past the Tofton trees and houses—on between the silent sunny fields and pastures, which seemed filled with a natural joy that had no reproach for theirs. The breath of the young, unwearied day, the delicious rhythmic dip of the oars, the fragmentary song of a passing bird heard now and then, as if it were only the overflowing of brim-full gladness, the sweet solitude of a twofold consciousness that was mingled into one by that grave untiring gaze which need not be averted—what else could there be in their minds for the first hour? Some low, subdued, languid exclamation of love came from Stephen from time to time, as he went on rowing idly, half automatically: otherwise, they spoke no word; for what could words have been but an inlet to thought? and thought did not belong to that enchanted haze in which they were enveloped—it belonged to the past and the future that lay outside the haze. Maggie was only dimly conscious of the banks, as they passed them, and dwelt with no recognition on the villages: she knew there were several to be passed before they reached Luckreth, where they always stopped and left the boat. At all times she was so liable to fits of absence, that she was likely enough to let her way-marks pass unnoticed.

But at last Stephen, who had been rowing more and more idly, ceased to row, laid down the oars, folded his arms, and looked down on the water as if watching the pace at which the boat glided without his help. This sudden change roused Maggie. She looked at the far-stretching fields—at the banks close by—and felt that they were entirely strange to her. A terrible alarm took possession of her.

'O, have we passed Luckreth—where we were to stop?' she exclaimed, looking back to see if the place were out of sight. No village was to be seen. She turned round again, with a look of distressed questioning at Stephen.

He went on watching the water, and said, in a strange, dreamy, absent tone, 'Yes—a long way.'

'O what shall I do?' cried Maggie, in an agony. 'We shall not get home for hours—and Lucy—O God, help me!'

She clasped her hands and broke into a sob, like a frightened child: she thought of nothing but of meeting Lucy, and seeing her look of pained surprise and doubt—perhaps of just upbraiding.

Stephen moved and sat near her, and gently drew down the clasped hands.

'Maggie,' he said, in a deep tone of slow decision, 'let us never go home again—till no one can part us—till we are married.'

The unusual tone, the startling words, arrested Maggie's sob, and she sat quite still—wondering: as if Stephen might have seen some possibilities that would alter everything, and annul the wretched facts.

'See, Maggie, how everything has come without our seeking—in spite of all our efforts. We never thought of being alone together again: it has all been done by others. See how the tide is carrying us out—away from all those unnatural bonds that we have been trying to make faster round us—and trying in vain. It will carry us on to Torby, and we can land there, and get some carriage, and hurry on to York and then to Scotland—and never pause a moment till we are bound to each other, so that only death can part us. It is the only right thing, dearest: it is the only way of escaping from this wretched entanglement. Everything has concurred to point it out to us. We have contrived nothing, we have thought of nothing ourselves.'

Stephen spoke with deep, earnest pleading. Maggie

listened—passing from her startled wonderment to the yearning after that belief, that the tide was doing it all—that she might glide along with the swift, silent stream, and not struggle any more. But across that stealing influence came the terrible shadow of past thoughts; and the sudden horror lest now, at last, the moment of fatal intoxication was close upon her, called up feelings of angry resistance towards Stephen.

'Let me go!' she said, in an agitated tone, flashing an indignant look at him, and trying to get her hands free. 'You have wanted to deprive me of any choice. You knew we were come too far—you have dared to take advantage of my thoughtlessness. It is unmanly to bring me into such a position.'

Stung by this reproach, he released her hands, moved back to his former place, and folded his arms, in a sort of desperation at the difficulty Maggie's words had made present to him. If she would not consent to go on, he must curse himself for the embarrassment he had led her into. But the reproach was the unendurable thing: the one thing worse than parting with her was, that she should feel he had acted unworthily towards her. At last he said, in a tone of suppressed rage:

'I didn't notice that we had passed Luckreth till we had got to the next village; and then it came into my mind that we would go on. I can't justify it: I ought to have told you. It is enough to make you hate me—since you don't love me well enough to make everything else indifferent to you, as I do you. Shall I stop the boat, and try to get you out here? I'll tell Lucy that I was mad—and that you hate me—and you shall be clear of me for ever. No one can blame you, because I have behaved unpardonably to you.'

Maggie was paralysed: it was easier to resist Stephen's pleading, than this picture he had called up of himself suffering while she was vindicated—easier even to turn away from his look of tenderness than from this look of angry misery, that seemed to place her in selfish isolation from him. He had called up a state of feeling in which the reasons which had acted on her conscience seemed to be transmuted into mere self-regard. The indignant fire in her eyes was quenched, and she began to look at him with timid distress. She had reproached him for being hurried into irrevocable trespass—she, who had been so weak herself.

'As if I shouldn't feel what happened to you—just the same,' she said, with reproach of another kind—the reproach of love, asking for more trust. This yielding to the idea of Stephen's suffering was more fatal than the other yielding, because it was less distinguishable from that sense of others' claims which was the moral basis of her resistance.

He felt all the relenting in her look and tone—it was heaven opening again. He moved to her side, and took her hand, leaning his elbow on the back of the boat, and saying nothing. He dreaded to utter another word, he dreaded to make another movement, that might provoke another reproach or denial from her. Life hung on her consent: everything else was hopeless, confused, sickening misery. They glided along in this way, both resting in that silence as in a haven, both dreading lest their feelings should be divided again—till they became aware that the clouds had gathered, and that the slightest perceptible freshening of the breeze was growing and growing, so that the whole character of the day was altered.

'You will be chill, Maggie, in this thin dress. Let me raise the cloak over your shoulders. Get up an instant, dearest.'

Maggie obeyed: there was an unspeakable charm in being told what to do, and having everything decided for her. She sat down again covered with the cloak, and Stephen took to his oars again, making haste; for they must try to get to Torby as fast as they could. Maggie was hardly conscious of having said or done anything decisive. All yielding is attended with a less vivid consciousness than resistance; it is the partial sleep of thought; it is the submergence of our own personality by another. Every influence tended to lull her into acquiescence: that dreamy gliding in the boat, which had lasted for four hours, and had brought some weariness and exhaustion—the recoil of her fatigued sensations from the impracticable difficulty of getting out of the boat at this unknown distance from home, and walking for long miles—all helped to bring her into more complete subjection to that strong mysterious charm which made a last parting from Stephen seem the death of all joy, and made the thought of wounding him like the first touch of the torturing iron before which resolution shrank. And then there was the present happiness of being with him, which was enough to absorb all her languid energy.

Presently Stephen observed a vessel coming after them. Several vessels, among them the steamer to Mudport, had passed them with the early tide, but for the last hour they had seen none. He looked more and more eagerly at this vessel, as if a new thought had come into his mind along with it, and then he looked at Maggie hesitatingly.

'Maggie, dearest,' he said, at last, 'if this vessel should be going to Mudport, or to any convenient place on the coast northward, it would be our best plan to get them to take us on board. You are fatigued—and it may soon rain—it may be a wretched business, getting to Torby in this boat. It's only a trading-vessel, but I daresay you can be made tolerably comfortable. We'll take the cushions out of the boat. It is really our best plan. They'll be glad enough to take us: I've got plenty of money about me; I can pay them well.'

Maggie's heart began to beat with reawakened alarm at this new proposition; but she was silent—one course seemed as difficult as another.

Stephen hailed the vessel. It was a Dutch vessel going to Mudport, the English mate informed him, and, if this wind held, would be there in less than two days.

'We had got out too far with our boat,' said Stephen. 'I was trying to make for Torby. But I'm afraid of the weather; and this lady—my wife—will be exhausted with fatigue and hunger. Take us on board—will you?—and haul up the boat. I'll pay you well.'

Maggie, now really faint and trembling with fear, was taken on board, making an interesting object of contemplation to admiring Dutchmen. The mate feared the lady would have a poor time of it on board, for they had no accommodation for such entirely unlooked-for passengers— no private cabin larger than an old-fashioned church-pew. But at least they had Dutch cleanliness, which makes all other inconveniences tolerable; and the boat-cushions were spread into a couch for Maggie on the poop with all alacrity. But to pace up and down the deck leaning on Stephen— being upheld by his strength—was the first change that she needed: then came food, and then quiet reclining on the cushions, with the sense that no new resolution *could* be taken that day. Everything must wait till to-morrow. Stephen sat beside her with her hand in his; they could only speak to each other in low tones: only look at each other now and then, for it would take a long while to dull the curiosity of the five men on board, and reduce these handsome young strangers to that minor degree of interest, which belongs, in a sailor's regard, to all objects nearer than the horizon. But Stephen was triumphantly happy. Every other thought or care was thrown into unmarked perspective by the certainty that Maggie must be his. The leap had been taken now: he had been tortured by scruples, he had fought fiercely with overmastering inclination, he had hesitated; but repentance was impossible. He murmured forth in fragmentary sentences his happiness—his adoration—his tenderness—his belief that their life together must be heaven—that her presence with him would give rapture to every common day—that to satisfy her lightest wish was dearer to him than all other bliss—that everything was easy for her sake, except to part with her, and now they never *would* part; he would belong to her for ever, and all that was his was hers—had no value for him except as it was hers. Such things, uttered in low broken tones by the one voice that has first stirred the fibre of young passion, have only a feeble effect—on experienced minds at a distance from them. To poor Maggie they were very near: they were like nectar held close to thirsty lips: there was, there *must* be, then, a life for mortals here below which was not hard and chill—in which affection would no longer be self-sacrifice. Stephen's passionate words made the vision of such a life more fully present to her than it had ever been before; and the vision for the time excluded all realities—all except the returning sun-gleams which broke out on the waters as the evening approached, and mingled with the visionary sunlight of promised happiness—all except the hand that pressed hers, and the voice that spoke to her, and the eyes that looked at her with grave, unspeakable love.

There was to be no rain, after all; the clouds rolled off to the horizon again, making the great purple rampart and long purple isles of that wondrous land which reveals itself to us when the sun goes down—the land that the evening star watches over. Maggie was to sleep all night on the poop; it was better than going below, and she was covered with the warmest wrappings the ship could furnish. It was still early, when the fatigues of the day brought on a drowsy longing for perfect rest, and she laid down her head, looking at the faint dying flush in the west, where the one golden lamp was getting brighter and brighter. Then she looked up at Stephen, who was still seated by her, hanging over her as he leaned his arm against the vessel's side. Behind all the delicious visions of these last hours, which had flowed over her like a soft stream, and made her entirely passive, there was the dim consciousness that the condition was a transient one, and that the morrow must bring back the old life of struggle—that there were thoughts which would presently avenge themselves for this oblivion. But now nothing was distinct to her: she was being lulled to sleep with that soft stream still flowing over her, with those delicious visions melting and fading like the wondrous aërial land of the west.

XIV

WAKING

WHEN Maggie was gone to sleep, Stephen, weary too with his unaccustomed amount of rowing, and with the intense inward life of the last twelve hours, but too restless to sleep, walked and lounged about the deck with his cigar far on into midnight, not seeing the dark water—hardly conscious there were stars—living only in the near and distant future. At last fatigue conquered restlessness, and he rolled himself up in a piece of tarpauling on the deck near Maggie's feet.

She had fallen asleep before nine, and had been sleeping for six hours before the faintest hint of a mid-summer day-break was discernible. She awoke from that vivid dreaming which makes the margin of our deeper rest: She was in a boat on the wide water with Stephen, and in the gathering darkness something like a star appeared, that grew and grew till they saw it was the Virgin seated in St. Ogg's boat, and it came nearer and nearer, till they saw the Virgin was Lucy and the boatman was Philip—no, not Philip, but her brother, who rowed past without looking at her; and she rose to stretch out her arms and call to him, and their own boat turned over with the movement, and they began to sink, till with one spasm of dread she seemed to awake, and find she was a child again in the parlour at evening twilight, and Tom was not really angry. From the soothed sense of that false waking she passed to the real waking—to the plash of water against the vessel, and the sound of a footstep on the deck, and the awful starlit sky. There was a moment of utter bewilderment before her mind could get disentangled from the confused web of dreams; but soon the whole terrible truth urged itself upon her. Stephen was not by her now: she was alone with her own memory and her own dread. The irrevocable wrong that must blot her life had been committed: she had brought sorrow into the lives of others—into the lives that were knit up with hers by trust and love. The feeling of a few short weeks had hurried her into the sins her nature had most recoiled from—breach of faith and cruel selfishness; she had rent the ties that had given meaning to duty, and had made herself an outlawed soul, with no guide but the wayward choice of her own passion. And where would that lead her?—where had it led her now? She had said she would rather die than fall into that temptation. She felt it now—now that the consequences of such a fall had come before the outward act was completed. There was at least this fruit from all her years of striving after the highest and best—that her soul, though betrayed, beguiled, ensnared, could never deliberately consent to a choice of the lower. And a choice of what? O God—not a choice of joy, but of conscious cruelty and hardness; for could she ever cease to see before her Lucy and Philip, with their murdered trust and hopes? Her life with Stephen could have no sacredness: she must for ever sink and wander vaguely, driven by uncertain impulse; for she had let go the clue of life—that clue which once in the far-off years her young need had clutched so strongly. She had renounced all delights then, before she knew them, before they had come within her reach. Philip had been right when he told her that she knew nothing of renunciation: she had thought it was quiet ecstasy; she saw it face to face now—that sad patient loving strength which holds the clue of life—and saw that the thorns were for ever pressing on its brow. The yesterday, which could never be revoked—if she could have changed it now for any length of inward silent endurance, she would have bowed beneath that cross with a sense of rest.

Daybreak came and the reddening eastern light, while her past life was grasping her in this way, with that tightening clutch which comes in the last moments of possible rescue. She could see Stephen now lying on the deck still fast asleep, and with the sight of him there came a wave of anguish that found its way in a long-suppressed sob. The worst bitterness of parting—the thought that urged the sharpest inward cry for help, was the pain it must give to *him*. But surmounting everything was the horror at her own possible failure, the dread lest her conscience should be benumbed again, and not rise to energy till it was too late.—Too late! it was too late already not to have caused misery: too late for everything, perhaps, but to rush away from the last act of baseness—the tasting of joys that were wrung from crushed hearts.

The sun was rising now, and Maggie started up with the sense that a day of resistance was beginning for her. Her eyelashes were still wet with tears, as with her shawl over her head, she sat looking at the slowly-rounding sun. Something roused Stephen too, and, getting up from his hard bed, he came to sit beside her. The sharp instinct of anxious love saw something to give him alarm in the very first glance. He had a hovering dread of some resistance in Maggie's nature that he would be unable to overcome. He had the uneasy consciousness that he had robbed her of perfect freedom yesterday: there was too much native honour in him, for him not to feel that, if her will should recoil, his conduct would have been odious, and she would have a right to reproach him.

But Maggie did not feel that right: she was too conscious of fatal weakness in herself—too full of the tenderness that comes with the foreseen need for inflicting a wound. She let him take her hand when he came to sit down beside her, and smiled at him—only with rather a sad glance; she could say nothing to pain him till the moment of possible parting was nearer. And so they drank their cup of coffee together, and walked about the deck, and heard the captain's assurance that they should be in at Mudport by five o'clock, each with an inward burthen; but in him it was an undefined fear, which he trusted to the coming hours to dissipate; in her it was a definite resolve on which she was trying silently to tighten her hold. Stephen was continually, through the morning, expressing his anxiety at the fatigue and discomfort she was suffering, and alluded to landing and to the change of motion and repose she would have in a carriage, wanting to assure himself more completely by presupposing that everything would be as he had arranged it. For a long while Maggie contented herself with assuring him that she had had a good night's rest, and that she didn't mind about being on the vessel—it was not like being on the open sea—it was only a little less pleasant than being in a boat on the Floss. But a suppressed resolve will betray itself in the eyes, and Stephen became more and more uneasy as the day advanced, under the sense that Maggie had entirely lost her passiveness. He longed, but did not dare, to speak of their marriage—of where they would go after it, and the steps he would take to inform his father, and the rest, of what had happened. He longed to assure himself of a tacit assent from her. But each time he looked at her, he gathered a stronger dread of the new, quiet sadness with which she met his eyes. And they were more and more silent.

'Here we are in sight of Mudport,' he said, at last. 'Now, dearest,' he added, turning towards her with a look that was half-beseeching, 'the worst part of your fatigue is over. On the land we can command swiftness. In another hour and a half we shall be in a chaise together—and that will seem rest to you after this.'

Maggie felt it was time to speak: it would only be unkind now to assent by silence. She spoke in the lowest tone, as he had done, but with distinct decision.

'We shall not be together—we shall have parted.'

The blood rushed to Stephen's face.

'We shall not,' he said. 'I'll die first.'

It was as he had dreaded—there was a struggle coming. But neither of them dared to say another word, till the boat was let down, and they were taken to the landing-place. Here there was a cluster of gazers and passengers awaiting the departure of the steamboat to St. Ogg's. Maggie had a dim sense, when she had landed, and Stephen was hurrying her along on his arm, that someone had advanced towards her from that cluster as if he were coming to speak to her. But she was hurried along, and was indifferent to everything but the coming trial.

A porter guided them to the nearest inn and posting-house, and Stephen gave the order for the chaise as they passed through the yard. Maggie took no notice of this, and only said, 'Ask them to show us into a room where we can sit down.'

When they entered, Maggie did not sit down, and Stephen, whose face had a desperate determination in it, was about to ring the bell, when she said, in a firm voice:

'I'm not going: we must part here.'

'Maggie,' he said, turning round towards her, and speaking in the tones of a man who feels a process of torture beginning, 'do you mean to kill me? What is the use of it now? The whole thing is done.'

'No, it is not done,' said Maggie. 'Too much is done—

more than we can ever remove the trace of. But I will go no farther. Don't try to prevail with me again. I couldn't choose yesterday.'

What was he to do? He dared not go near her—her anger might leap out, and make a new barrier. He walked backwards and forwards in maddening perplexity.

'Maggie,' he said at last, pausing before her and speaking in a tone of imploring wretchedness, 'have some pity—hear me—forgive me for what I did yesterday. I will obey you now—I will do nothing without your full consent. But don't blight our lives for ever by a rash perversity that can answer no good purpose to anyone—that can only create new evils. Sit down, dearest; wait—think what you are going to do. Don't treat me as if you couldn't trust me.'

He had chosen the most effective appeal; but Maggie's will was fixed unswervingly on the coming wrench. She had made up her mind to suffer.

'We must not wait,' she said, in a low but distinct voice; 'we must part at once.'

'We *can't* part, Maggie,' said Stephen, more impetuously. 'I can't bear it. What is the use of inflicting that misery on me? the blow—whatever it may have been—has been struck now. Will it help anyone else that you should drive me mad?'

'I will not begin any future, even for you,' said Maggie tremulously, 'with a deliberate consent to what ought not to have been. What I told you at Basset I feel now: I would rather have died than fall into this temptation. It would have been better if we had parted for ever then. But we must part now.'

'We will *not* part,' Stephen burst out, instinctively placing his back against the door—forgetting everything he had said a few moments before; 'I will not endure it. You'll make me desperate—I shan't know what I do.'

Maggie trembled. She felt that the parting could not be effected suddenly. She must rely on a slower appeal to Stephen's better self—she must be prepared for a harder task than that of rushing away while resolution was fresh. She sat down. Stephen, watching her with that look of desperation which had come over him like a lurid light, approached slowly from the door, seated himself close beside her, and grasped her hand. Her heart beat like the heart of a frightened bird; but this direct opposition helped her. She felt her determination growing stronger.

'Remember what you felt weeks ago,' she began, with beseeching earnestness—'remember what we both felt— that we owed ourselves to others, and must conquer every inclination which could make us false to that debt. We have failed to keep our resolutions; but the wrong remains the same.'

'No, it does *not* remain the same,' said Stephen. 'We have proved that it was impossible to keep our resolutions. We have proved that the feeling which draws us towards each other is too strong to be overcome: that natural law surmounts every other; we can't help what it clashes with.'

'It is not so, Stephen—I'm quite sure that is wrong. I have tried to think it again and again; but I see, if we judged in that way, there would be a warrant for all treachery and cruelty—we should justify breaking the most sacred ties that can ever be formed on earth. If the past is not to bind us, where can duty lie? We should have no law but the inclination of the moment.'

'But there are ties that can't be kept by mere resolution,' said Stephen, starting up and walking about again. 'What is outward faithfulness? Would they have thanked us for anything so hollow as constancy without love?'

Maggie did not answer immediately. She was undergoing an inward as well as an outward contest. At last she said, with a passionate assertion of her conviction, as much against herself as against him:

'That seems right—at first; but when I look further, I'm sure it is *not* right. Faithfulness and constancy mean something else besides doing what is easiest and pleasantest to ourselves. They mean renouncing whatever is opposed to the reliance others have in us—whatever would cause misery to those whom the course of our lives has made dependent on us. If we—if I had been better, nobler, those claims would have been so strongly present with me—I should have felt them pressing on my heart so continually, just as they do now in the moments when my conscience is awake—that the opposite feeling would never have grown in me, as it has done: it would have been quenched at once—I should have prayed for help so earnestly—I should have rushed away as we rush from hideous danger. I feel no excuse for myself—none. I should never have failed towards Lucy and Philip as I have done, if I had not been weak, selfish, and hard—able to think of their pain without a pain to myself that would have destroyed all temptation. O, what is Lucy feeling now? She believed in me—she loved me—she was so good to me. Think of her. . . .'

Maggie's voice was getting choked as she uttered these last words.

'I *can't* think of her,' said Stephen, stamping as if with pain. 'I can think of nothing but you, Maggie. You demand of a man what is impossible. I felt that once; but I can't go back to it now. And where is the use of *your* thinking of it, except to torture me? You can't save them from pain now; you can only tear yourself from me, and make my life worthless to me. And even if we could go back, and both fulfil our engagements—if that were possible now—it would be hateful—horrible, to think of your ever being Philip's wife—of your ever being the wife of a man you didn't love. We have both been rescued from a mistake.'

A deep flush came over Maggie's face, and she couldn't speak. Stephen saw this. He sat down again, taking her hand in his, and looking at her with passionate entreaty.

'Maggie! Dearest! If you love me, you are mine. Who can have so great a claim on you as I have? My life is bound up in your love. There is nothing in the past that can annul our right to each other: it is the first time we have either of us loved with our whole heart and soul.'

Maggie was still silent for a little while—looking down. Stephen was in a flutter of new hope: he was going to triumph. But she raised her eyes and met his with a glance that was filled with the anguish of regret—not with yielding.

'No—not with my whole heart and soul, Stephen,' she said, with timid resolution. 'I have never consented to it with my whole mind. There are memories, and affections, and longings after perfect goodness, that have such a strong hold on me; they would never quit me for long; they would come back and be pain to me—repentance. I couldn't live in peace if I put the shadow of a wilful sin between myself and God. I have caused sorrow already—I know—I feel it; but I have never deliberately consented to it: I have never said, "They shall suffer, that I may have joy." It has never been my will to marry you: if you were to win consent from the momentary triumph of my feelings for you, you would not have my whole soul. If I could wake back again into the time before yesterday, I would choose to be true to my calmer affections, and live without the joy of love.'

Stephen loosed her hand, and, rising impatiently, walked up and down the room in suppressed rage.

'Good God!' he burst out at last, 'what a miserable thing a woman's love is to a man's! I could commit crimes for you—and you can balance and choose in that way. But you *don't* love me; if you had a tithe of the feeling for me that I have for you, it would be impossible to you to think for a moment of sacrificing me. But it weighs nothing with you that you are robbing me of *my* life's happiness.'

Maggie pressed her fingers together almost convulsively as she held them clasped on her lap. A great terror was upon her, as if she were ever and anon seeing where she stood by great flashes of lightning, and then again stretched forth her hands in the darkness.

'No—I don't sacrifice you—I couldn't sacrifice you,' she said, as soon as she could speak again; 'but I can't believe in a good for you, that I feel—that we both feel is a wrong towards others. We can't choose happiness either for ourselves or for another: we can't tell where that will lie. We can only choose whether we will indulge ourselves in the present moment, or whether we will renounce that, for the sake of obeying the divine voice within us—for the sake of being true to all the motives that sanctify our lives.

I know this belief is hard: it has slipped away from me again and again; but I have felt that if I let it go for ever, I should have no light through the darkness of this life.'

'But, Maggie,' said Stephen, seating himself by her again, 'is it possible you don't see that what happened yesterday has altered the whole position of things? What infatuation is it—what obstinate prepossession that blinds you to that? It is too late to say what we might have done or what we ought to have done. Admitting the very worst view of what has been done, it is a fact we must act on now; our position is altered; the right course is no longer what it was before. We must accept our own actions and start afresh from them. Suppose we had been married yesterday? It is nearly the same thing. The effect on others would not have been different. It would only have made this difference to ourselves,' Stephen added bitterly, 'that you might have acknowledged then that your tie to me was stronger than to others.'

Again a deep flush came over Maggie's face, and she was silent. Stephen thought again that he was beginning to prevail—he had never yet believed that he should *not* prevail: there are possibilities which our minds shrink from too completely for us to fear them.

'Dearest,' he said, in his deepest, tenderest tone, leaning towards her, and putting his arm round her, 'you *are* mine now—the world believes it—duty must spring out of that now: in a few hours you will be legally mine, and those who had claims on us will submit—they will see that there was a force which declared against their claims.'

Maggie's eyes opened wide in one terrified look at the face that was close to hers, and she started up—pale again.

'O, I can't do it,' she said, in a voice almost of agony—'Stephen—don't ask me—don't urge me. I can't argue any longer—I don't know what is wise; but my heart will not let me do it. I see—I feel their trouble now: it is as if it were branded on my mind. *I* have suffered, and had no one to pity me; and now I have made others suffer. It would never leave me; it would embitter your love to me. I *do* care for Philip—in a different way: I remember all we said to each other; I know how he thought of me as the one promise of his life. He was given to me that I might make his lot less hard; and I have forsaken him. And Lucy—she has been deceived—she who trusted me more than anyone. I cannot marry you: I cannot take a good for myself that has been wrung out of their misery. It is not the force that ought to rule us—this that we feel for each other; it would rend me away from all that my past life has made dear and holy to me. I can't set out on a fresh life, and forget that: I must go back to it, and cling to it, else I shall feel as if there were nothing firm beneath my feet.'

'Good God, Maggie!' said Stephen, rising too and grasping her arm, 'you rave. How can you go back without marrying me? You don't know what will be said, dearest. You see nothing as it really is.'

'Yes, I do. But they will believe me. I will confess everything. Lucy will believe me—she will forgive you, and—and—O, *some* good will come by clinging to the right. Dear, dear Stephen, let me go!—don't drag me into deeper remorse. My whole soul has never consented—it does not consent now.'

Stephen let go her arm, and sank back on his chair, half stunned by despairing rage. He was silent a few moments, not looking at her; while her eyes were turned towards him yearningly, in alarm at this sudden change. At last he said, still without looking at her:

'Go, then—leave me—don't torture me any longer—I can't bear it.'

Involuntarily she leaned towards him and put out her hand to touch his. But he shrank from it as if it had been burning iron, and said again:

'Leave me.'

Maggie was not conscious of a decision as she turned away from that gloomy averted face, and walked out of the room: it was like an automatic action that fulfils a forgotten intention. What came after? A sense of stairs descended as if in a dream—of flagstones—of a chaise and horses standing—then a street, and a turning into another street where a stage-coach was standing, taking in passengers—and the darting thought that that coach would take her away, perhaps towards home. But she could ask nothing yet; she only got into the coach.

Home—where her mother and brother were—Philip—Lucy—the scene of her very cares and trials—was the haven towards which her mind tended—the sanctuary where sacred relics lay—where she would be rescued from more falling. The thought of Stephen was like a horrible throbbing pain, which yet, as such pains do, seemed to urge all other thoughts into activity. But among her thoughts, what others would say and think of her conduct was hardly present. Love and deep pity and remorseful anguish left no room for that.

The coach was taking her to York—farther away from home; but she did not learn that until she was set down in the old city at midnight. It was no matter: she could sleep there, and start home the next day. She had her purse in her pocket, with all her money in it—a bank-note and a sovereign: she had kept it in her pocket from forgetfulness, after going out to make purchases the day before yesterday.

Did she lie down in the gloomy bedroom of the old inn that night with her will bent unwaveringly on the path of penitent sacrifice? The great struggles of life are not so easy as that; the great problems of life are not so clear. In the darkness of that night she saw Stephen's face turned towards her in passionate, reproachful misery; she lived through again all the tremulous delights of his presence with her that made existence an easy floating in a stream of joy, instead of a quiet resolved endurance and effort. The love she had renounced came back upon her with a cruel charm, she felt herself opening her arms to receive it once more; and then it seemed to slip away and fade and vanish, leaving only the dying sound of a deep thrilling voice that said, 'Gone—for ever gone.'

BOOK SEVENTH

THE FINAL RESCUE

I

THE RETURN TO THE MILL

BETWEEN four and five o'clock on the afternoon of the fifth day from that on which Stephen and Maggie had left St. Ogg's, Tom Tulliver was standing on the gravel-walk outside the old house at Dorlcote Mill. He was master there now: he had half-fulfilled his father's dying wish, and by years of steady self-government and energetic work he had brought himself near to the attainment of more than the old respectability which had been the proud inheritance of the Dodsons and Tullivers.

But Tom's face, as he stood in the hot still sunshine of that summer afternoon, had no gladness, no triumph in it. His mouth wore its bitterest expression, his severe brow its hardest and deepest fold, as he drew down his hat farther over his eyes to shelter them from the sun, and, thrusting his hands deep into his pockets, began to walk up and down the gravel. No news of his sister had been heard since Bob Jakin had come back in the steamer from Mudport, and put an end to all improbable suppositions of an accident on the water by stating that he had seen her land from a vessel with Mr. Stephen Guest. Would the next news be that she was married—or what? Probably that she was not married: Tom's mind was set to the expectation of the worst that could happen—not death, but disgrace.

As he was walking with his back towards the entrance gate, and his face towards the rushing mill-stream, a tall dark-eyed figure, that we know well, approached the gate, and paused to look at him, with a fast-beating heart. Her brother was the human being of whom she had been most afraid, from her childhood upwards: afraid with that fear which springs in us when we love one who is inexorable, unbending, unmodifiable—with a mind that we can never mould ourselves upon, and yet that we cannot endure to alienate from us. That deep-rooted fear was shaking Maggie now; but her mind was unswervingly bent on returning to her brother, as the natural refuge that had been given her. In her deep humiliation under the retrospect of her own weakness—in her anguish at the injury she had inflicted—she almost desired to endure the severity of Tom's reproof, to submit in patient silence to that harsh disapproving judgment against which she had so often rebelled: it seemed no more than just to her now—who was weaker than she was? She craved that outward help to her better purpose which would come from complete, submissive confession—from being in the presence of those whose looks and words would be a reflection of her own conscience.

Maggie had been kept on her bed at York for a day with that prostrating headache which was likely to follow on the terrible strain of the previous day and night. There was an expression of physical pain still about her brow and eyes, and her whole appearance, with her dress so long unchanged, was worn and distressed. She lifted the latch of the gate and walked in—slowly. Tom did not hear the gate; he was just then close upon the roaring dam: but he presently turned, and lifting up his eyes, saw the figure whose worn look and loneliness seemed to him a confirmation of his worst conjectures. He paused, trembling and white with disgust and indignation.

Maggie paused too—three yards before him. She felt the hatred in his face: felt it rushing through her fibres; but she must speak.

'Tom,' she began faintly, 'I am come back to you—I am come back home—for refuge—to tell you everything.'

'You will find no home with me,' he answered, with tremulous rage. 'You have disgraced us all. You have disgraced my father's name. You have been a curse to your best friends. You have been base—deceitful; no motives are strong enough to restrain you. I wash my hands of you for ever. You don't belong to me.'

Their mother had come to the door now. She stood paralysed by the double shock of seeing Maggie and hearing Tom's words.

'Tom,' said Maggie, with more courage, 'I am perhaps not so guilty as you believe me to be. I never meant to give way to my feelings. I struggled against them. I was carried too far in the boat to come back on Tuesday. I came back as soon as I could.'

'I can't believe in you any more,' said Tom, gradually passing from the tremulous excitement of the first moment to cold inflexibility. 'You have been carrying on a clandestine relation with Stephen Guest—as you did before with another. He went to see you at my aunt Moss's; you walked alone with him in the lanes; you must have behaved as no modest girl would have done to her cousin's lover, else that could never have happened. The people at Luckreth saw you pass—you passed all the other places; you knew what you were doing. You have been using Philip Wakem as a screen to deceive Lucy—the kindest friend you ever had. Go and see the return you have made her: she's ill—unable to speak—my mother can't go near her, lest she should remind her of *you*.'

Maggie was half-stunned—too heavily pressed upon by her anguish even to discern any difference between her actual guilt and her brother's accusations, still less to vindicate herself.

'Tom,' she said, crushing her hands together under her cloak, in the effort to speak again. 'Whatever I have done, I repent it bitterly. I want to make amends. I will endure anything. I want to be kept from doing wrong again.'

'What *will* keep you?' said Tom, with cruel bitterness. 'Not religion; not your natural feelings of gratitude and honour. And he—he would deserve to be shot, if it were not—— But you are ten times worse than he is. I loathe your character and your conduct. You struggled with your feelings, you say. Yes! *I* have had feelings to struggle with; but I conquered them. I have had a harder life than you have had; but I have found *my* comfort in doing my duty. But I will sanction no such character as yours: the world shall know that *I* feel the difference between right and wrong. If you are in want, I will provide for you—let my mother know. But you shall not come under my roof. It is enough that I have to bear the thought of your disgrace: the sight of you is hateful to me.'

Slowly Maggie was turning away with despair in her heart. But the poor frightened mother's love leaped out now, stronger than all dread.

'My child! I'll go with you. You've got a mother.'

O the sweet rest of that embrace to the heart-stricken Maggie! More helpful than all wisdom is one draught of simple human pity that will not forsake us.

Tom turned and walked into the house.

'Come in, my child,' Mrs. Tulliver whispered. 'He'll let you stay and sleep in my bed. He won't deny that, if I ask him.'

'No, mother,' said Maggie, in a low tone, like a moan. 'I will never go in.'

'Then wait for me outside. I'll get ready and come with you.'

When his mother appeared with her bonnet on, Tom came out to her in the passage, and put money into her hands.

'My house is yours, mother, always,' he said. 'You will come and let me know everything you want—you will come back to me.'

Poor Mrs. Tulliver took the money, too frightened to say anything. The only thing clear to her was the mother's instinct, that she would go with her unhappy child.

Maggie was waiting outside the gate; she took her mother's hand, and they walked a little way in silence.

'Mother,' said Maggie, at last, 'we will go to Luke's cottage. Luke will take me in. He was very good to me when I was a little girl.'

'He's got no room for us, my dear, now; his wife's got so many children. I don't know where to go, if it isn't to one o' your aunts; and I hardly durst,' said poor Mrs. Tulliver, quite destitute of mental resources in this extremity.

Maggie was silent a little while, and then said:

'Let us go to Bob Jakin's, mother: his wife will have room for us, if they have no other lodger.'

So they went on their way to St. Ogg's—to the old house by the river-side.

Bob himself was at home, with a heaviness at heart which resisted even the new joy and pride of possessing a two months old baby, quite the liveliest of its age that had ever been born to prince or packman. He would perhaps not so thoroughly have understood all the dubiousness of Maggie's appearance with Mr. Stephen Guest on the quay at Mudport, if he had not witnessed the effect it produced on Tom when he went to report it; and since then, the circumstances which in any case gave a disastrous character to her elopement, had passed beyond the more polite circles of St. Ogg's, and had become matter of common talk, accessible to the grooms and errand-boys. So that when he opened the door and saw Maggie standing before him in her sorrow and weariness, he had no questions to ask, except one, which he dared only ask himself, Where was Mr. Stephen Guest? Bob, for his part, hoped he might be in the warmest department of an asylum understood to exist in the other world for gentlemen who are likely to be in fallen circumstances there.

The lodgings were vacant, and both Mrs. Jakin the larger and Mrs. Jakin the less were commanded to make all things comfortable for 'the old Missis and the young Miss' —alas! that she was still 'Miss.' The ingenious Bob was sorely perplexed as to how this result could have come about —how Mr. Stephen Guest could have gone away from her, or could have let her go away from him, when he had the chance of keeping her with him. But he was silent, and would not allow his wife to ask him a question: would not present himself in the room, lest it should appear like intrusion and a wish to pry; having the same chivalry towards dark-eyed Maggie, as in the days when he had bought her the memorable present of books.

But after a day or two Mrs. Tulliver was gone to the Mill again for a few hours to see to Tom's household matters.

Maggie had wished this: after the first violent outburst of feeling, which came as soon as she had no longer any active purpose to fulfil, she was less in need of her mother's presence; she even desired to be alone with her grief. But she had been solitary only a little while in the old sitting-room that looked on the river, when there came a tap at the door, and turning round her sad face as she said, 'Come in,' she saw Bob enter with the baby in his arms and Mumps at his heels.

'We'll go back, if it disturbs you, Miss,' said Bob.

'No,' said Maggie, in a low voice, wishing she could smile.

Bob, closing the door behind him, came and stood before her.

'You see, we've got a little un, Miss, and I wanted you to look at it, and take it in your arms, if you'd be so good. For we made free to name it after you, and it 'ud be better for your takin' a bit o' notice on it.'

Maggie could not speak, but she put out her arms to receive the tiny baby, while Mumps snuffed at it anxiously, to ascertain that this transference was all right. Maggie's heart had swelled at this action and speech of Bob's: she knew well enough that it was a way he had chosen to show his sympathy and respect.

'Sit down, Bob,' she said presently, and he sat down in silence, finding his tongue unmanageable in quite a new fashion, refusing to say what he wanted it to say.

'Bob,' she said, after a few moments, looking down at the baby, and holding it anxiously, as if she feared it might slip from her mind and her fingers, 'I have a favour to ask of you.'

'Don't you speak so, Miss,' said Bob, grasping the skin of Mumps's neck; 'if there 's anything I can do for you, I should look upon it as a day's earnings.'

'I want you to go to Dr. Kenn's, and ask to speak to him, and tell him that I am here, and should be very grateful if he would come to me while my mother is away. She will not come back till evening.'

'Eh, Miss—I'd do it in a minute—it is but a step; but Dr. Kenn's wife lies dead—she 's to be buried to-morrow

—died the day I come from Mudport. It's all the more pity she should ha' died just now, if you want him. I hardly like to go a-nigh him yet.'

'O no, Bob,' said Maggie, 'we must let it be—till after a few days, perhaps—when you hear that he is going about again. But perhaps he may be going out of town—to a distance,' she added, with a new sense of despondency at this idea.

'Not he, Miss,' said Bob. '*He*'ll none go away. He isn't one o' them gentlefolks as go to cry at waterin'-places when their wives die: he's got summat else to do. He looks fine an' sharp after the parish—he does. He christened the little un; an' he was *at* me to know what I did of a Sunday, as I didn't come to church. But I told him I was upo' the travel three parts o' the Sundays—an' then I'm so used to bein' on my legs, I can't sit so long on end—"an' lors, sir," says I, "a packman can do wi' a small 'lowance o' church: it tastes strong," says I; "there's no call to lay it on thick." Eh, Miss, how good the little un is wi' you! It's like as if it knowed you: it partly does, I'll be bound—like the birds know the mornin'.'

Bob's tongue was now evidently loosed from its unwonted bondage, and might even be in danger of doing more work than was required of it. But the subjects on which he longed to be informed were so steep and difficult of approach, that his tongue was likely to run on along the level rather than to carry him on that unbeaten road. He felt this, and was silent again for a little while, ruminating much on the possible forms in which he might put a question. At last he said, in a more timid voice than usual:

'Will you give me leave to ask you only one thing, Miss?'

Maggie was rather startled, but she answered, 'Yes, Bob, if it is about myself—not about any one else.'

'Well, Miss, it's this: *Do* you owe anybody a grudge?'

'No, not any one,' said Maggie, looking up at him inquiringly. 'Why?'

'O, lors, Miss,' said Bob, pinching Mumps's neck harder than ever, 'I wish you did—an' 'ud tell me—I'd leather him till I couldn't see—I would—an' the Justice might do what he liked to me arter.'

'O Bob,' said Maggie, smiling faintly, 'you're a very good friend to me. But I shouldn't like to punish any one, even if they'd done me wrong: I've done wrong myself too often.'

This view of things was puzzling to Bob, and threw more obscurity than ever over what could possibly have happened between Stephen and Maggie. But further questions would have been too intrusive, even if he could have framed them suitably, and he was obliged to carry baby away again to an expectant mother.

'Happen you'd like Mumps for company, Miss,' he said when he had taken the baby again. 'He's rare company—Mumps is—he knows iverything, an' makes no bother about it. If I tell him, he'll lie before you an' watch you—as still —just as he watches my pack. You'd better let me leave him a bit; he'll get fond on you. Lors, it's a fine thing to hev a dumb brute fond on you; it'll stick to you, an' make no jaw.'

'Yes, do leave him, please,' said Maggie. 'I think I should like to have Mumps for a friend.'

'Mumps, lie down there,' said Bob, pointing to a place in front of Maggie, 'an' niver do you stir till you're spoke to.'

Mumps lay down at once, and made no sign of restlessness when his master left the room.

II

ST. OGG'S PASSES JUDGMENT

It was soon known throughout St. Ogg's that Miss Tulliver was come back: she had not, then, eloped in order to be married to Mr. Stephen Guest—at all events, Mr. Stephen Guest had not married her—which came to the same thing, so far as her culpability was concerned. We judge others according to results; how else ?—not knowing the process by which results are arrived at. If Miss Tulliver, after a few months of well-chosen travel, had returned as Mrs. Stephen Guest—with a post-marital *trousseau*, and all the advantages possessed even by the most unwelcome wife of an only son, public opinion, which at St. Ogg's, as elsewhere, always knew what to think, would have judged in strict consistency with those results. Public opinion, in these cases, is always of the feminine gender—not the world, but the world's wife: and she would have seen, that two handsome young people—the gentleman of quite the first family in St. Ogg's—having found themselves in a false position, had been led into a course which, to say the least of it, was highly injudicious, and productive of sad pain and disappointment, especially to that sweet young thing, Miss Deane. Mr. Stephen Guest had certainly not behaved well; but then, young men were liable to those sudden infatuated attachments; and bad as it might seem in Mrs. Stephen Guest to admit the faintest advances from her cousin's lover (indeed it *had* been said that she was actually engaged to young Wakem—old Wakem himself had mentioned it), still she was very young—'and a deformed young man, you know!—and young Guest so very fascinating; and, they say, he positively worships her (to be sure, that can't last!) and he ran away with her in the boat quite against her will—and what could she do? She couldn't come back then: no one would have spoken to her; and how very well that maize-coloured satinette becomes her complexion! It seems as if the folds in front were quite come in; several of her dresses are made so;—they say he thinks nothing too handsome to buy for her. Poor Miss Deane! She is very pitiable; but then, there was no positive engagement; and the air at the coast will do her good. After all, if young Guest felt no more for her than *that*, it was better for her not to marry him. What a wonderful marriage for a girl like Miss Tulliver—quite romantic! Why, young Guest will put up for the borough at the next election. Nothing like commerce nowadays! That young Wakem nearly went out of his mind—he always *was* rather queer; but he's gone abroad again to be out of the way—quite the best thing for a deformed young man.

Miss Unit declares she will never visit Mr. and Mrs. Stephen Guest—such nonsense! pretending to be better than other people. Society couldn't be carried on if we inquired into private conduct in that way—and Christianity tells us to think no evil—and my belief is, that Miss Unit had no cards sent her.'

But the results, we know, were not of a kind to warrant this extenuation of the past. Maggie had returned without a *trousseau*, without a husband—in that degraded and outcast condition to which error is well known to lead; and the world's wife, with that fine instinct which is given her for the preservation of Society, saw at once that Miss Tulliver's conduct had been of the most aggravated kind. Could anything be more detestable? A girl so much indebted to her friends—whose mother as well as herself had received so much kindness from the Deanes—to lay the design of winning a young man's affections away from her own cousin, who had behaved like a sister to her! Winning his affections? That was not the phrase for such a girl as Miss Tulliver: it would have been more correct to say that she had been actuated by mere unwomanly boldness and unbridled passion. There was always something questionable about her. That connection with young Wakem, which, they said, had been carried on for years, looked very ill—disgusting, in fact! But with a girl of that disposition!—To the world's wife there had always been something in Miss Tulliver's very physique that a refined instinct felt to be prophetic of harm. As for poor Mr. Stephen Guest, he was rather pitiable than otherwise: a young man of five-and-twenty is not to be too severely judged in these cases—he is really very much at the mercy of a designing bold girl. And it was clear that he had given way in spite of himself: he had shaken her off as soon as he could; indeed, their having parted so soon looked very black indeed—*for her.* To be sure, he had written a letter, laying all the blame on himself, and telling the story in a romantic fashion so as to try and make her appear quite innocent: of course he would do that! But the refined instinct of the world's wife was not to be deceived:

providentially!—else what would become of Society? Why, her own brother had turned her from his door: he had seen enough, you might be sure, before he would do that. A truly respectable young man—Mr. Tom Tulliver: quite likely to rise in the world! His sister's disgrace was naturally a heavy blow to him. It was to be hoped that she would go out of the neighbourhood—to America, or anywhere— so as to purify the air of St. Ogg's from the taint of her presence, extremely dangerous to daughters there! No good could happen to her: it was only to be hoped she would repent, and that God would have mercy on her: He had not the care of Society on His hands—as the world's wife had.

It required nearly a fortnight for fine instinct to assure itself of these inspirations; indeed, it was a whole week before Stephen's letter came, telling his father the facts, and adding that he was gone across to Holland—had drawn upon the agent at Mudport for money—was incapable of any resolution at present.

Maggie, all this while, was too entirely filled with a more agonising anxiety to spend any thought on the view that was being taken of her conduct by the world of St. Ogg's: anxiety about Stephen—Lucy—Philip—beat on her poor heart in a hard, driving, ceaseless storm of mingled love, remorse, and pity. If she had thought of rejection and injustice at all, it would have seemed to her that they had done their worst—that she could hardly feel any stroke from them intolerable since the words she had heard from her brother's lips. Across all her anxiety for the loved and the injured, those words shot again and again, like a horrible pang that would have brought misery and dread even into a heaven of delights. The idea of ever recovering happiness never glimmered in her mind for a moment; it seemed as if every sensitive fibre in her were too entirely preoccupied by pain ever to vibrate again to another influence. Life stretched before her as one act of penitence, and all she craved, as she dwelt on her future lot, was something to guarantee her from more falling: her own weakness haunted her like a vision of hideous possibilities, that made no peace conceivable except such as lay in the sense of a sure refuge.

But she was not without practical intentions: the love of independence was too strong an inheritance and a habit for her not to remember that she must get her bread; and when other projects looked vague, she fell back on that of returning to her plain sewing, and so getting enough to pay for her lodging at Bob's. She meant to persuade her mother to return to the Mill by-and-by, and live with Tom again; and somehow or other she would maintain herself at St. Ogg's. Dr. Kenn would perhaps help her and advise her. She remembered his parting words at the bazaar. She remembered the momentary feeling of reliance that had sprung in her when he was talking with her, and she waited with yearning expectation for the opportunity of confiding everything to him. Her mother called every day at Mr Deane's to learn how Lucy was: the report was always sad —nothing had yet roused her from the feeble passivity which had come on with the first shock. But of Philip, Mrs. Tulliver had learned nothing: naturally, no one whom she met would speak to her about what related to her daughter. But at last she summoned courage to go and see sister Glegg, who of course would know everything, and had been even to see Tom at the Mill in Mrs. Tulliver's absence, though he had said nothing of what had passed on the occasion.

As soon as her mother was gone, Maggie put on her bonnet. She had resolved on walking to the Rectory and asking to see Dr. Kenn: he was in deep grief—but the grief of another does not jar upon us in such circumstances. It was the first time she had been beyond the door since her return; nevertheless her mind was so bent on the purpose of her walk, that the unpleasantness of meeting people on the way, and being stared at, did not occur to her. But she had no sooner passed beyond the narrower streets which she had to thread from Bob's dwelling, than she became aware of unusual glances cast at her; and this consciousness made her hurry along nervously, afraid to look to right or left. Presently, however, she came full on Mrs. and Miss Turnbull, old acquaintances of her family; they both looked at her strangely, and turned a little aside without speaking. All hard looks were pain to Maggie, but her self-reproach was too strong for resentment: 'No wonder they will not speak to me,' she thought—'they are very fond of Lucy.' But now she knew that she was about to pass a group of gentlemen, who were standing at the door of the billiard-rooms, and she could not help seeing young Torry step out a little with his glass at his eye, and bow to her with that air of nonchalance which he might have bestowed on a friendly bar-maid. Maggie's pride was too intense for her not to feel that sting, even in the midst of her sorrow; and for the first time the thought took strong hold of her that she would have other obloquy cast on her besides that which was felt to be due to her breach of faith towards Lucy. But she was at the Rectory now; there, perhaps, she would find something else than retribution. Retribution may come from any voice: the hardest, cruellest, most imbruted urchin at the street-corner can inflict it: surely help and pity are rarer things—more needful for the righteous to bestow.

She was shown up at once, after being announced, into Dr. Kenn's study, where he sat amongst piled-up books, for which he had little appetite, leaning his cheek against the head of his youngest child, a girl of three. The child was sent away with the servant, and when the door was closed, Dr. Kenn said, placing a chair for Maggie:

'I was coming to see you, Miss Tulliver; you have anticipated me; I am glad you did.'

Maggie looked at him with her childlike directness as she had done at the bazaar, and said:

'I want to tell you everything.'

But her eyes filled fast with tears as she said it, and all the pent-up excitement of her humiliating walk would have its vent before she could say more.

'Do tell me everything,' Dr. Kenn said, with quiet kindness in his grave firm voice. 'Think of me as one to whom a long experience has been granted, which may enable him to help you.'

In rather broken sentences, and with some effort at first, but soon with the greater ease that came from a sense of relief in the confidence, Maggie told the brief story of a struggle that must be the beginning of a long sorrow. Only the day before, Dr. Kenn had been made acquainted with the contents of Stephen's letter, and he had believed them at once, without the confirmation of Maggie's statement. That involuntary plaint of hers, '*O, I must go,*' had remained with him as the sign that she was undergoing some inward conflict.

Maggie dwelt the longest on the feeling which had made her come back to her mother and brother, which made her cling to all the memories of the past. When she had ended, Dr. Kenn was silent for some minutes: there was a difficulty on his mind. He rose, and walked up and down the hearth with his hands behind him. At last he seated himself again, and said, looking at Maggie:

'Your prompting to go to your nearest friends—to remain where all the ties of your life have been formed—is a true prompting, to which the Church in its original constitution and discipline responds—opening its arms to the penitent—watching over its children to the last—never abandoning them until they are hopelessly reprobate. And the Church ought to represent the feeling of the community, so that every parish should be a family knit together by Christian brotherhood under a spiritual father. But the ideas of discipline and Christian fraternity are entirely relaxed—they can hardly be said to exist in the public mind: they hardly survive except in the partial, contradictory form they have taken in the narrow communities of schismatics; and if I were not supported by the firm faith that the Church must ultimately recover the full force of that constitution which is alone fitted to human needs, I should often lose heart at observing the want of fellowship and sense of mutual responsibility among my own flock. At present everything seems tending towards the relaxation of ties—towards the substitution of wayward choice for the adherence to obligation, which has its roots in the past. Your conscience and your heart have given you true light on this point, Miss Tulliver; and I have said all this that you may know what my wish about you—what my advice to you—would be, if they sprang from my own feeling and opinion unmodified by counteracting circumstances.'

Dr. Kenn paused a little while. There was an entire absence of effusive benevolence in his manner; there was something almost cold in the gravity of his look and voice. If Maggie had not known that his benevolence was persevering in proportion to its reserve, she might have been chilled and frightened. As it was, she listened expectantly, quite sure that there would be some effective help in his words. He went on:

'Your inexperience of the world, Miss Tulliver, prevents you from anticipating fully the very unjust conceptions that will probably be formed concerning your conduct—conceptions which will have a baneful effect, even in spite of known evidence to disprove them.'

'O, I do—I begin to see,' said Maggie, unable to repress this utterance of her recent pain. 'I know I shall be insulted: I shall be thought worse than I am.'

'You perhaps do not yet know,' said Dr. Kenn, with a touch of more personal pity, 'that a letter is come which ought to satisfy everyone who has known anything of you, that you chose the steep and difficult path of a return to the right, at the moment when that return was most of all difficult.'

'O—where is he?' said poor Maggie, with a flush and tremor that no presence could have hindered.

'He is gone abroad: he has written of all that passed to his father. He has vindicated you to the utmost; and I hope the communication of that letter to your cousin will have a beneficial effect on her.'

Dr. Kenn waited for her to get calm again before he went on:

'That letter, as I said, ought to suffice to prevent false impressions concerning you. But I am bound to tell you, Miss Tulliver, that not only the experience of my whole life, but my observation within the last three days, makes me fear that there is hardly any evidence which will save you from the painful effect of false imputations. The persons who are the most incapable of a conscientious struggle such as yours, are precisely those who will be likely to shrink from you; because they will not believe in your struggle. I fear your life here will be attended not only with much pain, but with many obstructions. For this reason—and for this only—I ask you to consider whether it will not perhaps be better for you to take a situation at a distance, according to your former intention. I will exert myself at once to obtain one for you.'

'O, if I could but stop here!' said Maggie. 'I have no heart to begin a strange life again. I should have no stay. I should feel like a lonely wanderer—cut off from the past. I have written to the lady who offered me a situation to excuse myself. If I remained here, I could perhaps atone in some way to Lucy—to others: I could convince them that I'm sorry. And,' she added, with some of the old proud fire flashing out, 'I will not go away because people say false things of me. They shall learn to retract them. If I must go away at last, because—because others wish it, I will not go now.'

'Well,' said Dr. Kenn, after some consideration, 'if you determine on that, Miss Tulliver, you may rely on all the influence my position gives me. I am bound to aid and countenance you by the very duties of my office as a parish priest. I will add, that personally I have a deep interest in your peace of mind and welfare.'

'The only thing I want is some occupation that will enable me to get my bread and be independent,' said Maggie. 'I shall not want much. I can go on lodging where I am.'

'I must think over the subject maturely,' said Dr. Kenn, 'and in a few days I shall be better able to ascertain the general feeling. I shall come to see you: I shall bear you constantly in mind.'

When Maggie had left him, Dr. Kenn stood ruminating with his hands behind him, and his eyes fixed on the carpet, under a painful sense of doubt and difficulty. The tone of

Stephen's letter, which he had read, and the actual relations of all the persons concerned, forced upon him powerfully the idea of an ultimate marriage between Stephen and Maggie as the least evil; and the impossibility of their proximity in St. Ogg's on any other supposition, until after years of separation, threw an insurmountable prospective difficulty over Maggie's stay there. On the other hand, he entered with all the comprehension of a man who had known spiritual conflict, and lived through years of devoted service to his fellow-men, into that state of Maggie's heart and conscience which made the consent to the marriage a desecration to her: her conscience must not be tampered with: the principle on which she had acted was a safer guide than any balancing of consequences. His experience told him that intervention was too dubious a responsibility to be lightly incurred: the possible issue either of an endeavour to restore the former relations with Lucy and Philip, or of counselling submission to this irruption of a new feeling, was hidden in a darkness all the more impenetrable because each immediate step was clogged with evil.

The great problem of the shifting relation between passion and duty is clear to no man who is capable of apprehending it: the question whether the moment has come in which a man has fallen below the possibility of a renunciation that will carry any efficacy, and must accept the sway of a passion against which he had struggled as a trespass, is one for which we have no master-key that will fit all cases. The casuists have become a byword of reproach; but their perverted spirit of minute discrimination was the shadow of a truth to which eyes and hearts are too often fatally sealed—the truth, that moral judgments must remain false and hollow, unless they are checked and enlightened by a perpetual reference to the special circumstances that mark the individual lot.

All people of broad, strong sense have an instinctive repugnance to the men of maxims; because such people early discern that the mysterious complexity of our life is not to be embraced by maxims, and that to lace ourselves up in formulas of that sort is to repress all the divine promptings and inspirations that spring from growing insight and sympathy. And the man of maxims is the popular representative of the minds that are guided in their moral judgment solely by general rules, thinking that these will lead them to justice by a ready-made patent method, without the trouble of exerting patience, discrimination, impartiality—without any care to assure themselves whether they have the insight that comes from a hardly-earned estimate of temptation, or from a life vivid and intense enough to have created a wide fellow-feeling with all that is human.

III

SHOWING THAT OLD ACQUAINTANCES ARE CAPABLE OF SURPRISING US

WHEN Maggie was at home again, her mother brought her news of an unexpected line of conduct in aunt Glegg. As long as Maggie had not been heard of, Mrs. Glegg had half closed her shutters and drawn down her blinds: she felt assured that Maggie was drowned: that was far more probable than that her niece and legatee should have done anything to wound the family honour at the tenderest point. When, at last, she learned from Tom that Maggie had come home, and gathered from him what was her explanation of her absence, she burst forth in severe reproof of Tom for admitting the worst of his sister until he was compelled. If you were not to stand by your 'kin' as long as there was a shread of honour attributable to them, pray what were you to stand by? Lightly to admit conduct in one of your own family that would force you to alter your will, had never been the way of the Dodsons; and though Mrs. Glegg had always augured ill of Maggie's future at a time when other people were perhaps less clear-sighted, yet fair play was a jewel, and it was not for her own friends to help to rob the girl of her fair fame, and to cast her out from family shelter to the scorn of the outer world, until she had become unequivocally a family disgrace. The circumstances were unprecedented in Mrs. Glegg's experience—nothing of that kind had happened among the Dodsons before; but it was a case in which her hereditary rectitude and personal strength of character found a common channel along with her fundamental ideas of clanship, as they did in her life-long regard to equity in money matters. She quarrelled with Mr. Glegg, whose kindness, flowing entirely into compassion for Lucy, made him as hard in his judgment of Maggie as Mr. Deane himself was; and, fuming against her sister Tulliver because she did not at once come to her for advice and help, shut herself up in her own room with Baxter's 'Saints' Rest' from morning till night, denying herself to all visitors, till Mr. Glegg brought from Mr. Deane the news of Stephen's letter. Then Mrs. Glegg felt that she had adequate fighting-ground—then she laid aside Baxter, and was ready to meet all comers. While Mrs. Pullet could do nothing but shake her head and cry, and wish that cousin Abbot had died, or any number of funerals had happened rather than this, which had never happened before, so that there was no knowing how to act, and Mrs. Pullet could never enter St. Ogg's again, because 'acquaintances' knew of it all,—Mrs. Glegg only hoped that Mrs. Wooll, or anyone else, would come to her with their false tales about her own niece, and she would know what to say to that ill-advised person!

Again she had a scene of remonstrance with Tom, all the more severe in proportion to the greater strength of her present position. But Tom, like other immovable things, seemed only the more rigidly fixed under that attempt to shake him. Poor Tom! he judged by what he had been able to see; and the judgment was painful enough to himself. He thought he had the demonstration of facts observed through years by his own eyes which gave no warning of their imperfection, that Maggie's nature was utterly untrustworthy, and too strongly marked with evil tendencies to be safely treated with leniency: he would act on that demonstration at any cost; but the thought of it made his days bitter to him. Tom, like every one of us, was imprisoned within the limits of his own nature, and his education had simply glided over him, leaving a slight deposit of polish: if you are inclined to be severe on his severity, remember that the responsibility of tolerance lies with those who have the wider vision. There had arisen in Tom a repulsion towards Maggie that derived its very intensity from early childish love in the time when they had clasped tiny fingers together, and their later sense of nearness in a common duty and a common sorrow: the sight of her, as he had told her, was hateful to him. In this branch of the Dodson family aunt Glegg found a stronger nature than her own— a nature in which family feeling had lost the character of clanship by taking on a doubly deep dye of personal pride. Mrs. Glegg allowed that Maggie ought to be punished—she was not a woman to deny that—she knew what conduct was; but punished in proportion to the misdeeds proved against her, not to those which were cast upon her by people outside her own family, who might wish to show that their own kin were better.

'Your aunt Glegg scolded me so as niver was, my dear,' said poor Mrs. Tulliver, when she came back to Maggie, 'as I didn't go to her before—she said it wasn't for her to come to me first. But she spoke like a sister, too: *having* she allays was, and hard to please—O dear!—but she's said the kindest word as has ever been spoke by you yet, my child. For she says, for all she's been so set again' having one extry in the house, and making extry spoons and things, and putting her about in her ways, you shall have a shelter in her house, if you'll go to her dutiful, and she'll uphold you against folks as say harm of you when they've no call. And I told her I thought you couldn't bear to see anybody but me, you were so beat down with trouble; but she said, "*I* won't throw ill words at her—there's them out o' th' family 'ull be ready enough to do that. But I'll give her good advice; an' she must be humble." It's wonderful o' Jane; for I'm sure she used to throw everything I did wrong at me—if it was the raisin wine as turned out bad, or the pies too hot—or whativer it was.'

'O mother,' said poor Maggie, shrinking from the thought

of all the contact her bruised mind would have to bear, 'tell her I'm very grateful—I'll go to see her as soon as I can; but I can't see anyone just yet, except Dr. Kenn. I've been to him—he will advise me, and help me to get some occupation. I can't live with anyone, or be dependent on them, tell aunt Glegg; I must get my own bread. But did you hear nothing of Philip—Philip Wakem? Have you never seen anyone that has mentioned him?'

'No, my dear: but I've been to Lucy's, and I saw your uncle, and he says they got her to listen to the letter, and she took notice o' Miss Guest, and asked questions, and the doctor thinks she's on the turn to be better. What a world this is—what trouble, O dear! The law was the first beginning, an' it's gone from bad to worse, all of a sudden, just when the luck seemed on the turn.' This was the first lamentation that Mrs. Tulliver had let slip to Maggie, but old habit had been revived by the interview with sister Glegg.

'My poor, poor mother!' Maggie burst out, cut to the heart with pity and compunction, and throwing her arms round her mother's neck, 'I was always naughty and troublesome to you. And now you might have been happy if it hadn't been for me.'

'Eh, my dear,' said Mrs. Tulliver, leaning towards the warm young cheek; 'I must put up wi' my children—I shall never have no more; and if they bring me bad luck, I must be fond on it—there's nothing else much to be fond on, for my furnitur' went long ago. And you'd got to be very good once; I can't think how it's turned out the wrong way so!'

Still two or three more days passed, and Maggie heard nothing of Philip; anxiety about him was becoming her predominant trouble, and she summoned courage at last to inquire about him of Dr. Kenn, on his next visit to her. He did not even know if Philip was at home. The elder Wakem was made moody by an accumulation of annoyance: the disappointment in this young Jetsome, to whom, apparently, he was a good deal attached, had been followed close by the catastrophe to his son's hopes after he had done violence to his own strong feeling by conceding to them, and had incautiously mentioned this concession in St. Ogg's—and he was almost fierce in his brusqueness when anyone asked him a question about his son. But Philip could hardly have been ill, or it would have been known through the calling in of the medical man; it was probable that he was gone out of the town for a little while. Maggie sickened under this suspense, and her imagination began to live more and more persistently in what Philip was enduring. What did he believe about her?

At last Bob brought her a letter, without a post-mark, directed in a hand which she knew familiarly in the letters of her own name—a hand in which her name had been written long ago, in a pocket Shakespeare which she possessed. Her mother was in the room, and Maggie, in violent agitation, hurried up-stairs that she might read the letter in solitude. She read it with a throbbing brow:

'MAGGIE,—

'I believe in you—I know you never meant to deceive me—I know you tried to keep faith to me, and to all. I believed this before I had any other evidence of it than your own nature. The night after I last parted from you I suffered torments. I had seen what convinced me that you were not free; that there was another whose presence had a power over you which mine never possessed; but through all the suggestions—almost murderous suggestions—of rage and jealousy, my mind made its way to belief in your truthfulness. I was sure that you meant to cleave to me, as you had said; that you had rejected him; that you struggled to renounce him, for Lucy's sake and for mine. But I could see no issue that was not fatal for *you*; and that dread shut out the very thought of resignation. I foresaw that he would not relinquish you, and I believed then, as I believe now, that the strong attraction which drew you together proceeded only from one side of your characters, and belonged to that partial, divided action of our nature which makes half the tragedy of the human lot. I have felt the vibration of chords in your nature that I have continually felt the want of in his. But perhaps I am wrong;

perhaps I feel about you as the artist does about the scene over which his soul has brooded with love: he would tremble to see it confided to other hands; he would never believe that it could bear for another all the meaning and the beauty it bears for him.

'I dared not trust myself to see you that morning; I was filled with selfish passion; I was shattered by a night of conscious delirium. I told you long ago that I had never been resigned even to the mediocrity of my powers: how could I be resigned to the loss of the one thing which had ever come to me on earth, with the promise of such deep joy as would give a new and blessed meaning to the foregoing pain—the promise of another self that would lift my aching affection into the divine rapture of an ever-springing, ever-satisfied want?

'But the miseries of that night had prepared me for what came before the next. It was no suprise to me. I was certain that he had prevailed on you to sacrifice everything to him, and I waited with equal certainty to hear of your marriage. I measured your love and his by my own. But I was wrong, Maggie. There is something stronger in you than your love for him.

'I will not tell you what I went through in that interval. But even in its utmost agony—even in those terrible throes that love must suffer before it can be disembodied of selfish desire—my love for you sufficed to withhold me from suicide, without the aid of any other motive. In the midst of my egoism, I yet could not bear to come like a death-shadow across the feast of your joy. I could not bear to forsake the world in which you still lived and might need me; it was part of the faith I had vowed to you—to wait and endure. Maggie, that is a proof of what I write now to assure you of—that no anguish I have had to bear on your account has been too heavy a price to pay for the new life into which I have entered in loving you. I want you to put aside all grief because of the grief you have caused me. I was nurtured in the sense of privation; I never expected happiness; and in knowing you, in loving you, I have had, and still have, what reconciles me to life. You have been to my affections what light, what colour is to my eyes—what music is to the inward ear; you have raised a dim unrest into a vivid consciousness. The new life I have found in caring for your joy and sorrow more than for what is directly my own, has transformed the spirit of rebellious murmuring into that willing endurance which is the birth of strong sympathy. I think nothing but such complete and intense love could have initiated me into that enlarged life which grows and grows by appropriating the life of others; for before, I was always dragged back from it by ever-present painful self-consciousness. I even think sometimes that this gift of transferred life which has come to me in loving you, may be a new power to me.

'Then—dear one—in spite of all, you have been the blessing of my life. Let no self-reproach weigh on you because of me. It is I who should rather reproach myself for having urged my feelings upon you, and hurried you into words that you have felt as fetters. You meant to be true to those words; you *have* been true. I can measure your sacrifice by what I have known in only one half-hour of your presence with me, when I dreamed that you might love me best. But, Maggie, I have no just claim on you for more than affectionate remembrance.

'For some time I have shrunk from writing to you, because I have shrunk even from the appearance of wishing to thrust myself before you, and so repeating my original error. But you will not misconstrue me. I know that we must keep apart for a long while; cruel tongues would force us apart, if nothing else did. But I shall not go away. The place where you are is the one where my mind must live, wherever I might travel. And remember that I am unchangeably yours: yours—not with selfish wishes, but with a devotion that excludes such wishes.

'God comfort you,—my loving, large-souled Maggie. If everyone else has misconceived you, remember that you have never been doubted by him whose heart recognised you ten years ago.

'Do not believe anyone who says I am ill, because I am not seen out of doors. I have only had nervous headaches

—no worse than I have sometimes had them before. But the overpowering heat inclines me to be perfectly quiescent in the daytime. I am strong enough to obey any word which shall tell me that I can serve you by word or deed.

'Yours, to the last,

'PHILIP WAKEM.'

As Maggie knelt by the bed sobbing, with that letter pressed under her, her feelings again and again gathered themselves in a whispered cry, always in the same words:

'O God, is there any happiness in love that could make me forget *their* pain?'

IV

MAGGIE AND LUCY

By the end of the week Dr. Kenn had made up his mind that there was only one way in which he could secure to Maggie a suitable living at St. Ogg's. Even with his twenty years' experience as a parish priest, he was aghast at the obstinate continuance of imputations against her in the face of evidence. Hitherto he had been rather more adored and appealed to than was quite agreeable to him; but now, in attempting to open the ears of women to reason, and their consciences to justice, on behalf of Maggie Tulliver, he suddenly found himself as powerless as he was aware he would have been if he had attempted to influence the shape of bonnets. Dr. Kenn could not be contradicted; he was listened to in silence; but when he left the room, a comparison of opinions among his hearers yielded much the same result as before. Miss Tulliver had undeniably acted in a blamable manner; even Dr. Kenn did not deny that: how, then, could he think so lightly of her as to put that favourable interpretation on everything she had done? Even on the supposition that required the utmost stretch of belief—namely, that none of the things said about Miss Tulliver were true—still, since they *had* been said about her, they had cast an odour round her which must cause

her to be shrunk from by every woman who had to take
care of her own reputation—and of Society. To have taken
Maggie by the hand and said, 'I will not believe unproved
evil of you: my lips shall not utter it; my ears shall be closed
against it; I, too, am an erring mortal, liable to stumble,
apt to come short of my most earnest efforts; your lot has
been harder than mine, your temptation greater; let us
help each other to stand and walk without more falling;'—
to have done this would have demanded courage, deep
pity, self-knowledge, generous trust—would have demanded
a mind that tasted no piquancy in evil-speaking, that felt
no self-exaltation in condemning, that cheated itself with
no large words into the belief that life can have any moral
end, any high religion, which excludes the striving after
perfect truth, justice, and love towards the individual men
and women who come across our own path. The ladies of St.
Ogg's were not beguiled by any wide speculative conceptions; but they had their favourite abstraction, called
Society, which served to make their consciences perfectly
easy in doing what satisfied their own egoism—thinking
and speaking the worst of Maggie Tulliver, and turning
their backs upon her. It was naturally disappointing to
Dr. Kenn, after two years of superfluous incense from his
feminine parishioners, to find them suddenly maintaining
their views in opposition to his; but then, they maintained
them in opposition to a Higher Authority, which they had
venerated longer. That Authority had furnished a very
explicit answer to persons who might inquire where their
social duties began, and might be inclined to take wide
views as to the starting-point. The answer had not turned
on the ultimate good of Society, but on 'a certain man'
who was found in trouble by the wayside.

Not that St. Ogg's was empty of women with some
tenderness of heart and conscience: probably it had as fair
a proportion of human goodness in it as any other small
trading town of that day. But until every good man is
brave, we must expect to find many good women timid:
too timid even to believe in the correctness of their own
best promptings, when these would place them in a minority.

And the men at St. Ogg's were not all brave by any means: some of them were even fond of scandal—and to an extent that might have given their conversation an effeminate character, if it had not been distinguished by masculine jokes, and by an occasional shrug of the shoulders at the mutual hatred of women. It was the general feeling of the masculine mind at St. Ogg's that women were not to be interfered with in their treatment of each other.

And thus every direction in which Dr. Kenn had turned in the hope of procuring some kind recognition and some employment for Maggie, proved a disappointment to him. Mrs. James Torry could not think of taking Maggie as a nursery governess, even temporarily—a young women about whom 'such things had been said,' and about whom 'gentlemen joked;' and Miss Kirke, who had a spinal complaint, and wanted a reader and companion, felt quite sure that Maggie's mind must be of a quality with which she, for her part, could not risk *any* contact. Why did not Miss Tulliver accept the shelter offered her by her aunt Glegg?—it did not become a girl like her to refuse it. Or else, why did she not go out of the neighbourhood, and get a situation where she was not known? (It was not, apparently, of so much importance that she should carry her dangerous tendencies into strange families unknown at St. Ogg's.) She must be very bold and hardened to wish to stay in a parish where she was so much stared at and whispered about.

Dr. Kenn, having great natural firmness, began, in the presence of this opposition, as every firm man would have done, to contract a certain strength of determination over and above what would have been called forth by the end in view. He himself wanted a daily governess for his younger children; and though he had hesitated in the first instance to offer this position to Maggie, the resolution to protest with the utmost force of his personal and priestly character against her being crushed and driven away by slander, was now decisive. Maggie gratefully accepted an employment that gave her duties as well as a support: her days would be filled now, and solitary evenings would be a welcome rest. She no longer needed the sacrifice her mother made in staying with her, and Mrs. Tulliver was persuaded to go back to the Mill.

But now it began to be discovered that Dr. Kenn, exemplary as he had hitherto appeared, had his crotchets—possibly his weaknesses. The masculine mind of St. Ogg's smiled pleasantly, and did not wonder that Kenn liked to see a fine pair of eyes daily, or that he was inclined to take so lenient a view of the past; the feminine mind, regarded at that period as less powerful, took a more melancholy view of the case. If Dr. Kenn should be beguiled into marrying that Miss Tulliver! It was not safe to be too confident, even about the best of men: an apostle had fallen, and wept bitterly afterwards; and though Peter's denial was not a close precedent, his repentance was likely to be.

Maggie had not taken her daily walks to the Rectory for many weeks, before the dreadful possibility of her some time or other becoming the Rector's wife had been talked of so often in confidence, that ladies were beginning to discuss how they should behave to her in that position. For Dr. Kenn, it had been understood, had sat in the school-room half an hour one morning, when Miss Tulliver was giving her lessons; nay, he had sat there every morning; he had once walked home with her—he almost *always* walked home with her—and if not, he went to see her in the evening. What an artful creature she was! What a *mother* for those children! It was enough to make poor Mrs. Kenn turn in her grave, that they should be put under the care of this girl only a few weeks after her death. Would he be so lost to propriety as to marry her before the year was out? The masculine mind was sarcastic, and thought *not*.

The Miss Guests saw an alleviation to the sorrow of witnessing a folly in their Rector: at least their brother would be safe; and their knowledge of Stephen's tenacity was a constant ground of alarm to them, lest he should come back and marry Maggie. They were not among those who disbelieved their brother's letter; but they had no confidence in Maggie's adherence to her renunciation of him; they suspected that she had shrunk rather from the elopement than from the marriage, and that she lingered in St. Ogg's, relying on his return to her. They had always thought her disagreeable; they now thought her artful and proud; having quite as good grounds for that judgment as you and I probably have for many strong opinions of the same kind. Formerly they had not altogether delighted in the contemplated match with Lucy, but now their dread of a marriage between Stephen and Maggie added its momentum to their genuine pity and indignation on behalf of the gentle forsaken girl, in making them desire that he should return to her. As soon as Lucy was able to leave home, she was to seek relief from the oppressive heat of this August by going to the coast with the Miss Guests; and it was in their plans that Stephen should be induced to join them. On the very first hint of gossip concerning Maggie and Dr. Kenn, the report was conveyed in Miss Guest's letter to her brother.

Maggie had frequent tidings through her mother, or aunt Glegg, or Dr. Kenn, of Lucy's gradual progress towards recovery, and her thoughts tended continually towards her uncle Deane's house: she hungered for an interview with Lucy, if it were only for five minutes—to utter a word of penitence, to be assured by Lucy's own eyes and lips that she did not believe in the willing treachery of those whom she had loved and trusted. But she knew that even if her uncle's indignation had not closed his house against her, the agitation of such an interview would have been forbidden to Lucy. Only to have seen her without speaking, would have been some relief; for Maggie was haunted by a face cruel in its very gentleness: a face that had been turned on hers with glad sweet looks of trust and love from the twilight time of memory; changed now to a sad and weary face by a first heart-stroke. And as the days passed on, that pale image became more and more distinct; the picture grew and grew into more speaking definiteness under the avenging hand of remorse; the soft hazel eyes, in their look of pain, were bent for ever on Maggie, and pierced her the more because she could see no anger in them. But Lucy was not yet able to go to church, or any place where Maggie could see her; and even the hope of that departed when the news was told her by aunt Glegg that Lucy was really going away in a few days to Scarborough with the Miss Guests, who had been heard to say that they expected their brother to meet them there.

Only those who have known what hardest inward conflict is, can know what Maggie felt as she sat in her loneliness the evening after hearing that news from Mrs. Glegg—only those who have known what it is to dread their own selfish desires as the watching mother would dread the sleeping-potion that was to still her own pain.

She sat without candle in the twilight, with the window wide open towards the river; the sense of oppressive heat adding itself undistinguishably to the burthen of her lot. Seated on a chair against the window, with her arm on the window-sill, she was looking blankly at the flowing river, swift with the backward-rushing tide—struggling to see still the sweet face in its unreproaching sadness, that seemed now from moment to moment to sink away and be hidden behind a form that thrust itself between, and made darkness. Hearing the door open, she thought Mrs. Jakin was coming in with her supper, as usual; and with that repugnance to trivial speech which comes with languor and wretchedness, she shrank from turning round and saying she wanted nothing: good little Mrs. Jakin would be sure to make some well-meant remarks. But the next moment, without her having discerned the sound of a footstep, she felt a light hand on her shoulder, and heard a voice close to her saying, 'Maggie!'

The face was there—changed, but all the sweeter: the hazel eyes were there, with their heart-piercing tenderness.

'Maggie!' the soft voice said.

'Lucy!' answered a voice with a sharp ring of anguish in it; and Lucy threw her arms round Maggie's neck, and leaned her pale cheek against the burning brow.

'I stole out,' said Lucy, almost in a whisper, while she sat down close to Maggie and held her hand, 'when papa and the rest were away. Alice is come with me. I asked her to help me. But I must only stay a little while, because it is so late.'

It was easier to say that at first than to say anything else. They sat looking at each other. It seemed as if the interview must end without more speech, for speech was very difficult. Each felt that there would be something scorching in the words that would recall the irretrievable wrong. But soon, as Maggie looked, every distinct thought began to be overflowed by a wave of loving penitence, and words burst forth with a sob.

'God bless you for coming, Lucy.'

The sobs came thick on each other after that.

'Maggie, dear, be comforted,' said Lucy now, putting her cheek against Maggie's again. 'Don't grieve.'

And she sat still, hoping to soothe Maggie with that gentle caress.

'I didn't mean to deceive you, Lucy,' said Maggie, as soon as she could speak. 'It always made me wretched that I felt what I didn't like you to know. . . . It was because I thought it would all be conquered, and you might never see anything to wound you.'

'I know, dear,' said Lucy. 'I know you never meant to make me unhappy. . . . It is a trouble that has come on us all:—you have more to bear than I have—and you gave him up, when . . . you did what it must have been very hard to do.'

They were silent again a little while, sitting with clasped hands, and cheeks leaned together.

'Lucy,' Maggie began again, '*he* struggled too. He wanted to be true to you. He will come back to you. Forgive him —he will be happy then. . . .'

These words were rung forth from Maggie's deepest soul, with an effort like the convulsed clutch of a drowning man. Lucy trembled and was silent.

A gentle knock came at the door. It was Alice, the maid, who entered and said:

'I daredn't stay any longer, Miss Deane. They'll find it out, and there'll be such anger at your coming out so late.'

Lucy rose and said:

'Very well, Alice—in a minute.'

'I'm to go away on Friday, Maggie,' she added, when Alice had closed the door again. 'When I come back, and am strong, they will let me do as I like. I shall come to you when I please then.'

'Lucy,' said Maggie, with another great effort, 'I pray to God continually that I may never be the cause of sorrow to you any more.'

She pressed the little hand that she held between hers, and looked up into the face that was bent over hers. Lucy never forgot that look.

'Maggie,' she said, in a low voice, that had the solemnity of confession in it, 'you are better than I am. I can't. . . .'

She broke off there, and said no more. But they clasped each other again in a last embrace.

V

THE LAST CONFLICT

In the second week of September, Maggie was again sitting in her lonely room, battling with the old shadowy enemies that were for ever slain and rising again. It was past midnight, and the rain was beating heavily against the window, driven with fitful force by the rushing, loud moaning wind. For, the day after Lucy's visit, there had been a sudden change in the weather: the heat and drought had given way to cold variable winds, and heavy falls of rain at intervals; and she had been forbidden to risk the contemplated journey until the weather should become more settled. In the counties higher up the Floss, the rains had been continuous, and the completion of the harvest had been arrested. And now, for the last two days, the rains on this lower course of the river had been incessant, so that the old men had shaken their heads and talked of sixty years ago, when the same sort of weather, happening about the equinox, brought on the great floods, which swept the bridge away, and reduced the town to great misery. But the younger generation, who had seen several small floods, thought lightly of these sombre recollections and forebodings; and Bob Jakin, naturally prone to take a hopeful view of his own luck, laughed at his mother when she regretted their having taken a house by the river-side; observing that but for that they would have had no boats, which were the most lucky of possessions in case of a flood that obliged them to go to a distance for food.

But the careless and the fearful were alike sleeping in their beds now. There was hope that the rain would abate by the morrow; threatenings of a worse kind, from sudden thaws after falls of snow, had often passed off in the experience of the younger ones; and at the very worst, the banks would be sure to break lower down the river when the tide came in with violence, and so the waters would be carried off, without causing more than temporary inconvenience, and losses that would be felt only by the poorer sort, whom charity would relieve.

All were in their beds now, for it was past midnight: all, except some solitary watchers such as Maggie. She was seated in her little parlour towards the river with one candle, that left everything dim in the room, except a letter which lay before her on the table. That letter which had come to her to-day, was one of the causes that had kept her up far on into the night—unconscious how the hours were going—careless of seeking rest—with no image of rest coming across her mind, except of that far, far off rest, from which there would be no more waking for her into this struggling earthly life.

Two days before Maggie received that letter, she had been to the Rectory for the last time. The heavy rain would have prevented her from going since; but there was another reason. Dr. Kenn, at first enlightened only by a few hints as to the new turn which gossip and slander had taken in relation to Maggie, had recently been made more fully aware of it by an earnest remonstrance from one of his male parishioners against the indiscretion of persisting in the attempt to overcome the prevalent feeling in the parish by a course of resistance. Dr. Kenn, having a conscience void of offence in the matter, was still inclined to persevere—was still averse to give way before a public sentiment that was odious and contemptible; but he was finally wrought upon by the consideration of the peculiar responsibility attached to his office, of avoiding the appearance of evil—an 'appearance' that is always dependent on the average quality of surrounding minds. Where these minds are low and gross, the area of that 'appearance' is proportionately widened. Perhaps he was in danger of acting from obstinacy; perhaps it was his duty to succumb: conscientious people are apt to see their duty in that which is the most painful course; and to recede was always painful to Dr. Kenn. He made up his mind that he must advise Maggie to go away from St. Ogg's for a time; and he performed that difficult task with as much delicacy as he could, only stating in vague terms that he found his attempt to countenance her stay was a source of discord between himself and his parishioners, that was likely to obstruct his usefulness as a clergyman. He begged her to allow him to write to a clerical friend of his, who might possibly take her into his own family as governess; and, if not, would probably know of some other available position for a young woman in whose welfare Dr. Kenn felt a strong interest.

Poor Maggie listened with a trembling lip: she could say nothing but a faint 'thank you—I shall be grateful;' and she walked back to her lodgings, through the driving rain, with a new sense of desolation. She must be a lonely wanderer; she must go out among fresh faces, that would look at her wonderingly, because the days did not seem joyful to her; she must begin a new life, in which she would have to rouse herself to receive new impressions—and she was so unspeakably, sickeningly weary! There was no home, no help for the erring: even those who pitied were constrained to hardness. But ought she to complain? Ought she to shrink in this way from the long penance of life, which was all the possibility she had of lightening the load to some other sufferers, and so changing that passionate error into a new force of unselfish human love? All the next day she sat in her lonely room, with a window darkened by the cloud and the driving rain, thinking of that future, and wrestling for patience:—for what repose could poor Maggie ever win except by wrestling?

And on the third day—this day of which she had just sat out the close—the letter had come which was lying on the table before her.

The letter was from Stephen. He was come back from Holland: he was at Mudport again, unknown to any of his friends; and had written to her from that place, enclosing the letter to a person whom he trusted in St. Ogg's. From beginning to end it was a passionate cry of reproach: an appeal against her useless sacrifice of him—of herself: against that perverted notion of right which led her to crush all his hopes, for the sake of a mere idea, and not any substantial good—*his* hopes, whom she loved, and who loved her with that single overpowering passion, that worship, which a man never gives to a woman more than once in his life.

'They have written to me that you are to marry Kenn. As if I should believe that! Perhaps they have told you some such fables about me. Perhaps they tell you I have been "travelling." My body has been dragged about somewhere; but *I* have never travelled from the hideous place where you left me—where I started up from the stupor of helpless rage to find you gone.

'Maggie! whose pain can have been like mine? Whose injury is like mine? Who besides me has met that long look of love that has burnt itself into my soul, so that no other image can come there? Maggie, call me back to you! —call me back to life and goodness! I am banished from both now. I have no motives: I am indifferent to everything. Two months have only deepened the certainty that I can never care for life without you. Write me one word— say "Come!" In two days I should be with you. Maggie —have you forgotten what it was to be together?—to be within reach of a look—to be within hearing of each other's voice?'

When Maggie first read this letter she felt as if her real temptation had only just begun. At the entrance of the chill dark cavern, we turn with unworn courage from the warm light; but how, when we have trodden far in the damp darkness, and have begun to be faint and weary—how, if there is a sudden opening above us, and we are invited back again to the life-nourishing day? The leap of natural longing from under the pressure of pain is so strong, that all less immediate motives are likely to be forgotten—till the pain has been escaped from.

For hours Maggie felt as if her struggle had been in vain. For hours every other thought that she strove to summon was thrust aside by the image of Stephen waiting for the single word that would bring him to her. She did not *read* the letter: she heard him uttering it, and the voice shook her with its old strange power. All the day before she had been filled with the vision of a lonely future through which she must carry the burthen of regret, upheld only by clinging faith. And here—close within her reach—urging itself upon her even as a claim—was another future, in which hard endurance and effort were to be exchanged for easy delicious leaning on another's loving strength! And yet that promise of joy in the place of sadness did not make the dire force of the temptation to Maggie. It was Stephen's tone of misery, it was the doubt in the justice of her own resolve, that made the balance tremble, and made her once start from her seat to reach the pen and paper, and write 'Come!'

But close upon that decisive act, her mind recoiled; and the sense of contradiction with her past self in her moments of strength and clearness, came upon her like a pang of conscious degradation. No—she must wait; she must pray; the light that had forsaken her would come again: she should feel again what she had felt, when she had fled away, under an inspiration strong enough to conquer agony—to conquer love: she should feel again what she had felt when Lucy stood by her, when Philip's letter had stirred all the fibres that bound her to the calmer past.

She sat quite still, far on into the night: with no impulse to change her attitude, without active force enough even for the mental act of prayer: only waiting for the light that would surely come again. It came with the memories that no passion could long quench: the long past came back to her, and with it the fountains of self-renouncing pity and affection, of faithfulness and resolve. The words that were marked by the quiet hand in the little old book that she had long ago learned by heart, rushed even to her lips, and found a vent for themselves in a low murmur that was quite lost in the loud driving of the rain against the window and the loud moan and roar of the wind: 'I have received the Cross, I have received it from Thy hand; I will bear it, and bear it till death, as Thou hast laid it upon me.'

But soon other words rose that could find no utterance but in a sob: 'Forgive me, Stephen! It will pass away. You will come back to her.'

She took up the letter, held it to the candle, and let it burn slowly on the hearth. To-morrow she would write to him the last word of parting.

'I will bear it, and bear it till death. . . . But how long it will be before death comes! I am so young, so healthy. How shall I have patience and strength? Am I to struggle and fall and repent again?—has life other trials as hard for me still?'

With that cry of self-despair, Maggie fell on her knees against the table, and buried her sorrow-stricken face. Her soul went out to the Unseen Pity that would be with her to the end. Surely there was something being taught her by this experience of great need; and she must be learning a secret of human tenderness and long-suffering, that the less erring could hardly know? 'O God, if my life is to be long, let me live to bless and comfort——'

At that moment Maggie felt a startling sensation of sudden cold about her knees and feet: it was water flowing under her. She started up: the stream was flowing under the door that led into the passage. She was not bewildered for an instant—she knew it was the flood!

The tumult of emotion she had been enduring for the last twelve hours seemed to have left a great calm in her: without screaming, she hurried with the candle up-stairs to

Bob Jakin's bedroom. The door was ajar; she went in and shook him by the shoulder.

'Bob, the flood is come! it is in the house! let us see if we can make the boats safe.'

She lighted his candle, while the poor wife, snatching up her baby, burst into screams; and then she hurried down again to see if the waters were rising fast. There was a step down into the room at the door leading from the staircase; she saw that the water was already on a level with the step. While she was looking, something came with a tremendous crash against the window, and sent the leaded panes and the old wooden framework inwards in shivers,—the water pouring in after it.

'It is the boat!' cried Maggie. 'Bob, come down to get the boats!'

And without a moment's shudder of fear, she plunged through the water, which was rising fast to her knees, and by the glimmering light of the candle she had left on the stairs, she mounted on to the window-sill, and crept into the boat, which was left with the prow lodging and protruding through the window. Bob was not long after her, hurrying without shoes or stockings, but with the lanthorn in his hand.

'Why, they're both here—both the boats,' said Bob, as he got into the one where Maggie was. 'It's wonderful this fastening isn't broke too, as well as the mooring.'

In the excitement of getting into the other boat, unfastening it, and mastering an oar, Bob was not struck with the danger Maggie incurred. We are not apt to fear for the fearless, when we are companions in their danger, and Bob's mind was absorbed in possible expedients for the safety of the helpless in-doors. The fact that Maggie had been up, had waked him, and had taken the lead in activity, gave Bob a vague impression of her as one who would help to protect, not need to be protected. She too had got possession of an oar, and had pushed off, so as to release the boat from the overhanging window-frame.

'The water's rising so fast,' said Bob, 'I doubt it'll be in at the chambers before long—th' house is so low. I've more mind to get Prissy and the child and the mother into the boat, if I could, and trusten to the water—for th' old house is none so safe. And if I let go the boat . . . but *you*,' he exclaimed, suddenly lifting the light of his lanthorn on Maggie, as she stood in the rain with the oar in her hand and her black hair streaming.

Maggie had no time to answer, for a new tidal current swept along the line of the houses, and drove both the boats out on to the wide water, with a force that carried them far past the meeting current of the river.

In the first moments Maggie felt nothing, thought of nothing, but that she had suddenly passed away from that life which she had been dreading: it was the transition of death, without its agony—and she was alone in the darkness with God.

The whole thing had been so rapid—so dream-like—that the threads of ordinary association were broken: she sank down on the seat clutching the oar mechanically, and for a long while had no distinct conception of her position. The first thing that waked her to fuller consciousness was the cessation of the rain, and a perception that the darkness was divided by the faintest light, which parted the overhanging gloom from the immeasurable watery level below. She was driven out upon the flood:—that awful visitation of God which her father used to talk of—which had made the nightmare of her childish dreams. And with that thought there rushed in the vision of the old home— and Tom—and her mother—they had all listened together.

'O God, where am I? Which is the way home?' she cried out, in the dim loneliness.

What was happening to them at the Mill? The flood had once nearly destroyed it. They might be in danger—in distress: her mother and her brother, alone there, beyond reach of help! Her whole soul was strained now on that thought; and she saw the long-loved faces looking for help into the darkness, and finding none.

She was floating in smooth water now—perhaps far on the over-flooded fields. There was no sense of present danger to check the outgoing of her mind to the old home;

and she strained her eyes against the curtain of gloom that she might seize the first sight of her whereabout—that she might catch some faint suggestion of the spot towards which all her anxieties tended.

O how welcome, the widening of that dismal watery level—the gradual uplifting of the cloudy firmament—the slowly defining blackness of objects above the glassy dark! Yes—she must be out on the fields—those were the tops of hedgerow trees. Which way did the river lie? Looking behind her, she saw the lines of black trees: looking before her, there were none: then, the river lay before her. She seized an oar and began to paddle the boat forward with the energy of wakening hope: the dawning seemed to advance more swiftly, now she was in action; and she could soon see the poor dumb beasts crowding piteously on a mound where they had taken refuge. Onward she paddled and rowed by turns in the growing twilight: her wet clothes clung round her, and her streaming hair was dashed about by the wind, but she was hardly conscious of any bodily sensations—except a sensation of strength, inspired by mighty emotion. Along with the sense of danger and possible rescue for those long-remembered beings at the old home, there was an undefined sense of reconcilement with her brother: what quarrel, what harshness, what unbelief in each other can subsist in the presence of a great calamity, when all the artificial vesture of our life is gone, and we are all one with each other in primitive mortal needs? Vaguely, Maggie felt this;—in the strong resurgent love towards her brother that swept away all the later impressions of hard, cruel offence and misunderstanding, and left only the deep, underlying, unshakable memories of early union.

But now there was a large dark mass in the distance, and near to her Maggie could discern the current of the river. The dark mass must be—yes, it was—St. Ogg's. Ah, now she knew which way to look for the first glimpse of the well-known trees—the grey willows, the now yellowing chestnuts—and above them the old roof! But there was no colour, no shape yet: all was faint and dim. More and more strongly the energies seemed to come and put themselves forth, as if her life were a stored-up force that was being spent in this hour, unneeded for any future.

She must get her boat into the current of the Floss, else she would never be able to pass the Ripple and approach the house: this was the thought that occurred to her, as she imagined with more and more vividness the state of things round the old home. But then she might be carried very far down, and be unable to guide her boat out of the current again. For the first time distinct ideas of danger began to press upon her; but there was no choice of courses, no room for hesitation, and she floated into the current. Swiftly she went now, without effort; more and more clearly in the lessening distance and the growing light she began to discern the objects that she knew must be the well-known trees and roofs; nay, she was not far off a rushing muddy current that must be the strangely altered Ripple.

Great God! there were floating masses in it, that might dash against her boat as she passed, and cause her to perish too soon. What were those masses?

For the first time Maggie's heart began to beat in an agony of dread. She sat helpless—dimly conscious that she was being floated along—more intensely conscious of the anticipated clash. But the horror was transient: it passed away before the oncoming warehouses of St. Ogg's: she had passed the mouth of the Ripple, then: *now*, she must use all her skill and power to manage the boat and get it if possible out of the current. She could see now that the bridge was broken down: she could see the masts of a stranded vessel far out over the watery field. But no boats were to be seen moving on the river—such as had been laid hands on were employed in the flooded streets.

With new resolution, Maggie seized her oar, and stood up again to paddle; but the now ebbing tide added to the swiftness of the river, and she was carried along beyond the bridge. She could hear shouts from the windows overlooking the river, as if the people there were calling to her. It was not till she had passed on nearly to Tofton that she could get the boat clear of the current. Then with one yearning look towards her uncle Deane's house that lay farther down the river, she took to both her oars and rowed with all her might across the watery fields, back towards the Mill. Colour was beginning to awake now, and as she approached the Dorlcote fields, she could discern the tints of the trees—could see the old Scotch firs far to the right, and the home chestnuts—Oh! how deep they lay in the water: deeper than the trees on this side the hill. And the roof of the Mill—where was it? Those heavy fragments hurrying down the Ripple —what had they meant? But it was not the house—the house stood firm; drowned up to the first story, but still firm—or was it broken in at the end towards the Mill?

With panting joy that she was there at last—joy that overcame all distress—Maggie neared the front of the house. At first she heard no sound: she saw no object moving. Her boat was on a level with the up-stairs windows.

She called out in a loud piercing voice:

'Tom, where are you? Mother, where are you? Here is Maggie!'

Soon, from the window of the attic in the central gable, she heard Tom's voice:

'Who is it? Have you brought a boat?'

'It is I, Tom—Maggie. Where is mother?'

'She is not here: she went to Garum, the day before yesterday. I'll come down to the lower window.'

'Alone, Maggie?' said Tom, in a voice of deep astonishment, as he opened the middle window on a level with the boat.

'Yes, Tom: God has taken care of me, to bring me to you. Get in quickly. Is there no one else?'

'No,' said Tom, stepping into the boat, 'I fear the man is drowned: he was carried down the Ripple, I think, when part of the Mill fell with the crash of trees and stones against it: I've shouted again and again, and there has been no answer. Give me the oars, Maggie.'

It was not till Tom had pushed off and they were on the wide water—he face to face with Maggie—that the full meaning of what had happened rushed upon his mind. It came with so overpowering a force—it was such a new revelation to his spirit, of the depths in life, that had lain beyond his vision which he had fancied so keen and clear —that he was unable to ask a question. They sat mutely gazing at each other: Maggie with eyes of intense life looking out from a weary, beaten face—Tom pale with a certain awe and humiliation. Thought was busy though the lips were silent: and though he could ask no questions, he guessed a story of almost miraculous divinely-protected effort. But at last a mist gathered over the blue-grey eyes, and the lips found a word they could utter: the old childish—'Magsie!'

Maggie could make no answer but a long deep sob of that mysterious wondrous happiness that is one with pain.

As soon as she could speak, she said, 'We will go to Lucy, Tom: we'll go and see if she is safe, and then we can help the rest.'

Tom rowed with untired vigour, and with a different speed from poor Maggie's. The boat was soon in the current of the river again, and soon they would be at Tofton.

'Park House stands high up out of the flood,' said Maggie. 'Perhaps they have got Lucy there.'

Nothing else was said; a new danger was being carried towards them by the river. Some wooden machinery had just given way on one of the wharves, and huge fragments were being floated along. The sun was rising now, and the wide area of watery desolation was spread out in dreadful clearness around them—in dreadful clearness floated onwards the hurrying, threatening masses. A large company in a boat that was working its way along under the Tofton houses, observed their danger, and shouted, 'Get out of the current!'

But that could not be done at once, and Tom, looking before him, saw death rushing on them. Huge fragments, clinging together in fatal fellowship, made one wide mass across the stream.

'It is coming, Maggie!' Tom said, in a deep hoarse voice, loosing the oars, and clasping her.

The next instant the boat was no longer seen upon the water—and the huge mass was hurrying on in hideous triumph.

But soon the keel of the boat reappeared, a black speck on the golden water.

The boat reappeared—but brother and sister had gone down in an embrace never to be parted: living through again in one supreme moment the days when they had clasped their little hands in love, and roamed the daisied fields together.

CONCLUSION

NATURE repairs her ravages—repairs them with her sunshine, and with human labour. The desolation wrought by that flood, had left little visible trace on the face of the earth, five years after. The fifth autumn was rich in golden corn-stacks, rising in thick clusters among the distant hedgerows; the wharves and warehouses on the Floss were busy again, with echoes of eager voices, with hopeful lading and unlading.

And every man and woman mentioned in this history was still living—except those whose end we know.

Nature repairs her ravages—but not all. The up-torn trees are not rooted again; the parted hills are left scarred: if there is a new growth, the trees are not the same as the old, and the hills underneath their green vesture bear the marks of the past rending. To the eyes that have dwelt on the past, there is no thorough repair.

Dorlcote Mill was rebuilt. And Dorlcote churchyard,— where the brick grave that held a father whom we know, was found with the stone laid prostrate upon it after the flood,—had recovered all its grassy order and decent quiet.

Near that brick grave there was a tomb erected, very soon after the flood, for two bodies that were found in close embrace; and it was visited at different moments by two men who both felt that their keenest joy and keenest sorrow were for ever buried there.

One of them visited the tomb again with a sweet face beside him—but that was years after.

The other was always solitary. His great companionship was among the trees of the Red Deeps, where the buried joy seemed still to hover—like a revisiting spirit.

The tomb bore the names of Tom and Maggie Tulliver, and below the names it was written:

In their death they were not divided.'